Mrs Halliburton's Troubles by

Ellen Price was born on 17th January 1814 in Worcester.

In 1836 she married Henry Wood, whose career in banking and shipping meant living in Dauphiné, in the South of France, for two decades. During their time there they had four children.

Henry's business collapsed and he and Ellen together with their four children returned to England and settled in Upper Norwood near London.

Ellen now turned to writing and with her second book 'East Lynne' enjoyed remarkable popularity. This enabled her to support her family and to maintain a literary career.

It was a career in which she would write over 30 novels including 'Danesbury House', 'Oswald Cray', 'Mrs. Halliburton's Troubles', 'The Channings' and 'The Shadow of Ashlydyat'.

Sadly, her husband, Henry died in 1866.

Ellen though continued to strive on. In 1867, she purchased the magazine 'Argosy', founded two years previously by Alexander Strahan. She was a prolific writer and wrote much of the magazine herself although she had some very respected contributors, amongst them Hesba Stretton and Christina Rossetti. Although she would gradually pare down writing for the magazine she continued to write novel after novel. Such was her talent that for a time she was, in Australia, more popular than Charles Dickens.

Apart from novels she was an excellent translator and a writer of short stories. 'Reality or Delusion?' is a staple of supernatural anthologies to this day.

Ellen Wood died of bronchitis on 10th February 1887. He estate was valued at a very considerable £36,000.

She is buried in Highgate Cemetery, London.

A monument to her in Worcester Cathedral was unveiled in 1916.

Index of Contents

PART THE FIRST

CHAPTER I

THE CLERGYMAN'S DAUGHTER

In a very populous district of London, somewhat north of Temple Bar, there stood, many years ago, a low, ancient church amidst other churches—for you know that London abounds in them. The doors of this church were partially open one dark evening in December, and a faint, glimmering light might be observed inside by the passers-by.

It was known well enough what was going on within, and why the light was there. The rector was giving away the weekly bread. Years ago a benevolent person had left a certain sum to be spent in twenty weekly loaves, to be given to twenty poor widows at the discretion of the minister. Certain curious provisos were attached to the bequest. One was that the bread should not be less than two days old, and should have been deposited in the church at least twenty-four hours before distribution. Another, that each recipient must attend in person. Failing personal attendance, no matter how unavoidable her absence, she lost the loaf: no friend might receive it for her, neither might it be sent to her. In that case, the minister was enjoined to bestow it upon "any stranger widow who might present herself, even as should seem expedient to him:" the word "stranger" being, of course, used in contra-distinction to the twenty poor widows who were on the books as the charity's recipients. Four times a year, one shilling to each widow was added to the loaf of bread.

A loaf of bread is not very much. To us, sheltered in our abundant homes, it seems as nothing. But, to many a one, toiling and starving in this same city of London, a loaf may be almost the turning-point between death and life. The poor existed in those days as they exist in these: as they always will exist: therefore it was no matter of surprise that a crowd of widow women, most of them aged, all in poverty, should gather round the church doors when the bread was being given out, each hoping that, of the twenty poor widows, some one might fail to appear, and the clerk would come to the door and call out her own particular name as the fortunate substitute. On the days when the shilling was added to the loaf, this waiting and hoping crowd would be increased four-fold.

Thursday was the afternoon for the distribution. And on the day we are now writing about, the rector entered the church at the usual hour: four o'clock. He had to make his way through an unusual number of outsiders; for this was one of the shilling days. He knew them all personally; was familiar with their names and homes; for the Rev. Francis Tait was a hard-working clergyman. And hard-working clergymen were more rare in those days than they are in these.

Of Scottish birth, but chiefly reared in England, he had taken orders at the usual age, and become curate in a London parish, where the work was heavy and the stipend small. Not that the duties attached to the church itself were onerous; but it was a parish filled with poor. Those familiar with such parishes know what this means, when the minister is sympathising and conscientious. For twenty years he remained a curate, toiling in patience, cheerfully hoping. Twenty years! It seems little to write; but to live it is a great deal; and Francis Tait, in spite of his hopefulness, sometimes found it so. Then promotion came. The living of this little church that you now see open was bestowed upon him. A poor living as compared with some others; and a poor parish, speaking of the social condition of its inhabitants. But the living seemed wealth compared with what he had earned as a curate; and as to his flock being chiefly composed of the poor, he had not been accustomed to anything else. Then the Rev. Francis Tait married; and another twenty years went by.

He stood in the church this evening; the loaves resting on the shelf overhead, against the door of the vestry, all near the entrance. A flaring tallow candle stood on the small table between him and the widows who clustered opposite. He was sixty-five years old now; a spare man of middle height, with a clear, pale skin, an intelligent countenance, and a thoughtful, fine grey eye. He had a pleasant word, a kind inquiry for all, as he put the shilling into their hands; the lame old clerk at the same time handing over the loaf of bread.

"Are you all here to-night?" he asked, as the distribution went on.

"No, sir," was the answer from several who spoke at once. "Betty King's away."

"What is the matter with her?"

"The rheumaticks have laid hold on her, sir. She couldn't get here nohow. She's in her bed."

"I must go and see her," said he. "What, are you here again, Martha?" he continued, as a little deformed woman stepped from behind the rest, where she had been hidden. "I am glad to see you."

"Six blessed weeks this day, and I've not been able to come!" exclaimed the woman. "But I'm restored wonderful."

The distribution was approaching its close, when the rector spoke to his clerk. "Call in Eliza Turner."

The clerk placed on the table the four or five remaining loaves, that each woman might help herself during his absence, and went out to the door.

"'Liza Turner, his reverence has called for you."

A sigh of delight from Eliza Turner, and a groan of disappointment from those surrounding her, greeted the clerk in answer. He took no notice—he often heard it—but turned and limped into the church again. Eliza Turner followed; and another woman slipped in after Eliza Turner.

"Now, Widow Booth," cried the clerk, sharply, perceiving the intrusion, "what business have you here? You know it's again the rules."

"I must see his reverence," murmured the woman, pressing on—a meek, half-starved woman; and she pushed her way into the vestry, and told her pitiful tale.

"I'm worse off than Widow Turner," she moaned piteously, not in tones of complaint, but of entreaty. "She has a daughter in service as helps her; but me, I've my poor unfortunate daughter lying in my place weak with fever, sick with hunger! Oh, sir, couldn't you give the bounty this time to me? I've not had a bit or drop in my mouth since morning; and then it was but a taste o' bread and a drain o' tea, that a neighbour give me out o' charity."

It was absolutely necessary to discountenance these personal applications. The rector's rule was, never to give the spare bounty to those who applied for it: otherwise the distribution might have become a weekly scene of squabbling and confusion. He handed the shilling and bread to Eliza Turner; and when she had followed the other women out, he turned to the Widow Booth, who was sobbing against the wall; speaking kindly to her.

"You should not have come in, Mrs. Booth. You know that I do not allow it."

"But I'm starving, sir," was the answer. "I thought maybe as you'd divide it between me and Widow Turner. Sixpence for her, sixpence for me, and the loaf halved."

"I have no power to divide the gifts: to do so would be against the terms of the bequest. How is it you are so badly off this week? Has your work failed?"

"I couldn't do it, sir, with my sick one to attend to. And I've a gathering come on my thimble finger, and that has hindered me. I took ninepence the day before yesterday, sir, but last night it was every farthing of it gone."

"I will come round and see you by-and-by," said the clergyman.

She lifted her eyes yearningly. "Oh, sir! if you could but give me something for a morsel of bread now! I'd be grateful for a penny loaf."

"Mrs. Booth, you know that to give here would be altogether against my rule," he replied with unmistakable firmness. "Neither am I pleased when any of you attempt to ask it. Go home quietly: I have said that I will come to you by-and-by."

The woman thanked him and went out. Had anything been needed to prove the necessity of the rule, it would have been the eagerness with which the crowd of women gathered round her. Not one of them had gone away. "Had she got anything?" To reply that she had something, would have sent the whole crowd flocking in to beg in turn of the rector.

Widow Booth shook her head. "No, no. I knowed it before. He never will. He says he'll come round."

They dispersed; some in one direction, some in another. The rector blew out the candle, and he and the clerk came forth; and the church was closed for the distribution of bread until that day week. Mr. Tait took the keys himself to carry them home: they were kept at his house. Formerly the clerk had carried them there; but since he had become old and lame, Mr. Tait would not give him the trouble.

It was a fine night overhead, but the streets were sloppy; and the clergyman put his foot unavoidably in many a puddle. The streets through which his road lay were imperfectly lighted. The residence apportioned to the rector of this parish was adjoining a well-known square, fashionable in that day. It was a very good house, with a handsome outward appearance. If you judged by it, you would have said the living must be worth five hundred a year at least. It was not worth anything like that; and the parish treated their pastor liberally in according him so good a residence. A quarter of an hour's walk from the church brought Mr. Tait to it.

Until recently, a gentleman had shared this house with Mr. Tait and his family. The curate of a neighbouring parish, the Rev. John Acton, had been glad to live with them as a friend, admitted to their society and their table. It was a little help: and but for that, Mr. and Mrs. Tait would scarcely have thought themselves justified in keeping two servants, for the educational expenses of their children ran away with a large portion of their income. But Mr. Acton had now been removed to a distance, and they hoped to receive some one or other in his place.

On this evening, as Mr. Tait was picking his way through the puddles, the usual sitting-room of his house presented a cheerful appearance, ready to receive him. It was on the ground floor, looking upon the street, large and lofty, and bright with firelight. Two candles, not yet lighted, stood on the table behind the tea-tray, but the glow of the fire was sufficient for all the work that was being done in the room.

It was no work at all: but play. A young lady was quietly whirling round the room with a dancing step— quietly, because her feet and movements were gentle; and the tune she was humming, and to which she kept time, was carolled in an undertone. She was moving thus in the happy innocence of heart and youth. A graceful girl of middle height; one whom it gladdened the eye to look upon. Not for her beauty, for she had no very great beauty to boast of; but it was one of those countenances that win their own way to favour. A fair, gentle face, openly candid, with the same earnest, honest grey eye that so pleased you in Francis Tait, and brown hair. She was that gentleman's eldest child, and looked about eighteen. In reality she was a year older, but her face and dress were both youthful. She wore a violet silk frock, made with a low body and short sleeves: girls did not keep their pretty necks and arms covered up then. By daylight the dress would have appeared old, but it looked very well by candle-light.

The sound of the latch-key in the front door brought her dancing to an end. She knew who it was—no inmate of that house possessed a latch-key except its master—and she turned to the fire to light the candles.

Mr. Tait came into the room, removing neither overcoat nor hat. "Have you made tea, Jane?"

"No, papa; it has only just struck five."

"Then I think I'll go out again first. I have to call on one or two of the women, and it will be all one wetting. My feet are soaked already"—looking down at his buckled shoes and black gaiters. "You can get my slippers warmed, Jane. But"—the thought apparently striking him—"would your mamma care to wait?"

"Mamma had a cup of tea half an hour ago," replied Jane. "She said it might do her good; if she could get some sleep after it, she might be able to come down for a little before bedtime. The tea can be made whenever you like, papa. There's only Francis at home, and he and I could wait until ten, if you pleased."

"I'll go at once, then. Not until ten, Miss Jane, but until six, or about that time. Betty King is ill, but does not live far off. And I must step in to the Widow Booth's."

"Papa," cried Jane as he was turning away, "I forgot to tell you. Francis says he thinks he knows of a gentleman who would like to come here in Mr. Acton's place."

"Ah! who is it?" asked the rector.

"One of the masters at the school. Here's Francis coming down. He only went up to wash his hands."

"It is our new mathematical master, sir," cried Francis Tait, a youth of eighteen, who was being brought up to the Church. "I overheard him ask Dr. Percy if he could recommend him to a comfortable house where he might board, and make one of the family: so I told him perhaps you might receive him here. He said he'd come down and see you."

Mr. Tait paused. "Would he be a desirable inmate, think you, Francis? Is he a gentleman?"

"Quite a gentleman, I am sure," replied Francis. "And we all like what little we have seen of him. His name's Halliburton."

"Is he in Orders?"

"No. He intends to be, I think."

"Well, of course I can say nothing about it, one way or the other," concluded Mr. Tait, as he went out.

Jane stood before the fire in thought, her fingers unconsciously smoothing the parting of the glossy brown hair on her well-shaped head as she looked at it in the pier-glass. To say that she never did such a thing in vanity would be wrong; no pretty girl ever lived but was conscious of her good looks. Jane, however, was neither thinking of herself nor of vanity just then. She took a very practical part in home duties: with her mother, a practical part amidst her father's poor: and at this moment her thoughts were running on the additional work it might bring her, should this gentleman come to reside with them.

"What did you say his name was, Francis?" she suddenly asked of her brother.

"Whose?"

"That gentleman's. The new master at your school."

"Halliburton. I don't know his Christian name."

"I wonder," mused Jane aloud, "whether he will wear out his stockings as Mr. Acton did? There was always a dreadful amount of darning to be done to his. Is he an old guy, Francis?"

"Isn't he!" responded Francis Tait. "Don't faint when you see some one come in old and fat, with green rims to his spectacles. I don't say he's quite old enough to be papa's father, but—"

"Why! he must be eighty then, at least!" uttered Jane, in dismay. "How could you propose it to him? We should not care to have any one older than Mr. Acton."

"Acton! that young chicken!" contemptuously rejoined Francis. "Put him by the side of Mr. Halliburton! Acton was barely fifty."

"He was forty-eight, I think," said Jane. "Oh, dear! how I should like to have gone with Margaret and Robert this evening!" she exclaimed, forgetting the passing topic in another.

"They were not polite enough to invite me," said Francis. "I shall pay the old lady out."

Jane laughed. "You are growing too old now, Francis, to be admitted to a young ladies' breaking-up party. Mrs. Chilham said so to mamma—"

Jane's words were interrupted by a knock at the front door, apparently that of a visitor. "Jane!" cried her brother, in some trepidation, "I should not wonder if it's Mr. Halliburton! He did not say when he should come!"

Another minute, and one of the servants ushered a gentleman into the room. It was not an old guy, however, as Jane saw at a glance with a distinct feeling of relief. A tall, gentlemanlike man of five or six and twenty, with thin aquiline features, dark eyes, and a clear, fresh complexion. A handsome man, very prepossessing.

"You see I have soon availed myself of your permission to call," said he, in pleasant tones, as he took Francis Tait's hand, and glanced towards Jane with a slight bow.

"My sister Jane, sir," said Francis. "Jane, this is Mr. Halliburton."

Jane for once lost her self-possession. So surprised was she—in fact perplexed, for she did not know whether Francis was playing a trick upon her now, or whether he had previously played it; in short, whether this was, or was not, Mr. Halliburton—that she could only look from one to the other. "Are you Mr. Halliburton?" she said, in her straightforward simplicity.

"I am Mr. Halliburton," he answered, bending to her politely. "Can I have the pleasure of seeing Mr. Tait?"

"Will you take a seat?" said Jane. "Papa is out, but I do not think he will be very long."

"Where did he go to—do you know, Jane?" cried Francis, who was smothering a laugh.

"To Betty King's; and to Widow Booth's. He may have been going elsewhere also. I think he was."

"At any rate, I'll just run there and see. Jane, you can tell Mr. Halliburton all about it whilst I am away. Explain to him exactly how he will be here, and how we live. And then you can decide for yourself, sir," concluded Francis.

To splash through the wet streets to Betty King's or elsewhere was an expedition rather agreeable to Francis, in his eagerness; otherwise there was no particular necessity for his going.

"I am sorry mamma is not up," said Jane. "She suffers from occasional sick-headaches, and they generally keep her in bed for the day. I will give you any information in my power."

"Your brother Francis thought—that it might not be disagreeable to Mr. Tait to receive a stranger into his family," said Mr. Halliburton, speaking with some hesitation. But the young lady before him looked so lady-like, the house altogether seemed so well appointed, that he almost doubted whether the proposal would not offend her.

"We wish to receive some one," said Jane. "The house is sufficiently large to do so, and papa would like it for the sake of society: as well as that it would help in our housekeeping," she added, in her candour. "A friend of papa's was with us—I cannot remember precisely how many years, but he came when I was a little girl. It was the Rev. Mr. Acton. He left us last October."

"I feel sure that I should like it very much: and I should think myself fortunate if Mr. Tait would admit me," spoke the visitor.

Jane remembered the suggestion of Francis, and deemed it her duty to speak a little to Mr. Halliburton of "how he would be there," as it had been expressed. She might have done so without the suggestion, for she could not be otherwise than straightforward and open.

"We live very plainly," she observed. "A simple joint of meat one day; cold, with a pudding, the next."

"I should consider myself fortunate to get the pudding," replied Mr. Halliburton, smiling. "I have been tossed about a good deal of late years, Miss Tait, and have not come in for too much comfort. Just now I am in very uncomfortable lodgings."

"I dare say papa would like to have you," said Jane, frankly, with a sort of relief. She had thought he looked one who might be fastidious.

"I have neither father nor mother, brother nor sister," he resumed. "In fact, I may say that I am without relatives; for almost the only one I have has discarded me. I often think how rich those people must be who possess close connections and a happy home," he added, turning his bright glance upon her.

Jane dropped her work, which she had taken up. "I don't know what I should do without all my dear relatives," she exclaimed.

"Are you a large family?"

"We are six. Papa and mamma, and four children. I am the eldest, and Margaret is the youngest; Francis and Robert are between us. It is breaking-up night at Margaret's school, and she has gone to it with Robert," continued Jane, never doubting but the stranger must take as much interest in "breaking-up nights" as she did. "I was to have gone; but mamma has been unusually ill to-day."

"Were you disappointed?"

Jane bent her head while she confessed the fact, as though feeling it a confession to be ashamed of. "It would not have been kind to leave mamma," she added, "and I dare say some other pleasure will arise soon. Mamma is asleep now."

"What a charming girl!" thought Mr. Halliburton to himself. "How I wish she was my sister!"

"Margaret is to be a governess," observed Jane, "and is being educated for it. She has great talent for music, and also for drawing; it is not often the two are united. Her tastes lie quite that way—anything clever; and as papa has no money to give us, it was well to make her a governess."

"And you?" said Mr. Halliburton. The question might have been thought an impertinent one by many, but he spoke it only in his deep interest, and Jane Tait was of too ingenuous a disposition not to answer it as openly.

"I am not to be a governess. I am to stay at home with mamma and help her. There is plenty to do. Margaret cannot bear domestic duties, or sewing either. Dancing excepted, I have not learnt a single accomplishment—unless you call French an accomplishment."

"I am sure you have been well educated!" involuntarily spoke Mr. Halliburton.

"Yes; in all things solid," replied Jane. "Papa has taken care of that. He still directs my reading. I know a good bit—of—Latin"—she added, bringing out the concluding words with hesitation, as one who repents his sentence—"though I do not like to confess it to you."

"Why do you not?"

"Because I think girls who know Latin are laughed at. I did not regularly learn it, but I used to be in the room when papa or Mr. Acton was teaching Francis and Robert, and I picked it up unconsciously. Mr. Acton often took Francis; he had more time on his hands than papa. Francis is to be a clergyman."

"Miss Jane," said a servant, entering the room, "Mrs. Tait is awake, and wishes to see you."

Jane left Mr. Halliburton with a word of apology, and almost immediately after Mr. Tait came in. He was a little taken to when he saw the stranger. His imagination had run, if not upon an "old guy" in spectacles, certainly upon some steady, sober, middle-aged mathematical master. Would it be well to admit this young, good-looking man to his house.

If Jane Tait had been candid in her revelations to Mr. Halliburton, that gentleman, in his turn, was not less candid to her father. He, Edgar Halliburton, was the only child of a country clergyman, the Rev. William Halliburton, who had died when Edgar was sixteen, leaving nothing behind him. Edgar—he had previously lost his mother—found a home with his late mother's brother, a gentleman named Cooper, who resided in Birmingham. Mr. Cooper was a man in extensive wholesale business, and wished Edgar to go into his counting-house. Edgar declined. His father had lived long enough to form his tastes: his greatest wish had been to see him enter the Church; and the wish had become Edgar's own. Mr. Cooper thought there was nothing in the world like business: and looked upon that most sacred of all callings, God's ministry, only in the light of a profession. He had carved out his own career, step by step, attaining wealth and importance, and wished his nephew to do the same. "Which is best, lad?" he coarsely asked: "To rule as a merchant prince, or starve and toil as a curate? I'm not quite a merchant prince yet, but you may be." "It was my father's wish," pleaded Edgar in answer, "and it is my own. I cannot give it up, sir." The dispute ran high—not in words, but in obstinacy. Edgar would not yield, and at length Mr. Cooper discarded him. He turned him out of doors: told him that, if he must become a parson, he might get some one else to pay his expenses at Oxford, for he never would. Edgar Halliburton proceeded to London, and obtained employment as an usher in a school, teaching classics and mathematics. From that he became a private teacher, and had so earned his living up to the present time: but he had never succeeded in getting to college. And Mr. Tait, before they had talked together five minutes, was charmed with his visitor, and invited him to take tea with him, which Jane came down to make.

"Has your uncle never softened towards you?" Mr. Tait inquired.

"Never. I have addressed several letters to him, but they have been returned to me."

"He has no family, you say. You ought—in justice, you ought to inherit some of his wealth. Has he other relatives?"

"He has one standing to him in the same relationship as I—my Cousin Julia. It is not likely that I shall ever inherit a shilling of it, sir. I do not expect it."

"Right," said Mr. Tait, nodding his head approvingly. "There's no work so thriftless as that of waiting for legacies. Wearying, too. I was a poor curate, Mr. Halliburton, for twenty years—indeed, so far as being poor goes, I am not much else now—but let that pass. I had a relative who possessed money, and who had neither kith nor kin nearer to her than I was. For the best part of those twenty years I was giving covert hopes to that money; and when she died, and NOTHING was left to me, I found out how foolish and wasteful my hopes had been. I tell my children to trust to their own honest exertions, but never to trust to other people's money. Allow me to urge the same upon you."

Mr. Halliburton's lips and eyes alike smiled, as he looked gratefully at the rector, a man so much older than himself. "I never think of it," he earnestly said. "It appears, for me, to be as thoroughly lost as though it did not exist. I should not have mentioned it, sir, but that I consider it right you should know all particulars respecting me; if, as I hope, you will admit me to your home."

"I think we should get on very well together," frankly acknowledged Mr. Tait, forgetting the prudent ideas which had crossed his mind.

"I am sure we should, sir," warmly replied Edgar Halliburton. And the bargain was made.

CHAPTER II

THE SHADOW BECOMES SUBSTANCE

And yet it had perhaps been well that those prudent ideas had been allowed to obtain weight. Mr. Halliburton took up his abode with the Taits; and, the more they saw of him, the more they liked him. In which liking Jane must be included.

It was a possible shadow of the future, the effects the step would bring forth, which had whispered determent to Mr. Tait: a very brief shadow, which had crossed his mind imperfectly, and flitted away again. Where two young and attractive beings are thrown into daily companionship, the result too frequently is that a mutual regard arises, stronger than any other regard can ever be in this world. This result arrived here.

A twelvemonth passed over from the time of Mr. Halliburton's entrance—how swiftly for him and for Jane Tait they alone could tell. Not a word had been spoken to her by Mr. Halliburton that he might not have spoken to her mother or her sister Margaret; not a look on Jane's part had been given by which he could infer that he was more to her than the rest of the world. And yet both were inwardly conscious of the feelings of the other; and when the twelvemonth had gone by it had seemed to them but a span, for the love they bore each other.

One evening in December Jane stood in the dining-room waiting to make tea just as she had so waited that former evening. For any outward signs, you might have thought that not a single hour had elapsed since their first introduction—that it was the same evening as of old. It was sloppy outside, it was bright within. The candles stood on the table unlighted, the fire blazed, the tea-tray was placed, and only Jane was there. Mrs. Tait was upstairs with one of her frequent sick-headaches, Margaret was with her, and the others had not come in.

Jane stood in a reverie—her elbow resting on the mantel-piece, and the blaze from the fire flickering on her gentle face. She was fond of these few minutes of idleness on a winter's evening, between the twilight hour and lighting the candles.

The clock in the kitchen struck five. It did not arouse her: she heard it in a mechanical sort of manner, without taking note of it. Scarcely had the sound of the last stroke died away when there was a knock at the front door.

That aroused her—for she knew it. She knew the footsteps that came in when it was answered, and a rich damask arose to her cheeks, and the pulses of her heart went on a little quicker than they had been going before.

She took her elbow from the mantel-piece, and sat down quietly on a chair. No need to look who entered. Some one, taller by far than any in that house, came up to the fire, and bent to warm his hands over the blaze.

"It is a cold night, Jane. We shall have a severe frost."

"Yes," she answered; "the water in the barrel is already freezing over."

"How is your mamma now?"

"Better, thank you. Margaret has gone up to help her to dress. She is coming down to tea."

Mr. Halliburton remained silent a minute, and then turned to Jane, his face glowing with satisfaction. "I have had a piece of preferment offered me to-day."

"Have you?" she eagerly said. "What is it?"

"Dr. Percy proposes that, from January, I shall take the Greek classes as well as the mathematics, and he doubles my salary. Of course I shall have to give closer attendance, but I can readily do that. My time is not fully employed."

"I am very glad," said Jane.

"So am I," he answered. "Taking all my sources of income together, I shall now be earning two hundred and eighty-three pounds a year."

Jane laughed. "Have you been reckoning it up?"

"Ay; I had a motive in doing so."

His tone was peculiar, and it caused her to look at him, but her eyelids drooped under his gaze. He drew nearer, and laid his hand gently on her shoulder, bending down before her to speak.

"Jane, you have not mistaken me. I feel that you have read what has been in my heart, what have been my intentions, as surely as though I had spoken. It is not a great income, but it is sufficient, if you can think it so. May I speak to Mr. Tait?"

What Jane would have contrived to answer she never knew, but at that moment her mother's step was heard approaching. All she did was to glance shyly up at Mr. Halliburton, and he bent his head lower and kissed her. Then he walked rapidly to the door and opened it for Mrs. Tait—a pale, refined, delicate-looking lady, wrapped in a shawl. These violent headaches, from which she so frequently suffered, did not affect her permanent health, but on the days she suffered she would be utterly prostrated. Mr. Halliburton gave her his arm, and led her to a seat by the fire, his voice low and tender, his manner sympathizing. "I am already better," she said to him, "and shall be much better after tea. Sometimes I am tempted to envy those who do not know what a sick-headache is."

"They may know other maladies as painful, dear Mrs. Tait."

"Ay, indeed. None of us can expect to be free from pain of one sort or another in this world."

"Shall I make the tea, mamma?" asked Jane.

"Yes, dear; I shall be glad of it, and your papa is sure to be in soon. There he is!" she added, as the latch-key was heard in the door. "The boys are late this evening."

The rector came in, and, ere the evening was over, the news was broken to him by Mr. Halliburton. He wanted Jane.

It was the imperfect, uncertain shadow of twelve months ago become substance. It had been a shadow of the future only, you understand—not a shadow of evil. To Mr. Halliburton, personally, the rector had no objection—he had learned to love, esteem, and respect him—but it is a serious thing to give away a child.

"The income is very small to marry upon," he observed. "It is also uncertain."

"Not uncertain, sir, so long as I am blessed with health and strength. And I have no reason to fear that these will fail."

"I thought you were bent on taking Orders."

Mr. Halliburton's cheek slightly flushed. "It is a prospect I have fondly cherished," he said; "but its difficulties alarm me. The cost of the University is great; and were I to wait until I had saved sufficient money to go to college, I should be obliged, in a great degree, to give up my present means of living. Who would employ a tutor who must frequently be away for weeks? I should lose my connection, and perhaps never regain it. A good teaching connection is more easily lost than won."

"True," observed Mr. Tait.

"Once in Orders, I might remain for years a poor curate. I should most likely do so. I have neither interest nor influence. Sir, in that case Jane and I might be obliged to wait for years: perhaps go down to our graves waiting."

The Rev. Francis Tait threw back his thoughts. How he had waited; how he was not able to marry until years were advancing upon him; how in four years now he should have attained threescore years and ten—the term allotted to the life of man—whilst his children were still growing up around him! No! never, never would he counsel another to wait as he had been obliged to wait.

"I have not yet given up hope of eventually entering the Church," continued Mr. Halliburton; "though it must be accomplished, if at all, slowly and patiently. I think I may be able to keep one term, or perhaps two terms yearly, without damage to my teaching. I shall try to do so; try to find the necessary means and time. My marriage will make no difference to that, sir."

Many might have suggested to Edgar Halliburton that he might keep his terms first and marry afterwards. Mr. Tait did not: possibly the idea did not occur to him. If it occurred to Edgar Halliburton himself, he drove it from him. It would have delayed his marriage to an indefinite number of years; and he loved Jane too well to do that willingly. "I shall still get much better preferment in teaching than that which I now hold," he urged aloud to the rector. "It is not so very small to begin upon, sir, and Jane is willing to risk it."

"I will not part you and Jane," said Mr. Tait, warmly. "If you have made up your minds to share life and its cares together, you shall do so. Still, I cannot say that I think your prospects golden."

"Prospects that appear to have no gold at all in them sometimes turn out very brightly, sir."

"I can give Jane nothing, you know."

"I have never cast a thought to it, sir; have never imagined she would have a shilling," replied Mr. Halliburton, his face flushing with eagerness. "It is Jane herself I want; not money."

"Beyond a twenty-pound note which I may give her to put into her purse on her wedding morning, that she may not leave my house absolutely penniless, she will have nothing," cried the rector, in his straightforward manner. "Far from saving, I and her mother have been hardly able to make both ends meet at the end of the year. I might have saved a few pounds yearly, had I chosen to do so; but you know what this parish is; and the reflection has always been upon me: how would my Master look upon my putting by small sums of money, when many of those over whom I am placed were literally starving for bread? I have given what I could; but I have not saved for my children."

"You have done well, sir."

Mr. Tait sought his daughter. "Jane," he began—"Nay, child, do not tremble so! There is no need for trembling, or for tears, either: you have done nothing to displease me. Jane, I like Edgar Halliburton; I like him much. There is no one to whom I would rather give you. But I do not like his prospects. Teaching is very precarious."

Jane raised her timid eyes. "Precarious for him, papa? For one learned and clever as he!"

"It is badly paid. See how he toils—and he will have to toil more when the new year comes in—and only to earn two or three hundred a year!—in round numbers."

Tears gathered in Jane's eyes. Toil as he did, badly paid as he might be, she would rather have him than any other in the world, though that other might have revelled in thousands. The rector read somewhat of this in her downcast face.

"My dear, the consideration lies with you. If you choose to venture upon it, you shall have my consent, and I know you will have your mother's, for she thinks Edgar Halliburton has not his equal in the world. But it may bring you many troubles."

"Papa, I am not afraid. If troubles come, they—you—told us only last night—"

"What, child?"

"That troubles, regarded rightly, only lead us nearer to God," whispered Jane, simply and timidly.

"Right, child. And trouble must come before that great truth can be realized. Consider the question well, Jane—whether it may not be better to wait—and give your answer to-morrow. I shall tell Mr. Halliburton not to ask for it to-night. As you decide, so shall it be."

Need you be told what Jane's decision was? Two hundred and eighty-three pounds a year seems a large sum to an inexperienced girl; quite sufficient to purchase everything that might be wanted for a fireside.

And so she became Jane Halliburton.

CHAPTER III

THE REV. FRANCIS TAIT

A hot afternoon in July. Jane Halliburton was in the drawing-room with her mother, both sewing busily. It was a large room, with three windows, more pleasant than the dining-room beneath, and they were fond of sitting in it in summer. Jane had been married some three or four months now, but looked the same young, simple, placid girl that she ever did; and, but for the wedding-ring upon her finger, no stranger would have supposed her to be a wife.

An excellent arrangement had been arrived at—that she and her husband should remain inmates of Mr. Tait's house; at any rate, for the present. When plans were being discussed, before making the necessary arrangements for the marriage, and Mr. Halliburton was spending all his superfluous minutes hunting for a suitable house near to the old home, and not too dear, Francis Tait had given utterance to a remark—"I wonder who we shall get here in Mr. Halliburton's place, if papa takes any one else?" and Margaret, looking up from her drawing, had added, "Why can't Mr. Halliburton and Jane stay on with us? It would be so much pleasanter."

It was the first time the idea had been presented in any shape to the rector, and it seemed to go straight to his wishes. He put down a book he was reading, and spoke impulsively. "It would be the best thing; the very best thing! Would you like it, Halliburton?"

"I should, sir; very much. But it is Jane who must be consulted, not me."

Jane, her pretty cheeks covered with blushes, looked up and said she should like it also; she had thought of it, but had not liked to mention it, either to her mother or to Mr. Halliburton. "I have been quite troubled to think what mamma and the house will do without me," she added, ingenuously.

"Let Jane alone for thinking and planning, when difficulties are in the way," laughed Margaret. "My opinion is that we shall never get another pudding, or papa have his black silk Sunday hose darned, if Jane goes from us."

Mrs. Tait burst into tears. Like Margaret she was a bad manager, and had mourned over Jane's departure, secretly believing she should be half worried to death. "Oh! Jane, dear, say you'll remain!" she cried. "It will be such a relief to me! Margaret's of no earthly use, and everything will fall on my shoulders. Edgar, I hope you will remain with us! It will be pleasant for all. You know the house is sufficiently large."

And remain they did. The wedding took place at Easter, and Mr. Halliburton took Jane all the way to Dover to see the sea—a long way in those days—and kept her there for a week. And then they came back again, Jane to her old home duties, just as though she were Jane Tait still, and Mr. Halliburton to his teaching.

It was July now and hot weather; and Mrs. Tait and Jane were sewing in the drawing-room. They were working for Margaret. Mr. Halliburton, through some of his teaching connections, had obtained an excellent situation for Margaret in a first-rate school. Margaret was to enter as resident pupil, and receive every advantage towards the completion of her own education; in return for which she was to teach the younger pupils music, and pay ten pounds a year. Such an arrangement was almost unknown then, though it has been common enough since, and Mr. and Mrs. Tait thought of it very highly. Margaret Tait was only sixteen; but, as if in contrast to Jane, who looked younger than her actual years, Margaret looked older. In appearance, in manners, and also in advancement, Margaret might have been eighteen.

She was to enter the school, which was near Harrow, in another week, at the termination of the holidays, and Mrs. Tait and Jane had their hands full, getting her things ready.

"Was this slip measured, mamma?" Jane suddenly asked, after attentively regarding the work she had on her knee.

"I think so," replied Mrs. Tait. "Why?"

"It looks too short for Margaret. At least it will be too short when I have finished this fourth tuck. It must have been measured, though, for here are the pins in it. Perhaps Margaret measured it herself."

"Then of course it must be measured again. There's no trusting to anything Margaret does in the shape of work. And yet, how clever she is at music and drawing—in fact at all her studies!" added Mrs. Tait. "It is well, Jane, that we are not all gifted alike."

"I think it is," acquiesced Jane. "I will go up to Margaret's room for one of her slips, and measure this."

"You need not do that," said Mrs. Tait. "There's an old slip of hers amongst the work on the sofa."

Jane found the slip, and measured the one in her hand by it. "Yes, mamma! It is just the length without the tuck. Then I must take out what I have done of it. It is very little."

"Come hither, Jane. Your eyes are younger than mine. Is not that your papa coming towards us from the far end of the square?"

Jane approached the window nearest to her, not the one at which Mrs. Tait was sitting. "Oh, yes, that's papa. You might tell him by his dress, if by nothing else, mamma."

"I could tell him by himself, if I could see," said Mrs. Tait, quaintly. "I don't know how it is, Jane, but my sight grows very imperfect for a distance."

"Never mind that, mamma, so that you can continue to see well to work and read," said Jane cheerily. "How fast papa is walking!"

Very fast for the Rev. Francis Tait, who was not in general a quick walker. He entered his house, and came up to the drawing-room. He had not been well for the last few days, and threw himself into a chair, wearily.

"Jane, is there any of that beef-tea left, that was made for me yesterday?"

"Yes, papa," she said, springing up that she might get it for him. "I will bring it to you immediately."

"Stay, stay, child, not so fast," he interrupted. "It is not for myself. I can do without it. I have been pained by a sad sight," he added, looking at his wife. "There's that daughter of the Widow Booth's come home again. I called in upon them and there she was, lying on a mattress, dying from famine, as I verily believe. She returned last night in a dreadful state of exhaustion, the mother says, and has had nothing within her lips since but cold water. They tried her with solid food, but she could not swallow it. That beef-tea will just do for her. Have it warmed, Jane."

"She is a sinful, ill-doing girl, Francis," remarked Mrs. Tait, "and does not really deserve compassion."

"All the more reason, wife, that she should be rescued from death," said the rector, almost sternly. "The good may dare to die: the evil may not. Don't waste time, Jane. Put it into a bottle, warm, and I'll carry it round."

"Is there nothing else we can send her, papa, that may do for her equally well?" asked Jane. "A little wine, perhaps? There is very little of the beef-tea left, and it ought to be kept for you."

"Never mind; I wish to take it to her," said the rector. "A little wine afterwards may do her good."

Jane hastened to the kitchen, disturbing a servant who was doing something over the fire. "Susan, papa wants the remainder of the beef-tea warmed. Will you make haste and do it, whilst I search for a bottle to put it into? It is to be taken round to Charity Booth."

"What! is she back again?" exclaimed the servant, slightingly, which betrayed that her estimation of Charity Booth was no higher than was that of her mistress. "It's just like the master," she continued, proceeding to do what was required of her. "It's not often that anything's made for himself; but if it is, he never gets the benefit of it; he's sure to drop across somebody that he fancies wants it worse than he does. It's not right, Miss Jane."

Jane was searching a cupboard, and brought forth a clean green bottle, which held about half-a-pint. "This will be quite large enough, I think."

"I should think it would!" grumbled Susan, who could not be brought to look upon the giving away of her master's own peculiar property as anything but a personal grievance. "There's barely a gill of it left, and he ought to have had it himself, Miss Jane."

"Susan," she said, turning her bright face laughingly towards the woman, "it is a good thing that you went to church and saw me married, or I might think you meant to reflect upon me. How can I be 'Miss Jane,' with this ring on?"

"It's of no good my trying to remember it, ma'am. All the parish knows you are Mrs. Halliburton, fast enough; but it don't come ready to me."

Jane laughed pleasantly. "Where is Mary?" she asked.

"In the back room, going on with some of Miss Margaret's things. It's cooler, sitting there, than in this hot kitchen."

Jane carried the little bottle of beef-tea to her father, and gave it into his hand. He looked very pale, and rose from his chair slowly.

"Oh, papa, you do not seem well!" she involuntarily exclaimed. "Let me run and beat you up an egg. I will not be a minute."

"I can't wait, child. And I question if I could eat it, were it ready before me. I do not feel well, as you say."

"You ought to have taken this beef-tea yourself, papa. It was made for you."

Jane could not help laying a stress upon the word. Mr. Tait placed his hand gently upon her smoothly parted hair. "Jane, child, had I thought of myself before others throughout life, how should I have been following my Master's precepts?"

She ran down the stairs before him, opening the front door for him to pass through, that even that little exertion should be spared him. A loving, dutiful daughter was Jane; and it is probable that the thought of her worth especially crossed the mind of the rector at that moment. "God bless you, my child!" he aspirated, as he passed her.

Jane watched him across the square. Their house, though not actually in the square, commanded a view of it. Then she returned upstairs to her mother. "Papa thinks he will not lose time," she observed. "He is walking fast."

"I should call it running," responded Mrs. Tait, who had seen the speed from the window. "But, my dear, he'll do no good with that badly conducted Charity Booth."

About an hour passed away, and it was drawing towards dinner-time. Jane and Mrs. Tait were busy as ever, when Mr. Halliburton's well-known knock was heard.

"Edgar is home early this morning!" Jane exclaimed.

He came springing up the stairs, two at a time, in great haste, opened the drawing-room door, and just put in his head. Mrs. Tait, sitting with her back to the door and her face to the window, did not turn round, and consequently did not see him. Jane did; and was startled. Every vestige of colour had forsaken his face.

"Oh, Edgar! You are ill!"

"Ill! Not I," affecting to speak gaily. "I want you for a minute, Jane."

Mrs. Tait had looked round at Jane's exclamation, but Mr. Halliburton's face was then withdrawn. He was standing outside the door when Jane went out. He did not speak; but took her hand in silence and drew her into the back room, which was their own bedroom, and closed the door. Jane's face had grown as white as his.

"My darling, I did not mean to alarm you," he said, holding her to him. "I thought you had a brave heart, Jane. I thought that if I had a little unpleasant news to impart it would be best to tell you, that you may help me break it to the rest."

Jane's heart was not feeling very brave. "What is it?" she asked, scarcely able to speak the words from her ghastly lips.

"Jane," he said, tenderly and gravely, "before I say any more, you must strive for calmness."

"It is not about yourself! You are not ill?"

The question seemed superfluous. Mr. Halliburton was evidently not ill; but he was agitated. Jane was frightened and perplexed: not a glimpse of the real truth crossed her. "Tell me what it is at once, Edgar," she said, in a calmer tone. "I can bear certainty better than suspense."

"Why, yes, I think you are becoming brave already," he answered, looking straight into her eyes and smiling—which was intended to reassure her. "I must have my wife show herself a woman to-day; not a child. See what a bungler I am! I thought to tell you all quietly and smoothly, without alarming you; and see what I have done!—startled you to terror."

Jane smiled faintly. She knew all this was only the precursor of tidings that must be very ill and grievous. By a great effort she schooled herself to calmness. Mr. Halliburton continued:

"One, whom you and I love very much, has—has—met with an accident, Jane."

Her fears went straight to the right quarter at once. With that one exception by her side, there was no one she loved as she loved her father.

"Papa?"

"Yes. We must break it to Mrs. Tait."

Her heart beat wildly against his hand, and the livid hue was once more overspreading her face. But she strove urgently for calmness: he whispered to her of its necessity for her own sake.

"Edgar! is it death?"

It was death; but he would not tell her so yet. He plunged into the attendant details.

"He was hastening along with a small bottle in his hand, Jane. It contained something good for one of the sick poor, I am sure, for he was in their neighbourhood. Suddenly he was observed to fall; and the spectators raised him and took him to a doctor's. That doctor, unfortunately, was not at home, and they took him to another, so that time was lost. He was quite unconscious."

"But you do not tell me!" she wailed. "Is he dead?"

Mr. Halliburton asked himself a question—What good would be done by delaying the truth? He thought he had performed his task very badly. "Jane, Jane!" he whispered, "I can only hope to help you to bear it better than I have broken it to you."

She could not shed tears in that first awful moment: physically and mentally she leaned on him for support. "How can we tell my mother?"

It was necessary that Mrs. Tait should be told, and without delay. Even then the body was being conveyed to the house. By a curious coincidence, Mr. Halliburton had been passing the last doctor's surgery at the very moment the crowd was round its doors. Unusual business had called him there; or it was a street he did not enter once in a year. "The parson has fallen down in a fit," said some of them, recognizing and arresting him.

"The parson!" he repeated. "What! Mr. Tait?"

"Sure enough," said they. And Mr. Halliburton pressed into the surgeon's house just as the examination was over.

"The heart, no doubt, sir," said the doctor to him.

"He surely is not dead?"

"Quite dead. He must have died instantaneously."

The news had been wafted to the mob outside, and they were already taking a shutter from its hinges. "I will go on first and prepare the family," said Mr. Halliburton to them. "Give me a quarter of an hour's start, and then come on."

So that he had only a quarter of an hour for it all. His thoughts naturally turned to his wife: not simply to spare her alarm and pain, so far as he might, but he believed her, young as she was, to possess more calmness and self-control than Mrs. Tait. As he sped to the house he rehearsed his task; and might have accomplished it better but for his tell-tale face. "Jane," he whispered, "let this be your consolation ever: he was ready to go."

"Oh yes!" she answered, bursting into a storm of most distressing tears. "If any one here was ever fit for heaven, it was my dear father."

"Hark!" exclaimed Mr. Halliburton.

Some noise had arisen downstairs—a sound of voices speaking in undertones. There could be no doubt that people had come to the house with the news, and were imparting it to the two trembling servants.

"There's not a moment to be lost, Jane."

How Jane dried her eyes and suppressed all temporary sign of grief and emotion, she could not tell. A sense of duty was strong within her, and she knew that the most imperative duty of the present moment was the support and solace of her mother. She and her husband entered the drawing-room together, and Mrs. Tait turned with a smile to Mr. Halliburton.

"What secrets have you and Jane been talking together?" Then, catching sight of Jane's white and quivering lips, she broke into a cry of agony. "Jane! what has happened? What have you both come to tell me?"

The tears poured from Jane's fair young face as she clasped her mother fondly to her, tenderly whispering: "Dearest mamma, you must lean upon us now! We will all love you and take care of you as we have never yet done."

CHAPTER IV

NEW PLANS

The post-mortem examination established beyond doubt the fact that the Rev. Francis Tait's death was caused by heart disease. In the earlier period of his life it had been suspected that he was subject to it, but of late years unfavourable symptoms had not shown themselves.

With him died of course almost all his means; and his family, if not left utterly destitute, had little to boast in the way of wealth. Mrs. Tait enjoyed, and had for some time enjoyed, an annuity of fifty pounds a year; but it would cease at her death, whenever that event should take place. What was she to do with her children? Many a bereaved widow, far worse off than Mrs. Tait, has to ask the same perplexing question every day. Mrs. Tait's children were partially off her hands. Jane had her husband; Francis was earning his own living as an under-master in a school; with Margaret ten pounds a year must be paid; and there was still Robert.

The death had occurred in July. By October they must be away from the house. "You will be at no loss for a home, Mrs. Tait," Mr. Halliburton took an opportunity of kindly saying to her. "You must allow me and Jane to welcome you to ours."

"Yes, Edgar," was Mrs. Tait's unhesitating reply; "it will be the best plan. The furniture in this house will do for yours, and you shall have it, and you must take me and my small means into it—an incumbrance to you. I have pondered it all over, and I do not see anything else that can be done."

"I have no right whatever to your furniture," he replied, "and Jane has no more right to it than have your other children. The furniture shall be put into my house if you please; but you must either allow me to pay you for it, or it shall remain your own, to be removed again at any time you may please."

A house was looked for and taken. The furniture was valued, and Mr. Halliburton bought it—a fourth part of the sum Mrs. Tait positively refusing to take, for she declared that so much belonged to Jane. Then they quitted the old house of many years, and moved into the new one: Mr. and Mrs. Halliburton, Mrs. Tait, Robert, and the two servants.

"Will it be prudent for you, my dear, to retain both the servants?" Mrs. Tait asked of her daughter.

Jane blushed vividly. "We could do with one at present, mamma; but the time will be coming that I shall require two. And Susan and Mary are both so good that I do not care to part with them. You are used to them, too."

"Ah, child! I know that in all your plans and schemes you and Edgar think first of my comfort. Do you know what I was thinking of last night as I lay in bed?"

"What, mamma?"

"When Mr. Halliburton first spoke of wanting you, I and your poor papa felt inclined to hesitate, thinking you might have made a better match. But, my dear, I was wondering last night what we should have done in this crisis but for him."

"Yes," said Jane, gently. "Things that appear untoward at the time frequently turn out afterwards to have been the very best that could have happened. God directs all things, you know, mamma."

A contention arose respecting Robert, some weeks after they had been in their new house—or it may be better to call it a discussion. Robert had never taken very kindly to what he called book-learning. Mr. Tait's wish had been that both his sons should enter the Church. Robert had never openly opposed this wish, and for the calling itself he had a liking; but particularly disliked the study and application necessary to fit him for it. Silent while his father lived, he was so no longer; but took every opportunity of urging the point upon his mother. He was still attending Dr. Percy's school daily.

"You know, mother," dropping down one day in a chair, close to his mother and Jane, and catching up one leg to nurse—rather a favourite action of his—"I shall never earn salt at it."

"Salt at what, Robert?" asked Mrs. Tait.

"Why, at these rubbishing classics. I shall never make a tutor, as Mr. Halliburton and Francis do; and what on earth's to become of me? As to any chance of my being a parson, of course that's over: where's the money to come from?"

"What is to become of you, then?" cried Mrs. Tait. "I'm sure I don't know."

"Besides," went on Robert, lowering his voice, and calling up the most effectual argument he could think of, "I ought to be doing something for myself. I am living here upon Mr. Halliburton."

"He is delighted to have you, Robert," interrupted Jane, quickly. "Mamma pays—"

"Be quiet, Mrs. Jane! What sort of a wife do you call yourself, pray, to go against your husband's interests in that manner? I heard you preaching up to the charity children the other day about its being sinful to waste time."

"Well?" said Jane.

"Well! what's waste of time for other people is not waste of time for me, I suppose?" went on Robert.

"You are not wasting your time, Robert."

"I am. And if you had the sense people give you credit for, Madam Jane, you'd see it. I shall never, I say, earn my salt at teaching; and—just tell me yourself whether there seems any chance now that I shall enter the Church."

"At present I do not see that there is," confessed Jane.

"There! Then is it waste of time, or not, my continuing to study for a career which I can never enter upon?"

"But what else can you do, Robert?" interposed Mrs. Tait. "You cannot idle your time away at home, or be running about the streets all day."

"No," said Robert, "better stop at school for ever than do that. I want to see the world, mother."

"You—want—to—see—the—world!" echoed Mrs. Tait, bringing out the words slowly in her astonishment, whilst Jane looked up from her work, and fixed her eyes upon her brother.

"It's only natural that I should," said Robert, with equanimity. "I have an invitation to go down into Yorkshire."

"What to do?" cried Mrs. Tait.

"Oh, lots of things. They keep hunters, and—"

"Why, you were never on horseback in your life, Robert," laughed Jane. "You would come back with your neck broken."

"I do wish you'd be quiet, Jane!" returned Robert, reddening. "I am talking to mamma, not to you. Winchcombe has invited me to spend the Christmas holidays with him down at his father's place in Yorkshire. And, mother, I want to go; and I want you to promise that I shall not return to school when the holidays are over. I will do anything else that you choose to put me to. I'll learn to be a man of business, or I'll go into an office, or I'd be apprenticed to a doctor—anything you like, rather than stop at these everlasting school-books. I am sick of them."

"Robert, you take my breath away!" uttered Mrs. Tait. "I have no interest anywhere. I could not get you into any of these places."

"I dare say Mr. Halliburton could. He knows lots of people. Jane, you talk to him: he'll do anything for you."

There ensued, I say, much discussion about

Robert. But it is not with Robert Tait that our story has to do; and only a few words need be given to him here and there. It appeared to them all that it would be inexpedient for him to continue at school; both with regard to his own wishes and to his prospects. He was allowed to pay the visit with his schoolfellow, and (as he came back with neck unbroken) Mr. Halliburton succeeded in placing him in a large wholesale warehouse. Robert appeared to like it very much at first, and always came home to spend Sunday with them.

"He may rise in time to be one of the first mercantile men in London," observed Mr. Halliburton to his wife; "one of our merchant-princes, as my uncle used to say by me, if only—"

"If what? Why do you hesitate?" she asked.

"If he will only persevere, I was going to say. But, Jane, I fear perseverance is a quality that Robert does not possess."

Of course all that had to be proved. It lay in the future.

CHAPTER V

MARGARET

From two to three years passed away, and the Midsummer holidays were approaching. Margaret was expected as usual for them, and Jane, delighted to receive her, went about her glad preparations. Margaret would not return to the school, in which she had been a paid teacher for the last year; but was to enter a family as governess. For one efficient, well-educated, accomplished governess to be met with in those days, scores may be counted now—or who profess to be so; and Margaret Tait, though barely nineteen, anticipated a salary of seventy or eighty guineas a year.

A warm, bright day in June, that on which Mr. Halliburton went to receive Margaret. The coach brought her to its resting-place, the "Bull and Mouth," in St. Martin's-le-Grand, and Mr. Halliburton reached the inn as St. Paul's clock was striking midday. One minute more, and the coach drove in.

There she was, inside; a tall, fine girl, with a handsome face: a face full of resolution and energy. Margaret Tait had her good qualities, and she had also her faults: a great one, speaking of the latter, was self-will. She opened the door herself and leaped out before any one could help her, all joy and delight.

"And what about your boxes, Margaret?" questioned Mr. Halliburton, after a few words of greeting. "Have they come this time or not?"

Margaret laughed. "Yes, they really have. I have not lost them on the road, as I did at Christmas. You will never forget to tell me of that, I am sure! But it was more the guard's fault than mine."

A few minutes, and Mr. Halliburton, Margaret, and the boxes were lumbering along in one of the old glass coaches.

"And now tell me about every one," said Margaret. "How is dear mamma?"

"She is quite well. We are all well. Jane's famous."

"And my precious little Willy?"

"Oh," said Mr. Halliburton, quaintly, "he is a great deal too troublesome for anything to be the matter with him. I tell Jane she will have to begin the whipping system soon."

"And much Jane will attend to you! Is it a pretty baby?"

Mr. Halliburton raised his eyebrows. "Jane thinks so. I wonder she has not had its likeness taken."

"Is it christened?" continued Margaret.

"It is baptized. Jane would not have the christening until you were at home."

"And its name?"

"Jane."

"What a shame! Jane promised me it should be Margaret. Why did she decide upon her own name?"

"I decided upon it," said Mr. Halliburton. "Yours can wait until the next, Margaret."

Margaret laughed. "And how are you getting on?"

"Very well. I have every hour of the day occupied."

"I don't think you are looking well," rejoined Margaret. "You look thin and fagged."

"I am always thin, and mine is a fagging profession. Sometimes I feel terribly weary. But I am pretty well upon the whole, Margaret."

"Will Francis be at home these holidays?"

"No. He passes them at a gentleman's house in Norfolk—tutor to his sons. Francis is thoroughly industrious and persevering."

"A contrast to poor Robert, I suppose?"

"Well—yes; in that sense."

"There has been some trouble about Robert, has there not?" asked Margaret, her tone becoming grave. "Did he not get discharged?"

"He received notice of discharge. But I saw the principals and begged him on again. I would not talk about it to him if I were you, Margaret. He is sensitive upon the point. Robert's intentions are good, but his disposition is fickle. He has grown tired of his work and idles his time away; no house of business will put up with that."

The coach arrived at Mr. Halliburton's. Margaret rushed out of it, giving no one time to assist her, as she had done out of the other coach at the "Bull and Mouth." There was a great deal of impetuosity in Margaret Tait's character. She was quite a contrast to Jane—as she had just remarked there was a contrast between Francis and Robert upon other points—to sensible, lady-like, self-possessed Jane, who came forward so calmly to greet her, a glad depth of affection in her quiet eyes.

A boisterous embrace to her mother, a boisterous embrace to Jane, all in haste, and then Margaret caught up a little gentleman of some two years old, or more, who was standing holding on to Jane's dress, his great grey eyes, honest, loving, intelligent as were his mother's, cast up in a broad stare at Margaret.

"You naughty Willy! Have you forgotten Aunt Margaret? Oh, you darling child! Who's this?"

She carried the boy up to the end of the room, where stood their old servant Mary, nursing an infant of two months old. The baby had great grey eyes also, and they likewise were bent on noisy Margaret. "Oh, Willy, she is prettier than you! I won't nurse you any more. Mary, I'll shake hands with you presently. I must take that enchanting baby first."

Dropping discarded Willy upon the ground, snatching the baby from Mary's arms, Margaret kissed its pretty face until she made it cry. Jane came to the rescue.

"You don't understand babies, Margaret. Let Mary take her again. Come upstairs to your room, and make yourself ready for dinner. I think you must be hungry."

"So hungry that I shall frighten you. Of course, with the thought of coming home, I could not touch breakfast. I hope you have something especially nice!"

"Your favourite dinner," said Jane, smiling. "Loin of veal and broccoli."

"How thoughtful you are, Jane!" Margaret could not help exclaiming.

"Margaret, my dear," called out her mother, as she was leaving the room with Jane.

Margaret looked back. "What, mamma?"

"I hope you will not continue to go on with these children as you have begun; otherwise we shall have a quiet house turned into a noisy one."

"Is it a quiet house?" said Margaret, laughing.

"As if any house would not be quiet, regulated by Jane!" replied Mrs. Tait. And Margaret, laughing still, followed her sister.

It is curious to remark how differently things sometimes turn out from what we intended. Had any one asked Mrs. Tait, the day that Margaret came home, what Margaret's future career was to be, she had wondered at the question. "A governess, certainly," would have been her answer; and she would have thought that no power, humanly speaking, could prevent it. And yet, Margaret Tait, as it proved, never did become a governess.

The holidays were drawing to an end, and a very desirable situation, as was believed, had been found for Margaret by Mr. Halliburton, the negotiations for which were nearly completed. Mr. Halliburton gave private lessons in sundry well-connected families, and thus enabled to hear where ladies were required as governesses, he had recommended Margaret. The recommendation was favourably received, and a day was appointed for Margaret to make a personal visit at the town house of the people in question, when she would most probably be engaged.

On the previous evening at twilight Mr. Halliburton came home from one of his numerous engagements. Jane was alone. Mrs. Tait, not very well, had retired to rest early, and Margaret was out with Robert. In this, a leisure season of the year, Robert had most of his evenings to himself, after eight o'clock. He generally came home, and he and Margaret would go out together. Mr. Halliburton sat down at one of the windows in silence.

Jane went up to him, laying her hand affectionately on his shoulder. "You are very tired, Edgar?"

He did not reply: only drew her hand between his, and kept it there.

"You shall have supper at once," said Jane, glancing at the tray which stood ready on the table. "I am sure you must want it. And it is not right to indulge Margaret every night by waiting for her."

"Scarcely, when she does not come in until ten or half-past," said Mr. Halliburton. "Jane," he added confidentially, "do you think it well that Margaret should be out so frequently in an evening?"

"She is with Robert."

"She may not always be with Robert alone."

Jane felt her face flush. She knew her husband; knew that he was not one to speak unless he had some reason for doing so. "Edgar! why do you say this? Do you know anything? Have you seen Margaret?"

"I saw her a quarter of an hour ago—"

"With Robert?" interrupted Jane, more impulsively than she was in the habit of speaking.

"Robert was by her side. But she was walking arm in arm with Mr. Murray."

Jane did not much like the information. This Mr. Murray was in the same house as Robert, holding a better position. Robert had occasionally brought him home, and he had taken tea with them. Mrs.

Halliburton felt surprised at Margaret: it appeared, to her well-regulated mind, very like a clandestine proceeding. What would she have said, or thought, had she known that Margaret and Mr. Murray were in the habit of thus walking together constantly? Robert's being with them afforded no sufficient excuse.

Later they saw Margaret coming home with Robert alone. He left her at the door as usual, and then hastened away to his own home. Jane said nothing then, but she went to Margaret's room that evening.

"Oh, Edgar has been bringing home tales, has he?" was Margaret's answer, when the ice was broken; and her defiant tone brought Jane hardly knew what of dismay to her ear. "I saw him staring at us."

"Margaret!" gasped Jane, "what can have come to you? You are completely changed; you—you seem to speak no longer as a lady."

"Then why do you provoke me, Jane? Is it high treason to take a gentleman's arm, my brother being with me?"

"It is not right to do it in secret, Margaret. If you go out ostensibly to walk with Robert—"

"Jane, I will not listen," Margaret said, with flashing eyes. "Because you are Mrs. Halliburton, you assume a right to lecture me. I have committed no grievous wrong. When I do commit it, you may take your turn then."

"Oh, Margaret! why will you misjudge me?" asked Jane, her voice full of pain. "I speak to you in love, not in anger; I would not speak at all but for your good. If the Chevasneys were to hear of this, they might think you an unsuitable mistress for their children."

"Compose yourself," said Margaret, scoffingly. Never had she shown such a temper, so undesirable a disposition, as on this night; and Jane might well look at her in amazement, and hint that she was "changed." "I shall be found sufficiently suitable by the Chevasney family—when I consent to enter it."

Her tone was strangely significant, and Jane Halliburton's heart beat. "What do you imply, Margaret?" she inquired. "You appear to have some peculiar meaning."

Margaret, who had been standing before the glass all this time twisting her hair round her fingers, turned and looked her sister full in the face. "Jane, I'll tell you, if you will undertake to make things straight for me with mamma. I am not going to the Chevasneys—or anywhere else—as governess."

"Yes,"—said Jane faintly, for she had a presentiment of what was coming.

"I am going to be married instead."

"Oh, Margaret!"

"There is nothing to groan about," retorted Margaret. "Mr. Murray is coming to speak to mamma to-morrow, and if any of you have anything to say against him, you can say it to his face. He is a very respectable man, and has a good income; where's the objection to him?"

Jane could not say. Personally, she did not very much like Mr. Murray; and certain fond visions had pictured a higher destiny for handsome, accomplished Margaret. "I hope and trust you will be happy, if you do marry him, Margaret!" was all she said.

"I hope I shall. I must take my chance of that, as others do. Jane, I beg your pardon for my crossness, but you put me out of temper."

As others do. Ay! it was all a lottery. And Margaret Tait entered upon her hastily-chosen married life, knowing that it was so.

Several years went on; and years rarely go on without bringing changes with them. Jane had now four children. William, the eldest, was close upon thirteen; Edgar, the youngest, going on for nine; Jane and Frank were between them. Mrs. Tait was dead: and Francis Tait was the Reverend Francis Tait. By dint of hard work and perseverance, he had succeeded in qualifying for Orders, and was half starving upon a London curacy, as his father had done for so many years before him. In saying "half starving," I don't mean that he had not bread and cheese to eat; but when a clergyman's stipend is under a hundred a year, the expression "half starving" is justifiable. He hungers after many things that he is unable to obtain, and he cannot maintain his position as a gentleman. Francis Tait hungered. Over one want, especially, he hungered with an intensely ravenous hunger; and that was, the gratification of his taste for literature. The books he coveted to read were expensive; impossibilities to him; he could not purchase them, and libraries were then scarce. Had Francis Tait not been gifted with very great conscientiousness, he would have joined teaching with his ministry. But the wants of his parish required all his time; and he had inherited that large share of the monitor, conscience, from his father. "I suppose I shall have a living some time," he would think to himself: "when I am growing an old man, probably, as he was when he gained his."

So the Reverend Francis Tait plodded on at his curacy, and was content to await that remote day when fortune should drop from the skies.

Where was Margaret? Margaret had bidden adieu to old England for ever. Her husband, who had not been promoted in his house of business as rapidly as he thought he ought to have been, had thrown up his situation, home and home ties, and gone out to the woods of Canada to become a settler. Did Margaret repent her hasty marriage then? Did she find that her finished education, her peculiar tastes and habits, so unfitted for domestic life, were all lost in those wild woods? Music, drawing, languages, literature, of what use were they to her now? She might educate her own children, indeed, as they grew up: the only chance of education it appeared likely they would have. That Margaret found herself in a peculiarly uncongenial atmosphere, there could be no doubt; but, like a brave woman as she proved herself, not a hint of it, in writing home, ever escaped her, not a shadow of complaint could be gathered there. It was not often that she wrote, and her letters grew more rare as the years went on. Robert had accompanied them, and he boasted that he liked the life much; a thousand times better than that of the musty old warehouse.

Mr. Halliburton's teaching was excellent—his income good. He was now one of the professors at King's College; but had not yet succeeded in carrying out his dream—that of getting to Oxford or Cambridge. Edgar Halliburton had begun at the wrong end of the ladder: he should have gone to college first and married afterwards. He married first: and to college he never went. A man of moderate means, with a home to keep, a wife, children, servants, to provide for, has enough to do with his money and time, without spending them at college. He had quite given up the idea now; and perhaps had grown not to regret it very keenly: his home was one of refinement, comfort, and thorough happiness.

But about this period, or indeed some time prior to it, Mr. Halliburton had reason to believe that he was overtaxing his strength. For a long, long while, almost ever since he had been in London, he was aware that he had not felt thoroughly well. Hot weather affected him and rendered him languid; the chills of winter gave him a cough; the keen winds of spring attacked his chest. He would throw off his ailments bravely and go on again, not heeding them or thinking that they might ever become serious. Perhaps he never gave a thought to that until one evening when, upon coming in after a hard day's toil, he sat down in his chair and quietly fainted away.

Jane and one of the servants were standing over him when he recovered—Jane's face very pale and anxious.

"Do not be alarmed," he said, smiling at her. "I suppose I dropped asleep; or lost consciousness in some way."

"You fainted, Edgar."

"Fainted, did I? How silly I must have been! The room's warm, Jane: it must have overpowered me."

Jane was not deceived. She saw that he was making light of it to quiet her alarm, and brought him a glass of wine. He drank it, but could not eat anything: frequently could not eat now.

"Edgar," she said, "you are doing too much. I have seen it for a long time past."

"Seen what, Jane?"

"That your strength is not equal to your work. You must give up a portion of your teaching."

"My dear, how can I do so? Does it not take all I earn to meet expenses? When accounts are settled at the end of the year, have we a shilling to spare?"

It was so, and Jane knew it; but her husband's health was above every consideration in the world. "We must reduce our expenses," she said. "We must cease to live as we are living now. We will move into a smaller house, and keep one servant, and I will turn maid-of-all-work."

She laughed quite merrily; but Mr. Halliburton detected a serious meaning in her tone. He shook his head.

"No, Jane; that time, I hope, will never come."

He lay awake all that night buried in reflection. Do you know what this night-reflection is, when it comes to us in all its racking intensity? Surging over his brain, like the wild waves that chase each other on the ocean, came the thought, "What will become of my wife and children if I die?" Thought after thought, they all resolved themselves into that one focus:—"I have made no provision for my wife and children: what will become of them if I am taken?"

Mr. Halliburton had one good habit—it was possible that he had learnt it from his wife, for it was hers in no ordinary degree—the habit of looking steadfastly into the face of trouble. Not to groan and grumble at it—to sigh and lament that no one else's trouble ever was so great before—but to see how it might best be met and contended with; how the best could be made of it.

The only feasible way he could see, was that of insuring his life. He possessed neither lands nor money. Did he attempt to put by a portion of his income, it would take years and years to accumulate into a sum worth mentioning. Why, how long would it take him to economise only a thousand pounds? No. There was only one way—that of life insurance. It was an idea that would have occurred to most of us. He did not know how much it would take from his yearly income to effect it. A great deal, he was afraid; for he was approaching what is called middle life.

He had no secrets from his wife. He consulted her upon every point; she was his best friend, his confidante, his gentle counsellor, and he had no intention of concealing the step he was about to take. Why should he?

"Jane," he began, when they were at breakfast the next morning, "do you know what I have been thinking of all night?"

"Trouble, I am sure," she answered. "You have been very restless."

"Not exactly trouble"—for he did not choose to acknowledge, even to himself, that a strange sense of trouble did seem to rest on his heart and to weigh it down. "I have been thinking more of precaution than trouble."

"Precaution?" echoed Jane, looking at him.

"Ay, love. And the astonishing part of the business, to myself, is that I never thought of the necessity for this precaution before."

Jane divined now what he meant. Often and often had the idea occurred to her—"Should my husband's health or life fail, we are destitute." Not for herself did she so much care, but for her children.

"That sudden attack last night has brought me reflection," he resumed. "Life is uncertain with the best of us. It may be no more uncertain with me than with others; but I feel that I must act as though it were so. Jane, were I taken, there would be no provision for you."

"No," she quietly said.

"And therefore I must set about making one without delay, as far as I can. I shall insure my life."

Jane did not answer immediately. "It will take a great deal of money, Edgar," she presently said.

"I fear it will: but it must be done. What's the matter, Jane? You don't look hopeful over it."

"Because, were you to insure your life, to pay the yearly premium, and our home expenses, would necessitate your working as hard as you do now."

"Well?" said he. "Of course it would."

"In any case, our expenses shall be much reduced; of that I am determined," she went on somewhat dreamily, more it seemed in soliloquy than to her husband. "But, with this premium to pay in addition—"

"Jane," he interrupted, "there's not the least necessity for my relaxing my labours. I shall not think of doing it. I may not be very strong, but I am not ill. As to reducing our expenses, I see no help for that, inasmuch as I must draw from them for the premium."

"If you only can keep your health, Edgar, it is certainly what ought to be done—to insure your life. The thought has often crossed me."

"Why did you never suggest it?"

"I scarcely know. I believe I did not like to do so. And I really did not see how the premium was to be paid. How much shall you insure it for?"

"I thought of two thousand pounds. Could we afford more?"

"I think not. What would be the yearly premium for that sum?"

"I don't know. I will ascertain all particulars. What are you sighing about, Jane?"

Jane was sighing heavily. A weight seemed to have fallen upon her. "To talk of life-insurance puts me too much in mind of death," she murmured.

"Now, Jane, you are never going to turn goose!" he gaily said. "I have heard of persons who will not make a will, because it brings them a fancy they must be going to die. Insuring my life will not bring death any the quicker to me: I hope I shall be here many a year yet. Why, Jane, I may live to pay the insurance over and over again in annual premiums! Better that I had put by the money in a bank, I shall think then."

"The worst of putting by money in a bank, or in any other way, is, that you are not compelled to put it," observed Jane, looking up a little from her depression. "What ought to be put by—what is intended to be put by—too often goes in present wants, and putting by ends in name only: whereas, in life-assurance, the premium must be paid. Edgar," she added, passing to a different subject, "I wonder what we shall make of our boys?"

Mr. Halliburton's cheek flushed. "They shall go to college, please God—though I have not been able to get there myself."

"Oh, I hope so! One or two of them, at any rate."

Little difficulty did there appear to be in the plan to Mr. Halliburton.

His boys should enter the University, although he had not done so: the future of our children appears hopeful and easy to most of us. William and Frank were in the school attached to King's College: of which you hear Mr. Halliburton was now a professor. Edgar—never called anything but "Gar"—went to a private school, but he would soon be entered at King's College. Remarkably well-educated boys for their years, were the young Halliburtons. Mr. Halliburton and Jane had taken care of that. Home teaching was more efficient than school: both combined had rendered them unusually intelligent and advanced. Naturally intellectual, gifted with excellent qualities of mind and heart, Mrs. Halliburton had not failed to do her duty by them. She spared no pains; she knew how children ought to be brought up, and she did her duty well. Ah, my friends! only lay a good foundation in their earlier years, and your children will grow up to bless you.

"Jane, I wonder which office will be the best to insure in?"

Jane began to recall the names of some that were familiar to her.

"The Phoenix?" suggested she.

Mr. Halliburton laughed. "I think that's only for fire, Jane. I am not sure, though." In truth, he knew little about insurance offices himself.

"There's the Sun; and the Atlas; and the Argus—oh, and ever so many more," continued Jane.

"I'll inquire all about it to-day," said he.

"I wonder if the premium will take a hundred a year, Edgar?"

He could not tell. He feared it might. "I wish Jane," he observed, "that I had insured my life when I first married. The premium would have been small then, and we might have managed to spare it."

"Ay," she answered. "Sometimes I look back to things that I might have done in the past years: and I did not do them. Now, the time has gone by!"

"Well, it has not gone by for insuring," said Mr. Halliburton, rising from the breakfast-table and speaking in gay tones. "Half-past eight!" he cried, looking at his watch. "Good-bye, Jane," said he, bending to kiss her. "Wish me luck."

"A weighty insurance and a small premium," she said, laughing. "But you are not going about it now?"

"Of course not. The offices would not be open. I shall take an opportunity of doing so in the course of the day."

Mr. Halliburton departed on his usual duties. It was a warm day in April. His first attendance was King's College, and there he remained for the morning. Then he proceeded to gain information about the various offices and their respective merits: finally fixed upon the one he should apply to, and bent his steps towards it.

It was situated in the heart of the City, in a very busy part of it. The office also appeared to be busy, for several people were in it when Mr. Halliburton entered. A young man came forward to know his business.

"I wish to insure my life," said Mr. Halliburton. "How must I proceed about it?"

"Oh yes, sir. Mr. Procter, will you attend to this gentleman?"

Mr. Halliburton was marshalled to an inner room, where a gentlemanly man received him. He explained his business in detail, stated his age, and the sum he wished to insure for. Every information was politely afforded him; and a paper, with certain printed questions, was given him to fill up at his leisure, and then to be returned.

Mr. Halliburton glanced over it. "You require a certificate of my birth from the parish register where I was baptized, I perceive," he remarked. "Why so? In stating my age, I have stated it correctly."

The gentleman smiled. "Of that I make no doubt," he said, "for you look younger than the age you have given me. Our office makes it a rule in most cases to require the certificate from the register. All applicants are not scrupulous about telling the truth, and we have been obliged to adopt it in self-defence. We have had cases, we have indeed, sir, where we have insured a life, and then found—though perhaps not until the actual death has taken place—that the insurer was ten years older than he asserted. Therefore we demand a certificate. It does occasionally happen that applicants can bring well-known men to testify to their age, and then we do not mind dispensing with it."

Mr. Halliburton sent his thoughts round in a circle. There was no one in London who knew his age of their own positive knowledge; so it was useless to think of that. "There will be no difficulty in the matter," he said aloud. "I can get the certificate up from Devonshire in the course of two or three days by writing for it. My father was rector of the church where I was christened. This will be all, then? To fill up this paper and bring you the certificate."

"All; with the exception of being examined by our physician."

"What! is it necessary to be examined by a physician?" exclaimed Mr. Halliburton. "The paper states that I must hand in a report from my ordinary medical attendant. He will not give you a bad report of me," he added, smiling, "for it is little enough I have troubled him. I believe the worst thing he has attended me for has been a bad cold."

"So much the better," remarked the gentleman. "You do not look very strong."

"Very strong I don't think I am. I am too hard worked; get too little rest and recreation. It was suspecting that I am not so strong as I might be that set me thinking it might be well to insure my life for the sake of my wife and children," he ingenuously added, in his straightforward manner. "If I could count upon living and working on until I am an old man, I should not do so."

Again the gentleman smiled. "Looks are deceitful," he observed. "Nothing more so. Sometimes those who look the most delicate live the longest."

"You cannot say I look delicate," returned Mr. Halliburton.

"I did not say it. I consider that you do not look robust; but that is not saying that you look delicate. You may be a perfectly healthy man for all I can say to the contrary."

He ran his eyes over Mr. Halliburton as he spoke; over his tall, fine form, his dark hair, amidst which not a streak of grey mingled, his clearly-cut features, and his complexion, bright as a woman's. Was there suspicion in that complexion? "A handsome man, at any rate," thought the gazer, "if not a robust one."

"It will be necessary, then, that I see your physician?" asked Mr. Halliburton.

"Yes. It cannot be dispensed with. We would not insure without it. He attends here twice a week. In the intervening days, he may be seen in Savile-row, from three to five. It is Dr. Carrington. His days for coming here are Mondays and Thursdays."

"And this is Friday," remarked Mr. Halliburton. "I shall probably go up to him."

Mr. Halliburton said good morning, and came away with his paper. "It's great nonsense, my seeing this doctor!" he said to himself as he hastened home to dinner, which he knew he must have kept waiting. "But I suppose it is necessary as a general rule; and of course they won't make me an exception."

Hurrying over his dinner, in a manner that prevented its doing him any good—as Jane assured him—he sat down to his desk when it was over and wrote for the certificate of his birth. Folding and sealing the letter, he put on his hat to go out again.

"Shall you go to Savile-row this afternoon?" Jane inquired.

"If I can by any possibility get my teaching over in time," he answered. "Young Finchley's hour is four o'clock, but I can put him off until the evening. I dare say I shall get up there."

By dint of hurrying, Mr. Halliburton contrived to reach Savile-row, and arrived there in much heat at half-past four. There was no necessity for hurrying there on this particular day, but he felt impatient to get the business over; as if speed now could atone for past neglect. Dr. Carrington was at home but engaged, and Mr. Halliburton was shown into a room. Three or four others were waiting there; whether ordinary patients, or whether mere applicants of form like himself, he could not tell; and it was their turn to go in before it was his.

But his turn came at last, and he was ushered into the presence of the doctor—a little man, fair and reserved, with powder on his head.

Reserved in ordinary intercourse, but certainly not reserved in asking questions. Mr. Halliburton had never been so rigidly questioned before. What disorders had he had, and what had he not had? What were his habits, past and present? One question came at last: "Do you feel thoroughly strong?—healthy, elastic?"

"I feel languid in hot weather," replied Mr. Halliburton.

"Um! Appetite sound and good?"

"Generally speaking. It has not been so good of late."

"Breathing all right?"

"Yes; it is a little tight sometimes."

"Um! Subject to a cough?"

"I have no settled cough. A sort of hacking cough comes on at night occasionally. I attribute it to fatigue."

"Um! Will you open your shirt? Just unbutton it here"—touching the front—"and your flannel waistcoat, if you wear one."

Mr. Halliburton bared his chest in obedience and the doctor sounded it, and then put down his ear. Apparently his ear did not serve him sufficiently, for he took a small instrument out of a drawer, placed it on the chest, and then put his ear to that, changing the position of the instrument three or four times.

"That will do," he said at length.

He turned to put up his stethoscope again, and Mr. Halliburton drew the edges of his shirt together and buttoned them.

"Why don't you wear flannel waistcoats?" asked the doctor, with quite a sharp accent, his head down in the drawer.

"I do wear them in winter; but in warm weather I leave them off. It was only last week that I discarded them."

"Was ever such folly known!" ejaculated Dr. Carrington. "One would think people were born without common sense. Half the patients who come to me say they leave off their flannels in summer! Why, it is in summer they are most needed! And this warm weather won't last either. Go home, sir, and put one on at once."

"Certainly, if you think it right," said Mr. Halliburton with a smile. "I thank you for telling me."

He took up his hat and waited. The doctor appeared to wait for him to go. "I understood at the office that you would give me a paper testifying that you had examined me," explained Mr. Halliburton.

"Ah—but I can't give it," said the doctor.

"Why not, sir?"

"Because I am not satisfied with you. I cannot recommend you as a healthy life."

Mr. Halliburton's pulses quickened a little. "Sir!" he repeated. "Not a healthy life?"

"Not sufficiently healthy for insurance."

"Why! what is the matter with me?" he rejoined.

Dr. Carrington looked him full in the face for the space of a minute before replying. "I have had that question asked me before by parties whom I have felt obliged to decline as I am now declining you," he said, "and my answer has not always been palatable to them."

"It will be palatable to me, sir; in so far as that I desire to be made acquainted with the truth. What do you find amiss with me?"

"The lungs are diseased."

A chill fell over Mr. Halliburton. "Not extensively, I trust? Not beyond hope of recovery?"

"Were I to say not extensively, I should be deceiving you; and you tell me that you wish for the truth. They are extensively diseased—"

A mortal pallor overspread Mr. Halliburton's face, and he sank into a chair. "Not for myself," he gasped, as Dr. Carrington drew nearer to him. "I have a wife and children. If I die, they will want bread to eat."

"But you did not hear me out," returned the doctor, proceeding with equanimity, as if he had not been interrupted. "They are extensively diseased, but not beyond a hope of recovery. I do not say it is a strong hope; but a hope there is, as I judge, provided you use the right means and take care of yourself."

"What am I to do? What are the means?"

"You live, I presume, in this stifling, foggy, smoky London."

"Yes."

"Then got away from it. Go where you can have pure air and a clear atmosphere. That's the first and chief thing; and that's most essential. Not for a few weeks or months, you understand me—going out for a change of air, as people call it—you must leave London entirely; go away altogether."

"But it will be impossible," urged Mr. Halliburton. "My work lies in London."

"Ah!" said the doctor; "too many have been with me with whom it was the same case. But, I assure you that you must leave it; or it will be London versus life. You appear to me to be one who never ought to have come to London—You were not born in it?" he abruptly added.

"I never saw it until I was eighteen. I was born and reared in Devonshire."

"Just so. I knew it. Those born and reared in London become acclimatized to it, generally speaking, and it does not hurt them. It does not hurt numbers who are strangers: they find London as healthy a spot for them as any on the face of the globe. But there are a few who cannot and ought not to live in London; and I judge you to be one of them."

"Has this state of health been coming on long?"

"Yes, for some years. Had you remained in Devonshire, you might have been a sound man all your life. My only advice to you is—get away from London. You cannot live long if you remain in it."

Mr. Halliburton thanked Dr. Carrington and went out. How things had changed for him! What had gone with the day's beauty?—with the blue sky, the bright sun? The sky was blue still, and the sun shining; but darkness seemed to intervene between his eyes and outward things. Dying? A shiver went through him as he thought of Jane and the children, and a sick feeling of despair settled on his spirit.

CHAPTER VII

LATER IN THE DAY

The man was utterly prostrated. He felt that the fiat of death had gone forth, and there settled an undercurrent of conviction in his mind that for him there would be no recovery, take what precaution he would. He could not shake it off. There lay the fact and the fear, as a leaden weight.

He bent his steps towards home, walking the whole way; he moved along the streets mechanically. The crowds passed and repassed him, but he seemed far away. Once or twice he lifted his head to them with a yearning gesture. "Oh! that I were like you! bent on business, on pleasure, on social intercourse!" passed through his mind. "I am not as you; and for me you can do nothing. You cannot give me health; you cannot give me life."

He entered his home, and was conscious of merry voices and flitting footsteps. A little scene of gaiety was going on: he knew of this, but had forgotten it until that instant. It was the birthday of his little girl, and a few young friends had been invited to make merry. Jane, looking almost as young, quite as pretty, as when she married him, sat at the far end of their largest room before a well-spread tea-table. She wore festival attire. A dress of pearl-grey silk, and a thin gold chain round her neck. The little girls were chiefly in white, and the boys were on their best behaviour. Jane was telling them that tea was ready, and her two servants were helping to place the little people, and to wait upon them.

"Oh, and here's papa, too! just in time," she cried, lifting her eyes gladly at her husband. "That is delightful!"

Mr. Halliburton welcomed the children. He kissed some, he talked to others, just as if he had not that terrible vulture, care, within him. They saw nothing amiss; neither did Jane. He took his seat, and drank his tea; all, as it were, mechanically. It did not seem to be himself; he thought it must be some one else. In the last hour, his whole identity appeared to have changed. Bread and butter was handed to him. He took a slice and left it. Jane put some cake on to his plate: he left that also. Eat! with that awful fiat racking his senses! No, it was not possible.

Ho looked round on his children. His. William, a gentle boy, with his mother's calm, good face and her earnest eyes; Jane, a lovely child, with fair curls flowing and a bright colour, consciously vain this evening in her white birthday robes and her white ribbons; Frank, a slim, dark-eyed boy, always in mischief, his features handsome and clearly cut as were his father's; Gar, a delicate little chap, with fair curls like his sister Jane's. Must he leave those children?—abandon them to the mercies of a cold and cruel world?—bequeath them no place in it; no means of support? "Oh, God! Oh, God!" broke from his bitter heart, "if it be Thy will to take me, mayst Thou shelter them!"

"Edgar!"

He started palpably; so far in thought was he away. Yet it was only his wife who spoke to him.

"Edgar, have you been up to Dr. Carrington's?" she whispered, bending towards him.

In his confusion he muttered some unintelligible words, which she interpreted into a denial; there was a great deal of buzzing just then from the young voices around. Two of the gentlemen, Frank being one, were in hot contention touching a third gentleman's rabbits. Mrs. Halliburton called Frank to order, and said no more to her husband for the present.

"We are to dance after tea," said Jane. "I have been learning one quadrille to play. It is very easy, and mamma says I play it very well."

"Oh, we don't want dancing," grumbled one of the boys. "We'd rather have blindman's-buff."

Opinions were divided again. The girls wanted dancing, the boys blindman's-buff. Mrs. Halliburton was appealed to.

"I think it must be dancing first and blindman's-buff afterwards," said she.

Tea over, the furniture was pushed aside to clear a space for the dancers. Mr. Halliburton, his back against the wall, stood looking at them. Looking at them as was supposed; but had they been keen observers, they would have known that his eyes in reality saw not: they, like his thoughts, were far away.

His wife did presently notice that he seemed particularly abstracted. She came up to him; he was standing with his arms folded, his head bent. "Edgar, are you well?"

"Well? Oh yes, dear," he replied, making an effort to rouse himself.

"I hope you have no more teaching to-night?"

"I ought to go to young Finchley. I put him off until seven o'clock."

"Then"—was her quick rejoinder—"if you put off young Finchley, how was it you could not get to Savile-row?"

"I have been occupied all the afternoon, Jane," he said. Wanting the courage to say how the matter really stood, he evaded the question.

But, to go to young Finchley or to any other pupil that night, Mr. Halliburton felt himself physically unequal. Teach! Explain abstruse Greek and Latin rules, with his mind in its present state! It seemed to him that it mattered little—if he was to be taken from them so soon—whether he ever taught again. He was in the very depths of depression.

Suddenly, as he stood looking on, a thought came flashing over him as a ray of light. As a ray of light? Nay, as a whole flood of it. What if Dr. Carrington were wrong?—if it should prove that, in reality, nothing was the matter with him? Doctors—and very clever ones—were, he knew, sometimes mistaken. Perhaps Dr. Carrington had been so!

It was scarcely likely, he went on to reason, that a mortal disease should be upon him, and he have lived in ignorance of it! Why, he seemed to have had very little the matter with him; nothing to talk of, nothing to lie up for; comparatively speaking, he had been a healthy man—was in health then. Yes, the belief did present itself that Dr. Carrington was deceived. He, in the interests of the insurance office, might be unnecessarily cautious.

Mr. Halliburton left the wall, and grew cheerful and gay, and talked freely to the children. One little lady asked if he would dance with her. He laughed, and felt half inclined to do so.

Which was the true mood—that sombre one, or this? Was there nothing false about this one—was there no secret consciousness that it did not accord with his mind's actual belief; that he was only forcing it? Be it as it would, it did not last; in the very middle of a laughing sentence to his own little Janey, the old agony, the fear, returned—returned with terrific violence, as a torrent that has burst its bounds.

"I cannot bear this uncertainty!" he murmured to himself. And he went out of the room and took up his hat. Mrs. Halliburton, who at that moment happened to be crossing from another room, saw him open the hall-door.

"Are you going to young Finchley, Edgar?"

"No. I shall give him holiday for to-night. I shall be in soon, Jane."

He went straight to their own family doctor; a Mr. Allen, who lived close by. They were personal friends.

To the inquiry as to whether Mr. Allen was at home, the servant was about to usher him into the family sitting-room, but Mr. Halliburton stepped into the dusky surgery. He was in no mood for ladies' company. "I will wait here," he said. "Tell your master I wish to say a word to him."

The surgeon came immediately, a lighted candle in his hand. He was a dark man with a thin face. "Why won't you come in?" he asked. "There's only Mrs. Allen and the girls there. Is anything the matter?"

"Yes, Allen, something is the matter," was

Mr. Halliburton's reply. "I want a friend to-night: one who will deal with me candidly and openly: and I have come to you. Sit down."

They both sat down; and Mr. Halliburton gave him the history of the past four and twenty hours: commencing with the fainting-fit, and ending with his racking doubts as to whether Dr. Carrington's opinion was borne out by facts, or whether he might have been deceived. "Allen," he concluded, "you must see what you can make out of my state: and you must report to me without disguise, as you would report to your own soul."

The surgeon looked grave. "Carrington is a clever man," he said. "One whom it would be difficult to deceive."

"I know his reputation. But these clever men are not infallible. Put his opinion out of your mind: examine me yourself, and tell me what you think."

Mr. Allen proceeded to do so. He first of all asked Mr. Halliburton a few general questions as to his present state of health, as he would have done by any other patient, and then he sounded his lungs.

"Now then—the truth," said Mr. Halliburton.

"The truth is—so far as I can judge—that you are in no present danger whatever."

"Neither did Dr. Carrington say I was—in present danger," hastily replied Mr. Halliburton. "Are my lungs sound?"

"They are not sound: but neither do I think they are extensively diseased. You may live for many years, with care."

"Would any insurance office take me?"

"No. I do not think it would."

"It is just my death-knell, Allen."

"If you look at it in that light I shall be very sorry to have given you my opinion," observed the surgeon. "I repeat that, by taking care of yourself, you may stave off disease and live many years. I would not say this unless I thought it."

"And would your opinion be the same as the doctor's—that I must leave London for the country?"

"I think you would have a far better chance of getting well in the country than you have here. You have told me over and over again, you know, that you were sure London air was bad for you."

"Ay, I have," replied Mr. Halliburton. "I never have felt quite well in it, and that's the truth. Well, I must see what can be done. Good evening."

If the edict did not appear to be so irrevocably dark as that of Dr. Carrington, it was yet dark enough; and Mr. Halliburton, striving to look it full in the face, as he was in the habit of doing by troubles less grave, endeavoured to set himself to think "what could be done." There was no possible chance of keeping it from his wife. If it was really necessary that their place of residence should be changed, she must be taken into counsel; and the sooner she was told the better. He went home, resolved to tell her before he slept.

The little troop departed, the children in bed, they sat together over the fire; though the weather had become warm, an evening fire was pleasant still. He sat nervous and fidgety. Now the moment had arrived, he shrunk from his task.

"Edgar, I am sure you are not well!" she exclaimed. "I have observed it all the evening."

"Yes, Jane, I am well. Pretty well, that is. The truth is, my darling, I have some bad news for you, and I don't like to tell it."

Her own family were safe and well under her roof, and her fears flew to Francis, to Margaret, to Robert. Mr. Halliburton stopped her.

"It does not concern any of them, Jane. It is about myself."

"But what can it be, about yourself?"

"They—will—not—Will you listen to the news with a brave heart?" he broke off, with a smile, and the most cheering look he could call up to his face.

"Oh yes." She smiled too. She thought it could be nothing very bad.

"They will not insure my life, Jane."

Her heart stood still. "But why not?"

"They consider it too great a risk. They fancy I am not strong."

A sudden flush to her face; a moment's stillness; and then Jane Halliburton clasped her hands with a faint cry of despair. She saw that more remained behind.

CHAPTER VIII

SUSPENSE

Mrs. Halliburton sat in her chair, still enough except for the wailing cry which had just escaped her lips. Her husband would not look at her in that moment. His gaze was bent on the fire, and his cheek lay in his hand. As she cried out, he stretched forth his other hand and let it fall lightly upon hers.

"Jane, had I thought you would look at the dark side of the picture, I should have hesitated to tell you. Why, my dear child, the very fact of my telling you at all, should convince you that there's nothing very serious the matter," he added, in cheering tones of reasoning. Now that he had spoken, he deemed it well to make the very best he could of it.

"You say they will not insure your life?"

"Well, Jane, perhaps that expression was not a correct one. They have not declined as yet to do so; but Dr. Carrington says he cannot give the necessary certificate as to my being a thoroughly sound and healthy man."

"Then you did go up to Dr. Carrington?"

"I did. Forgive me, Jane: I could not enter upon it before all the children."

She leaned over and laid her head upon his shoulder. "Tell me all about it, Edgar," she whispered; "as much as you know yourself."

"I have told you nearly all, Jane. I saw Dr. Carrington, and he asked me a great many questions, and examined me here"—touching his chest. "He fancies the organs are not sound, and declined giving the certificate."

"That your chest is not sound?" asked Jane.

"He said the lungs."

"Ah!" she uttered. "What else did he say?"

"Well, he said nothing about heart, or liver, or any other vital part, so I conclude they are all right, and that there was nothing to say," replied Mr. Halliburton, attempting to be cheerful. "I could have told him my brain was strong enough had he asked about that, for I'm sure it gets its full share of work. I need not have mentioned this to you at all, Jane, but for a perplexing bit of advice the doctor gave me."

Jane sat straight in her chair again, and looked at Mr. Halliburton. The colour was beginning to return to her face. He continued:

"Dr. Carrington earnestly recommends me to remove from London. Indeed—he said—that it was necessary—if I would get well. No wonder that you found my manner absent," he continued very rapidly after his hesitation, "with that unpalatable counsel to digest."

"Did he think you very ill?" she breathed.

"He did not say I was 'very ill,' Jane. I am not very ill, as you may see for yourself. My dear, what he said was that my lungs were—were—"

"Diseased?" she put in.

"Diseased. Yes, that was it," he truthfully replied. "It is the term that medical men apply when they wish to indicate delicacy. And he strenuously recommended me to leave London."

"For how long? Did he say?"

"He said for good."

Jane felt startled. "How could it be done, Edgar?"

"In truth I do not know. If I leave London I leave my living behind me. Now you see why I was so absorbed at tea-time. When you saw me go out, I was going round to Allen's."

"And what does he say?" she eagerly interrupted.

"Oh, he seems to think it a mere nothing, compared with Dr. Carrington. He agreed with him on one point—that I ought to live out of London."

"Edgar, I will tell you what I think must be done," said Jane, after a pause. "I have not had time to reflect much upon it: but it strikes me that it would be advisable for you to see another doctor, and take his opinion: some man who is clever in affections of the lungs. Go to him to-morrow, without any delay. Should he say that you must leave London, of course we must leave it, no matter what the sacrifice."

The advice corresponded with Mr. Halliburton's own opinion, and he resolved to follow it. A conviction amounting to a certainty was upon him, that, go to what doctor he might, the fiat would be the same as Dr. Carrington's. He did not say so to Jane. On the contrary, he spoke of these insurance-office doctors as being over-fastidious in the interests of the office; and he tried to deceive his own heart with the sophistry.

"Shall you apply to another office to insure your life?" Jane asked.

"I would, if I thought it would not be useless."

"You think it would be useless?"

"The offices all keep their own doctors, and those doctors, it is my belief, are unnecessarily particular. I should call them crotchety, Jane."

"I think it must amount to this," said Jane; "that if there is anything seriously the matter with you, no office will be found to do it; but if the affection is only trifling or temporary you may be accepted."

"That is about it. Oh, Jane!" he added, with an irrepressible burst of anguish, "what would I not give to have insured my life before this came upon me! All those past years! They seem to have been allowed to run to waste, when I might have been using them to lay up in store for the children!"

How many are there of us who, looking back, can feel that our past years, in some way or other, have not been allowed to run to waste?

What a sleepless night that was for him! What a sleepless night for his wife! Both rose in the morning equally unrefreshed.

"To what doctor will you go?" Jane inquired as she was dressing.

"I have been thinking of Dr. Arnold of Finsbury," he replied.

"Yes, you could not go to a better. Edgar, you will let me accompany you?"

"No, no, Jane. Your accompanying me would do no good. You could not go into the room with me."

She saw the force of the objection. "I shall be so very anxious," she said, in a low tone.

He laughed at her; he was willing to make light of it if it might ease her fears. "My dear, I will come home at once and report to you: I will borrow Jack's seven-leagued boots, that I may come to you the quicker."

"You know that I shall be anxious," she repeated, feeling vexed.

"Jane," he said, his tone changing: "I see that you are more anxious already than is good for you. It is not well that you should be so."

"I wish I could be with you! I wish I could hear, as you will, Dr. Arnold's opinion from his own lips!" was all she answered.

"I will faithfully repeat it to you," said Mr. Halliburton.

"Faithfully—word for word? On your honour?"

"Yes, Jane, I will. You have my promise. Good news I shall be only too glad to tell you; and, should it be the worst, it will be necessary that you should know it."

"You must be there before ten o'clock," she observed; "otherwise there will be little chance of seeing him."

"I shall be there by nine, Jane. To spare time later would interfere too much with my day's work."

A thought crossed Jane's mind—if the fiat were unfavourable what would become of his day's work then—all his days? But she did not utter it.

"Oh, papa," cried Janey at breakfast, "was it not a beautiful party! Did you ever enjoy yourself so much before?"

"I don't suppose you ever did, Janey," he replied, in kindly tones.

"No, that I never did. Alice Harvey's birthday comes in summer, and she says she knows her mamma will let her give just such another! Mamma!"—turning to Mrs. Halliburton.

"Well, Jane?"

"Shall you let me have a new frock for it? You know I tore mine last night."

"All in good time, Janey. We don't know where we may all be then."

No, they did not. A foreshadowing of it was already upon the spirit of Mrs. Halliburton. Not upon the children: they were spared it as yet.

"Do not be surprised if you see me waiting for you when you come out of Dr. Arnold's," said Jane to her husband, in low tones, as he was going out.

"But, Jane, why? Indeed, I think it would be foolish of you to come. My dear, I never knew you like this before."

Perhaps not. But when, before, had there been cause for this apprehension?

Jane watched him depart. Calm as she contrived to remain outwardly, she was in a terribly restless, nervous state; little accustomed as she was so to give way. A sick feeling was within her, a miserable sensation of suspense; and she could scarcely battle with it. You may have felt the same, in the dread approach of some great calamity. The reading over, Janey got her books about, as usual. Mrs. Halliburton took charge of her education in every branch, excepting music: for that she had a master. She would not send Jane to school. The child sat down to her books, and was surprised at seeing her mother come into the room with her things on.

"Mamma! Are you going out?"

"For a little time, Jane."

"Oh, let me go! Let me go too!"

"Not this morning, dear. You will have plenty of work—preparing the lessons that you could not prepare last night."

"So I shall," said Janey. "I thought perhaps you meant to excuse them, mamma."

It was almost impossible for Jane to remain in the house, in her present state of agitation. She knew that it did appear absurdly foolish to go after her husband; but, walk somewhere she must: how could she turn a different way from that which he had taken? It was some distance to Finsbury; half an hour's walk at least. Should she go, or should she not, she asked herself as she went out of the house. She began to think that she might have remained at home had she exercised self-control. She had a great mind to turn back, and was slackening her pace, when she caught sight of Mr. Allen at his surgery window.

An impulse came over her that she would go in and ask his opinion of her husband. She opened the door and entered. The surgeon was making up some pills.

"You are out early, Mrs. Halliburton!"

"Yes," she replied. "Mr. Halliburton has gone to Finsbury Square to see Dr. Arnold, and I—Do you think him very ill?" she abruptly broke off.

"I do not, myself. Carrington—Did you know he had been to Dr. Carrington?" asked Mr. Allen, almost fearing he might be betraying secrets.

"I know all about it. I know what the doctor said. Do you think Dr. Carrington was mistaken?"

"In a measure. There's no doubt the lungs are affected, but I believe not to the grave extent assumed by Dr. Carrington."

"He assumed, then, that they were affected to a grave extent?" she hastily repeated, her heart beating faster.

"I thought you said you knew all about it, Mrs. Halliburton?"

"So I do. He may possibly not have told me the very worst said by Dr. Carrington; but he told me quite sufficient. Mr. Allen, you tell me—do you think that there is a chance of his recovery?"

"Most certainly I do," warmly replied the surgeon. "Every chance, Mrs. Halliburton. I see no reason whatever why he should not keep as well as he is now, and live for years, provided he takes care of himself. It appears that Dr. Carrington very strongly urged his removing into the country; he went so far as to say that it was his only chance for life—and in that I think he went too far again. But the country would undoubtedly do for him what London will not."

"You think that he ought to remove to the country?" she inquired, showing no sign of the terror those incautious words brought her—"his only chance for life."

"I do. If it be possible for him to manage his affairs so as to get away, I should say let him do so by all means."

"It must be done, you know, Mr. Allen, if it is essential."

"In my judgment it should be done. Many and many a time I have said to him myself, 'It's a pity but that you could be out of this heavy London!' Fogs affect him, and smoke affects him—the air altogether affects him: and I only wonder it has not told upon him before. As Dr. Carrington observed to him, there are some constitutions which somehow will not thrive here."

Mrs. Halliburton rose with a sigh. "I am glad you do not think so very seriously of him," she breathed.

"I do not think seriously of him at all," was the surgeon's answer. "I confess that he is not strong, and that he must have care. The pure air of the country, and relaxation from some of his most pressing work, may do wonders for him. If I might advise, I should say, Let no pecuniary considerations keep him here. And that is very disinterested advice, Mrs. Halliburton," concluded the doctor, laughing, "for, in losing you, I should lose both friends and patients."

Jane went out. Those ominous words were still ringing in her ears—"his only chance for life."

Forcing herself to self-control, she did not go to meet Mr. Halliburton. She returned home and took off her things, and gave what attention she could to Jane's lessons. But none can tell the suspense that was agitating her: the ever-restless glances she cast to the window, to see him pass. By-and-by she went and stood there.

At last she saw him coming along in the distance. She would have liked to fly to meet him—to say, What is the news? but she did not. More patience, and then, when he came in at the front door, she left the room she was in, and went with him into the drawing-room, her face white as death.

He saw how agitated she was, strive as she would for calmness. He stood looking at her with a smile.

"Well, Jane, it is not so very formidable, after all."

Her face grew hot, and her heart bounded on. "What does Dr. Arnold say? You know, Edgar, you promised me the truth without disguise."

"You shall have it, Jane. Dr. Arnold's opinion of me is not unfavourable. That the lungs are to a certain extent affected, is indisputable, and he thinks they have been so for some time. But he sees nothing to indicate present danger to life. He believes that I may grow into an old man yet."

Jane breathed freely. A word of earnest thanks went up from her heart.

"With proper diet—he has given me certain rules for living—and pure air and sunshine, he considers that I have really little to fear. I told you, Jane, those insurance doctors make the worst of things."

"Dr. Arnold, then, recommends the country?" observed Jane, paying no attention to the last remark.

"Very strongly. Almost as strongly as Dr. Carrington."

Jane lifted her eyes to her husband's face. "Dr. Carrington said, you know, that it was your only chance of life."

"Not quite as bad as that, Jane," he returned, never supposing but he must himself have let the remark slip, and wondering how he came to do so. "What Dr. Carrington said was, that it was London versus life."

"It is the same thing, Edgar. And now, what is to be done? Of course we have no alternative; into the country we must go. The question is, where?"

"Ay, that is the question," he answered. "Not only where, but what to do? I cannot drop down into a fresh place, and expect teaching to surround me at once, as if it had been waiting for me. But I have not time to talk now. Only fancy! it is half-past ten."

Mr. Halliburton went out and Jane remained, fastened as it were to her chair. A hundred perplexing plans and schemes were already working in her brain.

CHAPTER IX

SEEKING A HOME

Plans and schemes continued to work in Mrs. Halliburton's brain for days and days to come. Many and many an anxious consultation did she and her husband hold together—where should they go? What should they do? That it was necessary to do something, and speedily, events proved, independently of what had been said by the doctors. Before another month had passed over his head, Mr. Halliburton had become so much worse that he had to resign his post at King's College. But, to the hopeful minds of himself and Jane, the country change was to bring its remedy for all ills. They had grown to anticipate it with enthusiasm.

His thoughts naturally ran upon teaching, as his continued occupation. He knew nothing of any other. All England was before him; and he supposed he might obtain a living at it, wherever he might go. Such testimonials as his were not met with every day. His cousin Julia had married a man of some local influence (as Mr. Halliburton had understood) in the city in which they resided, the chief town of one of the midland counties: and a thought crossed his mind more than once, whether it might not be well to choose that same town to settle in.

"They might be able to recommend me, you see, Jane," he observed to his wife, one evening as they were sitting together, after the children were in bed. "Not that I should much like to ask any favour of Julia."

"Why not?" said Jane.

"Because she is not a pleasant person to ask a favour of: it is many years since I saw her, but I well remember that. Another reason why I feel inclined to that place is that it is a cathedral town. Cathedral towns have many of the higher order of the clergy in them; learning is sure to be considered there, should it not be anywhere else. Consequently there would be an opening for classical teaching."

Jane thought the argument had weight.

"And there's yet another thing," continued Mr. Halliburton. "You remember Peach?"

"Peach?—Peach?" repeated Jane, as if unable to recall the name.

"The young fellow I had so much trouble with, a few years ago—drilling him between his terms at Oxford. But for me, he never would have passed either his great or his little go. He did get plucked the first time he went up. You must remember him, Jane: he has often taken tea with us here."

"Oh, yes—yes! I remember him now. Charley Peach."

"Well, he has recently been appointed to a minor canonry in that same cathedral," resumed Mr. Halliburton. "Dr. Jacobs told me of it the other day. Now I am quite sure that Peach would be delighted to say a word for me, or to put anything in my way. That is another reason why I am inclined to go there."

"I suppose the town is a healthy one?"

"Ay, that it is; and it is seated in one of the most charming of our counties. There'll be no London fogs or smoke there."

"Then, Edgar, let us decide upon it."

"Yes, I think so—unless we should hear of an opening elsewhere that may promise better. We must be away by Midsummer, if we can, or soon after. It will be sharp work, though."

"What trouble it will be to pack the furniture!" she exclaimed.

"Pack what furniture, Jane? We must sell the furniture."

"Sell the furniture!" she uttered, aghast.

"My dear, it would never do to take the furniture down. It would cost almost as much as it is worth. There's no knowing, either, how long it might be upon the road, or what damage it might receive. I expect it would have to go principally by water."

"By water!" cried Mrs. Halliburton.

"I fancy so—by barge, I mean. Waggons would not take it, except by paying heavily. A great deal of the country traffic is done by water. This furniture is old, Jane, most of it, and will not bear rough travelling. Consider how many years your father and mother had it in use."

"Then what should we do for furniture when we get there?" asked Jane.

"Buy new with the money we receive from the sale of this. I have been reflecting upon it a good deal, Jane, and fancy it will be the better plan. However, if you care for this old furniture, we must take it."

Jane looked round upon it. She did care for the time-used furniture; but she knew how old it was, and was willing to do whatever might be best. A vision came into her mind of fresh, bright furniture, and it looked pleasant in imagination. "It would certainly be a great deal to pack and carry," she acknowledged. "And some of it is not worth it."

"And it would be more than we should want," resumed Mr. Halliburton. "Wherever we go we must be content with a small house; at any rate at first. But it will be time enough to go into these details, Jane, when we have finally decided upon our destination."

"Oh, Edgar! I shall be so sorry to take the boys from King's College."

"Jane," he said, a flash of pain crossing his face as he spoke, "there are so many things connected with it altogether that cause me sorrow, that my only resource is not to think upon them. I might be tempted to repine to ask in a spirit of rebellion why this affliction should have come upon us. It is God's decree, and it is my duty to submit as patiently as I can."

It was her duty also: and she knew it as she laid her hand upon her weary brow. A weary, weary brow from henceforth, that of Jane Halliburton!

CHAPTER X

A DYING BED

In a handsome chamber of a handsome house in Birmingham, an old man lay dying. For most of his life he had been engaged in a large wholesale business—had achieved local position, had accumulated moderate wealth. But neither wealth nor position can ensure peace to a death-bed; and the old man lay on his, groaning over the past.

The season was that of mid-winter. Not the winter following the intended removal of Mr. Halliburton from London, as spoken of in the last chapter, but the winter preceding it—for it is necessary to go back a little. A hard, sharp, white day in January: and the fire was piled high in the sick room, and the large flakes of snow piled themselves outside on the window frames and beat against the glass. The room was fitted up with every comfort the most fastidious invalid could desire; and yet, I say, nothing seemed to bring comfort to the invalid lying there. His hands were clenched as in mortal agony; his eyes were apparently watching the falling snow. The eyes saw it not: in reality they were cast back to where his mind was—the past.

What could be troubling him? Was it that loss, only two years ago, by which one-half of his savings had been engulfed? Scarcely. A man dying—as he knew he was—would be unlikely to care about that now. Ample competence had remained to him, and he had neither son nor daughter to inherit. Hark! what is it that he is murmuring between his parched lips, to the accompaniment of his clenched hands?

"I see it all now; I see it all! While we are buoyed up with health and strength, we continue hard, selfish, obstinate in our wickedness. But when death comes, we awake to our error; and death has come to me, and I have awakened to mine. Why did I turn him out like a dog? He had neither kith nor kin, and I sent him adrift on the world, to fight with it or to starve! He was the only child of my sister, and she was gone. She and I were of the same father and mother; we shared the same meals in childhood, the same home, the same play, the same hopes. She wrote to me when she was dying, as I am dying now: 'Richard, should my poor boy be left fatherless—for my husband's health seems to be failing—be his friend and protector for Helen's sake, and may Heaven bless you for it!' And I scoffed at the injunction when the boy offended me, and turned him out. Shall I have to answer for it?"

The last anxious doubt was uttered more audibly than the rest; it escaped from his lips with a groan. A woman who was dozing over the fire started up.

"Did you call, sir?"

"No. Go out and leave me."

"But—"

"Go out and leave me," he repeated, with anger little fitted to his position. And the woman was speeding from the room, when he caught at the curtain and recalled her.

"Are they not come?"

"Not yet, sir. But, with this heavy fall, it's not to be wondered at. The highways must be almost impassable. With good roads they might have been here hours ago."

She went out. He lay back on his pillow: his eyes wide open, but wearing the same dreamy look. You may be wondering who he is; though you probably guess, for you have heard of him once before as Mr. Cooper, the uncle who discarded Edgar Halliburton.

I must give you a few words of retrospect. Richard Cooper was the eldest of three children; the others were a brother and a sister: Richard, Alfred, and Helen. Alfred and Helen both married; Richard never did marry. It was somewhat singular that the brother and sister should both die, each leaving an orphan; and that the orphans should find a home in the house of their Uncle Richard. Julia Cooper, the brother's orphan, was the first to come to it, a long time before Edgar Halliburton came. Helen had married the Rev. William Halliburton, and she died at his rectory in Devonshire—sending that earnest prayer to her brother Richard which you have just heard him utter. A little while, and her husband, the rector, also died; and then it was that Edgar went up to his Uncle Richard's. Fortunate for these two orphan children, it appeared to be, that their uncle had not married and could give them a good home.

A good home he did give them. Julia left it first to become the wife of Anthony Dare, a solicitor in large practice in a distant city. She married him very soon after her cousin Edgar came to his uncle's. And it was after the marriage of Julia that Edgar was discarded and turned adrift. Years, many years, had gone by since then; and here lay Richard Cooper, stricken for death and repenting of the harshness, which he had not repented of or sought to atone for all through those long years. Ah, my friends! whatsoever may lie upon our consciences, however we may have contrived to ignore it during our busy lives, be assured that it will find us out on our death-bed!

Richard Cooper lay back on his pillow, his eyes wide open with their inward tribulation. "Who knows but there would be time yet?" he suddenly murmured. And the thought appeared to rouse his mind and flush his cheek, and he lifted his hand and grasped the bell-rope, ringing it so loudly as to bring two servants to the room.

"Go up, one of you, to Lawyer Weston's," he uttered. "Bring him back with you. Tell him I want to alter my will, and that there may yet be time. Don't send—one of you go," he repeated in tones of agonising entreaty. "Bring him; bring him back with you!"

As the echo of his voice died away there came a loud summons at the street door, as of a hasty arrival. "Sir," cried one of the maids, "they're come at last! I thought I heard a carriage drawing up in the snow."

"Who's come?" he asked in some confusion of mind. "Weston?"

"Not him, sir; Mr. and Mrs. Dare," replied the servant as she hurried out.

A lady and gentleman were getting out of a coach at the door. A tall, very tall man, with handsome features, but an unpleasantly free expression. The lady was tall also, stout and fair, with an imperious look in her little turned-up nose. "Are we in time?" the latter asked of the servants.

"It's nearly as much as can be said, ma'am," was the answer. "But he has roused up in the last hour, and is growing excited. The doctors thought it might be so: that he'd not continue in the lethargy to the last."

They went on at once to the sick chamber. Every sense of the dying man appeared to be on the alert. His hands were holding back the curtain, his eyes were strained on the door. "Why have you been so long?" he cried in a voice of strength they were surprised to hear.

"Dear uncle," said Mrs. Dare, bending over the bed and clasping the feeble hands, "we started the very moment the letter came. But we could not get along—the roads are dreadfully heavy."

"Sir," whispered a servant in the invalid's ear, "are we to go now for Lawyer Weston?"

"No, there's no need," was the prompt answer. "Anthony Dare, you are a lawyer," continued Mr. Cooper; "you'll do what I want done as well as another. Will you do it?"

"Anything you please, sir," was Mr. Dare's reply.

"Sit down, then; Julia, sit down. You may be hungry and thirsty after your journey; but you must wait. Life's not ebbing out of you, as it is out of me. We'll get this matter over, that my mind may be so far at rest; and then you can eat and drink of the best that my house affords. I am in mortal pain, Anthony Dare."

Mrs. Dare was silently removing some of her outer wrappings, and whispering with the servant at the extremity of the roomy chamber; but Mr. Dare, who had taken off his great-coat and hat in the hall, continued to stand by the sick bed.

"I am sorry to hear it, sir," he said, in reply to Mr. Cooper's concluding sentence. "Can the medical men afford you no relief?"

"It is pain of mind, Anthony Dare, not pain of body. That pain has passed from me. I would have sent for you and Julia before, but I did not think until yesterday that the end was so near. Never let a man be guilty of injustice!" broke forth Mr. Cooper, vehemently. "Or let him know that it will come home to him to trouble his dying bed."

"What can I do for you, sir?" questioned Mr. Dare.

"If you will open that bureau, you'll find pen, ink, and paper. Julia, come here: and see that we are alone."

The servant left the room, and Mrs. Dare came forward, divested of her cloaks. She wore a handsome dark-blue satin dress (much the fashion at that time) with a good deal of rich white lace about it, a heavy gold chain, and some very showy amethysts set in gold. The jewellery was real, however, not sham; but altogether her attire looked somewhat out of place for a death-chamber.

The afternoon was drawing to a close. What with that and the dense atmosphere outside, the chamber had grown dim. Mr. Dare disposed the writing materials on a small round table at the invalid's elbow, and then looked towards the distant window.

"I fear I cannot see, sir, without a light."

"Call for it, Julia," said the invalid.

A lamp was brought in and placed on the table, so that its rays should not affect those eyes so soon to close to all earthly light. And Mr. Dare waited, pen in hand.

"I have been hard and wilful," began Mr. Cooper, putting up his trembling hands. "I have been obdurate, and selfish, and unjust; and now it is keeping peace from me—"

"But in what way, dear uncle?" softly put in Mrs. Dare; and it may as well be remarked that whenever Mrs. Dare attempted to speak softly and kindly it seemed to bear an unnatural sound to others' ears.

"In what way?—why, with regard to Edgar Halliburton," said Mr. Cooper, the dew breaking out upon his brow. "In seeking to follow the calling marked out for him by his father, he only did his duty; and I should have seen it in that light but for my own obstinate pride and self-will. I did wrong to discard him: I have done wrong ever since in keeping him from me, in refusing to be reconciled. Are you listening, Anthony Dare?"

"Certainly, sir. I hear."

"Julia, I say that there was no reason for my turning him away. There has been no reason for my keeping him away. I have refused to be reconciled: I have sent back his letters unopened; I have held him at contemptuous defiance. When I heard that he had married, I cast harsh words to him because he had not asked my consent, though I was aware all the time, that I had given him no opportunity to ask it—I had harshly refused all overtures, all intercourse. I cast harsh words to his wife, knowing her not. But I see my error now. Do you see it, Julia? Do you see it, Anthony Dare?"

"Would you like to have him sent for, sir?" suggested Mr. Dare.

"It is too late. He could not be here in time. I don't know, either, where he lives in London, or what his address may be. Do you?"—looking at his niece.

"Oh dear, no," she replied, with a slightly contemptuous gesture of the shoulders. As much as to imply that to know the address of her cousin Edgar was quite beneath her.

"No, he could not get here," repeated the dying man, whilst Mrs. Dare wiped the dews that had gathered on his pallid and wrinkled brow. "Julia! Anthony! Anthony Dare!"

"Sir, what is it?"

"I wish you both to listen to me. I cannot die with this injustice unrepaired. I have made my will in Julia's favour. It is all left to her, except a few trifles to my servants. When the property comes to be realised, there will be at least sixteen thousand pounds, and but for that late mad speculation I entered into there would have been nearly forty thousand."

He paused. But neither Mr. nor Mrs. Dare answered.

"You are a lawyer, Anthony, and could draw up a fresh will. But there's no time, I say. What is darkening the room?" he abruptly broke off to ask.

Mr. Dare looked hastily up. Nothing was darkening the room, except the gradually increasing gloom of evening.

"My sight is growing dim, then," said the invalid. "Listen to me, both of you. I charge you, Anthony and Julia Dare, that you divide this money with Edgar Halliburton. Give him his full share; the half, even to a farthing. Will you do so, Anthony Dare?"

"Yes, I will, sir."

"Be it so. I charge you both solemnly—do not fail. If you would lay up peace for the time when you shall come to be where I am—do not fail. There's no time legally to do what is right; I feel that there is not. Ere the deed could be drawn up I should be gone, and could not sign it. But I leave the charge upon you; the solemn charge. The half of my money belongs of right to Edgar Halliburton: Julia has claim only to the other half. Be careful how you divide it: you are sole executor, Anthony Dare. Have you your paper ready?"

"Yes, sir."

"Then dot down a few words, as I dictate, and I will sign them. 'I, Richard Cooper, do repent of my injustice to my dear nephew, Edgar Halliburton. And I desire, by this my last act on my death-bed, to bequeath to him the half of the money and property I shall die possessed of; and I charge Anthony Dare, the executor of my will, to carry out this act and wish as strictly as though it were a formal and legal one. I desire that whatever I shall die possessed of, save the bequests to my servants, may be equally divided between my nephew Edgar and my niece Julia.'"

The dying man paused. "I think that's all that need be said," he observed. "Have you finished writing it, Anthony Dare?"

Mr. Dare wrote fast and quickly, and was concluding the last words. "It is written, sir."

"Read it."

Mr. Dare proceeded to do so. Short as the time was which it took to accomplish this, the old man had fallen into a doze ere it was concluded; a doze or a partial stupor. They could not tell which; but, in leaning over him, he woke up with a start.

"I can't die with this injustice unrepaired!" he cried, his memory evidently ignoring what had just been done. "Anthony Dare, your wife has no right to all my money. I shall leave half of it to Edgar. I want you to write it down."

"It is done, sir. This is the paper."

"Where? where? Why don't you get light into the room? It's dark—dark. This? Is this it?"—as Mr. Dare put it into his hand. "Now, mind!" he added, his tone changing to one of solemn enjoinder; "mind you act upon it. Julia has no right to more than her half share; she must not take more: money kept by wrong, acquired by injustice, never prospers. It would not bring you good, it would not bring a blessing. Give Edgar his legal half; and give him his old uncle's love and contrition. Tell him, if the past could come over again there should be no estrangement between us."

He lay panting for a few minutes, and then spoke again, the paper having fallen unnoticed from his hand.

"Julia, when you see Edgar's wife—Did I sign that paper?" he broke off.

"No, sir," said Mr. Dare. "Will you sign it now?"

"Ay. But, signed or not signed, you'll equally act upon it. I don't put it forth as a legal document; I suppose it would not, in this informal state, stand good in law. It is only a reminder to you, Anthony Dare, that you may not forget my wishes. Hold me up in bed, and have lights brought in."

Anthony Dare drew the curtain back, and the rays of the lamp flashed upon the dying man. Mr. Dare looked round for a book on which to place the paper while it was signed.

"I want a light," came again from the bed, in a pleading tone. "Julia, why don't you tell them to bring in the lamp?"

"The lamp is here, uncle. It is close to you."

"Then there's no oil in it," he cried. "Julia, I will have lights here. Tell them to bring up the dining-room lamps. Don't ring; go and see that they are brought."

Unwilling to oppose him, and doubting lest his sight should really have gone, Mrs. Dare went out, and returned with one of the servants and more light. Mr. Cooper was then lying back on his pillow, dozing and unconscious.

"Has he signed the paper?" Mrs. Dare whispered to her husband.

He shook his head negatively, and pointed to it. It was lying on the bed, just as Mrs. Dare had left it. Mrs. Dare caught it up from any prying eyes that might be about, folded it, and held it securely in her hand.

"He will wake up again presently, and can sign it then," observed Mr. Dare, just as a gentle ring was heard at the house door.

"It's the doctor," said the servant; "I know his ring."

But the old man never did sign the paper, and never woke up again. He lay in a state of lethargy throughout the night. Mr. and Mrs. Dare watched by his bedside; the servants watched; and the doctors came in at intervals. But there was no change in his state; until the last great change. It occurred at daybreak; and when the neighbours opened their windows to the cold and the snow, the house of Richard Cooper remained closed. Death was within it.

CHAPTER XI

HELSTONLEIGH

I believe that most of the readers of "The Channings" will not like this story less because its scene is laid in the same place, Helstonleigh.

I narrate to you, as you may have already discovered, a great deal of truth: of events that have actually happened, combined with fiction. I can only do this from my own personal experience, by taking you to the scenes and places where I have lived. Of this same town, Helstonleigh, I could relate to you volumes. No place in the world holds so green a spot in my memory. Do you remember Longfellow's poem—"My Lost Youth"?

"Often I think of the beautiful town,
That is seated by the sea;
Often in thought go up and down
The pleasant streets of that dear old town,
And my youth comes back to me.
And a verse of a Lapland song
Is haunting my memory still:
'A boy's will is the wind's will,
And the thoughts of youth are long, long thoughts.'

"I remember the gleams and glooms that dart
Across the schoolboy's brain;
The song and the silence in the heart,
That in part are prophecies, and in part
Are longings wild and vain.
And the voice of that fitful song
Sings on, and is never still:
'A boy's will is the wind's will,
And the thoughts of youth are long, long thoughts.'

"There are things of which I may not speak;
There are dreams that cannot die;
There are thoughts that make the strong heart weak,
And bring a pallor into the cheek,
And a mist before the eye.
And the words of that fatal song
Come over me like a chill:
'A boy's will is the wind's will,
And the thoughts of youth are long, long thoughts.'

"Strange to me now are the forms I meet
When I visit the dear old town;
But the native air is pure and sweet,
And the trees that o'ershadow each well-known street,
As they balance up and down,
Are singing the beautiful song,
Are sighing and whispering still:
'A boy's will is the wind's will,

And the thoughts of youth are long, long thoughts.'

"And Deering's woods are fresh and fair,
And with joy that is almost pain
My heart goes back to wander there,
And among the dreams of the days that were
I find my lost youth again.
And the music of that old song
Throbs in my memory still:
'A boy's will is the wind's will,
And the thoughts of youth are long, long thoughts.'"

Those are some of its verses, and what "Deering" is to Longfellow, "Helstonleigh" is to me.

The Birmingham stage-coach came into Helstonleigh one summer's night, and stopped at its destination, the Star-and-Garter Hotel, bringing with it some London passengers. The direct line of rail to Helstonleigh from London was not then opened; and this may serve to tell you how long it is ago. A lady and a little girl stepped from the inside of the coach, and a gentleman and three boys got down from the outside. The latter were soaking. Almost immediately after leaving Birmingham, to which place the rail had conveyed them, the rain had commenced to pour in torrents, and those outside received its full benefit. The coach was crammed, inside and out, but with the other passengers we have nothing to do. We have with these; they were the Halliburtons.

For the town which Mr. Halliburton had been desirous to remove to, the one in which his cousin, Mrs. Dare, resided, was no other than Helstonleigh.

Mrs. Halliburton drew a long face when she set eyes on her husband's condition. "Edgar! you must be wet through and through!"

"Yes, I am. There was no help for it."

"You should have come inside when I wanted you to do so," she cried, in a voice of distress. "You should indeed."

"And have suffered you to take my place outside? Nonsense, Jane!"

Jane looked at the hotel. "We had better remain here for the night. What do you think?"

"Yes, I think so," he replied. "It is too wet to go about looking after anything that might be less expensive. Inquire if we can have rooms, Jane, whilst I see after the luggage."

Mrs. Halliburton went in, leading Janey, and was confronted by the barmaid, a smart young woman in a smart cap. "Can we sleep here to-night?" she inquired.

"Yes, certainly. How many beds?"

"I will go up with you and see," said Mrs. Halliburton. "Be so kind as not to put us in your more expensive rooms," she added, in a lower tone.

The barmaid looked at her from top to toe, as it is much in the habit of barmaids to do when such a request is preferred. She saw a lady in a black silk dress, a cashmere shawl, and a plain straw bonnet, trimmed with white. Simple as the attire was, quiet as was the demeanour, there was that about Mrs. Halliburton, in her voice, her accent, her bearing altogether, which proclaimed her the gentlewoman; and the barmaid condescended to be civil.

"I have nothing to do with the rooms," she said; "I'll call the chambermaid. My goodness! You had better get those wet things off, sir, unless you want to be laid up with cold."

The words were uttered in surprise, as her eyes encountered Mr. Halliburton. He looked taller, and thinner, and handsomer than ever; but he had a hollow cough now, and his cheek was hectic, and he was certainly wet through.

The chambermaid allotted them rooms. Mr. Halliburton, after rubbing himself dry with towels, got into a warmed bed, and had warm drink supplied to him. Jane, after unpacking what would be wanted for the night, returned to the sitting-room, to which her children had been shown. A good-natured maid, seeing the boys' clothes were damp, had lighted a fire, and they were kneeling round it, having been provided with bread and butter and milk. Intelligent, truthful, good-looking boys they were, with clear skins and bright, honest eyes, and open countenances. Janey had fallen asleep on a chair, her flaxen curls making her a pillow on its elbow. The boys crowded to one side of the fireplace when their mother came in, leaving the larger space for her; and William rose and gave her a chair. Mrs. Halliburton sat down, having laid on the table a Book of Common Prayer, which she had brought in her hand.

"Mamma, I hope papa will not be ill!"

"Oh, William, I fear it. Such a terrible wetting! And to be so long in it! How is it that he was so much worse than you are?"

"Because he sat at the end, and the gentleman next him did not hold the umbrella over him at all. When it came on to rain, some of the passengers had umbrellas and some had not, so they were divided for the best. We three had one between us, and we were wedged in between two fat old men, who helped to keep us dry. What a pity there was not a place for papa inside!"

"Yes; or if he would only have taken mine!" cried Mrs. Halliburton. "A wetting would not have hurt me, as it may hurt him. What place did they call that, William, where I got out to ask him to change?"

"Bromsgrove Lickey. Mamma, you have had no tea!"

"I do not care for any," she sighed. Hers was a hopeful nature; but something within her, this evening, seemed to whisper of trial for the future. She turned to the table, where stood the remains of the children's meal, cut a piece of bread from the loaf, and slowly spread it with butter. Then she poured out a little milk.

"Dear mamma, do have some tea!" cried William; "that's nothing but our milk and water."

She shook her head and took the milk. Tea would only be an additional expense, and she was too completely dispirited to care what she drank.

"I will read now," she said, taking up the Prayer-book. "And afterwards, I think, you had better say your prayers here, near the fire, as you have been so wet."

She chose a short psalm, and read it aloud. Then the children knelt down, each at a separate chair, to say their prayers in silence. Not as children's prayers are sometimes hurried over, knelt they; but with lowly reverence, their heads bowed, their young hearts lifted, never doubting but they were heard by God. They had been trained in a good school.

Did you ever have a sale of old things? Goods and chattels which may have served your purpose and looked well in their places, seem so old when they come to be exhibited that you feel half-ashamed of them? And as to the sum they realise—you will not have much trouble in hoarding it. Had Mr. Halliburton known the small sum that would be the result of his sale; had Jane dreamt that they would go for an "old song," they had never consented to part with them. Better have been at the cost of carrying them to Helstonleigh. Their bedding, blankets, etc., they did take: and it was well they did so.

I feel almost afraid to tell you how very little money they had in hand when they arrived. All their worldly wealth was little more than a hundred and twenty pounds. Debts had to be paid before leaving London; and it cost money to give up their house without notice, for their landlord was severe.

One hundred and twenty pounds! And with this they had to buy fresh furniture, and to live until teaching came in. A forlorn prospect on which to recommence the world! No wonder that Jane shunned even tea at the inn, or any other expense that might lessen their funds! But hope is buoyant in the human heart: and unless it were so, half the world might lay themselves down to die.

Morning came: a bright, sunny, beautiful morning after the rain. Not, apparently, had Mr. Halliburton suffered. His limbs felt a little stiff, but that would go off before the day closed. Their plans were to take a small house, as cheap a one as they could find, in accordance with—you really must for once excuse the word—gentility. That—a tolerably fair appearance—was necessary to Mr. Halliburton's success as a teacher.

"A dry, healthy spot, a little way out of the town," mused the landlord of the "Star," to whom they communicated their desire. "The London Road would be the place then. And you probably will find there such a house as you require."

They found their way to the London Road—a healthy suburb of the town; and there discovered a house they thought might suit them: a semi-detached house of good appearance, inclosed by iron railings, and standing a little back from the road. A sitting-room was on either side the entrance, a kitchen at the back. Three bedrooms were above; and above these again was a garret. A small garden was behind the house; and beyond that was a field, which did not belong to them. The adjoining house was similar to this one; but that possessed a large and productive garden. An inmate of that house showed them over this one, dressed as a Quakeress. Her features were plain, but her complexion was fair and delicate, and she had calm blue eyes.

"The rent of the house is thirty-two pounds per annum," she said, in reply to Mrs. Halliburton's question. "It belongs to Thomas Ashley; but thee must not apply to him. I will furnish thee with the address of the agent, who has the letting of Friend Ashley's houses. It is Anthony Dare. You will find the house pleasant and healthy, if you decide upon it," she added, speaking to both of them.

The latter name had struck upon Mr. Halliburton's ear. "Jane!" he whispered to his wife, "that must be the Mr. Dare who married my cousin, Julia Cooper. His name was Anthony Dare."

Mr. Halliburton proceeded alone to the office of Mr. Dare, the gentleman you met at Mr. Cooper's; Mrs. Halliburton returning to her children at the hotel. They had decided to take the house. Mr. Dare was not at home. "In London, with his wife," the head clerk said. But the clerk had power to let the house. Mr. Halliburton gave him some particulars with regard to himself, and they were considered satisfactory; but he did not mention that he was related to Mrs. Dare.

The next thing was about furniture. The clerk directed Mr. Halliburton to a warehouse where both new and second-hand things might be obtained, and he proceeded to it, calling in at the "Star" for his wife. She knew a great deal more about furniture than he. They did the best they could, spending about fifty pounds. A Kidderminster carpet was bought for the best sitting-room. The other room, which was to be Mr. Halliburton's study, and the bedrooms, went for the present without any. "We will buy all those things when we have succeeded a bit," said Mr. Halliburton.

CHAPTER XII

ANNA LYNN

They slept that night again at the "Star," and the following morning early, they and their furniture took possession together of the house. A busy day they found it, arranging things. Jane—who had determined, as the saying runs, "to put her shoulder to the wheel," not only on this day, but on future days—did not intend to engage a regular servant. That, like the carpets, might be indulged in as they succeeded; but in the mean time she thought a young girl might be found who would come in for a few hours daily, and do what they wanted done.

In the course of the morning, the fair, pleasant face of the Quakeress was seen approaching the back door from the garden. She wore a lilac print gown, a net kerchief crossed under it on her neck, and the peculiar net cap, with its high caul and neat little border.

"I have stepped in to ask if I can help thee with thy work," she began. "Thee hast plenty to do, setting things straight, and thy husband does not look strong. I will aid if thee pleasest."

"You are very kind to be so thoughtful for a stranger," replied Jane, charmed with the straightforward frankness of the Quakeress. "I hope you will first tell me to whom I am indebted."

"Thee can call me Patience," was the ready reply. "I live next door, with Samuel Lynn and his daughter Anna. His wife died soon after the child was born. I was related to Anna Lynn; and when she was departing she sent for me, and begged me not to leave her child, unless Samuel should take unto himself another wife. But that appears to be far from his thoughts. He loves the child much; she is as the apple of his eye."

"Is Mr. Lynn in business?" asked Jane.

"Not on his own account now. He was a glove manufacturer, as a young man, but he had not a large capital; and when the British ports were opened for the admission of gloves from the French, it ruined him—as it did many others in the city. Only the rich masters could stand that. Numbers went then."

"Went!" echoed Jane. "Went where?"

"To ruin. Ah! I remember it: though it is a long time ago now. It was, I think, in the year 1825. I cannot describe to thee the distress and destruction it brought upon this city, until then so flourishing. The manufacturers had to close their works, and the men went about the streets starving."

"Did the distress continue long?"

"For weeks, and months, and years. The town will never be again, in that respect, what it has been. Samuel Lynn was a man of integrity, and he gave up business while he could pay everyone, and accepted the post of manager in the manufactory of Thomas Ashley. Thomas Ashley is one of the first manufacturers in the city, as his father was before him. When thee shall know the place and the people better, thee will find that there is not a name more respected throughout Helstonleigh than that of Thomas Ashley."

"I suppose he is a rich man?"

"Yes, he is rich," replied Patience, who was as busy with her hands as she was in talking. "His household is expensive, and he keeps his open and his close carriages; but for all that he must be putting by money. It is not for his riches that Thomas Ashley is respected, but for his high character. There is not a more just man living than Thomas Ashley; there is not a manufacturer in the town who is so considerate and kind to his workmen. His rate of wages is on the highest scale, and he is incapable of oppression. He has a son and daughter. He, the boy, causes him much uneasiness and cost."

"Is he—not steady?" hastily asked Jane.

"Bless thee, it is not that!" was the laughing answer of Patience. "He is but a young boy yet. When he was fourteen months old, the nurse let him fall from her arms, from the first landing to the hall below. At first they thought he was not hurt: Margaret Ashley herself thought it; the doctors thought it. But in a little time injury grew apparent. It lay in one of the hips; he is often in great pain, and will be lame for life. Abscess after abscess forms in the hip. They take him to the sea-side; to doctors in London; but nothing cures him. A beautiful boy as you ever saw; but his hurt renders him peevish. He is fond of books; and David Byrne, who is a Latin and Greek scholar, goes daily to instruct him; but the boy is thrown back by his fits of illness. It is a great grief to Thomas and Margaret Ashley. They—Why, Anna, is it thee? What dost thou do here?"

Mrs. Halliburton turned from the kitchen cupboard, where she and Patience were arranging crockery, to behold a little girl who was no doubt Anna Lynn. Dark blue eyes were deeply set beneath their long lashes, which lay on a damask and dimpled cheek; her pretty teeth shone like pearls between her smiling lips, and her chestnut hair fell in a mass of careless curls upon her neck. Never, Mrs. Halliburton thought, had she seen a face so lovely. Jane was a pretty child; but Jane faded into nothing in comparison with the vision standing there.

"Thee has thy cap off again, Anna!" cried the Quakeress, with some asperity of tone. "Art thee not ashamed to be so bold?—going about with thy head uncovered!"

"The cap came off, Patience," gently responded Anna. She had a sweetly timid manner; a modest expression.

"Thee need not tell me what is untrue. When the cap is tied on, it will not come off, unless purposely removed. Go home and put it on. Thee may come back again. Perhaps Friend Halliburton will permit thee to stay awhile with her children, who are arranging their books in the study. Is thy French lesson learnt?"

"Not quite," replied Anna, running away.

She returned with a pretty little white net cap on, the model of that worn by Patience. Her luxuriant curls were pushed under it, and the crimped border rested on the fair forehead.

"Nay, there is no call to put all thy hair out of sight, child," said Patience. "Where are thy combs."

"In my hair, Patience."

Patience took off the cap, formed two flat curls, by means of the combs, on either side the temples, put the cap on again, and tucked the rest of the hair smoothly under it. Mrs. Halliburton then took Anna's hand, and led her to her own children.

"What a pity it is to hide her hair!" she said afterwards to Patience.

"Dost thee think so? It is the custom with our people. Anna's hair is fine, and of a curly nature. Brush it as I will, it curls; and she has acquired a habit of taking her cap off when I am not watching. Her father, I grieve to say, will let her sit by the hour together, her hair down, as thee saw it now, and her cap anywhere. I believe he thinks nothing she does is wrong. I talk to him much."

"I never saw a more beautiful child!" said Jane, warmly.

"I grant thee that she is fair; but she is eleven years old now, and her vanity should be checked. She is sometimes invited to the Ashleys', where she sees the mode in which Mary Ashley is dressed, according to the fashion of the world, and it sets her longing. Samuel Lynn will not listen to me. He is pleased that his child should be received there as Mary Ashley's equal; he cannot forget the time when he was in a good position himself."

"Who teaches Anna?"

"She attends a small school for Friends, kept by Ruth Darby. It is the holidays now. Her father educates her well. She learns French and drawing, and other branches of study suitable for girls. Take care! let me help thee with that heavy table."

Presently they went to see how things were getting on in the study. Jane could not keep her eyes from the face of that lovely child. It partly hindered her work, which there was little need of on that busy day; a day so busy that they were all glad when it was over, and they were at liberty to retire to rest.

Rarely had Jane witnessed so beautiful a view as that which met her sight the following morning, when she drew up her blind. The previous day had been hazy—nothing was to be seen; now the atmosphere had cleared. The great extent of scenery spread around, the green fields, the growing corn, the sparkling rivulets, the woods with their darker and their brighter trees, the undulating slopes—all were charming. But beyond all, and far more charming, bounding the landscape in the distant horizon, stretched the long chain of the far-famed Malvern Hills. As the sun cast upon them its light and shade, their outline so clearly depicted against the sky, and their white villas peeping out from the trees at their base—Jane felt that she could have gazed for ever. A wondrous picture is that of Malvern, as seen from Helstonleigh in the freshness of the early morning.

"Edgar!" she impulsively exclaimed, turning to the bed—for Mr. Halliburton had not risen—"you never saw anything more beautiful than the view from this window. I am sure half the Londoners never dreamt of anything like it."

There was no reply. "Perhaps he may be still asleep," she thought. But upon approaching the bed, she saw that his eyes were open.

"Jane," he gasped, "I am ill."

"Ill!" she repeated, a spasm darting through her heart.

"Every limb is paining me. My head aches, and I am burning with fever. I have felt it coming on all night."

She bent down; she felt his hands and his hot face—all burning, as he said, with fever.

"We must call in a doctor," she quietly said, suppressing every sign of dismay, that it might not agitate him. "I will ask Patience to recommend one."

"Yes; better have a doctor at once. What will become of us? If I should be going to have an illness—"

"Stay, Edgar; do not give way to sad anticipations," she gently said. "A brave mind, you know, goes half way towards a cure. It is the effect of that wetting; the cold must have been smouldering within you."

Smouldering only to burst out the fiercer for delay. Patience spoke in favour of their own medical man, a Mr. Parry, who lived near them and had a large practice. He came; and pronounced the malady to be rheumatic fever.

CHAPTER XIII

ILLNESS

For nine weeks Mr. Halliburton never left his bed. His wife was worn to a shadow; what with waiting upon him, and battling with her anxiety. Her body was weary, her heart was sick. Do you know the cost of illness? Jane knew it then.

In two weeks more he could leave his easy-chair and crawl about the room; and by that time he was all eagerness to commence his operations for the future.

"I must have some cards printed, Jane," he cried, one morning. "'Mr. Halliburton, Professor of Classics and Mathematics, late of King's Col—'—or should it be simply 'Edgar Halliburton?'" he broke off, to deliberate. "I wonder what the custom may be, down here?"

"I think you should wait until you are stronger, before you order your cards," was Jane's reply.

"But I can be getting things in train, Jane. I have been—how many weeks is it now?"

"Eleven."

"To be sure. It was June when we came; it is now September. I have been obliged to neglect the boys' lessons, too!"

"They have been very good and quiet; have gone on with their lessons themselves. If we have trouble in other ways, we have a blessing in our children, Edgar. They are thoroughly loving and dutiful."

"I don't know the ordinary terms of the neighbourhood," he resumed, after an interval of silence. "And—I wonder if people will want references? Jane"—after another silence—"you must put your things on, and go to Mrs. Dare's."

"To Mrs. Dare's!" she echoed. "Now? I don't know her."

"Never mind about not knowing her," he eagerly continued. "She is my cousin. You must ask whether they will allow themselves to be referred to. Peach will allow it also, I am quite certain. Do go, Jane."

Invalids in the weak state of Mr. Halliburton are apt to be restlessly impatient when the mind is set upon any plan or project. Jane found that it would vex him much if she declined to go to Mrs. Dare, and she prepared for the visit. Patience directed her to their residence.

It was situated at the opposite end of Helstonleigh. A handsome house, inclosed in a high wall, and bearing the imposing title of "Pomeranian Knoll." Jane entered the iron gates, walked round the carriage drive that inclosed the lawn, and rang the house bell. A showy footman in light blue livery, with a bunch of cords on his shoulder, answered it.

"Can I see Mrs. Dare?"

"What name, ma'am?"

Jane gave in one of her visiting cards, wondering whether that was not too grand a proceeding, considering the errand upon which she had come. She was shown into an elegant room, to the presence of Mrs. Dare. That lady was in a costly morning dress, with chains, rings, bracelets, and other glittering jewellery about her: as she had worn the evening you saw her beside Mr. Cooper's death-bed.

"Mrs. Halliburton?" she was repeating in doubt, when Jane entered, her eyes strained on the card. "What Mrs. Halliburton?" she added, not very civilly, turning her eyes upon Jane.

Jane explained. The wife of Edgar Halliburton, Mrs. Dare's cousin.

Mrs. Dare's presence of mind wholly forsook her. She grew deathly white; she caught at a chair for support; she was utterly unable to speak or to conceal her agitation. Jane could only look at her in amazement, wondering whether she was seized with sudden illness.

A few moments and she recovered herself. She took a seat, motioned Jane to another, and asked, as she might have asked of any stranger, what her business might be. Jane explained it, somewhat at length.

Mrs. Dare's surprise was great. She could not or would not understand; and her face flushed a deep red, and again grew deadly pale. "Edgar Halliburton come to live in Helstonleigh!" she repeated. "And you say you are his wife?"

"I am his wife," was the reply of Jane, spoken with quiet dignity.

"What is it that you say he has in view, in coming here?"

"I beg your pardon; I thought I had explained." And Jane went over the ground again—why he had been obliged to leave London, and his reasons for settling in Helstonleigh.

"You could not have come to a worse place," said Mrs. Dare, who appeared to be annoyed almost beyond repression. "Masters of all sorts are so plentiful here that they tread on each other's heels."

Discouraging news! And Jane's heart beat fast on hearing it. "My husband thought you and Mr. Dare would kindly interest yourselves for him. He knows that Mr. Peach will—"

"No," interrupted Mrs. Dare, in decisive tones. "For Edgar Halliburton's own sake I must decline to recommend him; or, indeed, to interfere at all. It would only encourage fallacious hopes. Masters are here in abundance—I speak of private masters; they don't find half enough to do. Schools are also plentiful. The best thing will be to go to some place where there is a better opening, and not to settle himself here at all!"

"But we have already settled here," replied Jane.

A thought suddenly struck Mrs. Dare. "It can never be Edgar who has taken Mr. Ashley's cottage in the London Road? I remember the name was said to be Halliburton."

"The same. It was let to us by Mr. Dare's clerk."

Mrs. Dare sat biting her lips. That she was grievously annoyed was evident, but in deference to good manners, which were partially returning to her, she strove to repress its signs. "I presume your husband is poor, Mrs. Halliburton?"

"We are very poor."

"It is generally the case with teachers, as I have observed. Well, I can only give one answer to your application—that we must decline all interference. I hope Edgar will not think of applying again to us upon the subject."

Jane rose. Mrs. Dare remained seated. And yet she prided herself upon her good breeding!

"I had forgotten a question which my husband particularly desired me to ask," Jane said, turning back, as she was moving to the door. "Edgar saw by the papers that his uncle, Mr. Cooper, died the beginning of the year. Did he remember him on his death-bed, so far as to send a message of reconciliation?"

Strange to say, the countenance of Mrs. Dare again changed; now to a burning heat, now to a livid pallor. She hesitated in her answer.

"Yes," she said at length. "Mr. Cooper so far relented as to send him his forgiveness. 'Tell my nephew Edgar, if you ever see him, that I am sorry for my harshness; that I would treat him differently were the time to come over again.' I do not remember the precise words; but they were to that effect. There is no doubt that he would have wished to be reconciled; but time did not allow it. I should have written to Edgar of this, had I been acquainted with his address."

"A letter addressed to King's College would always have found him. But he will be glad to hear this. He also bade me ask how Mr. Cooper's money was left—if you would kindly give him the information."

Mrs. Dare bent her head. She was busy playing with her bracelet. "The will was proved in Doctors' Commons. Edgar Halliburton may see it by paying a shilling there."

It was not a gracious answer, and Jane paused. "He cannot go to Doctors' Commons; he is not in London," she gently said.

Mrs. Dare raised her head. A look, speaking plainly of defiance, had settled itself on her features. "It was left to me; the whole of it, except a few trifling legacies to his servants. What could Edgar Halliburton expect?"

"I am sure that he did not expect anything," observed Jane. "Though I believe a hope has sometimes crossed his mind that Mr. Cooper might at the last relent, and remember him."

"Nay," said Mrs. Dare, "he had behaved too disobediently for that. First, in opposing his uncle's wishes that he should enter into business; secondly, in his marriage."

"In his marriage!" echoed Jane, a flush rising to her own face.

"It was so. Mr. Cooper was exceedingly exasperated when he heard that Edgar had married. He looked upon the marriage, I believe, as undesirable for him in a pecuniary point of view. You must pardon my speaking of this to you personally. You appear to wish for the truth."

The flush on Jane's face deepened to crimson.

"It is true that I had no money," she said. "But I am the daughter of a clergyman, and was reared a gentlewoman!"

"I suppose my uncle thought Edgar Halliburton should have married a fortune. However all that is past and gone, and it will do no good to recall it. I am sorry that you should have been so ill-advised for your own interests as to fix on this place to come to."

Mrs. Dare rose. She had sat all this time; Jane had stood. "Tell Edgar, from me, that I am sorry to hear of his illness. Tell him there is no possible chance of success for him in Helstonleigh; no opening whatever! When I say that I hope he will speedily remove to some place less overdone with masters, I speak only in his own interest!"

She rang the bell as she spoke, and gave Jane the tips of two of her fingers. The footman held open the hall door, and bowed her out. Jane went down the gravel sweep, determined never again to trouble Mrs. Dare.

"Joseph!" cried Mrs. Dare, sharply.

"Ma'am?"

"Should that lady ever call again, I am not at home, remember!"

"Very well, ma'am," was the man's reply.

Mrs. Dare did not stay to hear it. She had flown upstairs to her room in trepidation. There she attired herself hastily and went out, bending her steps towards Mr. Dare's office. It was situated at the end of the town; and the door displayed a brass plate: "Mr. Dare, Solicitor."

Mrs. Dare entered the outer room. "Is Mr. Dare alone?" she asked of the clerks.

"No, ma'am. Mr. Ashley is with him."

Chafing at the answer, for she was in a mood of great impatience, of inward tremor, Mrs. Dare waited for a few minutes. Mr. Ashley came out. A man of nearly forty years, rather above the middle height, with a fresh complexion, dark eyes, and well-formed features. A benevolent-looking, good man. His wife was a cousin of Mr. Dare's.

Mr. Dare was seated at his table in his own room when his wife came in. She had turned again of an ashy paleness, and she dropped into a chair near to him.

"What is the matter?" he asked in astonishment. "Are you ill?"

"I think I shall die," she gasped. "I have had a mortal fright, Anthony."

Mr. Dare rose. He was about to get her some water, or to call for it, but she caught his arm. "Stay, and hear me! Stay! Anthony, those Halliburtons have come to Helstonleigh. Come to live here!"

Mr. Dare's mouth opened. "What Halliburtons?" he presently asked.

"They. He has come here to settle. He wants to teach; and his wife has been with me, asking us to be referees. Of course I put the stopper upon that. The idea of our having poor relations in the town who get their living by teaching!"

A very disagreeable idea indeed; for those who were playing first fiddle in the place, and expected to play it still. But not for that did the man and wife stand gazing at each other; and the naturally bold look on Mr. Dare's face had faded considerably just then.

"She asked about the will," said Mrs. Dare, dropping her voice to a whisper, and looking round with a shiver. "I thought I should have died with fear."

Mr. Dare rallied his courage. Any little reminiscence that may have momentarily disturbed his equanimity he shook off, and was his own bold self again.

"Nonsense, Julia! What is there to fear? The will is proved and acted upon. Whatever the old man may have uttered to us in his death ramblings was heard by ourselves alone. If any one had heard it, I should not much care. A will's a will all the world over; and to act against it would be illegal."

Mrs. Dare sat wiping her brow and gathering up her courage. It came back by slow degrees.

"Anthony, we must get them out of Helstonleigh. For more reasons than one we must get them out. They are in that house of Mr. Ashley's."

He looked surprised. "They! Ay, to be sure: the name in the books is Halliburton. It never occurred to me that it could be they. I wonder if they are poor?"

"Very poor, the wife said."

"Just so," said Mr. Dare, with a pleasant smile. "I'll not ask for the rent this quarter, but let it go on a bit. We may get them out, Mrs. Dare."

You need not be told that Anthony Dare and his wife had omitted to act upon Mr. Cooper's dying injunction. At the time they did really intend to fulfil it; they were not thieves or forgers. But Edgar Halliburton was not present to remind them of his claims: and, when the money came to be realised, to be in their own hands, there it was suffered to remain. Waiting for him, of course; they did not know precisely where to find him, and did not take any trouble to inquire. Very tempting and useful they found the money. A large portion of their own share went in paying back debts, for they lived at an extravagant rate; and—and in short they had intrenched upon that other share, and could not now have paid it over had they been ever so willing to do so. No wonder that Mrs. Dare had felt as one in mortal fear when she met Jane Halliburton face to face!

CHAPTER XIV

A CHRISTMAS DREAM

Winter had come to Helstonleigh: frost hovered in the air and rested on the ground. How was Mr. Halliburton? He had never once been out since his illness, and he sat by the fire when he did not lie in bed, and his cough was racking him. He might, and probably would, have recovered health under more favourable auspices, but anxiety of mind was killing him. Their money was dwindling to a close, and delicacies they dared not get for him. Mr. Halliburton would say he did not require them; could not eat them if they were procured. Poor man! he craved for them in his inmost heart. Strange to say, he did not see his own danger. Or, rather, it would have been strange but that similar cases are met with every day. "When this cold weather has passed, and spring is in, then I shall get up my strength," was his constant cry. "Then I shall set about my work in earnest, and make my arrival and my plans known to Peach. It has been of no use troubling him beforehand." False, false hopes! fond, delusive hopes!

Dr. Carrington had said that if he took care of himself, he might live and be well. The other doctors had said the same. And there was no reason to doubt their judgment. But they had not bargained for an attack of rheumatic fever, or for the increased injury to the lungs which the same cause, that past soaking, had induced.

On Christmas Eve, he and Jane were sitting over the fire in the twilight. He could come downstairs now; indeed, he did not appear to be so ill as he really was. The surgeon who attended him in the fever had been discharged long ago. "There's nothing the matter with me now but debility; and, only time will bring me out of that," Mr. Halliburton said, when he dismissed him. Jane was hopeful; more hopeful by fits and starts than continuously so; but she did really believe he might get well when winter had passed. They were sitting beside the fire, when a great bustle interrupted them. All the children trooped in at once, with the noise it is the delight of children not to stir without. Frank, who had been out, had entered the house with his arms full of holly and ivy, his bright face glowing with excitement. The others were attending him to show off the prize.

"Look at all this Christmas, mamma!" cried he. "I have bought it."

"Bought it?" repeated Jane. "My dear Frank, did I not tell you we must do without Christmas this year?"

"But it cost nothing, mamma. Only a penny!"

Jane sighed. She did not say to the children that even a penny was no longer "nothing."

"You know that penny I have kept in my pocket a long while," went on Frank in excitement, addressing the assemblage. "Well, I thought if mamma would not buy some Christmas, I would."

"But you did not buy all that for a penny, Frank? We should pay sixpence for it in London."

"I did, though, mamma. I had it of that old man who lives in the cottage higher up the road, with the big garden to it. He was going to cut me more, but I told him this was plenty. You should have seen the heaps he gave a woman for twopence: she wanted a wheelbarrow to carry it away."

Janey clapped her hands, and began to dance. "I shall help you to dress the rooms! We must have a merry Christmas!"

Mr. Halliburton drew her to him. "Yes, we must have a merry Christmas, must we not, Janey? Jane"— turning to his wife—"can you manage to have a nice dinner for us? Christmas only comes once a year."

He looked up with his haggard face: very much as though he were longing for a nice dinner then.

"I will see what I can do," said Jane in reply, smothering down another sigh. "I am going out presently to the butcher's. A joint of beef will be best; and though the pudding's a plain one, I hope it will be good. Yes, we must keep Christmas."

Christmas-day dawned, and in due time they assembled as usual. Jane intended to go to church that day. During her husband's illness she had been obliged to send the children alone. They had been trained to know what church meant, and did not require some one with them to keep them in order there. A good thing if the same could be said of all children!

It was a clear, bright morning, cold and frosty. Mr. Halliburton came down just as they were starting.

"I feel so much better to-day!" he exclaimed. "I could almost go with you myself. Jane"—smiling at her look of consternation—"you need not be startled: I do not intend to attempt it. William, you are not ready."

"Mamma said I was to stay with you, papa."

"Stay with me! There's not the least necessity for that. I tell you all I am feeling better to-day—quite well. You can go with the rest, William."

William looked at his mother, and for a moment Jane hesitated. Only for a moment. "I would rather he remained, Edgar," she said. "Betsy will be gone by twelve o'clock. Indeed, I should not feel comfortable at the thought of your being alone."

"Oh, very well," replied Mr. Halliburton, quite gaily. "I suppose you must remain, William, or we shall have mamma leaving when the service is only half over to see whether I have not fallen into the fire."

Jane had all the household care upon her shoulders now, and a great portion of the household work. Though an active domestic manager, she had known nothing practically of the more menial work of a house; she knew it only too well now. The old saying is a very true one: "Necessity makes us acquainted with strange bedfellows." This young girl, Betsy, who came in part of each day to assist, was almost as much trouble as profit. She had said to Jane on Christmas Eve: "If you please, mother says I am to be at home to-morrow, if it's convenient." I am! However, Jane and the young lady came to a compromise. She was to go home at twelve and come back later to wash up the dishes. Of course it entailed upon Jane all the trouble of preparing dinner.

Have you ever known one of these cases yourself? Where a lady—a lady, mind you, as Jane was—has had to put aside her habits of refinement, pin up her gown, and turn to and cook; roast the meat and boil potatoes, and all the ether essential items? Many a one is doing it now in real life. Jane Halliburton was not a solitary example. The pudding had been made the day before and partly boiled: it was now on the fire, boiling again, and the rest of the dinner she would do on her return from church.

It was something wonderful, the improvement in Mr. Halliburton's health that day. He took his part with William in reading the psalms and lessons while the rest were at church: it was what he had been unable to do for a long time in consequence of his cough and laboured breathing. The duty over, he lay back in his chair; in thought apparently, not exhaustion.

"Peace on earth, and good will towards men!" he repeated presently, in a fervent, but somewhat absent tone. "William, my boy, I think peace must be coming to me at last. I do feel so well."

"What peace, papa?" asked William, puzzled.

"The peace of renewed health, of hope; freedom from worry. The Christmas season and the bright day have taken away all my despondency. Let me go on like this, and in another month I shall be out and at work."

William's eyes sparkled. He fully believed it all. Boys are sanguine.

They were to dine at three o'clock, and Jane did her best to prepare it. During the process, Patience appeared at the back door with a plate of oranges. "Will thee accept of these for thy children?" asked she.

"How kind you are!" exclaimed Jane, in a grateful impulse, as she thought of her children. Of such little treats they had latterly enjoyed a scanty share. "Patience, I hope you did not buy them purposely?"

"Had I had to buy them, thee would not have seen them," returned the candid Quakeress. "A friend of Samuel Lynn's, who lives at Bristol, sends us a small case every winter. When I was unpacking it this morning I said to him, 'The young ones at the next door would be pleased with a few of these'; but he did not answer. Thee must not think him selfish; he is not a selfish man; but he cannot bear to see anything go beside the child. Anna looked at him eagerly; she would have been pleased to send half the box: and he saw it. 'Take in a few, Patience,' he cried."

"I am much obliged to him, and to you also," repeated Jane. "Patience, Mr. Halliburton is so much better to-day! Go in, and see him."

Patience went into the parlour, carrying the oranges with her. When she came out again there was a grave expression on her serene face.

"Thee will do well not to count upon this apparent improvement in thy husband."

Jane's heart went down considerably. "I do not exactly count upon it, Patience," she confessed; "but he does seem to have changed so much for the better that I feel in greater spirits than I have felt this many a day. His cough seems almost well."

"I do not wish to throw a damp upon thee; still, were I thee, I would not reckon upon it. These sudden improvements sometimes turn out to have been deceitful. Fare thee well!"

Jane went into the parlour. The children were gathered round the plate of oranges. "Mamma, do look!" cried Janey. "Are they not good? There are six: one apiece for us all. I wonder if papa could eat one? Gar, you are not to touch. Papa, could you eat an orange?"

Unseen by the children, Mr. Halliburton had been straining his eager gaze upon the oranges. His mouth parched with inward fever, his throat dry, they appeared, coming thus unexpectedly before him, what the long-wished-for spring of water is to the fainting traveller in the desert. Jane caught the look, and handed the plate to him. "You would like one, Edgar?"

"I am thirsty," he said, in tones savouring of apology, for the oranges seemed to belong to the children rather than to him. "I think I must eat mine before dinner. Cut it into four, will you?"

He took up one of the quarters. "It is delicious!" he exclaimed. "It is so refreshing!"

The children stood around and watched him. They enjoyed oranges, but scarcely with a zest so intense as that.

When Jane returned to the kitchen, she found a helpmate. The maid from next door, Grace, a young Quakeress, fair and demure, was standing there. She had been sent by Patience to do what she could for half an hour. "How considerate she is!" thought grateful Jane.

They dined in comfort, Grace waiting on them. Afterwards the oranges were placed upon the table. Master Gar caught up the plate, and presented it to his mother. "Papa has had his," quoth he.

"Not for me, Gar," said Jane. "I do not eat oranges. I will give mine to papa."

The three younger children speedily attacked theirs. William did not. He left his by the side of the one rejected by his mother, and set the plate by Mr. Halliburton.

"Do you intend these for me, William?"

"Yes, papa."

Frank looked surprised. "William, you don't mean to say you are not going to eat your orange? Why, you were as glad as any of us when they came."

"I eat oranges when I want them," observed William, with an affectation of carelessness, which betrayed a delicacy of feeling that might have done honour to one older than he. "I have had too good a dinner to care about oranges."

Mr. Halliburton drew William towards him, and looked steadfastly into his face with a meaning smile. "Thank you, my darling," he whispered: and William coloured excessively as he sat down.

Mr. Halliburton ate the oranges, and appeared as if he could have eaten as many more. Then he leaned his head back on the pillow which was placed over his chair, and presently fell asleep.

"Be very still, dear children," whispered Jane.

They looked round, saw why they were to be still, and hushed their busy voices. William pulled a stool to his mother's feet, and took his seat on it, holding her hand between his.

"Papa will soon be well again now," he softly said. "Don't you think so, mamma?"

"Indeed I hope he will," she answered.

"But don't you think it?" he persisted; and Jane detected an anxiety in his tone. Could there have been a shadow of fear upon the boy's own heart? "He said mamma, whilst you were at church, that in another month he should be strong again."

"Not quite so soon as that, I fear, William. He has been so much reduced, you know. Later: if he goes on as well as he appears to be going on now."

Jane set the children to that renowned game. "Cross questions and crooked answers." You may have had the pleasure of playing it: if so, you will remember that it consists chiefly of whispering. It is difficult to keep children quiet long together.

"Where am I?" cried a sudden voice, startling the children in the midst of their silent whispers.

It came from Mr. Halliburton. He had slept about half an hour, and was now looking round in bewilderment, his head starting away from the pillow. "Where am I?" he repeated.

"You have been asleep, papa," cried Frank.

"Asleep! Oh, yes! I remember. You are all here, and it is Christmas Day. I have been dreaming."

"What about, papa?"

Mr. Halliburton let his head fall back on the pillow again. He fixed his eyes on vacancy, and there ensued a silence. The children looked at him.

"Singular things are dreams," he presently exclaimed. "I thought I was on a broad, wide road—an immense road, and it was crowded with people. We were all going one way, stumbling and tripping along—"

"What made you stumble, papa?" interrupted Janey, whose busy tongue was ever ready to talk.

"The road was full of impediments," continued Mr. Halliburton, in a dreamy tone, as if his mental vision were buried in the scene and he was relating what had actually occurred. "Stones, and hillocks, and brambles, and pools of shallow water, and long grass that got entangled round our feet: nothing but difficulties and hindrances. At the end, in the horizon, as far as the eye could reach—very, very far away indeed—a hundred times as far away as the Malvern Hills appear to be from us—there shone a brilliant light. So brilliant! You have never seen anything like it in life, for the naked eye could not bear such light. And yet we seemed to look at it, and our sight was not dazzled!"

"Perhaps it was fireworks?" interrupted Gar. Mr. Halliburton went on without heeding him.

"We were all pressing on to get to the light, though the distant journey seemed as if it could never end. So long as we kept our eyes fixed on the light, we could see how we walked, and we passed over the rough places without fear. Not without difficulty. But still we did pass them, and advanced. But the moment we took our eyes from the light, then we were stopped; some fell; some wandered aside, and would not try to go forward; some were torn by the brambles; some fell into the water; some stuck in the mud; in short, they could not get on any way. And yet they knew—at least, it seemed that they knew—that if they would only lift their eyes to the light, and keep them steadfastly on it, they were certain to be helped, and to make progress. The few who did keep their eyes on it—very few they were!—steadily bore onwards. The same hindrances, the same difficulties were in their path, so that at times they also felt tempted to despair—to fear they could not get on. But their fears were groundless. So long as they did not take their eyes from the light, it guided them in certainty and safety over the rough places. It was a helper that could not fail; and it was ready to guide every one—all those millions and millions of travellers. To guide them throughout the whole of the way until they had gained it."

The children had become interested and were listening with hushed lips. "Why did they not all let it guide them?" breathlessly asked William. "Nothing can be more easy than to keep our eyes on a light that does not dazzle. What did you do, papa?"

"It seemed that the light would only shine on one step at a time," continued Mr. Halliburton, not in answer to William, but evidently absorbed in his own thoughts. "We could not see further than the one step, but that was sufficient; for the moment we had taken it, then the light shone upon another. And so we passed on, progressing to the end, the light seeming brighter and brighter as we drew near to it."

"Did you get to it, papa?"

"I am trying to recollect, William. I seemed to be quite close to it. I suppose I awoke then."

Mr. Halliburton paused, still in thought: but he said no more. Presently he turned to his wife. "Is it nearly tea-time, Jane? I cannot think what makes me so thirsty."

"We can have tea now, if you like," she replied. "I will go and see about it."

She left the room, and Janey ran after her. In the kitchen, making a great show and parade of being at work amidst plates and dishes, was a damsel of fifteen, her hair curiously twisted about her head, and her round, green eyes wide open. It was Betsy.

"That was good pudding," cried she, turning her face to Mrs. Halliburton. "Better than mother's."

She alluded to a slice which had been given her. Jane smiled. "We want tea, Betsy."

"Have it in directly, mum," was Miss Betsy's acquiescent response.

Scarcely were the words spoken, when a commotion was heard in the sitting-room. The door was flung open, and the boys called out, the tone of their voices one of utter alarm. Jane, the child, and the maid, made but one step to the room. All Jane's fears had flown to "fire."

Fire had been almost less startling. Mr. Halliburton was lying back on the pillow with a ghastly face, his mouth, and shirt-front stained with blood. He could not speak, but he asked assistance with his imploring eyes. In coughing he had broken a blood-vessel.

Jane did not faint; did not scream. Her whole heart turned sick, and she felt that the end had come. Janey sank down on the floor with a faint cry, and hid her face on the sofa. One glimpse was sufficient for Betsy. The moment she had taken it, she subsided into a succession of shrieks; flew out of the house and burst into that of Mr. Lynn. There she terrified the sober family by announcing that Mr. Halliburton was lying with his throat cut.

Mr. Lynn and Patience hurried in, ordering Anna to remain where she was. They saw what was the matter, and placed him in a better position: Patience helping Mrs. Halliburton to sponge his face.

"Shall I get the doctor for thee, friend?" asked the Quaker of Jane. "I shall bring him quicker, maybe, than one of thy lads would."

"Oh! yes, yes!"

"I warned thee not to be sanguine," whispered Patience, when Mr. Lynn had gone. "I feared it might be only the deceitfulness of the ending."

The ending! what a confirmation of Jane's own fears! She turned her eyes despairingly on Patience.

Mr. Halliburton opened his trembling lips, as though he would have spoken. Patience stopped him.

"Thee must not talk, friend. If thee hast need of anything, can thee not make a sign?"

He gave them to understand that he wanted water. This was given to him, and he appeared to be more composed.

"There is nothing else that I can do just now," observed Patience. "I will go back and take thy little girl with me. See her, hiding there!"

Patience did so. Betsy cowered over the fire in the kitchen, and the three boys and their mother stood round the dying man.

"Children!" he gasped.

"Oh, Edgar! do not speak!" interrupted Jane.

He smiled as he looked at her, very much as though he knew that it did not matter whether he spoke or remained silent. "I am at the journey's end, Jane; close to the light. Children," he panted at slow intervals, "when I told you my dream, I little thought it was only a type of the present reality. I think it was sent to me that I might tell it you, for I now see its meaning. You are travelling on to that light, as I thought I was—as I have been. You will have the same stumbling-blocks to walk over; none are exempt from them; trials, and temptations, and sorrows, and drawbacks. But the light is there, ever shining to guide you, for it is Heaven. Will you always look up to it?"

He gathered their hands together, and held them between his. The boys, awe-struck, bewildered with terror and grief, could only gaze in silence and listen.

"The light is God, my children. He is above you, and below you, and round about you everywhere. He is ready to help you at every step and turn. Make Him your guide; put your whole dependence upon Him, implicitly trust to Him to lighten your path, so that you may see to walk in it. He cannot fail. Look up to

Him, and you will be unerringly guided, though it may be—though it probably will be—only step by step. Never lose your trust in God, and then rest assured He will conduct you to His own bright ending. Jane, let them take it to their hearts! May God bless you, my dear ones! and bring you to me hereafter!"

He ceased, and lay exhausted; his eyes fondly seeking Jane's, her hand clasped in his. Jane's own eyes were dry and burning, and she appeared to be unnaturally calm. Gradually the fading eyes closed. In a very short time the knock of Samuel Lynn was heard at the door. He had brought the doctor. William, passing his handkerchief over his wet face, went to open it.

Mr. Parry stepped into the room, and Jane moved from beside her husband to give place to him. "He sighed heavily a minute or two ago," she whispered.

The surgeon looked at him. He bent his ear to the open mouth, and then gently unbuttoned the waistcoat, and listened for the beating of the heart. "His life passed away in that sigh," murmured the doctor to Jane.

It was even so. Edgar Halliburton had gone into the light.

CHAPTER XV

THE FUNERAL

Jane looked around her—looked at all the terrors of her situation. The first burst of grief over, and a day or two gone on, she could only look at it. She did not know which way to turn or what to do. It is true she placed implicit trust in God—in the LIGHT spoken of by her husband when he was passing away. Throughout her life she had borne an ever-present, lively trust in God's unchanging care; and she had incessantly striven to implant the same trust in the minds of her children. But in this season of dread anxiety, of hopeless bereavement, you will not think less well of her for hearing that she did give way to despondency, almost to despair.

From tears for him who had been the dear partner of her life, to anxiety for the future of his children—from anxiety for them, to pecuniary distress and embarrassment—so passed on her hours from Christmas night. Calm she had contrived to be in the presence of others; but it was the calm of an aching heart. She dreaded her own reflections. When she rose in the morning she said, "How shall I bear up through the day?" and when she went to her bed, it would be, "How shall I drag through the right?" Tossing, turning, moaning; walking the room in the darkness when no eye was upon her; kneeling, almost without hope, to pour forth her tribulations to God—who would believe that, in the daytime, before others, she could be so apparently serene? Only once did she give way, and that was the day before the funeral.

Patience sympathised with her in a reasoning sort of way. It had been next to impossible for Jane to keep her pecuniary anxiety from Patience, who advised and assisted her in making the various arrangements. It was necessary to go to work in the most sparing manner possible; and it ended in Jane's taking Patience into her full confidence.

"If thee can but keep a house over thy head, so as to retain thy children with thee, thee wilt get along. Do not be cast down."

"Oh, Patience, that is what I have been thinking about—how am I to keep the house together. I do not see that I can do it."

"The furniture is thine," observed Patience. "Thee might let two or three of thy rooms, so as to cover the rent."

"I have thought all that over and over again to myself," sighed Jane. "But, Patience—allowing that the rent were made in that way—how are we to live?"

"Thee must occupy thy time in some way. Thee can sew! Dost thee know dress-making?"

"No—only sufficient of it to make my own plain gowns and Jane's frocks. As to plain sewing, I could never earn food at it—it is so badly paid. And there will be the education of my boys, and their clothing."

"Thee hast anxiety before thee—I see it," said Patience, in a grave tone. "Still, I would not have thee be cast down. Thee will make thyself ill, and that will not be the way to mend thy condition."

Jane sat down, her hands clasped on her knees, her mind viewing her dark troubles. "If I were but clear, I should have better hope," she said, lifting her face in its sad sorrow. "Patience, we owe half a year's rent; and there will be the funeral expenses besides."

"Hast thee no kindred that would aid thee in thy strait?"

Jane shook her head. The only "kindred" she possessed in the whole world was one who had barely enough for his own poor wants—her brother Francis.

"Hast thee no little property to dispose of?" continued Patience. "Watches, or things of that kind?"

There was her husband's watch. But Jane's pale face crimsoned at the idea of parting with it in that manner. It was a good watch, and had long ago been promised to William.

"I can understand thy flush of aversion," said Patience, kindly. "I would not be the one to suggest aught to hurt thy feelings; but thy necessities may leave no alternative."

A conviction that they would leave none was already stealing over Jane. She possessed a few trinkets herself, not of much value, and a little silver. All might have to go, not excepting the watch. "Would there be a difficulty in disposing of them, Patience?" she asked aloud.

"None at all: there is the pawn-shop," said the plain-speaking Quakeress. "I do not know what many would do without it. I can tell thee that some of the great ones of this city send their plate to it on occasion. Thee would not like to go to such a place thyself, but thy servant's mother, Elizabeth Carter, is a discreet woman: she would render thee this little service. As I tell thee, if thee can only surmount present difficulties, so as to secure a start, thee may get on."

Surmount present difficulties! It seemed to Jane next door to an impossibility. She had the merest trifle of money left, was in debt, and without means, so far as she saw, of earning even food. She paid her last night visit to the room which contained the coffin, and went thence up to her bed, to toss the night through on her wet pillow, with a burning brow and an aching heart.

It was a sad funeral to see, and one of the plainest of the plain. The clerk of the church, who had condescended to come up to escort it—a condescension he did not often vouchsafe to poor funerals, for they afforded nothing good to eat and drink—walked first, without a hatband. Then came the coffin, covered with a pall, and William and Frank behind it. Jane had not sent Gar, poor little fellow! She thought he might be better away. That was all; there were no attendants: the clerk, the two boys, the coffin, and the men who bore it.

It was sad to see. The people stopped to look as it went along the streets, following with their eyes the poor fatherless children. One young man stood aside, raised his hat, and held it in his hand until the coffin had passed. But the young man had lived in foreign countries, where it is the custom to remain uncovered whilst a funeral goes by.

He was buried at St. Martin's Church; and, singular to say, the officiating minister was the Rev. Mr. Peach. Mr. Peach did not know who he was interring: he had taken the service for St. Martin's rector. William heard his name: how many times had he heard his poor father mention the name in connection with his hopeful prospects! He burst into wailing sobs at the thought. Mr. Peach glanced off his book to look compassionately at the sobbing boy.

The funeral was over, the last word of the service spoken, the first shovel of earth flung rattling on to the coffin. The clerk did not pay the compliment of his escort back again; indeed, there was nothing to escort but the two boys. They walked alone, with no company but their hatbands.

In the evening, at dusk, they were gathered together—Jane and all the children. Tears seemed to have a respite: they had been shed of late all too plentifully.

"I must speak to you, children," said Jane, lifting her head, and breaking the silence. "I may as well speak now, as let the days go on first. You are young, but you are old enough to understand me. Do you know, my darlings, how very sad our position is?"

"In losing papa?" said Janey, catching her breath.

"Yes, yes, in losing him," wailed Jane. "For that includes more than you suspect. But I wish to allude more particularly to the future. My dears, I do not see what is to become of us. We have no money; and we have no one to give us any or to lend us any; no one in the wide world."

The children did not interrupt; only William moved his chair nearer to hers. She looked so young in her widow's cap: nearly as young as when, years ago, she had married him who had that day been put out of her sight for ever.

"If we can only keep a roof over our heads," continued Jane, speaking very softly from the effort to subdue her threatening emotion, "we may perhaps struggle on. Perhaps. But it will be struggling; and you do not know half that the word implies. We may not have enough to eat. We may be cold and hungry—not once, but constantly; and we shall certainly have to encounter and endure the slights and humiliations attendant on extreme poverty. I do not know that we can retain a home; for we may, in a week or two, be turned from this."

"But why be turned from this, mamma?"

"Because there is rent owing, and I have not the means to pay it," she answered. "I have written to your uncle Francis, but I do not believe he will be able to help me. He—"

"Why can't we go back to London to live?" eagerly interrupted little Gar. "It was so nice there! It was a better home than this."

"You forget, Gar, that—that—" here she almost broke down, and had to pause a minute—"that our income there was earned by papa. He would not be there to earn it now. No, my dear ones; I have thought the future over in every way—thought until my brain has become confused—and the only possible chance that I can see, of our surmounting difficulties, so as to enable us to exist, is by endeavouring to keep this home. Patience suggests that I should let part of it. I had already thought of that; and I shall endeavour to do so. It may cover the rent and taxes. And I must try and do something else that will find us food."

The children looked perfectly thunderstruck, especially the two elder ones, William and Jane. "Do something to find food!" they uttered, aghast. "Mamma, what do you mean?"

It is so difficult to make children understand these unhappy things—those who have been brought up in comfort. Jane sighed, and explained further. Little desolate hearts they were who listened to her.

"William," she resumed, "your poor papa's watch was to have been yours; but—I scarcely like to tell you—I fear I shall be obliged to dispose of it to help our necessities."

A spasm shot across William's face. But, brave-hearted boy that he was, he would not let his mother see his disappointment, and looked cheerfully at her.

"There is one thought that weighs more heavily on my mind than all—your education. How I shall manage to continue it I do not know. My darlings, I look upon this only in a degree less essential to you than food: you know that learning is better than house and land. I do not yet see my way clear in any way: it is very dark—almost as dark as it can be; and but for one Friend, I should despair."

"What friend is that, mamma? Do you mean Patience?"

"I mean God," replied Jane. "I know that He is a sure refuge to those who trust in Him. In my saddest moments, when I think how certain that refuge is, a ray of light flashes over me, bright as that glorious light in your papa's dream. Oh, my dear children! Perhaps we shall be helped to struggle on!"

"Who will buy us new clothes?" cried Frank, dropping upon another phase of the difficulty. Jane sighed: it was all terribly indistinct.

"In all the tribulation that will probably come upon us, the humiliations, the necessities, we must strive for patience to bear them. You do not yet understand the meaning of the term, to bear; but you will learn it all too soon. You must bear not only for your own sakes, because it is your lot, and you cannot go from it; not only for mine, but chiefly because it is the will of God. This affliction could not have come upon us unless God had permitted it, and I am quite sure, therefore, that it is in some way sent for our good. We shall not be utterly miserable if we can keep together in our house. You will aid me in it, will you not?"

"In what way, mamma?" they eagerly asked, as if wishing to begin something then. "What can we do?"

"You can aid me by being dutiful and obedient; by giving me no unnecessary anxiety or trouble; by cheerfully making the best of our privations; and you can strive to retain what you have already learnt by going diligently over your lessons together. All this will aid and comfort me."

William's tears burst forth, and he laid his head on his mother's lap. "Oh, mamma dear, I will try and do for you all I can," he sobbed. "I will indeed."

"Take comfort, my boy," she whispered, leaning tenderly over him. "Remember that your last act to your father was a loving sacrifice, in giving to him the orange that you would have enjoyed. I marked it, William. My darling children, let us all strive to bear on steadfastly to that far-off light, ever looking unto God."

CHAPTER XVI

TROUBLE

A week elapsed, after the burial of Mr. Halliburton. By that time Jane had looked fully into the best and worst of her condition, and had, so to say, organised her plans. By the disposal of the watch, with what little silver they possessed, and ornaments of her own, she had been enabled to discharge the expenses of the funeral and other small debts, and to retain a trifle in hand for present wants.

On the last day of the week, Saturday, she received an application for the rent. A stylish-looking stripling of some nineteen years, with light eyes and fair hair, called from Mr. Dare to demand it. Jane told him she could not pay him then, but would write and explain to Mr. Dare. Upon which the gentleman, whose manners were haughtily condescending, turned on his heel and left the house, not deigning to say good morning. As he was swinging out at the gate, Patience, coming home from market with a basket in her hand, met him. "How dost thee?" said she in salutation. But there was no response from the other, except that his head went a shade higher.

"Do you know who that is?" inquired Jane, afterwards.

"Of a surety. It is young Anthony Dare."

"He has not pleasing manners."

"Not to us. There is not a more arrogant youth in the town. But his private character is not well spoken of."

Jane sat down to write to Mr. Dare. Her brother Francis, to whom she had explained her situation, had promised her the rent for the half-year due, sixteen pounds, by the middle of February. He could not let her have it before that period, he said, but she might positively count upon it then. She begged Mr. Dare to accord her the favour of waiting until then. Sealing her note, she sent it to him.

On the Monday following, all was in readiness to let; and Jane was full of hope, looking for the advent of lodgers. The best parlour and the two best bedrooms had been vacated, and were in order. Jane slept now with her little girl, and the boys had mattresses laid down for them on the floor at the top of the house. They were to make the study their sitting-room from henceforth; and a card in the window displayed the announcement "Lodgings." The more modern word "apartments" had not then come into fashion at Helstonleigh.

Patience came in after breakfast with a piece of grey merino in her hand.

"Would thee like to make a frock for Anna?" asked she of Mrs. Halliburton. "Sarah Locke does them for her mostly, for it is work that I am not clever at; but Sarah sends me word she is too full of work this week to undertake it. I heard thee say thee made Janey's frocks. If thee can do this, and earn half-a-crown, thee art welcome. It is what I should pay Sarah."

Jane took the merino in thankfulness. It was as a ray of hope, come to light up her heart. Only the instant before Patience entered she was wishing that something could arrive for her to do, never supposing that it would arrive. And now it had come!—and would bring her in two-and-sixpence! "Two-and-sixpence!" we may feel inclined to echo, in undisguised contempt for the trifle. Ay! but we may never have known the yearning want of two-and-sixpence, or of ten-and-sixpence either!

Jane cut out the skirt by a pattern frock, and sat down to make it, her mind ruminating on the future. The children were at their lessons, round the table. "I have just two pounds seventeen and sixpence left," deliberated Jane. "This half-crown will make it three pounds. I wonder how long we can live upon that? We have good clothes, and for the present the boys' boots are good. If I can let the rooms we shall have the rent, so that food is the chief thing to look to. We must spin the money out; must live upon bread and potatoes and a little milk, until something comes in. I wonder if five shillings a week would pay for bare food, and for coals? I fear—"

Jane's dreams were interrupted. The front gate was swung open, and two people, men or gentlemen, approached the house door and knocked. Their movements were so quick that Jane caught only a glimpse of them. "See who it is, will you, William?"

She heard them walk in and ask if she was at home. Putting down her work, she shook the threads from her black dress and went out to them, William returning to his lessons.

The visitors were standing in the passage—one well-dressed man and one shabby one. The former made a civil demand for the half-year's rent due. Jane replied that she had written to Mr. Dare on the previous Saturday, explaining things to him, and asking him to wait a short time.

"Mr. Dare cannot wait," was the rejoinder of the applicant, still speaking civilly. "You must allow me to remark, ma'am, that you are strangers to the town, that you have paid no rent since you entered the house—"

"We believed it was the custom to pay half-yearly, as Mr. Dare did not apply for it at the Michaelmas quarter," interrupted Jane. "We should have paid then, had he asked for it."

"At any rate, it is not paid," was the reply. "And—I am sorry, ma'am, to be under the necessity of leaving this man in possession until you do pay!"

They walked deliberately into the best parlour; and Jane, amidst a rushing feeling of despair that turned her heart to sickness, knew that a seizure had been put into the house.

As she stood in her bewilderment, Patience entered by the back door, the way she always did enter, and caught a glimpse of the shabby man. She drew Jane into the kitchen.

"What does that man do here?" she inquired.

For answer Jane sank into a chair and burst into sobs so violent as to surprise the calm Quakeress. She turned and shut the door.

"Hush thee! Now hush thee! Thy children will hear and be terrified. Art thee behind with thy taxes?"

For some minutes Jane could not reply. "Not for taxes," she said; "they are paid. Mr. Dare has put him in for the rent."

Patience revolved the news in considerable astonishment. "Nay, but I think thee must be in error. Thomas Ashley would not do such a thing."

"He has done it," sobbed Jane.

"It is not in accordance with his character. He is a humane and considerate man. Verily I grieve for thee! That man is not an agreeable inmate of a house. We had him in ours last year!"

"You!" uttered Jane, surprise penetrating even to her own grief. "You!"

"They force us to pay church-rates," explained Patience. "We have a scruple to do so, believing the call unjust. For years Samuel Lynn had paid the claim to avert consequences; but last year he and many more Friends stood out against it. The result was, that that man, now in thy parlour, was put into our house. The amount claimed was one pound nine shillings; and they took out of our house, and sold, goods which had cost us eleven pounds, and which were equal to new."

"Oh, Patience, tell me what I had better do!" implored Jane, reverting to her own trouble. "If we are turned out and our things sold, we must go to the workhouse. We cannot be in the streets."

"Indeed, I feel incompetent to advise thee. Had thee not better see Anthony Dare, and try thy persuasion that he would remove the seizure and wait?"

"I will go to him at once," feverishly returned Jane. "You will allow Janey to remain with you, Patience, while I do so?"

"Of a surety I will. She—"

At that moment the children burst into the kitchen, one after the other. "Mamma, who is that shabby-looking man come into the study? He has seated himself right in front of the fire, and is knocking it about. And the other is looking at the tables and chairs."

It was Frank who spoke; impetuous

Frank. Mrs. Halliburton cast a despairing look around her, and Patience drew their attention.

"That man is here on business," she said to them. "You must not be rude to him, or he will be ten times more rude to you. The other will soon be gone. Your mother is going abroad for an hour; perhaps when she returns she will rid the house of him. Jane, child, thee can come with me and take thy dinner with Anna."

Mrs. Halliburton waited until the better-looking of the two men was gone, and then started. It was a raw, cold day—what some people call a black frost. Black and gloomy it all looked to her, outwardly and inwardly, as she traversed the streets to the office of Mr. Dare. Patience had directed her, and the plate on the door, "Mr. Dare, Solicitor," showed her the right house. She stepped inside that door, which stood open, and knocked at one to the right of the passage. "Clerks' Room" was inscribed upon it.

"Come in."

Three or four clerks were in it. In one of them she recognized him who had just left her house. The other clerks appeared to defer to him, and called him "Mr. Stubbs." Jane, giving her name, said she wished to see Mr. Dare, and the request was conveyed to an inner room. It brought forth young Anthony.

"My father is busy and cannot see you," was his salutation. "I can hear anything you may have to say. It will be the same thing."

"Thank you," replied Jane, in courteous tones, very different from his. "But I would prefer to see Mr. Dare."

"He is engaged, I say," sharply repeated Anthony.

"I will wait, then. I must see him."

Anthony Dare stalked back again. Jane, seeing a bench against the wall, sat down. It was about half-past twelve when she arrived there, and when the clock struck two, there she was still. Several clients, during that time, had come and gone; they were admitted to Mr. Dare, but she sat on, neglected. At two o'clock Anthony came through the room with his hat on. He appeared to be going out.

"What! are you here still?" he exclaimed, in genuine or affected surprise; never, in his ill-manners, removing his hat—he of whom it was his delight to hear it said that he was the most complete gentleman in Helstonleigh. "I assure you it is not of the least use your waiting. Mr. Dare will not be able to see you."

"Mr. Dare can surely spare me a minute when he has done with others."

"He cannot to-day. Can you not say to me what you want to say?"

"Indeed I must see Mr. Dare himself. I will wait on, if you will allow me, hoping to do so."

Anthony Dare vouchsafed no reply, and went out. One or two of the clerks looked round. They appeared not to understand why she sat on so persistently, or why Mr. Dare refused to see her.

In about an hour's time the inner door opened. A tall man, with a bold, free countenance, looked into the room. Supposing it to be Mr. Dare, Jane rose and approached him. "Will you allow me a few minutes' conversation?" she asked. "I presume you are Mr. Dare?"

He put up his hands as if to fence her off. "I have no time, I have no time," he reiterated, and shut the door in her face. Jane sat down again on the bench. "Stubbs, I want you," came forth from Mr. Dare's voice, as he opened the door an inch to speak it.

Stubbs went in, remained a few minutes, and then returned, put on his hat, and walked out. His departure was the signal for considerable relaxation in the office duties. "When the cat's away—" you know the rest. Yawning, stretching, whispering, and laughing supervened. One of the clerks took from his pocket a paper of the biscuits called "Union" in Helstonleigh, and began eating them. Another pulled out a bottle, and solaced himself with some of its contents—whatever they might be. Suddenly the man with the biscuits got off his stool, and offered them to Mrs. Halliburton. Her pale, sad face may have prompted his good nature to the act.

"You have waited a good while, ma'am, and perhaps have lost your dinner through it," he said.

Jane took one of them. "You are very kind. Thank you," she faintly said.

But not a crumb of it could she swallow. She had taken a slice of dry toast for her breakfast that morning, with half a cup of milk; and it was long since she had had a sufficiency of food at any meal. She felt weak, sick, faint; but anxiety and suspense were at work within, parching her throat, destroying her appetite. She held the biscuit in her fingers, resting on her lap, and, in spite of her efforts, the rebellious tears forced themselves to her eyes. Raising her hand, she quietly let fall her widow's veil.

A poor-looking man came in, and counted out eight shillings, laying them upon the desk. "I couldn't make up the other two this week; I couldn't, indeed," he said, with trembling eagerness. "I'll bring twelve next week, please to say."

"Mind you do," responded one of the clerks; "or you know what will be in store for you."

The man shook his head. He probably did know; and, in going out, was nearly knocked over by a handsome lad of seventeen, who was running in. Very handsome were his features; but they were marred by the free expression which characterized Mr. Dare's.

"I say, is the governor in?" cried he, out of breath.

"Yes, sir. Lord Hawkesley's with him."

"The deuce take Lord Hawkesley, then!" returned the young gentleman. "Where's Stubbs? I want my week's money, and I can't wait. Walker, I say, where's Stubbs?"

"Stubbs is gone out, sir."

"What a bother! Halloa! Here's some money! What is this?" continued the speaker, catching up the eight shillings.

"It is some that has just been paid in, Master Herbert."

"That's all right then," said he, slipping five of them into his jacket pocket. "Tell Stubbs to put it down as my week's money."

He tore off. Jane sat on, wondering what she was to do. There appeared to be little probability that she would be admitted to Mr. Dare; and yet, how could she go home as she came—hopeless—to the presence of that man? No; she must wait still; wait until the last. She might catch a word with Mr. Dare as he was leaving. Jane could not help thinking his behaviour very bad in refusing to see her.

The office was being lighted when Mr. Stubbs returned. One of the clerks pointed to the three shillings with his pen. "Kinnersley has brought eight shillings. He will make it twelve next week. Couldn't manage the ten this, he says."

"Where are the eight shillings?" asked Stubbs. "I see only three."

"Oh, Master Herbert came in, and took off five. He said you were to put it down as his week's money."

"He'll take a little too much some day, if he's not checked," was the cynical reply of the senior clerk. "However, it's no business of mine."

He put the three shillings into his own desk, and made an entry in a book. After that he went in to Mr. Dare, who was now alone. A large room, handsomely fitted up. Mr. Dare's table was near one of the windows: a desk, at which Anthony sometimes sat, was at the other. Mr. Dare looked up.

"I could not do anything, sir," said Stubbs. "The other party will listen to no proposal at all. They say they'll throw it into Chancery first. An awful rage they are in."

"Tush!" said Mr. Dare. "Chancery, indeed! They'll tell another tale in a day or two. Has Kinnersley been in?"

"Kinnersley has brought eight shillings, and promises to bring twelve next Monday. Master Herbert carried off five of them, and left word it was for his week's money."

"A smart blade!" cried Mr. Dare, apostrophizing his son with personal pride. "'Take it when I can,' is his motto. He'll make a good lawyer, Stubbs."

"Very good," acquiesced Stubbs.

"Is that woman gone yet?"

"No, sir. My opinion is, she means to wait until she sees you."

"Then send her in at once, and let's get it over," thundered Mr. Dare.

In what lay his objection to seeing her? A dread lest she should put forth their relationship as a plea for his clemency? If so, he was destined to be agreeably disappointed. Jane did not allude to it; would not allude to it. After that interview held with Mrs. Dare, some three or four months before, she had dropped all remembrance of the connection: even the children did not know of it. She only solicited Mr. Dare's leniency now, as any other stranger might have solicited it. Little chance was there of Mr. Dare's acceding to her prayer: he and his wife both wanted Helstonleigh to be free of the Halliburtons.

"It will be utter ruin," she urged. "It will turn us, beggars, into the streets. Mr. Dare, I promise you the rent by the middle of February. Unless it were certain, my brother would not have promised it to me. Surely you may accord me this short time."

"Ma'am, I cannot—that is, Mr. Ashley cannot. It was a reprehensible piece of carelessness on my part to suffer the rent to go on for half a year, considering that you were strangers. Mr. Ashley will look to me to see him well out of it."

"There is sufficient furniture in my house, new furniture, to pay what is owing three times over."

"May be, as it stands in it. Things worth forty pounds in a house, won't fetch ten at a sale."

"That is an additional reason why I—"

"Now, my good lady," interrupted Mr. Dare, with imperative civility, "one word is as good as a thousand; and that word I have said. I cannot withdraw the seizure, except on receipt of the rent and costs. Pay them, and I shall be most happy to do it. If you stop here all night I can give you no other answer; and my time is valuable."

He glanced at the door as he spoke. Jane took the hint, and passed out of it. As much by the tone, as by the words, she gathered that there was no hope whatever.

The streets were bright with gas as she hurried along, her head bent, her veil over her face, her tears falling silently. But when she left the town behind her, and approached a lonely part of the road where no eye was on her, no ear near her, then the sobs burst forth uncontrolled.

"No eye on her? no ear near her?" Ay, but there was! There was one Eye, one Ear, which never closes. And as Jane's dreadful trouble resolved itself into a cry for help to Him who ever listens, there seemed to come a feeling of peace, of trust, into her soul.

CHAPTER XVII

THOMAS ASHLEY

Frank met her as she went in. It was dark; but she kept her veil down.

"Oh, mamma, that's the most horrible man!" he began, in a whisper. "You know the cheese you brought in on Saturday, that we might not eat our bread quite dry; well, he has eaten it up, every morsel, and half a loaf of bread! And he has burnt the whole scuttleful of coal! And he swore because there was no meat; and he swore at us because we would not go to the public-house and buy him some beer. He said we were to buy it and pay for it."

"I said you would not allow us to go, mamma," interrupted William, who now came up. "I told him that if he wanted beer he must go and get it for himself. I spoke civilly, you know, not rudely. He went into such a passion, and said such things! It is a good thing Jane was out."

"Where is Gar?" she asked.

"Gar was frightened at the man, and the tobacco-smoke made him sick, and he cried; and then he lay down on the floor, and went to sleep."

She felt sick. She drew her two boys into the parlour—dark there, except for the lamp in the road, which shone in. Pressing them in her arms, completely subdued by the miseries of her situation, she leaned her forehead upon William's shoulder, and burst once more into a most distressing flood of tears.

They were alarmed. They cried with her. "Oh, mamma! what is it? Why don't you order the man to go away?"

"My boys, I must tell you; I cannot keep it from you," she sobbed. "That man is put here to remain, until I can pay the rent. If I cannot pay it, our things will be taken and sold."

William's pulses and heart alike beat, but he was silent, Frank spoke. "Whatever shall we do, mamma?"

"I do not know," she wailed. "Perhaps God will help us. There is no one else to do it."

Patience came in, for about the sixth time, to see whether Jane had returned, and how the mission had sped. They called her into the cold, dark room. Jane gave her the history of the whole day, and Patience listened in astonishment.

"I cannot but believe that Thomas Ashley must have been mis-informed," said she, presently. "But that you are strangers in the place, I should say you had an enemy who may have gone to him with a tale that thee can pay, but will not. Still, even in that case, it would be unlike Thomas Ashley. He is a kind and a good man; not a harsh one."

"Mr. Dare told me he was expressly acting for Mr. Ashley."

"Well, I say that I cannot understand it," repeated Patience. "It is not like Thomas Ashley. I will give thee an instance of his disposition and general character. There was a baker rented under him, living in a house of Thomas Ashley's. The baker got behind with his rent; other bakers were more favoured than he; but he kept on at his trade, hoping times would mend. Year by year he failed in his rent—Thomas Ashley, mark thee, still paying him regularly for the bread supplied to his family. 'Why do you not stop his bread-money?' asked one, who knew of this, of Thomas Ashley. 'Because he is poor, and looks to my weekly money, with that of others, to buy his flour,' was Thomas Ashley's answer. Well, when he owed several years' rent, the baker died, and the widow was going to move. Anthony Dare hastened to Thomas Ashley. 'Which day shall I levy a distress upon the goods?' asked he. 'Not at all,' replied Thomas Ashley. And he went to the widow, and told her the rent was forgiven, and the goods were her own, to take with her when she left. That is Thomas Ashley."

Jane bent her head in thought. "Is Mr. Lynn at home?" she asked. "I should like to speak to him."

"He has had his tea and gone back to the manufactory, but he will be home soon after eight. I will keep Jane till bedtime. She and Anna are happy over their puzzles."

"Patience, am I obliged to find that man in food?"

"That thee art. It is the law."

The noise made by Patience in going away, brought the man forth from the study, a candle in his hand. "When is that mother of yours coming back?" he roared out to the boys. Jane advanced. "Oh, you are here!" he uttered, wrathfully. "What are you going to give me to eat and drink? A pretty thing this is, to have an officer in, and starve him!"

"You shall have tea directly. You shall have what we have," she answered, in a low tone.

The kettle was boiling on the study fire. Jane lighted a fire in the parlour, and sent Frank out for butter. The man smoked over the study fire, as he had done all the afternoon, and Gar slept beside him on the floor, but William went now and brought the child away. Jane sent the man his tea in, and the loaf and butter.

The fare did not please him. He came to the parlour and said he must have meat; he had had none for his dinner.

"I cannot give it you," replied Jane. "We are eating dry toast and bread, as you may see. I sent butter to you."

He stood there for some minutes, giving vent to his feelings in rather strong language; and then he went back to revenge himself upon the butter for the want of meat. Jane laid her hand upon her beating throat: beating with its tribulation.

Between eight and nine Jane went to the next door. Samuel Lynn had come home for the evening, and was sitting at the table in his parlour, helping the two little girls with a geographical puzzle, which had baffled their skill. He was a little man, quiet in movement, pale and sedate in feature, dry and unsympathising in manner.

"Thee art in trouble, friend, I hear," he said, placing a chair for Jane, whilst Patience came and called the children away. "It is sad for thee."

"In great trouble," answered Jane. "I came in to ask if you would serve me in my trouble. I fancy perhaps you can do so if you will."

"In what way, friend?"

"Would you interest yourself for me with Mr. Ashley? He might listen to you. Were he assured that the money would be forthcoming in February, I think he might agree to give me time."

"Friend, I cannot do this," was the reply of the Quaker. "My relations with Thomas Ashley are confined to business matters, and I cannot overstep them. To interfere with his private affairs would not be seemly; neither might he deem it so. I am but his servant, remember."

The words fell upon her heart as ice. She believed it her only chance—some one interceding for her with Mr. Ashley. She said so.

"Why not go to him thyself, friend?"

"Would he hear me?" hastily asked Jane. "I am a stranger to him."

"Thee art his tenant. As to hearing thee, that he certainly would. Thomas Ashley is of a courteous nature. The poorest workman in our manufactory, going to the master with a grievance, is sure of a patient hearing. But if thee ask me would he grant thy petition, there I cannot inform thee. Patience opines that thee, or thy intentions, may have been falsely represented to him. I never knew him resort to harsh measures before."

"When would be the best time to see him? Is it too late to-night?"

"To-night would not be a likely time, friend, to trouble him. He has not long returned from a day's journey, and is, no doubt, cold and tired. I met James Meeking driving down as I came home; he had left the master at his house. They have been out on business connected with the manufactory. Thee might see him in the morning, at his breakfast hour."

Jane rose and thanked the Quaker. "I will certainly go," she said.

"There is no need to say to him that I suggested it to thee, friend. Go as of thy own accord."

Jane went home with her little girl. Their undesirable visitor looked out at the study door, and began a battle about supper. It ought to comprise, in his opinion, meat and beer. He insisted that one of the boys should go out for beer. Jane steadily refused. She was tempted to tell him that the children of a gentleman were not despatched to public-houses on such errands. She offered him the money to go and get some for himself.

It aroused his anger. He accused her of wanting to get him out of the house by stratagem, that she might lock him out; and he flung the pence back amongst them. Janey screamed, and Gar burst out crying. As Patience had said, he was not a pleasant inmate. Jane ran upstairs, and the children followed her.

"Where is he to sleep?" inquired William.

It is a positive fact that, until that moment, Jane had forgotten all about the sleeping. Of course he must sleep there, though she had not thought of it. Amidst the poor in her father's parish in London, Jane had seen many phases of distress; but with this particular annoyance she had never been brought into contact. However, it had to be done.

What a night that was for her! She paced her room nearly throughout it, with quiet movement, Janey sleeping placidly—now giving way to all the dark appearances of her position, to uncontrollable despondency; now kneeling and crying for help in her heartfelt anguish.

Morning came; the black frost had gone, and the sun shone. After breakfast Jane put on her shawl and bonnet.

Mr. Ashley's residence was very near to them—only a little higher up the road. It was a large house, almost a mansion, surrounded by a beautiful garden. Jane had passed it two or three times, and thought what a nice place it was. She repeatedly saw Mr. Ashley walk past her house as he went to or came from the manufactory: she was not a bad reader of countenances, and she judged him to be a thorough gentleman. His face was a refined one, his manner pleasant.

She found that she had gone at an untoward time. Standing before the hall door was Mr. Ashley's open carriage, the groom standing at the horse's head. Even as Jane ascended the steps the door opened, and Mr. and Mrs. Ashley were coming forth. Feeling terribly distressed and disappointed, she scarcely defined why, Jane accosted the former, and requested a few minutes' interview.

Mr. Ashley looked at her. A fair young widow, evidently a lady. He did not recognise her. He had seen her before, but she was in a different style of dress now.

Mr. Ashley raised his hat as he replied to her. "Is your business with me pressing? I was just going out."

"Indeed it is pressing," she said; "or I would not think of asking to detain you."

"Then walk in," he returned. "A little delay will not make much difference."

Opening the door of a small sitting-room, apparently his own, he invited her to a seat near the fire. As she took it, Jane untied the crape strings of her bonnet and threw back her heavy veil. She was as white as a sheet, and felt choking.

"I fear you are ill," Mr. Ashley remarked. "Can I get you anything?"

"I shall be better in a minute, thank you," she panted. "Perhaps you do not know me, sir. I live in your house, a little lower down. I am Mrs. Halliburton."

"Oh, I beg your pardon, madam; I did not remember you at first. I have seen you in passing."

His manner was perfectly kind and open. Not in the least like that of a landlord who had just put a distress into his tenant's house.

"I have come here to beseech your mercy," she began in agitation. "I have not the rent now, but if you will consent to wait until the middle of February, it will be ready. Oh, Mr. Ashley, do not oppress me for it! Think of my situation."

"I never oppressed any one in my life," was the quiet rejoinder of Mr. Ashley, spoken, however, in a somewhat surprised tone.

"Sir, it is oppression. I beg your pardon for saying so. I promise that the rent shall be paid to you in a few weeks: to force my furniture from me now, is oppression."

"I do not understand you," returned Mr. Ashley.

"To sell my furniture under the distress will be utter ruin to me and my children," she continued. "We have no resource, no home; we shall have to lie in the streets, or die. Oh, sir, do not take it!"

"But you are agitating yourself unnecessarily, Mrs. Halliburton. I have no intention of taking your furniture."

"No intention, sir!" she echoed. "You have put in a distress."

"Put in a what?" cried he, in unbounded surprise.

"A distress. The man has been in since yesterday morning."

Mr. Ashley looked at her a few moments in silence. "Did the man tell you where he came from?"

"It was Mr. Dare who put him in—acting for you. I went to Mr. Dare, and he kept me waiting nearly five hours in his outer office before he would see me. When he did see me, he declined to hear me. All he would say was, that I must pay the rent or he should take the furniture: acting for Mr. Ashley."

A strangely severe expression darkened Mr. Ashley's face. "First of all, my dear lady, let me assure you that I knew nothing of this, or it should never have been done. I am surprised at Mr. Dare."

Could she fail to trust that open countenance—that benevolent eye? Her hopes rose high within her. "Sir, will you withdraw the man, and give me time?"

"I will."

The revulsion of feeling, from despair and grief, was too great. She burst into tears, having struggled against them in vain. Mr. Ashley rose and looked from the window; and presently she grew calmer. When he sat down again she gave him the outline of her situation; of her present dilemma; of her hopes—poor hopes that they were!—of getting a scanty living through letting her rooms and doing some sewing, or by other employment. "Were I to lose my furniture, it would take from me this only chance," she concluded.

"You shall not lose it through me," warmly spoke Mr. Ashley. "The man shall be dismissed from your house in half an hour's time."

"Oh, thank you, thank you!" she breathed, rising to leave. "I have not been able to supply him with great things in the shape of food, and he uses very bad language in the hearing of my children. Thank you, Mr. Ashley."

He shook hands with her cordially, and attended her to the hall door. Mrs. Ashley, a pretty, lady-like woman, somewhat stately in general, stood there still. Well wrapped in velvet and furs, she did not care to return to the warm rooms. Jane said a few words of apology for detaining her, and passed on.

Mr. Ashley turned back to his room, drew his desk towards him, and began to write. His wife followed him. "Who was that, Thomas?"

"Mrs. Halliburton: our widowed tenant, next door to Samuel Lynn's. You remember I told you of meeting the funeral. Two little boys were following alone."

"Oh, poor little things! yes. What did she want?"

Mr. Ashley made no reply: he was writing rapidly. The note, when finished, was sealed and directed to Mr. Dare. He then helped his wife into the carriage, took the reins, and sat down beside her. The groom took his place in the seat behind, and Mr. Ashley drove round the gravel drive, out at the gate, and turned towards Helstonleigh.

"Thomas, you are going the wrong way!" said Mrs. Ashley, in consternation. "What are you thinking of?"

"I shall turn directly," he answered. There was a severe look upon his face, and he drove very fast, by which signs Mrs. Ashley knew something had put him out. She inquired, and he gave her the outline of what he had just heard.

"How could Anthony Dare act so?" involuntarily exclaimed Mrs. Ashley.

"I don't know. I shall give him a piece of my mind to-morrow more plainly than he will like. This is not the first time he has attempted a rascally action under cover of my name."

"Shall you lose the rent?"

"I think not, Margaret. She said not, and she carries sincerity in her face. I am sure I shall not lose it if she can help it. If I do, I must, that's all. I never yet added to the trouble of those in distress, and I never will."

He pulled up at Mrs. Halliburton's house, which she had just reached also. The groom came to the horse, and Mr. Ashley entered. The "man" was comfortably stretched before the study fire, smoking his short pipe. Up he jumped when he saw Mr. Ashley, and smuggled his pipe into his pocket. His offensive manner had changed to humble servility.

"Do you know me?" shortly inquired Mr. Ashley.

The man pulled his hair in token of respect. "Certainly, sir. Mr. Ashley."

"Very well. Carry this note to Mr. Dare."

The man received the note in his hand, and held it there, apparently, in some perplexity. "May I leave, sir, without the authority of Mr. Dare?"

"I thought you said you knew me," was Mr. Ashley's reply, haughty displeasure in his tone.

"I beg pardon, sir," replied the man, pulling his hair again, and making a movement of departure. "I suppose I bain't a-coming back, sir?"

"You are not."

He took up a small bundle tied in a blue handkerchief, which he had brought with him and appeared excessively careful of, caught at his battered hat, ducked his head to Mr. Ashley, and left the house, the note held between his fingers. Would you like to see what it contained?

"Dear Sir,—I find that you have levied a distress on Mrs. Halliburton's goods for rent due to me. That you should have done so without my authority astonishes me much; that you should have done so at all, knowing what you do of my principles, astonishes me more. I send the man back to you. The costs of this procedure you will either set down to me, or pay out of your own pocket, whichever you may deem the more just; but you will not charge them to Mrs. Halliburton. Have the goodness to call upon me to-morrow morning in East Street.

"THOMAS ASHLEY."

"He will not trouble you again, Mrs. Halliburton," observed Mr. Ashley, with a pleasant smile, as he went out to his carriage.

Jane stood at her window. She watched the man go towards Helstonleigh with the note; she watched Mr. Ashley step into his seat, turn his horse, and drive up the road. But all things were looking misty to her, for her eyes were dim.

"God did hear me," was her earnest thought.

CHAPTER XVIII

HONEY FAIR

Helstonleigh abounded with glove manufactories. It was a trade that might be said to be a blessing to the localities where it was carried on, since it was one of the very few employments that furnished to the poor female population easy, clean, and profitable work at their own homes. The evils arising to women who go out to work in factories have been rehearsed over and over again; and the chief evil—we will put others out of sight—is, that it takes the married woman from her home and her family. Her young children drag themselves up in her absence, for worse or for better; alone they must do it, for she has to be away, toiling for daily bread. There is no home privacy, no home comfort, no home happiness; the factory is their life, and other interests give way to it. But with glove-making the case was different. Whilst the husbands were at the manufactories pursuing their day's work, the wives and elder daughters were earning money easily and pleasantly at home. The work was clean and profitable; all that was necessary for its accomplishment being common skill as a seamstress.

Not five minutes' walk from Mrs. Halliburton's house, and nearer to Helstonleigh, a turning out of the main road led you to quite a colony of workwomen—gloveresses, as they were termed in the local phraseology. It was a long, wide lane; the houses, some larger, some smaller, built on either side of it. A road quite wide enough for health if the inhabitants had only kept it as it ought to have been kept: but they did not do so. The highway was made a common receptacle for refuse. It was so much easier to open the kitchen door (most of the houses were entered at once by the kitchen), and to "chuck" things out, pêle-mêle, rather than be at the trouble of conveying them to the proper receptacle, the dust-bin at the back. Occasionally a solitary policeman would come, picking his way through the dirt and dust, and order it to be removed; upon which some slight improvement would be visible for a day or two. The name of this charming place was Honey Fair; though, in truth, it was redolent of nothing so pleasant as honey.

Of the occupants of these houses, the husbands and elder sons were all glove operatives; several of them in the manufactory of Mr. Ashley. The wives sewed the gloves at home. Many a similar colony to Honey Fair was there in Helstonleigh, but in hearing of one you hear of all. The trade was extensively pursued. A very few of the manufactories were of the extent that was Mr. Ashley's; and they gradually descended in size, until some comprised not half a score workmen, all told; but whose masters alike dignified themselves by the title of "manufacturer."

There flourished a shop in the general line in Honey Fair kept by a Mrs. Buffle, a great gossip. Her husband, a well-meaning, steady little man, mincing in his speech and gait, scrupulously neat and clean in his attire, and thence called "the dandy," was chief workman at one of the smallest of the establishments. He had three men and two boys under him; and so he styled himself the "foreman." No one knew half so much of the affairs of their neighbours as did Mrs. Buffle; no one could tell of the ill-doings and shortcomings of Honey Fair as she could. Many a gloveress girl, running in at dusk for a halfpenny candle, did not receive it until she had first submitted to a lecture from Mrs. Buffle. Not that her custom was all of this ignoble description: some of the gentlemen's houses in the neighbourhood would deal with her in a chance way, when out of articles at home. Her wares were good; her home-cured bacon was particularly good. Amidst other olfactory treats indigenous to Honey Fair was that of pigs and pig-sties, kept by Mrs. Buffle.

Occasionally Mrs. Halliburton would go to this shop; it was nearer to her house than any other; and, in her small way, had been extensively patronised by her. Of all her customers, Mrs. Halliburton was the one who most puzzled Mrs. Buffle. In the first place, she never gossiped; in the second, though evidently a lady, she would carry her purchases home herself. The very servants from the very large houses, coming flaunting in their smart caps, would loftily order their pound of bacon or shillingsworth of eggs sent home for them. Mrs. Halliburton took hers away in her own hand; and this puzzled Mrs. Buffle. "But her pays ready money," observed that lady, when relating this to another customer, "so 'tain't my place to grumble."

During the summer weather, whenever Jane had occasion to walk through Honey Fair, on her way to this shop, she would linger to admire the women at their open doors and windows, busy over their nice clean work. Rocking the cradle with one foot, or jogging the baby on their knees, to a tune of their own composing, their hands would be ever active at their employment. Some made the gloves; that is, seamed the fingers together and put in the thumbs, and these were called "makers." Some welted, or hemmed the gloves round at the edge of the wrist; these were called "welters." Some worked the three ornamental lines on the back; and these were called "pointers." Some of the work was done in what was called a patent machine, whereby the stitches were rendered perfectly equal. And some of the stouter gloves were stitched together, instead of being sewn: stitching so beautifully regular and neat, that a stranger would look at it in admiration. In short, there were different branches in the making and sewing of gloves, as there are in most trades.

It now struck Jane that she might find employment at this work until better times should come round. True, she had never worked at it; but she was expert with her needle, and it was easily acquired. She possessed a dry, cool hand, too; a great thing where sewing-silk, sometimes floss silk, has to be used. What cared she for lowering herself to the employment only dealt out to the poor? Was she not poor herself? And who knew her in Helstonleigh?

The day that Mr. Ashley removed the dreaded visitor from her house, Jane had occasion to speak to Elizabeth Carter, her young servant's mother. At dusk, putting aside the frock she was making for Anna, Jane proceeded to Honey Fair, in which perfumed locality Mrs. Carter lived. An agreement had been entered into that Betsy should still go to Mrs. Halliburton's to do the washing (after her own fashion, but Jane could not afford to be fastidious now), and also what was wanted in the way of scouring—Betsy being paid a trifle in return, and instructed in the mysteries of reading and writing.

"'Taint no profit," observed Mrs. Carter to a crony, "but 'taint no loss. Her won't do nothing at home, let me cry after her as I will. Out her goes, gampusing to this house, gampusing to that; but not a bit of work'll her stick to at home. If these new folks can keep her to work a bit, so much the better; it'll be getting her hand in; and better still, if they teaches her to read and write. Her wouldn't learn nothing from the school-missis."

Not a very favourable description of Miss Betsy. But, what the girl chiefly wanted was a firm hand over her. Her temper and disposition were good; but she was an only child, and her mother, though possessing a firm hand, and a firm tongue, too, in general—none more so in Honey Fair—had spoilt and indulged Miss Betsy until her authority was gone.

After her business was over this evening with Mrs. Carter, Jane, who wanted some darning cotton, turned into Mrs. Buffle's shop. That priestess was in her accustomed place behind the counter. She curtseyed twice, and spoke in a low, subdued tone, in deference to the widow's cap and bonnet—to the deep mourning altogether, which Mrs. Buffle's curiosity had not had the gratification of beholding before.

"Would you like it fine or coarse, mum? Here's both. 'Taint a great assortment, but it's the best quality. I don't have much call for darning cotton, mum; the folks round about is always at their gloving work."

"But they must mend their stockings," observed Jane.

"Not they," returned Mrs. Buffle. "They'd go in naked heels, mum, afore they'd take a needle and darn 'em up. They have took to wear them untidy boots to cover the holes, and away they go with 'em unlaced; tongue hanging, and tag trailing half a mile behind 'em. Great big slatterns, they be!"

"They seem always at work," remarked Jane.

"Always at work!" repeated Mrs. Buffle. "You don't know much of 'em, mum, or you'd not say it. They'll play one day, and work the next; that's their work. It's only a few of the steady ones that'll work regular, all the week through."

"What could a good, steady workwoman earn a week at the glove-making?"

"That depends, mum, upon how close she stuck to it," responded Mrs. Buffle.

"I mean, sitting closely."

"Oh, well," debated Mrs. Buffle carelessly, "she might earn ten shillings a week, and do it comfortable."

Ten shillings a week! Jane's heart beat hopefully. Upon ten shillings a week she might manage to exist, to keep her children from starvation, until better days arose. She, impelled by necessity, could sit longer and closer, too, than perhaps those women did. Mrs. Buffle continued, full of inward gratulation that her silent customer had come round to gossip at last.

"They be the improvidentest things in the world, mum, these gloveress girls. Sundays they be dressed up as grand as queens, flowers inside their bonnets, and ribbuns out, a-setting the churches and chapels alight with their finery; and then off for walks with their sweethearts, all the afternoon and evening. Mondays is mostly spent in waste, gathering of themselves at each other's houses, talking and laughing, or, may be, off to the fields again—anything for idleness. Tuesdays is often the same, and then the rest of the week they has to scout over their work, to get it in on the Saturday. Ah! you don't know 'em, mum."

Jane paid for her darning cotton and came away, much to Mrs. Buffle's regret. "Ten shillings a week," kept ringing in her ears.

CHAPTER XIX

MRS REECE AND DOBBS

Jane was busy that evening; but the following morning she went into Samuel Lynn's. Patience was in the kitchen, washing currants for a pudding; the maid upstairs at her work. Jane held the body of Anna's frock in her hand. She wished to try it on.

"Anna is not at home," was the reply of Patience. "She is gone to spend the day with Mary Ashley."

Jane felt sorry; she had been in hopes of finishing it that day. "Patience," said she, "I want to ask your advice. I have been thinking that I might get employment at sewing gloves. It seems easy work to learn."

"Would thee like the work?" asked Patience. "Ladies have a prejudice against it, because it is the work supplied to the poor. Not but that some ladies in this town, willing to eke out their means, do work at it in private. They get the work brought out to them and taken in."

"That would be the worst for me," observed Jane: "taking in the work. I do fear I should not like it."

"Of course not. Thee could not go to the manufactory and stand amid the crowd of women for thy turn to be served as one of them. Wait thee an instant."

Patience dried her hands upon the roller-towel, and took Jane into the best parlour, the one less frequently used. Opening a closet, she reached from it a small, peculiar-looking machine, and some unmade gloves: the latter were in a basket, covered over with a white cloth.

"This is different work from what the women do," said she. "It is what is called the French point, and is confined to a few of the chief manufacturers. It is not allowed to be done publicly, lest all should get hold of the stitch. Those who employ the point have it done in private."

"Who does it here?" exclaimed Jane.

"I do," said Patience, laughing. "Did thee think I should be like the fine ladies, ashamed to put my hand to it? I and James Meeking's wife do all that is at present being done for the Ashley manufactory. But now, look thee. Samuel Lynn was saying only last night, that they must search out for some other hand who would be trustworthy, for they want more of the work done. It is easy to learn, and I know they would give it thee. It is a little better paid than the other work, too. Sit thee down and try it."

Patience fixed the back of the glove in the pretty little square machine, took the needle—a peculiar one—and showed how it was to be done. Jane, in a glow of delight, accomplished some stitches readily.

"I see thee would be handy at it," said Patience. "Thee can take the machine indoors to-day and practise. I will give thee a piece of old leather to exercise upon. In two or three days thee may be quite perfect. I do not work very much at it myself, at which Samuel Lynn grumbles. It is all my own profit, what I earn, so that he has no selfish motive in urging me to work, except that they want more of it done. But I have my household matters to attend to, and Anna takes up my time. I get enough for my clothes, and that is all I care for."

"I know I could do it! I could do it well, Patience."

"Then I am sure thee may have it to do. They will supply thee with a machine, and Samuel Lynn will bring thy work home and take it back again, as he does mine. He—"

William was bursting in upon them with a beaming face. "Mamma, make haste home. Two ladies are asking to see the rooms."

Jane hurried in. In the parlour sat a pleasant-looking old lady in a large black silk bonnet. The other, smarter, younger (but she must have been forty at least), and very cross-looking, wore a Leghorn bonnet with green and scarlet bows. She was the old lady's companion, housekeeper, servant, all combined in one, as Jane found afterwards.

"You have lodgings to let, ma'am," said the old lady. "Can we see them?"

"This is the sitting-room," Jane was beginning; but she was interrupted by the smart one in a snappish tone.

"This the sitting-room! Do you call this furnished?"

"Don't be hasty, Dobbs," rebuked her mistress. "Hear what the lady has to say."

"The furniture is homely, certainly," acknowledged Jane. "But it is new and clean. That is a most comfortable sofa. The bedrooms are above."

The old lady said she would see them, and they proceeded upstairs. Dobbs put her head into one room, and withdrew it with a shriek. "This room has no bedside carpets."

"I am sorry to say that I have no bedside carpets at present," said Jane, feeling all the discouragement of the avowal. "I will get some as soon as I possibly can, if any one taking the rooms will kindly do without them for a little while."

"Perhaps we might, Dobbs," suggested the old lady, who appeared to be of an accommodating, easy nature; readily satisfied.

"Begging your pardon, ma'am, you'll do nothing of the sort," returned Dobbs. "We should have you doubled up with cramp, if you clapped your feet on to a cold floor. I am not going to do it."

"I never do have cramp, Dobbs."

"Which is no reason, ma'am, why you never should," authoritatively returned Dobbs.

"What a lovely view from these back windows!" exclaimed the old lady. "Dobbs, do you see the Malvern Hills?"

"We don't eat and drink views," testily responded Dobbs.

"They are pleasant to look at though," said her mistress. "I like these rooms. Is there a closet, ma'am, or small apartment that we could have for our trunks, if we came?"

"We are not coming," interrupted Dobbs, before Jane could answer. "Carpetless floors won't suit us, ma'am."

"There is a closet here, over the entrance," said Jane to the old lady, as she opened the door. "Our own boxes are in it now, but I can have them moved upstairs."

"So there's a cock-loft, is there?" put in Dobbs.

"A what?" cried Jane, who had never heard the word. "There is nothing upstairs but an attic. A garret, as it is called here."

"Yes," burst forth Dobbs, "it is called a garret by them that want to be fine. Cock-loft is good enough for us decent folk: we've never called it anything else. Who sleeps up there?" she summarily demanded.

"My little boys. This was their room, but I have put them upstairs that I may let this one."

"There ma'am!" said Dobbs, triumphantly, as she turned to her mistress. "You'll believe me another time, I hope! I told you I knew there was a pack of children. One of 'em opened the door to us."

"Perhaps they are quiet children," said the old lady, who had been so long used to the grumbling and domineering of Dobbs, that she took it as a matter of course.

"They are, indeed," said Jane, "quiet, good children. I will answer for it that they will not disturb you in any way."

"I should like to see the kitchen, ma'am," said the old lady.

"We only want the use of it," snapped Dobbs. "Our kitchen fire goes out after dinner, and I boil the kettle for tea in the parlour."

"Would attendance be required?" asked Jane of the old lady.

"No, it wouldn't," answered Dobbs, in the same tart tone. "I wait upon my missis, and I wait upon myself, and we have a woman in to do the cleaning, and the washing goes out."

The answer gave Jane great relief. Attending upon lodgers had been a dubious prospect in more respects than one.

"It's a very good kitchen," said the old lady, as they went in, and she turned round in it.

"I'll be bound it smokes," said Dobbs.

"No, it does not," replied Jane.

"Where's the coalhouse?" asked Dobbs. "Is there two?"

"Only one," said Jane. "It is at the back of the kitchen."

"Then—if we did come—where could our coal be put?" fiercely demanded Dobbs. "I must have my coalhouse to myself, with a lock and key. I don't want the house's fires supplied from my missis's coal."

Jane's cheeks flushed as she turned to the old lady. "Allow me to assure you that your property—of whatever nature it may be—will be perfectly sacred in this house. Whether locked up or not, it will be left untouched by me and mine."

"To be sure, ma'am," pleasantly returned the old lady. "I'm not afraid. You must not mind what Dobbs says: she means nothing."

"And our safe for meat and butter," proceeded that undaunted functionary. "Is there a key to it?"

"And now about the rent?" said the old lady, giving Jane no time to answer that there was a key.

Jane hesitated. And then, with a flush, asked twenty shillings a week.

"My conscience!" uttered Dobbs. "Twenty shillings a week. And us finding spoons and linen!"

"Dobbs," said the old lady. "I don't see that it is so very out of the way. A parlour, two bedrooms, a closet, and the kitchen, all furnished—"

"The closet's an empty, dark hole, and the kitchen's only the use of it, and the bedrooms are carpetless," reiterated Dobbs, drowning her mistress's voice. "But, if anybody asked you for your head, ma'am, you'd just cut it off and give it, if I wasn't at hand to stop you."

"Well, Dobbs, we have seen nothing else to suit us up here. And you know I want to settle myself at this end of the town, on account of it being high and dry. Parry says I must."

"We have not half looked yet," said Dobbs.

"A pound a-week is a good price, ma'am; and we have not paid quite so much where we are: but I don't know that it's unreasonable," continued the old lady to Jane. "What shall we do, Dobbs?"

"Do, ma'am! Why, of course you'll come out, and try higher up. To take these rooms without looking out for others, would be as bad as buying a pig in a poke. Come along, ma'am. Bedrooms without carpets won't do for us at any price," she added to Jane by way of a party salutation.

They left the house, the lady with a cordial good morning, Dobbs with none at all; and went quarrelling up the road. That is, the old lady reasoning, and Dobbs disputing. The former proposed, if they saw nothing to suit them better, to purchase bedside carpeting: upon which Dobbs accused her of wanting to bring herself to the workhouse.

Patience, who had watched them away, from her parlour window, came in to learn the success. She brought in with her the machine, a plain piece of leather, the size of the back of a glove, neatly fixed in it. Jane's tears were falling.

"I think they would have taken them had there been bedside carpets," sighed she. "Oh, Patience, what a help it would been! I asked a pound a week."

"Did thee? That was a good price, considering thee would not have to give attendance."

"How do you know I should not?" asked Jane.

"Because I know Hannah Dobbs waits upon her mistress," replied Patience. "She is the widow of Joseph Reece, and he left her well off. I heard they were coming to live up this way. Did they quite decline them? Because, I can tell thee what. We have some strips of bedside carpet not being used, and I would not mind lending them till thee can buy others. It is a pity thee should lose the letting for the sake of a bit of carpet."

Jane looked up gratefully. "What should I have done without you, Patience?"

"Nay, it is not much: thee art welcome. I would not risk the carpet with unknown people, but Hannah Dobbs is cleanly and careful."

"She has a very repelling manner," observed Jane.

"It is not agreeable," assented Patience, with a smile; "but she is attached to her mistress, and serves her faithfully."

Jane sat down to practise upon the leather, watching the road at the same time. In about an hour she saw Mrs. Reece and Dobbs returning. William went out, and asked if they would step in.

They were already coming. They had seen nothing they liked so well. Jane said she believed she could promise them bedside carpets.

"Then, I think we will decide, ma'am," said the old lady. "We saw one set of rooms, very nice ones; and they asked only seventeen shillings a-week: but they have a young man lodger, a pupil at the infirmary, and he comes home at all hours of the night. Dobbs questioned them till they confessed that it was so."

"I know what them infirmary pupils is," indignantly put in Dobbs. "I am not going to suffer my missis to come in contact with their habits. There ain't one of 'em as thinks anything of stopping out till morning light. And before the sun's up they'll have a pipe in their mouths, filling the house with smoke! It's said, too, that there's mysterious big boxes brought to 'em, for what they call the 'furtherance of science': perhaps some of the churchyard sextons could tell what's in 'em!"

"Well, Dobbs. I think we may take this good lady's rooms. I'm sure we shan't get better suited elsewhere."

Dobbs only grunted. She was tired with her walk, and had really no objection to the rooms; except as to price: that, she persisted in disputing as outrageous.

"I suppose you would not take less?" said the old lady to Jane.

Jane hesitated; but it was impossible for her to be otherwise than candid and truthful. "I would take a trifle less, sooner than not let you the rooms; but I am very poor, and every shilling is a consideration to me."

"Well, I will take them at the price," concluded the good-natured old lady. "And Dobbs, if you grumble, I can't help it. Can we come in—let me see?—this is Wednesday—"

"I won't come in on a Friday for anybody," interrupted Dobbs fiercely.

"We will come in on Tuesday next, ma'am," decided the old lady. "Before that, I'll send in a trolley of coal, if you'll be so kind as to receive it."

"And to lock it up," snapped Dobbs.

CHAPTER XX

THE GLOVE OPERATIVES

At the hours of going to and leaving work, the Helstonleigh streets were alive with glove operatives, some being in one branch of the trade, some in another. There were parers, grounders, leather-sorters, dyers, cutters, makers-up, and so on: all being necessary, besides the sewing, to turn out one pair of gloves; though, I dare say, you did not think it. The wages varied according to the particular work, or the men's ability and industry, from fifteen shillings a week to twenty-five: but all could earn a good living. If a man gained more than twenty-five, he had a stated salary; as was the case with the foremen. These wages, joined to what was earned by the women, were sufficient to maintain a comfortable home, and to bring up children decently. Unfortunately the same drawbacks prevailed in Helstonleigh that are but too common elsewhere; and they may be classed under one general head—improvidence. The men were given to idling away at the public-houses more time than was good for them: the women to scold and to quarrel. Some were slatterns; and a great many gave their husbands the welcome of a home of discomfort, ill-management, and dirt: which, of course, had the effect of sending them out all the more surely.

Just about this period, the men had their especial grievance—or thought they had: and that was, a low rate of wages and not full employment. Had they paid a visit to other places and compared their wages with some earned by operatives of a different class, they had found less cause to complain. The men were rather given to comparing present wages with those they had earned before the dark crisis (dark as far as Helstonleigh's trade was concerned) when the British ports were opened to foreign gloves. But few, comparatively speaking, of the manufacturers had weathered that storm. Years have elapsed since then: but the employment remained scarce, and the wages (I have quoted them to you) low. Altogether, the men were, many of them, dissatisfied. They even went so far as to talk of a "strike"; strikes being less common in those days than they are in these.

It was Saturday night, and the streets were crowded. The hands were pouring out of the different manufactories; clean-looking, respectable workmen, as a whole: for the branches of glove-making are for the most part of a cleanly nature. Some wore their white aprons; some had rolled them up round their waists. A few—very few, it must be owned—were going to their homes, but the greater portion were bound for the public-house.

One of the most extensively patronised of the public-houses was The Cutters' Arms. On a Saturday night, when the men's pockets were lined, this would be crowded. The men flocked into it now and filled it, although its room for entertainment was very large. The order from most of them was a pint of mild ale and some tobacco.

"Any news, Joe Fisher?" asked a man, when the pipes were set going.

Joe Fisher tossed his head and growled. He was a tall, dark man; clothes and condition both dilapidated. The questioner took a few whiffs, and repeated his question. Joe growled again, but did not speak.

"Well, you might give a chap a civil answer, Fisher."

"What's the matter, you two?" cried a third.

"Ben Wilks asks me is there any news!" called out Fisher, indignantly. "I thought he might ha' heered on't without asking. Our pay was docked again to-night; that's the news."

"No!" uttered Wilks.

"It were," said Fisher savagely. "A shilling a week less, good. Who's a-going to stand it?"

"There ain't no help for standing it," interposed a quiet-looking man named Wheeler. "I suppose the masters is forced to lower. They say so."

"Have your master forced hisself to it?" angrily retorted Fisher.

"Well, Fisher, you know I'm fortunate. As all is that gets in to work at Ashley's."

"And precious good care they take to stop in!" cried Fisher, much aggravated. "No danger that Ashley's hands'll give way and afford outsiders a chance."

"Why should they give way?" sensibly asked Wheeler. "You need never think to get in at Ashley's, Fisher, so there's no cause for you to grumble."

A titter went round at Fisher's expense. He did not like it. "I might stand my chance with others, if there was room. Who says I couldn't? Come, now!"

A man laughed. "You had better ask Samuel Lynn that question, Fisher. Why, he wouldn't look at you! You are not steady enough for him."

"Samuel Lynn may go along for a ill-natured broadbrim!" was Fisher's retort. "There'd not be half the difficulty in getting in with Mr. Ashley hisself."

"Yes, there would," said Wheeler, quietly. "Mr. Ashley pays first wages, and he'll have first hands. Quaker Lynn knows what he's about."

"Don't dispute about nothing, Fisher," interrupted a voice, borne through the clouds of smoke from the far end of the room. "To lose a shilling a week is bad, but not so bad as losing all. I have heard ill news this evening."

Fisher stretched up his long neck. "Who's that a-talking? Is it Mr. Crouch?"

It was Stephen Crouch; the foreman in a large firm, and a respectable, intelligent man. "Do you remember, any of you, that a report arose some time ago about Wilson and King? A report that died away again?"

"That they were on their last legs," replied several voices. "Well?"

"Well, they are off them now," continued Stephen Crouch.

Up rose a man, his voice shaking with emotion. "It's not true, Mr. Crouch, sure—ly!"

"It is, Vincent. Wilson and King are going to wind up. It will be announced next week."

"Mercy help us! There'll be forty more hands throwed out! What's to become of us all?"

A dead silence fell on the room. Vincent broke it. Hope is strong in the human heart. "Mr. Crouch, I don't think it can be true. Our wages was all paid up to-night. And we have not heard a breath on't."

"I know all that," said Stephen Crouch. "I know where the money came from to pay them. It came from Mr. Ashley."

The assertion astonished the room. "From Mr. Ashley! Did he tell it abroad?"

"He tell it!" indignantly returned Stephen Crouch. "Mr. Ashley is an honourable man. No. Wilson and King have a tattler too near to them; that's how it came out. Not but what it would have been known all over Helstonleigh on Monday, all particulars. Every sixpence, pretty near, that Wilson and King have, is locked up in their stock. They expected remittances by the London mail this morning, and they did not come. They went to the bank. The bank was shy, and would not make advances; and they had nothing in hand for wages. They went to Mr. Ashley and told him their perplexity, and he drew a cheque. The bank cashed that, with a bow. And if it had not been for Mr. Ashley, Ned Vincent, you and the rest of their hands would have gone home to-night with empty pockets."

"Will Mr. Ashley lose the money?"

"Not he. He knew there was no danger of that, when he lent it. Nobody will lose by Wilson and King. They have more than enough to pay everybody in full; only their money's locked up."

"Why are they giving up?"

"Because they can't keep on. They have been losing a long while. What do you ask—what will they do? They must do as others have done before them, who have been unable to keep on. If Wilson and King had given up ten years ago, they had then each a nice little bit of property to retire upon. But it has been sunk since. There are too many others in this city in the same ease."

"And what's to become of us hands that's throwed out?" asked Vincent, returning to his own personal grievance.

"You must try and get taken on somewhere else, Vincent," observed Stephen Crouch.

"There ain't a better cutter than Ned Vincent going," cried another voice. "He won't wait long."

"I don't know about that," returned Vincent gloomily. "The masters is overdone with hands."

"Of all the bad luck as ever fell upon a town, the opening of the ports to them foreign French was the worst for Helstonleigh," broke in the intemperate voice of Fisher.

"Hold th' tongue, Fisher!" exclaimed a sensible voice. "We won't get into them discussions again. Didn't we go over 'em, night after night, and year after year, till we were heart-sick?—and what did they ever bring us but ill-feeling? It's done, and it can't be undone. The ports be open, and they'll never be closed again."

"Did the opening of 'em ruin the trade of Helstonleigh, or didn't it? Answer me that," said Fisher.

"It did. We know it to our cost," was the sad answer. "But there's no help for it."

"Oh," returned Fisher ironically. "I thought you were going to hold out that the opening of 'em was a boon to the place, and the keeping 'em open a blessing. That 'ud be a new dodge. Why do they keep 'em open?"

"Just hark at Fisher!" said Mr. Buffle in a mincing tone. "He wants to know why Government keeps open the British ports. Don't every dozen of gloves that comes into the country pay a heavy duty? Is it likely Government would give up that, Fisher?"

"What did they do afore they had it?" roared Fisher. "If they did without the duty then, they could do without it now."

"I have heered of some gents as never tasted sugar," returned Mr. Buffle; "but I never heered of one, who had the liking for it, as was willing to forego the use of it. It's a case in pint; the Government have tasted the sweets of the glove-duty, and they stick to it."

"Avaricious wolves!" growled Fisher. "But you are a fool, dandy, for all that. What's a bit of paltry duty, alongside of our wants? If a few of them great Government lords had to go on empty stomachs for a month, they'd know what the opening of ports means."

"In all political changes, such as this, certain localities must suffer," broke in the quiet voice of Stephen Crouch. "It will be the means of increasing commerce wonderfully; and we, that the measure crushed, must be content to suffer for the general good. The effects to us can never be undone. I know what you say, Fisher," he continued, silencing Fisher by a gesture. "I know that the ports might be re-closed to-morrow, if Government so willed it. But it could not undo for us what has been done. It could not repair the ruin that was wrought on Helstonleigh. It could not reinstate firms in business; or refund to the masters their wasted capital; or collect the hands it scattered over the country, to find a bit of work, to beg, or to starve; or bring the dead back to life. It could not do any of this. Neither would it restore a flourishing trade to those of us who are left."

"What's that last, Crouch?"

"It never would," emphatically repeated Stephen Crouch. "A shattered trade cannot be brought together again. It is like a shattered glass: you may mourn over the pieces, but you cannot put them together. Believe me, or not, as you please, my friends, but the only thing remaining is, to make the best of what is left to us. There are other trades a deal worse off than we are."

"I have talked to ye about that there move—a strike," resumed Fisher, after a pause. "We shall get no good till we try it—"

"Fisher, don't you be a fool and show it," was the imperative interruption of Stephen Crouch. "I have explained to you till I am tired, what would be the effects of a strike. It would just finish you bad workmen up, and send you and your children into the nearest dry ditch for a floor, with the open skies above you for a roof."

"We have never tried a strike in Helstonleigh," answered Fisher, holding to his own opinion.

"And I trust we never shall," returned the intelligent foreman. "Other trades may have their strikes if they choose, and it's not our business to find fault with them for it; but the glove trade has hitherto kept itself aloof from strikes, and it's to be hoped it always will. You cannot understand how a strike works, Joe Fisher, or you'd not let your head be running on it."

"Others' heads be running on it as well as mine, Master Crouch," said Fisher, nodding significantly.

"It is not improbable," was the equable rejoinder of Stephen Crouch. "Go and strike next week, half a dozen of you. I mean the operatives of half a dozen firms."

"Every firm in the place must strike," interrupted Fisher hastily. "A few on us doing it would only make bad worse."

Stephen Crouch smiled. "Exactly. But the difficulty, Fisher, will be, that all the firms won't strike. Ask the men in our firm to strike; ask those in Ashley's; ask others that we could name—and what would their answer be? Why, that they know when they are well off. Suppose, for argument's sake, that we did all strike; suppose all the hands in Helstonleigh struck next Monday morning, and the manufactories had to be closed? Who would have the worst of it?—we or the masters?"

"The masters," returned Fisher in an obstinate tone.

"No. The masters have good houses over their heads, and their bankers' books to supply their wants while they are waiting—and their orders are not so great that they need fear much pressure on that score. The London houses would dispatch a few extra orders to Paris and Grenoble, and the masters here might enjoy a nice little trip to the sea-side while our senses were coming back to us. But where should we be? Out at elbows, out at pocket, out at heart; some starving, some in the workhouse. If you want to avoid those contingencies, Joe Fisher, you'll keep from strikes."

Fisher answered by an ironical cheer. "Here, missis," said he to the landlady, who was then passing him, "let's have another pint, after that."

"That'll make nine pints you owe for since Monday night, Joe Fisher," responded the landlady.

"What if I do?" grunted Fisher irascibly. "I am able to pay. I ain't out of work."

CHAPTER XXI

THE LADIES OF HONEY FAIR

It was Saturday night in Honey Fair. A night when the ladies were at leisure to abandon themselves to their private pursuits. The work of the past week had gone into the warehouses; and the fresh work brought out would not be begun until Monday morning. Some of them, as Mrs. Buffle has informed us, did not begin it then. The women chiefly cleaned their houses and mended their clothes; some washed and ironed—Honey Fair was not famous for its management—not going to bed till Sunday morning; some did their marketing; and a few, careless and lazy, spent it in running from house to house, or congregated in the road to gossip.

About half-past eight, one of the latter suddenly lifted the latch of a house door and thrust in her head. It was Joe Fisher's wife. Her face was red, and her cap in tatters.

"Is our Becky in here, Mrs. Carter?"

Mrs. Carter was busy. She was the maternal parent of Miss Betsy. Her kitchen fire was out, her furniture was heaped one thing upon another; a pail of water stood ready to wash the brick floor, when she should have finished rubbing up the grate, and her hands and face were as grimy as the black-lead.

"There's no Becky here," snapped she.

"I can't find her," returned Mrs. Fisher. "I thought her might be along of your Betsy. I say, here's your husband coming round the corner. There's Mark Mason and Robert East and Dale along of him. And— my! what has that young 'un of East's been doing to hisself? He's black from head to foot. Come and look."

Mrs. Carter disdained the invitation. She was a hard-working, thrifty woman, but a cross one. Priding herself upon her cleanliness, she perpetually returned loud thanks that she was not as the dirty ones around her. She was the Pharisee amidst many publicans.

"If I passed my time staring and gossiping as some does, where 'ud my work be?" was her rebuke. "Shut the door, Suke Fisher."

Suke Fisher did as she was bid. She turned her wrists back upon her hips, and walked to meet the advancing party, having discerned their approach by the light of the gas-lamps. "Be you going to be sold for a blackamoor?" demanded she of the boy.

The boy laughed. His head, face, shoulders, hands, were ornamented with a thick, black liquid, not unlike blacking. He appeared to enjoy the treat, as if he had been anointed with some fragrant oil.

"He is not a bad spectacle, is he, Dame Fisher?" remarked the young man, whom she had called Robert East.

"What's a-done it?" questioned she.

"Him and Jacky Brumm got larking, and upset the dye-pot upon themselves. We rubbed 'em down with the leather shreds, but it keeps on dripping from their hair."

"Won't Charlotte warm his back for him!" apostrophised Mrs. Fisher.

The boy threw a disdainful look at her, in return for the remark. "Charlotte's not so fond of warming backs. She never even scolds for an accident."

The boy and Robert East were half-brothers. They entered one of the cottages. Robert East and his sister were between twenty and thirty, and the boy was ten. Their mother had died early, and the young boy's mother, their father's second wife, died when the child was born. The father also died. How Robert and his sister, the one then seventeen, the other fourteen, had struggled to make a living for themselves, and to bring up the baby, they alone knew. The manner in which they had succeeded was a marvel to many; none were more respectable now than they were in all Honey Fair.

Charlotte, neat and nice, sat by her bright kitchen fire, a savoury stew cooking on the hob beside it. It was her custom to have something good for supper on a Saturday night. Did she make home attractive on that night to draw her brother from the seductions of the public-house? Most likely. And she had her reward: for Robert never failed to come. The cloth was laid, the red bricks of the floor were clean, and Charlotte's face, as she looked up from her stocking-mending, was bright. It darkened to consternation, however, when she cast her eyes on the boy.

"Tom, what have you been doing?"

"Jacky Brumm threw a pot of dye over me, Charlotte."

"There's not much real damage, Charlotte," interposed her brother. "It looks worse than it is. I'll get it out of his hair presently, and put his clothes into a pail of water. What have you got to-night? It smells good."

He alluded to supper, and took off the lid of the saucepan to peep in. She had some stewed beef, with carrots, and the savoury steam ascended to Robert's pleased face.

Very few in Honey Fair managed as did Charlotte East. How she did her housework no one knew. Not a woman, married or single, got through more glove-sewing than Charlotte. Not one kept her house in better order: and her clothes and her brother's were neat and respectable, week-days as well as Sundays. Her work was taken into the warehouse on Saturday mornings, and her marketing was done. In the afternoon she cleaned her house, and by four o'clock was ready to sit down to her mending. No one ever saw her in a bustle, and yet all her work was done; and well done. Perhaps one great secret of it was that she rose very early in the morning, winter and summer.

"Look, Robert, here is a nice book I have bought," said she, putting a periodical into his hands. "It comes out weekly. I shall take it in."

Robert turned over the leaves. "It seems very interesting," he said presently. "Here's a paper that tells all about the Holy Land. And another that tells us how glass is made; I have often wondered."

"You can read it to us of an evening while I work," said she. "It will be quite a help to our getting on Tom: almost as good as sending him to school. I gave—"

The words were interrupted. The door was violently burst open, and a woman entered the kitchen; knocking at doors before entering was not the fashion in Honey Fair. The intruder was Mrs. Brumm.

"I say, Robert East, did you see anything of my husband?"

"I saw him go into the Horned Ram."

"Then I wish the Horned Ram was into him!" wrathfully retorted Mrs. Brumm. "He vowed faithfully he'd come home with his wages the first thing after leaving work. He knows I have not a thing in the place for to-morrow—and Dame Buffle looking out for her money. I have a good mind to go down to the Horned Ram, and be on to him!"

Robert East offered no opinion upon this delicate point. He remembered the last time Mrs. Brumm had gone to the Horned Ram to be "on" to her husband, and what it had produced. A midnight quarrel that disturbed the slumbers of Honey Fair.

"Who was along of him?" pursued she.

"Three or four of them. Hubbard and Jones, I saw go in: and Adam Thorneycroft."

A quick rising of the head, as if startled, and a faint accession of colour, told that one of those names had struck, perhaps unpleasantly, on the ear of Charlotte East. "Where are your own earnings?" she asked of Mrs. Brumm.

"I have had to take them to Bankes's," was the rueful reply. "It's a good deal now, and they're in a regular tantrum this week, and wouldn't even wait till Monday. They threatened to tell Brumm, and it frightened me out of my seventeen senses. And now, for him to go into that dratted Horned Ram with his wages! and me without a pennypiece! It's not more for the necessaries I want to get in, than for the things that is in pawn. I can't iron nothing: the irons is there."

Charlotte, busy still, turned round. "I would not put in irons, and such things, that I wanted to use."

"I dare say you wouldn't!" tartly responded Mrs. Brumm. "One has to put in what one's got, and the things our husbands won't miss the sight of. It's fine to be you, Charlotte East, setting yourself up for a lady, and never putting your foot inside the pawn-shop, with your clean hands and your clean kitchen on a Saturday night, sitting down to a hot supper, while the rest of us is a-scrubbing!"

Charlotte laughed good-humouredly. "If I tried to set myself up for a lady, I could not be one. I work as hard as anybody; only I get it done betimes."

Mrs. Brumm sniffed—having no ready answer at hand. And at that moment Tom East, encased in black, peeped out of the brewhouse, where he had been sent by Charlotte to wash the dye off his hands. "Sakes alive!" uttered Mrs. Brumm, aghast at the sight.

"Jacky's worse than me," responded Tom, rather proud of having to say so much. Robert explained to her how it had happened.

"And our Jacky's as bad as that!" she cried. "Won't I wring it out of him!"

"Nonsense," said Robert; "it was an accident. Boys will be boys."

"Yes, they will: and it's not the men that have to wash for 'em and keep 'em clean!" retorted Mrs. Brumm, terribly wrathful. "And me at a standstill for my irons! And that beast of a Brumm stopping out."

"I will lend you my irons," said Charlotte.

"I won't take 'em," was the ungracious reply. "If I don't get my own, I won't borrow none. Brumm, he'll be looking out for his Sunday clean shirt to-morrow, and he won't get it; and that'll punish him more than anything else. There's not a man in Honey Fair as likes to go sprucer on a Sunday than Brumm."

"So much the better," said Charlotte. "When men lose pride in their appearance, they are apt to lose it in their conduct."

"You must always put in your word for folks, Charlotte East, let 'em be ever so bad," was Mrs. Brumm's parting salutation, as she went off and shut the door with a bang.

Meanwhile Timothy Carter, Mrs. Carter's husband, had turned into his own dwelling, after leaving Robert East. The first thing to greet him was the pail of water. Mrs. Carter had completed her grate, and was dashing her water on to the floor. Timothy received it on his legs.

"What's that for?" demanded Timothy, who was a meek and timid little man.

"Why do you brush in so sharp, then?" cried she. "Who was to know you was a-coming?"

Timothy had not "brushed in sharp;" he had gone in quietly. He stood ruefully shaking the wet from his legs, first one, then the other, and afterwards began to pick his way on tiptoe towards the fireplace.

"Now, it's of no use your attempting to sit down yet," rebuked his wife, in her usual cross accents. "There ain't no room for you at the fire, and there ain't no warmth in it; it's but this blessed minute lighted. Sit yourself on that table, again the wall, and then your legs'll be in the dry."

"And there I may sit for an hour, for you'll be all that time before you have finished, by the looks on't," he ventured to remonstrate.

"And half another hour to the end of it," answered she. "There's Betsy, as ought to be helping, gadding out somewhere ever since she came home at seven o'clock."

"You says to me, says you, 'You come home to-night, Tim, as soon as work's over, and don't go drinking!' You know you did," repeated Timothy in an injured tone.

"And it's a good thing as you have come, or you'd have heard my tongue in a way you wouldn't like!" was Mrs. Carter's reply.

Timothy sighed. That tongue was the two-edged sword of his life: how dreaded, none but himself could tell. He had mounted the table in obedience to orders, but he now got off again.

"What are you after now?" shrilly demanded Mrs. Carter, who was on her knees, scouring the bricks.

"I want my pipe and 'baccy."

"You stop where you are," was the imperative answer, "and wait till I have time to get it;" and Timothy humbly sat down again.

"You might get this done afore night, 'Lizabeth, as I've said over and over again," cried he, plucking up a little spirit. "When a man comes home tired, even if there ain't a bit o' supper for him, he expects a morsel o' fire to sit down to, so as he can smoke his pipe in quiet. It cows him, you see, to find his place in this ruck, where there ain't a dry spot to put the sole of his foot on, and nothing but a table with unekal legs to sit upon, and—"

"I might get it done afore?" shrieked Mrs. Carter. "Afore! When, through that Betsy's laziness, leaving everything on my shoulders, I couldn't get in my gloving till four o'clock this afternoon! Every earthly thing have I had to do since then. I raked out my fire—"

"What's the good of raking out the fire?" interposed Timothy.

"Goodness help the simpleton! Wanting to know the good of raking out the fire—as if he was born yesterday! Can a grate be black-leaded while it's hot, pray?"

"It might be black-leaded at some other time," debated he. "In a morning, perhaps."

"I dare say it might, if I had not my gloving to do," she answered, trembling with wrath. "When folks takes out shop work, they has to get on with that—and is glad to do it. Where would you be if I earned nothing? It isn't much of a roof we should have over our heads, with your paltry fifteen or sixteen shillings a-week. You be nothing but a parer, remember."

"There's no need to disparage of me, 'Lizabeth," he rejoined, with a meek little cough. "You knowed I was a parer before you ventured on me."

"Just take your legs up higher, or you'll be knocking my cap with your dirty boots," said Mrs. Carter, who was nearing the table in her scrubbing.

"I'll stand outside the door a bit, I think," he answered. "I am in your way everywhere."

"Sit where you are, and lift up your legs," was the reiterated command. And Timothy obeyed.

Cold and dreary, on he sat, watching the cleaning of the kitchen. The fire gave out no heat, and the squares of bricks did not dry. He took some silver from his pocket, and laid it in a stack on the table beside him, for his wife to take up at her leisure. She allowed him no chance of squandering his wages.

A few minutes, and Mrs. Carter rose from her knees and went into the yard for a fresh supply of water. Timothy did not wait for a second ducking. He slipped off the table, took a shilling from the heap, and stole from the house.

Back came Mrs. Carter, her pail brimming. "You go over to Dame Buffle's, Tim, and—Why, where's he gone?"

He was not in the kitchen, that was certain; and she opened the staircase door, and elevated her voice shrilly. "Are you gone tramping up my stairs, with your dirty boots? Tim Carter, I say, are you upstairs?"

Of course Tim Carter was not upstairs: or he had never dared to leave that voice unanswered.

"Now, if he has gone off to any of them sotting publics, he shan't hear the last of it," she exclaimed, opening the door and gazing as far as the nearest gas-light would permit. But Timothy was beyond her eye and reach, and she caught up the money and counted it. Fourteen shillings. One shilling of it gone.

She knew what it meant, and dashed the silver into a wide-necked canister on the high mantelshelf, which contained also her own earnings for the week. It would have been as much as meek Tim Carter's life was worth to touch that canister, and she kept it openly on the mantel-piece. Many unfortunate wives in Honey Fair could not keep their money from their husbands even under lock and key. As she was putting the canister in its place again, Betsy came in. Mrs. Carter turned sharply upon her.

"Now, miss! where have you been?"

"Law, mother, how you fly out! I have only been to Cross's."

"You ungrateful piece of brass, when you know there's so much to be done on a Satur-night that I can't turn myself round! You shan't go gadding about half your time. I'll put you from home entire, to a good tight service."

Betsy had heard the same threat so often that its effect was gone. Had her mother only kept her in one-tenth of the subjection that she did her husband, it might have been better for the young lady. "I was only in at Cross's," she repeated.

"What's the good of telling me that falsehood? I went to Cross's after you, but you wasn't there, and hadn't been there. You want a good sound shaking, miss."

"If I wasn't at Cross's, I was at Mason's," was the imperturbable reply of Miss Betsy. "I was at Mason's first. Mark Mason came home and turned as sour as a wasp, because the place was in a mess. She was washing her children, and she's got the kitchen to do, and he began blowing up. I left 'em then, and went in to Cross's. Mason went back down the hill; so he'll come home tipsy."

"Why can't she get her children washed afore he comes home?" retorted Mrs. Carter, who could see plenty of motes in her neighbours' eyes, though utterly blind to the beam in her own. "Such wretched management! Children ought to be packed out of the way by seven o'clock."

"You don't get your cleaning over, any more than she does," remarked Miss Betsy boldly.

Mrs. Carter turned an angry gaze upon her; a torrent of words breaking from her lips. "I get my cleaning over! I, who am at work every moment of my day, from early morning till late at night! You'd liken me to that good-for-nothing Het Mason, who hardly makes a dozen o' gloves in a week, and keeps her house like a pigsty! Where would you and your father be, if I didn't work to keep you, and slave to make the place sweet and comfortable? Be off to Dame Buffle's and buy me a besom, you ungrateful monkey: and then you turn to and dust these chairs."

Betsy did not wait for a second bidding. She preferred going for besoms, or for anything else, to her mother's kitchen and her mother's scolding. Her coming back was another affair; she would be just as likely to propel the besom into the kitchen and make off herself, as to enter.

She suddenly stopped now, door in hand, to relate some news.

"I say, mother, there's going to be a party at the Alhambra tea-gardens."

"A party at the Alhambra tea-gardens, with frost and snow on the ground!" ironically repeated Mrs. Carter. "Be off, and don't be an oaf."

"It's true," said Betsy. "All Honey Fair's going to it. I shall go too. 'Melia and Mary Ann Cross is going to have new things for it, and—"

"Will you go along and get that besom?" cried angry Mrs. Carter. "No child of mine shall go off to their Alhambras, catching their death on the wet grass."

"Wet grass!" echoed Betsy. "Why, you're never such a gaby as to think they'd have a party on the grass! It is to be in the big room, and there's to be a fiddle and a tam—"

"—bourine" never came. Mrs. Carter sent the wet mop flying after Miss Betsy, and the young lady, dexterously evading it, flung-to the door and departed.

A couple of hours later, Timothy Carter was escorted home, his own walking none of the steadiest. The men with him had taken more than Timothy; but it was that weak man's misfortune to be overcome by a little. You will allow, however, that he had taken enough, having spent his shilling and gone into debt besides. Mrs. Carter received him—Well, I am rather at a loss to describe it. She did not actually beat him, but her shrill voice might be heard all over Honey Fair, lavishing hard names upon helpless Tim. First of all, she turned out his pockets. The shilling was all gone. "And how much more tacked on to it?" asked she, wise by experience. And Timothy was just able to understand and answer. He felt himself as a lamb in the fangs of a wolf. "Eightpence halfpenny."

"A shilling and eightpence halfpenny chucked away in drink in one night!" repeated Mrs. Carter. She gave him a short, emphatic shake, and propelled him up the stairs; leaving him without a light, to get to bed as he could. She had still some hours' work downstairs, in the shape of mending clothes.

But it never once occurred to Mrs. Carter that she had herself to thank for his misdoings. With a tidy room and a cheerful fire to receive him, on returning from his day's work, Timothy Carter would no more have thought of the public-houses than you or I should. And if, as did Charlotte East, she had welcomed him with a good supper and a pleasant tongue, poor Tim in his gratitude had forsworn public-houses for ever.

Neither, when Mark Mason staggered home, and his wife raved at and quarrelled with him, to the further edification of Honey Fair, did it strike that lady that she could be in fault. As Mrs. Carter had said, Henrietta Mason did not overburden herself with work of any sort; but she did make a pretence of washing her four children in a bucket on a Saturday night, and her kitchen afterwards. The ceremony was delayed through idleness and bad management to the least propitious part of the evening. So sure as she had the bucket before the fire, and the children collected round it; one in, one just out roaring to be dried, and the two others waiting their turn for the water, all of them stark naked—for Mrs. Mason made a point of undressing them at once to save trouble—so sure, I say, as these ablutions were in progress, the children frantically crying, Mrs. Mason boxing, storming, and rubbing, and the kitchen swimming, in would walk the father. Words invariably ensued: a short, sharp quarrel; and he would turn out again for the nearest public-house, where he was welcomed by a sociable room and a glowing fire. Can any one be surprised that it should be so?

You must not think these cases overdrawn; you must not think them exceptional cases. They are neither the one nor the other. They are truthful pictures, taken from what Honey Fair was then. I very much fear the same pictures might be taken from some places still.

CHAPTER XXII

MR BRUMM'S SUNDAY SHIRT

But there's something to say yet of Mrs. Brumm. You saw her turning away from Robert East's door, saying that her husband, Andrew, had promised to come home that night and to bring his wages. Mrs. Brumm, a bad manager, as were many of the rest, would probably have received him with a sloppy kitchen, buckets, and besoms. Andrew had had experience of this, and, disloyal knight that he was, allowed himself to be seduced into the Horned Ram. He'd just take one pint and a pipe, he said to his conscience, and be home in time for his wife to get what she wanted. A little private matter of his own would call him away early. Pressed for a sum of money in the week which was owing to his club, and not possessing it, he had put his Sunday coat in pledge: and this he wanted to get out. However, a comrade sitting in the next chair to him at the Horned Ram had to get his coat out of the same accommodating receptacle. Nothing more easy than for him to bring out Andrew's at the same time; which was done. The coat on the back of his chair, his pipe in his mouth, and a pint of good ale before him, the outer world was as nothing to Andrew Brumm.

At ten o'clock, the landlord came in. "Andrew Brumm, here's your wife wanting to see you."

Now Andrew was not a bad sort of man by any means, but he had a great antipathy to being looked after. A joke went round at Andrew's expense; for if there was one thing the men in general hated more than another, it was that their wives should come in quest of them to the public-houses. Mrs. Brumm received a sharp reprimand; but she saw that he was, as she expressed it, "getting on," so she got some money from him and kept her scolding for another opportunity.

She did not go near the pawnbroker's to get her irons out. She bought a bit of meat and what else she wanted, and returned to Honey Fair. Robert East was closing his door for the night as she passed it. "Has Brumm come home?" he asked.

"Not he, the toper! He is stuck fast at the Horned Ram, getting in for it nicely. I have been after him for some money."

"Have you got your irons out?" inquired Charlotte, coming to the door.

"No, nor nothing else; and there's pretty near half the kitchen in. It's him that'll suffer. He has been getting out his own coat, but he can't put it on. Leastways, he won't without a clean collar and shirt; and let him fish for them. Wait till to-morrow comes, Mr. 'Drew Brumm!"

"Was his coat in?" returned Charlotte, surprised.

"That it was. Him as goes on so when I puts a thing or two in! He owed some money at his club, and he went and put his coat in for four shillings, and Adam Thorneycroft has been and fetched it out for him."

"Adam Thorneycroft!" involuntarily returned Charlotte.

"Thorneycroft's coat was in too, and he went for it just now, and Brumm gave him the ticket to get out his. Smith's daughter told me that. She was serving with her mother in the bar."

"Is Adam Thorneycroft at the Horned Ram still?"

"That he is: side by side with Brumm. A nice pair of 'em! Charlotte East, take my advice; don't you have anything to say to Thorneycroft. A woman had better climb up to the top of her topmost chimbley and pitch herself off, head foremost, than marry a man given to drink."

Charlotte East felt vexed at the allusion—vexed that her name should be coupled openly with that of Adam Thorneycroft by the busy tongues of Honey Fair. That an attachment existed between herself and Adam Thorneycroft was true; but she did not wish the fact to become too apparent to others. Latterly she had been schooling her heart to forget him, for he was taking to frequent public-houses.

Mrs. Brumm went home, and was soon followed by her husband. He was not much the worse for what he had taken: he was a little. Mrs. Brumm reproached him with it, and a wordy war ensued.

They arose peaceably in the morning. Andrew was a civil, well-conducted man, and but for Horned Rams would have been a pattern to three parts of Honey Fair. He liked to be dressed well on Sunday and to attend the cathedral with his two children: he was very fond of listening to the chanting Mrs. Brumm—as was the custom generally with the wives of Honey Fair—stayed at home to cook the dinner. Andrew was accustomed to do many odd jobs on the Sunday morning, to save his wife trouble. He cleaned the boots and shoes, brushed his clothes, filled the coal-box, and made himself useful in sundry other ways. All this done, they sat down to breakfast with the two children, the unfortunate Jacky less black than he had been the previous night.

"Now, Jacky," said Brumm, when the meal was over, "get yourself ready; it has gone ten. Polly too."

"It's a'most too cold for Polly this morning," said Mrs. Brumm.

"Not a bit on't. The walk'll do her good, and give her an appetite for dinner. What is for dinner, Bell? I asked you before, but you didn't answer."

"It ain't much thanks to you as there's anything," retorted Mrs. Brumm, who rejoiced in the aristocratic name of Arabella. "You plant yourself again at the Horned Ram, and see if I worries myself to come after you for money. I'll starve on the Sunday first."

"I can't think what goes of your money," returned Andrew. "There had not used to be this fuss if I stopped out for half an hour on the Saturday night, with my wages in my pocket. Where does yours go to?"

"It goes in necessaries," shortly answered Mrs. Brumm. But not caring for reasons of her own to pursue this particular topic, she turned to that of the dinner. "I have half a shoulder of mutton, and I'm going to take it to the bake'us with a batter pudden under it, and to boil the taters at home."

"That's capital!" returned Andrew, gently rubbing his hands. "There's nothing nicer than baked mutton and a batter pudden. Jacky, brush your hair well: it's as rough as bristles."

"I had to use a handful of soda to get the dye out," said Mrs. Brumm. "Soda's awful stuff for making the hair rough."

Andrew slipped out to the Honey Fair barber, who did an extensive business on Sunday morning, to be shaved. When he returned he went up to wash and dress, and finally uncovered a deal box where he was accustomed to find his clean shirt. With all Mrs. Brumm's faults she had neat ways. The shirt was not there.

"Bell, where's my clean shirt?" he called out from the top of the stairs.

Mrs. Bell Brumm had been listening for the words and received them with satisfaction. She nodded, winked, and went through a little pantomime of ecstasy, to the intense delight of the children, who were in the secret, and nodded and winked with her. "Clean shirt?" she called back again, as if not understanding.

"My Sunday shirt ain't here."

"You haven't got no Sunday shirt to-day."

Andrew Brumm descended the stairs in consternation. "No Sunday shirt!" he repeated.

"No shirt, nor no collar, nor no handkercher," coolly affirmed Mrs. Brumm. "There ain't none ironed. They be all in the wet and the rough, wrapped up in an old towel. Jacky and Polly haven't nothing either."

Brumm stared considerably. "Why, what's the meaning of that?"

"The irons are in pawn," shortly answered Mrs. Brumm. "You know you never came home with the money, so I couldn't get 'em out."

Another wordy war. Andrew protested she had no "call" to put the irons in any such place. She impudently retorted that she should put the house in if she liked.

A hundred such little episodes could be related of the domestic life of Honey Fair.

CHAPTER XXIII

THE MESSRS BANKES

On the Monday morning, a troop of the gloveress girls flocked into Charlotte East's. They were taking holiday, as was usual with them on Mondays. Charlotte was a favourite. It is true, she "bothered" them, as they called it, with good advice, but they liked her in spite of it. Charlotte's kitchen was always tidy and peaceful, with a bright fire burning in it: other kitchens would be full of bustle and dirt. Charlotte never let them hinder her; she worked away at her gloves all the time. Charlotte was a glove-maker; that is, she sewed the fingers together, and put in the thumbs, forgits, and quirks. Look at your own gloves, English made. The long strips running up inside the fingers are the forgits; and the little pieces between, where the fingers open, are the quirks. The gloves Charlotte was occupied with now were of a very dark green colour, almost black, called corbeau in the trade, and they were sewn with white silk. Charlotte's stitches were as beautifully regular as though she had used a patent machine. The white silk and the fellow glove to the one she was making, lay inside a clean white handkerchief doubled upon her lap; other gloves, equally well covered, were in a basket at her side.

The girls had come in noisily, with flushed cheeks and eager eyes. Charlotte saw that something was exciting them. They liked to tell her of their little difficulties and pleasures. Betsy Carter had informed her mother that there was going to be a "party at the Alhambra tea-gardens," if you remember; and this was the point of interest to-day. These "Alhambra tea-gardens," however formidable and perhaps suggestive the name, were very innocent in reality. They belonged to a quiet roadside inn, half a mile from the town, and comprised a large garden and extensive lawn. The view from them was beautiful; and many a party from Helstonleigh, far higher in the scale of society than these girls, would go there in summer to take tea and enjoy the view. A young, tall, handsome girl of eighteen had drawn her chair close to Charlotte's. She was the half-sister of Mark Mason, and had her home with him and his wife; supporting herself after a fashion by her work. But she was always in debt to them, and she and Mrs. Mark did not get along well together. She wore a new shawl, and straw bonnet trimmed with blue ribbons: and her dark hair fell in glossy ringlets—as was the fashion then. Two other girls perched themselves on a table. They were sisters—Amelia and Mary Ann Cross; others placed themselves where they could. Somewhat light were they in manner, these girls; free in speech. Nothing farther. If an unhappy girl did, by mischance, turn out badly, or, as the expressive phrase had it, "went wrong," she was forthwith shunned, and shunned for ever. Whatever may have been the faults and failings prevailing in Honey Fair, this sort of wrong-doing was not common amongst them.

"Why, Caroline, that is new!" exclaimed Charlotte East, alluding to the shawl.

Caroline Mason laughed. "Is it not a beauty?" cried she. And it may be remarked that in speech and accent she was superior to some of the girls.

Charlotte took a corner of it in her hand. "It must have cost a pound at least," she said. "Is it paid for?"

Again Caroline laughed. "Never you mind whether it's paid for or not, Charlotte. You won't be called upon for the money for it. As I told my sister-in-law yesterday."

"You did not want it, Caroline; and I am quite sure you could not afford it. Your winter cloak was good yet. It is so bad a plan, getting goods on credit. I wish those Bankeses had never come near the place!"

"Don't you run down Bankes's, Charlotte East," interposed Eliza Tyrrett, a very plain girl, with an ill-natured expression of face. "We should never get along at all if it wasn't for Bankes's."

"You would get along all the better," returned Charlotte. "How much are they going to charge you for this shawl, Caroline?"

Caroline and Eliza Tyrrett exchanged peculiar glances. There appeared to be some secret between them, connected with the shawl. "Oh, a pound or so," replied Caroline. "What was it, Eliza?"

Eliza Tyrrett burst into a loud laugh, and Caroline echoed it. Charlotte East did not press for the answer. But she did press the matter against dealing with Bankes's; as she had pressed it many a time before.

A twelvemonth ago, some strangers had opened a linen-draper's shop in a back street of Helstonleigh; brothers of the name of Bankes. They professed to do business upon credit, and to wait upon people at their own homes, after the fashion of hawkers. Every Monday would one of them appear in Honey Fair, a great pack of goods on his back, which would be opened for inspection at each house. Caps, shawls, gown-pieces, calico, flannel, and finery, would be displayed in all their fascinations. Now, you who are reading this, only reflect on the temptation! The women of Honey Fair went into debt; and it was three parts the work of their lives to keep the finery, and the system, from the knowledge of their husbands.

"Pay us so much weekly," Bankes's would say. And the women did so: it seemed like getting a gown for nothing. But Bankes's were found to be strict in collecting the instalments; and how these weekly payments told upon the wages, I will leave you to judge. Some would have many shillings to pay weekly. Charlotte East and a few more prudent ones spoke against this system; but they made no impression. The temptation was too great. Charlotte assumed that this was how Caroline Mason's shawl had been obtained. In that, however, she was mistaken.

"Charlotte, we are going down to Bankes's. There'll be a better choice in his shop than in his pack. You have heard of the party at the Alhambra. Well, it is to be next Monday, and we want to ask you what we shall wear. What would you advise us to get for it?"

"Get nothing," replied Charlotte. "Don't go to Bankes's, and don't go to the Alhambra."

The whole assembly sat in wonder, with open eyes. "Not go to the party!" echoed pert Amelia Cross. "What next, Charlotte East?"

"I told you what it would be, if you came into Charlotte East's," said Eliza Tyrrett, a sneer on her countenance.

"I am not against proper amusement, though I don't much care for it myself," said Charlotte. "But when you speak of going to a party at the Alhambra, somehow it does not sound respectable."

The girls opened their eyes wider. "Why, Charlotte, what harm do you suppose will come to us? We can take care of ourselves, I hope?"

"It is not that," said Charlotte. "Of course you can. Still it does not sound nice. It is like going to a public-house—you can't call the Alhambra anything else. It is quite different, this, from going there to have tea in the summer. But that's not it, I say. If you go to it, you would be running into debt for all sorts of things at Bankes's, and get into trouble."

"My sister-in-law says you are a croaker, Charlotte; and she's right," cried Caroline Mason, with good-humour.

"Charlotte, it is not a bit of use your talking," broke in Mary Ann Cross vehemently. "We shall go to the party, and we shall buy new things for it. Bankes's have some lovely sarcenets, cross-barred; green, and pink, and lilac; and me and 'Melia mean to have a dress apiece off 'em. With a pink bow in front, and a white collar—my! wouldn't folks stare at us!—Twelve yards each it would take, and they are one-and-eightpence a yard."

"Mary Ann, it would be just madness! There'd be the making, the lining, and the ribbon: five or six-and-twenty shillings each, they would cost you. Pray don't!"

"How you do reckon things up, Charlotte! We should pay off weekly: we have time afore us."

"What would your father say?"

"Charlotte, just hold your noise about father," quickly returned Amelia Cross, in a hushed and altered tone. "You know we don't tell him about Bankes's."

Charlotte found she might as well have talked to the winds. The girls were bent upon the evening's pleasure, and also upon the smart things they deemed necessary for it. A few minutes more and they left her; and trooped down to the shop of the Messrs. Bankes.

Charlotte was coming home that evening from an errand to the town, when she met Adam Thorneycroft. He was somewhat above the common run of workmen.

"Oh, is it you, Charlotte?" he exclaimed, stopping her. "I say, how is it that you'll never have anything to say to me now?"

"I have told you why, Adam," she replied.

"You have told me a pack of nonsense. I wouldn't lose you, Charlotte, to be made king of England. When once we are married, you shall see how steady I'll be. I will not enter a public-house."

"You have been saying that you will not for these twelve months past, Adam," she sadly rejoined; and, had her face been visible in the dark night, he would have seen that it was working with agitation.

"What does it hurt a man, to go out and take a quiet pipe and a glass after his work's over? Everybody does it."

"Everybody does not. But I do not wish to contend. It seems to bring you no conviction. Half the miseries around us in Honey Fair arise from so much of the wages being wasted at the public-houses. I know what you would say—that the wives are in fault as well. So they are. I do not believe people were sent into the world to live as so many of us live: nothing but scuffle and discomfort, and—I may almost say it—sinfulness. One of these wretched households shall never be mine."

"My goodness, Charlotte! How seriously you speak!"

"It is a serious subject. I want to try to live so as to do my duty by myself and by those around me; to pass my days in peace with the world and with my conscience. A woman beaten down, cowed by all sorts of ills, could not do so; and, where the husband is unsteady, she must be beaten down. Adam, you know it is not with a willing heart I give you up, but I am forced to it."

"How can you bring yourself to say this to me?" he rejoined.

"I don't deny that it is hard," she faintly said, suppressing with difficulty her emotion. "This many a week I and duty have been having a conflict with each other: but duty has gained the mastery. I knew it would from the first—"

"Duty be smothered!" interrupted Adam Thorneycroft. "I shall think you a born natural presently, Charlotte."

"Yes, I know. I can't help it. Adam, we should never pull together, you see. Good-bye! We can be friends in future, if you like; nothing more."

She held out her hand to him for a parting salutation. Adam, hurt and angry, flung it from him, and turned towards Helstonleigh: and Charlotte continued her way home, her tears dropping in the dusky night.

CHAPTER XXIV

HARD TO BEAR

Mrs. Halliburton struggled on. A struggle, my reader, that it is to be hoped, for your comfort's sake, you have never experienced, and never will. She had learnt the stitch for the back of the gloves, and Mr. Lynn supplied her with a machine and with work. But she could not do it quickly as yet; though it was a hopeful day for her when she found that her weekly earnings amounted to six shillings.

Mrs. Reece paid her twenty shillings a week. Or rather, Dobbs: for Dobbs was paymaster-general. Of that, Jane could use (she had made a close calculation) six shillings, putting by fourteen for rent and taxes. Her taxes were very light, part of them being paid by the landlord, as was the custom with some houses in Helstonleigh. But for this, the rent would have been less. Sorely tempted as she was, by hunger, by cold, almost by starvation, Jane was resolute in leaving the fourteen shillings intact. She had suffered too much from non-payment of the last rent, not to be prepared with the next. But—the endurance and deprivation!—how great they were! And she suffered far more for her children than for herself.

One night, towards the middle of February, she felt very downhearted: almost as if she could not struggle on much longer. With her own earnings and the six shillings taken from Mrs. Reece's money she could count little more than twelve shillings weekly, and everything had to be found out of it. Coals, candles, washing—that is, the soap, firing, etc., necessary for Miss Betsy Carter to do it with; the boys' shoe-mending and other trifles, besides food. You will not, therefore, be surprised to hear that on this night they had literally nothing in the house but part of a loaf of bread. Jane was resolute in one thing— not to go into debt. Mrs. Buffle would have given credit, probably other shops also; but Jane believed that her sole chance of surmounting the struggle eventually was by keeping debt, even trifling debt, away. They had this morning eaten bread for breakfast; they had eaten potatoes and salt for dinner; and now, tea-time, there was bread again. All Jane had in her pocket was twopence, which must be kept for milk for the following morning; so they were drinking water now.

They were round the fire; two of the boys kneeling on the ground to get the better blaze, thankful they had a fire at all. Their lessons were over for the day. William had been thoroughly well brought on by his father, in Greek, Latin, Euclid, and in English generally—in short, in the branches necessary to a good education. Frank and Gar were forward also; indeed, Frank, for his age, was a very good Latin scholar. But how could they do much good or make much progress by themselves? William helped his brothers as well as he could, but it was somewhat profitless work; and Jane was all too conscious that they needed to be at school. Altogether, her heart was sore within her.

Another thing was beginning to worry her—a fear lest her brother should not be able to send the rent. She had fully counted upon it; but, now that the time of its promised receipt was at hand, fears and doubts arose. She was dwelling on it now—now, as she sat there at her work, in the twilight of the early spring evening. If the money did not come, all she could do would be to go to Mr. Ashley, tell him of her ill luck, and that he must take the things at last. They must turn out, wanderers on the wide earth; no—

A plaintive cry interrupted her dream and recalled her to reality. It came from Jane, who was seated on a stool, her head leaning against the side of the mantel-piece.

"She is crying, mamma," cried quick Frank; and Janey whispered something into Frank's ear, the cry deepening into sobs.

"Mamma, she's crying because she's hungry."

"Janey, dear, I have nothing but bread. You know it. Could you eat a bit?"

"I want something else," sobbed Janey. "Some meat, or some pudding. It is such a long time since we had any. I am tired of bread; I am very hungry."

There came an echoing cry from the other side of the fireplace. Gar had laid his head down on the floor, and he now broke out, sobbing also.

"I am hungry too. I don't like bread any more than Janey does. When shall we have something nice?"

Jane gathered them to her, one in each arm, soothing them with soft caresses, her heart aching, her own sobs choked down, one single comfort present to her—that God knew what she had to bear.

Almost she began to fear for her own health. Would the intense anxiety, combined with the want of sufficient food, tell upon her? Would her sleepless nights tell upon her? Would her grief for the loss of her husband—a grief not the less keenly felt because she did not parade it—tell upon her? All that lay in the future.

She rose the next morning early to her work; she always had to rise early—the boys and Jane setting the breakfast. Breakfast! Putting the bread upon the table and taking in the milk. For twopence they had a quart of skimmed milk, and were glad to get it. Her head was heavy, her frame hot, the result of inward fever, her limbs were tired before the day began; worse than all, there was that utter weariness of mind which predisposes a sufferer from it to lie down and die. "This will never do," thought Jane; "I must bear up."

A dispute between Frank and Gar! They were good, affectionate boys; but little tempers must break out now and then. In trying to settle it, Jane burst into tears. It put an end to the fray more effectually than anything else could have done. The boys looked blank with consternation, and Janey burst into hysterical sobs.

"Don't, Jane, don't," said the poor mother; "I am not well; but do not you cry."

"I am not well, either," sobbed Janey. "It hurts me here, and here." She put her hand to her head and chest, and Jane knew that she was weak from long-continued insufficiency of food. There was no remedy for it. Jane only wished she could bear for them all.

Some time after breakfast there came the postman's knock at the door. A thickish letter—twopence to pay. The penny postal system had come in, but letters were not so universally prepaid then as they are now.

Jane glanced over it with a beating heart. Yes, it was her brother's handwriting. Could the promised rent have really arrived? She felt sick with agitation.

"I have no money at all, Frank. Ask Dobbs if she will lend you twopence."

Away went Frank, in his quick and not very ceremonious manner, penetrating to the kitchen, where Dobbs happened to be. "Dobbs, will you please to lend mamma twopence? It is for a letter."

"Dobbs, indeed! Who's 'Dobbs'?" retorted that functionary in wrath. "I am Mrs. Dobbs, if you please. Take yourself out of my sight till you can learn manners."

"Won't you lend it? The postman's waiting."

"No, I won't," returned Dobbs.

Back ran Frank. "She won't lend it, mamma. She says I was rude to her, and called her Dobbs."

"Oh, Frank!" But the postman was impatient, demanding whether he was to be kept there all day. Jane was fain to apply to Dobbs herself, and procured the loan. Then she ran upstairs with the letter, and her trembling fingers broke the seal. Two banknotes, for 10£. each, fell out of it. The promised loan had been sixteen pounds. The Rev. Francis Tait had contrived to spare four pounds more.

Before Jane had recovered from her excitement—almost before a breath of thanks had gone up from her heart—she saw Mr. Ashley on the opposite side of the road, going towards Helstonleigh. Being in no state to weigh her actions, only conscious that the two notes lay in her hand—actual realities—she threw on her bonnet and shawl, and went across the road to Mr. Ashley. In her agitation, she scarcely knew what she did or said.

"Oh, sir—I beg your pardon—but I have at this moment received the money for the back rent. May I give it to you now?"

Mr. Ashley looked at her in surprise. A scarlet spot shone on her thin cheeks—a happy excitement was spread over her face of care. He read the indications plainly—that she was an eager payer, but no willing debtor. The open letter in her hand, and the postman opposite, told the tale.

"There is no such hurry, Mrs. Halliburton," he said, smiling. "I cannot give you a receipt here."

"You can send it to me," she said. "I would rather pay you than Mr. Dare."

She held out the notes to him. He felt in his pocket whether he had sufficient change, found he had, and handed it to her. "That is it, madam—four sovereigns. Thank you."

She took them hesitatingly, but did not close her hand. "Was there not some expense incurred when—when that man was put in?"

"Not for you to pay, Mrs. Halliburton," he pointedly returned. "I hope you are getting pretty well through your troubles?"

The tears came into her eyes, and she turned them away. Getting pretty well through her troubles! "Thank you for inquiring," she meekly said. "I shall, I believe, have the quarter's rent ready in March, when it falls due."

"Do not put yourself out of the way to pay it," he replied. "If it would be more convenient to you to let it go on to the half-year, it would be the same to me."

Her heart rose to the kindness. "Thank you, Mr. Ashley, thank you very much for your consideration; but I must pay as I go on, if I possibly can."

Patience stood at her gate, smiling as she recrossed the road. She had seen what had passed.

"Thee hast good news, I see. But thee wert in a hurry, to pay thy rent in the road."

"My brother has sent me the rent and four pounds over. Patience, I can buy bedside carpets now."

Patience looked pleased. "With all thy riches thee will scarcely thank me for this poor three and sixpence," holding out the silver to her. "Samuel Lynn left it; it is owing thee for thy work."

Jane smiled sadly as she took it. Her riches! "How is Anna?" she asked.

"She is nicely, thank thee, and is gone to school. But she was wilful over her lessons this morning. Farewell. I am glad thee art so far out of thy perplexities."

Very far, indeed; and a great relief it was. Can you realize these troubles of Mrs. Halliburton's? Not, I think, as she realized them. We pity the trials and endurance of the poor; but, believe me, they are as nothing compared with the bitter lot of reduced gentlepeople. Jane had not been brought up to poverty, to scanty and hard fare, to labour, to humiliations, to the pain of debt. But for hope—and some of us know how strong that is in the human heart—and for that better hope, trust, Jane never could have gone through her trials. Her physical privations alone were almost too hard to bear. Can you wonder that an unexpected present of four pounds seemed as a mine of wealth?

CHAPTER XXV

INCIPIENT VANITY

But four pounds, however large a sum to look at, dwindles down sadly in the spending; especially when bedside carpets, and boys' boots—new ones and the mending of old ones—have to be deducted from it at the commencement. An idea had for some time been looming in Jane's mind; looming ominously, for she did not like to speak of it. It was, that William must go out and enter upon some employment, by which a little weekly money might be added to their stock. He was eager enough; indulging, no doubt, boy-like, peculiar visions of his own, great and grand. But these Jane had to dispel; to explain that for young boys, such as he, earning money implied hard work.

His face flushed scarlet. Jane drew him to her and pressed her cheek upon his.

"There would be no real disgrace in it, my darling. No work in itself brings disgrace; be it carrying out parcels or sweeping out a shop. So long as we retain our refinement of tone, of manner, our courteous conduct one to the other, we shall still be gentlepeople, let us work at what we may. William, I think it is your duty to help in our need."

"Yes, I see, mamma," he answered. "I will try and do it; anything that may turn up."

Jane had not much faith in things "turning up." She believed that they must be sought for. That same evening she went into Mr. Lynn's, with the view to asking his counsel. There she found Anna in trouble. The cause was as follows.

Patience, leaving Anna alone at her lessons, had gone into the kitchen to give some directions to Grace. Anna seized the opportunity to take a little recreation: not that it was greatly needed, for—spoilt child that she was!—she had merely looked at her books with vacant eyes, not having in reality learned a single word. First of all, off went her cap. Next, she drew from her pocket a small mirror, about the size of a five-shilling piece. Propping this against her books on the table before her, so that the rays of the lamp might fall upon it, she proceeded to admire herself, and twist her flowing hair round her pretty fingers to make a shower of ringlets. Sad vanity for a little born Quakeress! But it must be owned that never did mirror, small or large, give back a more lovely image than that child's. She had just arranged her curls, and was contemplating their effect to her entire satisfaction, when back came Patience sooner than she was expected, and caught the young lady at her impromptu toilette. What with the curls and what with the mirror, Anna did not know which to hurry away first.

"Thee naughty child! Thee naughty, naughty child! What is to become of thee? Where did thee get this?"

Anna burst into tears. In her perplexity she said she had "found" the mirror.

"That thee did not," said Patience calmly. "I ask thee where thee got it from?"

Of a remarkably pliant nature, wavering and timid, Anna never withstood long the persistent questioning of Patience. Amid many tears the truth came out. Lucy Dixon had brought it to school in her workbox. It was a doll's mirror, and she, Anna, had given her sixpence for it.

"The sixpence that thy father bestowed upon thee yesterday for being a good girl," retorted Patience. "I told him thee would likely not make a profitable use of it. Come up to bed with thee! I will talk to thee after thee are in it."

Of all things, Anna disliked to be sent to bed before her time. She sobbed, expostulated, and promised all sorts of amendment for the future. Patience, firm and quiet, would have carried her point, but for the entrance of Samuel Lynn. The fault was related to him by Patience, and the mirror exhibited. Anna clung around him in a storm of sobs.

"Dear father! Dear, dear father, don't thee let me go to bed! Let me sit by thee while thee hast thy supper. Patience may keep the glass, but don't thee let me go."

It was quite a picture—the child clinging there with her crimsoned cheeks, her wet eyelashes, and her soft flowing hair. Samuel Lynn, albeit a man not given to demonstration, strained her to him with a loving movement. Perhaps the crime of looking into a doll's glass and toying with her hair appeared to him more venial than it did to Patience; but then, she was his beloved child.

"Will thee transgress again, Anna?"

"No, I never will," sobbed Anna.

"Then Patience will suffer thee to sit up this once. But thee must be careful."

He placed her in a chair close to him. Patience, disapproving very much but saying nothing, left the room. Grace appeared with the supper-tray, and a message that Patience would take her supper in the kitchen. It was at this juncture that Mrs. Halliburton came in. She told the Quaker that she had come to consult him about William; and mentioned her intentions.

"To tell thee the truth, friend, I have marvelled much that thee did not, under thy circumstances, seek to place out thy eldest son," was the answer. "He might be helping thee."

"He is young to earn anything, Mr. Lynn. Do you see a chance of my getting him a place?"

"That depends, friend, upon the sort of place he may wish for. I could help him to a place to-morrow. But it is one that may not accord with thy notions."

"What is it?" eagerly asked Jane.

"It is in Thomas Ashley's manufactory. We are in want of another boy, and the master told me to-day I had better inquire for one."

"What would he have to do?" asked Jane. "And what would he earn?"

"He would have to do anything he may be directed to do. Thy son is older than are our boys who come to us ordinarily, and he has been differently brought up; therefore I might put him to somewhat better employment. He might also be paid a trifle more. They sweep and dust, go on outdoor errands, carry messages indoors, black the gloves, get in coal; and they earn, if they are sharp, half-a-crown a week."

Jane's heart sank within her.

"But thy son, I say, might be treated somewhat differently. Not that he must be above doing any of these duties, should he be put to them. I can assure thee, friend, that some of the first manufacturers of this town have thus begun their career. A thoroughly practical knowledge of the business is only to be acquired by beginning at the first step of the ladder, and working upwards."

"Did Mr. Ashley so begin?" She could scarcely tell why she asked the question. Unless it was that a feeling came over her that if Mr. Ashley had done these things, she would not mind William's doing them.

"No, friend. Thomas Ashley's father was a man of means, and Thomas was bred up a classical scholar and a gentleman. He has never taken a practical part in the working of the business: I do that for him. His labours are chiefly confined to the correspondence and the keeping of the books. His father wished him to embrace a profession rather than be a glove manufacturer: but Thomas preferred to succeed his father. If thee would like thy son to enter our manufactory, I will try him."

Jane was dubious. She felt quite sure that William would not like it. "He has been thinking of a counting-house, or a lawyer's or conveyancer's office," she said aloud. "He would like to employ his time in writing. Would there be difficulty in getting him into one?"

"I do not opine a lawyer would take a boy of his size. They require their writing to be well and correctly done. About that, I cannot tell thee much, for I have nothing to do with lawyers. He can inquire."

Jane rose. She stood by the table, unconsciously stroking Anna's flowing curls—for the cap had never been replaced, and Samuel Lynn found no fault with the omission. "I will speak candidly," said Jane. "I fear that the place you have kindly offered me would not be liked by William. Other employments, writing for example, would be more palatable. Nevertheless, were he unable to obtain anything else I should be glad to accept this. Will you give me three or four days for consideration?"

"To oblige thee, I will, friend. When Thomas Ashley gives orders, he is prompt in having them attended to; and he spoke, as I have informed thee, about a fresh boy to-day. Would it not be a help to thee, friend, if thee got thy other two boys into the school attached to the cathedral?"

"But I have no interest," said Jane. "I hear that education there is free; but I do not possess the slightest chance."

"Thee may get a chance, friend. There's nothing like trying. I must tell thee that the school is not thought highly of, in consequence of the instruction being confined exclusively to Latin and Greek. In the old days this was thought enough; but people are now getting more enlightened. Thomas Ashley was educated there; but he had a private tutor at home for the branches not taught at the college; he had also masters for what are called accomplishments. He is one of the most accomplished men of the day.

Few are so thoroughly and comprehensively educated as Thomas Ashley. I have heard say thy sons have begun Latin. It might be a help to them if they could get in."

"I should desire nothing better," Jane breathlessly rejoined, a new hope penetrating her heart. "I have heard of the collegiate school here; but, until very recently I supposed it to be an expensive institution."

"No, friend; it is free. The best way to get a boy in is by making interest with the head-master of the school, or with some of the cathedral clergy."

A recollection of Mr. Peach flashed into Jane's mind as a ray of light. She bade good-night to Samuel Lynn and Anna, and to Patience as she passed the kitchen. Patience had been crying.

"I am grieved about Anna," she explained. "I love the child dearly, but Samuel Lynn is blind to her faults; and it argues badly for the future. Thee cannot imagine half her vanity; I fear me, too, she is deceitful. I wish her father could see it! I wish he would indulge her less and correct her more! Good night to thee."

Before concluding the chapter, it may as well be mentioned that a piece of good fortune about this time befell Janey. She found favour with Dobbs! How it came about perhaps Dobbs could not herself have told. Certainly no one else could.

Mrs. Reece had got into the habit of asking Jane into her parlour to tea. She was a kind-hearted old lady and liked the child. Dobbs would afterwards be at work, generally some patching and mending to her own clothes; and Dobbs, though she would not acknowledge it to herself or to any one else, could not see to thread her needle. Needle in one hand and thread in the other, she would poke the two together for five minutes, no result supervening. Janey hit upon the plan of threading her a needle in silence, whilst Dobbs used the one; and from that time Jane kept her in threaded needles. Whether this conciliated Dobbs must remain a mystery, but she took a liking for Jane; and the liking grew into love. Henceforth Janey wanted for nothing. While the others starved, she lived on the fat of the land. Meat and pudding, fowls and pastry, whatever dinner in the parlour might consist of, Janey had her share of it, and a full share too. At first Mrs. Halliburton, from motives of delicacy, would not allow Jane to go in; upon which Dobbs would enter, boiling over with indignation, red with the exertion of cooking, and triumphantly bear her off. Jane spoke seriously to Mrs. Reece about it, but the old lady declared she was as glad to have the child as Dobbs was.

Once, Janey came to a standstill over some apple pudding, which had followed upon veal cutlets and bacon. "I am quite full," said she, more plainly than politely: "I can't eat a bit more. May I give this piece upon my plate to Gar?"

"No, you may not," snapped Dobbs, drowning Mrs. Reece's words, that she might give it and welcome. "How dare you, Janey? You know that boys is the loadstones of my life."

Dobbs probably used the word loadstones to indicate a heavy weight. She seized the plate of pudding and finished it herself, lest it should find its way to the suggested quarter—a self-sacrifice which served to show her earnestness in the cause. Nothing gave Dobbs indigestion like apple pudding, and she knew she should be a martyr for four-and-twenty hours afterwards.

Thus Jane, at least, suffered from henceforth no privations, and for this Mrs. Halliburton was very thankful. The time was to come, however, when she would have reason to be more so.

CHAPTER XXVI

MR ASHLEY'S MANUFACTORY

The happy thought, suggested by Samuel Lynn, Jane carried out. She applied in person to Mr. Peach, and he obtained an immediate entrance for Frank to the college school, with a promise for Gar to enter at quarter-day, the 25th of March. He was perfectly thunderstruck when he found that his old friend and tutor, Mr. Halliburton, was dead; had died in Helstonleigh; and that he—he!—had buried him. There was no need to ask him twice, after that, to exert his interest for the fatherless children. The school (I have told you what it was many years ago) was not held in the highest repute, from the reason spoken of by Samuel Lynn; vacancies often occurred, and admission was easy. It was one great weight off Jane's mind.

William was not so fortunate. He was at that period very short for his age, timid in manner, and no office could be persuaded to take him. Nothing in the least congenial to him presented itself or could be found; and the result was that he resigned himself to Samuel Lynn, who introduced him to Mr. Ashley's extensive manufactory—to be initiated by degrees into all the mysteries necessary to convert a skin into a glove. And although his interest and curiosity were excited by what he saw, he pronounced it a "hateful" business.

When the skins came in from the leather-dressers they were washed in a tub of cold water. The next day warm water, mixed with yolks of eggs, was poured on them, and a couple of men, bare-legged to the knee, got into the tub, and danced upon them, skins, eggs, and water, for two hours. Then they were spread in a field to dry, till they were as hard as lantern horn; then they were "staked," as it was called—a long process, to smooth and soften them. To the stainers next, to be stained black or coloured; next to the parers, to have the loose flesh pared from the inside, and to be smoothed again with pumice-stone—all this being done on the outside premises. Then they came inside, to the hands of one of the foremen, who sorted and marked them for the cutters. The cutters cut the skins into tranks (the shape of the hand in outline) with the separate thumbs and forgits, and sent them in to the slitters. The slitters slit the four fingers, and shaped the thumbs and forgits: after that, they were ready for the women—three different women, you may remember, being necessary to turn out each glove, so far as the sewing went; for one woman rarely worked at more than her own peculiar branch, or was capable of working at it. This done, and back in the manufactory again, they had to be pulled straight, and "padded," or rubbed, a process by which they were brightened. If black gloves, the seams were washed over with a black dye, or else glazed; then they were hung up to dry. This done, they went into Samuel Lynn's room, a large room next to Mr. Ashley's private room, and here they were sorted into firsts, seconds, or thirds; the sorting being always done by Samuel Lynn, or by James Meeking the head foreman. It was called "making-up." Next they were banded round with a paper in dozens, labelled, and placed in small boxes, ready for the warehouses in London. A great deal, you see, before one pair of gloves could be turned out.

The first morning that William went at six o'clock with Samuel Lynn, he was ordered to light the fire in Mr. Ashley's room, sweep it out, and dust it, first of all sprinkling the floor with water from a watering-pot. And this was to be part of his work every morning at present; Samuel Lynn giving him strict charge never to disturb anything on Mr. Ashley's desk. If he moved things to dust the desk, he was to lay them down again in the same places and in the same position. The duster consisted of some leather shreds tied up into a knot, the ends loose. He found he should have to wait on Mr. Ashley and Samuel Lynn, bring things they wanted, carry messages to the men, and go out when sent. A pair of shears, which he could not manage, was put into his hand, and he had to cut a damaged skin, useless for gloves, into narrow strips, standing at one of the counters in Samuel Lynn's room. William wondered whether they were to make another duster, but he found they were used in the manufactory in place of string. That done, a round, polished stick was handed to him, tapered at either end, which he had to pass over and over some small gloves to make them smooth, after the manner of a cook rolling out paste for a pie. He looked with dismay at the two young errand boys of the establishment, who were black with dye. But Samuel Lynn had distinctly told him that he would not be expected to place himself on their level. The rooms were for the most part very light, one or two sides being entirely of glass.

On the evening of this first day, William, after he got home, sat there in sad heaviness. His mother asked how he liked his employment, and he returned an evasive answer. Presently he rose to go to bed, saying he had a headache. Up he went to the garret, and flung himself down on the mattress, sobbing as if his heart would break. Jane, suspecting something of this, followed him up. She caught him in her arms.

"Oh, my darling, don't give way! Things may grow brighter after a time."

"It is such a dreadful change!—from my books, my Latin and Greek, to go there and sweep out places like those two black boys!" he said hysterically, all his reticence gone.

"My dear boy! my darling boy! I know not how to reconcile you, how to lessen your cares. Your experience of the sorrow of life is beginning early. You are hungry, too."

"I am always hungry," answered William, quite unable to affect concealment in that hour of grief. "I heard one of those black boys say he had boiled pork and greens for dinner. I did so envy him."

Jane checked her tears; they were rising rebelliously. "William, darling your lot seems just now very dark and painful, but it might be worse."

"Worse!" he echoed in surprise. "How could it be worse? Mamma, I am no better than an errand-boy there."

"It would be worse, William, if you were one of those poor black boys. Unenlightened; no wish for higher things; content to remain as they are for ever."

"But that could never be," he urged. "To be content with such a life is impossible."

"They are content, William."

He saw the drift of the argument. "Yes, mamma," he acknowledged; "I did not reflect. It would be worse if I were quite as they are."

"William, we can only bear our difficulties, and make the best of them, trusting to surmount them in the end. You and I must both do this. Trust is different from hope. If we only hope, we may lose courage; but if we fully and freely trust, we cannot. Patience and perseverance, endurance and trust, they will in the end triumph; never fear. If I feared, William, I should go into the grave with despair. I never lose my trust. I never lose my conviction, firm and certain, that God is watching over me, that He is permitting these trials for some wise purpose, and that in His own good time we shall be brought through them."

William's sobs were growing lighter.

"The time may come when we shall be at ease again," continued Jane; "when we shall look back on this time of trial, and be thankful that we did bear up and surmount it, instead of fainting under the burden. God will take care that the battle is not too hot for us, if we only resign ourselves, in all trust, to do the best. The future is grievously dim and indistinct. As the guiding light in your father's dream shone only on one step at a time, so can I see only one step before me."

"What step is that?" he asked somewhat eagerly.

"The one obvious step before me is to persevere, as I am now doing, to try and retain this home for you, my children; to work as I can, so as to keep you around me. I must strive to keep you together, and you must help me. Bear up bravely, William. Make the best of this unpleasant employment and its mortifications, and strive to overcome your repugnance to it. Be resolute, my boy, in doing your duty in it, because it is your duty, and because, William—because it is helping your mother."

A shadow of the trust, so firm in his mother's heart, began to dawn in his. "Yes, it is my duty," he resolutely said. "I will try to do it—to hope and trust."

Jane strained him to her. "Were you and I to give way now, darling, our past troubles would have been borne for nothing. Let us, I repeat, look forward to the time when we may say, 'We did not faint; we battled on, and overcame.' It will come, William. Only trust to God."

She quitted him, leaving him to reflection and resolve scarcely befitting his young years.

The week wore on to its close. On the Saturday night, William, his face flushed, held out four shillings to his mother. "My week's wages, mamma."

Jane's face flushed also. "It is more than I expected, William," she said. "I fancied you would have three."

"I think the master fixed the sum," said William.

"The master? Do you mean Mr. Ashley?"

"We never say 'Mr. Ashley' in the manufactory; we say 'the master.' Mr. Lynn was paying the wages to-night. I heard them say that sometimes Mr. Lynn paid them, and sometimes James Meeking. Those two black boys have half-a-crown apiece. He left me to the last, and when the rest were gone, he looked at me and took up three shillings. Then he seemed to hesitate, and suddenly he locked the desk, went into the master's room, and spoke with him. He came back in a minute, unlocked the desk, and gave me four shillings. 'Thee hast not earned it,' he said, 'but I think thee has done thy best. Thee will have the same each week, so long as thee does so.'"

Jane held the four shillings, and felt that she was growing quite rich. The rest crowded round to look. "Can't we have a nice dinner to-morrow with it?" said one.

"I think we must," said Jane cheerily. "A nice dinner for once in a way. What shall it be?"

"Roast beef," called out Frank.

"Pork with crackling," suggested Janey. "That of Mrs. Reece's yesterday was so good."

"Couldn't we have fowls and a jam pudding?" asked Gar.

Jane smiled and kissed him. All the suggestions were beyond her purse. "We will have a meat pudding," she said; "that's best." And the children cheerfully acquiesced. They had implicit faith in their mother; they knew that what she said was best, would be best.

On this same Saturday night Charlotte East was returning home from Helstonleigh, an errand having taken her thither after dark. Almost opposite to the turning to Honey Fair, a lane branched off, leading to some farm-houses; a lane, green and pleasant in summer, but bare and uninviting now. Two people turned into it as Charlotte looked across. She caught only a glance; but something in the aspect of both struck upon her as familiar. A gas-lamp at the corner shed a light upon the spot, and Charlotte suddenly halted, and stood endeavouring to peer further. But they were soon out of view. A feeling of dismay had stolen over Charlotte. She hoped she was mistaken; that the parties were not those she had fancied; and she slowly continued her way. A few paces more, she turned up the road leading to Honey Fair and found herself nearly knocked over by one who came running against her, apparently in some excitement and in a great hurry.

"Who's this?" cried the voice of Eliza Tyrrett. "Charlotte East, I declare! I say, have you seen anything of Caroline Mason?"

Charlotte hesitated. She hoped she had not seen her; though the misgiving was upon her that she had. "Did you think I might have seen her?" she returned. "Has she come this way?"

"Yes, I expect she has come this way, and I want to find her," returned Eliza Tyrrett vehemently. "I saw her making off out of Honey Fair, and I saw who was waiting for her round the corner. I knew my company wasn't wanted then, and turned into Dame Buffle's for a talk; and there I found that Madam Carry has been telling falsehoods about me. Let me set on to her, that's all! I shall say what she won't like."

"Who do you mean was waiting for her?" inquired Charlotte East.

Eliza Tyrrett laughed. She was beginning to recover her temper. "You'd like to know, wouldn't you?" said she pertly. "But I'm not going to tell tales out of school."

"I think I do know," returned Charlotte quietly. "I fear I do."

"Do you? I thought nobody knew nothing about it but me. It has been going on this ten weeks. Did you see her, though, Charlotte?"

"I thought I saw her, but I could not believe my eyes. She was with—with—some one she has no business to be with."

"Oh, as to business, I don't know about that," carelessly answered Eliza Tyrrett. "We have a right to walk with anybody we like."

"Whether it is good or bad for you?" returned Charlotte.

"There's no 'bad' in it," cried Eliza Tyrrett indignantly. "I never saw such an old maid as you are, Charlotte East, never! Carry Mason's not a child, to be led into mischief."

"Carry's very foolish," was Charlotte's comment.

"Oh, of course you think so, or it wouldn't be you. You'll go and tell upon her at home, I suppose, now."

"I shall tell her," said Charlotte. "Folks should choose their acquaintances in their own class of life, if they want things to turn out pleasantly."

"Were you not all took in about that shawl!" uttered Eliza Tyrrett, with a laugh. "You thought she went in debt for it at Bankes's, and her people at home thought so. Het Mason shrieked on at her like anything, for spending money on her back while she owed it for her board. He gave her that."

"Eliza!"

"He did. Law, where's the harm? He is rich enough to give all us girls in Honey Fair one apiece, and who'd be the worse for it? Only his pocket; and that can afford it. I wish he would!"

"I wish you would not talk so, Eliza. She is not a fit companion for him, even though it is but to take a walk; and she ought to remember that she is not."

"He wants her for a longer companion than that," observed Eliza Tyrrett; "that is, if he tells true. He wants her to marry him."

"He—wants her to marry him!" repeated Charlotte, speaking the words in sheer amazement. "Who says so?"

"He does. I should hardly think he can be in earnest, though."

"Eliza Tyrrett, we cannot be speaking of the same person," cried Charlotte, feeling bewildered. "To whom have you been alluding?"

"To the same that you have, I expect. Young Anthony Dare."

CHAPTER XXVII

THE FORGOTTEN LETTER

It was the last day of March, and five o'clock in the afternoon. The great bell had rung in Mr. Ashley's manufactory, the signal for the men to go to their tea. Scuffling feet echoed to it from all parts, and clattered down the stairs on their way out. The ground floor was not used for the indoor purposes of the manufactory, the business being carried on in the first and second floors. The first flight of stairs opened into what was called the serving-room, a very large apartment; through this, on the right, branched off Mr. Ashley's room and Samuel Lynn's. On the left, various passages led to other rooms, and the upper flight of stairs was opposite to the entrance-stairs. The serving-counter, running completely across the room, formed a barrier between the serving-room and the entrance staircase.

The men flocked into the serving-room, passed it, and rattled down the stairs. Samuel Lynn was changing his coat to follow, and William Halliburton was waiting for him, his cap on, for he walked to and fro with the Quaker, when Mr. Ashley's voice was heard from his room: the counting-house, as it was frequently called.

"William!" It was usual to distinguish the boys by their Christian name only; the men by both their Christian and surnames. Samuel Lynn was "Mr. Lynn."

"Did thee not hear the master calling to thee?"

William had certainly heard Mr. Ashley's voice; but it was so unusual to be called by it, that he had paid no attention. He had very little communication with Mr. Ashley; in the three or four weeks he had now been at the manufactory Mr. Ashley had not spoken to him a dozen words. He hastened into the counting-house, taking off his cap in the presence of Mr. Ashley.

"Have the men gone to tea?" inquired Mr. Ashley, who was sealing a letter.

"Yes, sir," replied William.

"Is George Dance gone?" George Dance was an apprentice, and it was his business to take the letters to the post.

"They are all gone, sir, except Mr. Lynn; and James Meeking, who is waiting to lock up."

"Do you know the post-office?"

"Oh, yes, sir. It is in West Street, at the other end of the town."

"Take this letter, and put it carefully in."

William received the letter from Mr. Ashley, and dropped it into his jacket pocket. It was addressed to Bristol; the London mail-bags were already made up. Mr. Ashley put on his hat and departed, followed by Samuel Lynn and William. James Meeking locked up, as it was his invariable business to do, and carried the keys into his own house. He inhabited part of the ground floor of the premises.

"Are thee not coming home with me this evening?" inquired Samuel Lynn of William, who was turning off the opposite way.

"No; the master has given me a letter to post. I have also an errand to do for my mother."

It happened (things do happen in a curious sort of way in this world) that Mrs. Halliburton had desired William to bring her in some candles and soap at tea-time, and to purchase them at Lockett's shop. Lockett's shop was rather far off; there were others nearer; but Lockett's goods were of the best quality, and his extensive trade enabled him to sell a halfpenny a pound cheaper. A halfpenny was a halfpenny with Jane then. William went on his way, walking fast.

As he was passing the cathedral, he came into contact with the college boys, then just let out of school. It was the first day that Gar had joined; he had received his appointment, according to promise. Very thankful was Jane; in spite of the drawback of having to provide them with linen surplices. William halted to see if he could discern Gar amidst the throng: it was not unnatural that he should look for him.

One of the boys caught sight of William standing there. It was Cyril Dare, the third son of Mr. Dare, a boy older and considerably bigger than William.

"If there's not another of that Halliburton lot posted there!" cried he, to a knot of those around. "Perhaps he will be coming amongst us next—because we have not enough with the two! Look at the fellow, staring at us! He is a common errand-boy at Ashley's."

Frank Halliburton, who, little as he was, wanted neither for spirit nor pluck, heard the words and confronted Cyril Dare. "That is my brother," said he. "What have you to say against him?"

Cyril Dare cast a glance of scorn on Frank, regarding him from top to toe. "You audacious young puppy! I say he is a snob. There!"

"Then I say he is not," retorted Frank. "You are one yourself, for saying it."

Cyril Dare, big enough to have crushed Frank to death, speedily had him on the ground, and treated him not very mercifully when there. William, a witness to this, but not understanding it, pushed his way through the crowd to protect Frank. All he saw was that Frank was down, and two big boys were kicking him.

"Let him alone!" cried he. "How can you be so cowardly as to attack a little fellow? And two of you! Shame!"

Now, if there was one earthly thing that the college boys would not brook, it was being interfered with by a stranger. William suffered. Frank's treatment had been nothing to what he had to submit to. He was knocked down, trampled on, kicked, buffeted, abused; Cyril Dare being the chief and primary aggressor. At that moment the under-master came in view, and the boys made off—all except Cyril Dare.

Reined in against the wall, at a few yards' distance, was a lad on a pony. He had delicately expressive features, large soft brown eyes, a complexion too bright for health, and wavy dark hair. The face was beautiful; but two upright lines were indented in the white forehead, as if worn there by pain, and the one ungloved hand was white and thin. He was as old as William within a year; but, slight and fragile, would be taken to be much younger. Seeing and hearing—though not very clearly—what had passed, he touched his pony, and rode up to Cyril Dare. The latter was beginning to walk away leisurely, in the wake of his companions; the upper boys were rather fond of ignoring the presence of the under-master. Cyril turned at hearing himself called.

"What! Is it you, Henry Ashley? Where did you spring from?"

"Cyril Dare," was the answer, "you are a wretched coward."

Cyril Dare was feeling anger yet, and the words did not lessen it. "Of course you can say so!" he cried. "You know that you can say what you like with impunity. One can't chastise a cripple like you."

The brilliant, painful colour flushed into the face of Henry Ashley. To allude openly to infirmity such as this is as iron entering into the soul. Upon a sensitive, timid, refined nature (and those suffering from this sort of affliction are nearly sure to possess that nature), it falls with a bitterness that can neither be conceived by others nor spoken of by themselves. Henry Ashley braved it out.

"A coward, and a double coward!" he repeated, looking Cyril Dare full in the face, whilst the transparent flush grew hotter on his own. "You struck a young boy down, and then kicked him; and for nothing but that he stood up like a trump at your abuse of his brother."

"You couldn't hear," returned Cyril Dare roughly.

"I heard enough. I say that you are a coward."

"Chut! They are snobs out-and-out."

"I don't care if they are chimney-sweeps. It does not make you less a coward. And you'll be one as long as you live. If I had my strength, I'd serve you out as you served them out."

"Ah, but you have not your strength, you know!" mocked Cyril. "And as you seem to be going into one of your heroic fits, I shall make a start, for I have no time to waste on them."

He tore away. Henry Ashley turned his pony and addressed William. Both boys had spoken rapidly, so that scarcely a minute had passed, and William had only just risen from the ground. He leaned against the wall, giddy, as he wiped the blood from his face. "Are you much hurt?" asked Henry, kindly, his large dark eyes full of sympathy.

"No, thank you; it is nothing," replied William. "He is a great coward, though, whoever he is."

"It is Cyril Dare," called out Frank.

"Yes, it is Cyril Dare," continued Henry Ashley. "I have been telling him what a coward he is. I am ashamed of him: he is my cousin, in a remote degree. I am glad you are not hurt."

Henry Ashley rode away towards his home. Frank followed in the same direction; as did Gar, who now came in view. William proceeded up the town. He was a little hurt, although he had disowned it to Henry Ashley. His head felt light, his arms ached; perhaps the sensation of giddiness was as much from the want of food as anything. He purchased what was required for his mother; and then made the best of his way home again. Mr. Ashley's letter had gone clean out of his head.

Frank, in the manner usual with boys, carried home so exaggerated a story of William's damages, that Jane expected to see him arrive half-killed. Samuel Lynn heard of it, and said William might stop at home that evening. It has never been mentioned that his hours were from six till eight in the morning, from nine till one, from two till five, and from six till eight. These were Mr. Lynn's hours, and William was allowed to keep the same; the men had half-an-hour less allowed for breakfast and tea.

William was glad of the rest, after his battle, and the evening passed on. It was growing late, almost bedtime, when suddenly there flashed into his memory Mr. Ashley's letter. He put his hand into his jacket-pocket. There it lay, snug and safe. With a few words of explanation to his mother, so hasty and incoherent that she did not understand a syllable, he snatched his cap, and flew away in the direction of the town.

Boys have good legs and lungs; and William scarcely slackened speed until he gained the post-office, not far short of a mile. Dropping the letter into the box, he stood against the wall to recover breath. A clerk was standing at the door whistling; and at that moment a gentleman, apparently a stranger, came out of a neighbouring hotel, a letter in hand.

"This is the head post-office, I believe?" said he to the clerk.

"Yes."

"Am I in time to post a letter for Bristol?"

"No, sir. The bags for the Bristol mail are made up. It will be through the town directly."

William heard this with consternation. If it was too late for this gentleman's letter, it was too late for Mr. Ashley's.

He said nothing to any one that night; but he lay awake thinking over what might be the consequences of his forgetfulness. The letter might be one of importance; Mr. Ashley might discharge him for his neglect—and the weekly four shillings had grown into an absolute necessity. William possessed a large share of conscientiousness, and the fault disturbed him much.

When he came down at six, he found his mother up and at work. He gave her the history of what had happened. "What can be done?" he asked.

"Nay, William, put that question to yourself. What ought you to do? Reflect a moment."

"I suppose I ought to tell Mr. Ashley."

"Do not say 'I suppose,' my dear. You must tell him."

"Yes, I know I must," he acknowledged. "I have been thinking about it all night. But I don't like to."

"Ah, child! we have many things to do that we 'don't like.' But the first trouble is always the worst. Look it fully in the face, and it will melt away. There is no help for it in this matter, William; your duty is plain. There's Mr. Lynn looking out for you."

William went out, heavy with the thought of the task he should have to accomplish after breakfast. He knew that he must do it. It was a duty, as his mother had said; and she had fully impressed upon them all, from their infancy, the necessity of looking out for their duty and doing it, whether in great things or in small.

Mr. Ashley entered the manufactory that morning at his usual hour, half-past nine. He opened and read his letters, and then was engaged for some time with Samuel Lynn. By ten o'clock the counting-house was clear. Mr. Ashley was alone in it, and William knew that his time was come. He went in, and approached Mr. Ashley's desk.

Mr. Ashley, who was writing, looked up. "What is it?"

William's face grew red and white by turns. He was of a remarkably sensitive nature; and these sensitive natures cannot help betraying their inward emotion. Try as he would, he could not get a word out. Mr. Ashley was surprised. "What is the matter?" he wonderingly asked.

"If you please, sir—I am very sorry—it is about the letter," he stammered, and was unable to get any further.

"The letter!" repeated Mr. Ashley. "What letter? Not the letter I gave you to post?"

"I forgot it, sir,"—and William's own voice sounded to his ear painfully clear.

"Forgot to post it! That was unpardonably careless. Where is the letter?"

"I forgot it, sir, until night, and then I ran to the post-office and put it in. Afterwards I heard the clerk say that the Bristol bags were made up, so of course it would not go. I am very sorry, sir," he repeated, after a pause.

"How came you to forget it? You ought to have gone direct from here, and posted it."

"So I did go, sir. That is I was going, but—"

"But what?" returned Mr. Ashley, for William had made a dead standstill.

"The college boys set on me, sir. They were ill-using my brother, and I interfered; and then they turned upon me. It made me forget the letter."

"It was you who got into an affray with the college boys, was it?" cried Mr. Ashley. He had heard his son's version of the affair, without suspecting that it related to William.

William waited by the desk. "If you please, sir, was it of great consequence?"

"It might have been. Do not be guilty of such carelessness again."

"I will try not, sir."

Mr. Ashley looked down at his writing. William waited. He did not suppose it was over, and he wanted to know the worst. "Why do you stay?" asked Mr. Ashley.

"I hope you will not turn me away for it, sir," he said, his colour changing again.

"Well—not this time," replied Mr. Ashley, smiling to himself. "But I'll tell you what I should have felt inclined to turn you away for," he added—"concealing the fact from me. Whatever fault, omission, or accident you may commit, always acknowledge it at once; it is the best plan, and the easiest. You may go back to your work now."

William left the room with a lighter step. Mr. Ashley looked after him. "That's an honest lad," thought he. "He might just as well have kept it from me; calculating on the chances of its not coming out: many boys would have done so. He has been brought up in a good school."

Before the day was over, William came again into contact with Mr. Ashley. That gentleman sometimes made his appearance in the manufactory in an evening—not always. He did not on this one. When Samuel Lynn and William entered it on their return from tea, a gentleman was waiting in the counting-house on business. Samuel Lynn, who was, on such occasions, Mr. Ashley's alter ego, came out of the counting-house presently, with a note in his hand.

"Thee put on thy cap, and take this to the master's house. Ask to see him, and say that I wait for an answer."

William ran off with the note: no fear of his forgetting this time. It was addressed in the plain form used by the Quakers, "Thomas Ashley;" and could William have looked inside, he would have seen, instead of the complimentary "Sir," that the commencement was, "Respected Friend." He observed his mother sitting close at her window, to catch what remained of the declining light, and nodded to her as he passed.

"Can I see Mr. Ashley?" he inquired, when he reached the house.

The servant replied that he could. He left William in the hall, and opened the door of the dining-room; a handsome room, of lofty proportions. Mr. Ashley was slowly pacing it to and fro, whilst Henry sat at a table, preparing his Latin exercise for his tutor. It was Mr. Ashley's custom to help Henry with his Latin, easing difficulties to him by explanation. Henry was very backward with his classics; he had not yet begun Greek: his own private hope was, that he never should begin it. His sufferings rendered learning always irksome, sometimes unbearable. The same cause frequently made him irritable—an irritation that could not be checked, as it would have been in a more healthy boy. The servant told his master he was wanted, and Mr. Ashley looked into the hall.

"Oh, is it you, William?" he said. "Come in."

William advanced. "Mr. Lynn said I was to see yourself, sir, and to say that he waited for an answer."

Mr. Ashley opened the note, and read it by the lamp on Henry's table. It was not dark outside, and the chandelier was not lighted, but Henry's lamp was. "Sit down," said Mr. Ashley to William, and left the room, note in hand.

William felt it was something, Mr. Ashley's recognizing a difference between him and those black boys in the manufactory: they would scarcely have been told to sit in the hall. William sat down on the first chair at hand. Henry Ashley looked at him, and he recognized him as the boy who had been maltreated by the college boys on the previous day; but Henry was in no mood to be sociable, or even condescending—he never was, when over his lessons. His hip was giving him pain, and his exercise was making him fractious.

"There! it's always the case! Another five minutes, and I should have finished this horrid exercise. Papa is sure to go away, or be called away, when he's helping me! It's a shame."

Mrs. Ashley opened the door at this juncture, and looked into the room. "I thought your papa was here, Henry."

"No, he is not here. He has gone to his study, and I am stuck fast. Some blessed note has come, which he has to attend to: and I don't know whether this word should be put in the ablative or the dative! I'll run the pen through it!"

"Oh, Henry, Henry! Do not be so impatient."

Mrs. Ashley shut the door again; and Henry continued to worry himself, making no progress, except in fretfulness. At length William approached him. "Will you let me help you?"

Surprise brought Henry's grumbling to a standstill. "You!" he exclaimed. "Do you know anything of Latin?"

"I am very much farther in it than what you are doing. My brother Gar is as far as that. Shall I help you? You have put that wrong; it ought to be in the accusative."

"Well, if you can help me, you may, for I want to get it over," said Henry, with a doubting stress upon the "can." "You can sit down, if you wish to," he patronizingly added.

"Thank you, I don't care about sitting down," replied William, beginning at once upon his task.

The two boys were soon deep in the exercise, William not doing it, but rendering it easy to Henry; in the same manner that Mr. Halliburton, when he was at that stage, used to make it clear to him.

"I say," cried Henry, "who taught you?"

"Papa. He gave a great deal of time to me, and that got me on. I can see a wrong word there," added William, casting his eyes to the top of the page. "It ought to be in the vocative, and you have put it in the dative."

"You are mistaken, then. Papa told me that: and he is not likely to be wrong. Papa is one of the best classical scholars of the day—although he is a manufacturer," added Henry, who, through his relatives, the Dares, had been infected with a contempt for business.

"It should be in the vocative," repeated William.

"I shan't alter it. The idea of your finding fault with Mr. Ashley's Latin! Let us get on. What case is this?"

The last word of the exercise was being written, when Mr. Ashley opened the door and called to William. He gave him a note for Mr. Lynn, and William departed. Mr. Ashley returned to complete the interrupted exercise.

"I say, papa, that fellow knows Latin," began Henry.

"What fellow?" returned Mr. Ashley.

"Why, that chap of yours who has been here. He has helped me through my exercise. Not doing it for me: you need not be afraid; but explaining to me how to do it. He made it easier to me than you do, papa."

Mr. Ashley took the book in his hand, and saw that it was correct. He knew Henry could not, or would not, have made it so himself. Henry continued:

"He said his papa used to explain it to him. Fancy one of your manufactory errand-boys saying 'papa.'"

"You must not class him with the ordinary errand-boys, Henry. The boy has been as well brought up as you have."

"I thought so; for he has impudence about him," was Master Henry's retort.

"Was he impudent to you?"

"To me? Oh no. He is as civil a fellow as ever I spoke to. Indeed, but for remembering who he was, I should call him a gentlemanly fellow. Whilst he was telling me, I forgot who he was, and talked to him as an equal, and he talked to me as one. I call him impudent, because he found fault with your Latin."

"Indeed!" returned Mr. Ashley, an amused smile parting his lips.

"He says this word's wrong. That it ought to be in the vocative case."

"So it ought to be," assented Mr. Ashley, casting his eyes on the word to which Henry pointed.

"You told me the dative, papa."

"That I certainly did not, Henry. The mistake must have been your own."

"He persisted that it was wrong, although I told him it was your Latin. Papa, it is the same boy who had the row yesterday with Cyril Dare. What a pity it is, though, that a fellow so well up in his Latin should be shut up in a manufactory!"

"The only 'pity' is, that he is in it too early," was the response of Mr. Ashley. "His Latin would not be any detriment to his being in a manufactory, or the manufactory to his Latin. I am a manufacturer myself, Henry. You appear to ignore that sometimes."

"The Dares go on so. They din it into my ears that a manufacturer cannot be a gentleman."

"I shall cause you to drop the acquaintance of the Dares, if you allow yourself to listen to all the false and foolish notions they may give utterance to. Cyril Dare will probably go into a manufactory himself."

Henry looked up curiously. "I don't think so, papa."

"I do," returned Mr. Ashley, in a significant tone. Henry was surprised at the news. He knew his father never advanced a decided opinion unless he had good grounds for it. He burst into a laugh. The notion of Cyril Dare's going into a manufactory tickled his fancy amazingly.

PART THE SECOND

CHAPTER I

A SUGGESTED FEAR

One morning, towards the middle of April, Mrs. Halliburton went up to Mr. Ashley's. She had brought him the quarter's rent.

"Will you allow me to pay it to yourself, sir—now, and in future?" she asked. "I feel an unconquerable aversion to having further dealings with Mr. Dare."

"I can understand that you should have," said Mr. Ashley. "Yes, you can pay it to me, Mrs. Halliburton. Always remembering you know, that I am in no hurry for it," he added with a smile.

"Thank you. You are very kind. But I must pay as I go on."

He wrote the receipt, and handed it to her. "I hope you are satisfied with William?" she said, as she folded it up.

"Quite so. I believe he gives satisfaction to Mr. Lynn. I have little to do with him myself. Mr. Lynn tells me that he finds him a remarkably truthful, open-natured boy."

"You will always find him that," said Jane. "He is getting more reconciled to the manufactory than he was at first."

"Did he not like it at first?"

"No, he did not. He was disappointed altogether. He had hoped to find some employment more suited to the way in which he had been brought up. He cannot divest himself of the idea that he is looked upon as on a level with the poor errand-boys of your establishment, and therefore has lost caste. He had wished also to be in some office—a lawyer's, for instance—where the hours for leaving are early, so that he might have had the evening for his studies. But he is growing more reconciled to the inevitable."

"I suppose he wished to continue his studies?"

"He did so naturally. The foundation of an advanced education has been laid, and he expected it was to go on to completion. His brothers are now in the college school, occupied all day long with their studies, and of course William feels the difference. He gets to his books for an hour when he returns home in an evening; but he is weary, and does not do much good."

"He appears to be a more persevering, thoughtful boy than are some," remarked Mr. Ashley.

"Very thoughtful—very persevering. It has been the labour of my life, Mr. Ashley, to foster good seed in my children; to reason with them, to make them my companions. They have been endowed, I am thankful to say, with admirable qualities of head and heart, and I have striven unweariedly to nourish the good in them. It is not often that boys are brought into contact with sorrow so early as they. Their father's death and my adverse circumstances have been real trials."

"They must have been," rejoined Mr. Ashley.

"While others of their age think only of play," she continued, "my boys have been obliged to learn the sad experiences of life; and it has given them a thought, a care, beyond their years. There is no necessity to make Frank and Edgar apply to their lessons unremittingly; they do it of their own accord, with their whole abilities, knowing that education is the only advantage they can possess—the one chance of their getting on in the world. Had William been a boy of a different disposition, less tractable, less reflective, less conscientious, I might have found some difficulty in inducing him to work as he is doing."

"Does he complain?" inquired Mr. Ashley.

"Oh no, sir! He feels that it is his duty to work, to assist as far as he can, and he does it without complaining. I see that he cannot help feeling it. He would like to be in the college with his brothers; but I cheer him up, and tell him it may all turn out for the best. Perhaps it will."

She rose as she spoke. Mr. Ashley shook hands with her, and attended her through the hall. "Your sons deserve to get on, Mrs. Halliburton, and I hope they will do so. It is an admirable promise for the future man when a boy displays thought and self-reliance."

"Mamma!" suddenly exclaimed Janey, as they sat at breakfast the morning after this, "do you remember what to-day is? It is my birthday."

Jane had remembered it. She had been almost in hopes that the child would not remember it. One year ago that day the first glimpse of the shadow so soon to fall upon them had shown itself. What a change! The contrast between last year and this was almost incredible. Then they had been in possession of a good home, were living in prosperity, in apparent security. Now—Jane's heart turned sick at the thought. Only one short year!

"Yes, Janey dear," she replied in sadly subdued tones. "I did not forget it. I—"

A double knock at the door interrupted what she would have further said. They heard Dobbs answer it: visitors were chiefly for Mrs. Reece.

Who should be standing there but Samuel Lynn! He did not choose the familiar back way, as Patience did, had he occasion to call, but knocked at the front.

"Is Jane Halliburton within?"

"You can go and see," said crusty, disappointed Dobbs, flourishing her hand towards the study door. "It's not often that she's out."

Jane rose at his entrance; but he declined to sit, standing while he delivered the message with which he had been charged.

"Friend, thee need not send thy son to the manufactory again in an evening, except on Saturdays. On the other evenings he may remain at home from tea-time and pursue his studies. His wages will not be lessened."

And Jane knew that the considerate kindness emanated from Thomas Ashley.

She managed better with her work as the months went on. By summer she could do it quickly; the days were long then, and, by dint of sitting closely to it, she could earn twelve shillings a week. With William's earnings, and the six shillings taken from Mrs. Reece's payments, that made twenty-two. It was quite a fortune compared with what had been. But like most good fortunes it had its drawbacks. In the first place, she could not always earn it; she was compelled to steal unwilling time to mend her own and the children's clothes. In the second place, a large portion of it had to be devoted to buying their clothes, besides other incidental expenses; so that in the matter of housekeeping they were not much better off than before. Still, Jane did begin to think that she should see her way clearer. But there was sorrow of a different nature looming in the distance.

One afternoon, which Jane was obliged to devote to plain sewing, she was sitting alone in the study when there came a hard short thump at it, which was Dobbs's way of making known her presence there.

"Come in!"

Dobbs came in and sat herself down opposite Jane. It was summer weather, and the August dust blew in at the open window. "I want to know what's the matter with Janey," began she, without circumlocution.

"With Janey?" repeated Mrs. Halliburton. "What should be the matter with her? I know of nothing."

"Of course not," sarcastically answered Dobbs. "Eyes appear to be given to some folks only to blind 'em—more's the pity! You can't see it; my missis can't see it; but I say that the child is ill."

"Oh, Dobbs! I think you must be mistaken."

"Now I'd thank you to be civil, if you please, Mrs. Halliburton," retorted Dobbs. "You don't take me for a common servant, I hope. Who's 'Dobbs'?"

"I had no wish to be uncivil," said Jane. "I am so accustomed to hearing Mrs. Reece call you Dobbs, that—"

"My missis is one case, and other folks is another," burst forth Dobbs, by way of interruption. "I have a handle to my name, I hope, which is Mrs. Dobbs, and I'd be obleeged to you not to forget it again. What's the reason that Janey's always tired now, I ask—don't want to stir—gets a bright pink in the cheeks and inside the hands?"

"It is only the effect of the hot weather."

The opinion did not please Dobbs. "There's not a earthly thing happens but it's laid to the weather," she angrily cried. "The weather, indeed! If Janey is not going off after her pa, it's an odd thing to me."

Jane's heart-pulse stood still.

"Does she have night-perspirations, or does she not?" demanded Dobbs. "She tells me she's hot and damp; so I conclude it is so."

"Only from the heat—only from the heat," panted Jane eagerly. She dared not admit the fear.

"Well, the first time I go down to the town, I shall take her to Parry. It won't be at your cost," she hastened to add in ungracious tones, for Jane was about to interrupt. "If she wants to know what she is took to the doctor for, I shall tell her it is to have her teeth looked at. She has a nasty cough upon her: perhaps you haven't noticed that! Some can't see a child decaying under their very nose, while strangers can see it palpable."

"She has coughed since last week, the day of the rain, when she went with Anna Lynn into the field at the back, and they got their feet wet. Oh, I am sure there is nothing seriously the matter with her," added Jane, resolutely endeavouring to put the suggested fear from her. "I want her in: she must help me with my sewing."

"Then she's not a-going to help," resolutely returned Dobbs. "She has had a good dinner of roast lamb, sparrow-grass and kidney potatoes, and she's sitting back in my easy chair, opposite to my missis in hers. Her wanting always to rest might have told some folks that she was ailing. When children are in health, their legs and wings and tongue are on the go from morning till night. You never need pervide 'em with a seat but for their meals; and, give 'em their way, they'd eat them standing. Jane's always wanting to rest now, and she shall rest."

"But, indeed she must help me to-day," urged Jane. "She can sew straight seams, and hem. Look at this heap of mending! and it must be finished to-night. I cannot afford to be about it to-morrow."

"What sewing is it you want done?" questioned Dobbs, lifting up the work with a jerk. "I'll do it myself sooner than the child shall be bothered."

"Oh no, thank you. I should not like to trouble you with it."

"Now, I make the offer to do the work," crossly responded Dobbs; "and if I didn't mean to do it, I shouldn't make it. You'd do well to give it me, if you want it done. Janey shan't work this afternoon."

Taking her at her word, and indeed glad to do so, Jane showed Dobbs a task, and Dobbs swung off with it. Jane called after her that she had not taken a needle and cotton. Dobbs retorted that she had needles and cotton of her own, she hoped, and needn't be beholden to anybody else for 'em.

Jane sat on, anxious, all the afternoon. Janey remained in Mrs. Reece's parlour, and revelled in an early tea and pikelets. Jane was disturbed from her thoughts by the boisterous entrance of Frank and Gar; more boisterous than usual. Frank was a most excitable boy, and had been told that evening by the head master of the college school, the Reverend Mr. Keating, that he might be one of the candidates for the vacant place in the choir. This was enough to set Frank off for a week. "You know what a nice voice you say I have, mamma; what a good ear for music!" he reiterated. "As good, you tell us, as Aunt Margaret's used to be. I shall be sure to gain the post if you will let me try. We have to be at college for an hour morning and afternoon daily, but we can easily get that up if we are industrious. Some of the best Helstonleigh scholars who have shone at Oxford and Cambridge were choristers. And I should have about ten pounds a-year paid to me."

Ten pounds a-year! Jane listened with a beating heart. It would more than keep him in clothes. She inquired more fully into particulars.

The result was that Frank had permission to try for the vacant choristership, and gained it. His voice was the best of those tried. He went home in a glow. "Now, mamma, the sooner you set about a new surplice for me the better."

"A new surplice, Frank!" Ah, it was not all profit.

"A chorister must have two surplices, mamma. King's scholars can do with one, having them washed between the Sundays: choristers can't. We must have them always in wear, you know, except in Lent, and on the day of King Charles the Martyr."

Jane smiled; he talked so fast. "What is that you are running on about?"

"Goodness, mamma, don't you understand? All the six weeks of Lent, and on the 30th of January, the cathedral is hung with black, and the choristers have to wear black cloth surplices. They don't find the black ones: the college does that."

Frank's success in gaining the place did not give universal pleasure to the college school. Since the day of the disturbance in the spring, in which William was mixed up, the two young Halliburtons had been at a discount with the desk at which Cyril Dare sat; and this desk pretty well ruled the school.

"It's coming to a fine pass!" exclaimed Cyril Dare, when the result of the trial was carried into the school. "Here's the town clerk's own son passed over as nobody, and that snob of a Halliburton put in! Somebody ought to have told the dean what snobs they are."

"What would the dean have cared?" grumbled another, whose young brother had been amongst the rejected ones. "To get good voices in the choir is all he cares for in the matter."

"I say, where do they live—that set?"

"In a house of Ashley's, in the London Road," answered Cyril Dare. "They couldn't pay the rent, and my father put a bum in."

"Bosh, Dare!"

"It's true," said Cyril Dare. "My father manages Ashley's rents, you know. They'd have had every stick and stone sold, only Ashley—he is a regular soft over some things—took and gave them time. Oh, they are a horrid lot! They don't keep a servant!"

The blank astonishment this last item of intelligence caused at the desk, can't be described. Again Cyril's word was disputed.

"They don't, I tell you," he repeated. "I taxed Halliburton senior with it one day, and he told me to my face they could not afford one. He possesses brass enough to set up a foundry, does that fellow. The eldest one is at Ashley's manufactory, errand-boy. Errand-boy! And here's this one promoted to the choir, over gentlemen's heads! He ought to be pitched into, ought Halliburton senior."

In the school, Frank was Halliburton senior; Gar, Halliburton junior. "How is it that he says he was at King's College before he came here? I heard him tell Keating so," asked a boy.

At this moment Mr. Keating's voice was heard. "Silence!" Cyril Dare let a minute elapse, and then began again.

"Such a low thing, you know, not to keep servants! We couldn't do at all without five or six. I'll tell you what: the school may do as it likes, but our desk shall cut the two fellows here."

And the desk did so; and Frank and Gar had to put up with many mortifications. There was no help for it. Frank was brave as a young lion; but against some sorts of oppression there is no standing up. More than once was the boy in tears, telling his griefs to his mother. It fell more on Frank than it did on Gar.

Jane could only strive to console him, as she did William. "Patience and forbearance, my darling Frank! You will outlive it in time."

CHAPTER II

SHADOWS IN HONEY FAIR

August was hot in Honey Fair. The women sat at their open doors, or even outside them; the children tumbled in the gutters; the refuse in the road was none the better for the month's heat.

Charlotte East sat in her kitchen one Tuesday afternoon, busy as usual. Her door was shut, but her window was open. Suddenly the latch was lifted and Mrs. Cross came in: not with the bold, boisterous movements that were common to Honey Fair, but with creeping steps that seemed afraid of their own echoes, and a scared face.

Mrs. Cross was in trouble. Her two daughters, Amelia and Mary Ann, to whom you have had the honour of an introduction, had purchased those lovely cross-barred sarcenets, green, pink, and lilac, and worn them at the party at the Alhambra: which party went off satisfactorily, leaving nothing behind it but some headaches for the next day, and a trifle of pecuniary embarrassment to Honey Fair in general. What with the finery for the party, and other finery, and what with articles really useful, but which perhaps might have been done without, Honey Fair was pretty deeply in with the Messrs. Bankes. In Mrs. Cross's family alone, herself and her daughters owed, conjointly, so much to these accommodating tradesmen that it took eight shillings a week to keep them quiet. You can readily understand how this impoverished the weekly housekeeping; and the falsehoods that had to be concocted, by way of keeping the husband, Jacob Cross, in the dark, were something alarming. This was the state of things in many of the homes of Honey Fair.

Mrs. Cross came in with timid steps and a scared face. "Charlotte, lend me five shillings for the love of goodness!" cried she, speaking as if afraid of the sound of her own voice. "I don't know another soul to ask but you. There ain't another that would have it to lend, barring Dame Buffle, and she never lends."

"You owe me twelve shillings already," answered Charlotte, pausing for a moment in her sewing.

"I know that. I'll pay you off by degrees, if it's only a shilling a week. I am a'most drove mad. Bankes's folks was here yesterday, and me and the girls had only four shillings to give 'em. I'm getting in arrears frightful, and Bankes's is as cranky over it as can be. It's all smooth and fair so long as you're buying of Bankes's and paying 'em; but just get behind, and see what short answers and sour looks you'll have!"

"But Amelia and Mary Ann took in their work on Saturday and had their money?"

"My patience! I don't know what us should do if they hadn't! We have to pay up everywhere. We're in debt at Buffle's, in debt to the baker, in debt for shoes; we're in debt on all sides. And there's Cross spending three shilling good of his wages at the public-house! It takes what me and the girls earn to pay a bit up here and there, and stop things from coming to Cross's ears. Half the house is in the pawn-shop, and what'll become of us I don't know. I can't sleep o' nights, hardly, for thinking on't."

Charlotte felt sure that, were it her case, she should not sleep at all.

"The worst is, I have to keep the little 'uns away from school. Pay for 'em I can't. And a fine muck they get into, playing in the road all day. 'What does these children do to theirselves at school, to get into this dirty mess?' asks Cross, when he comes in. 'Oh, they plays a bit in the gutter coming home,' says I. 'We plays a bit, father,' cries they, when they hears me, a-winking at each other to think how we does their father."

Charlotte shook her head. "I should end it all."

"End it! I wish we could end it! The girls is going to slave theirselves night and day this week and next. But it's not for my good: it's for their'n. They want to get their grand silks out o' pawn! Nothing but outside finery goes down with them, though they've not an inside rag to their backs. They leave care to me. Fools to be sure, they was, to buy them silks! They have been in the pawn-shop ever since, and Bankes's a-tearing 'em to pieces for the money!"

"I should end it by confessing to Jacob," said Charlotte, when she could get in a word. "He is not a bad husband—"

"And look at his passionate temper!" broke in Mrs. Cross. "Let it get to his ears that we have gone on tick to Bankes's and elsewhere, and he'd rave the house out of winders."

"He would be angry at first, no doubt; but when he cooled down he would see the necessity of something being done, and help in it. If you all set on and put your shoulders to the wheel you might soon get clear. Live upon the very least that will satisfy hunger—the plainest food—dry bread and potatoes. No beer, no meat, no finery, no luxuries; and with the rest of the week's money begin to pay up. You'd be clear in no time."

Mrs. Cross stared in consternation. "You be a Job's comforter, Charlotte! Dry bread and taters! who could put up with that?"

"When poor people like us fall into trouble, it is the only way that I know of to get out of it. I'd rather mortify my appetite for a year than have my rest broken by care."

"Your advice is good enough for talking, Charlotte, but it don't answer for acting. Cross must have his bit o' meat and his beer, his butter and his cheese, his tea and his sugar—and so must the rest on us. But about this five shillings?—do lend it me, Charlotte! It is for the landlord: we're almost in a fix with him."

"For the landlord!" repeated Charlotte involuntarily. "You must keep him paid, or it would be the worst of all."

"I know we must. He was took bad yesterday—more's the blessing!—and couldn't get round; but he's here to-day as burly as beef. We haven't paid him for this three weeks," she added, dropping her voice to an ominous whisper; "and I declare to you, Charlotte East, that the sight of him at our door is as good to me as a dose of physic. Just now, round he comes, a-lifting the latch, and me turning sick the minute I sees him. 'Ready, Mrs. Cross?' asks he, in his short, surly way, putting his brown wig up. 'I'm sorry I ain't, Mr. Abbott, sir,' says I; 'but I'll have some next week for certain.' 'That won't do for me,' says he: 'I must have it this. If you can't give me some money, I shall apply to your husband.' The fright this put me into I've not got over yet, Charlotte; for Cross don't know but what the rent's paid up regular. 'I know what's going on,' old Abbott begins again, 'and I have knowed it for some time. You women in this Honey Fair, you pay your money to them Bankeses, which is the blight o' the place, and then you can't pay me.' Only fancy his calling Bankeses a blight!"

"That's just what they are," remarked Charlotte.

"For shame, Charlotte East! When one's way is a bit eased by being able to get a few things on trust, you must put in your word again it! Some of us would never get a new gown to our backs if it wasn't for Bankeses. Abbott's gone off to other houses, collecting; warning me as he'd call again in half an hour, and if some money wasn't ready for him then he'd go straight off to Jacob, to his shop o' work. If you can let me have one week for him, Charlotte—five shillings—I'll be ever grateful."

Charlotte rose, unlocked a drawer, and gave five shillings to Mrs. Cross, thinking in her own mind that the kindest course would be for the landlord to go to Cross, as he had threatened.

Mrs. Cross took the money. Her mind so far relieved, she could indulge in a little gossip; for Mr. Abbott's half-hour had not yet expired.

"I say, Charlotte, what d'ye think? I'm afraid Ben Tyrrett and our Mary Ann is a-going to take up together."

"Indeed!" exclaimed Charlotte. "That's new."

"Not over-new. They have been talking together on and off, but I never thought it was serious till last Sunday. I have set my face dead against it. He has a nasty temper of his own; and he's nothing but a jobber at fifteen shillings a week, and his profits of the egg-whites. Our Mary Ann might do better than that."

"I think she might," assented Charlotte. "And she is over-young to think of marrying."

"Young!" wrathfully repeated Mrs. Cross. "I should think she is young! Girls are as soft as apes. The minute a chap says a word to 'em about marrying, they're all agog to do it, whether it's fit, or whether it's unfit. Our Mary Ann might look inches over Ben Tyrrett's head, if she had any sense in her. Hark ye, Charlotte! When you see her, just put in a word against it; maybe it'll turn her. Tell her you'd not have Tyrrett at a gift."

"And that's true," replied Charlotte, with a laugh, as her guest departed.

A few minutes, and Charlotte received another visitor. This was the wife of Mark Mason—a tall, bony woman, with rough black hair and a loud voice. That voice and Mark did not get on very well together. She put her hands back upon her hips, and used it now, standing before Charlotte in a threatening attitude.

"What do you do, keeping our Carry out at night?"

Charlotte looked up in surprise. She was thinking of something else, or her answer might have been more cautious, for she was one of those who never willingly make mischief.

"I do not keep Caroline out. She is here of an evening now and then—not often."

Mrs. Mason laughed—a low derisive laugh of mockery. "I knew it was a falsehood when she told it me! There she goes out, night after night, night after night; so I set Mark on to her, for I couldn't keep her in, neither find out where she went to. Mark was in a passion—something had put him out, and Carry was frightened, for he had hold of her arm savage-like. 'I am at Charlotte East's of a night, Mark,' she said. 'I shall take no harm there.'"

Charlotte did not lift her eyes from her work. Mrs. Mason stood defiantly.

"Now, then! Where is it she gets to?"

"Why do you apply to me?" returned Charlotte. "I am not Caroline Mason's keeper."

"If you bain't her keeper, you be her adviser," retorted Mrs. Mason. "And that's worse."

"When I advise Caroline at all, I advise her for her good."

"My eyes are opened now, if they was blind before," continued Mrs. Mason, apostrophizing in no gentle terms the offending Caroline. "Who gave Carry that there shawl?—who gave, her that there fine gown?—who gave her that gold brooch, with a stone in it 'twixt red and yaller, and a naked Cupid in white aflying on it? 'A nice brooch you've got there, miss,' says I to her. 'Yes,' says she, 'they call 'em cameons.' 'And where did you get it, pray?' says I. 'And that's my business,' answers she. Next there was a neck-scarf, green and lavender, with yaller fringe at its ends, as deep as my forefinger. 'You're running up a tidy score at Bankes's, my lady,' says I. 'I shan't come to you to pay for it,' says she. 'No,' thinks I to myself, 'but you be living in our house, and you may bring Mark into trouble over it,' for he's a soft-hearted gander at times. So down I goes to Bankes's place last night. 'Just turn to the debt-book, young man,' says I to the gentleman behind the counter—it were the one with the dark hair—'and tell me how much is owed by Caroline Mason.' 'Come to settle it?' asks he. 'Maybe, and maybe not,' says I. 'I wants my question answered, whether or no.' Are you listening, Charlotte East?"

Charlotte lifted her eyes from her work. "Yes."

"He lays hold of a big book," continues Mrs. Mason, who was talking her face crimson, "and draws his finger down its pages. 'Caroline Mason—Caroline Mason,' says he. 'I don't think we have anything against her. No: it's crossed off. There was a trifle against her, but she paid it last week.' Well, I stood staring at the man, thinking he was deceiving me, saying she had paid. 'When did she pay for that shawl she had in the winter, and how much did it cost?' asks I. 'Shawl?' says he. 'Caroline Mason hasn't had no shawl of us.' 'Nor a gown at Easter—a fancy sort of thing, with stripes?' I goes on: 'nor a cameon brooch last week? nor a scarf with yaller fringe?' 'Nothing o' the sort,' says he, decisive. 'Caroline Mason hasn't bought any of those things from us. She had some bonnet ribbon, and that she paid for.' Now, what was I to think?" concluded Mrs. Mason.

Charlotte did not know.

"I comes home a-pondering, and at the corner of the lane I catches sight of a certain gentleman loitering about in the shade. The truth flashed into my mind. 'He's after our Caroline,' says I to myself; 'and it's him that has given her the things, and we shall just have her a world's spectacle!' I accused Eliza Tyrrett of being the confidant. 'It isn't me,' says she; 'it's Charlotte East.' So I bottled up my temper till now, and now I've come to learn the rights on't."

"I cannot tell you the rights," replied Charlotte. "I do not know them. I have striven to give Caroline some good advice lately, and that is all I have had to do with it. Mrs. Mason, you know that I should never advise Caroline, or any one else, but for her good."

Mrs. Mason would have acknowledged this in a cooler moment. "Why did that Tyrrett girl laugh at me, then? And why did Carry say she spent her evenings here?" cried she. "The gentleman I see was young Anthony Dare: and Carry had better bury herself alive than be drawn aside by his nonsense."

"Much better," acquiesced Charlotte. "Where is Caroline?"

"Under lock and key," said Mrs. Mason.

"Under lock and key!" echoed Charlotte.

"Yes; under lock and key; and there she shall stop. She was out all this blessed morning with Eliza Tyrrett, and never walked herself in till after Mark had had his dinner and was gone. So then I began upon her. My temper was up, and I didn't spare her. I vowed I'd tell Mark what I had seen and heard, and what sort of a wolf she allowed to make her presents of fine clothes. With that she turned wild and flung up to her room in the cock-loft, and I followed and locked her in."

"You have done very wrong," said Charlotte. "It is not by harshness that any good will be done with Caroline. You know her disposition: a child might lead her by kindness, but she rises up against harshness. My opinion is that she never would have given the least trouble at all had you made her a better home."

This bold avowal took away Mrs. Mason's breath. "A better home!" cried she, when she could speak. "A better home! Fed upon French rolls and lobster salad and apricot tarts, and give her a lady's maid to hook-and-eye her gown for her! My heart! that beats all."

"I don't speak of food, and that sort of thing," rejoined Charlotte. "If you had treated her with kind words instead of cross ones she would have been as good a girl as ever lived. Instead of that you have made your home unbearable; and so driven her out, with her dangerous good looks, to be told of them by the first idler who came across her: and that seems to have been Anthony Dare. Go home and let her out of where you have locked her in; do, Hetty Mason! Let her out, and speak kindly to her, and treat her as a sister; and you'll undo all the bad yet."

"I shan't then!" was the passionate reply. "I'll see you and her hung first, before I speak kind to her to encourage her in her loose ways!"

Mrs. Mason flung out of the house as she concluded, giving the door a bang which only had the effect of sending it open again. Charlotte sighed as she rose to close it: not only for any peril that Caroline Mason might be in, but for the general blindness, the distorted views of right and wrong, which seemed to obtain amidst the women of Honey Fair.

CHAPTER III

THE DARES AT HOME

A profusion of glass and plate glittered on the dining-table of Mr. Dare. It was six o'clock, and they had just sat down. Mrs. Dare, in a light gauze dress and blonde head-dress, sat at the head of the table. There was a large family of them; four sons and four daughters; and all were present; also Miss Benyon, the governess. Anthony and Herbert sat on either side Mrs. Dare; Adelaide and Julia, the eldest daughters, near their father; the four other children, Cyril and George, Rosa and Minny, were between them.

Mr. Dare was helping the salmon. In due course, a plate, followed by the sauce, was carried to Anthony.

"What's this! Melted butter! Where's the lobster sauce?"

"There is no lobster sauce to-day," said Mrs. Dare. "We sent late, and the lobsters were all gone. There was a small supply. Joseph, take the anchovy to Mr. Anthony."

Mr. Anthony jerked the anchovy sauce off the salver, dashed some on to his plate, and jerked the bottle back again. Not with a very good grace: his palate was a dainty one. Indeed, it was a family complaint.

"I wouldn't give a fig for salmon without lobster sauce," he cried. "I hope you won't send late again."

"It was the cook's fault," said Mrs. Dare. "She did not fully understand my orders."

"Deaf old creature!" exclaimed Anthony.

"Anthony, there's cucumber," said Julia, looking down the table at her brother. "Ann, take the cucumber to Mr. Anthony."

"You know I never eat cucumber with salmon," grumbled Anthony, in reply. And it was not graciously spoken, for the offer had been dictated by good-nature.

A pause ensued. It was at length broken by Mrs. Dare.

"Herbert, are you growing more reconciled to office-work?"

"No; and never shall," returned Herbert. "From ten till five is an awful clog upon one's time; it's as bad as school."

Mr. Dare looked up from his plate. "You might have been put to a profession that would occupy a great deal more time than that, Herbert. What calls have you upon your time, pray, that it is so valuable? Will you take some more fish?"

"Well, I don't know. I think I will. It is good to-day; very good with the cucumber, that Anthony despises."

Ann took his plate up to Mr. Dare.

"Anthony," said that gentleman, as he helped the salmon, "where were you this afternoon? You were away from the office altogether, after two o'clock."

"Out with Hawkesley," shortly replied Anthony.

"Yes; it is all very well to say, 'Out with Hawkesley,' but the office suffers. I wish you young men were not quite so fond of taking your pleasure."

"A little more fish, sir?" asked Joseph of Anthony.

"Not if I know it."

The second course came in. A quarter of lamb, asparagus and other vegetables. Herbert looked cross. He had recently taken a dislike to lamb, or fancied he had done so.

"Of course there's something coming for me!" he said.

"Oh, of course," said Mrs. Dare. "Cook knows you don't like lamb."

Nothing, however, came in. Ann was sent to inquire the reason of the neglect. The cook had been unable to procure veal cutlet, and Master Herbert had said if she ever sent him up a mutton-chop again he should throw it at her head. Such was the message brought back.

"What an old story-teller she must be to say she could not get veal cutlet!" exclaimed Herbert. "I hate mutton and lamb, and I am not going to eat either one or the other."

"I heard the butcher say this morning that he had no veal, Master Herbert," interposed Ann. "This hot weather they don't kill much meat."

"Why have you taken this dislike to lamb, Herbert?" asked Mr. Dare. "You have eaten it all the season."

"That's just it," answered Herbert. "I have eaten so much of it that I am sick of it."

"Never mind, Herbert," said his mother. "There's a cherry tart coming and a delicious lemon pudding. I don't think you can be so very hungry; you went twice to salmon."

Herbert was not in a good humour. All the Dares had been culpably pampered, and of course it bore its fruits. He sat drumming with his silver fork upon the table, condescending to try a little asparagus, and a great deal of both pie and pudding. Cheese, salad, and dessert followed, of which Herbert partook plentifully. Still he thought he was terribly used in not having had different meat specially provided for him; and he could not recover his good humour. I tell you the Dares had been most culpably indulged. The house was one of luxury and profusion, and every little whim and fancy had been studied. It is one of the worst schools a child can be reared in.

The three younger daughters and the governess withdrew, after taking each a glass of wine. Cyril and George went off likewise, to their lessons or to play. It was their own affair, and Mr. Dare made it no concern of his. Presently Mrs. Dare and Adelaide rose.

"Hawkesley's coming in this evening," called out Anthony, as they were going through the door.

Adelaide turned. "What did you say, Anthony?"

"Lord Hawkesley's coming. At least he said he would look in for an hour. But there's no dependence to be placed on him."

"We must be in the large drawing-room, mamma, this evening," said Adelaide, as they crossed the hall. "Miss Benyon and the children can take tea in the school-room."

"Yes," assented Mrs. Dare. "It is bad form to have one's drawing-room cucumbered with children, and Lord Hawkesley understands all that. Let them be in the school-room."

"Julia also?"

Mrs. Dare shrugged her shoulders. "If you can persuade her into it. I don't think Julia will consent to take tea in the school-room. Why should she?"

Adelaide vouchsafed no reply. Dutiful children they were not—affectionate children they were not—they had not been brought up to be so. Mrs. Dare was of the world, worldly: very much so: and that leaves very little time upon the hands for earnest duties. She had taken no pains to train her children: she had given them very little love. This conversation had taken place in the hall. Mrs. Dare went upstairs to the large drawing-room, a really handsome room. She rang the bell and gave sundry orders, the moving motive for all being the doubtful visit of Viscount Hawkesley—ices from the pastrycook's, a tray of refreshments, the best china, the best silver. Then Mrs. Dare reclined in her chair for her after-dinner nap—an indulgence she much favoured.

Adelaide Dare entered the smaller drawing-room, an apartment more commonly used, and opening from the hall. Julia was reading a book just brought in from the library. Miss Benyon was softly playing, and the two little ones were quarrelling. Miss Benyon turned round from the piano when Adelaide entered.

"You must make tea in the school-room this evening, Miss Benyon, for the children. Julia, you are to take yours there."

Julia looked up from her book. "Who says so?"

"Mamma. Lord Hawkesley's coming, and we cannot have the drawing-room crowded."

"I am not going to keep out of the drawing-room for Lord Hawkesley," returned Julia, a quiet girl in appearance and manner. "Who is Lord Hawkesley, that he should disarrange the economy of the house? There's so much ceremony and parade observed when he comes that it upsets all comfort. Your lordship this, and your lordship that; and papa my-lording him to the skies. I don't like it. He looks down upon us—I know he does—although he condescends to make a sort of friend of Anthony."

Adelaide Dare's dark eyes flashed and her face crimsoned. She was a handsome girl. "Julia! I do think you are an idiot!"

"Perhaps I am," composedly returned Julia, who was of a careless, easy temper; "but I am not going to be kept out of the drawing-room for my Lord Hawkesley. Let me go on with my book in peace, Adelaide: it is a charming one."

Meanwhile Herbert Dare, seeing no prospect of more wine in store—for Mr. Dare, with wonderful prudence, told Herbert that two glasses of port were sufficient for him—left his seat, and bolted out at the dining-room window, which opened on to the ground. He ran into the hall for his hat, and then, speeding across the lawn, passed into the high-road. Anthony remained alone with his father; and Anthony was plucking up courage to speak upon a subject that was causing him some perplexity. He plunged into it at once.

"Father, I am in a mess. I have managed to outrun the constable."

Mr. Dare was at that moment holding his glass of wine between his eye and the light. The words quite scared him. He set his glass down and looked at Anthony.

"How's that? How have you managed that?"

"I don't know how it has come about," was Anthony's answer. "It is so, sir; and you must be so good as to help me out of it."

"Your allowance is sufficient—amply so. Do you forget that I set you clear of debt at the beginning of the year? What money do you want?"

Anthony Dare began pulling the fringe out of the dessert napkin, to the great detriment of the damask. "Two hundred pounds, sir."

"Two hundred pounds!" echoed Mr. Dare, a dark expression clouding his handsome face. "Do you want to ruin me, Anthony? Look at my expenses! Look at the claims upon me! I say that your allowance is a liberal one, and you ought to keep within it."

Anthony sat biting his lip. "I would not have applied to you, sir, if I could have helped it; but I am driven into a corner and must find money. I and Hawkesley drew some bills together. He has taken up two, and I—"

"Then you and Hawkesley were a couple of fools for your pains," intemperately interrupted Mr. Dare. "There's no game so dangerous, so delusive, as that of drawing bills. Have I not told you so, over and over again? Simple debt may be put off from month to month, and from year to year; but bills are nasty things. When I was a young man I lived for years upon promises to pay, but I took care not to put my name to a bill."

"Hawkesley—"

"Hawkesley may do what you must not," interrupted Mr. Dare, drowning his son's voice. "He has his father's long rent-roll to turn to. Recollect, Anthony, this must not occur again. It is impossible that I can be called upon periodically for these sums. Herbert is almost a man, and Cyril and George are growing up. A pretty thing, if you were all to come upon me in this manner. I have to exert my wits as it is, I can tell you. I'll give you a cheque to-morrow; and I should serve you right if I were to put you upon half allowance until I am repaid."

Mr. Dare finished his wine, rang for the table to be cleared, and left the room. Anthony remained standing against the side of the window, half in, half out, buried in a brown study, when Herbert came up, leaping over the grass. Herbert was nearly as tall as Anthony. He had been for some time articled to his father, but had only joined the office the previous Midsummer. He looked into the room and saw it was empty.

"Where's the governor?"

"Gone somewhere. Into the drawing-room, perhaps," replied Anthony.

"What a nuisance!" ejaculated Herbert. "One can't talk to him before the girls. I want twenty-five shillings from him. Markham has the primest fishing-rod to sell, and I must have it."

"Twenty-five shillings for a fishing-rod!" cried Anthony.

"And cheap at the price," answered Herbert. "You don't often see so complete a thing as this. Markham would not part with it—it's a relic of his better days, he says—only his old mother wants some comfort or other which he can't otherwise afford. The case—"

"You have half-a-dozen fishing-rods already."

"Half a dozen rubbish! That's what they are, compared with this one. It's no business of yours, Anthony."

"Not at all. But you'll oblige me, Herbert, by not bothering the governor for money to-night. I have been asking him for some, and it has put him out."

"Did you get it?"

Anthony nodded.

"Then you'll let me have the one-pound-five, Anthony?"

"I can't," returned Anthony. "I shall have a cheque to-morrow, and I must pay it away whole. That won't clear me. But I didn't dare to tell of more."

"If I don't get that fishing-rod to-night, Markham may sell it to some one else," grumbled Herbert.

"Go and get it," replied Anthony. "Promise him the money for to-morrow. You are not obliged to give it, you know. The governor has just said that he lived for years upon promises to pay."

"Markham wants the money down."

"He'll think that as good as down if you tell him he shall have it to-morrow. Bring the fishing-rod away; possession's nine points of the law, you know."

"He'll make such an awful row afterwards, if he finds he does not get the money."

"Let him. You can row again. It's the easiest thing on earth to fence off little paltry debts like that. People get tired of asking for them."

Away vaulted Herbert for the fishing-rod. Anthony yawned, stretched himself, and walked out just as twilight was fading. He was going out to keep an appointment.

Herbert Dare went back to Markham's. The man—though, indeed, so far as birth went he might be called a gentleman—lived a little way beyond Mr. Dare's. The cottage was situated in the midst of a large garden, in which Markham worked late and early. He had a very, very small patrimony upon which he lived and kept his mother. He was bending over one of the beds when Herbert returned. "He would take the fishing-rod then, and bring the money over at nine in the morning, before going to the office.

Mr. Dare was gone out, or he would have brought it at once," was the substance of the words in which Herbert concluded the negotiation.

Could they have looked behind the hedge at that moment, Herbert Dare and Markham, they would have seen two young gentlemen suddenly duck down under its shelter, creep silently along, heedless of the ditch, which, however, was tolerably dry at that season, make a sudden bolt across the road, when they got opposite Mr. Dare's entrance, and whisk within its gates. They were Cyril and George. That they had been at some mischief and were trying to escape detection, was unmistakable. Under cover of the garden-wall, as they had previously done under cover of the hedge, crept they; sprang into the house by the dining-room window, tore up the stairs, and took refuge in the drawing-room, startlingly arousing Mrs. Dare from her after-dinner slumbers.

In point of fact, they had reckoned upon finding the room unoccupied.

CHAPTER IV

THROWING AT THE BATS

Aroused thus abruptly out of sleep, cross and startled, Mrs. Dare attacked the two boys with angry words. "I will know what you have been doing," she exclaimed, rising and shaking out the flounces of her dress. "You have been at some mischief! Why do you come violently in, in this manner, looking as frightened as hares?"

"Not frightened," replied Cyril. "We are only hot. We had a run for it."

"A run for what?" she repeated. "When I say I will know a thing, I mean to know it. I ask you what you have been doing?"

"It's nothing very dreadful, that you need put yourself out," replied George. "One of old Markham's windows has come to grief."

"Then that's through throwing stones again!" exclaimed Mrs. Dare. "Now I am certain of it, and you need not attempt to deny it. You shall pay for it out of your own pocket-money if he comes here, as he did the last time."

"Ah, but he won't come here," returned Cyril. "He didn't see us. Is tea not ready?"

"You can go to the school-room and see. You are to take it there this evening."

The boys tore away to the school-room. Unlike Julia, they did not care where they took it, provided they had it. Miss Benyon was pouring out the tea as they entered. They threw themselves on a sofa, and burst into a fit of laughter so immoderate and long that their two young sisters crowded round eagerly, asking to hear the joke.

"It was the primest fun!" cried Cyril, when he could speak. "We have just smashed one of Markham's windows. The old woman was at it in a nightcap, and I think the stone must have touched her head. Markham and Herbert were holding a confab together and they never saw us!"

"We were chucking at the leathering bats," put in George, jealous that his brother should have all the telling to himself, "and the stone—"

"It is leather-winged bat, George," interrupted the governess. "I corrected you the other night."

"What does it matter?" roughly answered George. "I wish you wouldn't put me out. A leathering-bat dipped down nearly right upon our heads, and we both heaved at him, and one of the stones went through the window, nearly taking, as Cyril says, old Mother Markham's head. Won't they be in a temper at having to pay for it! They are as poor as charity."

"They'll make you pay," said Rosa.

"Will they?" retorted Cyril. "No catch, no have! I'll give them leave to make us pay when they find us out. Do you suppose we are donkeys, you girls? We dipped down under the hedge, and not a soul saw us. What's for tea?"

"Bread and butter," replied the governess.

"Then those may eat it that like! I shall have jam."

Cyril rang the bell as he spoke. Nancy, the maid who waited on the school-room, came in answer to it. "Some jam," said Cyril. "And be quick over it."

"What sort, sir?" inquired Nancy.

"Sort? oh—let's see: damson."

"The damson jam was finished last week, sir. It is nearly the season to make more."

Cyril replied by a rude and ugly word. After some cogitation, he decided upon black currant.

"And bring me up some apricot," put in George.

"And we'll have some gooseberry," called out Rosa. "If you boys have jam, we'll have some too."

Nancy disappeared. Cyril suddenly threw himself back on the sofa, and burst into another ringing laugh. "I can't help it," he exclaimed. "I am thinking of the old woman's fright, and their dismay at having to pay the damage."

"Do you know what I should do in your place, Cyril?" said Miss Benyon. "I should go back to Markham, and tell him honourably that I caused the accident. You know how poor they are; they cannot afford to pay for it."

Cyril stared at Miss Benyon. "Where'd be the pull of that?" asked he.

"The 'pull,' Cyril, would be, that you would repair a wrong done to an unoffending neighbour, and might go to sleep with a clear conscience."

The last suggestion amused Cyril amazingly he and conscience had not a great deal to do with each other. He was politely telling Miss Benyon that those notions were good enough for old maids, when Nancy appeared with the several sorts of jam demanded. Cyril drew his chair to the table, and Nancy went down.

"Ring the bell, Rosa," said Cyril, before the girl could well have reached the kitchen. "I can't see one sort from another; we must have candles."

"Ring it yourself," retorted Rosa.

"George, ring the bell," commanded Cyril.

George obeyed. He was under Cyril in the college school, and accustomed to obey him.

"You might have told Nancy when she was here," remarked Miss Benyon to Cyril. "It would have saved her a journey."

"And if it would?" asked Cyril. "What were servants' legs made for, but to be used?"

Nancy received the order for the candles, and brought them up. It was to be hoped her legs were made to be used, for scarcely had Cyril begun to enjoy his black currant jam when they were heard coming up the stairs again.

"Master Cyril, Mr. Markham wants to see you."

Cyril and the rest exchanged looks. "Did you say I was at home?"

"Yes, sir."

"Then you were an idiot for your pains! I can't come down, tell him. I am at tea."

Down went Nancy accordingly. And back she came again. "He says he must see you, Master Cyril."

"Be a man, Cyril, and face it," whispered Miss Benyon in his ear.

Cyril jerked his head rudely away from her. "I won't go down. There! Nancy, you may tell Markham so."

"He has sat down on the garden bench, sir, outside the window to wait," explained Nancy. "He says, if you won't see him he shall ask for Mr. Dare."

Cyril appeared to be in for it. He dashed his bread and jam on the table, and clattered down. "Who's wanting me?" called out he, when he got outside. "Oh!—is it you, Markham?"

"How came you to throw a stone just now, and break my window, Cyril Dare?"

The words threw Cyril into the greatest apparent surprise. "I throw a stone and break your window!" repeated he. "I don't know what you mean."

"Either you or your brother threw it; you were both together. It entered my mother's bedroom window, and went within an inch of her head. I'll trouble you to send a glazier round to put the pane in."

"Well, of all strange accusations, this is about the strangest!" uttered Cyril. "We have not been near your window; we are upstairs at our tea."

At this juncture, Mr. Dare came out. He had heard the altercation in the house. "What's this?" asked he. "Good evening, Markham."

Markham explained. "They crouched down under the hedge when they had done the mischief," he continued, "thinking, no doubt, to get away undetected. But, as it happened, Brooks the nurseryman was in his ground behind the opposite hedge, and he saw the whole. He says they were throwing at the bats. Now I should be sorry to get them punished, Mr. Dare; we have been boys ourselves; but if young gentlemen will throw stones, they must pay for any damage they do. I have requested your son to send a glazier round in the morning. I am sorry he should have denied the fact."

Mr. Dare turned to Cyril. "If you did it, why do you deny it?"

Cyril hesitated for the tenth part of a second. Which would be the best policy? To give in, or to hold out? He chose the latter. His word was as good as that confounded Brooks's, and he'd brave it out! "We didn't do it," he angrily said; "we have not been near the place this evening. Brooks must have mistaken others for us in the dusk."

"They did do it, Mr. Dare. There's no mistake about it. Brooks had been watching them, and he thinks it was the bigger one who threw that particular stone. If I had set a house on fire," Markham added to Cyril, "I'd rather confess the accident, than deny it by a lie. What sort of a man do you expect to make?"

"A better one than you!" insolently retorted Cyril.

"Wait an instant," said Mr. Dare. He proceeded to the school-room to inquire of George. That young gentleman had been an admiring hearer of the colloquy from a staircase-window. He tore back to the school-room on the approach of his father; hastily deciding that he must bear out Cyril in the denial. "Now, George," said Mr. Dare, sternly, "did you and Cyril do this, or did you not?"

"Of course we did not, papa," was the ready reply. "We have not been near Markham's. Brooks must be a fool."

Mr. Dare believed him. He was leaving the room when Miss Benyon interposed.

"Sir, I should be doing wrong to allow you to be deceived. They did break the window."

The address caused Mr. Dare to pause. "How do you know it, Miss Benyon?"

Miss Benyon related what had passed. Mr. Dare cast his eyes sternly upon his youngest son. "It is you who are the fool, George, not Brooks. A lie is sure to get found out in the end; don't attempt to tell another."

Mr. Dare went down. "I cannot come quite to the bottom of this business, Markham," said he, feeling unwilling to expose his sons more than they had exposed themselves. "At all events you shall have the window put in. A pane of glass is not much on either side."

"It is a good deal to my pocket, Mr. Dare. But that's all I ask. And you know my character too well to fear I would make a doubtful claim. Brooks is open to inquiry."

He departed; and Mr. Dare touched Cyril on the arm. "Come with me."

He took him into the room, and there ensued an angry lecture. Cyril thought George had confessed, and stood silent before his father. "What a sneak he must have been!" thought Cyril. "Won't I serve him out!"

"If you have acquired the habit of speaking falsely, you had better relinquish it," resumed Mr. Dare. "It will not be a recommendation in the eyes of Mr. Ashley."

"I am not going to Ashley's," burst forth Cyril; for the mention of the subject was sure to anger him. "Turn manufacturer, indeed! I'd rather—"

"You'd rather be a gentleman at large," interrupted Mr. Dare. "But," he sarcastically added, "gentlemen require something to live upon. Listen, Cyril. One of the finest openings that I know of in this city, for a young man, is in Ashley's manufactory. You may despise Mr. Ashley as a manufacturer; but others respect him. He was reared a gentleman—he is regarded as one; he is wealthy, and his business is large and flourishing. Suppose you could drop into this, after him?—succeed to this fine business, its sole proprietor? I can tell you that you would occupy a better position, and be in receipt of a far larger income than either Anthony or Herbert will be."

"But there's no such chance as that, for me," debated Cyril.

"There is the chance: and that's why you are to be placed there. Henry, from his infirmity, is not to be brought up to business, and there is no other son. You will be apprenticed to Mr. Ashley, with a view to succeeding, as a son would, first of all to a partnership with him, eventually to the whole. Now, this is the prospect before you, Cyril; and prejudiced though you are, you must see that it is a fine one."

"Well," acknowledged Cyril, "I wouldn't object to drop into a good thing like that. Has Mr. Ashley proposed it?"

"No, he has not distinctly proposed it. But he did admit, when your apprenticeship was being spoken of, that he might be wanting somebody to succeed him. He more than hinted that whoever might be chosen to succeed him, or to be associated with him, must be rendered fit for the connection by being an estimable and a good man; one held in honour by his fellow citizens. No other could be linked with the name of Ashley. And now, sir, what do you think he, Mr. Ashley, would say to your behaviour to-night?"

Cyril looked rather shame-faced.

"You will go to Mr. Ashley's, Cyril. But I wish you to remember, to remember always, that the ultimate advantages will depend upon yourself and your conduct. Become a good man, and there's little doubt they will be yours; turn out indifferently, and there's not the slightest chance for you."

"I shan't succeed to any of Ashley's money, I suppose?" complacently questioned Cyril, who somewhat ignored the conditions, and saw himself in prospective Mr. Ashley's successor.

"It is impossible to say what you may succeed to," replied Mr. Dare, in so significant a tone as to surprise Cyril. "Henry Ashley's I should imagine to be a doubtful life; should anything happen to him, Mary Ashley will, of course, inherit all. And he will be a fortunate man who shall get into her good graces and marry her."

It was a broad hint to a boy like Cyril. "She's such a proud thing, that Mary Ashley!" grumbled he.

"She is a very sweet child," was the warm rejoinder of Mr. Dare. And Cyril went upstairs again to his jam and his interrupted tea.

Meanwhile the evening went on, and the drawing-room was waiting for Lord Hawkesley. Mrs. Dare and Adelaide were waiting for him—waiting anxiously in elegant attire. Mr. Dare did not seem to care whether he came or not; and Julia, who was buried in an easy chair with her book, would have preferred, of the two, that he stayed away. Between eight and nine he arrived. A little man; young, fair, with light eyes and sharp features, a somewhat cynical expression habitually on his lips. Helstonleigh, in its gossip, conjectured that he must be making young Anthony Dare useful to him in some way or other, or he would not have condescended to the intimacy. For Lord Hawkesley, a proud man by nature, had been reared as an earl's son and heir; which meant an exclusiveness far greater in those days than it is in these. This was the third evening visit he had paid to Mrs. Dare. Had Adelaide's good looks any attraction for him? She was beginning to think so, and to weave visions upon the strength of it. Entrenched as the Dares were in their folly and assumption, Adelaide was blind to the wide social gulf that lay between herself and Viscount Hawkesley.

She sat down at the piano at his request and sang an Italian song. She had a good voice, and her singing was better than her Italian accent. Lord Hawkesley stood by her and looked over the music.

"I like your style of singing very much," he remarked to her when the song was over. "You must have learnt of a good master."

"Comme ça," carelessly rejoined Adelaide. As is the case with many more young ladies who possess a superficial knowledge of French, she thought it the perfection of good taste to display as much of it as she did know. "I had the best professor that Helstonleigh can give; but what are Helstonleigh professors compared with those of London? We cannot expect first-rate talent here."

"Do you like London?" asked Lord Hawkesley.

"I was never there," replied Adelaide, feeling the confession, when made to Lord Hawkesley, to be nothing but a humiliation.

"Indeed! You would enjoy a London season."

"Oh, so much! I know nothing of the London season, except from books. A contrast to your lordship, you will say," she added, with a laugh. "You must be almost tired of it; désillusionné."

"What's that in English?" inquired Lord Hawkesley, whose French studies, as far as they had extended, had been utterly thrown away upon him. Labouring under the deficiency, he had to make the best of it, and did it with a boast. "Used up, I suppose you mean?"

Adelaide coloured excessively. She wondered if he was laughing at her, and made a mental vow never to speak French to a lord again.

"Will you think me exacting, Miss Dare, if I trespass upon you for another song?"

Adelaide did not think him exacting in the least. She was ready to sing as long as he pleased.

CHAPTER V

CHARLOTTE EAST'S PRESENT

Towards dusk, that same evening, Charlotte East went over to Mrs. Buffle's for some butter. After she was served, Mrs. Buffle—who was a little shrimp of a woman, with a red nose—crossed her arms upon the counter and bent her face towards Charlotte's. "Have you heered the news?" asked she. "Mary Ann Cross is going to make a match of it with Ben Tyrrett."

"Is she?" said Charlotte. "They had better wait a few years, both of them, until they shall have put by something."

"They're neither of them of the putting-by sort," returned Mrs. Buffle. "Them Crosses is the worst girls to spend in all the Fair: unless it's Carry Mason. She don't spare her back, she don't. The wonder is, how she gets it."

"Young girls will dress," observed Charlotte, carelessly.

Mrs. Buffle laughed. "You speak as if you were an old one."

"I feel like one sometimes, Mrs. Buffle. When children are left, as I and Robert were, with a baby brother to bring up, and hardly any means to do it upon, it helps to steady them. Tom—"

Eliza Tyrrett burst in at the door, with a violence that made its bell twang and tinkle. "Half-a-pound o' dips, long-tens, Dame Buffle, and be quick about it," was her order. "There's such a flare-up, in at Mason's."

"A flare-up!" repeated Mrs. Buffle, who was always ripe and ready for a dish of scandal, whether it touched on domestic differences, or on young girls' improvidence in the shape of dress. "Is Mason and her having a noise?"

"It's not him and her. It's about Carry. Hetty Mason locked Carry up this afternoon, and Mason never came home at all to tea; he went and had some beer instead, and a turn at skittles, and she wouldn't let Carry out. He came in just now, and his wife told him a whole heap about Carry, and Mason went up to the cock-loft, undid the door, and threatened to kick Carry down. They're having it out in the kitchen, all three."

"What has Carry done?" asked Mrs. Buffle eagerly.

"Perhaps Charlotte East can tell," said Eliza Tyrrett, slyly. "She has been thick with Carry lately. I am not a-going to spoil sport."

Charlotte took up her butter, and bending a severe look of caution on the Tyrrett girl, left the shop. Anthony Dare's reputation was not a brilliant one, and the bare fact of Caroline Mason's allowing herself to walk with him would have damaged her in the eyes of Honey Fair. As well keep it, if possible, from Mrs. Buffle and other gossips.

As Charlotte crossed to her own door, she became conscious that some one was flying towards her in the dusk of the evening: a woman with a fleet foot and panting breath. Charlotte caught hold of her. "Caroline, where are you going?"

"Let me alone, Charlotte East"—and Caroline's nostrils were working, her eyes flashing. "I have left their house for ever, and am going to one who will give me a better."

Charlotte held her tight. "You must not go, Caroline."

"I will," she defiantly answered. "I have chosen my lot this night for better or for worse. Will I stay to be taunted without a cause? To be told I am what I am not? No! If anything should happen to me, let them reproach themselves, for they have driven me on to it."

Charlotte tried her utmost to restrain the wild girl. "Caroline," she urged, "this is the turning-point in your life. A step forward, and you may have passed it beyond recall; a step backwards, and you may be saved for ever. Come home with me."

Caroline in her madness—it was little else—turned her ghastly face upon Charlotte. "You shan't stop me, Charlotte East! You go your way, and I'll go mine. Shall Mark and she go on at me without cause, I say, calling me false names?"

"Come home with me, Caroline. You shall stay with me to-night; you shan't go back to Hetty. My bed's not large, but it will hold us."

"I won't, I won't!" she uttered, struggling to be free.

"Only for a minute," implored Charlotte. "Come in for a minute until you are calm. You are mad just now."

"I am driven to it. There!"

With a jerk she wrenched herself from Charlotte's grasp, passion giving her strength: and she flew onwards and was lost in the dark night. Charlotte East ran home. Her brothers were there. "Tom," said she, "put this butter in the cupboard for me;" and out she went again. At the end of Honey Fair, a road lay each way. Which should she take? Which had Caroline taken?

She chose the one to the right—it was the most retired—and went groping about it for twenty minutes. As it happened, as such things generally do happen, Caroline had taken the other.

In a sheltered part of that, which lay back, away from the glare of the gas lamps, Caroline had taken refuge. She had expected some one would be there to meet her; but she found herself mistaken. Down she sat on a stone, and her wild passion began to diminish.

Nearly half an hour afterwards, Charlotte found her there. Caroline was talking to Anthony Dare, who had just come up. Charlotte grasped Caroline.

"You must come with me, Caroline."

"Who on earth are you, and what do you want intruding here?" demanded Anthony Dare, turning round with a fierce stare on Charlotte.

"I am Charlotte East, sir, if it is any matter to you to know my name, and I am a friend of Caroline Mason's. I am here to take her out of harm's way."

"There's nothing to harm her here," haughtily answered young Anthony. "Mind your own business."

"I am afraid there is one thing to harm her, sir, and that's you," said brave Charlotte. "You can't come among us people in Honey Fair for any good. Folks bent on good errands don't need to wait till dark before they pay their visits. You had better give up prowling about this place, Mr. Anthony Dare. Stay with your equals, sir; with those that will be a match for you."

"The woman must be deranged!" uttered Anthony, going into a terrible passion. "How dare you presume to say such things to me?"

"How dare you, sir, set yourself out to work ill?" retorted Charlotte. "Come along, Caroline," she added to the girl, who was now crying bitterly. "As for you, sir, if you mean no harm, as you say, and it is necessary that you should condescend to visit Honey Fair, please to pay your visits in the broad light of day."

No very pleasant word broke from Anthony Dare. He would have liked to exterminate Charlotte. "Caroline," foamed he, "order this woman away. If I could see a policeman, I'd give her in charge."

"Sir, if you dare attempt to detain her, I'll appeal to the first passer-by. I'll tell them to look at the great and grand Mr. Anthony Dare, and to ask him what he wants here, night after night."

Even as Charlotte spoke, footsteps were heard, and two gentlemen, talking together, advanced. The voice of one fell familiarly on the ear of Anthony Dare, familiarly on that of Charlotte East. The latter uttered a joyful cry.

"There's Mr. Ashley! Loose her, sir, or I'll call to him."

To have Mr. Ashley "called to" on the point would not be altogether agreeable to the feelings of young Anthony. "You fool!" he exclaimed to Charlotte East, "what harm do you suppose I meant, or thought of? You must be a very strange person yourself, to get such a thing into your imagination. Good night, Caroline."

And turning on his heel haughtily, Anthony Dare stalked off in the direction of Helstonleigh. Mr. Ashley passed on, having noticed nothing, and Charlotte East wound her arm round the sobbing girl, subdued now, and led her home.

Anthony went straight to Pomeranian Knoll, and threw himself on to a sofa in a very ill humour. Lord Hawkesley was occupied with Adelaide and her singing, and paid little attention to him.

At the close of the evening they left together, Anthony going out with Lord Hawkesley, and linking arms as they proceeded towards the Star Hotel, Lord Hawkesley's usual quarters when in Helstonleigh.

"I have got two hundred out of the governor," began Anthony in a confidential tone. "He will give me the cheque to-morrow."

"What's two hundred, Dare?" slightingly spoke his lordship. "It's nothing."

"It was of no use trying for more to-night. The two hundred will stop present worry, Hawkesley; the future must be provided for when it comes." And they walked on with a quicker step.

Mrs. Dare had looked at her watch as they departed. It was half-past eleven. She said she supposed they might as well be going to bed, and Mr. Dare roused himself. For the last half-hour he had been half-asleep; quite asleep he did not choose to fall, in the young man's presence. A viscount to Lawyer Dare was a viscount. "Where's Herbert?" asked he, stretching himself. Master Herbert, Joseph answered, had had supper served (not being able to recover from the short allowance at dinner), and had gone to bed. The rest, excepting Adelaide, had gone before, free from want, from care, full of the good things of this life. The young Halliburtons, their cousins once removed, had knelt and thanked God for the day's good, even though that day to them had been what all their days were now, one of poverty and privation. Not so the Dares. As children, for they were not in a heathen land, they had been taught to say their prayers at night; but as they grew older, the custom was suffered to fall into disuse. The family attended church on Sundays, fashionably attired, and there ended their religion.

To bed and to sleep went they, all the household, old and young—Joseph, the manservant, excepted. Sleepy Joseph stretched himself in a large chair to wait the return of Mr. Anthony: sleepy Joseph had so to stretch himself most nights. Mr. Anthony might come in in an hour's time, or Mr. Anthony might not come in until it was nearly time to commence the day's duties in the morning. It was all a chance; as poor Joseph knew to his cost.

Nine o'clock was the breakfast hour at Mr. Dare's, and the family were in general pretty punctual at it. On the following morning they were all assembled at the meal, Anthony rather red about the eyes, when Ann, the housemaid, entered.

"Here's a parcel for you, Mr. Anthony."

She held in her arms a large untidy sort of bundle, done round with string. Anthony turned his wondering eyes upon it.

"That! It can't be for me."

"A boy brought it and said it was for you, sir," returned Ann, letting the cumbersome parcel fall on a chair. "I asked if there was any answer, and he said there was not."

"It must be from your tailor, Anthony," said Mrs. Dare.

Anthony's consequence was offended at the suggestion. "My tailor send me a parcel done up like that!" repeated he. "He had better! He would get no more of my custom."

"What an extraordinary direction!" exclaimed Julia, who had got up, and drawn near, in her curiosity: "'Young Mister Antony Dare!' Just look, all of you."

Anthony rose, and the rest followed, except Mr. Dare, who was busy with a county paper, and paid no attention. A happy thought darted into Minny's mind. "I know!" she cried, clapping her hands. "Cyril and George are playing Anthony a trick, like the one they played Miss Benyon."

Anthony, too hastily taking up the view thus suggested, and inwardly vowing a not agreeable chastisement to the two, as soon as they should rush in to breakfast from school, took out his penknife and severed the string. The paper fell apart, and the contents rolled on to the floor.

What on earth were they? What did they mean? A woman's gown, tawdry but pretty; a shawl; a neck-scarf, with gold-coloured fringe; two pairs of gloves, the fingers worn into holes; a bow of handsome ribbon; a cameo brooch, fine and false; and one or two more such articles, not new, stood disclosed. The party around gazed in sheer amazement.

"If ever I saw such a collection as this!" exclaimed Mrs. Dare. "It is a woman's clothing. Why should they have been sent to you, Anthony?"

Anthony's cheek wore rather a conscious colour just then. "How should I know?" he replied. "They must have been directed to me by mistake. Take the rags away, Ann"—spurning them with his foot—"and throw them into the dust-bin. Who knows what infected place they may have come from?"

Mrs. Dare and the young ladies shrieked at the last suggestion, gathered their skirts about them, and retired as far as the limits of the room allowed. Some enemy of malicious intent must have done it, they became convinced. Ann—no more liking to be infected with measles or what not than they—seized the tongs, gingerly lifted the articles inside the paper, dragged the whole outside the door, and called Joseph to carry them to the receptacle indicated by Mr. Anthony.

Charlotte East had thought she would not do her work by halves.

CHAPTER VI

We must leap over some months. A story, you know, cannot stand still, any more than we can.

Spring had come round. The sofa belonging to Mrs. Reece's parlour was in Mrs. Halliburton's, and Janey was lying on it—her blue eyes bright, her cheeks hectic, her fair curls falling in disorder. Through autumn, through winter, it had appeared that Dobbs's prognostications of evil for Jane were not to be borne out, for she had recovered from the temporary indications of illness, and had continued well; but, with the early spring weather, Jane failed, and failed rapidly. The cough came back, and great weakness grew upon her. She was always wanting to be at rest, and would lie about anywhere. Spreading a cloak on the floor, with a pillow for her head, Janey would plant herself between her mother and the fire, pulling the cloak up on the side near the door. One day Dobbs came in and saw her there.

"My heart alive!" uttered Dobbs, when she had recovered her surprise; "what are you lying down there for?"

"I am tired," replied Janey; "and there's nowhere else to lie. If I put three chairs together, it is not comfortable, and the pillow rolls off."

"There's the sofa in our room," said Dobbs. "Why don't you lie on that?"

"So I do, you know, Dobbs; but I want to talk to mamma sometimes."

Dobbs disappeared. Presently there was a floundering and thumping heard in the passage, and the sofa was propelled in by Dobbs, very red with the exertion. "My missis is indignant to think that the child should be upon the floor," cried she, wrathfully. "One would suppose some folks were born without brains, or the sofa might have been asked for."

"But, Dobbs," said Janey—and she was allowed to "Dobbs" as much as she pleased, unreproved—"what am I to lie on in your room?"

"Isn't there my easy chair, with the high foot-board in front—as good as a bed when you let it out?" returned Dobbs, proceeding to place Janey comfortably on the sofa. "And now let me say what I came in to say, when the sight of that child on the cold floor sent me shocked out again," she added, turning to Jane. "My missis's leg is no better to-day, and she has made up her mind to have Parry. It's erysipelas, as sure as a gun. Every other spring, about, she's laid up with it in her legs, one or the other of 'em. Ten weeks I have known her in bed with it—"

"The very best preventive to erysipelas is to take an occasional warm bath," interrupted Jane.

The suggestion gave immense offence to Dobbs. "A warm bath!" she uttered, ironically. "And how, pray, should my missis take a warm bath? Sit down in a mashing-tub, and have a furnace of boiling water turned on to her? Those new-fangled notions may do for Londoners, but they are not known at Helstonleigh. Warm baths!" repeated Dobbs, with increased scorn: "hadn't you better propose a water-bed at once? I have heard that they are inventing them also."

"I have heard so, too," pleasantly replied Jane.

"Well, my missis is going to have Parry up, and she intends that he shall see Janey and give her some physic—if physic will be of use," added Dobbs, with an incredulous sniff. "My missis says it will. She puts faith in Parry's physic as if it was gold; it's a good thing she's not ill often, or she'd let herself be poisoned if quantity could poison her! And, Janey, you'll take the physic, like a precious lamb; and heaps of nice things you shall have after it, to drive the taste out. Warm baths!" ejaculated Dobbs, as she went out, returning to the old grievance. "I wonder what the world's coming to?"

Mr. Parry was called in, and soon had his two regular patients there. Mrs. Reece was confined to her bed with erysipelas in her leg; and if Janey seemed better one day, she seemed worse the next. The surgeon did not say what was the matter with Jane. He ordered her everything good in the shape of food; he particularly ordered port wine. An hour after the latter order had been given Dobbs appeared, with a full decanter in her hand.

"It's two glasses a day that she is to take—one at eleven and one at three," cried she without circumlocution.

"But, indeed, I cannot think of accepting so costly a thing from Mrs. Reece as port wine," interrupted Jane, in consternation.

"You can do as you like, ma'am," said Dobbs with equanimity. "Janey will accept it; she'll drink her two glasses of wine daily, if I have to come and drench her with it. And it won't be any cost out of my missis's pocket, if that's what you are thinking of," logically proceeded Dobbs. "Parry says it will be a good three months before she can take her wine again; so Janey can drink it for her. If my missis grudged her port wine or was cramped in pocket, I should not take my one glass a day, which I do regular."

"I can never repay you and Mrs. Reece for your kindness and generosity to Jane," sighed Mrs. Halliburton.

"You can do it when you are asked," was Dobbs's retort. "There's the wing and merrythought of a fowl coming in for her dinner, with a bit of sweet boiled pork. I don't give myself the ceremony of cloth-laying, now my missis is in bed, but just eat it in the rough; so the child had better have hers brought in here comfortably, till my missis is down again. And, Janey, you'll come upstairs to tea to us; I have taken up the easy chair."

"Thank you very much, Dobbs," said Janey.

"And don't you let them cormorants be eating her dinners or drinking her wine," said Dobbs, fiercely, as she was going out. "Keep a sharp look-out upon 'em."

"They would not do it!" warmly replied Jane. "You do not know my boys yet, if you think they would rob their sick sister."

"I know that boys' stomachs are always on the crave for anything that's good," retorted Dobbs. "You might skin a boy if you were forced to it, but you'd never drive his nature out of him; and that's to be always eating!"

So she had even this help—port wine! It seemed almost beyond belief, and Jane lost herself in thought.

"Mamma, you don't hear me!"

"Did you speak, Janey?"

"I say I think Dobbs got that fowl for me. Mrs. Reece is not taking meat, and Dobbs would not buy a fowl for herself. She will give me all the best parts, and pick the bones herself. You'll see. How kind they are to me! What should I have done, mamma, if I had only our plain food? I know I could not eat it now."

"God is over us, my dear child," was Jane's reply. "It is He who has directed this help to us: never doubt it, Jane. Whether we live or die," she added pointedly, "we are in His hands, and He orders all things for the best."

"Can to die be for the best?" asked Janey, sitting up to think over the question.

"Why, yes, my dear girl; certainly it is, if God wills it. How often have I talked to you about the REST after the grave! No more tears, no more partings. Which is best—to be here, or to go to that rest? Oh, Janey! we can put up surely with illness and with crosses here, if we may only attain to that. This world will last only for a little while at best; but that other will abide for ever and for ever."

A summons from Mr. Parry's boy: Miss Halliburton's medicine had arrived. Miss Halliburton made a grievous face over it, when her mamma poured the dose out. "I never can take it! It smells so nasty!"

Jane held the wine-glass towards her, a grave, kind smile upon her face. "My darling, it is one of earth's little crosses; try and not rebel against it. Here's a bit of Patience's jam left, to take after it."

Janey smiled bravely as she took the glass. "It was not so bad as I thought, mamma," said she, when she had swallowed it.

"Of course not, Janey; nothing is that we set about with a brave heart."

But, with every good thing, Janey did not improve. Her mother shrank from admitting the fact that was growing only too palpable; and Dobbs would come in and sit looking at Janey for a quarter of an hour together, never speaking.

"Why do you look at me so, Dobbs?" asked Janey, one day, suddenly. "You were crying when you looked at me last night at dusk."

Dobbs was rather taken to. "I had been peeling onions," said she.

"Why do you shrink from looking at the truth?" an inward voice kept repeating in Mrs. Halliburton's heart. "Is it right, or wise, or well to do so?" No; she knew that it could not be.

That same day, after Mr. Parry had paid his visit to Mrs. Reece, he looked in upon Janey. "Am I getting better?" she asked him. "I want to go into the green fields again, and run about."

"Ah," said he, "we must wait for that, little maid."

Jane went out to the door with him. When he put out his hand to say good morning, he saw that she was white with emotion, and could not speak readily. "Will she live or die, Mr. Parry?" was the whispered question that came at last.

"Now don't distress yourself, Mrs. Halliburton. In these lingering cases we must be content to wait the issue, whatever it may be."

"I have had so much trouble of one sort or another, that I think I have become inured to it," she continued, striving to speak more calmly. "These several days past I have been deciding to ask you the truth. If I am to lose her, it will be better that I should know it beforehand: it will be easier for me to bear. She is in danger, is she not?"

"Yes," he replied; "I fear she is."

"Is there any hope?"

"Well, you know, Mrs. Halliburton, while there is life there is hope."

His tone was kindly; but she could not well mistake that, of human hope, there was none. Her lips were pale—her bosom was heaving. "I understand," she murmured. "Tell me one other thing: how near is the end?"

"That I really cannot tell you," he more readily replied. "These cases vary much in their progression. Do not be downcast, Mrs. Halliburton. We must every one of us go, sooner or later. Sometimes I wish I could see all mine gone before me, rather than leave them behind to the cares of this troublesome world."

He shook hands and departed. Jane crept softly upstairs to her own room, and was shut in for ten minutes. Poor thing! she could not spare time for the indulgence of grief, as others might! she must hasten to her never-ceasing work. She had her task to do; and ten minutes lost from it in the day must be made up at night.

As she was going downstairs, with red eyes, Mrs. Reece heard her footstep and called to her from her bed. "Is that you, ma'am?"

So Jane had to go in. "Are you better?" she inquired.

"No, ma'am, I don't see much improvement," replied the old lady. "Mr. Parry is going to change the lotion; but it's a thing that will have its course. How is Janey? Does he say?"

"She is much the same," said Jane. "She grows no better. I fear she never will."

"Ay! so Dobbs says; and it strikes me Parry has told her so. Now, ma'am, you spare nothing that can do her good. Whatever she fancies, tell Dobbs, and it shall be had. I would not for the world have a dying child stinted while I can help it. Don't spare wine; don't spare anything."

"A dying child!" The words, in spite of Jane's previous convictions; nay, her knowledge; caused her heart to sink with a chill. She proceeded, as she had done many times before, to express a tithe of her gratitude to Mrs. Reece for the substantial kindness shown to Janey.

"Don't say anything about it, ma'am," returned the old lady in her simple, straightforward way. "I have neither chick nor child of my own, and both I and Dobbs have taken a liking for Janey. We can't think anything we can do too much for her. I have spoken to Parry—therefore don't spare his services; at any hour of the day or night send for him if you deem it necessary."

With another attempt at heartfelt thanks, Jane went down. Full as her cup was to the brim, she was yet overwhelmed with the sense of kindness shown. From that time she set herself to the task of preparing Janey for the great change by gradual degrees—a little now, a little then: to make her long for the translation to that better land.

One evening, about eight o'clock, Patience entered—partly to inquire after Janey, partly to ask William if he would go to bring Anna from Mrs. Ashley's, where she had been taking tea. Samuel Lynn was detained in the town on business, and Grace had been permitted to go out: therefore Patience had no one to send. William left his books, and went out with alacrity. Patience sat down by Janey's sofa.

"I get so tired, Patience. I wish I had some pretty books to read! I have read all Anna's over and over again."

"And she won't eat solids now, and she grows tired of mutton-broth, and sago, and egg-flip, and those things," put in Dobbs, in an injured tone, who was also sitting there.

"I would try her with a little beef-tea, made with plenty of carrots and thickened with arrowroot," said Patience.

"Beef-tea, made with carrots and thickened with arrowroot!" ungraciously responded Dobbs, who held in contempt every one's cooking except her own.

"I can tell thee that it is one of the nicest things taken," said Patience. "It might be a change for the child."

"How's it made?" asked Dobbs. "It might do for my missis: she's tired of mutton broth."

"Slice a pound of lean beef, and let it soak for two hours in a quart of cold water," replied Patience. "Then put meat and water into a saucepan, with a couple of large carrots scraped and sliced. Let it warm gradually, and then simmer for about four hours, thee putting salt to taste. Strain it off; and, when cold, take off the fat. As the broth is wanted, stir it up, and take from it as much as may be required, boiling the portion, for a minute, with a little arrowroot."

Dobbs condescended to intimate that perhaps she might try it; though she'd be bound it was poor stuff.

William had hastened to Mr. Ashley's. He was shown into a room to wait for Anna, and his attention was immediately attracted by a shelf full of children's story-books. He knew they were just what Janey was longing for. He had taken some in his hand, when Anna came in, ready for him, accompanied by Mrs. Ashley, Mary, and Henry. Then William became aware of the liberty he had taken in touching the things, and, in his self-consciousness, the colour, as usual, rushed to his face. It was a frank, ingenuous face, with its fair, open forehead, and its earnest, dark grey eyes; and Mrs. Ashley thought it so.

"Were you looking at our books?" asked Henry, who was in a remarkably good humour.

"I am sorry to have touched them," replied William. "I was thinking of something else."

"I would be nearly sure thee were thinking of thy sister," cried Anna, who had an ever-ready tongue.

"Yes, I was," replied William candidly. "I was wishing she could read them."

"I have told her about the books," said Anna, turning from William to the rest. "I related to her as much as I could remember of 'Anna Ross:' that book which thee had in thy hand, William. She would so like to read them; she is always ill."

"Is she very ill?" inquired Mrs. Ashley.

"She is dying," replied Anna.

It was the first intimation William had received of the great fear. His countenance changed, his heart beat wildly. "Oh, Anna! who says it?" he cried out, in a low, wailing tone.

There was a dead silence. Anna's announcement sounded sufficiently startling, and Mrs. Ashley looked with sympathy at the evidently agitated boy.

"There! that's my tongue!" cried Anna repentantly. "Patience says she wonders some one does not cut it out for me."

Mary Ashley—a fair, gentle little girl, with large brown eyes, like Henry's—stepped forward, full of sympathy. "I have heard of your sister from Anna," she said. "She is welcome to read all my books; you can take some to her now, and change them as often as you like."

How pleased William was! Mary selected four, and gave them to him. "Anna Ross," "The Blind Farmer," "Theophilus and Sophia," and "Margaret White." Very old, some of the books, and childish; but admirably suited to what people were beginning to call Jane—a dying child.

"I say," cried out Henry, a little aristocratic patronage in his tone, as William was departing, "how do you get on with your Latin?"

"I get on very well. Not quite so fast as I should with a master. I have to puzzle out difficulties for myself, and I am not sure but that's one of the best ways to get on. I go on with my Greek, too; and Euclid, and—"

"How much time do you work?" burst forth Henry.

"From six o'clock till half-past nine. A little of the time I am helping my brothers."

"There's perseverance, Henry!" cried Mrs. Ashley; and Master Henry shrugged his shoulders.

"Anna," began William, as they walked along, "how do you know that Janey is so ill?"

"Now, William, thee must ask thy mother whether she is ill or not. She may get well—how do I know? She was ill last summer, and Hannah Dobbs would have it she was in a bad way then; but she recovered. Dost thee know what Patience says?"

"What?" asked William eagerly.

"Patience says I have ten ears where I ought to have two; and I think thee hast the same. Fare thee well," she added, as they reached her door. "Thank thee for coming for me."

William waited at the gate until Anna was admitted, and then hastened home. Jane was alone, working as usual.

"Mamma, is it true that Janey is dying?"

Jane's heart gave a leap; and poor William, as she saw, could scarcely speak for agitation. "Who told you that?" she asked in low tones.

"Anna Lynn. Is it true?"

"William, I fear it may be. Don't grieve, child! don't grieve!"

William had laid his head down upon the table, the sobs breaking forth. His poor mother left her seat, and bent her head down beside him, sobbing also.

"William, for my sake don't grieve!" she whispered. "God alone knows what is good. He would not take her unless it were for the best."

CHAPTER VII

THE END

April passed. May was passing; and the end of Jane Halliburton was at hand. There was no secret now about her state; but she was going away very peacefully.

In this month, May, there occurred another vacancy in the choir of the cathedral. Little Gar—but he was growing too big now to be called Little Gar—proved to be the successful candidate; so that both boys were now in the choir.

"It will be such a help to me, learning to chant, should I ever try for a minor canonry," boasted Gar, who never tired of telling them that he meant to be a clergyman.

"Gar, dear, did you ever sit down and count the cost?" asked Mrs. Halliburton. "I fear it will not be your luck to go to college."

"Labor omnia vincit," cried out Gar. "You have heard us stumbling over our Latin often enough, mamma, to know what that means. Frank will need to count the cost, too, if he is ever to make himself into a barrister; and he says he will be one."

"Oh, you two vain boys!" cried Jane, laughing.

"Mamma," spoke up Janey from the sofa—and her breathing was laboured now—"is there harm in their wishing this?"

"Not at all. They are laudable aims. Only Frank and Gar are so poor and friendless that I fear the hopes are too ambitious to end in anything but disappointment."

Janey called Gar to her, and pulled his face down to a level with hers, whispering softly, "Strive well, Gar, and trust in God."

Later, when Jane had to be out on an indispensable errand, Dobbs came in to sit with Janey. She brought her some jelly in a saucer.

"I am nearly tired of it, Dobbs," said Janey. "I grow tired of everything. And I don't like to say so, because it seems so ungrateful."

"It's the nature of illness to get tired of things," responded Dobbs, who thought it was her mission never to cease buoying Janey up with hope. "You'll be better when the hot weather comes in."

"No, I shan't, Dobbs. I shall never get better now."

A combination of feelings, indignation predominating, nearly took away Dobbs's breath. "Who on earth has been putting that grim notion in your head?" asked she.

"It is true, Dobbs."

"True!" ejaculated Dobbs. "Who has been saying it to you? I want to know that."

"Mamma for one. She—"

"Of all the stupids!" burst forth Dobbs, drowning what Janey was about to say. "To frighten the child by telling her she's going to die!"

"It does not frighten me, Dobbs. I like to lie and think of it."

Dobbs fell into a doubt whether Janey was in her senses. "Like to lie and think of being screwed down in a coffin, and put into the cold ground, and left there till the judgment day!" uttered she.

"Oh, but, Dobbs, you must know better than that," returned Jane. "We are not put into the coffin; it is only our bodies that are put into the coffin; we go into the world of departed spirits."

"De-par-ted what?" ejaculated Dobbs, whose notions of the future—the life after this life—were not very definite; and who could not have been more astonished had Jane begun to talk to her in Greek.

"Mamma has always tried to explain these things to us," said Jane. "She has made them as clear to us as they can be made, and she has taught us not to fear death. She says a great mistake is often made by those who bring up children. They are taught to run away from death as something gloomy and frightful, instead of being shown its bright side."

"Well, I never heard the like!" exclaimed Dobbs, lost in wonder. "How can there be a bright side to death?—in a horrid coffin, with brass nails and tin-tacks that screw you down?"

Tears filled Janey's eyes. "Oh, Dobbs, you must learn better than that, or how will you ever be reconciled to death? Don't you know that when we die, we—our spirit, that is, for it is our spirit that lives and thinks—leave our body behind us? There's no more consciousness in our body, and it is put into the grave till the last day. It is like the shell that the silkworm casts away when it comes into the moth: the life is in the moth: not in the cast-off shell. You cannot think what trouble mamma has taken with us always to explain these things; and she has talked to me so much lately."

"And where does the spirit go—by which, I suppose, you mean the soul?" asked Dobbs.

Janey shook her head, to express her ignorance at the best. "It is all a mystery," she said; "but mamma has taught us to believe that there's a place for the departed, and that we shall be there. It is not to be supposed that the soul, a thing of life, could be boxed up in a coffin, Dobbs. When Jesus Christ said to the thief on the cross, 'To-day shalt thou be with me in paradise,' he meant that world. It is a place of light and rest."

"And the good and bad are there together?"

Again Janey shook her head. "Don't you remember, in the parable of the rich man and the beggar, there was a great gulf between them, and Abraham said that it could not be passed? I dare say it will be very peaceful and happy there: quite different from this world, where there's so much trouble and sickness. Why should I be afraid of death, Dobbs?"

Dobbs sat looking at her, and was some minutes before she spoke. "Not afraid to die!" she slowly said. "Well, I should be."

Janey's eyes were wet. "Nobody need be afraid to die when they have learnt to trust in God. Don't you know," she answered with something like enthusiasm, "that many people, when dying, have seen Jesus waiting for them? What does it matter, then, where our bodies are put? We are going to be with Jesus. Indeed, Dobbs, there's nothing sad in dying, if you only can look at it in the right way. It is those who look at it in the wrong way that are afraid to die."

"The child's as learned as a minister!" was Dobbs's inward comment. "Ours told us last Sunday evening at Chapel that we were all on the high road to perdition. I'd rather listen to her creed than to his: it sounds more encouraging. Their ma hasn't brought 'em up amiss; and that's the truth!"

The soliloquy was interrupted by the return of Mrs. Halliburton. Almost immediately afterwards some visitors came in—Mary Ashley and Anna Lynn. It was the first time Mary had been there, and she had come to bring Janey some more books. She was one of those graceful children whom it is pleasant to look at. A contrast in attire she presented to the little Quakeress, with her silk dress, her straw hat, trimmed with a wreath of flowers and white ribbons, her dark curls falling beneath it. She was much younger than her brother Henry; but there was a great resemblance between them—in the refined features, the bright complexion, and the soft dark eyes. Somehow, through a remark made by Dobbs, the conversation turned upon Jane's inability to recover; and Mary Ashley heard with extreme wonder that death was not dreaded. "Her ma has taught her different," was Dobbs's comment.

"Mamma takes great pains with us," observed Mary; "but I should not like to die. How is it?" she added, turning to Mrs. Halliburton. "Jane is not much older than I, and yet she does not dread it!"

"My dear," was the reply, "I think it is simply this. Those whom God is intending to take from the world, He often, in His mercy and wisdom, weans from the love of it. You are healthy and strong, and the world is pleasant to you. Jane has been so long weak and ill that she no longer finds enjoyment in it; and this naturally causes her to look beyond this world to the rest and peace of the next. All things are well ordered."

Mary Ashley began to think they must be. Chattering Anna, vain Anna, sat gazing at Mary's pretty hat, her drooping curls; none, except Anna herself, knew with what envious longing. Anna, at any rate, was not tired of the world.

The end grew nearer and nearer. There came a day when Jane did not get up; there came a second, and a third. On the fourth morning, Janey, who had passed a comfortable night, compared with some nights which had preceded it, was sitting up in bed when her brothers came in from school. They hurried over their breakfast and ran up to her, carrying the remains of it in their hands.

The first few minutes after breakfast had always been devoted by Jane to reading to her children; in spite of her necessity for close working they were so devoted still. "I will read here this morning," she observed, as the boys stood around the bed.

"Mamma," interrupted Janey, "read about the holy city, in the Book of Revelation."

Mrs. Halliburton turned to the twenty-first chapter, and had read to the twenty-third verse—"And the city had no need of the sun, neither of the moon, to shine in it: for the glory of God did lighten it, and the Lamb is the light thereof"—when Jane suddenly started forward in bed, her eyes fixed on some opposite point. Mrs. Halliburton paused, and endeavoured to put her gently back again.

"Oh, mamma, don't keep me!" she said in a strangely thrilling tone; "don't keep me! I see the light! I see papa!"

There was a strange light, not as of earth, in her own face, an ineffable smile on her lip, that told more of heaven. Her arms dropped; and she sank back on the pillow. Jane Halliburton had gone to her Heavenly Father; it may be also to her earthly one. Gar screamed.

Dobbs arrived in the midst of the commotion. And when Dobbs saw what had happened, she fell into a storm of anger, of passionate sobs, half ready to knock down Mrs. Halliburton with words, and the poor boys with blows. Why was she not called to see the last of her? The only young thing she had cared for in all the world, and yet she could not be allowed to wish her farewell! She'd never love another again as long as her days lasted! In vain they strove to explain to her that it was sudden, unexpected, momentary: Dobbs would not listen.

Mrs. Halliburton stole away from Dobbs's storm—anywhere. Her heart was brimful. Although she had known that this must be the ending, now that it had come she was as one unprepared. In her grief and sorrow, she was tempted for a moment—but only for a moment—to question the goodness and wisdom of God.

Some one called to her from the foot of the stairs, and she went down. She had to go down; she could not shut herself up, as those can who have servants to be their deputies. Anna Lynn stood there, dressed for school.

"Friend Jane Halliburton, Patience has sent me to ask after Janey this morning. Is she better?"

"No, Anna. She is dead."

Jane spoke with unnatural calmness. The child, scared at the words, backed away out at the garden door, and then flew to Patience with the news. It brought Patience in. Jane was nearly prostrate then.

"Nay, but thee art grieving sadly! Thee must not take on so."

"Oh, Patience! why should it be?" she wailed aloud in her despair and bereavement. "Anna left in health and joyousness; my child taken! Surely God is dealing hardly with me."

"Thee must not say that," returned Patience gravely. "But thee art not thyself just now. What truth was it that I heard thee impress upon thy child not a week ago? That God's ways are not as our ways."

CHAPTER VIII

A WEDDING IN HONEY FAIR

But that such contrasts are all too common in life, you might think it scarcely seemly to go direct from a house of death to a house of marriage. This same morning which witnessed the death of Jane Halliburton, witnessed also the wedding of Mary Ann Cross and Ben Tyrrett. Upon which there was wonderful rejoicing at the Crosses' house.

Of course, whether a wedding was a good one or a bad one (speaking from a pecuniary point of view), it was equally the custom to feast over it in Honey Fair. Benjamin Tyrrett was only what is called a jobber in the glove trade, earning fifteen or sixteen shillings a week; but Mary Ann Cross made up her mind to have him—in defiance of parental and other admonitions that she ought to look over Ben's head. They had gone to work Honey Fair fashion, preparing nothing. Every shilling that Mary Ann Cross could spare went in finery—had long gone in finery. In vain Charlotte East impressed upon her the necessity of saving: of waiting. Mary Ann would do neither one nor the other.

"All that you can spare from back debts, and from present actual wants, you should put by," Charlotte had urged. "You don't know how many more calls there are for money after marriage than before it."

"There'll be two of us to earn it then," logically replied Mary Ann.

"And two of you to live," said Charlotte. "To marry upon nothing is to rush into trouble."

"How you do go on, Charlotte East! He'll earn his wages, and I shall earn mine. Where'll be the trouble? I shan't want to spend so much upon my back when I am married."

"To marry as you are going to do, must bring trouble," persisted Charlotte. "He will manage to get together a few bits of cheap furniture, just what you can't do without, to put into one room; and there you will be set up, neither of you having one sixpence laid by to fall back upon; and perhaps the furniture unpaid, hanging like a log upon you. What shall you do when children come, Mary Ann?"

Mary Ann Cross giggled. "If ever I heard the like of you, Charlotte! If children do come, they must come, that's all. We can't send 'em back again."

"No, you can't," said Charlotte. "They generally arrive in pretty good troops: and sometimes there's little to welcome them on. Half the quarrels between man and wife, in our class of life, spring from nothing but large families and small means. Their tempers get soured with each other, and never get pleased again."

"Folks must take their chance, Charlotte."

"There's no must in it. You are nineteen, Ben Tyrrett's twenty-three; suppose you made up your minds to wait two or three years. You would be quite young enough then: and meanwhile, if both of you laid by, you would have something in hand to meet extra expenses, or sickness if it came."

"Opinions differs," shortly returned Mary Ann. "If folks tell true, you were putting by ever so long for your marriage, and it all ended in smoke. I'd rather make sure of a husband when I can get him."

An expression of pain crossed the face of Charlotte East. "Whether I marry or not," she answered calmly, "I shall be none the worse for having laid money by instead of squandering it. If the best man that ever was born came to me, I would not marry him if we had made no better provision for a rainy day than you and Tyrrett have. What can come of such unions, Mary Ann?"

"It's the way most of us girls do marry," returned Mary Ann.

"And what comes of it, I ask? Blows sometimes, Mary Ann; the workhouse sometimes; trouble always."

"Is it true that you put by, Charlotte?"

"Yes. I put by what I can."

"But how in wonder do you manage it? You dress as well as we do. I'm sure our backs take all our money; father pretty nigh keeps the house."

"I dress better than you in one sense, Mary Ann. I don't have on a silk gown one day and a petticoat in rags the next. No one ever sees me otherwise than neat and clean, and my clothes keep good a long while. It's the finery that runs away with your money. I am not ashamed to make a bonnet last two years; you'd have two in a season. Another thing, Mary Ann: I do not waste my time—I sit to my work; and I dare say I earn double what you do."

"Let us hear what you earned last week, if it isn't impertinent," was Mary Ann's answer.

"Ten and ninepence."

"Look at that!" cried the girl, lifting her hands. "I brought out but five and twopence, and I left no money for silk, and am in debt two quarterns. 'Melia was worse. Hers came to four and eleven. That surly old foreman says to me when he was paying, 'What d'ye leave for silk, Mary Ann Cross? There's two quarterns down.' 'I know there is, sir,' says I, 'but I don't leave nothing to-day.' He gave a grunt at that, the old file did."

"And I suppose you spent your five shillings in some useless thing?"

"I had to pay up at Bankes's, and the rest went in a new peach bonnet-ribbon."

"Peach! You should have bought white, if you must be married."

"Thank you, Charlotte! What next? Do you suppose I'm going to be married in that shabby old straw, that I've worn all the spring? Not if I know it."

"Where's your money to come from for a new one? There will be other things wanted, more essential than a bonnet."

"I'll have a new one if I go in trust for it," returned Mary Ann. "Tyrrett buys the ring. And it is of no use for you to preach, Charlotte; if you preach your tongue out, it'll do no good."

Charlotte might, indeed, have preached a very long sermon before she could effect any change in the system of improvidence obtaining in Honey Fair. Neither Benjamin Tyrrett nor Mary Ann Cross was gifted with forethought, and they took no pains to acquire it.

The marriage was carried out, and this was the happy day. Mrs. Cross gave an entertainment in honour of the event, at which the bride and bridegroom assisted—as the French say—with as many others as the kitchen would hold. Tea for the ladies, pipes and ale for the gentlemen, supper for all, with spirits-and-water handed round.

How Mrs. Cross had contrived to go on so long without an exposé, she scarcely knew herself. The wonder was, that she had gone on at all. It took the energies of her life to patch up her embarrassments, and hide her difficulties from her husband. The evil day, however, was only delayed. It could not be averted.

CHAPTER IX

AN EXPLOSION FOR MRS CROSS

The evil day, hinted at in the last chapter, was not long in coming. It might not have fallen quite so soon but for a misfortune which overtook Jacob Cross. The manufacturer for whom he worked died suddenly, and the business was immediately given up—the made gloves being bought by up a London house, and the stock in trade, leather machines, etc., sold by auction. He had been a first-class manufacturer, doing nearly as large a business as Mr. Ashley; and not only Jacob Cross, but many more men in Honey Fair were thrown out of work—one of whom was Andrew Brumm; another, Timothy Carter. This happened only a few months after Mary Ann Cross's marriage.

It struck terror to the heart of Mrs. Cross. Though she had paid some of her debts, she had incurred others: indeed, the very fact of her having to pay had caused her to incur fresh ones. Her position was ominous. She and Amelia had worked for this same manufacturer, now dead, and of course they were at a standstill. Mary Ann Tyrrett had likewise worked for him; but she had left the paternal home; and with her we have nothing just now to do. The position of others was ominous, as well as that of Mrs. Cross. It was the autumn season, and trade was flat. Winter orders had gone in, and there was no necessity to hurry those for the spring; so that the hands thrown out of work, both men and women, stood every chance of remaining out.

A gloom overspread Honey Fair. In many a household the articles least needed went, week after week, to the pawnbrokers, without being redeemed on the Saturday night, as in more prosperous times. Upon the proceeds the families had to exist. It was bad enough for those who were free from debt; but for those already labouring under it—above all, labouring under secret debt—it was something not to be told. Mrs. Cross had nightmares regularly every night. Visions would come over her now and again of running away, if she had only known where to run to. The men would stand or sit at their doors all day, with pipes in their mouths: money was sure to be found for tobacco, by hook or by crook. There they would lounge in gloomy silence, varied by an occasional wordy war with their wives, who wished them anywhere else; or they and their pipes would saunter up and down the road, forming into groups to condole with each other and to abuse the glove trade.

One Monday afternoon there was a small assemblage in the kitchen of Jacob Cross—himself, Andrew Brumm, and Timothy Carter. Brumm and Carter were, in one sense, more fortunate than Cross; inasmuch as that their respective wives worked each for another house, not the one which had closed; therefore they retained their employment. The fact, however, appeared to afford little consolation to the two men, for they were keeping up a chorus of grumbling, when Joe Fisher staggered in—if you have not forgotten him.

Fisher had hitherto managed, to the intense surprise of every one, to keep out of the workhouse. He would be taken on for a job of work now and then; but manufacturers were chary of employing Joe Fisher. For one thing, he gave way to drink. A disreputable-looking object had he become: a tattered coat and waistcoat, pantaloons in rags, and not the ghost of a shirt. People wondered how he found money for drink.

"Who'll give us house-room?" was his salutation, as he pushed himself in, his eyes haggard, his legs unsteady, his face thin from incipient famine. "Will nobody give us a corner to lie in?"

The men took their pipes from their mouths. "Turned out at last, Joe?"

"Turned out," replied Joe. "And my missis close upon her down-lying."

Mrs. Cross, who was at the back of the kitchen, washing out her potato saucepan, of which frugal edible, seasoned with salt, the family dinner had consisted, put in her word.

"You couldn't expect nothing else, Joe Fisher. There you have been, in them folks' furnished room, paying nothing, and paying nothing, and you drinking everlasting. They have threatened you long enough. Last week, you know, they took a vow you should go this."

"Where's the wife and little 'uns?" asked meek Timothy Carter.

"You can look at 'em," responded Fisher. "They're not a hundred miles off. They bain't out of view."

He gave a flourish of his hand towards the road, and the men and Mrs. Cross crowded to the door to reconnoitre. In the middle of the lane, crouched down in its mud, for the weather had been bad, and it was very wet under foot, was untidy Sukey Fisher—a woman all skin and bone now, her face hopeless and desperate. She wore no cap, and her matted hair fell on to her gown—such a gown! all tatters and dirt. Several young children huddled around her.

"Untidy creature!" muttered Mrs. Cross to herself. "She is as fond of a drop as her lazy, quarrelsome husband; and this is what they have brought it to between 'em! Them poor little objects of young 'uns 'ud be as well dead as alive."

"Look at 'em!" began Fisher. "And they call this a free country! They call it a country as is a pattern to others and a refuge for the needy. Why don't Government, that opened our ports to them foreign French and keeps 'em open, come down and take a look at my wife squatting there?—turned out of our room without a place to put our heads into!"

"If you hadn't put quite as much inside your head, Joe Fisher, and been doing of it for years, you might have had more for the outside on't now," again spoke Mrs. Cross in her sharp tones. The woman was not naturally sharp, as were some in Honey Fair; but the miserable fear she lived in, added to their present privations, told upon her temper.

"Hold your magging," said Joe Fisher. "I never like to quarrel with petticuts, one's own belongings excepted. All as I say, Mother Cross, is, don't you mag."

Mrs. Cross made no reply to this, and Fisher resumed.

"This comes of letting the Government and the masters have their own way! If we had that there strike among us, that I've so often told ye on, things would be different. Let a man sit down a minute, Cross."

Cross civilly pushed a chair towards him, concentrating his attention afterwards upon Mrs. Fisher. A crowd had collected round her; and Mrs. Buffle, with a feeling of humanity that few had given that lady credit for possessing, sent out an old woollen shawl to the shivering woman, and a basin of hasty pudding. The mother could not feed the whining children fast enough with the one iron spoon.

A young man ran up to Cross's door. It was Adam Thorneycroft. He did not live in Honey Fair, but often found his way to it, although Charlotte had rejected him. "Is Joe Fisher here?" asked he. "Fisher, why don't you go to the workhouse and tell them the state your wife is in? She can't stop there."

"Her state is no concern of your'n, Master Thorneycroft," was the sullen answer.

Thorneycroft turned on his heel, a scornful gesture escaping him at Fisher's half-stupid condition. "I must be off to my work," he observed; "but can't one of you, who are gentlemen at large, just go to the workhouse and acquaint them with the woman's helplessness, and that of her children around her?"

Timothy Carter responded to it. "I'll go," said he; "I haven't nothing to do with myself this afternoon."

Timothy and Adam walked away together, Tim treading with gingerly feet past his own door, lest his wife should recognise his step, bolt out, and stop him. Charlotte East was standing at her door, and Adam halted. Timothy walked on: he did not feel himself perfectly safe yet.

"What a life that poor woman's is!" exclaimed Charlotte.

"Ay," assented Adam; "and all through Fisher's not sticking to his work."

Charlotte moved her face gravely towards him. "Say through his drinking, Adam."

"Do you speak that as a warning, Charlotte?" he continued. "I think you mean well by me, but you go just the wrong way to show it. If you wanted me to keep steady, you should have come and helped me in it. Good-bye. I am late."

"Gentlemen at large, young Thorney called us!" cried Jacob Cross to his friend Brumm, as Fisher went off and they sat down again. "He's not far out. What's to be the end on't?"

"Why, the work'us," responded Mrs. Cross, who rarely let an opportunity slip of putting in her own opinion. "The work'us for us as well as for the Fishers, unless things take a turn. When great, big, able-bodied men is throwed out o' work, and yet has to eat and drink, and other folks at home has to eat and drink, and nothing to stay their stomachs upon, the work'us can't be far off."

"Never for me!" said Andrew Brumm. "I'll work to keep me and mine out on it, if it is at breaking stones upon the road. I know one thing—if ever I do get into certain work again, I'll make my missis be a bit providenter than she was before."

"Bell Brumm ain't one of the provident sort," dissented Mrs. Cross. "How do you manage to get along at all, Drew, these bad times? You don't seem to get into trouble."

"Well, we manage somehow," replied Andrew. "But we have to pinch. My missis sticks at her work, now I be out on't. She hardly looks off it; and I does the house, and sees to the children. Nine shilling, all but her silk, she earned last week. And finding that we can exist on that after a fashion, has set me thinking that when my good wages was added to it we ought to have put by for a rainy day," he continued, after a pause. "Just let me get the chance again!"

"It's surprising the miracles wages works when folks ain't earning none!" put in Mrs. Cross in a tone of irony, who did not altogether like the turn the conversation was taking. "When you get into work again, Drew Brumm, your wife won't be more able to save than the rest of us."

"But she shall," returned Andrew. "And she sees for herself now that it might be done."

"I was a-making a calkelation yesterday how long we might hold out on our household things," observed Jacob Cross—a silent man, in general. "If none of us can get work, they'll have to go, piecemeal. One can't clam; one must live upon something."

"I'm resolved upon one point—that I won't have no underhand debt again," resumed Brumm. "Last spring I found out the flaring trade my missis was carrying on with them Bankes's—and the way I come to know of it was funny: but never mind that. 'Bell,' says I to her, 'I'd rather sell off all I've got and go tramping the country, than I'd live with a sword over my head'—which debt is. And I went down to Bankes's and said to 'em, 'If you let my wife get into debt again, I won't pay it, as I now give you notice, and I'll have you up before the justices for a pest.' I thought I'd make it strong, you see, Cross. And I paid off their bill, so much a week, and got shut of 'em. Them Bankes's does more mischief in Honey Fair than everything else put together."

"Why, what do Bankes's do?" asked Jacob, in happy ignorance.

"Do!" returned Brumm. "Don't you know—"

But at that critical moment, Mrs. Cross, in bustling behind Andrew Brumm's chair, which was on the tilt, contrived to get her foot entangled in it. Brumm, his chair, and his pipe, all came down together.

"Mercy on us!" uttered Jacob Cross, coming to the rescue. "How did you manage that, Brumm?"

Before Brumm could answer, or had well gathered himself up, there was another visitor—Mr. Abbott, the landlord of at least a third of Honey Fair. He had come on his usual Monday's errand. Jacob Cross put down his pipe and touched his hat, which, in the manners of Honey Fair, was worn indoors. It was not often that the landlord and the men came into contact with each other.

"Are you ready for me, Mrs. Cross?"

"We are not ready to-day, sir," interposed Jacob. "You must please to give us a little grace these hard times, sir. The moment I be in work again, I'll think of you, before I think of ourselves."

"I have given all the grace I can give," replied Mr. Abbott, a hard, surly man. "You must either pay, or turn out: I don't care which."

"I'll pay you as soon as I am in work, sir; you may count upon it. As to turning out, sir, where could I turn to? You'd not let me take out my furniture, and we can't sit down in the street, as Fisher's wife is doing."

Mr. Abbott turned to the door. When he came back, a man was with him. "I must trouble you to give this man house-room for a few days. As you won't go out, he must stop in, to see that your goods stop in."

Cross's spirit rose within him. "It's a hard way to treat a man, sir! I have lived under you for years, and you have had your rent regular."

"Regular!" exclaimed the landlord. "I have had more trouble to get it from your wife, since Bankes's came to Helstonleigh, than from anybody else in Honey Fair."

Cross did not understand this. He was too much absorbed by the point in question to ask an explanation. "There's only three weeks owing to you, sir, and—"

"Three weeks!" interrupted Mr. Abbott; "there are nine weeks owing to me. Nine weeks to-day."

Jacob Cross stood confounded. "Who says there's nine weeks?" asked he.

"I say so. Your wife can say so. Ask her."

But Mrs. Cross, with a scared face and white lips, whisked through the door and hurried down Honey Fair. The explosion had come.

Mr. Abbott, wasting no more words, departed, leaving the unwelcome visitor behind him. Andrew Brumm came in again from outside, where he had stood, out of delicacy, feeling thankful that his rent was all right. It was pinching work; but Andrew was beginning to learn that debt pinches the mind, more than hunger pinches the body.

"Comrade," whispered he, grasping Cross's hand, "it's all along of them Bankes's. The women buy their fal-lals and their finery, and the weekly payments to 'em must be kept up, whether or no, for fear Bankes's should let out on't to us, and ask us for the money. Of course the rent and other things gets behind. Half the women round us are knee-deep in Bankes's books."

"Why couldn't you have told me this before?" demanded Cross, in his astonishment.

"It's not my province to interfere with other men's wives," was Brumm's sensible answer.

"Where's she got to?" cried Jacob, looking round for his wife. "I'll come to the bottom of this. Nine weeks' rent owing; and her salving me up that it was only three!"

Jacob might well say, "Where's she got to?" Mrs. Cross had glided down Honey Fair into the first friendly door that happened to be open. That was Mrs. Carter's. "For mercy's sake, let's stop here a minute, Elizabeth Carter!" exclaimed she. "We have got the bums in!"

Mrs. Carter was rubbing up some brass candlesticks. Work ran short with her that week, and therefore she spent it in cleaning, which was her notion of taking holiday; scrubbing and scouring from morning till night. She turned round and stared at Mrs. Cross, who, with white face and gasping breath, had sunk down upon a chair.

"What on earth's the matter?"

"Abbott has brought it out to my husband that I owes nine weeks' rent, and he's telling him about Bankes's, and now he has gone and put a bum into the house!"

"More soft you, to have had to do with Bankes's!" was the sympathy offered by Mrs. Carter. "You couldn't expect nothing less."

"That old skinflint, Abbott—"

Mrs. Cross stopped short. She opened the staircase door about an inch, and humbly twisted herself through the aperture. Who should be standing there to hear her, having followed her in, but Mr. Abbott himself.

He had no need to say, "Ready, Mrs. Carter?" Mrs. Carter always was ready. She paid him weekly, and asked no favour. The payment made, he departed again, and Mrs. Cross emerged from her retreat.

"You can pay him!" she exclaimed, with some envy. "And Timothy's out o' work, too; and you be slack. How do you manage it?"

"I'm not a fool," was the logical response of Mrs. Carter. "If I spent my earnings when they are coming in regular, or let Tim keep his to his own cheek, where should we be in a time like this? I have my understanding about me."

Mrs. Carter did not praise her understanding without cause. Whatever social virtues she may have lacked, she was rich in thrift, in forethought. Had Timothy remained out of work for a twelvemonth, they would not have been put to shifts.

"I'm afraid to go back!" cried Mrs. Cross.

"So should I be, if I got myself into your mess."

The offered sympathy not being consolatory to her present frame of mind, Mrs. Cross departed. Home, at present, she dared not go. She went about Honey Fair, seeking the gossiping pity which Elizabeth Carter had declined to give, but which she was yearning for. Thus she spent an hour or two.

Meanwhile the news had been spreading through Honey Fair, "Crosses had the bums in;" and Mary Ann, hearing it, flew home to know whether it was correct. She—partly through fear, partly in the security from paternal correction, imparted to her by the feeling that she was Mary Ann Tyrrett, and no longer Mary Ann Cross—yielded to her father's questions, and made full confession. Debts here, debts there, debts everywhere. Cross was overwhelmed; and when his wife at length came in, he quietly knocked her down.

The broker advanced to the rescue. "If you dare to come between man and wife," raved Cross, lifting his arm menacingly, "I'll serve you the same." He was a quiet-tempered man, but this business had terribly exasperated him. "You'll come to die in the work'us," he uttered to his wife. "And serve you right! It's your doings that have broke up our home."

"No," retorted she passionately, as she lifted herself from the floor; "it's your squanderings in the publics o' nights, that have helped to break up our home."

It was a little of both.

The quarrel was interrupted by a commotion outside, and Mrs. Cross darted out to look—glad, perhaps, to escape from her husband's anger. An official from the workhouse had come down with an order for the admission of Susan Fisher instanter. Timothy Carter, in his meek and humane spirit, had so enlarged upon the state of affairs in general, touching Mrs. Fisher, that the workhouse bestirred itself. An officer was despatched to marshal them into it at once. The uproar was caused by her resistance: she was still sitting in the road.

"I won't go into the work'us," she screamed; "I won't go there to be parted from my children and my husband. If I'm to die, I'll die out here."

"Just get up and march, and don't let's have no row," said the officer. "Else I'll fetch a wheel-barrer, and wheel ye to it."

She resisted, shrieking and flinging her arms and her wild hair about her, as only a foolish woman would do; the children, alarmed, clung to her and cried, and all Honey Fair came out to look. Mr. Joe Fisher also staggered up, in a state not to be described. He had been invited by some friend, more sympathizing than judicious, to solace his troubles with strong waters; and down he fell in the mud, helpless.

"Well, here's a pretty kettle of fish!" cried the perplexed workhouse man. "A nice pair, they are! How I am to get 'em both there, is beyond me! She can walk, if she's forced to it; but he can't! They spend their money in sotting, and when they have no more to spend they come to us to keep 'em! I must get an open cart."

The cart was procured somewhere and brought to the scene, a policeman in attendance; and the children were lifted into it one by one. Next the man was thrown in, like a clod; and then came the woman's turn. With much struggling and kicking, with shrieks that might have been heard a mile off, she was at length hoisted into it. But she tumbled out again: raving that "no work'us shouldn't hold her." The official raved in turn; and Honey Fair hugged itself. It had not had the gratification of so exciting a scene for many a day; to say nothing of the satisfaction it derived from hearing the workhouse set at defiance.

The official and the policeman at length conquered. She was secured, and the cart started at a snail's pace with its load—Mrs. Fisher setting up a prolonged and dismal lamentation not unlike an Irish howl: and Honey Fair, in its curiosity, following the cart as its train.

CHAPTER X

A STRAY SHILLING

"Whose shilling is this on my desk?" inquired Mr. Ashley of Samuel Lynn, one morning towards the close of the summer.

"I cannot tell thee," was the reply of the Quaker. "I know nothing of it."

"It is none of mine, to my knowledge," remarked Mr. Ashley.

"What shilling is that on the master's desk?" repeated Samuel Lynn to William when he returned into his own room, where William was.

"I put a shilling on the desk this morning," replied William. "I found it in the waste-paper basket."

"Thee go in, then, and tell the master."

William did so. "The shilling rolled out of the waste-paper basket, sir," said he, entering the counting-house and approaching Mr. Ashley.

Mr. Ashley was remarkably exact in his accounts. He had missed no shilling, and he did not think it was his. "What should bring a shilling in the waste-paper basket?" he asked. "It may have rolled out of your own pocket."

William could have smiled at the remark. A shilling out of his pocket! "Oh, no, sir, it did not."

Mr. Ashley sat looking earnestly at William—as the latter fancied. In reality he was buried deep in his own thoughts. But William felt uncomfortable under the survey, and his face flushed to a glow. Why should he feel uncomfortable? What should cause the flush?

This. Since Janey's death, some months ago now, their circumstances had been more straitened than ever; of course, there had been expenses attending it, and Mrs. Halliburton was paying them off weekly. Bread and potatoes, and a little milk, would often be their food. On the previous night Jane had a sick headache. Some tea would have been acceptable, but she had neither tea nor money in the house; and she was firm in her resolution not to purchase on trust. On this morning early, when William rose, he found his mother down before him, at her work as usual. Her head felt better, she said; it might get quite well if she had only some tea; but she had not, and—there was an end of it. William went out, ardently wishing (in the vague profitless manner that he might have wished for Aladdin's lamp) that he had only a shilling to procure some for her. When, half an hour after, this shilling rolled out of the waste-paper basket, as he was shaking it in Mr. Ashley's counting-house, a strong temptation—not to take it, but to wish that he might take it, that it was not wrong to take it—rushed over him. He put it down on the desk and turned from it—turned from the temptation, for the shilling seemed to scorch his fingers. The remembrance of this wish—it sounded to him like a dishonest one—had brought the vivid colour to his face, under what he thought was Mr. Ashley's scrutiny. That gentleman observed it.

"What are you turning red for?"

This crowned all. William's face changed to scarlet.

Mr. Ashley was surprised. He came to the conclusion that some mystery must be connected with the shilling—something wrong. He determined to fathom it. "Why do you look confused?" he resumed.

"It was only at my own thoughts, sir."

"What are they? Let me hear them."

William hesitated. "I would rather not tell them, sir."

"But I would rather you did." Mr. Ashley spoke quietly, as usual; but there lay command in the quietest tone of Mr. Ashley's.

Implicit obedience had been enjoined upon the Halliburtons from their earliest childhood. In that manufactory Mr. Ashley was William's master, and he believed he had no resource but to comply with his desire. William was of a remarkably ingenuous nature; and if he had to impart a thing, he did not do it by halves, although it might tell against himself.

"When I found that shilling this morning, sir, the thought came over me to wish it was mine—to wish that I might take it without doing ill. The thought did not come over me to take it," he added, raising his truthful eyes to Mr. Ashley's, "only to wish that it was not wrong to do so. When you looked at me so earnestly, sir, I fancied you could see what my thoughts had been. And they were not honourable thoughts."

"Did you ever take money that was not yours?" asked Mr. Ashley, after a pause.

William looked surprised. "No, sir, never."

Mr. Ashley paused again. "I have known children help themselves to halfpence and pence, and think it little crime."

The boy shook his head. "We have been taught better than that, sir. And, besides the crime, money taken in that way would bring us no good, only trouble. It could not prosper."

"Tell me why you think that."

"My mother has always taught us that a bad action can never prosper in the end."

"I suppose you coveted the shilling for marbles; or for sweetmeats?"

"Oh no, sir. It was not for myself that I wished it."

"Then for whom? For what?"

This caused William's face to flush again. Mr. Ashley questioned till he drew from him the particulars—how that he had wished to buy some tea, and why he had wished it.

"I have heard," remarked Mr. Ashley, after listening, "that you have many privations to put up with."

"It is true, sir. But we don't so much care for them if we only can put up with them. My mother says she knows better days will be in store for us, if we only bear on patiently. I am sure we boys ought to do so, if she can. It is worse for her than for us."

There ensued another searching question from Mr. Ashley. "Have you ever, when alone in the egg-house, amidst its thousands of eggs, been tempted to pocket a few to carry home?"

For one moment William suffered a flash of resentment to cross his countenance. The next his eyes filled with tears. He felt deeply hurt.

"No, sir, I have not. I hope you do not fear that I am capable of it?"

"No, I do not," said Mr. Ashley. "Your father was a clergyman, I think I have heard?"

"He was intended for a clergyman, sir, but he did not get to the University. His father was a clergyman—a rector in Devonshire, and my mother's father was a clergyman in London. My uncle Francis is also a clergyman, but only a curate. We are gentlepeople, though we are poor. We would not take eggs or anything else."

Mr. Ashley suppressed a smile. "I conclude that you and your brothers live in hope some time of regaining your position in life?"

"Yes, sir. I think it is that hope that makes us put up with hard things so well."

"What do you think of being?"

William's countenance fell. "There is not so much chance of my getting on, sir, as there is for my brothers. Frank and Gar are hopeful enough; but I don't look forward to anything good for me. My mother says if I only help her I shall be doing my duty."

"Your sister died in a decline," remarked Mr. Ashley. "These home privations must have told upon her."

William's face brightened. "She had everything she wanted, sir; everything, even to port wine. Mrs. Reece and Dobbs took a liking to her when they first came, and they never let her want for anything. Mamma says that Jane's wants having been supplied in so extraordinary a manner, ought to teach us how certainly God is looking over us and taking care of us—that all things, when they come to be absolutely needed, will no doubt be supplied to us, as they were to her."

"What a perfect trust in God that boy seems to have!" mused Mr. Ashley, when he dismissed William. "Mrs. Halliburton must be a mother in a thousand. And he will make a man in a thousand, unless I am mistaken. Truthful, open, candid—I don't know a boy like him!"

About five minutes before the great bell was rung at one o'clock, William was called into the counting-house. "I have been casting up my cash and find I am a shilling short," observed Mr. Ashley, "therefore the shilling that you found is no doubt the missing one. I shall give it to you," he continued: "a reward for telling me the straightforward truth when I questioned you."

William took the shilling—as he supposed. "Here are two!" he exclaimed, in his surprise.

"You cannot buy much tea with one; and that is what you were thinking of. Would you like to be apprenticed to me?" Mr. Ashley resumed, drowning the boy's thanks.

The question took William by storm: he was at a loss what to answer. He would have been equally at a loss had he been accorded a whole week to deliberate upon it. He looked foolish, and said he could not tell.

"Would you like the business?" pursued Mr. Ashley.

"I like the business very well, sir, now I'm used to it. But I could not hope ever to get on to be a master."

"There's no knowing what you may get on to be, if you are steady and persevering. Masters don't begin at the top of the tree; they begin at the bottom and work up to it. At least, that is the case with a great many. In becoming an apprentice you would occupy a better position in the manufactory than you do now."

"Joe Stubbs is an apprentice, is he not, sir?"

"I will explain it to you, if you do not understand," said Mr. Ashley. "Joe Stubbs is apprenticed to one branch of the business, the cutting; John Braithwait is an apprentice to the staining, and so on. These lads expect to remain workmen all their lives, working at their own peculiar branch. You would not be apprenticed to any one branch, but to the whole, with a view to becoming hereafter a manager or a master; in the same manner that I might apprentice my son, were he intended for the business."

William thought he should like this. Suddenly his countenance fell.

"What now?" asked Mr. Ashley.

"I have heard, sir, that the apprentices do not earn wages at first. I—I am afraid we could not well do at home without mine."

"You need not concern yourself with what you hear, or with what others earn or don't earn. I should give you eight shillings a-week, instead of four, and you would retain your evenings for study, as you do now. I do not see any different or better opening for you," continued Mr. Ashley; "but should any arise hereafter, through your mother's relatives, or from any other channel, I would not stand in the way of your advancement, but would consent to cancel your indentures. Do you understand what I have been saying?"

"Yes, sir, I do. Thank you very much."

"You can speak to Mrs. Halliburton about it, and hear what her wishes may be," concluded Mr. Ashley.

The result was, that William was apprenticed to Mr. Ashley. "I can tell thee, thee hast found favour with the master," remarked Samuel Lynn to William. "He has made thee his apprentice, and has admitted thee, I hear, to the companionship of his son. They are proofs that he judges well of thee. Pay thee attention to deserve it."

It was quite true that William was admitted to the occasional companionship of Henry Ashley. Henry had taken a fancy to him, and would get him there to help him stumble through his Latin.

The next to be apprenticed to Mr. Ashley, and almost at the same time, was Cyril Dare. But when he found that he was to be the fellow-apprentice of William Halliburton, the two on a level in every respect, wages excepted—and of wages Master Cyril was at first to earn none—he was most indignant, and complained explosively to his father. "Can't you speak to Mr. Ashley, sir?"

"Where would be the use?" asked Mr. Dare. "There's not a man in Helstonleigh would brook interference in his affairs less than Thomas Ashley. If one of the two apprentices must leave, because they are too much for each other's company, it would be you, Cyril, rely upon it."

Cyril growled; but, as Mr. Dare said, there was no help for it. And he and William had to get on together in the best way they could. Cyril had thought that he should be the only gentleman-apprentice at Mr. Ashley's. There was a marked distinction observed in a manufactory between the common apprentices, who did the rough work, and what were called the gentleman-apprentices. It did not please Cyril that William should have been made one of the latter.

CHAPTER XI

THE SCHOOLBOYS' NOTES

As the time went on, Jane's brain grew very busy. Its care was the education of her boys—a perplexing theme. So far as the classics went, they were progressing. Frank and Gar certainly were not pushed on as they might have been, for Helstonleigh collegiate school was not at that time renowned for its pushing qualities; but the boys had a spur in themselves. Jane never ceased to urge them to attention, to strive after progress; not by the harsh reproaches some children have to hear, but by loving encouragement and gentle persuasion. She would call up pleasant pictures of the future, when they should have surmounted the difficulties of toil, and be reaping their reward. It had ever been her custom to treat her children as friends; as friends and companions, more than as children. I am not sure that it is not a good plan in all cases, but it undoubtedly is so where children are naturally well disposed and intelligent. Even when they were little, she would converse and reason with them, so far as their understandings would permit. The primary thing she inculcated was the habit of unquestioning obedience. This secured in their earliest childhood, she could afford to reason with them as they grew older; to appeal to their own sense of intelligence; to show them how to form and exercise a right judgment. Had the children been wilful, deceitful, or opposed to her, her plan must have been different; compulsion must have taken the place of reasoning. When they did anything wrong—all children will, or they are not children—she would take the offender to her alone. There would be no scolding; but in a grave, calm, loving voice she would say, "Was this right? Did you forget that you were doing wrong and would grieve me? Did you forget that you were offending God?" And so she would talk; and teach them to do right in all things, for the sake of right, for the sake of doing their duty to Heaven and to man. These lessons from a mother loved as Jane was, could not fail to take root and bear seed. The young Halliburtons were in fair training to make not only good, but admirable men.

Jane inculcated another valuable lesson. In all perplexity, trouble, or untoward misfortune, she taught them to look it full in the face; not to fly from it, as is the too-common custom, but to meet it and do the best with it. She knew that in trouble, as in terror, looking it in the face takes away half its sting: and so she was teaching them to look, not only by precept, but by example. With such minds, such training to work upon, there was little need to urge them to apply closely to their studies; they saw its necessity themselves, and acted upon it. "It is your only chance, my darlings, of getting on in life," she would say. "You wish to be good and great men; and I think perhaps you may be, if you persevere. It is a tempting thing, I know, to leave wearying tasks for play or idleness; but do not yield to it. Look to the future. When you feel tired, out of sorts, as if Latin were the greatest grievance upon earth, say to yourselves, 'It is my duty to keep on, and my duty I must do. If I turn idle now, my past application will be lost; but, if I persevere, I may go bravely on to the end.' Be brave, darlings, for my sake."

And the boys were so. Thus it would happen that when the rest of the school were talking, or idling, or being caned, the Halliburtons were at work. The head master could not fail to observe their steady application; and he more than once held them up as an example to the school.

So far so good. But though the classics are essential parts of a good education, they do not include all its requisites. And nothing else was taught in the college school. There certainly was a writing master, and something like an initiation into the first rules of arithmetic was attempted; but not a boy in the charity school, hard by, that could not have shamed the college boys in adding up a column of figures or in writing a page. As to their English—You should have seen them attempt to write a letter. In short, the college school ignored everything except Latin and Greek.

This state of affairs gave Jane great concern. "Unless I can organize some plan, my boys will grow up dunces," she said to herself. And a plan she did organize. None could remedy this so well as herself; she, so thoroughly educated in all essential branches. It would take two hours from her work, but for the sake of her boys she would sacrifice that. Every night, therefore, except Saturday, as soon as they had prepared their lessons for school—and in doing that they were helped by William—she left her work and became their instructor. History, geography, astronomy, composition, and so on. You can fill up the list.

And she had her reward. The boys advanced rapidly. As the months and quarters went on, it was only so much the more instruction gained by them.

I think you must be indulged with a glance at one of these college school notes. But, first of all, suppose we read one written by Frank.

"DEAR GLENN,—Thanks for wishing me to join your fishing expedition the day after to-morrow, but I can't come. My mother says, as I had a holiday from college one day last week, it will not do to ask for it again. You told me to send word this evening whether or not, so I drop you this note. I should like to go, and shall be thinking of you all day. Mind you let me have a look at the fish you bring home. Yours,

"FRANK HALLIBURTON."

The note was addressed "Glenn senior," and Gar was ordered to deliver it at Glenn senior's house. Glenn senior, who was a king's scholar, not a chorister, made a wry face over it when delivered, and sat down on the spur of the moment to answer it:

"DEER HALIBURTON,—Its all stuf about not asking for leve again what do the musty old prebens care who gets leve therell be enuff to sing without you tell your mother I cant excuse you from our party theirs 8 of us going and a stunning baxket of progg as good go out for a day's fishing has stop at home on a holiday for the benefit of that preshous colledge bring me word you'll come to-morrow at skool for we want to arrange our plans yours old fellow

"P GLENN."

Master P. Glenn was concluding his note when his father passed through the room and glanced over the boy's shoulder. He (Mr. Glenn) was a surgeon; one of the chief surgeons attached to the Helstonleigh infirmary, and in excellent practice. "At your exercise, Philip?"

"No, papa. I am writing a note to one of our fellows. I want him to be of our fishing party on Wednesday."

"Wednesday! Have you a holiday on Wednesday?"

"Yes. Don't you know it will be a saint's day?"

"Not I," said Mr. Glenn. "Saints' days don't concern me as they do you college boys. That's a pretty specimen of English!" he added, running his amused eyes over Philip's note.

"Are there any mistakes in it?" returned Philip. "But it's no matter, papa. We don't profess to write English in the college school."

"It is well you don't profess it," remarked Mr. Glenn. "But how is it your friend Halliburton can turn out good English?" He had taken up Frank's letter.

"Oh! they are such chaps for learning, the two Halliburtons. They stick at it like a horse-leech—never getting the cane for turned lessons. They have school at home in the evenings for English, and history, and such stuff that they don't get at college."

"Have they a tutor?"

"They are not rich enough for a tutor. Mrs. Halliburton's the tutor. What do you think Gar Halliburton did the other day? Keating was having a row with the fourth desk, and he gave them some extra verses to do. Up goes Gar Halliburton, before he had been a minute at his seat. 'If you please, sir,' says he to Keating, 'I had better have another piece.' 'Why so?' asks Keating. 'Because,' says Gar, 'I did these same verses with my brother at home a week ago.' He meant his eldest brother; not Frank. But, now, was not that honourable, papa?"

"Yes, it was," answered Mr. Glenn.

"That's just the Halliburtons all over. They are ultra-honourable."

"I should like to see your friend Frank, and inquire how he manages to pick up his English."

"Let me bring him to tea to-morrow night!" cried Philip eagerly.

"You may, if you like."

"Hurrah!" shouted Philip. "And you'll persuade him not to mind his mother, but to come to our fishing party?"

"Philip!"

"Well, papa, I don't mean that, exactly. But I do not see the use of boys listening to their mothers just in everything."

Philip Glenn seized his note, and added a postscript:—"My father sais you are to come to tea to-morrow we shall be so joly." And it was despatched to Frank by a servant in livery.

CHAPTER XII

A LESSON FOR PHILIP GLENN

Frank was as eager to accept the invitation as Philip had been to offer it. When the afternoon arrived, and school was over, Frank tore home, donned his best clothes, and then tore back again to Mr. Glenn's house. Philip received him in the small room, where he and his brother prepared their lessons.

"How is it that you and my boys write English so differently?" inquired Mr. Glenn, when he had made Frank's acquaintance.

Frank broke into a broad smile, suggested by the remembrance of Philip's English. "We study it at home, sir."

"But some one teaches you?"

"Mamma. She was afraid that we should grow up ignorant of everything except Latin and Greek; so she thought she would remedy the evil."

"And she takes you in an evening?"

"Yes, sir; every evening except Saturday, when she is sure to be busy. She comes to the table as soon as our lessons for school are prepared, and we commence English. The easier portions of our Latin and Greek we do in the day, I and Gar: we crib the time from play-hours; and my brother William helps us at night with the more difficult parts."

"Where is your brother at school?" asked Mr. Glenn.

"He is not at school, sir. He is at Mr. Ashley's, with Cyril Dare. William has not been to school since papa died. But he was well up in everything, for papa had taken great pains with him, and he has gone on by himself since."

"Can he do much good by himself?"

"Good!" echoed Frank, speaking bluntly in his eagerness; "I don't think you could find so good a scholar for his age. There's not one could come near him in the college school. At first he found it hard work. He had no one to explain difficult points for him, and was obliged to puzzle them out with his own brains. And it's that that has got him on."

Mr. Glenn nodded. "Where a good foundation has been laid, a hard-working boy may get on better without a master than with one, provided—"

"That is just what William says," interrupted Frank, his dark eyes sparkling with animation. "He would have given anything at one time to be at the college school with us; but he does not care about it now."

"Provided his heart is in his work, I was about to add," said Mr. Glenn, smiling at Frank's eagerness.

"Oh, of course, sir. And that's what William's is. He has such capital books, too—all the best that are published. They were papa's. I hardly know how I and Gar should get on, without William's help."

"Does he help you?"

"He has helped us ever since papa died; before we went to college, and since. We do algebra and Euclid with him."

"In—deed!" exclaimed Mr. Glenn, looking hard at Frank. "When do you contrive to do all this?"

"In the evening. Tea is over by half-past five, and we three—William, I, and Gar—turn at once to our lessons. In about two hours mamma joins us, and we work with her about two hours more. Of course we have different nights for different studies, Latin every night, Greek nearly every night, Euclid twice a week, algebra twice a week, and so on. And the lessons we do with mamma are portioned out; some one night, some another."

"You must be very persevering boys," cried Mr. Glenn. "Do you never catch yourselves looking off to play; to talk and laugh?"

"No, sir, never. We have got into the habit of sticking to our lessons; mamma brought us into it. And then, we are anxious to get on: half the battle lies in that."

"I think it does. Philip, my boy, here's a lesson for you, and for all other lazy scapegraces."

Philip shrugged his shoulders, with a laugh. "Papa, I don't see any good in working so hard."

"Your friend Frank does."

"We are obliged to work, sir," said Frank, candidly. "We have no money, and it is only by education that we can hope to get on. Mamma thinks it may turn out all for the best. She says that boys who expect money very often rely upon it and not upon themselves. She would rather turn us out into the world with our talents cultivated and a will to use them, than with a fortune apiece. There's not a parable in the Bible mamma is fonder of reading to us than that of the ten talents."

"No fortune!" repeated Mr. Glenn in a dreamy tone.

"Not a penny; mamma has to work to keep us," returned Frank, making the avowal as freely as though he had proclaimed that his mother was lady-in-waiting to the Queen, and he one of her pages. Jane had contrived to convince them that in poverty itself there lay no shame or stigma; but a great deal in paltry attempts to conceal it.

"Frank," said Mr. Glenn, "I was thinking that you must possess a fortune in your mother."

"And so we do!" said Frank. "When Philip's note came to me last night, and we were—were—"

"Laughing over it!" suggested Mr. Glenn, helping out Frank's hesitation, and laughing himself.

"Yes, that's it; only I did not like to say it," acknowledged Frank. "But I dare say you know, sir, how most of the college boys write. Mamma said then, how glad we ought to be that she can make time to teach us better, and that we have the resolution to persevere."

"I wish your mother would admit my sons to her class," said Mr. Glenn, half-seriously, half-jokingly. "I would give her any recompense."

"Shall I ask her?" cried Frank.

"Perhaps she would feel hurt?"

"Oh no, she wouldn't," answered Frank impulsively. "I will ask her."

"I should not like such a strict mother," avowed Philip Glenn.

"Strict!" echoed Frank. "Mamma's not strict."

"She must be. She says you shan't come fishing with us to-morrow."

"No, she did not. She said she wished me not to go, and thought I had better not, and then she left it to me."

Philip Glenn stared. "You told me at school this morning that it was decided you were not to come. And now you say Mrs. Halliburton left it to you."

"So she did," answered Frank. "She generally leaves these things to us. She shows us what we ought to do, and why it is right that we should do it, and then she leaves it to what she calls our own good sense. It is like putting us upon our honour."

"And you do as you know she wishes you would do?" interposed Mr. Glenn.

"Yes, sir, always."

"Suppose you were to take your own will for once against hers?" cried Philip in a cross tone. "What then?"

"Then I dare say she would decide herself the next time, and tell us we were not to be trusted. But there's no fear. We know her wishes are sure to be right; and we would not vex her for the world. The last time the dean was here there was a fuss about the choristers getting holiday so often; and he forbade its being done."

"But the dean's away," impatiently interrupted Philip Glenn. "Old Ripton is in residence, and he would give it you for the asking. He knows nothing about the dean's order."

"That's the very reason," returned Frank. "Mamma put it to me whether it would be an honourable thing to do. She said, if Dr. Ripton had known of the dean's order, then I might have asked him, and he could do as he pleased. She makes us wish to do what is right—not only what appears so."

"And you'll punish yourself by going without the holiday, for some rubbishing notion of 'doing right'! It's just nonsense, Frank."

"Of course we have to punish ourselves sometimes," acknowledged Frank. "I shall be wishing all day long to-morrow that I was with you. But when evening comes, and the day's over, then I shall be glad to have done right. Mamma says if we do not learn to act rightly and self-reliantly as boys we shall not do so as men."

Mr. Glenn laid his hand on Frank's shoulder. "Inculcate your creed upon my sons, if you can," said he, speaking seriously. "Has your mother taught it to you long?"

"She has always been teaching it to us; ever since we were little," rejoined Frank. "If we had to begin now, I don't know that we should make much of it."

Mr. Glenn fell into a reverie. As Mr. Ashley had once judged by some words dropped by William, so Mr. Glenn was judging now—that Mrs. Halliburton must be a mother in a thousand. Frank turned to Philip.

"Have you done your lessons?"

"Done my lessons! No. Have you?"

Frank laughed. "Yes, or I should not have come. I have not played a minute to-day—but cribbed the time. Scanning, and exercise, and Greek; I have done them all."

"It seems to me that you and your brothers make friends of your lessons, whilst most boys make enemies," observed Mr. Glenn.

"Yes, that's true," said Frank.

"Philip," said Mr. Glenn to his son that evening after Frank had departed, "I give you carte blanche to bring that boy here as much as you like. If you are wise, you will make a lasting friend of him."

"I like the Halliburtons," replied Philip. "The college school doesn't, though."

"And pray, why?"

"Well, I think Dare senior first set the school against them—that's Cyril, you know, papa. He was always going on at them. They were snobs for sticking to their lessons, he said, which gentlemen never did; and they were snobs because they had no money to spend, which gentlemen always had; and they were snobs for this, and snobs for the other; and he got his desk, which ruled the school, to cut them. They had to put up with a good deal then, but they are bigger now, and can fight their way; and, since Dare senior left, the school has begun to like them. If they are poor, they can't help it," concluded Philip, as if he would apologize for the fact.

"Poor!" retorted Mr. Glenn. "I can tell you, Master Philip, and the college school too, that they are rich in things that you want. Unless I am deceived, the Halliburtons will grow up to be men of no common order."

CHAPTER XIII

MAKING PROGRESS

Trifles, as we all know, lead to great events. When Frank Halliburton had gone home, in his usual flying, eager manner, plunging headlong into the subject of Mr. Glenn's request, and Jane consented to grant it, she little thought that it would lead to a considerable increase to her income, enabling them to procure several comforts, and rendering better private instruction than her own easy for her sons.

Not that she yielded to the request at once. She took time for consideration. But Frank was urgent; and she was one of those ever ready to do a good turn for others. The Glenns, as Frank said, did write English wretchedly; and if she could help to improve them without losing time or money, neither of which she could afford, why not do so? And she consented.

It certainly did occur to Mrs. Halliburton to wonder that Mr. Glenn had not provided private instruction for his sons, to remedy the deficiencies existing in the college school system. Mr. Glenn suddenly awoke to the same wonder himself. The fact was, that he, like many other gentlemen in Helstonleigh who had sons in the college school, had been content to let things take their chance: possibly he assumed that spelling and composition would come to his sons by intuition, as they grew older. The contrast Frank Halliburton presented to Philip aroused him from his neglect.

Jane consented to allow the two young Glenns to share the time and instruction she gave to her own boys. Mr. Glenn received the favour gladly; but, at first, there was great battling with the young gentlemen themselves. They could not be made to complete their lessons for school, so as to be at Mrs. Halliburton's by the hour appointed. At length it was accomplished, and they took to going regularly.

Before three months had elapsed, great improvement had become visible in their spelling. They were also acquiring an insight into English grammar; had learnt that America was not situated in the Mediterranean, or watered by the Nile; and that English history did not solely consist of two incidents— the beheading of King Charles, and the Gunpowder Plot. Improvement was also visible in their manners and in the bent of their minds. From being boisterous, self-willed, and careless, they became more considerate, more tractable; and Mr. Glenn actually once heard Philip decline to embark in some tempting scrape, because it would "not be right."

For it was impossible for Jane to have lads near her, and not gently try to counteract their faults and failings, as she would have done by her own sons; whilst the remarkable consideration and deference paid by the young Halliburtons to their mother, their warm affection for her, and the pleasant peace, the refinement of tone and manner distinguishing their home, told upon Philip and Charles Glenn with good influence. At the end of three months, Mr. Glenn wrote a note of warm thanks to Mrs. Halliburton, expressing a hope that she would still allow his sons the privilege of joining her own, and, in a delicate manner, begging grace for his act, enclosed four guineas; which was payment at the rate of sixteen guineas a year for the two.

Jane had not expected it. Nothing had been hinted to her about payment, and she did not expect to receive any: she did not understand that the boys had joined on those terms. It was very welcome. In writing back to Mr. Glenn, she stated that she had not expected to receive remuneration; but she spoke of her straitened circumstances and thanked him for the help it would be.

"That comes from a gentlewoman," was his remark to his wife, when he read the note. "I should like to know her."

"I hinted as much to Frank one day, but he said his mother was too much occupied to receive visits or to pay them," was Mrs. Glenn's reply.

As it happened, however, Mr. Glenn did pay her a visit. A friend of his, whose boys were in the college school, struck with the improvement in the Glenns, and hearing of its source, wondered whether his boys might not be received on the same terms, and Mr. Glenn undertook to propose it. The result of all this was, that in six months from the time of that afternoon when Frank first took tea at Mr. Glenn's, Jane had ten evening pupils, college boys. There she stopped. Others applied, but her table would not hold more, nor could she do justice to a greater number. The ten would bring her in eighty guineas a year; she devoted to them two hours, five evenings in the week.

Now she could command somewhat better food, and more liberal instruction for her own boys, William included, in those higher branches of knowledge which they could not, or had not, commenced for themselves. A learned professor, David Byrne, whose lodgings were in the London Road, was applied to, and he agreed to receive the young Halliburtons at a very moderate charge, three evenings in the week.

"Mamma," cried William, one day, with his thoughtful smile, soon after this agreement was entered upon, "we seem to be getting on amazingly. We can learn something else now, if you have no objection."

"What is that?" asked Jane.

"French. As I and Samuel Lynn were walking home to-day, we met Monsieur Colin. He said he was about to organize a French class, twelve in number, and would be glad if we would make three of the number. What do you say?"

"It is a great temptation," answered Jane. "I have long wished you could learn French. Would it be very expensive?"

"Very cheap to us. He said he considered you a sister professor—"

"The idea!" burst forth Frank, hotly. "Mamma a professor!"

"Indeed, I don't know that I can aspire to anything so formidable," said Jane, with a laugh. "A schoolmistress would be a better word."

Frank was indignant. "You are not a schoolmistress, mamma. I—"

"Frank," interrupted Jane, her tone changing to seriousness.

"What, mamma?"

"I am thankful to be one."

The tears rose to Frank's eyes. "You are a lady, mamma. I shall never think you anything else. There!"

Jane smiled. "Well, I hope I am, Frank; although I help to make gloves and teach boys English."

"How well Mr. Lynn speaks French!" exclaimed William.

"Does he speak it?"

"As a native. I cannot tell what his accent may be, but he speaks it as readily as Monsieur Colin. Shall we learn, mamma? It will be the greatest advantage to us, Monsieur Colin conversing with us in French."

"But what about the time, William?"

"Oh, if you will manage the money, we will manage the time," returned William, laughing. "Only trust to us, mother. We will make it, and neglect nothing."

"Then, William, you may tell Monsieur Colin that you shall learn."

"Fair and easy!" broke out Frank; a saying of his when pleased. "Mamma, I think, what with one thing and another turning up, we boys shall be getting quite first-class education."

"Although mamma feared we never should accomplish it," returned William. "As did I."

"Fear!" cried Frank. "I didn't. I knew that 'where there's a will there's a way.' Degeneres animos timor arguit," added he, finishing off with one of his favourite Latin quotations; but forgetting, in his flourish, that he was paying a poor compliment to his mother and his brother.

CHAPTER XIV

WILLIAM HALLIBURTON'S GHOST

This chapter may be said to commence the second part of this history, for some years have elapsed since the events last recorded.

Do you doubt that the self-denying patience displayed by Jane Halliburton, her persevering struggles, her never-fainting industry, joined to her all-perfect trust in the goodness and guidance of the Most High God, could fail to bring their reward? It is not possible. But do not fancy that it came suddenly in the shape of a coach-and-six. Rewards worth having are not acquired so easily. Have you met with the following lines? They are somewhat applicable.

"How rarely, friend, a good, great man inherits

Honour and wealth, with all his worth and pains!
It seems a fable from the land of spirits
When any man obtains that which he merits,
Or any merits that which he obtains.
For shame, my friend! renounce this idle strain:
What would'st thou have the good, great man obtain—
Wealth? title? dignity? a golden chain?
Or heaps of corpses which his sword hath slain?
Goodness and greatness are not means, but ends.
Hath he not always treasures, always friends,
The good, great man? Three treasures—
Love; and life; and calm thoughts, equable as infants' breath.
And three fast friends, more sure than day or night,
Himself; his Maker; and the angel, Death."

Jane's reward was in progress: it had not fully come. At present it was little more than that of an approving conscience for having fought her way through difficulties in the patient continuance of well-doing, and in the fulfilment, in a remarkable manner, of the subject she had had most at heart—that of giving her sons an education that would fit them to fulfil any part they might be called upon to play in the destinies of life—in watching them grow up full of promise to make good and great men.

In circumstances, Jane was tolerably at ease now. Time had wrought its changes. Mrs. Reece had gone—not into other lodgings, but to join Janey Halliburton on the long journey. And Dobbs—Dobbs!—was servant to Mrs. Halliburton! Dobbs had experienced misfortune. Dobbs had put by a good round sum in a bank, for Dobbs had been provident all her life; and the bank broke and swallowed up Dobbs's savings; and nearly all Dobbs's surly independence went with it. Misfortunes do not come alone; and Mrs. Reece died almost immediately after Dobbs's treacherous bank went. The old lady's will had been good to leave Dobbs something, but she had not the power to do so: the income she had enjoyed went at her death to her late husband's relatives. She had made Dobbs handsome presents from time to time, and these Dobbs had placed with the rest of her money. It had all gone.

Poor Dobbs, good for nothing in the first shock of the loss, paid Mrs. Halliburton for a bedroom weekly, and sat down to fret. Next, she tried to earn a living at making gloves—an employment Dobbs had followed in her early days. But, what with not being so young as she was, neither eyes nor fingers, Dobbs found she could make nothing of the work. She went about the house doing odd tasks for Mrs. Halliburton, until that lady ventured on a proposal (with as much deference as though she had been making it to an Indian Begum), that Dobbs should remain with her as her servant. An experienced, thoroughly good servant she required now; and that she knew Dobbs to be. Dobbs acquiesced; and forthwith went upstairs, moved her things into the dark closet, and obstinately adopted it as her own bedroom.

The death of Mrs. Reece had enabled Jane to put into practice a plan she had long thought of—that of receiving boarders into her house, after the manner of the dames at Eton. Some of the foundation boys in the college school lived at a distance, and it was a great matter with the parents to place them in families where they would find a good home. The wife of the head master, Mrs. Keating, took in half-a-dozen; Jane thought she might do the same. She had been asked to do so; but had not room while Mrs. Reece was with her. She still held her class in the evening. As one set of boys finished with her, others were only too glad to take their places: there was no teaching like Mrs. Halliburton's. Upon making it known that she could receive boarders, applications poured in; and six, all she had accommodation for, came. They, of course, attended the college school during the day. Thus she could afford to relinquish working at the gloves; and did so, to Samuel Lynn's chagrin: a steady, regular worker, as Jane had been, was valuable to the manufactory. Altogether, what with her evening class, and the sum paid by the boarders, her income was between two and three hundred a year, not including what was earned by William.

William had made progress at Mr. Ashley's, and now earned thirty shillings a week. Frank and Gar had not left the college school. Frank's time was out, and more than out: but when a scholar advanced in the manner that Frank Halliburton had done, Mr. Keating was not in a hurry to intimate to him that his time had expired. So Frank remained on, studying hard, one of the most finished scholars Helstonleigh Collegiate School had ever turned out.

There sat one great desire in Frank's heart; it had almost grown into a passion; it coloured his dreams by night and his thoughts by day—that of matriculating at one of the two Universities. The random and somewhat dim idea of Frank's early days—studying for the Bar—had become the fixed purpose of his life. That he was especially gifted with the tastes and qualifications necessary to make a good pleader, there could be no doubt about; therefore, Frank had probably not mistaken his vocation. Persevering in study, keen in perceptive intellect, equable in temper, fluent and persuasive in speech, a true type was he of an embryo barrister. He did not quite see his way yet to getting to college. Neither did Gar; and Gar had set his mind upon the Church.

One cold January evening, bright, clear, and frosty, Samuel Lynn stopped away from the manufactory. He had received a letter by the evening post saying that a friend, on his way from Birmingham to Bristol, would halt for a few hours at his house and go on by the Bristol mail, which passed through the city at eleven o'clock. The friend arrived punctually, was regaled with tea and other good things in the state parlour, and he and Samuel Lynn settled themselves to enjoy a pleasant evening together, Patience and Anna forming part of the company. Anna's luxuriant curls and her wondrous beauty—for, in growing up, that beauty had not belied the promise of her childhood—were shaded under the demure Quaker's cap. Something else had not belied the promise of her childhood, and that was her vanity.

Apparently, she did not find the evening or the visitor to her taste. He was old, as were her father and Patience: every one above thirty Anna was apt to class as "old." She fidgeted, was restless, and, just as the clock struck seven—as if the sound rendered any further inaction unbearable—she rose and was quietly stealing from the room.

"Where are thee going, Anna?" asked her father.

Anna coloured, as if taken by surprise. "Friend Jane Halliburton promised to lend me a book, father: I should like to fetch it."

"Sit thee still, child; thee dost not want to read to-night when friend Stanley is with us. Show him thy drawings. Meanwhile, I will get the chessmen. Thee'd like a game?" turning to his visitor.

"Ay, I should," was the ready answer. "Remember, friend Lynn, I beat thee last time."

"Maybe my skill will redeem itself to-night," nodded the Quaker, as he rose for the chessboard. "It shall try its best."

"Would thee like a candle?" asked Patience, who was busy sewing.

"Not at all. My chamber is light as day, with the moon so near the full."

Mr. Lynn went up to his room. The chessboard and men were kept on a table near the window. As he took them from it he glanced out at the pleasant scene. His window, at the back, faced the charming landscape, and the Malvern Hills in the horizon shone out almost as distinctly as by day. Not, however, on the landscape were Samuel Lynn's eyes fixed; they had caught something nearer, which drew his attention.

Pacing the field-path which ran behind his low garden hedge was a male figure in a cloak. To see a man, whether with a cloak or without it, abroad on a moonlight night, would not have been extraordinary; but Samuel Lynn's notice was drawn by this one's movements. Beyond the immediate space occupied by the house, the field-path was hidden: on one side, by the high hedge intervening between his garden and Mrs. Halliburton's; on the other, by a wall. The figure—whoever it might be—would come to one of these corners, stealthily peep at Samuel Lynn's house and windows, and then continue his way past it, until he reached the other corner, where he would halt and peep again, partially hiding himself behind the hedge. That he was waiting for something or some one was apparent, for he stamped his feet occasionally in an impatient manner.

"What can it be that he does there?" cried the Quaker, half aloud: "this is the second time I have seen him. He cannot be taking a sketch of my house by moonlight! Were it any other than thee, William Halliburton, I should say it wore a clandestine look."

He returned to the parlour, and took his revenge on his friend by checkmating him three times in succession. At nine o'clock supper came in, and at ten Mr. Stanley, accompanied by Samuel Lynn, left, to walk leisurely into Helstonleigh and await the Bristol mail. As they turned out of the house they saw William Halliburton going in at his own door.

"It is a cold night," William remarked to Mr. Lynn.

"Very. Good night to thee."

You cannot see what he is like by this light, especially in that disguising cloak, and the cap with its protecting ears. But you can see him the following morning, as he stands in Mr. Ashley's counting-house.

A well-grown, upright, noble form, a head taller than Samuel Lynn, by whose side he is standing, with a peculiarly attractive face. Not for its beauty—the face cannot boast of very much—but for its broad brow of intellect, its firm, sweet mouth, and its truthful dark-grey eyes. None could mistake William Halliburton for anything but a gentleman, although they had seen him, as now, with a white apron tied round his waist. William was making up gloves: a term, as you may remember, which means sorting them according to their qualities—work that was sometimes done in Mr. Ashley's room, on account of its steady light, for it bore a north aspect. A table, or counter, was fixed down one side, under its windows. Mr. Lynn stood by his side, looking on.

"Thee can do it tolerably well, William," he observed, after some minutes' close inspection.

William smiled. The Quaker never bestowed decided praise, and never thought any one could be trusted in the making-up department, himself and James Meeking excepted. William had been exercised in the making-up for the past eighteen months, and he thought he ought to do it pretty well by this time. Mr. Lynn was turning away, when his keen sight fell on several dozens at a little distance. He took up one of the top pairs with a hasty movement, knitted his brow, and then took up others.

"Thee has not exercised thy judgment or thy caution here, friend William."

"I did not make up those," replied William.

"Who did, then?"

"Cyril Dare."

"I have told Cyril Dare he is not to attempt the making-up," returned

Samuel Lynn, in severe tones. "When did he do these?"

"Yesterday afternoon."

"There, again! He knows the gloves are not made up in a winter's afternoon. I myself would not do it by so obscure a light. Thee go over these thyself when thee has finished the stack before thee."

Samuel Lynn was not one who spared work. He mixed the offending dozens together indiscriminately, and pushed them towards William. Then he turned to his own place, and went on with his work: he was also making up. Presently he spoke again.

"What does thee do at the back of my house of a night? Thee must find the walk cold."

William turned his head with a movement of surprise. "I don't do anything at the back of your house. What do you mean?"

"Not walk about there, watching it, as thee did last night?"

"Certainly not! I do not understand you."

Samuel Lynn's brows knit heavily. "William, I deemed thee truthful. Why deny what is a palpable fact?"

William Halliburton put down the pair of gloves he had in his hand, and turned to the Quaker. "In saying that I do not walk at the back of your house at night, or at the back of any house, I state the truth."

"Last night at seven o'clock, I saw thee parading there in thy cloak. I saw thee, I say, William. The night was unusually light."

"Last night, from tea-time until half-past nine, I never stirred out of my mother's parlour," rejoined William. "I was at my books as usual. At half-past nine I ran up to say a word to Henry Ashley. You saw me returning."

"But I saw thee at the back with my own eyes," persisted the Quaker. "I saw thy cloak. Thee had on that blue cap of thine: it was tied down over thy ears; and the collar of the cloak was turned up, to protect thee, as I surmised, from the cold."

"It must have been my ghost," responded William. "Should I be likely to pace up and down a cold field, for pastime, on a January night?"

"Will thee oblige me by putting on thy cloak?" was all the answer returned by Samuel Lynn.

"What—now?"

"Please."

William, laughing, went out of the room, and came back in his cloak. It was an old-fashioned cloak—a remarkable cloak—a dark plaid, its collar lined with red. Formerly worn by gentlemen, they had now become nearly obsolete; but William had picked this up for much less than half its value. He did not care much for fashion, and it was warm and comfortable in winter weather.

"Perhaps you wish me to put on my cap?" said William, in a serio-comic tone.

"Yes; and turn down the ears."

He obeyed, very much amused. "Anything more?" asked he.

"Walk thyself about an instant."

His lips smiling, his eyes dancing, William marched from one side of the room to the other. While this was in process Cyril Dare bustled in, and stood in amazement, staring at William. The Quaker paid no attention to his arrival, except that he took out his watch and glanced at it. He continued to address William.

"And thee can assure me to my face, that thee was not pacing the field last night in the moonlight, dressed as now?"

"I can, and do," replied William.

"Then, William, it is one of two things. My eyes or thy word must be false."

"Did you see my face?" asked William.

"Not much of that. With the ears down and the collar up, thy face was pretty effectually concealed. There's not another cloak like thine in all Helstonleigh."

"You are right there," laughed William; "there's not one half so handsome. Admire the contrast of the purple and green plaid and the scarlet collar."

"No, not another like it," emphatically repeated the Quaker. "I tell thee, William Halliburton, in the teeth of thy denial, that I saw thee, or a figure precisely similar to thee, parading the field-path last night, and stealthily watching my windows."

"It's a clear case of ghost," returned William, with an amused look at Cyril Dare. "How much longer am I to make a walking Guy of myself, for your pleasure and Cyril's astonishment?"

"Thee can take it off," replied the Quaker, his curt tone betraying dissatisfaction. Until that moment he had believed William Halliburton to be the very quintessence of truth. His belief was now shaken.

In the small passage between Mr. Ashley's room and Samuel Lynn's, William hung up the cloak and cap. The Quaker turned to Cyril Dare, who was taking off his great-coat, stern displeasure in his tone.

"Dost thee know the time?"

"Just gone half-past nine," replied Cyril.

Mr. Lynn held out his watch to Cyril. It wanted seventeen minutes to ten. "Nine o'clock is thy hour. I am tired of telling thee to be more punctual. And thee did not come before breakfast."

"I overslept myself," said Cyril.

"As thee dost pretty often, it seems. If thee can do no better than thee did yesterday, as well oversleep thyself for good. Look at these gloves."

"Well!" cried Cyril, who was a good-looking young man, in stature not far short of William. At least he would have been good-looking, but for his eyes; there was a look in them, almost amounting to a squint; and they did not gaze openly and honestly into another's eyes. His face was thin, and his features were well-formed. "Well!" cried he.

"It is well," repeated the Quaker; "well that I looked at them, for they must be done again. Firsts are mixed with seconds, thirds with firsts; I do not know that I ever saw gloves so ill made up. What have I told thee?"

"Lots of things," responded Cyril, who liked to set the manager at defiance, as far as he dared.

"I have desired thee never to attempt to make up the gloves. I now forbid thee again; and thee will do well not to forget it. Begin and band these gloves that William Halliburton is making ready."

Cyril jerked open the drawer where the paper bands were kept, took some out of it, and carried them to the counter, where William stood. Mr. Lynn interposed with another order.

"Thee will please put thy apron on."

Now, having to wear this apron was the very bugbear of Cyril Dare's life. "There's no need of an apron to paper gloves," he responded.

"Thee will put on thy apron, friend," calmly repeated Samuel Lynn.

"I hate the apron," fumed Cyril, jerking open another drawer, and jerking out his apron; for he might not openly disobey the authority of Samuel Lynn. "I should think I am the first gentleman that ever was made to wear one."

"If thee are practically engaged in a glove manufactory, thee must wear an apron, gentleman or no gentleman," equably returned the Quaker. "As we all do."

"All don't!" retorted Cyril. "The master does not."

"Thee are not in the master's position yet, Cyril Dare. And I would advise thee to exercise thy discretion more and thy tongue less."

The discussion was interrupted by the entrance of Mr. Ashley, and the room dropped into silence. There might be no presuming in the presence of the master. He sat down to his desk, and opened his morning letters. Presently a young man put his head in and addressed Samuel Lynn.

"Noaks, the stainer, has come in, sir. He says the skins given out to him yesterday would be better for coloured than blacks."

"Desire James Meeking to attend to him," said Mr. Lynn.

"James Meeking isn't here, sir. He's up in the cutters' room, or somewhere."

Samuel Lynn, upon this, went out himself. Cyril Dare followed him. Cyril was rather fond of taking short trips about the manufactory, as interludes to his work. Soon after, the master lifted his head.

"Step here, William."

William put down the gloves he was examining and approached the desk. "What sort of a French scholar are you?" inquired Mr. Ashley.

"A very good one, sir," he replied, after a pause given to surprise. "I know it thoroughly. I can read and write it as readily as I can English."

"But I mean as to speaking. Could you make yourself understood, for instance, if you were suddenly dropped down into a French town, where the natives spoke nothing but their own language?"

William smiled. "I don't think I should have much difficulty over it. I have been so much with Monsieur Colin that I talk as fast as he does. He stops me occasionally to grumble at what he calls l'accent anglais."

"I am not sure that I shall not send you on a mission to France," resumed Mr. Ashley. "You can be better spared than Samuel Lynn; and it must be one of you. Will you undertake it?"

"I will undertake anything that you wish me to do, sir, that I could accomplish," replied William, lifting his clear earnest eyes to those of his master.

"You are an exceedingly good judge of skins: even Samuel Lynn admits that. I want some intelligent, trustworthy person to go over to France, look about the markets there, and pick up what will suit us. The demand for skins is great at the present time, and the markets must be watched to select suitable bales before other bidders step in and pounce upon them. By these means we may secure some good bargains and good skins: we have succeeded lately in doing neither."

"At Annonay, I presume you mean, sir."

"Annonay and its neighbourhood; that's the chief market for dressed skins. The undressed pelts are to be met with best, as you are aware, in the neighbourhood of Lyons. You would have to look after both. I have talked the matter over with Mr. Lynn, and he thinks you may be trusted both as to ability and conduct."

"I will do my best if I am sent," replied William.

"Your stay might extend over two or three months. We can do with a great deal; both of pelts and dressed skins. The dressers at Annonay—Cyril, what are you doing there?"

Cyril could scarcely have told. He had come into the counting-house unnoticed, and his ears had picked up somewhat of the conversation. In his anger and annoyance, Cyril had remained, his face turned towards the speakers, listening for more.

For it had oozed out at Pomeranian Knoll, through a word dropped by Henry Ashley, that Mr. Ashley had it in contemplation to despatch some one from the manufactory on this mission to France, and that the some one would not be Samuel Lynn. Cyril received the information with avidity, never doubting that he would be the one fixed upon. To give him his due, he was really a good judge of skins—not better than William; but somehow Cyril had never given a thought to William in the matter. Greatly had he anticipated the journey to the land of pleasure, where he would be under no one's control but his own. In that moment, when he heard Mr. Ashley speaking to William upon the subject, not to him, Cyril felt at war with every one and everything; with the master, with William, and especially with the business, which he hated as much as he had ever done.

But Mr. Ashley was not one to do things in a hurry, and he had only broached the subject.

CHAPTER XV

"NOTHING RISK, NOTHING WIN"

It was Saturday night, the Saturday after the above conversation, and Mr. Lynn was making ready to pay the men. James Meeking was payer in a general way; but James Meeking was also packer; that is, he packed, with assistance, the goods destined for London. A parcel was being sent off this evening, so that it fell to Mr. Lynn's lot to pay the workmen. He stood before the desk in the serving-room, counting out the money in readiness. There was a quantity of silver in a bag, and a great many brown paper packets of halfpence; each packet containing five shillings. But they all had to be counted, for sometimes a packet would run a penny or twopence short.

The door at the foot of the stairs was heard to open, and a man's step came up. It proved to be a workman from a neighbouring manufactory.

"If you please, Mr. Lynn, could you oblige our people with twelve or fourteen pounds' worth of change?" he asked. "We couldn't get in enough to-day, try as we would. The halfpence seem as scarce as the silver."

Now it happened that the Ashley manufactory was that evening abundantly supplied. Samuel Lynn went into the counting-house to the master, who was seated at the desk. "The Dunns have sent in to know if we can oblige them with twelve or fourteen pounds' worth of change," said he. "We have plenty to-night; but to send away so much may run us very short. Dost thee happen to have any gold that thee can spare?"

Mr. Ashley looked at his own cash drawer. "Here are six, seven sovereigns."

"That will be sufficient," replied Samuel Lynn, taking them from his hand, and going back to the applicant in the serving-room. "How much has thee need of?" asked he.

"Fourteen pounds, please, sir. I have the cheque here, made out for it. Silver or copper, it doesn't matter which; or a little gold. I have brought a basket along with me."

Mr. Lynn gave the money, and took the cheque. The man departed, and the Quaker carried the cheque to Mr. Ashley.

Mr. Ashley put the cheque into one of the pigeon-holes of his desk. He had the account in duplicate before him, of the goods going off, and was casting it up. William and Cyril were both in the counting-house, but not engaged with Mr. Ashley. William was marking small figures on certain banded gloves; Cyril was looking on, an employment that suited Cyril amazingly. His want of occupation caught the Quaker's eye.

"If thee has nothing to do, thee can come and help me count the papers of coppers."

Cyril dared not say "No," before Mr. Ashley. He might have hesitated to say it to Samuel Lynn; nevertheless, it was a work he especially disliked. It is not pleasant to soil the fingers counting innumerable five-shilling brown-paper packets of copper money; to part them into stacks of twelve pence, or twenty-four halfpence. In point of fact, it was James Meeking's work; but there were times when Samuel Lynn, William, and Cyril had each to take his turn at it. Perhaps the two former liked it no better than did Cyril Dare.

Cyril ungraciously followed to the serving-room. In a few minutes James Meeking looked in at the counting-house. "Is the master ready?"

Mr. Ashley rose and went into the next room, carrying one of the duplicate lists. The men were waiting to pack—James Meeking and the other packer, a young man named Dance. The several papers of boxes were ready on a side counter; and Mr. Ashley stood with the list in his hand, ready to verify them. Had Samuel Lynn not been occupied with serving, he would have done this.

"Three dozen best men's outsizes, coloured," called out James Meeking, reading the marks on the first parcel he took up.

"Right," responded Mr. Ashley.

James Meeking laid it upon the packing-table—clear, except for an enormous sheet of brown paper as thick as card-board—turned to the side counter and took up another of the parcels.

"Three dozen best men's outsizes, coloured," repeated he.

"Right," replied Mr. Ashley.

And so on, till all the parcels were told through and were found to tally with the invoice. Then began the packing. It made a large parcel, about four feet square. Mr. Ashley remained, looking on.

"You will not have enough string there," he observed, as the men were placing the string round it in squares.

"I told you we shouldn't, Meeking," said George Dance.

"There's no more downstairs," was Meeking's answer, "I thought it might be enough."

Neither of the men could leave the parcel. They were mounted on steps on either side of it. Mr. Ashley called to William. "Light the lantern, and go upstairs to the string-closet. Bring down a ball."

Candles were not allowed to be carried about the premises. William came forth, lighted the lantern, and went upstairs. At the same moment, Cyril Dare, who had finished his disagreeable copper counting, strolled into the counting-house. Finding it empty, he thought he could not do better than take a survey of Mr. Ashley's desk, the lid of which was propped open. He had no particular motive in doing this, except that that receptacle might present some food or other to gratify his curiosity, which the glove-laden counters could not be supposed to do. Amidst other things his eyes fell on the Messrs. Dunns' cheque, which lay in one of the pigeon-holes.

"It would set me up for a fortnight, that fourteen pounds!" ejaculated he. "No one would find it out, either. Ashley would suspect any one in the manufactory before he'd suspect me!"

He stood for a moment in indecision, his hand stretched out. Should it be drawn back, and the temptation resisted; or, should he yield to it? "Here goes!" cried Cyril. "Nothing risk, nothing win!"

He transferred the cheque to his own pocket, and stole out of the counting-house into the small narrow passage which intervened between it and Mr. Lynn's room, where the parcel was being made up. Passing stealthily through the room, at the back of the huge parcel, which hid him from the eyes of the men and of Mr. Ashley, he emerged in safety into the serving-room, took up his position close to Samuel Lynn, and began assiduously to count over some shilling stacks which he had already verified. Samuel Lynn, his face turned to the crowd of men who were on the other side the counter receiving their wages, had not noticed the absence of Cyril Dare. Upon this probable fact Cyril had reckoned.

"Any more to count?" asked Cyril.

Samuel Lynn turned his head round. "Not if thee has finished all the packets." Had he seen what had just taken place, he might have entrusted packets of coppers to Mr. Cyril less confidently.

Cyril jumped upon the edge of the desk, and remained perched there. William Halliburton came back with the twine, which he handed to George Dance. Blowing out the lantern, he returned to the counting-house.

The parcel was completed, and James Meeking directed it in his plain, clerk-like hand—"Messrs. James Morrison, Dillon, and Co., Fore Street, London." It was then conveyed to a truck in waiting, to be wheeled to the parcels office. Mr. Ashley returned to his desk and sat down. Presently Cyril Dare came in.

"Halliburton, don't you want to be paid to-night? Every one's paid but you. Mr. Lynn's waiting to close the desk."

"Here is a letter for the post, William," called out Mr. Ashley.

"I am coming back, sir. I have not set the counter straight yet."

He received his money—thirty shillings a week now. He then put things straight in the counting-house, to do which was as much Cyril's work as his, and took a letter from the hands of Mr. Ashley. It contained one of the duplicate lists, and was addressed as the parcel had been. William generally had charge of the outward-bound letters now; he did not forget them as he had done in his first unlucky essay. He threw on the elegant cloak of which you have heard, took his hat, and went through the town, as far as the post-office, Cyril Dare walking with him. There they parted; Cyril continuing his way homewards, William retracing his steps.

All had left the manufactory except Mr. Ashley and Samuel Lynn. James Meeking had gone down. On a late night, as the present, when all had done except the master and Samuel Lynn, the latter would sometimes say to the foreman, "Thee can go on to thy supper; I will lock up, and bring thee the keys." Mr. Ashley was setting his desk straight—putting sundry papers in their places; tearing up others. He unlocked his cash drawer, and put his hand into the pigeon-hole for the cheque. It was not there. Neither there nor anywhere, that he could see.

"Why, where's that cheque?" he exclaimed.

It caused Samuel Lynn to turn. "Cheque?" he repeated.

"Dunns' cheque, that you brought me an hour ago."

"I saw thee put it in the second pigeon-hole," said the Quaker, advancing to the desk, and standing by Mr. Ashley.

"I know I did. But it is gone."

"Thee must have moved it. Perhaps it is in thy private drawer?"

Mr. Ashley shook his head: he was deep in consideration. "I have not touched it since I placed it there," he presently said. "Unless—surely I cannot have torn it up by mistake?"

He and Samuel Lynn both stooped over the waste-paper basket. They could detect nothing of the sort amidst its contents. Mr. Ashley was nonplussed. "This is a curious thing, Samuel," said he. "No one was in the room during my absence except William Halliburton."

"He would not meddle with thy desk," observed the Quaker.

"No: nor suffer any one else to meddle with it. I should like to see William. He may possibly throw some light upon the subject. The cheque could not vanish into thin air."

Samuel Lynn went down to James Meeking's, whom he disturbed at supper. He bade him watch at the entrance-gate for the return of William from the post-office, and request him to walk into the manufactory. William was not very long in making his appearance. He received the message—that the master and Mr. Lynn wanted him—and in he went with alacrity, having jumped to the conclusion that some conference was about to be held touching the French journey.

Considerably surprised was he to learn what the matter really was. He quite laughed at the idea of the cheque's being gone, and believed that Mr. Ashley must have torn it up. Very minutely went he over the contents of the paper-basket. Its relics were not there.

"It's like magic!" exclaimed William. "No one entered the counting-house; not even Mr. Lynn or Cyril Dare."

"Cyril Dare was with me," said the Quaker. "Verily it seems to savour of the marvellous."

It certainly did; and no conclusion could be come to. Neither could anything be done that night.

It was late when William reached home—a quarter past ten. Frank was sitting over the fire, waiting for him. Gar had gone to bed tired; Mrs. Halliburton with headache; Dobbs, because there was nothing more to do.

"How late you are!" was Frank's salutation; "just because I want to have a talk with you."

"Upon the old theme," said William, with a smile. "Oxford or Cambridge?"

"I say, William, if you are going to throw cold water upon it—But it won't put a damper upon me," broke off Frank, gaily.

"I would rather throw hot water on it than cold, Frank."

"Look here, William. I am growing up to be a man, and I can't bear the idea of living longer upon my mother. At my age I ought to be helping her. I am no nearer the University than I was years ago; and if I cannot get there, all my labour and my learning will be thrown away."

"Not thrown away," said William.

"Thrown away as far as my views are concerned. I must go to the Bar, or go to nothing—aut Cæsar, aut nullus. To the University I will go; and I see nothing for it but to do so as a servitor. I shan't care a fig for the ridicule of those who get there by a golden road. There's Lacon going to Christchurch at Easter, a gentleman commoner; Parr goes to Cambridge, to old Trinity."

"They are the sons of rich men."

"I am not envying them. We have not faced the difficulties of our position so long, and made the best of them, for me to begin envying others now. Wall's nephew goes up at Easter—"

"Oh, does he?" interrupted William. "I thought he could not manage it."

"Nor can he manage it in that sense. His father has too large a family to help him, and there's no chance of the exhibition. It is promised, Keating has announced. The exhibitions in Helstonleigh College don't go by right."

"Right or merit, do you mean, Frank?"

"I suppose I mean merit; but the one implies the other. They go by neither."

"Or you think that Frank Halliburton would have had it?"

"At any rate, he has not got it. Neither has Wall. Therefore, we have made up our minds, he and I, to go to Oxford as servitors."

"All right! Success to you both!"

Frank fell into a reverie. The friend of whom he spoke, Wall, was nephew of the under-master of the college school. "Of course I never expected to get to college in any other way," continued Frank, taking up the tongs and balancing them on his fingers. "If an exhibition did at odd moments cross my hopes, I would not dwell upon it. There are fellows in the school richer and greater than I. However, the exhibition is gone, and there's an end of it. The question now is—if I do go as a servitor, can my mother find the little additional expense necessary to keep me there?"

"Yes, I am sure she can: and will," replied William.

"There'll be the expenses of travelling, and sundry other little things," went on Frank. "Wall says it will cost each of us about fifteen pounds a year. We have dinner and supper free. Of course, I should never think of tea, and for breakfast I would take milk and plain bread. There'd be living at home between terms—unless I found something to do—and my clothes."

"It can be managed. Frank, you'll drop those tongs."

"What we shall have to do as servitors neither I nor Wall can precisely tell," continued Frank, paying no attention to the warning. "Wall says, brushing clothes, and setting tables for meals, and waiting on the other students at dinner, will be amongst the refreshing exercises. However it may be, my mind is made up to do. If they put me to black shoes, I shall only sing over it, and sit down to my studies with a better will when the shoes have come to an end."

William smiled. "Blacking shoes will be no new employment to you, Frank."

"No. And if ever I catch myself coveting the ease and dignity of the lordly hats, I shall just cast my thoughts back again to our early privations; to what my mother struggled through for us; and that will bring me down again. We owe all to her; and I hope she will owe something to us in the shape of comforts before she dies," warmly added Frank, the tears rising to his eyes.

"It is what I have hoped for years," replied William, in a low tone. "It is coming, Frank."

"Well, I think I do now see one step before me. You remember papa's dream, William?"

William simply bowed his head.

"Lately I have not even seen that step. Between ourselves, I was losing some of my hopefulness; and you know that is what I never lost, whatever the rest of you may have done."

"We none of us lost hope, Frank. It was hope that enabled us to bear on. You were over-sanguine."

"It comes to the same thing. The step I see before me now is to go to Oxford as a servitor. To St. John's if I can, for I should like to be with Wall. He is a good, plodding fellow, though I don't know that he is over-burthened with brains."

"Not with the quick brains of Frank Halliburton."

Frank laughed. "You know Perry, the minor canon? He also went to St. John's as a servitor. I shall get him to tell me—"

Frank stopped. The tongs had gone down with a clatter.

CHAPTER XVI

MRS DARE'S GOVERNESS

"There's such a row at our place!" suddenly announced Cyril Dare, at the Pomeranian Knoll dinner-table, one Monday evening.

"What about?" asked Mr. Dare.

"Some money's missing. At least, a cheque; which amounts to the same thing."

"Not quite the same," dissented Mr. Dare. "Unless it has been cashed."

"I mean the same as regards noise," continued Cyril. "There's as much fuss being made over it as if it had been fourteen pounds' weight of solid gold. It was a cheque of Dunns'; and the master put it into his desk, or says he did so. When he came to look for it, it was gone."

"Who took it?" inquired Mr. Dare.

"Who's to know? That's what we want to find out."

"What was the amount?"

"Fourteen pounds, I say. A paltry sum. Ashley makes a boast, and says it's not the amount that bothers him, but the feeling that we must have some one false near us."

"Don't speak so slightingly of money," rebuked Mr. Dare. "Fourteen pounds are not so easily picked up that it should be pleasant to lose them."

"I'm sure I don't want to speak slightingly of money," returned Cyril, rebelliously. "You keep me too short, sir, for me not to know the full value of it. But fourteen pounds cannot be much of a loss to Mr. Ashley."

"If I keep you short, you have forced me to it by your extravagances—you and the rest of you," responded Mr. Dare, in short, emphatic tones.

An unpleasant pause ensued. When the father of a family intimates that his income is diminishing, it is not a welcome announcement. The young Dares had been obliged to hear it often lately. Adelaide broke the silence.

"How was the cheque taken?"

"It was a cheque brought by Dunns' people on Saturday night, in exchange for money, and the master placed it in his open desk in the counting-house," explained Cyril. "He went into Lynn's room to watch the packing, and was away an hour. When he returned, the cheque was gone."

"Who was in the counting-house?"

"Not a soul except Halliburton. He was there all the time."

"And no one else went in?" cried Mr. Dare.

"No one," replied Cyril, sending up his plate for more meat.

"Why, then, it would look as if Halliburton took it?" exclaimed Mr. Dare.

Cyril raised his eyebrows. "No one would venture to suggest as much in the hearing of the manufactory. It appears to be impressed with the opinion that Halliburton, like kings, can do no wrong."

"Mr. Ashley is so?"

"Mr. Ashley, and downwards."

"But, Cyril, if the facts are as you state, Halliburton must have been the one to take it," objected Mr. Dare. "Possibly the cheque may have been only mislaid?"

"The counting-house underwent a thorough search this morning, and every corner of the master's desk was turned out, but nothing came of it. Halliburton appears to be in a world of surprise as to where it can have gone; but he does not seem to glance at the fact that suspicion may attach to him."

"Of course Mr. Ashley intends to investigate it officially?" said Mr. Dare.

"He does not say," replied Cyril. "He had the two packers before him this morning separately, inquiring if they saw any one pass through the room to the counting-house on Saturday night. He also questioned me. We had none of us seen anything of the sort."

"Where were you at the time, Cyril?" eagerly questioned Mr. Dare.

Knowing what we know, it may seem a pointed question. It was not, however, so spoken. Mr. Dare would probably have suspected the whole manufactory before casting suspicion upon his son. The thought that really crossed his mind was, that if his son had happened to be in the way and had seen the thief, whoever he might be, steal into the counting-house, so that through him he might be discovered, it would have been a feather in Cyril's cap in the sight of Mr. Ashley. And to find favour with Mr. Ashley Mr. Dare considered ought to be the ruling aim of Cyril's life.

"I was away from it all, as it happened," said Cyril, in reply to the question. "Old Lynn nailed me on Saturday to help to pay the men. While the cheque was disappearing, I was at the delightful employment of counting coppers."

"Did one of the packers get in?"

"Impossible. They were under Mr. Ashley's eye the whole time."

"Look here, Cyril," interrupted Mrs. Dare, the first word she had spoken: "is it sure that that yea-and-nay Simon of a Quaker has not helped himself to it?"

Cyril burst into a laugh. "He is not a Simon in the manufactory, I can tell you, ma'am. He is too much of a martinet."

"Will Mr. Ashley be at the manufactory this evening, Cyril?" questioned Mr. Dare.

"You may as well ask me whether the moon will shine," was the response of Cyril. "Mr. Ashley comes sometimes in an evening; but we never know whether he will or not, beforehand."

"Because he may be glad of legal assistance," remarked Mr. Dare, who rarely failed to turn an eye to business.

You may remember the party that formerly sat round Mr. Dare's dinner-table on that day, some years ago, when Herbert was pleased to fancy that he fared badly, not appreciating the excellences of lamb. Two of that party were now absent from it—Julia Dare and Miss Benyon. Julia had married, and had left England with her husband; and Miss Benyon had been discarded for a more fashionable governess.

This fashionable governess now sat at the table. She was called Mademoiselle Varsini. You must not mistake her for a French woman; she was an Italian. She had been a great deal in France, and spoke the language as a native—indeed, it was more easy to her now than her childhood's tongue; and French was the language she was required to converse in with her pupils, Rosa and Minny Dare. English also she spoke fluently, but with a foreign accent.

She was peculiar looking. Her complexion was of pale olive, and her eyes were light blue. It is not often that light blue eyes are seen in conjunction with so dark a skin. Strange eyes they were—eyes that glistened as if they were made of glass; they had at times a hard, glazed appearance. Her black hair was drawn from her face and twisted into innumerable rolls at the back of her head. It was smooth and beautiful, as if a silken rope had been coiled there. Her lips were thin and compressed in a remarkable degree, which may have been supposed to indicate firmness of character. Tall, and full across the bust for her years, her figure would have been called a fine one. She wore a closely-fitting dress of some soft, dark material, with small embroidered cuffs and collar.

What were her years? She said twenty-five: but she might be taken for either older or younger. It is difficult to guess with certainty the age of an Italian woman. As a rule they look much older than English women; and, when they do begin to show age, they show it rapidly. Mr. Dare had never approved of the engagement of this foreign governess. Mrs. Dare had picked her up from an advertisement, and had persisted in engaging her, in spite of the written references being in French and that she could only read one word in ten of them. Mr. Dare's scruples were solely pecuniary. The salary was to be fifty pounds a year; exactly double the amount paid to Miss Benyon; and he had great expenses on him now. "What did the girls want with a fashionable foreign governess?" he asked. But he made no impression upon Mrs. Dare. The lady was engaged, and arrived in Helstonleigh: and Mr. Dare had declared, from that hour to this, that he could not make her out. He professed to be a great reader of the human face, and of human character.

"Has there been any attempt made to cash the cheque?" resumed Mr. Dare to Cyril.

"Ashley said nothing about that," replied Cyril. "It was lost after banking hours on Saturday night; therefore he would be sure to stop it at the bank before Monday morning. It is Ashley's loss; Dunns, of course, have nothing to do with it."

"It would be no difficult matter to change it in the town," remarked Anthony Dare. "Anyone would cash a cheque of Dunns': it is as good as a banknote."

Cyril lifted his shoulders. "The fellow had better not be caught at it, though."

"What would be the punishment in Angleterre for such a crime?" spoke up the governess.

"Transportation for a longer or a shorter period," replied Mr. Dare.

"What you would phrase aux galères mademoiselle," struck in Herbert.

"Ah, ça!" responded mademoiselle.

As they called her "mademoiselle" we must do the same. There had been a discussion as to what she was to be called when she first came. Miss Varsini was not grand enough. Signora Varsini was not deemed familiar enough for daily use. Therefore "mademoiselle" was decided upon. It appeared to be all one to mademoiselle herself. She had been accustomed, she said, to be called mademoiselle in France.

Mr. Dare hurried over his dinner and his wine, and rose. He was going to find out Mr. Ashley. He was in hopes some professional business might arise to him in the investigation of the loss spoken of by Cyril. He was not a particularly covetous man, and had never been considered grasping, especially in business; but circumstances were rendering him so now. His general expenses were enormous—his sons contrived that their own expenses should be enormous; and Mr. Dare sometimes did not know which way to turn to meet them. Anthony drained him—it was Mr. Dare's own expression; Herbert drained him; Cyril wanted to drain him; George was working on for it. Small odds and ends arising in a lawyer's practice, that years ago Mr. Dare would scarcely have cared to trouble himself to undertake, were eagerly sought for by him now. He must work to live. It was not that his practice was a bad one; it was an excellent practice; but, do as Mr. Dare would, his expenses outran it.

He bent his steps to the manufactory. Had Mr. Ashley not been there, Mr. Dare would have gone on to his house. But Mr. Ashley was there. They were shut into the private room, and Mr. Ashley gave the particulars of the loss, more in detail than Cyril had given them.

"There is only one opinion to be formed," observed Mr. Dare. "Young Halliburton was the thief. The cheque could not go of itself; and no one else appears to have been near it."

In urging the case against William, Mr. Dare was influenced by no covert motive. He drew his inferences from the circumstances related to him, and spoke in accordance with them. The resentment he had once felt against the Halliburtons for coming to Helstonleigh (though the resentment was on Mrs. Dare's part rather than on his) had long since died away. They did not cross his path or he theirs; they did not presume upon the relationship; had not, so far as Mr. Dare knew, made it known abroad; therefore they were quite welcome to be in Helstonleigh for Mr. Dare. To do Mr. Dare justice, he was rather kindly disposed towards his fellow-creatures, unless self-interest carried him the other way. Cyril often amused himself at home by abusing William Halliburton: they were tolerable friends and companions when together, but Cyril could not overcome his feeling of dislike; a feeling to which jealousy was now added, for William found more favour with Mr. Ashley than he did. Cyril gave vent to his anger in explosions at home, and William was not spared in them: but Mr. Dare had learnt what his son's prejudices were worth.

"It must have been Halliburton," repeated Mr. Dare.

"No," replied Mr. Ashley. "There are four persons, of all those who were in my manufactory on Saturday night, for whom I will answer as confidently as I would for myself. James Meeking and George Dance are two. I believe them both to be honest as the day; and if additional confirmation that it was not they were necessary, neither of them stirred from beneath my own eye during the possible time of the loss. The other two are Samuel Lynn and William Halliburton. Samuel Lynn is above suspicion; and I have watched William grow up from boyhood—always upright, truthful and honourable; but more truthful, more honourable, year by year, as the years have passed."

"I dare say he is," acquiesced Mr. Dare. "Indeed, I like his look myself. There's something unusually frank about it. Of course you will have it officially investigated? I came down to offer you my services in the matter."

"You are very good," was the reply of Mr. Ashley. "Before entering farther into the affair, I must be fully convinced that the cheque's disappearance was not caused by myself. I—"

"By yourself?" interrupted Mr. Dare, in surprise.

"I do not think it was, mind; but there is a chance of it. I remember tearing up a paper or two after I received the cheque, and putting the pieces, as I believe, into the waste-paper basket. But I won't answer for it that I did not put them into the fire instead, as I passed it on my way to Mr. Lynn's room to call over the parcels bill."

"But you would not tear up the cheque?" cried Mr. Dare.

"Certainly not, intentionally. If I did it through carelessness, all I can say is, I have been very careless. No; I shall not stir in this matter for a day or two."

"But why wait?" asked Mr. Dare.

"If the cheque was stolen, it was probably changed somewhere in the town that same night; and this will soon be known. I shall wait."

Mr. Dare could not bring Mr. Ashley to a more business-like frame of mind. He left the manufactory, and went straight to the police-station, there to hold an interview with Mr. Sergeant Delves, a popular officer, with whom Mr. Dare had had dealings before. He stated the case to him, and desired Mr. Delves to ferret out what he could.

"Privately, you know, Delves," said he, winking at the sergeant, whom he held by the shoulder. "There's no doubt, in my opinion, that the cheque was changed that same night—probably at a public-house. Go to work sub rosâ—you understand; and any information you may obtain bring quietly to me. Don't take it to Mr. Ashley."

"I understand," replied Sergeant Delves, a portly man with a padded breast and a red face, who, in his official costume, always looked as if he were choking. "I'll see to it."

And he did so; and very effectively.

CHAPTER XVII

But the evening is not yet over at Pomeranian Knoll.

The dinner-table had broken up. Anthony Dare left the house soon after his father. Mrs. Dare turned to the fire for her after-dinner nap: the young ladies, Adelaide excepted, proceeded to the drawing-room. Adelaide Dare was thinner than formerly; and there was a worn, restless look upon her face, that told of care or of disappointment. She remained in her seat at the dessert-table, and, fencing herself round with a newspaper, lest Mrs. Dare's eyes should open, took a letter from her pocket and spread it on the table.

Viscount Hawkesley had never come forward to make her the Viscountess; but he had not given up his visits to Pomeranian Knoll, and Adelaide had never ceased hoping. It was one of his letters that she was poring over now. Two or three years ago she might have married well. A clergyman had desired to make her his wife. Adelaide declined. She had possibly her own private reasons for believing in the good faith of Lord Hawkesley. Adelaide Dare was not the first who has thrown away the substance to grasp the shadow.

Mademoiselle Varsini, on leaving the dinner-table, had gone up to the school-room. There she stirred the fire into a blaze, sat down in a chair, and bent her head in what seemed to be an attitude of listening.

She did not listen in vain. Soon, stealthy footsteps were heard ascending the stairs, and a streak of vermilion flashed into her olive cheek, and she pressed her hand upon her bosom, as if to still its beating. "Que je suis bête!" she murmured. French was far more familiar to her than her native tongue.

The footsteps proved to be those of Herbert Dare. A tall, handsome man now, better-looking than Anthony. He, Herbert, would have been very handsome indeed, but that his features were spoiled by the free expression they had worn in his youth—free as that which characterised the face of Mr. Dare. He was coming in to pay a visit to the governess. He paid her a good many visits: possibly thought it polite to do so. Some gentlemen are polite, and some are the contrary; some take every opportunity of improving their minds; some don't care whether they improve them or not. Herbert Dare we should place amidst the former: a thirst for foreign languages must, undoubtedly, be reckoned one of the desires for improvement. Minny Dare had one evening broken in upon a visit her brother was paying to mademoiselle, and she (very impertinently, it must be owned) inquired what he was doing there. "Taking an Italian lesson," Herbert answered, and he did not want Minny to bother him over it. Minny made a wry face at the books spread out between Herbert and mademoiselle, seated opposite each other at either end of the table, and withdrew with all speed lest the governess should press her to share in it. Minny did not like Italian lessons as much as Herbert appeared to do.

He came in with quiet footsteps, and the first thing he did was to—lock the door. The action may have been intended as a quiet reproof to Miss Minny: if so, it is a pity she was not there to profit by it.

"Have they asked for me in the salon?" began the governess.

"Not they," replied Herbert. "They are too much occupied with their own concerns."

"Herbert, why were you not here on Saturday night?" she asked.

"On Saturday night? Oh—I remember. I had to go out to keep an engagement."

"You might have spoken to me first, then," she answered resentfully. "Just one little word. I did come up here, and I waited—I waited! After the tea I came up, and I waited again. Ah! quelle patience!"

"Waited to give me my Italian lesson?"

Herbert Dare spoke in a voice of laughing raillery. The Italian girl did not seem inclined to laugh. She stood on one side the fire, and its blaze—it was the only light in the room—flickered on her compressed lips. More compressed than ever were they to-night.

"Now, what's the use of turning cross, Bianca?" continued Herbert, still laughing. "You are as exacting as if I paid you a guinea a lesson, and went upon a system of 'no lesson, no pay.' If—"

"Bah!" interrupted mademoiselle angrily: and it certainly was not respectful of Herbert, as pupil, to call her by her Christian name—if it was that which angered her. "I am getting nearly tired of it all."

"Tired of me! You might have a worse pupil—"

"Will you be quiet, then!" cried she, stamping her foot. "I am not inclined for folly to-night. You shall not say again you are coming here, if you don't come, mind, as you did on Saturday night."

"Well, I had an engagement, and I went straight off from the dinner-table to keep it," answered Herbert, becoming serious. "Upon my word of honour it was not my fault, Bianca; it was a business engagement. I had not time to come here before I went."

"Then you might have come when you returned," she said.

"Scarcely," replied he. "I was not home till two in the morning."

Bianca Varsini lifted her strange eyes to his. "Why tell me that?" she asked, her voice changing to one of mournful complaint. "I know you went out from dinner—I watched you out; and I saw you when you went out again. It was past ten. I saw you with my own eyes."

"You must have good eyes, Bianca. I went out from the dinner-table—"

"Not then—not then; I speak not of then," she vehemently interrupted. "You might have come here before you went out the second time."

"I declare I don't know what you mean," he said, staring at her. "I did not come in until two in the morning. It was past two."

"But I saw you," she persisted. "It was moonlight, and I saw you cross the lawn from the dining-room window, and go out. I was at this window, and I watched you go in the direction of the gate. It was long past ten."

"Bianca, you were dreaming! I was not near the house."

Again she stamped her foot. "Why you deceive me? Would I say I saw you if I did not?"

Herbert had once seen Bianca Varsini in a passion. He did not care to see her in one again. When he said that he had not come near the house, from the time of his leaving it on rising from dinner, until two in the morning, he had spoken the strict truth. What the Italian girl was driving at, he could not imagine: but he deemed it as well to drop the subject.

"You are a folle, Bianca, as you often call yourself," said he jestingly, taking her hands. "You go into a temper for nothing. I'd get rid of that haste, if I were you."

"It was my mother's temper," she answered, drawing her hands away and letting them fall by her side. "Do you know what she once did! She spit in the face of the Archevêque of Paris!"

"She was a lady!" cried Herbert ironically. "How was that?"

"He offended her. He was passing her in procession at the Fête Dieu, and he said something reproachful to her, and it put her in a temper, and she spit at him! She could do worse than that if she liked! She could have died for those who were kind to her; but let them offend her—je les en fais mes compliments!"

"I say, mademoiselle, who was your mother?"

"Never you mind! She was on the stage; not what you English call good. But she was good to me; and she wished me to be what she was not. When I was twelve she put me into a convent. La maudite place!"

Herbert laughed. He knew enough of French to understand the expression.

"It was maudite to me. I must not dance; I must not sing; I must not have my liberty to do the simplest thing on earth. I must be up in the morning to prayers; and then at my lessons all day; and then at prayers again. I did pray. I did pray to the Virgin to take me from it. I nearly prayed my heart out—and she never heard me! I had been there a year—figure to yourself, a year!—when my mother came to see me. She had been back in Italy. 'Take me away,' I said to her, 'before I die!' 'No, Bianca mia,' she answered, 'I leave you here that you may not die; that your life may be happier than mine is, for mine is the vraie misère.' I not tell you in Italian, as she spoke, for you not understand it," rapidly interrupted mademoiselle. "My mother, she continued to me: 'When you are instructed, you shall become a gouvernante in a family of the noblesse; you shall consort with the princes without shame; and perhaps you will make a good parti in marriage. Though you have no fortune, you will be accomplished; you will have the manière and the tournure; you will be belle.' Do you think me belle?" she abruptly broke off again.

"Enchanting!" answered Herbert. "Have I not told you so five hundred times?"

She stole a glance at the little old-fashioned oval glass which hung over the mantel-piece, and then went on.

"My mother would not take me out. Though I lay on the flagstones of the visitors' parlour, though I wept for it, she would not take me out. 'It is for your good, Bianca mia,' she said. And I remained there seven years. Seven years! Do you figure it?"

"But I suppose you grew reconciled?"

"We grow reconciled to the worst in time," she answered, dreamily gazing into the fire with her strange eyes. "I pressed down my despair into myself at first, and I looked out for the opportunity to run away. We were as closely kept as the nuns in their cells, in their barred rooms, in their grated chapel; but, sooner than not have had my will and get away, I would have set the place on fire!"

"I say, mademoiselle, don't you talk treason!" cried Herbert, laughing.

"Do you think I would not?" she answered, turning to him, a gleaming look in her eyes. "But I had to wait for the opportunity to escape; and, while I waited, news came that my mother had died. She caught cold one night when she was in her evening robe, and it settled in her throat, and formed a dépôt, and she died. And so it was all over with my escape! My mother gone, I had nowhere to fly to. And I stopped in that enfer seven years."

"You are complimentary to convents, Bianca. Maudite in one breath, enfer in another!"

"They are all that, and worse!" intemperately responded the Italian girl. "They are—mais n'importe; c'est fini pour moi. I had to beat down my heart then, and stop in one. Ah! I know not how I did it. I look back and wonder. Seven years!"

"But who paid for you all that time?"

"My mother was not poor. She had enough for that. She made the arrangements with a priest when she was dying, and paid the money to him. The convent educated me, and dressed me, and made me hard. Their cold rules beat down my rebellious heart; beat it down to hardness. I should not have been so hard but for that convent!"

"Oh, you are hard, then?" was the remark of Herbert Dare.

"I can be!" nodded Mademoiselle Varsini. "Better not cross me!"

"And how did you get out of the convent?"

"When I was nineteen, they sent me out into a situation, to teach music and my own language, and French and English. They taught well in the convent: I could speak English then as readily as I speak it now: and they gave me a box of clothes and four five-franc pieces, saying that was the last of my mother's effects. What cared I? Had they turned me out penniless, I should have jumped to go. I served in that first situation two years. It was easy, and it was good pay."

"French people?"

"But certainly: Parisians. It was not more than one mile from the convent. There was but one little pupil."

"Why did you leave?"

"I was put into a passion one day, and madame said after that she was frightened to keep me. Ah! I have had adventures, I can tell you. In the next place I did not stay three months; the ennui came to me, and I left it for another that I found; and the other one I liked—I had my liberty. I should have stayed in that, but one came and turned me out of it."

"A fresh governess?"

"No; a man. A hideous. He was madame's brother, and he was wrinkled and yellow, and his long skinny fingers were like claws. He wanted me to marry him; he said he was rich. Sell myself to that monster? No!—continue a governess, rather. One evening madame and my two pupils had gone to the Odéon, and he came to the little étude where I sat. He locked the door, and said he would not unlock it till I gave him a promise to be his wife. I stormed, and I stormed: he tried to take my hand, the imbécile! He laughed at me, and said I was caged—"

"Why did you not ring the bell?" interrupted Herbert.

"Bon! Do we have bells in every room in the old Parisian houses? I would have pulled open the window, but he stood against the fastening, laughing still; so I dashed my hand through a pane, and the glass clattered down to the court below, and the servants came out to look up. 'I cannot undo the étude door,' I called to them; 'come and break it open!' So that hideous undid it then, and the servants got some water and bathed my hand. 'But why need the signora have put her hand through the glass? Why not have opened the window?' said one. 'What is that to you?' I said. 'You will not have to pay for it. Bind my hand up.' They wrapped it in a handkerchief, and I put on my bonnet and cloak, and went out. Madeleine—she was the cook, and a good old soul—saw me. 'But where is the signorina going so late as this?' she asked. 'Where should I be going, but to the pharmacien's?' I answered; and I went my way."

"We say chemist's in England," observed Herbert. "Did he find your hand much damaged?"

"I did not go there. Think you I made attention to my hand? I went to the—what you call it?—cutler's shops, through the Rue Montmartre, and I bought a two-edged stiletto. It was that long"—pointing from her wrist to the end of her finger—"besides the handle. I showed it to that hideous the next day. 'You come to the room where I sit again,' I said to him, 'and you will see.' He told madame his sister, and she said I must leave."

Herbert Dare looked at her—at her pale face, which had gone white in the telling, her glistening, stony eyes, her drawn lips. "You would not have dared to use the stiletto, though!" he cried, in some wonder.

"I not dare! You do not know me. When I am roused, there's not a thing I would not dare to do. I am not ruffled at trifles: things that excite others do not trouble me. 'Bah! What matter trifles?' I say. My mother always told me to let the evil spirit lie torpid within me, or I should not die in my bed."

"I say," cried Herbert, half mockingly, "what religion do you call yourself?"

She took the question literally. "I am a Catholic or Protestant as is agreeable to my places," was the very candid answer. "I am not a dévote—a saint. Where's the use of it?"

"That is why you generally have those violent headaches on Sunday," said Herbert Dare, laughing. "You ought—"

There was an interruption. Rosa Dare's footsteps were heard on the stairs, and they halted at the door.

"Mademoiselle!" she called out.

Mademoiselle did not answer. Herbert Dare flung his handkerchief over the handle of the door in a manner that hid the key-hole. Rosa Dare tried the door, found it fastened, and went off grumbling.

"It's my belief mademoiselle locks herself in there to get a nap after dinner, as mamma does in the dining-room!"

She was heard to enter the drawing-room and slam the door. Herbert softly opened that of the school-room, and went down after his sister.

"I say, Herbert," cried Rosa, when he entered, "have you seen anything of mademoiselle?"

"I!" responded Herbert. "Do you think I keep mademoiselle in my pocket?"

"She goes and locks herself up in the school-room after dinner, and I can't think what she does there, or what she can be at," retorted Rosa.

"At her devotions, perhaps," suggested Herbert.

The words did not please Mrs. Dare, who had then joined the circle. "Herbert, I will not have Mademoiselle Varsini ridiculed," she said quite sternly. "She is a most efficient instructress for Rosa and Minny, and we must be careful not to give her offence, or she might leave."

"I'm sure I have heard of foreign women telling their beads till cock-crowing," persisted Herbert.

"Those are Roman Catholics. A Protestant, as is Mademoiselle Varsini—"

Mrs. Dare's angry words were cut short by the appearance of Mademoiselle Varsini herself. She, the governess, turned to Rosa. "What did you want just now when you came to the school-room door?"

"I wanted you here to show me that filet stitch," answered Rosa, slight impertinence peeping out in her tone. "And I don't see why you should not answer when I knock, mademoiselle."

"It may not always suit me to answer," was the calm reply of the governess. "My time is my own after dinner; and Madame Dare will agree with me that a governess should hold full control over her school-room."

"You are perfectly right, mademoiselle," acquiesced Mrs. Dare.

Mademoiselle went to the piano and dashed off a symphony. She was a brilliant player. Herbert, looking at his watch, and finding it later than he thought, hurried from the house.

CHAPTER XVIII

A VISION IN HONEY FAIR

The surmise that the missing cheque had been changed into good money on the Saturday night, proved to be correct. White, the butcher at the corner of the shambles, had given change for it, and locked up the cheque in the cash-box. Had he paid it into the bank on Monday, he would have found what it was worth. But he did not do so. Mr. White was a fat man with a good-humoured countenance and black hair. Sergeant Delves proceeded to his house some time on the Tuesday.

"I hear you cashed a cheque of the Messrs. Dunn on Saturday night," began he. "Who brought it to you?"

"Ah, what about that cheque?" returned the butcher. "One of your men has been in here, asking a lot of questions."

"A good deal about it," said the sergeant. "It was stolen from Mr. Ashley."

"Stolen from Mr. Ashley!" echoed the butcher, staring at Sergeant Delves.

"Stolen out of his desk. And you stand a nice chance, White, of losing the money. You should be more cautious. Who was it brought it here?"

"A gentleman. A respectable man, at any rate. Who says it's stolen?"

"I do," replied the sergeant, sitting himself down on the meat-block—rather a damp seat from its just having been washed with hot water. Delves liked to make himself familiar with his old friends in Helstonleigh in a patronising manner; it was only lately he had been promoted to sergeant. "Now! let's have the particulars, White."

"I had just shut up my shop, all but the door, when in come a gentleman in a cloak and cap. 'Could you oblige the Messrs. Dunn with change for a cheque, Mr. White?' says he, handing a cheque to me. 'Yes, sir,' said I, 'I can; very happy to oblige 'em. Would you like it in gold?' Well, he said he would like it in gold, and I gave it to him. 'Thank ye,' said he; 'I'd have got it nearer if I could, for I'm troubled to death with tooth-ache; but people are shut up:' and I noticed that he had kept his white handkerchief up to his mouth and nose. He went out with the gold, and I put up the cheque. And that's all I know about it, Delves."

"Don't you know who it was?"

"No, I don't. He had a cap on, with the ears coming down his cheeks; and, what with that, and the peak over his eyes, and the white handkerchief held up to his nose, I didn't so much as get a sight of his face. The shop was pretty near dark, too, for the gas was out. There was only a candle at the pay window."

"If a man came in disguised like that, asking to have a cheque changed into gold, it might have occurred to some tradesmen there'd be something wrong about it," cried the sergeant.

"I didn't know he was disguised," objected the butcher. "I saw it was a good cheque of the Messrs. Dunn, and I never gave a thought to anything else. I've had their cheques before to-day. Mr. William Dunn has dealt here this twenty year. But now that it's put into my head, I begin to think he was disguised," continued the butcher. "His voice was odd, thick and low, and he spoke as if he had plums in his mouth."

"Should you know him again?"

"Ay. That is if he came in dressed as he was then. I'd know the cloak out of a hundred. It was one of them old-fashioned plaid rockelows."

"Roquelaures," corrected the sergeant.

"Something of that. The collar was lined with red, with a little edge of fur on it. There's a few such shaped cloaks in the town now, made of blue serge or cloth."

"What time was it?" asked the sergeant.

"Just eleven. I was shutting up."

Sergeant Delves took possession of the cheque and proceeded to the office of Mr. Dare. A long conference ensued, and then they went out together towards Mr. Ashley's manufactory. On the road they happened to meet Cyril, and Mr. Dare drew him aside.

"Do you happen to know any one who wears an old-fashioned plaid cloak?" he asked.

"Halliburton wears one," replied Cyril: "the greatest object of a thing you ever saw. I say," continued Cyril, "what's old Delves doing with you?"

"Not much," carelessly said Mr. Dare. "He has been looking after a little private business for me."

"Oh, is that all?" and Cyril, feeling reassured, tore off on the errand he was bound for. For reasons best known to himself, it would not have pleased him that Sergeant Delves should be pressed into the affair of the cheque. At least, Cyril would have preferred that the matter should be allowed to rest.

He executed his commission, one that he had been charged with by Samuel Lynn, turned back, passed the manufactory, and took his way to Honey Fair on a little matter of his own. It was only the purchase of a dog—not to make a mystery of it. A dog that had taken Cyril's fancy, and for which he and the owner had not yet been able to come to terms. So he was going up again to try his powers of persuasion.

As he walked rapidly through Honey Fair, he saw a little bit of by-play on the opposite side. A young woman in a tattered gown, and a dirty bonnet drawn over her face, was walking along as rapidly as he. Her bent head, her humble attitude, her shrinking air, her haste to get out of sight of others, all betrayed that she, from some cause or other, was not in good odour with the world around. That she felt herself under a cloud, was only too apparent: it was a cloud of humiliation, for which she had only herself to thank. The women who met her hurried past with a toss of the head and then stood to peep after her as she disappeared in the distance.

She hurried—hurried past them—glad, it seemed, to be away from their stern looks and condemning eyes. Had you seen her, you would never have recognised her. In the dim eye, darker than of yore, the white cheek, the wasted form, no likeness remained of the once-blooming Caroline Mason.

Just as she passed opposite to Cyril, Eliza Tyrrett came out of a house and met her; and Eliza, picking up her skirts, lest they should become contaminated, swept past with a sidelong glance of reproach and a scornful gesture. Caroline's head only bent the lower as she glided away from her old companion.

It had been just as well that Charlotte East had not sent back that bundle, years ago, to surprise Anthony Dare. It was years now since Charlotte herself had come to the same conclusion.

CHAPTER XIX

THE DUPLICATE CLOAKS

Leaning back against the corner of the mantel-piece by the side of the blazing fire in his private room, calmly surveying those ranged before him, and listening to their tale with an impassive face, was Thomas Ashley. Sergeant Delves and Mr. Dare were giving him the account of the changing of the cheque, obtained from White the butcher. Samuel Lynn stood near the master's desk, his brow knit in perplexity, his countenance keen and anxious. The description of the cloak, tallying so exactly with the one worn by William Halliburton, led Mr. Dare to the conclusion, nay, to the positive conviction that the butcher's visitor could have been no other than William. The sergeant held the same view; but the sergeant adopted it with difficulty.

"It's an odd thing for him to turn thief," said he, reflectively. "I'd have trusted that young fellow, sir, with untold gold," he added, to Mr. Ashley. "Here's another proof how we may be deceived."

"I told you," said Mr. Dare, turning to Mr. Ashley, "that it could be no other than Halliburton."

"Thee will permit me to say, friend Dare, that I do not agree with thy deductions," interposed the Quaker, before Mr. Ashley could answer.

"Why, what would you have?" returned Mr. Dare. "Nothing can be plainer. Ask Sergeant Delves if he thinks further proof can be needed."

"Many a man has been hanged upon less," was the oracular answer of Sergeant Delves.

"What part of my deductions do you object to?" inquired Mr. Dare of the Quaker.

"Thee art assuming—if I understand thee correctly—that there is no other cloak in the city so similar to William's as to be mistaken for it."

"Just so."

"Then, friend, I tell thee that there is."

Mr. Dare opened his eyes. "Who wears it?" he asked.

"That is another question," said Samuel Lynn. "I should be glad to find out myself, for curiosity's sake."

Then Mr. Lynn told the story of his having observed a man, whom he had taken for William, walking at the back of his house, apparently waiting for something. "I saw him on two evenings," he observed, "at some considerable interval of time. The figure bore a perfect resemblance to William Halliburton; the height, the cloak, the cap—all appeared to be his. I taxed him with it. He denied it in toto, said he had not been walking there at all, and I believed he was attempting, for the first time since I have known him, to deceive me. I—"

"Are you sure he was not?" put in Mr. Dare.

"Thee should allow me to finish, friend. Last night I was home somewhat earlier than usual—thee can recollect why," the Quaker added, looking at Mr. Ashley. "I was up in my room, and I saw the same figure pacing about in precisely the same manner. William's denial had staggered me, otherwise I could have been ready to affirm that it was himself and no other. The moon was not up; but it was a very light night, and I marked every point in the cloak—it was as like William's as two peas are like each other. What he could want, pacing at the back of my house and of his, puzzled me much. I—"

"What time was this, Mr. Lynn?" interrupted the sergeant.

"Past eight o'clock. Later than the hour at which I had seen him on the two previous occasions. 'It is William Halliburton, of a surety,' I said to myself; and I thought I would pounce upon him, and so convict him of the falsehood he had told. I left my house by the front door, went down the road, past the houses, and entered the gate admitting into the field. I walked up quietly, keeping under the hedge as much as possible, and approached William—as I deemed him to be. He was then standing still, and gazing at the upper windows of my house. In spite of my caution, he heard me, and turned round. Whether he knew me or not, I cannot say; but he clipped the cloak around him with a hasty movement, and made off right across the field. I would not be balked if I could help it. I opened friend Jane Halliburton's back gate, and proceeded through the garden and house to the parlour, which I entered without ceremony. There sat William at his books."

"Then it was not he, after all!" cried Mr. Dare, interested in the tale.

"Of a surety it was not he. I tell thee, friend, he was seated quietly at his studies. 'Hast thee lent thy cloak to a friend to-night?' I asked him. He looked surprised, and said he had not. But, to be convinced, I requested to see his cloak, and he took me outside the door, and there was the cloak hanging up in the passage, his cap beside it. That is why I did not approve of thy deductions, friend Anthony Dare, in assuming that the cloak, which the man had on who changed the cheque, must be William Halliburton's," concluded Mr. Lynn.

"You say the man looked like William when you were close to him?" inquired Mr. Ashley, who thought the whole affair very curious, and now broke silence for the first time.

"Very much like him," answered Samuel Lynn. "But the resemblance may have been only in the cloak and cap. The face was not discernible; by accident or design, it was concealed. I think there need not be better negative proof that it was not William who changed the cheque."

Mr. Ashley smiled. "Without this evidence of Mr. Lynn's I could have told you it was waste of time to cast suspicion on William Halliburton to me," said he, addressing the sergeant and Mr. Dare. "Were you to come here and accuse myself, it would make just as much impression upon me. Wait an instant, gentlemen."

He went to the door, opened it, and called William. The latter came in, erect, courteous, noble—never suspecting the sergeant's business there could have anything to do with him.

"William," began his master, "who is it that wears a similar cloak to yours, in the town?"

"I am unable to say, sir," was William's ready reply. "Until last night," and he turned to Samuel Lynn with a smile, "I should have said there was not another like it. I suppose now there must be one."

"If there is one, there may be more," remarked Mr. Ashley. "The fact is, William, the cheque has been traced. It was changed at White's, the butcher; and the person changing it wore a cloak, it seems, very much like yours."

"Indeed!" cried William, with animation. "Well, sir, of course there may be many such cloaks in the town. All I can say is, I have not seen them."

"There can't be many," spoke up the sergeant, "if it be the old-fashioned sort of thing described to me."

William looked the sergeant full in the face with his open countenance, his honest eyes. No guilt there. "Would you like to see my cloak?" he asked. "It may be a guide, if you think the one worn resembled it."

The sergeant nodded. "I was going to ask you to bring it in, if it was here."

William brought it in. "It is one of the bygones," said he laughing. "I have some thoughts of forwarding it to the British Museum, as a specimen of antiquity. Stay! I will put it on, that you may see its beauties the better."

He threw the cloak over his shoulders, and exhibited himself off, as he had done once before in that counting-house for the benefit of Samuel Lynn. "I think the British Museum will get it," he continued, in the same joking spirit. "Not until winter's over, though. It is a good friend on a cold night."

Sergeant Delves' eyes were riveted on the cloak. "Where have I seen that cloak?" he mused, in a dreamy tone. "Lately, too!"

"You may have seen me in it," said William.

The sergeant shook his head. He lifted one hand to his temples, and proceeded to rub them gently, as if the process would assist his memory, never once relaxing his gaze.

"Did White say the changer of the cheque was a tall man?" asked Mr. Ashley.

"Yes," said Mr. Dare. "Whether he meant as tall as William Halliburton, I cannot say. There are not—why, I should think there are not a hundred men in the town who come up to that height," he added, looking at William.

"Yourself one of them," said William, turning to him with a smile.

Mr. Dare shook his head, a regret for his past youth crossing his heart. "Ay, once. I am beginning to grow downward now."

Mr. Ashley was buried in reflection. There was a curious sound of mystery about the tale altogether, to his ears. That there were many thieves in Helstonleigh, he did not doubt—people who would appropriate a cheque, or anything else that came in their way; but why the same person—if it was the same—should pace the cold field at night, watching Samuel Lynn's house, was inexplicable. "It may not be the same," he observed aloud. "Shall you watch for the man again?" he asked of Mr. Lynn.

"I shall not give myself much trouble over it now," was the reply. "While I was concerned to ascertain William's truthfulness—"

"I scarcely think you need have doubted it, Mr. Lynn," interrupted William.

"True. I have never doubted thee yet. But it appeared to be thy word against the sight of my own eyes. The master will understand—"

A most extraordinary interruption came from Sergeant Delves. He threw up his head with a start, and gave vent to a shrill, prolonged whistle. "It looks dark!" cried he.

"What didst thee say, friend Delves?"

"I beg pardon, gentlemen," answered the sergeant. "I was not speaking to any of you; I was following up the bent of mine own thoughts. It suddenly flashed into my mind who it is that I have seen in one of these cloaks."

"And who is it?" asked Mr. Dare.

"You must excuse me, sir, if I keep that to myself," was the answer.

"As tall a man as William Halliburton?"

The sergeant ran his eyes up and down William's figure. "A shade taller, I should say, if anything."

"And it struck me that the man who made off across the field was a shade taller," observed Samuel Lynn.

"Well, I can't make sense of it," resumed Mr. Dare, breaking a pause. "Let us allow, if you like, that there are fifty such cloaks in the town. Unless one, wearing such, had access to Mr. Ashley's counting-house, to this very room that we are now in, how does the fact of there being others remove the suspicion from William Halliburton?"

Mr. Dare had not intended wilfully to cause him pain. He had forgotten for the moment that William was a stranger to the doubt raised touching himself. Amidst the deep silence that ensued, William looked from one to the other.

"Who suspects me?" he asked, surprise the only emotion in his tone.

Sergeant Delves tapped him significantly on the shoulder. "Never you trouble yourself, young sir. If what has come into my mind be right, it isn't you who are guilty."

When he and Mr. Dare went out, Mr. Ashley followed them to the outer gate. As they stood there talking, Frank Halliburton passed. "Look here," thought the sergeant to himself, "there's not much doubt as to the black sheep—I see that: but it's as well, to be on the sure side. Young man," cried he aloud to Frank, in the authoritative, patronizing manner which Sergeant Delves was fond of assuming when he could, "what time did your brother William get home last Saturday night? I suppose you know, if you were at home yourself."

Frank looked at him rather haughtily. "I know," he replied. "I have yet to learn why you need know."

"Tell him, Frank," said Mr. Ashley, with a smile.

"It was a little after ten," said Frank.

"Did he go out again?" asked the sergeant.

"Out again at that time!" cried Frank. "No: he did not go out again. We sat talking together ever so long, and then went up to bed."

"Ah!" rejoined the sergeant. It was all he answered. And he wished Mr. Ashley good day, and departed with Mr. Dare.

"I am going to Oxford at Easter, Mr. Ashley," cried Frank with animation.

"I am pleased to hear it."

"But only as a servitor. I don't mind," he added, throwing back his head with pardonable pride. "Let me once get a start, and I hope to rise above some who go there as gentlemen-commoners. I intend to make this my circuit," he went on, half jokingly, half seriously.

"You are ambitious, Frank. I heartily wish you success. There's nothing like keeping a good heart."

"Oh yes, success is not doubtful. I'll do battle with all the obstructions in my course. Good afternoon, sir."

William, curious and anxious, could make nothing of his books that night at home. At length he threw up, put on the notable cloak, and went down to the manufactory. He found Mr. Ashley there; and the counting-house soon received an addition to its company in the person of Sergeant Delves. He had come in search of William. Not being aware that William was allowed the privilege of spending his evenings at home, he had supposed the manufactory was the place to find him in.

"I want you down at White's," said the sergeant. "Put on your cloak, will you be so good, Mr. Halliburton, and come with me?"

"Do you suspect me?" was William's answer.

"No, I don't," returned the sergeant. "I told you before, to-day, that I did not. The fact is"—dropping his voice to a mysterious whisper—"I want to do a little bit of private inquiry on my own account. I have a clue to the party: and I should like to work it out."

"If you have a sufficient clue, the party had better be arrested at once," observed Mr. Ashley.

"Ah, but it's not sufficient for that," nodded the sergeant. "No, Mr. Ashley, sir; my strong advice to you is, keep quiet a bit."

They started for the butcher's, William wearing his cloak and cap, and Mr. Ashley accompanying them. Mr. Ashley possessed his own curiosity upon various points; perhaps his own doubts.

"It is strange who this man can be who walks at the back of your house," observed Mr. Ashley to William, as they went along. "What can be his motive for walking there, dressed like you?"

"It is curious, sir."

"I should suppose it can only arise from a desire that he should be taken for you," continued Mr. Ashley. "But to what end? Why should he walk there at all?"

"Why, indeed!" responded William.

"What coloured gloves are you wearing?" abruptly interrupted Sergeant Delves.

William took his hands from beneath his cloak, and held them out. They were of the darkest possible colour, next to black; the shade called in the glove trade "corbeau." "These are all I have in use at present," he said. "They are nearly new."

"Have you worn any light gloves lately? Tan or fawn?"

"I scarcely ever wear tan gloves. I have not put on a pair for months."

They arrived at the butcher's and entered. White was standing at his block, chopping a bone in two. He lifted his head, and touched his hair to Mr. Ashley.

"Is this the gentleman who had the money of you for the cheque?" began Sergeant Delves, without circumlocution.

Mr. White put down his chopper, and took a survey of William. "It's like the cloak and cap that the other wore," said he.

Sergeants take up words quickly. "That the 'other' wore? Then you do not think it was this one?"

"No, I don't," decided the butcher. "The one who brought the cheque was a shorter man."

"Shorter!" repeated Mr. Ashley, remembering it had been said in his counting-house that the man who appeared to be personating William was thought to have the advantage the other way. "You mean taller, White."

"No, sir, I mean shorter. I am sure he was shorter. Not much, though."

There was a pause. "You observed that his gloves were tan, I think," said the sergeant.

"Something of that sort. Clean light gloves they were, such as gentlemen wear."

"Finally, then, White, you decide that this was not the gentleman?"

"Not he," said the butcher. "It's not the same voice."

"The voice goes for nothing," said Sergeant Delves. "The other one had plums in his mouth."

"Well," said the butcher, "I think I should have known Mr. Halliburton, in spite of any disguise, had he come in."

"Don't make too sure, White," said the sergeant, with one of his wise nods. "He who came might have turned out to be just as familiar to you as Mr. Halliburton, if he had let you see his face. The fact is, White, there's some one going about with a cloak like this, and we want to find out who it is. Mr. Halliburton would give a pound out of his pocket, I'm sure, to know."

"I'd give two," said Mr. Ashley, with a smile.

"Sir," asked the butcher of Mr. Ashley, "what about the money? Shall I lose it?"

"Now, White, just wait a bit," put in the sergeant. "If it was a gentleman that changed it, perhaps we shall get it out of him. Any way, you keep quiet."

They left the shop—standing a moment together before parting. The sergeant's road lay one way; Mr. Ashley's and William's another. "This only makes the matter more obscure," observed Mr. Ashley, alluding to what had passed.

"Not at all. It makes it all the more clear," was the cool reply of the sergeant.

"White says the man was shorter than Mr. Halliburton."

"It's just what I expected him to say," nodded the sergeant. "If I am on the right scent—and I'd lay a thousand pound on it!—the man who changed the cheque is shorter. I just wanted White's evidence on the point," he added, looking at William; "and that is why I asked you to come down, dressed in your cloak. Good night, gentlemen."

He turned up the Shambles. And Mr. Ashley and William walked away side by side.

The conversation at Mr. Dare's dinner-table again turned upon the loss of the cheque, and the proceedings thereon. It was natural that it should turn upon it. Mr. Dare's mind was full of it; and he gave utterance to various conjectures and speculations, as they occurred to him.

"In spite of what they say, I cannot help thinking that it must have been William Halliburton," he remarked with emphasis. "He alone was in the counting-house when the cheque disappeared; and the person changing it at White's, is proved to have borne the strongest possible resemblance to him; at all events, to his dress. The face was hidden—as of course it would be. People who attempt to pass off stolen cheques, take pretty good care that their features are not seen.

"But who hesitates to bring it home to Halliburton?" inquired Mrs. Dare.

"They all do—as it seems to me. Ashley won't hear a word: laughs at the idea of Halliburton's being capable of it, and says we may as well accuse himself. That's nothing: as Cyril says, Mr. Ashley appears to be imbued with the idea that Halliburton can do no wrong: but now Delves has veered round. He shifts the blame entirely off Halliburton."

"Upon whom does he shift it?" asked Anthony Dare.

"He won't say," replied Mr. Dare. "He has grown mysterious over it since the afternoon; nodding and winking, and giving no explanation. He says he knows who it is who possesses the second cloak."

"The second cloak!" The words were a puzzle to most at table, and Mr. Dare had to explain that another cloak, similar to that worn by William Halliburton, was supposed to be in existence.

Cyril looked up, with wonder marked on his face. "Does Delves say there are two such cloaks?" asked he.

"That there are two such cloaks appears to be an indisputable fact," replied Mr. Dare. "The one cloak was parading behind the Halliburtons' house last night. Samuel Lynn went up to it—"

"The cloak parading tout seul—alone?" interrupted Signora Varsini, with a perplexed air.

A laugh went round the table. "Accompanied by the wearer, mademoiselle," said Mr. Dare, continuing the account of Samuel Lynn's adventure. "Thus the fact of there being two cloaks is established," he proceeded. "Still, that tells nothing; unless the owner of the other has access to Mr. Ashley's counting-house. I pointed this fact out to them. But Delves—which is most unaccountable—differed from me; and when we parted he expressed an opinion, with that confident nod of his, that it was not Halliburton's cloak which had been in the mischief at the butcher's, but the other."

"What a thundering falsehood!" burst forth Herbert Dare.

"Sir!" cried Mr. Dare, while all around the table stared at Herbert's excited manner.

Herbert had the grace to feel ashamed of his abrupt and intemperate rudeness. "I beg your pardon, sir; I spoke in my surprise. I mean that Delves must be telling a falsehood, if he seeks to throw the guilt off Halliburton. The very fact of the fellow's wearing a strange cloak such as that, when he went to get rid of the cheque, must be proof positive of Halliburton's guilt."

"So I think," acquiesced Mr. Dare.

"What sort of a cloak is this that you laugh at, and call scarce?" inquired the governess.

"The greatest scarecrow of a thing you can conceive, mademoiselle," responded Mr. Dare. "I had the pleasure of seeing it to-day on Halliburton. It is a dark green-and-blue Scotch plaid, made very full, with a turned up collar lined with red, and a bit of fur edging it."

"Plaid? Plaid?" repeated mademoiselle. "Why it must be—"

"What?" asked Mr. Dare, for she had stopped.

"It must be very ugly," concluded she. But somehow Mr. Dare gathered an impression that it was not what she had been about to say.

"What is it that Delves says about the cloaks?" eagerly questioned Cyril. "I cannot make it out."

"Delves says he knows who it is that owns the other; and that it was the other which went to change the cheque at White's."

"What mysterious words, papa!" cried Adelaide. "The cloak went to change the cheque!"

"They were Delves' own words," replied Mr. Dare. "He did seem remarkably mysterious over it."

"Is he going to hunt up the other cloak?" resumed Cyril.

"I conclude so. He was pondering over it for some time before he could remember who it was that he had seen wear a similar cloak. When the recollection came to him, he started up with surprise. Sharp men, these police-officers!" added Mr. Dare. "They forget nothing."

"And they ferret out everything," said Herbert with some testiness. "Instead of wasting time over vain speculations touching cloaks, why does not he secure Halliburton? It is impossible that the other cloak—if there is another—could have had anything to do with the affair."

"I dropped a note to Delves after he left me, recommending him to follow up the suspicion on Halliburton, whether Mr. Ashley is agreeable or not," said Mr. Dare. "I have rarely in my life met with a stronger case of presumptive evidence."

So, many, besides Mr. Dare, would have felt inclined to say. Herbert, like his father, was firm in the belief that William Halliburton must have taken the money; that it must have been he who paid the visit to the butcher. What Cyril thought may be best inferred from his actions. A sudden fear had come over him that Sergeant Delves was really going to search out the other cloak. A most inconvenient procedure for Cyril, lest, in the process, the sergeant should search out him. He laid down his knife and fork. He had had quite enough dinner for one day.

"Are you not hungry, Cyril?" asked his mother.

"I had a tremendous lunch," answered Cyril. "I can't eat more now."

He sat at the table until they had finished, feeling that he was being choked with dread. But that a guilty conscience deprives us of free action, he would have left the table and gone about some work he was now eager to do.

He rose when the rest did, looked about for a pair of large scissors, and glided with them up the staircase, his eyes and ears on the alert, lest there should be any watching him. No human being in that house had the slightest knowledge of what Cyril was about to do, or that he was going to do anything; but to Cyril's guilty conscience it seemed that all must be on the look-out.

A candle and scissors in hand he stole up to Herbert's room and locked himself in. Inside a closet within the room hung a dark blue camlet cloak, and Cyril took it from the hook. It had a plaid lining: a lining of the precise pattern and colours that the material of William Halliburton's cloak was composed of. The cloak was of the same full, old-fashioned make; its collar was lined with red, tipped with fur: in short, the one cloak worn on the right side and the other worn on the wrong side, could not have been told apart. This cloak belonged to Herbert Dare; occasionally, though not often, he went out at dusk, wearing it wrong side outermost. It was he, no doubt, whom Sergeant Delves had seen wearing one. He was a little taller than William Halliburton, towering above six feet. What his motive had been in causing a cloak to be lined so that, turned, it should resemble William Halliburton's, or whether the similarity in the lining had been accidental, was only known to Herbert himself.

With trembling fingers, and sharp scissors that were not particular where they cut, Cyril began his task of taking out this plaid lining. That he had worn it to the butcher's, and that he feared it might tell tales of him, were facts only too apparent. Better put it out of the way for ever! Unpicking, cutting, snipping, Cyril tore away at the lining, and at length got it out, the cloak suffering considerable damage in the shape of cuts and rents, and loose threads. Hanging the cloak up again, he twisted the lining together.

He was thus engaged when the handle of the door was briskly turned, as if some one essayed to enter who had not expected to find it fastened. Cyril dashed the lining under the bed, and made a spring to the window. To leap out? surely not: for the fall would have killed him. But he had nearly lost all presence of mind in his perplexity and fear.

Another turn at the handle, and the steps went on their way. Cyril thought he recognized them for the housemaid's, Betsy. He supposed she was going her evening round of the chambers. Gathering the lining under his arm, he halted to think. His hands shook, and his face was white.

What should he do with this tell-tale thing? He could not eat it; he dared not burn it. There was no room, of those which had fires, where he might make sure of being alone: and the smell would alarm the house. What was he to do with it?

Dig a hole and bury it, came a prompting voice within him; and Cyril waited for no better suggestion, but crept with it down the stairs, and out to the garden.

Seizing a spade, he dug a hole rapidly in an unfrequented place; and when it was large enough thrust the stuff in. Then he covered it over again, to leave the spot apparently as he found it.

"I wish those stars would give a stronger light," grumbled Cyril, looking up at the dark blue canopy. "I must come again in the morning, I suppose, and see that it's all safe. It wouldn't do to bring a lantern."

Now it happened that Mr. Herbert Dare was bound on a private errand that evening. His intention was to go abroad in his cloak while he executed it. Just about the time that Cyril was putting the finishing touch to the hole, Herbert went up to his room to get the cloak.

To get the cloak, indeed! When Herbert opened the closet-door, nothing except the mutilated object just described met his eye. A torn, cut thing, the threads hanging from it loosely. Nothing could exceed Herbert's consternation as he stared at it. He thought he must be in a dream. Was it his cloak? Just before dinner, when he came up to wash his hands, he had seen his cloak hanging there, perfect. He shook it, he pulled it, he peered at it. His cloak it certainly was; but who had destroyed it? A suspicion flashed into his mind that it might be the governess. He made but a few steps to the school-room, carrying the cloak with him.

The governess was sitting there, listlessly enough. Perhaps she was waiting for him. "I say, mademoiselle," he began, "what on earth have you been doing to my cloak?"

"To your cloak!" responded she. "What should I have been doing to it?"

"Look here," he said, spreading it out before her. "Who or what has done this? It was all right when I went down to dinner."

She stared at it in astonishment great as Herbert's, and threw off a volley of surprise in her foreign tongue. But she was a shrewd woman. Ay, never was there a shrewder than Bianca Varsini. Mr. Sergeant Delves was not a bad hand at ferreting out conclusions; but she would have beaten the sergeant hollow.

"Tenez," cried she, putting up her forefinger in thought, as she gazed at the cloak. "Cyril did this."

"Cyril!"

She nodded her head. "You stood it out to me that you did not come in on Saturday evening and go out again between ten and eleven—"

"I did not," interrupted Herbert. "I told you truth, but you would not believe me."

"But this cloak went out. And it was turned the plaid side outwards, and your cap was on, tied down at the ears. Naturally I thought it was you. It must have been Cyril! Do you comprehend?"

"No, I don't," said Herbert. "How mysteriously you are speaking!"

"It must have been Cyril who robbed Mr. Ashley."

"Mademoiselle!" interrupted Herbert indignantly.

"Ecoutez, mon ami. He was blanched as white as a mouchoir, while your father spoke of it at dinner—did you see that he could not eat? 'You look guilty, Monsieur Cyril,' I said to myself, not really thinking him to be so. But be persuaded it was no other. He must have taken the paper-money—or what you call it—and come home here for your cloak and cap to wear, while he changed it for gold, thinking it would fall on that other one who wears the cloak; that William Hall—I cannot say the name; c'est trop dur pour les lèvres. It is Cyril, and no other. He has turned afraid now, and has torn the lining out."

Herbert could make no rejoinder at first, partly in dismay, partly in astonishment. "It cannot have been Cyril!" he reiterated.

"I say it is Cyril," persisted the young lady. "I saw him creep up the stairs after dinner, with a candle and your mother's great scissors in his hand. He did not see me. I was in the dark, looking out of my room. Depend he was going to do it then."

"Then, of all blind idiots, Cyril's the worst!—if he did take the cheque," uttered Herbert. "Should it become known, he is done for; and that for life. And my father helping to fan the flame!"

The governess shrugged her shoulders. "I not like Cyril," she said. "I have never liked him since I came."

"But you will not tell against him!" cried Herbert, in fear.

"No, no, no. Tell against your brother! Why should I? It is no concern of mine. Unless people meddle with me, I not meddle with them. Cyril is safe, for me."

"What on earth am I to do for my cloak to-night?" debated Herbert. "I was going—going where I want it."

"Why you want it so to-night?" asked mademoiselle sharply.

"Because it's cold," responded Herbert. "The cloak was warmer than my overcoat is."

"Last night you go out, to-night you go out, to-morrow you go out. It is always so now!"

"I have a lot of perplexing business upon me," answered Herbert. "I have no time to see about it in the day."

Some little time longer he remained talking with her, partially disputing. The Italian, from some cause or other, went into ill-humour and said some provoking things. Herbert, it must be confessed, received them with good temper, and she grew more affable. When he left her, she offered to pick the loose threads out of the cloak, and hem up the bottom.

"You'll lock the door while you do it?" he urged.

"I will take it to my chamber," she said. "No one will molest me there."

Herbert left it with her and went out. Cyril went out. Anthony had already gone out. Mr. Dare remained at home. He and his wife were conversing over the dining-room fire, in the course of the evening, when Joseph came in.

"You are wanted, please, sir," he said to his master.

"Who wants me?" asked Mr. Dare.

"It's Policeman Delves, sir."

"Oh, show him in here," said Mr. Dare. "I hope something will be done in this," he added to his wife. "It may turn out a good slice of luck for me."

Sergeant Delves came in. In point of fact, he had just returned from that interview with the butcher, where he had been accompanied by Mr. Ashley and William.

"Well, Delves, did you get my note?" asked Mr. Dare.

"Yes, sir, I did," said the sergeant, taking the seat offered him. "It's what I have come up about."

"Do you intend to act upon my advice?"

"Why—no, I think not," replied the sergeant. "Not, at any rate, until I have had a talk with you."

"What will you take?"

"Well, sir, the night's cold. I don't mind a drop of brandy-and-water."

It was brought, and Mr. Dare joined his visitor in partaking of it. He agreed with him that the night was cold. But nothing could Mr. Dare make of him. As often as he turned the conversation on the subject in hand, so often did the sergeant turn it off again. Mrs. Dare grew tired of listening to nothing; and she departed, leaving them together.

Then the manner of Sergeant Delves changed. He drew his chair forward; and bent towards Mr. Dare.

"You have been urging me to go against young Halliburton," he began. "It won't do. Halliburton no more fingered that cheque, or had anything to do with it, than you or I had. Mr. Dare, don't you stir in this matter any further."

"My present intention is to stir it to the bottom," returned Mr. Dare.

"Look here," said the sergeant in an undertone; "I am not obliged to take notice of offences that don't come legally in my way. Many a thing has been done in this town—ay, and is being done now—that I am obliged to wink at; it don't lay right in my duty to take notice of it, so I keep my eyes shut. Now that's just it in this case. So long as the parties concerned, Mr. Ashley, or White, don't put it into my hands officially, I am not obliged to take so-and-so into custody, or to act upon my own suspicions. And I won't do it upon suspicions of my own: I promise it. If I am forced, that's another matter."

"Are you alluding to Halliburton?"

"No. You are on the wrong scent, I say."

"And you think you are on the right one?"

"I could put my finger out this night and lay it on the fox. But I tell you, sir, I don't want to, unless I am compelled. Don't you compel me, Mr. Dare, of all people in the world."

Mr. Dare leaned back in his chair, his thumbs in his waistcoat armholes. No suspicion of the truth had crossed him, and he could not understand either the sergeant or his manner. The latter rose to depart.

"The other cloak, similar to young Halliburton's, belongs to your son Herbert," he whispered, as he passed Mr. Dare. "It was his brother, Cyril, who wore it on Saturday night, and who changed the cheque: therefore we may give a guess as to who took the cheque out of Mr. Ashley's desk. Now you be still over it, sir, for his sake, as I shall be. If I can, I'll call at your office to-morrow, Mr. Dare, and talk further. White must have the money refunded to him, or he won't be still."

Anthony Dare fell into a confusion of horror and consternation, leaving the sergeant to bow himself out. Mrs. Dare heard the departure, and returned to the room.

"Well," cried she briskly, "is he going to accuse Halliburton?"

Mr. Dare did not answer. He looked up in a beseeching, helpless sort of manner, as one who is stunned by a blow.

"What is the matter?" she questioned, gazing at him closely. "Are you ill?"

He rose up shaking, as if ague were upon him. "No—no."

"Perhaps you are cold," said Mrs. Dare. "I asked you what Delves was going to do. Will he accuse Halliburton?"

"Be still!" sharply cried Mr. Dare in a tone of pain. "The matter is to be hushed up. It was not Halliburton."

CHAPTER XXI

A PRESENT OF TEA-LEAVES

How went on Honey Fair? Better and worse, better and worse, according to custom; the worse prevailing over the better.

Of all its inhabitants, none had advanced so well as Robert East. Honestly to confess it, that is not saying much; since the greater portion, instead of advancing in the world's social scale, had retrograded. Robert had left the manufactory he had worked for and was now second foreman at Mr. Ashley's. He was also becoming through perseverance an excellent scholar in a plain way. He had had one friend to help him; and that was William Halliburton.

The Easts had removed to a better house; one of those which had a garden in front of it. No garden was more fragrant than theirs; and it was kept in order by Robert and Thomas East. The house was larger than they required, and part of it was occupied by Stephen Crouch and his daughter. It was known that the Easts were putting by money: and Honey Fair wondered: for none lived more comfortably, more respectably. Honey Fair—taking it as a whole—lived neither comfortably nor respectably. The Fishers had never come out of the workhouse, and Joe was dead. The Crosses, turned from their home, their furniture sold, had found lodgings; two rooms. Improvident as ever, were they. They did not attempt to rise even to their former condition; but grovelled on, living from hand to mouth. The Masons, man and wife, passed their time agreeably in quarrels. At least, that it was agreeable may be assumed, for the quarrels never ceased. Now and then they were diversified by a fight. The children were growing up without training; and Caroline—ah! I don't know that it will do much good to ask after her. Caroline, years ago, had taken a false step; and, try as she would, she could not regain her footing. She lived in a garret alone. She had so lived a long while; and she worked her fingers to the bone to keep body and soul together, and went about with her head down. Honey Fair looked askance at her, and gathered up its petticoats when they saw her coming, as you saw Eliza Tyrrett gather up hers, lest they should come into contact with those contaminations. The Carters thrived; the Brumms, also, were better off than they used to be; and the Buffles did so excellently that a joke went about that they would be retiring on their fortune: but the greater portion of Honey Fair was full of trouble and improvidence.

William Halliburton frequently found himself in Honey Fair. It was the most direct road from his house to that of Monsieur Colin, the French master. William, sociably inclined by nature, had sometimes dropped in at one or other of the houses. He would find Robert East labouring at his books much more than he need have laboured had some little assistance been given him in his progress. William good-naturedly undertook to supply it. It became quite a common thing for him to go round and pass an hour with the Easts and Stephen Crouch.

The unpleasant social features of Honey Fair thus obtruded themselves on William Halliburton's notice; it was impossible that any one passing much through Honey Fair should not be struck with them. Could nothing be done to rescue the people from this degraded condition?—and a degraded one it was, compared with what it might have been. Young and inexperienced as he was, it was a question that sometimes arose to William's mind. Dirty homes, scolding mothers, ragged and pining children, rough and swearing husbands! Waste, discomfort, evil. The women laid the blame on the men: reproached them with wasting their evenings and their money at the public-house. The men retorted upon the women, and said they had not a home "fit for a pig to come into." Meanwhile the money, whether earned by husband or wife, went. It went somehow, bringing apparently nothing to show for it, and the least possible return of good. Thus they struggled and squabbled on, their lives little better than one continued scene of scramble, discomfort, and toil. At a year's end they were not in the least bettered, not in the least raised, socially, morally, or physically, from their condition at the year's commencement. Nothing had been achieved; except that they were one year nearer to the great barrier which separates time from eternity.

Ask them what they were toiling and struggling for. They did not know. What was their end, their aim? They had none. If they could only rub on, and keep body and soul together (as poor Caroline Mason was trying to do in her garret), it appeared to be all they cared for. They did not endeavour to lift up their hopes or their aspirations above that; they were willing so to go on until death should come. What a life! what an end!

A feeling would now and then come over William that he might in some way help them to attempt better things. To do so was a duty which seemed to be lying across his path, that he might take it up and make it his. How to set about it, he knew no more than the Man in the Moon. Now and then disheartening moments would come upon him. To attempt to sweep away the evils of Honey Fair appeared a far more formidable task than to cleanse the Augean Stables could ever have appeared to Hercules. He knew that any endeavour, whether on his part or on that of others, who might be far more experienced and capable than he, would be utterly fruitless unless the incentive to exertion, to strive to do better, should be first born within themselves. Ah, my friends! the aid of others may be looked upon as a great thing; but without self-struggle and self-help little good will be effected.

One evening in passing the house partially occupied by the Crosses the door was flung violently open, a girl of fifteen flew shrieking out and a saucer of wet tea-leaves came flying after her. The tea-leaves alighted on the girl's neck, just escaping William's arm. It was the youngest girl of the family, Patty. The tea-leaves had come from Mrs. Cross. Her face was red with passion, her voice loud; the girl, on her part, was insulting and abusive. Mrs. Cross had her hands stretched out, to scratch, or tear, or pull hair, and a personal skirmish would inevitably have ensued but for the chance of William's being there. He received the hands upon his arm and contrived to detain them.

"What's the matter, Mrs. Cross?"

"Matter!" raved Mrs. Cross. "She's a idle, impedent wicked huzzy—that's what's the matter. She knows I've my gloving to get in for Saturday, and not a stroke'll she help. There's the dishes lying dirty from dinner, the tea-cups lying from tea, and touch 'em she won't. She expects me to do it, and me with my gloving to find 'em in food! I took hold of her arm to make her do it, and she turned and struck at me, the good-for-nothing faggot! I hope none on it didn't go on you, sir," added Mrs. Cross, somewhat modifying her voice, and pausing to recover breath.

"Better that it had gone on my coat than on Patty's neck," replied he, in a good-natured, half-joking tone; though, indeed, the girl, with her evil look at her mother, her insolent air, stood there scarcely worth his defence. "If my mother asked me to wash tea-things or do anything else, Patty, I should do it, and think it a pleasure to help her," he added, to the girl.

Patty pushed her tangled hair behind her ears, and turned a defiant look upon her mother. Hidden as she had thought it from William, he saw it.

"You just wait," nodded Mrs. Cross, in answer as defiant. "I'll make your back smart by-and-by."

Which of the two was the more in fault? It was hard to say. The girl had never been brought up to know her duty, or to do it. The mother from her earliest childhood had given abuse and blows; no kindly, persuasive words; no training. Little wonder, now Patty was growing up, that she turned again. It was the usual sort of maternal government throughout Honey Fair. In these, and similar cases, where could interference or counsel avail, unless the spirit of the mothers and daughters could be changed?

William walked on, after the little episode of the tea-leaves. He could not help contrasting these homes with his home; their life with his life. He was given to reflection beyond his years, and he wished these people could be aroused to improvement both of mind and body. They were living for no end; toiling only to satisfy the wants of the day—nay, to arrest the wants, rather than to satisfy them. How many of them were so much as thinking of another world? Their toil and turmoil in this was too great to enable them to cast a thought to the next.

"I wonder," mused William, as he stepped towards M. Colin's, "whether some of the better-conducted of the men might not be induced to come round to East's in an evening? It might be a beginning, at any rate. Once wean the men from the public-houses, and there's no knowing what reform might be effected. I would willingly give up an hour or two of my evenings to them!"

His visit to M. Colin over, he retraced his steps to Honey Fair and turned into Robert East's. It was past eight o'clock then. Robert and Stephen Crouch were home from work, and were getting out their books. Charlotte sat by, at work as usual, and Tom East was drawing Charlotte's head towards him, to whisper something to her.

"Robert," said William, speaking impulsively, the moment he entered, "I wonder whether you could induce a few of your neighbours to come here of an evening?"

"What for, sir?" asked Robert turning round from the book-shelves where he stood, searching for some volume.

"It might be so much better for them. It might end in being so. I wish," he added with sudden warmth, "we could get all Honey Fair here!"

"All Honey Fair!" echoed Stephen Crouch in astonishment.

"I mean what I say, Crouch."

"Why, sir, the room wouldn't hold a quarter or a tenth part, or a hundredth part of them."

William laughed. "No, that it would not, practically. There is so much discomfort around us, and—and ill-doing—I must call it so, for want of a better name—that I sometimes wish we could mend it a little."

"Who mend it, sir?"

"Any one who would try. You two might help towards it. If you could seduce a few round here, and get them to be interested in your own evening occupation—books and rational conversation—and so wean them from the public-houses, it would be a great thing."

"There'd never be any good done with the men, take them as a whole, sir. They are an ignorant, easy-going lot, and don't care to be better."

"That's just it, Crouch. They don't care to be better. But they might be taught to care. It would be a very great thing if Honey Fair could be brought to spend its evenings as you spend yours. If the men gave up spending their money, and reeling home after it; and the women kept tidy hearths and civil tongues. As Charlotte does," he added looking round at her.

"There's no denying that, sir."

"I think something might be done. By degrees, you understand; not in a hurry. Were you to take the men by storm—to say, 'We want you to lead changed lives, and are going to show you how to do it,' your movement would fail, and you would get laughed at into the bargain. Say to the men, 'You shan't go to the public-house, because you waste your time, your money, and your temper,' and, rely upon it, it would have as much effect as if you spoke to the wind. But get them to come here as a sort of change, and you may secure them for good if you make the evenings pleasant to them. In short, give them some employment or attraction that will outweigh the attractions of the public-house."

"It would certainly be a good thing," said Stephen Crouch, musingly. "They might be for trying to raise themselves then."

"Ay," spoke William, with enthusiasm. "Once let them find the day-spring within themselves, the wish to do right, to be raised above what they are now, and the rest will be easy. When once that day-spring can be found, a man is made. God never sent a man here, but he implanted that within him. The difficulty is, to awaken it."

"And it is not always done, sir," said Charlotte, lifting her face from her work with a kindling eye, a heightened colour. She had found it.

"Charlotte, I fear it is rarely done, instead of not always. It lies pretty dormant, to judge by appearances, in Honey Fair."

William was right. It is an epoch in a man's life, that finding what he had not inaptly called the day-spring. Self-esteem, self-reliance, the courage of long-continued patience, the striving to make the best of the mind's good gifts—all are born of it. He who possesses it may soar to a bright and, happy lot, bearing in mind—may he always bear it!—the rest and reward promised hereafter.

"At any rate, it would be giving them a chance, as it seems to me," observed William. "I think I know one who would come. Andrew Brumm."

"Ah, he would, and be glad to come," replied Robert East. "He is different from many of them. I know another who would, sir; and that's Adam Thornycroft."

Charlotte bent her head over her work.

"Since that cousin of his died of delirium tremens, Thornycroft has said good-bye to the public-houses. He spends his evenings at home with his mother: but I know he would like to spend them here. Tim Carter would come, sir."

"If Mrs. Tim will let him," put in Tom East saucily. And a laugh went round.

"Ever so few to begin with, will set the example to others," remarked William. "There's no knowing what it may grow to. Small beginnings make great endings. I have talked with my mother about Honey Fair. She has always said: 'Before Honey Fair's conduct can be improved, its minds must be improved.'"

"There will be the women yet, sir," spoke Charlotte. "If they are to remain as they are, it will be of little use the men doing anything for themselves."

"Charlotte, once begun, I say there's no knowing where the work may end," he gravely answered.

The rain, which had been threatening all the evening, was coming down pretty smartly as William walked through Honey Fair on his return. Standing against a shutter near his own door was Jacob Cross. "Good night, Jacob," said William.

"Goodnight, sir," answered Jacob sullenly.

"Are you standing in the rain that it may make you grow, as the children say?" asked William in his ever-pleasant tone.

"I'm standing here 'cause I've nowhere else to stand," said the man, his voice full of resentment. "I'm turned out of our room, and I have no money for the Horned Ram."

"A good thing you have not," thought William. "What has turned you out of your room?" he asked.

"I'm turned out, sir, by the row there is in it. Our Mary Ann's come home."

"Mary Ann?" repeated William, not quite understanding.

"Our Mary Ann, what took and married Ben Tyrrett. A fine market she have brought her pigs to!"

"What has she done?" questioned William.

"She's done enough," wrathfully answered Cross. "We told her when she married Tyrrett that he was nothing but a jobber at fifteen shillings a-week—and it's all he was, sir, as you know. 'Wait,' I says to her; 'somebody better than him'll turn up.' Her mother says 'Wait.' Others says 'Wait.' No, not she; the girls are all marrying mad. Well, she took her own way; she would take it; and they got married, and set up upon nothing. Neither of 'em had saved a two-penny-piece; and Ben fond of the public; and our Mary Ann fond of laziness and finery; and not knowing how to keep house any more than her young sister Patty did."

William remembered the little interlude of that evening in which Miss Patty had played her part. Jacob continued.

"It was all fine and sunshiny with 'em for a few days or a few weeks, till the novelty wears off, and then they finds things going cranky. The money, that begins to run short; and Mary Ann, she finds that Ben likes his glass; and Ben, he finds that she's just a doll, with no gumption or management inside her. They quarrels—naterally, and they comes to us to settle it. 'You was both red-hot for the bargain,' says I, 'and you must just make the best of it and of one another.' And so they went back: and it has gone on till this, quarrelling continual. And now he's took to beat her, and home she came to-night, not half an hour ago, with her three children and a black eye, vowing she'll stop at home and won't go back to him again. And she and her mother's having words over it, and the babies a-squalling—enough noise to raise the ceiling off, and I come out of it. I wish I was dead, I do!"

Jacob's account of the noise was scarcely exaggerated. It penetrated to where they stood, two or three houses off. William had moved closer, that the umbrella might give Cross part of its shelter. "Not a very sensible wish, that of yours, is it, Cross?" remarked he.

"I have wished it long, sir, sensible or not sensible. I slaves away my days and have nothing but a pigsty to step into at home, and angry words in it. A nice place for a tired man! I can't afford the public more than three or four nights a-week; not that, always. They're getting corky at the beer-shops, nowadays, and won't give trust. Wednesday this is; Thursday, to-morrow; Friday, next night: three nights, and me without a shelter to put my head in!"

"I should like to take you to one to-morrow night," said William. "Will you go with me?"

"Where to?" ungraciously asked Cross.

"To Robert East's. You know how he and Crouch spend their evenings. There's always something going on there interesting and pleasant."

"Crouch and East don't want me."

"Yes, they do. They will be only too glad if you, and a few more intelligent men, will join them. Try it, Cross. There's a warm room to sit in, at all events, and nothing to pay."

"Ah, it's all very fine for them Easts! We haven't their luck. Look at me! Down in the world."

William put his hand on the man's shoulder. "Why should you be down in the world?"

"Why should I?" repeated Cross, in surprise. "Because I am," he logically answered.

"That is not the reason. The reason is because you do not try to rise in the world."

"It's no use trying."

"Have you ever tried?"

"Why, no! How can I try?"

"You wished just now that you were dead. Would it not be better to wish to live?"

"Not such a life as mine."

"But to wish to live would seem to imply that it must be a better life. And why need your life be so miserable? You gain fair wages; your wife earns money. Altogether I suppose you must have twenty-six or twenty-eight shillings a week—"

"But there's no thrift with it," exclaimed Cross. "It melts away somehow. Before the middle of the week comes, it's all gone."

"You spend some at the Horned Ram, you know," said William, not in a reproving tone.

"She squanders away in rubbish more than that," was Jacob's answer, pointing towards his house, and not giving at all a complimentary stress upon the "she."

"And with nothing to show for it in return, either of you. Try another plan, Jacob."

"I'd not be backward—if I could see one to try," said he, after a pause.

"Be here at half-past eight to-morrow evening, and I will go in with you to East's. If you cannot see any better way, you can spend a pleasant evening. But now, Jacob, let me say a word to you, and do you note it. If you find the evening pass agreeably, go the next evening, and the next; go always. You can't tell all that may arise from it in time. I know of one thing that will."

"What's that, sir?"

"Why, that instead of wishing yourself dead, you will grow to think life too short, for the good you find in it."

He went on his way. Jacob Cross, deprived of the umbrella, stood in the rain as before and looked after him, indulging his reflections.

"He is a young man, and things wear their bright side to him. But he has a cordial way with him, and don't look at folks as if they was dirt."

And that had been the origin of the soirées held at Robert East's. By degrees ten or a dozen men took to going there, and—what was more—to like to go, and to find an interest in it. It was a great improvement upon the Horned Ram.

CHAPTER XXII

HENRY ASHLEY'S OBJECT IN LIFE

On one of the warm, bright days that we sometimes have in the month of February, all the brighter from their contrast to the passing winter, William Halliburton was walking home to tea from the manufactory, and overtook Henry Ashley limping along.

Henry was below the middle height, and slight in form, with the same beautiful face that had marked his boyhood, delicately refined in feature, brilliant in colour; the same upright lines of pain knit in the smooth white brow.

"Just the man I wanted," said he, linking his arm within William's. "You are a good help up a hill, and I am hot and tired."

"Wrapped up in that coat, with its fur lining, I should think you are! I have doffed my elegant cloak, you see, to-day."

"Is it off to the British Museum?"

William laughed. "I have not had time to pack it up."

"I am glad I met you. You must come home to tea with me. Well? Why are you hesitating? You have no engagement?"

"Nothing more than usual. My studies—"

"You are study mad!" interrupted Henry Ashley. "What do you want to be? A Socrates? An Admirable Crichton?"

"Nothing so formidable. I want to be useful."

"And you make yourself accomplished, as a preliminary step to it. Mary took up the fencing-sticks for you yesterday. Herbert Dare was at our house—some freak is taking him to be a pretty constant visitor just now—and the talk turned upon Frank. You know," broke off Henry in his quaint way, "I never use long words when short ones will do: you learned ones would say 'conversation.' Mr. Keating had said to my father that Frank Halliburton was a brilliant scholar, and I retailed it to Herbert. I knew it would put him up, and there's nothing I like half so much as to rile the Dares. Herbert sneered. 'And he owes it partly to William,' I went on, 'for if Frank's a brilliant scholar, William's a brillianter!' 'William Halliburton a brilliant scholar!' stormed scornful Herbert. 'Has he learnt to be one at the manufactory? So long as he knows how gloves are made, that's enough for him. What does he want with the requirements of gentlemen?' Up looked Miss Mary; her colour rising, her eyes flashing. She was at her drawing: at which, by the way, she makes no progress; nothing to be compared with Anna Lynn. 'William Halliburton has forgotten more than you ever learnt, Herbert Dare,' cried she; 'and there's more of the true gentleman in his little finger than there is in your whole body.' 'There's for you, Herbert Dare,' whistled I; 'but it's true, lad, like it or not as you may!' Herbert was riled."

Henry turned his head as he concluded, and looked up at William. A gleam like a sunbeam had flashed into William's eyes; a colour to his cheeks.

"Well?" cried Henry sharply, for William did not speak. "Have you nothing to say?"

"It was generous of Miss Ashley."

"I don't mean that. Oh dear!" sighed Henry, who appeared to be in one of his fitful moods; "who is to know whether things will turn out crooked or straight in this world of ours? What objection have you to coming home with me for the evening? That's what I mean."

"None. I can give up my books for a night, bookworm as you think me. But they will expect me at East's."

"Happy the man that expecteth nothing!" responded Henry. "Disappoint them."

"As for disappointing them, I shouldn't so much mind, but I can't abide to disappoint myself," returned William, quoting from Goldsmith's good old play, of which both he and Henry were fond.

"You don't mean to say it would be a disappointment to you, not giving the lesson, or whatever it is, to those working chaps!" uttered Henry Ashley.

"Not as you would count disappointment. When I do not get round for an hour, it seems as a night lost. I know the men like to see me; and I am always fearing that we are not sure of them."

"You speak as though your whole soul were in the business," returned Henry Ashley.

"I think my heart is in it."

Henry looked at him wistfully, and his tone grew serious. "William, I would give all I am worth, present, and to come, to change places with you."

"To change places with me!" echoed William, in surprise.

"Yes: for you have an object in life. You may have many. To be useful in your generation is one of them."

"And so may you have objects in life."

"With this encumbrance!" He stamped his lame leg, and a look of keen vexation settled itself in his face. "You can go forth into the world with your strong limbs, your unbroken health; you can work, or you can play; you can be active, or you can be still, at will. But what am I? A poor, weak creature; infirm of temper, tortured by pain, condemned half my days to the monotony of a sick-room. Compare my lot with yours!"

"There are those who would choose your lot in preference to mine, were the option given them," returned William. "I must work. It is a duty laid upon me. You can play."

"Thank you! How?"

"I am not speaking literally. Every good and pleasing thing that money can purchase is at your command. You have only to enjoy them, so far as you may. One, suffering as you do, bears not upon him the responsibility to use his time, that a healthy man does. Lots, in this world, Henry, are, as I believe, pretty equally balanced. Many would envy you your life of calm repose."

"It is not calm," was the abrupt rejoinder. "It is disturbed by pain, and aggravated by temper; and—and—tormented by uncertainty."

"At any rate, you can subdue the one."

"Which, pray?"

"The temper. Henry"—dropping his voice—"a victory over your own temper may be one of the few obligations laid upon you."

"I wish I could live for an object," grumbled Henry.

"Come round with me to East's, sometimes."

"I—daresay!" retorted Henry, when he could recover from his amazement. "Thank you again, Mr. Halliburton."

William laughed. But he soon resumed his seriousness. "I can understand that for you, the favoured son of Mr. Ashley, reared in refinement and exclusiveness—"

"Enshrined in pride—the failing that Helstonleigh is pleased to call my besetting sin; sheltered under care and coddling so great that the very winds of heaven are not suffered to visit my face too roughly!" was the impetuous interruption of Henry Ashley. "Come! bring it all out. Don't, from motives of delicacy, keep in any of my faults, virtues, or advantages!"

"I can understand, I say, why you are unwilling to break through the reserve of your home habits," William calmly continued. "But, if you did so, you might no longer have to complain of the want of an object in life."

At this moment they came in view of William's house. Mrs. Halliburton happened to be at one of the windows. William nodded his greeting, and Henry raised his hat. Presently Henry began again.

"Pray, do you join the town in its gratuitous opinion that Henry Ashley, of all in it, is the proudest amid the proud?"

"I do not find you proud," said William.

"You! As far as you and I are concerned, I think the boot might be on the other leg. You might set up for being proud over me."

William could not help laughing. "Putting joking aside, my opinion is, Henry, that your shyness and sensitiveness are in fault; not your pride. It is your reserved manner alone which has caused Helstonleigh to take up the impression that you are unduly proud."

"Right, old fellow!" returned Henry in emphatic tones. "If you knew how far I and pride stand apart—but let it pass."

Arrived at the entrance to Mr. Ashley's, William threw open the gate for Henry, retreating himself. "I must go home first, Henry. I won't be a quarter of an hour."

Henry looked cross. "Why on earth, then, did you not go in as we passed? What was the use of your coming up here to go back again?"

"I thought my arm was helping you."

"So it was. But—there! don't be an hour."

As William walked rapidly back, he met Mrs. Ashley's carriage. She and Mary were in it. Mrs. Ashley nodded as he raised his hat, and Mary glanced at him with a smile and a heightened colour. She had grown up to excessive beauty.

A few moments, and William met beauty of another style—Anna Lynn. Her cheeks were the flushed, dimpled cheeks of her childhood; the same sky-blue eyes gleaming from between their long dark lashes; the same profusion of silky, brown hair; the same gentle, sweetly modest manners. William stopped to shake hands with her.

"Out alone, Anna?"

"I am on my way to take tea with Mary Ashley."

"Are you? We shall meet there, then."

"That will be pleasant. Fare thee well for the present, William."

She continued her way. William ran in home, and to his chamber. Dressing himself hastily, he went to the room where his mother sat, and stood before her.

"Does my coat fit me, mother?"

"Why, where are you going?" she asked.

"To Mrs. Ashley's. I have put on my new coat. Does it do? It seems all right"—throwing up his arms.

"Yes, it fits you exactly. I think you are growing a dandy. Go along. I must not look at you too long."

"Why not?" he asked in surprise.

"In case I grow proud of my eldest son. And I would rather be proud of his goodness than of his looks."

William laughingly gave his mother a farewell kiss. "Tell Gar I am sorry he will not have me at his elbow this evening, to find fault with his Greek. Good-bye, mother dear."

In truth, there was something remarkably noble in William Halliburton's appearance. As he entered Mrs. Ashley's drawing-room, the fact seemed to strike upon Henry with unusual force, who greeted him from his distant sofa.

"So that's what you went back for!—to turn yourself into a buck!" he called out as William approached him. "As if you were not well enough before! Did you dress for me, pray?"

"For you!" laughed William. "That's good!"

"In saying 'me,' I include the family," returned Henry quaintly. "There's no one else to dress for."

"Yes, there is. There's Anna Lynn."

Now, in good truth, William had no covert meaning in giving this answer. The words rose to his lips, and he spoke them lightly. Perhaps he could have given a very different one, had he been compelled to speak out the inmost feeling of his heart. Strange, however, was the effect on Henry Ashley. He grasped William's arm with emotion, and pulled his face down to him as he lay.

"What do you say? What do you mean?"

"I mean nothing in particular. Anna is here."

"You shall not evade me," gasped Henry. "I must have it out, now or later. WHAT is it that you mean?"

William stood, almost confounded. Henry was evidently in painful excitement; every vestige of colour had forsaken his sensitive countenance, and his white hands shook as they held William.

"What do you mean?" William whispered. "I said nothing to agitate you thus, that I am aware of. Are we at cross-purposes?"

A spot, bright as carmine, began to flush into the invalid's pale cheeks, and he moved his face so that the light did not fall upon it.

"I'll have it out, I say. What is Anna Lynn to you?"

"Nothing," answered William, a smile parting his lips.

"What is she to you?" reiterated Henry, his tone painfully earnest.

William edged himself on to the sofa, so as to cover Henry from the gaze of any eyes that might be directed to him from the other parts of the room. "I like Anna very much," he said in a clear, low tone; "almost as I might like a sister; but I have no love for her, in the sense you would imply—if I am not mistaking your meaning. And I never shall have."

Henry looked at him wistfully. "On your honour?"

"Henry! was there need to ask it? On my honour, if you will."

"No, no; there was no need: you are always truthful. Bear with me, William! bear with my infirmities."

"My sister Anna Lynn might be, and welcome. My wife never."

Henry did not answer. His face was growing damp with physical pain.

"You have one of your fits of suffering coming on!" breathed William. "Shall I get you anything?"

"Hush! only sit there, to hide me from them: and be still."

William did as he was requested, sitting so as to screen him from Mrs. Ashley and the rest. He held his hands, and the paroxysm, sharp while it lasted, passed away. Henry's very lips had grown white with pain.

"You see what a poor wretch I am!"

"I see that you suffer," was William's compassionate answer.

"From henceforth there is a fresh bond of union between us, for you possess my secret. It is what no one else in the world does. William, that's my object in life."

William did not reply. Perplexity was crowding on his mind, shading his countenance.

"Well!" cried Henry, beginning to recover his equanimity, and with it his sharp retorts. "Why are you looking so blue?"

"Will it be smooth sailing for you, Henry, with Mr. Ashley?"

"Yes, I think it will," was the hasty rejoinder: its very haste, its fractious tone, proving that Henry was by no means so sure of it as he would imply. "I am not as others are: therefore he will let minor considerations yield to my happiness."

William looked uncommonly grave. "Mr. Ashley is not all," he said, arousing from a reverie. "There may be difficulties elsewhere. She must not marry out of their own society. Samuel Lynn is one of its strictest members."

"Rubbish! Samuel Lynn is my father's servant, and I am my father's son. If Samuel should take a strait-laced fit, and hold out, why, I'll turn broadbrim."

"Samuel Lynn is my father's servant!" In that very fact, William saw cause to fear that it might not be such plain sailing with Mr. Ashley as Henry wished to anticipate. He could not help looking the doubts he felt. Henry observed it.

"What's the matter now?" he peevishly asked. "I do think you were born to be the plague of my life! My belief is, you want her for yourself."

"I am only anxious for you, Henry. I wish you could have assured yourself that it would go well, before— before allowing your feelings to be irrevocably bound up in it. A blow, for you, might be hard to bear."

"How could I help my feelings?" retorted Henry. "I did not fix them purposely on Anna Lynn. Before I knew anything about it, they had fixed themselves. Almost before I knew that I cared for her, she was more to me than the sun in the heavens. There has been no help for it at all, I tell you. So don't preach."

"Have you spoken to her?"

Henry shook his head. "The time has not come for it. I must make it right with the master before I can stir a step: and I fear it is not quite ripe for that. Mind you don't talk."

William smiled. "I will mind."

"You'd better. If that Quaker society got a hint of it, there's no knowing what a hullabaloo they might make. They might be for reading Anna a public lecture at Meeting: or get Samuel Lynn to vow he'd not give his consent."

"I should argue in this way, were I you, Henry. With my love so firmly fixed on Anna Lynn—I beg your pardon, Miss Ashley."

William started up. Mary Ashley was standing close to the sofa. Had she caught the sense of the last words?

"Mamma spoke twice, but you were too busily engaged to hear," said Mary. "Henry, James is waiting to wheel your sofa to the tea-table."

Henry rose. Passing his arm through William's, he approached the group. The servant pushed the sofa after them. Standing together were Mary Ashley and Anna Lynn. They presented a great contrast to each other. Mary wore an evening dress of shimmering silk, its low body trimmed with rich white lace; white lace hung from its drooping sleeves: and she had on ornaments of gold. Anna was in grey merino, high in the neck, close at the wrists; not a bit of lace about her, not an ornament; nothing but a plain white linen collar. "Catch me letting her wear those Methodistical things when she shall be mine!" thought Henry. "I'll make a bonfire of the lot."

But the Quaker cap? Ah! it was not there. Anna had continued her habit at home of throwing it off, as formerly. Patience reprimanded in vain. She was not seconded by Samuel Lynn. "We are by ourselves, Patience; it does not much matter," he would say; "the child says she is cooler without it." But had Samuel Lynn known that Anna was in the habit of discarding it on every possible occasion when she was from home, he had been as severe as Patience. At Mr. Ashley's, especially, she would sit, as now, without it, her lovely face made more lovely by its falling curls. Anna did wrong, and she knew it; but she was a wilful girl, and a vain one. That pretty, timid, retiring manner concealed much self-will, much vanity; though in some things she was as easily swayed as a child.

She disobeyed Patience in another matter. Patience would say to her, "Should Mary Ashley be opening her instrument of music, thee will mind not to listen to her songs: thee can go into another room."

"Oh, yes, Patience," she would answer; "I will mind."

But, instead of not listening, Miss Anna would place herself near the piano, and drink in the songs as if her whole heart were in the music. Music had a great effect upon her; and there she would sit entranced, as though she were in some earthly Elysium. She said nothing of this at home; but the deceit was wrong.

They were sitting down to tea, when Herbert Dare came in. The hours for meals were early at Mr. Ashley's: the medical men considered it best for Henry. Herbert could be a gentleman when he chose; good-looking also; quite an addition to a drawing-room. He took his seat between Mary and Anna.

"I say, how is it you are not dining at home this evening?" asked Henry, who somehow did not regard the Dares with any great favour.

"I dined in the middle of the day," was Herbert's reply.

"The condescension! I thought only plebeians did that. James, is there a piece of chalk in the house? I must chalk that up."

"Henry! Henry!" reproved Mrs. Ashley.

"Oh, let him talk, Mrs. Ashley," said Herbert, with supreme good humour. "There's nothing he likes so well as a wordy war."

"Nothing in the world," acquiesced Henry. "Especially with Herbert Dare."

CHAPTER XXIII

ATTERLY'S FIELD

Laughing, talking, playing at proverbs, earning and paying forfeits, it was a merry group in Mrs. Ashley's drawing-room. That lady herself was not joining in the merriment. She sat apart at a small table, some work in her hand, speaking a word now and then, and smiling to herself in echo to some unusual burst of laughter. It was so surprising that only five voices could make so much noise. They were sitting in a circle; Mary Ashley between William Halliburton and Herbert Dare, Anna Lynn between Herbert Dare and Henry Ashley, Henry and William side by side.

Time, in these happy moments, passes rapidly. In due course, the hands of the French clock on the mantel-piece pointed to half-past eight, and its silver tones rang out the chimes. They were at the end of the game, and just settling themselves to commence another. The half-hour aroused William, and he glanced towards the clock.

"Half-past eight! who would have thought it? I had no idea it was so late. I must leave you just for half an hour," he added, rising.

"Leave for what?" cried Henry Ashley.

"To go as far as East's. I will not remain there."

Henry broke into a "wordy war," as Herbert Dare had called it earlier in the evening. William smiled, and overruled him in his quiet way.

"They have my promise to go round this evening," he said. "I gave it them unconditionally, and must just go round to tell them I cannot come—if that's not a contradiction. Don't look so cross, Henry."

"Of course, you don't mean to come back," resentfully spoke Henry. "When you get there, you'll stop there."

"No; I have told you I will not. But if I let them expect me all the evening, they will be looking and waiting, and do no good."

He went out as he spoke, and left the house. As he reached the gate Mr. Ashley was coming in. Mr. Ashley had been in the manufactory; he did not often go there after tea. "Going already, William?" Mr. Ashley exclaimed in accents of surprise.

"Not for long, sir. I must just look in at East's."

"Is that scheme likely to prosper? Can you keep the men?"

"Yes, indeed, I think so. My hopes are strong."

"Well, there's nothing like hope," answered Mr. Ashley, with a laugh. "But I shall wonder if you do keep them. William," he added, after a slight pause, his tone changing to a business one, "I have a few words to say to you. I was about to speak to you in the counting-house this afternoon, but something put it aside. I have changed my plans with respect to this Lyons journey. Instead of despatching you, as I had thought of doing, I believe I shall send Samuel Lynn."

Mr. Ashley paused. William did not immediately reply.

"Samuel Lynn's experience is greater than yours. It is a new thing, and he will see, better than you could do, what can and what cannot be done."

"Very well, sir," at length answered William.

"You speak as though you were disappointed," remarked Mr. Ashley.

William was disappointed. But his motive for the feeling lay far deeper than Mr. Ashley supposed. "I should like to have gone, sir, very much. But—of course, my liking, or not liking, has nothing to do with it. Perhaps it is as well that I should not go," he resumed, more in soliloquy, as if he were trying to reconcile himself to the disappointment by argument, than in observation to Mr. Ashley. "I do not see how the men would have done without me at East's."

"Ay, that's a grave consideration," replied Mr. Ashley jokingly, as he turned to walk to his own door.

William stood still, nailed as it were to the spot, looking after his master. A most unwelcome thought had flashed over him; and in the impulse of the moment he followed Mr. Ashley, to speak it out. Even in the night's obscurity, his emotion was perceptible.

"Mr. Ashley, the suspicion cast on me, at the time that cheque was lost, has not been the reason—the reason for your declining to intrust me with this commission?"

Mr. Ashley looked at him in surprise. But that William's agitation was all too real, he would have laughed at him.

"William, I think you are turning silly. No suspicion was cast on you."

"You have never stirred in the matter, sir; you have never spoken to me to tell me you were satisfied that I was not in any way guilty," was William's impulsive answer.

"Spoken to you! where was the need? Why, William, my whole life, my daily intercourse with you, is only so much proof that you have my full confidence. Should I admit you to my home, to the companionship of my children, if I had no more faith in you than that?"

"True," said William, beginning to recover himself. "It was a thought that flashed over me, sir, when you said I was not to be sent on this journey. I should not like you to doubt me; I could not live under it."

"William, you reproached me with not having stirred in—"

"I beg your pardon, sir. I never thought of such a thing as reproach. I would not presume to do it."

"I have not stirred in the matter," resumed Mr. Ashley. "A very disagreeable suspicion arises in my mind at times, as to how the cheque went; and I do not choose to stir in it. Have you no suspicion on the point?"

The question took William by surprise. He stammered in his answer; an unusual thing for him to do. "N—o."

"I ask if you have a suspicion?" quietly repeated Mr. Ashley, meaningly, as if he took William's answer for nothing, or had not heard it.

Then William spoke out readily. "A suspicion has crossed my mind, sir. But it is one I should not like to breathe to you."

"That's enough. I see. White voluntarily took the loss of the money on himself. He came to me to say so; therefore, I infer that it has in some private way been refunded to him. Mr. Dare veered round, and advised me not to investigate the affair, as I was no loser by it; Delves hinted the same thing. Altogether, I can see through the thing pretty clearly, and I am content to let it rest. Are you satisfied? If not—"

Mr. Ashley broke off abruptly. William waited.

"So, don't turn foolish again. You and I now understand each other. William!" he emphatically added, "I am growing to like you almost as I like my own children. I am proud of you; and I shall be prouder yet. God bless you, my boy!"

It was so very rare that the calm, dignified Thomas Ashley was betrayed into anything like demonstrativeness, that William could only stand and look. And while he looked, the door closed on his master.

He went way with all speed, calling at his home. Were the truth to be told, perhaps William was quite as anxious to be back again at Mr. Ashley's as Henry was that he should be there. Scarcely stopping for a word of greeting, he opened a drawer, took from it a small case of fossils, and then searched for something else; something which apparently he could not find.

"Have any of you seen my microscope?" he asked, turning to the group at the table bending over their books.

Jane looked round. "My dear, I lent it to Patience to-day. I suppose she forgot to return it. Gar, will you go and ask her for it?"

"Don't disturb yourself, Gar," said William. "I am going out, and will ask Patience myself."

Patience was alone in her parlour. She returned him the microscope, saying that the reason she had not sent it in was, that she had not had time to use it. "Thee art in evening dress!" she remarked to William.

"I am at Mrs. Ashley's. I have only come out for a few minutes. Thank you. Good night, Patience."

"Wait thee a moment, William. Is Anna ready to come home?"

"No, that she is not. Why?"

"I want to send for her. Samuel Lynn is spending the evening in the town, so I must send Grace. And I don't care to send her late. She will only get talking to John Pembridge, if she goes out after he is home from work."

William smiled. "It is natural that she should, I suppose. When are they going to be married?"

"Shortly," answered Patience, in a tone not quite so equable as usual. Patience saw no good in people getting married in general; and she was vexed at the prospect of losing Grace in particular. "She leaves us in a fortnight from this," she continued, alluding to Grace, "and all her thoughts seem to be bent now upon meeting John Pembridge. Could thee bring Anna home for me?"

"With pleasure," replied William.

"That is well, then. Grace does not deserve to go out to-night, for she wilfully crossed me to-day. Good evening, William."

Fossil-case in hand, and the microscope in his pocket, William made the best of his way to Honey Fair. Robert East, Stephen Crouch, Brumm, Thornycroft, Carter, Cross, and some half-dozen others, were crowded round Robert's table. William handed them the fossils and the microscope; told the men to amuse themselves with them for that night, and he would explain more about them on the morrow. He was ever anxious that the men should have some object of amusement as a rallying point on these evenings; anything to keep their interest awakened.

Before the half-hour had expired, he was back at Mr. Ashley's. Proverbs had been given up, and Mary was at the piano. Mr. Ashley had been accompanying her on the flute, on which instrument he was a brilliant player, and when William entered she was singing a duet with Herbert Dare. Anna—disobedient Anna—was seated, listening with all her ears and heart to the music, her up-turned countenance quite wonderful to look upon in its rapt delight.

"I think you could sing," spoke Henry Ashley to her, in an undertone, after watching her while the song lasted.

Anna shook her head. "I may not try," she said, raising her blue eyes to him for one moment, and then dropping them.

"The time may come when you may," returned Henry, in a deeper whisper.

She did not answer, she did not lift her eyes; but the faintest possible smile parted her rosy lips—a smile which seemed to express a consciousness that perhaps that time might come. And Henry, shy and sensitive, stood apart and gazed upon her, his heart beating.

"Young lady," said William, advancing, "do you know that a special honour has been assigned me to-night? One that concerns you."

Anna raised her eyes now. She felt as much at ease with William as she did with her father or Patience. "What dost thee say, William? An honour?"

"That of seeing you safely home. I—"

"What's that for?" interrupted Anna. "Where's my father?"

"He is not at home this evening. And Patience did not care to send out Grace. I'll take care of you."

William could not but observe the sudden flush, the glow of pleasure, or what looked like pleasure, that overspread Anna's countenance at the information. "What's that for?" he thought, echoing her recent words. But Mary began to sing again, and his attention was diverted.

Ten o'clock was the signal for departure. As they were going out—William, Anna, and Herbert Dare, who took the opportunity to leave with them—Henry Ashley limped after them, and drew William aside in the hall.

"Honour bright, mind, my friend!"

William did not understand. "Honour bright, always," said he. "But what do you mean?"

"You'll not get making love to her on your way home!"

William could not help laughing. He turned his amused face full on Henry. "Be at rest. I would not care to make love to her, had I full leave and license from the Quaker society, granted me in public meeting."

"Do you think I did not see her brightened countenance when you told her she was to go home with you?" retorted Henry.

"I saw it too. I conclude she was pleased that her father was not coming for her, little undutiful thing! However it may have been, rely upon it that brightening was not for me."

Pressing his hand warmly, with a pressure that no false friend ever gave, William hastened away. It was time. Herbert Dare and Anna had not waited for him, but were ever so far ahead.

"Very polite of you!" cried William, when he caught them up. "Anna, had you gone pitching into that part of the path they are mending, I should have been responsible, you know. You might have waited for me."

He spoke good-humouredly, making a joke of it. Herbert Dare did not appear to receive it as one. He retorted haughtily.

"Do you suppose I am not capable of taking care of Miss Lynn? As much so as you, at any rate."

"Possibly," coolly returned William, not losing his good-humoured tone. Herbert Dare had given Anna his arm. William walked near her on the other side. Thus they reached Mr. Lynn's.

"Good night," said Herbert, shaking hands with her. "Good night to you, Halliburton."

"Good night," replied William.

Herbert Dare set off running. William knocked at the door and waited until it was opened. Then he also shook hands with Anna, and saw her in.

Frank and Gar were putting up their books for the night when William entered. The boarders had gone to bed. Jane, a very unusual thing for her, was sitting by the fire, doing nothing.

"Am I not idle, William?" she said.

William bent to kiss her. "There's no need for you to be anything but idle now, mother."

"No need! William, you know better. There's great need that none should be idle: none in the world. But I have a bad headache to-night."

"William," called out Gar, "they brought this round for you from East's. Young Tom came with it."

It was the case of fossils and the microscope. William observed that they need not have sent them, as he should want them there the next evening. "Patience said she had not had time to use the microscope," he continued. "I think I will take it in to her. I suppose she has been buying linen, and wants to see if the threads are even."

"The Lynns will have gone to bed by this time," said Jane.

"Not to-night. I have only just seen Anna home from Mrs. Ashley's; and Mr. Lynn has gone out to supper."

He turned to leave the room with the microscope, but Gar was looking at the fossils and asked the loan of it. A few minutes, and William finally went out.

Patience came to the door, in answer to his knock. She thanked him for the microscope and stood a minute or two chatting. Patience was fond of a gossip; there was no denying it.

"Will thee not walk in?"

"Not now," he said, turning away. "Good night, Patience."

"Good night to thee. Thee send in Anna, please. She is having a pretty long talk with thy mother."

William was at a loss. "I saw Anna in from Mr. Ashley's."

"She did but ask whether her father was home, and then ran through the house," replied Patience. "She had a message for thy mother, she said, from Margaret Ashley."

"Mrs. Ashley does not send messages to my mother," returned William, in some wonder. "They have no acquaintance with each other—beyond a bow, in passing."

"She must have sent her one to-night—why else should the child go in to deliver it?" persisted Patience. "Not but that Anna is always running into thy house at nights. I fear she must trouble thy mother at her class."

"She never stays long enough for that," replied William. "When she does come in—and it is not often— she just opens the door; 'How dost thee, friend Jane Halliburton?' and out again."

"Then thee can know nothing about it, William. I tell thee she never stays less than an hour, and she is always there. I say to her that one of these evenings thy mother may likely be hinting to her that her room will be more acceptable than her company. Thee send her home now, please."

William turned away. Curious thoughts were passing through his mind. That Anna did not go in, in the frequent manner Patience intimated; that she rarely stayed above a minute or two, he knew. He knew— at least, he felt perfectly sure—that Anna was not at his house now; had not been there. And yet Patience said "Send her home."

"Has Anna been here?" he asked when he went in.

"Anna? No."

Not just that moment, to draw observation, but presently, William left the room, and went into the garden at the back. A very unpleasant suspicion had arisen in his mind. It might not have occurred to him, but for certain glances which he had observed pass that evening between Herbert Dare and Anna— glances of confidence—as if they had a private mutual understanding on some point or other. He had not understood them then: he very much feared he was about to understand them now.

Opening the gate leading to the field at the back, commonly called Atterly's Field, he looked cautiously around. For a moment or two he could see nothing. The hedge was thick on either side, and no living being appeared to be beneath its shade. But he saw farther when his eyes became accustomed to the obscurity.

Pacing slowly together, were Herbert Dare and Anna. Now moving on, a few steps; now pausing to converse more at ease. William drew a deep breath. He saw quite enough to be sure this was not the first time they had so paced together: and thought after thought crowded on his mind; one idea, one remembrance chasing another.

Was this the explanation of the plaid cloak, which had paraded stealthily on that very field-path during the past winter? There could not be a doubt of it. And was it in this manner that Anna's flying absences from home were spent—absences which she, in her unpardonable deceit, had accounted for to Patience by saying that she was with Mrs. Halliburton? Alas for Anna! Alas for all who deviate by an untruth from the path of rectitude! If the misguided child—she was little better than a child—could only have seen the future that was before her! It may have been very pleasant, very romantic to steal a march on Patience, and pace out there in the cold, chattering to Herbert Dare; listening to his protestations that he cared for no one in the world but herself; never had cared, never should care: but it was laying up for Anna a day of reckoning, the like of which had rarely fallen on a young head. William seemed to take it all in at a glance; and, rising tumultuously over other unpleasant thoughts, came the remembrance of Henry Ashley's misplaced and ill-starred love.

With another deep breath, that was more like a groan than anything else—for Herbert Dare never brought good to any one in his life, and William knew it—William set off towards them. Whether they heard footsteps, or whether they thought the time for parting had come, certain it was that Herbert was gone before William could reach them, and Anna was speeding towards her home with a fleet step. William placed himself in her way, and she started aside with a scream that went echoing through the field. Then they had not heard him.

"William, is it thee? Thee hast frightened me nearly out of my senses."

"Anna," he gravely said, "Patience is waiting for you."

Anna Lynn's imagination led her to all sorts of fantastic fears. "Oh, William, thee hast not been in to Patience!" she exclaimed, in sudden trembling. "Thee hast not been to our house to seek me!"

They had reached his gate now. He halted, and took her hand in his, his manner impressive, his voice firm. "Anna, I must speak to you as I would to my own sister; as I might to Janey, had she lived, and been drawn into this terrible imprudence. Though, indeed, I should not then speak, but act. What tales are they that Herbert Dare is deceiving you with?"

"Hast thee been in to Patience? Hast thee been in to Patience?" reiterated Anna.

"Patience knows nothing of this. She thinks you are at our house. I ask you, Anna, what foolish tales Herbert Dare is deceiving you with?"

Anna—relieved on the score of her fright—shook her head petulantly. "He is not deceiving me with any. He would not deceive."

"Anna, hear me. His very nature, as I believe, is deceit. I fear he has little truth, little honour within him. Is Herbert professing to—to love you?"

"I will not answer thee aught. I will not hear thee speak against Herbert Dare."

"Anna," he continued in a lower tone, "you ought to be afraid of Herbert Dare. He is not a good man."

How wilful she was! "It is of no use thy talking," she reiterated, putting her fingers to her ears. "Herbert Dare is good. I will not hear thee speak against him."

"Then, Anna, as you meet it in this way, I must inform your father or Patience of what I have seen. If you will not keep yourself out of harm's way, they must do it for you."

It terrified her to the last degree. Anna could have died rather than suffer her escapade to reach the ears of home. "How can thee talk of harm, William? What harm is likely to come to me? I did no more harm talking to Herbert Dare here, than I did, talking to him in Margaret Ashley's drawing-room."

"My dear child, you do not understand things," he answered. "The very fact of your stealing from your home to walk about in this manner, however innocent it may be in itself, would do you incalculable harm in the eyes of the world. And I am quite sure that in no shape or form can Herbert Dare bring you good, or contribute to your good. Tell me one thing, Anna: Have you learnt to care much for him?"

"I don't care for him at all," responded Anna.

"No! Then why walk about with him?"

"Because it's fun to cheat Patience."

"Oh, Anna, this is very wrong, very foolish. Do you mean what you say—that you do not care for him?"

"Of course I mean it," she answered. "I think he is very kind and pleasant, and he gave me a pretty locket. But that's all. William, thee wilt not tell upon me?" she continued, clinging to his arm, her tone changing to one of entreaty, as the terror, which she had been endeavouring to conceal with light words, returned upon her. "William! thee art kind and obliging—thee wilt not tell upon me! I will promise thee never to meet Herbert Dare again, if thee wilt not."

"It would be for your own sake, Anna, that I should speak. How do I know that you would keep your word?"

"I give thee my promise that I will! I will not meet Herbert Dare in this way again. I tell thee I do not care to meet him. Canst thee not believe me?"

He did believe her, implicitly. Her eyes were streaming; her pretty hands clung about him. He did like Anna very much, and he would not draw vexation upon her, if it could be avoided with expediency.

"I will rely upon you then, Anna. Believe me, you could not choose a worse friend in all Helstonleigh, than Herbert Dare. I have your word?"

"Yes. And I have thine."

He placed her arm within his own, and led her to the back door of her house. Patience was standing at it. "I have brought you the little truant," he said.

"It is well thee hast," replied Patience. "I had just opened the door to come after her. Anna, thee art worse than a wild thing. Running off in this manner!"

It had not been in William's way to see much of Anna's inner qualities. He had not detected her deceit; he did not know that she could be untruthful when it suited her to be so. He had firm faith in her word, never questioning that it might be depended upon. Nevertheless, when he came afterwards to reflect upon the matter, he thought it might be his duty to give Patience a little word of caution. And this he could do without compromising Anna.

He contrived to see Patience alone the very next day. She began talking of their previous evening at the Ashleys'.

"Yes," observed William, "it was a pleasant evening. It would have been all the pleasanter, though, but for one who was there—Herbert Dare."

"I do not admire the Dares," said Patience frigidly.

"Nor I. But I observed one thing, Patience—that he admires Anna. Were Anna my sister, I should not like her to be too much admired by Herbert Dare. So take care of her."

Patience looked steadily at him. William continued, his tone confidential.

"You know what Herbert Dare is said to be, Patience—fonder of leading people to ill than to good. Anna is giddy—as you yourself tell her twenty times a day. I would keep her carefully under my own eyes. I would not even allow her to run into our house at night, as she is fond of doing," he added with marked emphasis. "She is as safe there as she is here; but it is giving her a taste of liberty that she may not be the better for in the end. When she comes in, send Grace with her, or bring her yourself: I will see her home again. Tell her she is a grown-up young lady now, and it is not proper that she should go out unattended," he concluded, laughing.

"William, I do not quite understand thee. Hast thee cause to say this?"

"All I say, Patience, is—keep her out of the way of possible harm, of undesirable friendships. Were Anna to be drawn into a liking for Herbert Dare, I am sure it would not be agreeable to Mr. Lynn. He would never consider the Dares a desirable family for her to marry into—"

"Marry into the family of the Dares!" interrupted Patience hotly. "Art thee losing thy senses, William?"

"These likings sometimes lead to marriage," quietly continued William. "Therefore, I say, keep her away from all chance of forming them. Believe me, my advice is good."

"I think I understand," concluded Patience. "I thank thee kindly, William."

CHAPTER XXIV

ANNA'S EXCUSE

A very unpleasant part of the story has now to be touched upon. Unpleasant things occur in real life, and if true pictures have to be given of the world as it exists, as it goes on its round, day by day, allusion to them cannot be wholly avoided.

Certain words of William Halliburton to Patience had run in this fashion: "Were Anna to be drawn into a liking for Herbert Dare, I am sure it would not be agreeable to Mr. Lynn. He would never consider the Dares a desirable family for her to marry into." In thus speaking, William had striven to put the case in a polite sort of form to the ears of Patience. As to any probability of marriage between one of the Dares and Anna Lynn, he would scarcely have believed it within the range of possibility. The Dares, one and all, would have considered Anna far beneath them in position, whilst the difference of religion would on Anna's side be an almost insurmountable objection. The worst that William had contemplated was the "liking" he had hinted at. He cared for Anna's welfare as he would have cared for a sister's, and he believed it would not contribute to her happiness that she should become attached to Herbert Dare. But for compromising Anna—and he had given his word not to do it—he would have spoken out openly and said there was a danger of this liking coming to pass, if she met him as he feared she had been in the habit of doing. Certainly he would not have alluded to the remote possibility of marriage, the mention of which had so scared Patience.

What had William thought, what had Patience said, could they have known that this liking was already implanted in Anna's heart beyond recall? Alas! that it should have been so! Quiet, childish, timid as Anna outwardly appeared, the strongest affection had been aroused in her heart for Herbert Dare—was filling its every crevice. These apparently shy, sensitive natures are sometimes only the more passionate and wayward within. One evening a few months previously, Anna was walking in Atterly's Field, behind their house. Anna had been in the habit of walking there—nay, of playing there—since she was a child, and she would as soon have associated harm with their garden as with that field. Farmer Atterly kept his sheep in it, and Anna had run about with the lambs as long as she could remember. Herbert Dare came up accidentally—the path through it, leading along at the back of the houses, was public, though not much frequented—and he spoke to Anna. Anna knew him to say "Good day" when she passed him in the street; and she now and then saw him at Mrs. Ashley's. Herbert stayed talking with her a few minutes, and then went on his way.

Somehow, from that time, he and Anna encountered each other there pretty frequently; and that was how the liking had grown. If a qualm of conscience crossed Miss Anna at times that it was not quite the thing for a young lady to do, thus to meet a gentleman in secret, she conveniently put the qualm away. That harm should arise from it in any way never so much as crossed her mind for a moment; and to do Herbert Dare justice, real harm was probably as far from his mind as from hers.

He grew to like her, almost as she liked him. Herbert Dare did not, in the sight of Helstonleigh, stand out as a model of all the cardinal virtues; but he was not all bad. Anna believed him all good—all honour, truth, excellence; and her heart had flashed out a rebuke to William when he hinted that Herbert was not exactly a paragon. She only knew that the very sound of his footstep made her heart leap with happiness; she only knew that to her he appeared everything that was bright and fascinating. Her great dread was, lest their intimacy should become known and separation ensue. That separation would be inevitable, were her father or Patience to become cognizant of it, Anna rightly believed.

Cunning little sophist that she was! She would fain persuade herself that an innocent meeting out of doors was justifiable, where a meeting indoors was out of the question. They had no acquaintance with the Dares; consequently Herbert could plead no excuse for calling in upon them—none at least that would be likely to carry weight with Patience. And so the young lady reconciled her conscience in the best way she could, stole out as often as she was able to meet him, and left discovery to take care of itself.

Discovery came in the shape of William Halliburton. It was bad enough; but far less alarming to Anna than it might have been. Had her father dropped upon her, she would have run away and fallen into the nearest pond, in her terror and consternation.

Though guilty of certain trifling inaccuracies—such as protesting that she "did not care" for Herbert Dare—Anna, in that interview with William, fully meant to keep the promise she made, not to meet him again. Promises, however, given under the influence of terror or other sudden emotion, are not always kept. It would probably prove so with Anna's. One thing was indisputable—that where a mind could so far forget its moral rectitude as to practise deceit in one particular, as Anna was doing, it would not be very scrupulous to keep its better promises.

Anna's thoughts for many a morning latterly, when she arose, had been "This evening I shall see him," and the prospect seemed to quicken her fingers, as it quickened her heart. But on the morning after the discovery, her first thought was, "I must never see him again as I have done. How shall I warn him not to come?" That he would be in the field again that evening, unless warned, she knew: if William Halliburton saw him there a quarrel might ensue between them; at any rate, an unpleasant scene. Anna came down, feeling cross and petulant, and inclined to wish William had been at the bottom of the sea before he had found them out the previous evening.

"Where there's a will, there's a way," it is said. Anna Lynn contrived that day to exemplify it. Her will was set upon seeing Herbert Dare, and she did see him: it can scarcely be said by accident. Anna contrived to be sent into the town by Patience on an errand, and she managed to linger so long in the neighbourhood of Mr. Dare's office, gazing in at the shops in West Street (if Patience had only seen her!), that Herbert Dare passed.

"Anna!"

"Herbert, I have been waiting in the hope of seeing thee," she whispered, her manner timid as a fawn, her pretty cheeks blushing. "Thee must not come again in the evening, for I cannot meet thee."

"Why so?" asked Herbert.

"William Halliburton saw me with thee last night, and he says it is not right. I had to give him my promise not to meet thee again, or he would have told my father."

Herbert cast a word to William; not a complimentary one. "What business is it of his?" he asked.

"I dare not stay talking to thee, Herbert. Patience will likely be sending Grace after me, finding me so long away. But I was obliged to tell thee this, lest thee should be coming again. Fare thee well!"

Passing swiftly from him, Anna went on her way. Herbert did not choose to follow her in the open street. She went along, poor child, with her head down and her eyelashes glistening. It was little else than bitter sorrow thus to part with Herbert Dare.

Patience was standing at the door, looking out for her when she came in sight of home. Patience had given little heed to what William Halliburton had said the previous night, or she might not have sent Anna into Helstonleigh alone. In point of fact, Patience had thought William a little fanciful. But when, instead of being home at four o'clock, as she ought to have been, the clock struck five, and she had not made her appearance, Patience began to think she did let her have too much liberty.

"Now, where hast thee been?" was Patience's salutation, delivered in icy tones.

"I met so many people, Patience. They stayed to talk with me."

Brushing past Patience, deaf to her subsequent reproofs, Anna flew up to her own room. When she came down, her father had entered, and Patience was pouring out the tea.

"Wilt thee tell thy father where thee hast been?"

The command was delivered in Patience's driest tone. Anna, inwardly tormented, outwardly vexed, burst into tears. The Quaker looked up in surprise.

Patience explained. Anna had left home at three o'clock to execute a little commission: she might well have been home in three-quarters of an hour and she had only made her appearance now.

"What kept thee, child?" asked her father.

"I only looked in at a shop or two," pleaded Anna, through her tears. "There were the prettiest new engravings in at Thomas Woakam's! If Patience had wanted me to run both ways, she should have said so."

Notwithstanding the little spice of impertinence peeping out in the last sentence, Samuel Lynn saw no reason to correct Anna. That she could ever be wrong, he scarcely admitted to his own heart. "Dry thy tears, child, and take thy tea," said he. "Patience wanted thee, maybe, for some household matter; it can wait another opportunity. Patience," he added, as if to drown the sound of his words and their remembrance, "are my shirts in order?"

"Thy shirts in order?" repeated Patience. "Why dost thee ask that?"

"I should not have asked it without reason," returned he. "Wilt thee please give me an answer?"

"The old shirts are as much in order as things, beginning to wear, can be," replied Patience. "Thy new shirts I cannot say much about. They will not be finished this side Midsummer, unless Anna sits to them a little closer than she is doing now."

"Thy shirts will be ready quite in time, father; before the old ones are gone beyond wearing," spoke up Anna.

"I don't know that," said Mr. Lynn. "Had they been ready, child, I might have wanted them now. I am going a journey."

"Is it the French journey thee hast talked of once or twice lately?" interposed Patience.

"Yes," said Samuel Lynn. "The master was speaking to me about it this afternoon. We were interrupted, and I did not altogether gather when he wishes me to start; but I fancy it will be immediately—"

"Oh, father! couldst thee not take me?"

The interruption came from Anna. Her blue eyes were glistening, her cheeks were crimson; a journey to the interior of France wore charms for her as great as it did for Cyril Dare. All the way home from West Street she had been thinking how she should spend her miserable home days, debarred of the evening snatches of Mr. Herbert's charming society. Going to France would be something.

"I wish I could take thee, child! But thee art aware thee might as well ask me to take the Malvern Hills."

In her inward conviction, Anna believed she might. Before she could oppose any answering but most useless argument, Samuel Lynn's attention was directed to the road. Parting opposite to his house, as if they had just walked together from the manufactory, were Mr. Ashley and William Halliburton. The master walked on. William, catching Samuel Lynn's eye, came across and entered.

Mr. Ashley had been telling William some news. Though no vacillating man in a general way, it appeared that he had again reconsidered his determination with regard to despatching William to France. He had come to the resolve to send him, as well as Samuel Lynn. William could not help surmising that his betrayed emotion the previous night, his fears touching Mr. Ashley's reason for not sending him, may have had something to do with that gentleman's change of mind.

"Will you be troubled with me?" asked he of Mr. Lynn, when he had imparted this to him.

"If such be the master's fiat, I cannot help being troubled with thee," was the answer of Samuel Lynn; but the tone of his voice spoke of anything rather than dissatisfaction. "Why is he sending thee as well as myself?"

"He told me he thought it might be best that you should show me the markets, and introduce me to the skin merchants, as I should probably have to make the journey alone in future," replied William. "I had no idea, until the master mentioned it now, that you had ever made the journey yourself, Mr. Lynn; you never told me."

"There was nothing, that I am aware of, to call for the information," observed the Quaker, in his usual dry manner. "I went there two or three times on my own account when I was in business for myself. Did the master tell thee when he should expect us to start?"

"Not precisely. The beginning of the week, I think."

"I have been asking my father if he cannot take me," put in Anna, in plaintive tones, looking at William.

"And I have answered her, that she may as well ask me to take the Malvern Hills," was the rejoinder of Samuel Lynn. "I could as likely take the one as the other."

Likely or unlikely, Samuel Lynn would have taken her beyond all doubt—taken her with a greedy, sheltering grasp—had he foreseen the result of leaving her at home, the grievous trouble that was to fall upon her head.

"Thee wilt drink a dish of tea with us this evening, William?"

It was Patience who spoke. William hesitated, but he saw they would be pleased at his doing so, and he sat down. The conversation turned upon France—upon Samuel Lynn's experiences, and William's anticipations. Anna lapsed into silence and abstraction.

In the bustle of moving, when Samuel Lynn was departing for the manufactory, William, before going home to his books, contrived to obtain a word alone with Anna.

"Have you thought of our compact?"

"Yes," she said, freely meeting his eyes in honest truth. "I saw him this afternoon in the street; I went on purpose to try and meet him. He will not come again."

"That is well. Mind and take care of yourself, Anna," he added, with a smile. "I shall be away, and not able to give an eye to you, as I freely confess it had been my resolve to do."

Anna shook her head. "He does not come again," she repeated. "Thee may go away believing me, William."

And William did go away believing her—went away to France putting faith in her; thinking that the undesirable intimacy was at an end for ever.

CHAPTER XXV

PATIENCE COME TO GRIEF

In the early part of March, Samuel Lynn and William departed on their journey to France. And the first thought that occurred to Patience afterwards was one that is apt to occur to many thrifty housekeepers on the absence of the master—that of instituting a thorough cleansing of the house, from garret to cellar; or, as Anna mischievously expressed it, "turning the house inside out." She knew Patience did not like her wild phrases, and therefore she used them.

Patience was parting with Grace—the servant who had been with them so many years. Grace had resolved to get married. In vain Patience assured her that marriage, generally speaking, was found to be nothing better than a bed of thorns. Grace would not listen. Others had risked the thorns before her, and she thought she must try her chance with the rest. Patience had no resource but to fall in with the decision, and to look out for another servant. It appeared that she could not readily find one; at least, one whom she would venture to engage. She was unusually particular; and while she waited and looked out, she engaged Hester Dell, a humble member of her own persuasion, to come in temporarily. Hester lived with her aged mother, not far off, chiefly supporting herself by doing fine needlework at her own, or at the Friends' houses. She readily consented to take up her abode with Patience for a month or so, to help with the housework, and looked upon it as a sort of holiday.

"It's of no use to begin the house until Grace shall be gone," observed Patience to Anna. "She'd likely be scrubbing the paper on the walls, instead of the paint, for her head is turned just now."

"What fun, if she should!" ejaculated Anna.

"Fun for thee, perhaps, who art ignorant of cost and labour," rebuked Patience. "I shall wait until Grace has departed. The day that she goes, Hester comes in; and I shall have the house begun the day following."

"Couldn't thee have it begun the same day?" saucily asked Anna.

"Will thee attend to thy stitching?" returned Patience sharply. "Thy father's wristbands will not be done the better for thy nonsense."

"Shall I be turned out of my bedroom?" resumed Anna.

"For a night, perchance. Thee canst go into thy father's. But the top of the house will be done first."

"Is the roof to be scrubbed?" went on Anna. "I don't know how Hester will hold on while she does it."

"Thee art in one of thy wilful humours this morning," responded Patience. "Art thee going to set me at defiance now thy father's back is turned?"

"Who said anything about setting thee at defiance?" asked Anna. "I should like to see Hester scrubbing the roof!"

"Thee hadst better behave thyself, Anna," was the retort of Patience. And Anna, in her lighthearted wilfulness, burst into a merry laugh.

Grace departed, and Hester came in: a quiet little body, of forty years, with dark hair and defective teeth. Patience, as good as her word, was up betimes the following morning, and had the house up betimes, to institute the ceremony. Their house contained the same accommodation as Mrs. Halliburton's, with this addition—that the garret in the Quaker's had been partitioned off into two chambers. Patience slept in one; Grace had occupied the other. The three bedrooms on the floor beneath were used, one by Mr. Lynn, one by Anna; the other was kept as a spare room, for any chance visitor; the "best room" it was usually called. The house belonged to Mr. Lynn. Formerly, both houses had belonged to him; but at the time of his loss he had sold the other to Mr. Ashley.

The ablutions were in full play. Hester, with a pail, mop, scrubbing-brush, and other essentials, was ensconced in the top chambers; Anna, ostensibly at her wristband stitching (but the work did not get on very fast), was singing to herself in an undertone in one of the parlours, the door safely shut; while Patience was exercising a general superintendence, giving an eye everywhere. Suddenly there echoed a loud noise, as of a fall, and a scream resounded throughout the house. It appeared to come from what they usually called the bedroom floor. Anna flew up the stairs, and Hester Dell flew down the upper ones. At the foot of the garret stairs, her head against the door of Anna's chamber, lay Patience and a heavy bed-pole. In attempting to carry the pole down from her room, she had somehow overbalanced herself, and fallen heavily.

"Is the house coming down?" Anna was beginning to say. But she stopped in consternation when she saw Patience. Hester attempted to pick her up.

"Thee cannot raise me, Hester. Anna, child, thee must not attempt to touch me. I fear my leg is br—"

Her voice died away, her eyes closed, and a hue, as of death, overspread her countenance. Anna, more terrified than she had ever been in her life, flew round to Mrs. Halliburton's.

Dobbs, from her kitchen, saw her coming—saw the young face streaming with tears, heard the short cries of alarm—and Dobbs stepped out.

"Why, what on earth's the matter now?" asked she.

Anna seized Dobbs, and clung to her; partly that to do so seemed some protection in her great terror. "Oh, Dobbs, come in to Patience!" she cried. "I think she's dying."

The voice reached the ears of Jane. She came forth from the parlour. Dobbs was then running in to Samuel Lynn's, and Jane ran also, understanding nothing.

Patience was reviving when they entered. All her cry was, that they must not move her. One of her legs was in some manner doubled under her, and doubled over the pole. Jane felt a conviction that it was broken.

"Who can run fastest?" she asked. "We must have Mr. Parry here."

Hester waited for no further instruction. She caught up her fawn-coloured Quaker shawl and grey bonnet, and was off, putting them on as she ran. Anna, sobbing wildly, turned and hid her face on Jane, as one who wants to be comforted. Then, her mood changing, she threw herself down beside Patience, the tears from her own eyes falling on Patience's face.

"Patience, dear Patience, canst thee forgive me? I have been wilful and naughty, but I never meant to cross thee really. I did it only to tease thee; but I loved thee all the while."

Patience, suffering as she was, drew down the repentant face to kiss it fervently. "I know it, dear child; I know thee. Don't thee distress thyself for me."

Mr. Parry came, and Patience was carried into the spare room. Her leg was broken, and badly broken; the surgeon called it a compound fracture.

So there was an end to the grand cleansing scheme for a long time to come! Patience lay in sickness and pain, and Hester had to make her her first care. Anna's spirits revived in a day or two. Mr. Parry said a cure would be effected in time; that the worst of the business was the long confinement for Patience; and Anna forgot her dutiful fit of repentance. Patience would be well again, would be about as before; and, as to the present confinement, Anna rather grew to look upon it as the interposition of some good fairy, who must have taken her own liberty under its special protection.

Whether Anna would have succeeded in eluding the vigilance of Patience up cannot be told; she certainly did that of Patience down. Anna had told Herbert Dare that he was not to pay a visit to Atterly's field again, or expect her to pay one; but Herbert Dare was about the last person to obey such advice. Had William Halliburton remained to be—as Herbert termed it—a treacherous spy, there's no doubt that Herbert would have striven to set his vigilance at defiance: with William's absence, the field, both literally and figuratively, was open to him. In the absence of Samuel Lynn, it was doubly open. Herbert Dare knew perfectly well that if the Quaker once gained the slightest inkling of his secret acquaintance with Anna, it would effectually be put a stop to. To wear a cloak resembling William Halliburton's, on his visits to the field, had been the result of a bright idea. It had suddenly occurred to Mr. Herbert that if the Quaker's lynx eyes did by mischance catch sight of the cloak, promenading some fine night at the back of his residence, they would accord it no particular notice, concluding the wearer to be William Halliburton taking a moonlight stroll at the back of his residence. Nevertheless, Herbert had timed his visits so as to make pretty sure that Samuel Lynn was out of view, safely ensconced in Mr. Ashley's manufactory; and he had generally succeeded. Not quite always, as the reader knows.

Anna was of a most persuadable nature. In defiance of her promise to William, she suffered Herbert Dare to persuade her again into the old system of meeting him. Guileless as a child, never giving thought to wrong or to harm—beyond the wrong and harm of thus clandestinely stealing out, and that wrong she conveniently ignored—she saw nothing very grave in doing it. Herbert could not come indoors; Patience would be sure not to welcome him; and therefore, she logically argued to her own mind, she must go out to him.

She had learnt to like Herbert Dare a great deal too well not to wish to meet him, to talk with him. Herbert, on his part, had learnt to like her. An hour passed in whispering to Anna, in mischievously untying her sober cap, and letting the curls fall, in laying his own hand fondly on the young head, and telling her he cared for her beyond every earthly thing. It had grown to be one of his most favourite recreations; and Herbert was not one to deny himself any recreation that he took a fancy to. He intended no harm to the pretty child. It is possible that, had any one seriously pointed out to him the harm that might arise to Anna, in the estimation of Helstonleigh, should these stolen meetings be found out, Herbert might for once have done violence to his inclinations, and not have persisted in them. Unfortunately—very unfortunately, as it was to turn out—there was no one to give this word of caution. Patience was ill, William was away: and no one else knew anything about it. In point of fact, Patience could not be said to know anything, for William's warning had not made the impression upon her that it ought to have done. Patience's confiding nature was in fault. For Anna deliberately to meet Herbert Dare or any other "Herbert" in secret, she would have deemed a simple impossibility. In the judgment of Patience, it had been nothing less than irredeemable sin.

What did Herbert Dare promise himself, in thus leading Anna into this imprudence? Herbert promised himself nothing—beyond the passing gratification of the hour. Herbert had never been one to give any care to the future, for himself or for any one else; and he was not likely to begin to do it at present. As to seeking Anna for his wife, such a thought had never crossed his mind. In the first place, at the rate the Dares—Herbert and his brothers—were going on, a wife for any of them seemed amongst the impossibilities. Unless, indeed, she made the bargain beforehand to live upon air; there was no chance of their having anything else to live upon. But, had Herbert been in a position, pecuniarily considered, to marry ten wives, Anna Lynn would not have been one of them. Agreeable as it might be to him to linger with Anna, he considered her far beneath himself; and pride, with Herbert, was always in the ascendant. Herbert had been introduced to Anna Lynn at Mrs. Ashley's, and that threw a sort of prestige around her. She was also enshrined in the respectable Quaker body of the town. But for these facts, for being who she was, Herbert might have been less scrupulous in his behaviour towards her. He would not—it may be as well to say he dared not—be otherwise than considerate towards Anna Lynn; but, on the other hand, he would not have considered her worthy to become his wife. On the part of Samuel Lynn, he would far rather have seen his child in her coffin, than the wife of Herbert Dare. The young Dares did not bear a good name in Helstonleigh.

In this most uncertain and unsatisfactory state of things, what on earth—as Dobbs had said to Anna—did Herbert want with her at all? Far, far better that he had allowed Anna to fall in with the sensible advice of William Halliburton—"Do not meet him again." It was a sad pity; and it is very probable that Herbert Dare regretted it afterwards, in the grievous misery it entailed. Misery to both; and without positive ill conduct on the part of either.

But that time has not yet come, and we are only at the stage of Samuel Lynn's absence and Patience's broken leg. Anna had taken to stealing out again; and her wits were at work to concoct a plausible excuse for her absences to Hester Dell, that no tales might be carried to Patience.

"Hester, Patience is a fidget. Thee must see that. She would like me to keep at my work all day, all day, evening too, and never have a breath of fresh air! She'd like me to shut myself up in this parlour, as she has now to be shut up in her room; never to be in the garden in the lovely twilight; never to run and look at the pretty lambs in the field; never to go next door, and say 'How dost thee?' to Jane Halliburton! It's a shame, Hester!"

"Well, I think it would be, if it were true," responded Hester, a simple woman in mind and language, who loved Anna almost as well as did Patience. "But dost thee not think thee art mistaken, child? Patience seems anxious that thee should go out. She says I am to take thee."

"I dare say!" responded Anna; "and leave her all alone! How would she come downstairs with her broken leg, if any one knocked at the door? She's a dreadful fidget, Hester. She'd like to watch me as a cat watches a mouse. Look at last night! It's all on account of these shirts. She thinks I shan't get them done. I shall."

"Why, dear, I think thee wilt," returned Hester, casting her eyes on the work. "Thee art getting on with them."

"I am getting on nicely. I have done all the stitching, and nearly the plain part of the bodies; I shall soon be at the gathers. What did she say to thee last night?"

"She said, 'Go to the parlour, Hester, and See whether Anna does not want a light.' And I came and could not find thee. And then she said thee wast always running into the next door, troubling them, and she would not have it done. Thee came in just at the time, and she scolded thee."

"Yes, she did," resentfully spoke Anna. "I tell thee, Hester, she's the worst fidget breathing. I give thee my word, Hester, that I had not been inside the Halliburtons' door. I had been in this garden and in the field. I had been close at work all day—"

"Not quite all day, dear," interrupted Hester, willing to smooth matters to the child as far as she was able. "Thee hadst thy friend Mary Ashley here to call in the morning, and thee hadst Sarah Dixon in the afternoon."

"Well, I had been at work a good part of the day," corrected Anna, "and I wanted some fresh air after it. Where's the crime?"

"Crime, dear! It's only natural. If I had not my errands to go upon, and so take the air that way, I should like myself to run to the field, when my work was done."

"So would any one else, except Patience," retorted Anna. "Hester, look thee. When she asks after me again, thee hast no need to tell her, should I have run out. It only fidgets her, and she is not well enough to be fidgeted. Thee tell her I am at my sewing. But I can't be sewing for ever, Hester; I must have a few minutes' holiday from it now and then. Patience might have cause to grumble if I ran away and left it in the day."

"Well, dear, I think it is only reasonable," slowly answered Hester, considering the matter over. "I'll not tell her thee art in the garden again; for she must be kept tranquil, friend Parry says."

"She was just as bad when I was a little girl, Hester," concluded Anna. "She wouldn't let me run in the garden alone then, for fear I should eat the gooseberries. But it is not the gooseberry season now."

"All quite true and reasonable," thought Hester Dell.

And so the young lady contrived to enjoy a fair share of evening liberty. Not but that she would have done with more, had she known how to get it. And as the weeks went on, and the cold weather of early spring merged into summer days, more genial nights, she and Herbert Dare grew bold in their immunity from discovery, and scarcely an evening passed but they might have been seen, had any one been on the watch, in Farmer Atterly's field. Anna had reached the point of taking his arm now; and there they would pace under cover of the hedge, Herbert talking, and Anna dreaming that she was in Eden.

CHAPTER XXVI

THE GOVERNESS'S EXPEDITION

Herbert Dare sat enjoying the beauty of the April evening in the garden of Pomeranian Knoll. He was hoisted on the back of a garden bench, and balanced himself astride it, the tip of one toe resting on the seat, the other foot dangling. The month was drawing to its close, and the beams of the setting sun streamed athwart Herbert's face. It might be supposed that he had seated himself there to bask in the soft, still air and lovely sunset. In point of fact, he hardly knew whether the sun was rising or setting— whether the evening was fair or foul—so buried was he in deep thought and perplexing care.

The particular care which was troubling Herbert Dare, was one which has, at some time or other, troubled the peace of a great many of us. It was pecuniary embarrassment. Herbert had been in it for a long time; had, in fact, been sinking into it deeper and deeper. He had managed to ward it off hitherto in some way or other; but the time to do that much longer was going by. He was not given to forethought, it has been previously mentioned; but he could not conceal from himself that unpleasantness would ensue, and that speedily, unless something could be done. What was that something to be? He did not know; he could not imagine. His father protested that he had not the means to help him; and Herbert believed that Mr. Dare spoke the truth. Not that Mr. Dare knew of the extent of the embarrassment. Had he done so, it would have come to the same thing, so far as his help went. His sons, as he said, had drained him to the utmost.

Anthony passed the end of the walk. Whether he saw Herbert or not, certain it was, that he turned away from his direction. Herbert lifted his eyes, an angry light in them. He lifted his voice also, angry too.

"Here, you! Don't go skulking off because you see me sitting here. I want you."

Anthony was taken to. It is more than probable that he was skulking off, and that he had seen Herbert, for he did not particularly care then to come into contact with his brother. Anthony was in embarrassment on his own score; was ill at ease from more reasons than one; and when the mind is troubled, sharp words do not tend to soothe it. Little else than sharp words had been exchanged latterly between Anthony and Herbert Dare.

It was no temporary ill-feeling, vexed to-day, pleased to-morrow, which had grown up between them; the ill-will had existed a long time. Herbert believed that his brother had injured him, had wilfully played him false, and his heart bitterly resented it. That Anthony was in fault at the beginning was undoubted. He had drawn Herbert unsuspiciously—unsuspiciously on Herbert's part, you understand—into some mess with regard to bills. Anthony was fond of "bills;" Herbert, more wise in that respect, had never meddled with them: his opinion coincided with his father's: they were edged tools, which cut both ways. "Eschew bills if you want to die upon your own bed," was a saying of Mr. Dare's, frequently uttered for the benefit of his sons. Good advice, no doubt. Mr. Dare, as a lawyer, ought to know. Herbert had held by the advice; Anthony never had; and the time came when Anthony took care that his brother should not.

In a period of deep embarrassment for Anthony, he had persuaded Herbert to sign two bills for him, their aggregate amount being large; assuring him, in the most earnest and apparently truthful manner, that the money to meet them, when due, was already provided. Herbert, in his good nature, fell into the snare. It turned out not only that the bills were not met at all, but Anthony had so contrived it that Herbert should be responsible, not he himself. Herbert regarded it as a shameful piece of treachery, and never ceased to reproach his brother. Anthony, who was of a sullen, morose temper, resented the reproach; and they did not lead together the happiest of lives. The bills were not settled yet; indeed, they formed part of Herbert's most pressing embarrassments. This was one cause of the ill-feeling between them, and there were others, of a different nature. Anthony and Herbert Dare had never been cordial with each other, even in childhood.

Anthony, called by Herbert, advanced. "Who wants to skulk away?" asked he. "Are you judging me by yourself?"

"I hope not," returned Herbert, in tones of the most withering contempt and scorn. "Listen to me. I've told you five hundred times that I'll have some settlement, and if you don't come to it amicably, I'll force you to it. Do you hear, you? I'll force you to it."

"Try it," retorted Anthony, with a mocking laugh; and he coolly walked away.

Walked away, leaving Herbert in a towering rage. He felt inclined to follow him; to knock him down. Had Anthony only met the affair in a proper spirit, it had been different. Had he said, "Herbert, I am uncommonly vexed—I'll see what can be done," or words to that effect, half the sting in his brother's mind would have been removed; but, to taunt Herbert with having to pay—as he sometimes did—was almost unbearable. Had Herbert been of Anthony's temper, he would have proved that it was quite unbearable.

But Herbert's temper was roused now. It was the toss of a die whether he followed Anthony and struck him down, or whether he did not. The die was cast by the appearance of Signora Varsini; and Anthony, for that evening, escaped.

It was not very gallant of Herbert to remain where he was, in the presence of the governess, astride upon the garden bench. Herbert was feeling angry in no ordinary degree, and this may have been his excuse. She came up, apparently in anger also. Her brow was frowning, her compressed mouth drawn in until its lips were hidden.

There is good advice in the old song or saying: "It is well to be off with the old love, before you are on with the new." As good advice as that of Mr. Dare's, relative to the bills. Herbert might have sung it in character. He should have made things square with the Signora Varsini, before entering too extensively on his friendship with Anna Lynn.

Not that the governess could be supposed to occupy any position in the mind or heart of Herbert Dare, except as governess; governess to his sisters. Herbert would probably have said so, had you asked him. What she might have said, is a different matter. She looks angry enough to say anything just now. The fact appeared to be—so far as any one not personally interested in the matter could be supposed to gather it—that Herbert had latterly given offence to the governess, by not going to the school-room for what he called his Italian lessons. Of course he could not be in two places at once; and if his leisure hour after dinner was spent in Atterly's field, it was impossible that he could be in the school-room, learning Italian with the governess. But she resented it as a slight. She was of an exacting nature; probably of a jealous nature; and she regarded it as a personal slight, and resented it bitterly. She had been rather abrupt in speech and manner to Herbert, in consequence; and that, he resented. But, being naturally of an easy temper, Herbert was no friend to unnecessary disputes. He tried what he could towards soothing the young lady; and, finding he effected no good in that way, he adopted the other alternative—he shunned her. The governess perceived this, and worked herself up into a state of semi-fury.

She came down upon him in full sail. The moment Herbert saw her, he remembered having given her a half-promise the previous day to pay her a visit that evening. "Now for it," thought he to himself.

"Why you keep me waiting like this?" began she, when she was close to him.

"Have I kept you waiting?" civilly returned Herbert. "I am very sorry. The fact is, mademoiselle, I have a good deal of worry upon me, and I'm fit for nobody's company but my own to-night. You might not have thanked me for my visit, had I come."

"That is my own look-out," replied the governess. "When a gentleman makes a promise to me, I expect him to keep it. I go up to the school-room, and I wait, I wait, I wait! Ah, my poor patience, how I wait! I have that copy of Tasso, that you said you would like to see. Will you come?"

Herbert thought he was in for it. He glanced at the setting sun—at least, at the spot where the sun had gone down, for it had sunk below the horizon, leaving only crimson streaks in the grey sky to tell of what had been. Twilight was rapidly coming on, when he would depart to pay his usual evening visit: there was no time, he decided, for Tasso and the governess.

"I'll come another evening," said he. "I have an engagement, and I must go out to keep it."

A stony hardness settled on mademoiselle's face. "What engagement?" she imperatively demanded.

It might be thought that Herbert would have been justified in civilly declining to satisfy her curiosity. What was it to her? Apparently he thought otherwise. Possibly he was afraid of an outbreak.

"What engagement! Oh—I am going to play a pool at billiards with Lord Hawkesley. He is in Helstonleigh again."

"And that is what you go for, every evening—to play billiards with Lord Hawkesley?" she resumed, her eyes glistening ominously.

"Of course it is, mademoiselle. With Hawkesley or other fellows."

"A lie!" curtly responded mademoiselle.

"I say," cried Herbert, laughing good-humouredly: "do you call that orthodox language?"

"It nothing to you what I call it," she cried, clipping her words in her vehemence, as she would do when excited. "It not with Milord Hawkesley, not to billiards that you go! I know it is not."

"Then I tell you that I often play billiards," cried Herbert. "On my honour I do."

"May-be, may-be," answered she, very rapidly. "But it not to billiards that you go every evening. Every evening!—every evening! Not an evening now, but you go out, you go out! I bought Tasso—do you know that I bought Tasso?—that I have bought it with my money, that you may have the pleasure of hearing me read it, as you said—as you call it? Should I spend the money, had I thought you would not come when I had it—would not care to hear it read?"

Had she been in a more amiable mood, Herbert would have told her that she was a simpleton for spending her money; he would have told her that Tasso, read in the original, would have been to him unintelligible as Sanscrit. He had a faint remembrance of saying to mademoiselle that he should like to read Tasso, in answer to a remark that Tasso was her favourite of the Italian poets: but he had only made the observation carelessly, without seriously meaning anything. And she had been so foolish as to go and buy it!

"Will you come this evening and hear it begun?" she continued, breaking the pause, and speaking rather more graciously.

"Upon my word of honour, Bianca, I can't to-night," he answered, feeling himself, between the two—the engagement made, and the engagement sought to be made—somewhat embarrassed. "I will come another evening; you may depend upon me."

"You say to me yesterday that you would come this evening; that I might depend upon you. Much you care!"

"But I could not help myself. An engagement arose, and I was obliged to fall in with it. I was, indeed. I'll hear Tasso another evening."

"You will not break your paltry engagement at billiards to keep your word to a lady! C'est bien!"

"It—it is not altogether that," replied Herbert, getting out of the reproach in the best way he could. "I have some business as well."

She fastened her glistening eyes upon him. There was an expression in them which Herbert neither understood nor liked. "C'est très bien!" she slowly repeated. "I know where you are going, and for what!"

A smile—at her assumed knowledge, and what it was worth—flitted over Herbert Dare's face. "You are very wise," said he.

"Take care of yourself, mon ami! C'est tout ce que je vous dis."

"Now, mademoiselle, what is the matter, that you should look and speak in that manner?" he asked, still in the same good-humoured tone, as if he would fain pass the affair away in a joke. "I'm sure I have enough bother upon me, without your adding to it."

"What is your bother?"

"Never mind: it would give you no pleasure to know it. It is caused by Anthony—and be hanged to him!"

"Anthony is worth ten of you!" fiercely responded mademoiselle.

"Every one to his own liking," carelessly remarked Herbert. "It's well for me that all the world does not think as you do, mademoiselle."

Mademoiselle looked as though she would like to beat him. "So!" she foamed, drawing back her bloodless lips; "now that your turn is served, Bianca Varsini may just be sent to the enfer! Garde-toi, mon camarade!"

"Garde your voice," replied Herbert. "The cows yonder will think it's a tempest. I wish my turn was served, in more ways than one. What particular turn do you mean? If it's buying Tasso, I'll purchase it from you at double price."

He could not help giving her a little chaff. It was what he would have called it: chaff. Exacting people fretted his generally easy temper, and he was beginning to fear that she would detain him until it was too late to see Anna.

But, on the latter score, he was set at rest. With a few words, spoken in Italian, she nodded her head angrily at him, and turned away. Fierce words, in spite of their low tone, Herbert was sure they were, but he could not catch one of them. Had he caught them all, it would have come to the same, so far as his understanding went. Excellent as Signora Varsini's method of teaching Italian may have been, her lessons had not as yet been very efficient for Herbert Dare.

She crossed her hands before her, and went down the walk, taking the path to the house. Proceeding straight up to the school-room, she met Cyril on the stairs. He had apparently been dressing himself for the evening, and was going out to spend it. The governess caught him abruptly, pulled him inside the school-room, and closed the door.

"I say, mademoiselle, what's that for?" asked Cyril, believing, by the fierce look of the young lady, that she was about to take some summary vengeance upon him.

"Cyril! you tell me. Where is it that Herbert goes to of an evening? Every evening—every evening?"

Cyril stared excessively. "What does it concern you to know where he goes, mademoiselle?" returned he.

"I want to know for my own reasons, and that's enough for you, Monsieur Cyril. Where does he go?"

"He goes out," responded Cyril.

The governess stamped her foot petulantly. "I could tell you that he goes out. I ask you where it is that he goes?"

"How should I know?" was Cyril's answer. "It's not my business."

"Don't you know?" demanded mademoiselle.

"No, that I don't," heartily spoke Cyril. "Do you suppose I watch him, mademoiselle? He'd pretty soon pitch into me, if he caught me at that game. I dare say he goes to billiards."

The suggestion excited the ire of the governess. "He has been telling you to say so!" she said, menace in every tone of her voice, every gesture of her lifted hand.

Cyril opened his eyes to their utmost width. He could not understand why the governess should be asking him this, or why Herbert's movements should concern her. "I know nothing at all about it," he answered; and, so far, he spoke the truth. "I don't know that Herbert goes anywhere in particular of an evening. If he does, he would not tell me."

She laid her hand heavily on his shoulder; she brought her face—terrible in its livid earnestness—almost into contact with his. "Ecoutez, mon ami," she whispered to the amazed Cyril. "If you are going to play this game with me, I will play one with you. Who wore the cloak to that boucherie, and got the money?—who ripped out the écossais side afterwards, leaving it all mangled and open? Think you, I don't know? Ah, ha! Monsieur Cyril, you cannot play the farce with me!"

Cyril's face turned ghastly, drops of sweat broke out over his forehead. "Hush!" he cried, looking round in the instinct of terror, lest listeners should be at hand.

"Yes; you say, 'Hush!'" she resumed. "I will hush if you don't make me speak. I have hushed ever since. You tell me what I want to know, and I'll hush always."

"Mademoiselle Varsini!" he cried, his manner too painfully earnest for her to doubt now that he spoke the truth: "I declare that I know nothing of Herbert's movements. I don't know where he goes or what he does. When I told you I supposed he went to billiards, I said what I thought might be the case. He may go to fifty places of an evening, for all I can tell. Tell me what it is you want found out, and I will try and do it."

Cyril was not one to play the spy on his brother; in fact, as he had just classically observed to the young lady, Herbert would have "pitched into" him, had he found him attempting it. And serve him right! But Cyril saw that he was in her power; and that made all the difference. He would now have tracked Herbert to the ends of the earth at her bidding.

But she did not bid him. Quite the contrary. She took her hand from Cyril's shoulder, opened the door, and said she did not want him any longer. "It is no matter," cried she; "I wanted to learn something about Monsieur Herbert, for a reason; but if you do not know it, let it pass. It is no matter."

Cyril departed; first of all lifting his cowardly face. It looked a coward's then. "You'll keep counsel, mademoiselle?"

"Yes. When people don't offend me, I don't offend them."

She stood at the door after he had gone down, half in, half out of the room, apparently in deep thought. Presently footsteps were heard coming up, and she retreated and closed the door.

They were those of Herbert. He went on to his room, remained there a few minutes, and then came out again. Mademoiselle had the door ajar as he descended. Her quick eye detected that he had been giving a few finishing touches to his toilette—brushing his hair, pulling down his wristbands, and various other little odds and ends of dandyism.

"And you do that to play billiards!" nodded she, inwardly, as she looked after him. "I'll see, monsieur."

Upstairs with a soft step, went she, to her own chamber. She reached from her box a long and loose dark-green cloak, similar to those worn by the women of France and Flanders, and a black silk quilted bonnet. It was her travelling attire, and she put it on now. Then she locked her chamber door behind her, and slipped down into the dining-room, with as soft a step as she had gone up.

Passing out at the open window, she kept tolerably under cover of the trees, and gained the road. It was quite dusk then, but she recognized Herbert before her, walking with a quick step. She put on a quick step also, keeping a safe distance between herself and him. He went through the town, to the London road, and turned into Atterly's field. The governess turned into it after him.

There she stopped under the hedge, to reconnoitre. A few minutes, and she could distinguish that he was joined by some young girl, whom he met with every token of respect and confidence. A strange cry went forth on the evening air.

Herbert Dare was startled. "What noise was that?" he exclaimed.

Anna had heard nothing. "It must have been one of the lambs in the field, Herbert."

"It was more like a human voice in pain," observed Herbert. But they heard no more.

They began their usual walk—a few paces backward and forward, beneath the most sheltered part of the hedge, Anna taking his arm. Mademoiselle could see, as well as the darkness allowed her; but she could not hear. Her face, peeping out of the shadowy bonnet, was not unlike the face of a tiger.

She crawled away. She had noticed as she turned into the field an iron gate that led into the garden, which the hedge skirted. She crept round to it, found it locked, and mounted it. It had spikes on the top, but the signora would not have cared just then had she found herself impaled. She got safe over it, and then considered how to reach the spot where they stood without their hearing her.

Would she be baffled? She be baffled! No. She stooped down, unlaced her boots, and stole softly on in her stockings. And there she was! almost as close to them as they were to each other.

Where had the signora heard those gentle, timid tones before? A lovely girl, looking little more than a child, in her modest Quaker dress, rose to her mind's eye. She had seen her with Miss Ashley. She—the signora—knelt down upon the earth, the better to catch what was said.

"Listeners never hear any good of themselves." It is a proverb too often exemplified, as the signora could have told that night. Herbert Dare was accounting for his late appearance, which he laid to the charge of the governess. He gave a description of the interview she had volunteered him in the garden at home—more ludicrous, perhaps, than true, but certainly not complimentary to the signora. Anna laughed; and the lady on the other side gathered that this was not the first time she had formed a topic of merriment between them. You should have seen her face. Pour plaisir, as she herself might have said.

She stayed out the interview. When it was over, and Herbert Dare had departed, she put on her boots and mounted the gate again; but she was not so agile this time, and a spike entered her wrist. Binding her handkerchief round it, to arrest the blood, she returned to Pomeranian Knoll.

Five hundred questions were showered upon her when she entered the drawing-room, looking calm and impassible as ever. Not a tress of her elaborate braids of hair was out of place; not a fold awry in her dress. Much wonder had been excited by her failing to appear at tea; Minny had drummed a waltz on her chamber door, but mademoiselle would not open it, and would not speak.

"I cannot speak when I am lying down with those vilaine headaches," remarked mademoiselle.

"Have you a headache, mademoiselle?" asked Mrs. Dare. "Will you have a cup of tea brought up?"

Mademoiselle declined the tea. She was not thirsty.

"What have you done to your wrist, mademoiselle?" called out Herbert, who was stretched on a sofa, at the far end of the room.

"My wrist? Oh, I scratched it."

"How did you manage that?"

"Ah, bah! it's nothing," responded mademoiselle.

It is grievous, when ill-feeling arises between brothers, that that ill-feeling should be cherished instead of being subdued. But such was the case with Anthony and Herbert Dare. By the time the sunny month of May came in, matters had grown to such a height between them, that Mr. Dare found himself compelled to interfere. It was beginning to make things in the house uncomfortable. They would meet at meals, and not only abstain from speaking to each other, but take every possible opportunity of showing mutual and marked discourtesy. No positive outbreak between them had as yet taken place in the presence of the family: but it was only smouldering, and might be daily looked for.

Mr. Dare, so far as the original cause went, blamed his eldest son. Undoubtedly Anthony had been solely in fault. It was a dishonourable, ungenerous, unmanly act, to draw his brother into trouble, and to do it plausibly and deceitfully. At the present stage of the affair, Mr. Dare saw occasion to blame Herbert more than Anthony. "It is you who keep up the ball, Herbert," he said to him. "If you would suffer the matter to die away, Anthony would do so." "Of course he would," Herbert replied. "He has served his turn, and would be glad that it should end there."

It was in vain that Mr. Dare talked to them. A dozen times did he recommend them to "shake hands and make it up." Neither appeared inclined to take the advice. Anthony was sullen. He would have been content to let the affair drop quietly into oblivion: perhaps, as Herbert said, had been glad that it should so drop; but, make the slightest move towards it, he would not. Herbert openly said that he'd not shake hands. If Anthony wanted ever to shake hands with him again, let him pay up.

There lay the grievance; "paying up." The bills, not paid, were a terrible thorn in the side of Herbert Dare. He was responsible, and he knew not one hour from another but he might be arrested on them. To soothe matters between his sons, Mr. Dare would willingly have taken the charge of payment upon himself, but he had positively not the money to do it with. In point of fact, Mr. Dare was growing seriously embarrassed on his own score. He had had a great deal of trouble with his sons, with Anthony in particular, and he had grown sick and tired of helping them out of pecuniary difficulties. Still, he would have relieved Herbert of this one nightmare, had it been in his power. Herbert had been deluded into it, without any advantage to himself; therefore Mr. Dare had the will, could he have managed it, to help him out. He told Herbert that he would see what he could do after a while. The promise did not relieve Herbert of present fears; neither did it restore peace between the malcontents. Had Herbert been relieved of that particular embarrassment, others would have remained to him; but that fact did not in the least lessen his soreness, as to the point in question.

It was an intensely hot day; far hotter than is usual at the season; and the afternoon sun streamed full on the windows of Pomeranian Knoll, suggesting thoughts of July, instead of May. A gay party—at any rate, a party dressed in gay attire—were crossing the hall to enter a carriage that waited at the door. Mr. Dare, Mrs. Dare, and Adelaide. Mrs. Dare had always been given to gay attire, and her daughters had inherited her taste. They were going to dine at a friend's house, a few miles' distance from Helstonleigh. The invitation was for seven o'clock. It was now striking six, the dinner-hour at Mr. Dare's.

Minny, looking half melted, had perched herself upon the end of the balustrades to watch the departure.

"You'll fall, child," said Mr. Dare.

Minny laughed, and said there was no danger of her falling. She wondered what her father would think if he saw her sometimes at her gymnastics on the balustrades, taking a sweeping slide from the top to the bottom. She generally contrived that he should not see her; or mademoiselle either. Mademoiselle had caught sight of the performance once, and had given her a whole French fable to learn by way of punishment.

"Are we to have strawberries for dinner, mamma?" asked Minny.

"You will have what I have thought proper to order," replied Mrs. Dare rather sharply. She was feeling hot and cross. Something had put her out while dressing.

"I think you might wait for strawberries until they are ripe in our own garden; not buy them regardless of cost," interposed Mr. Dare, speaking for the general benefit, but not to any one in particular.

Minny dropped the subject. "Your dress is turned up, Adelaide," said she.

Adelaide looked languidly behind her, and a maid, who had followed them down, advanced and put right the refractory dress: a handsome dress of pink silk, glistening with its own richness. At that moment Anthony entered the hall. He had just come home to dinner, and looked in a very bad humour.

"How late you'll be!" he cried.

"Not at all. We shall drive there in an hour."

They swept out at the door, Mrs. Dare and Adelaide. Mr. Dare was about to follow them when a sudden thought appeared to strike him, and he turned back and addressed Anthony.

"You young men take care that you don't get quarrelling with each other. Do you hear, Anthony?"

"I hear," ungraciously replied Anthony, not turning to speak, but continuing his way up to his dressing-room. He probably regarded the injunction with contempt, for it was too much in Anthony Dare's nature so to regard all advice, of whatever kind. Nevertheless it had been well that he had given heed to it. It had been well that that last word to his father had been one of affection!

Dinner was served. Anthony, in the absence of Mr. and Mrs. Dare, took the head. Rosa, with a show of great parade and ceremony, assumed the seat opposite to him and said she should be mistress. Minny responded that Rosa was not going to be mistress over her, and the governess desired Miss Rosa not to talk so loudly. Rather derogatory checks, these, to the dignity of a "mistress."

Herbert was not at table. Irregular as the young Dares were in many of their habits, they were generally home to dinner. Minny wondered aloud where Herbert was. Anthony replied that he was "skulking."

"Skulking!" echoed Minny.

"Yes, skulking," angrily repeated Anthony. "He left the office at three o'clock, and has never been near it since. And the governor left at four!" he added, in a tone that seemed to say he considered that also a grievance.

"Where did Herbert go to?" asked Rosa.

"I don't know," responded Anthony. "I only know that I had a double share of work to do."

Anthony Dare was no friend to work. And having had to do a little more than he would have done had Herbert remained at his post, had considerably aggravated his temper.

"Why should Monsieur Herbert go away and leave you his work to do?" inquired the governess, lifting her eyes from her plate to Anthony.

"I shall take care to ask him why," returned Anthony.

"It is not fair that he should," continued mademoiselle. "I would not have done it for him, Monsieur Anthony."

"Neither should I, had I not been obliged," said Anthony, not in the least relaxing from his ill-humour, either in looks or tone. "It was work that had to be done before post-time, and one of our clerks is away on business to-day."

Dinner proceeded to its close. Joseph hesitated, unwilling to remove the cloth. "Is it to be left for Mr. Herbert?" he asked.

"No!" imperiously answered Anthony. "If he cannot come in for dinner, dinner shall not be kept for him."

"Cook is keeping the things by the fire, sir."

"Then tell her to save herself the trouble."

So the cloth was removed, and dessert put on. To Minny's inexpressible disappointment it turned out that there were no strawberries. This put her into an ill-humour, and she left the table and the room, declaring she would not touch anything else. Mademoiselle Varsini called her back, and ordered her to her seat; she would not permit so great a breach of discipline. Cyril and George, who were not under mademoiselle's control, gulped down a glass of wine, and hastened out to keep an engagement. It was a very innocent one; a cricket match had been organized for the evening, by some of the old college boys; and Cyril and George were amongst the players. It has never been mentioned that Mr. Ashley, in his strict sense of justice, had allowed Cyril the privilege of spending his evenings at home five nights in the week, as he did to William Halliburton.

The rest remained at table. Minny, per force; Rosa, to take an unlimited quantity of oranges; Mademoiselle Varsini, because it was the custom to remain. But mademoiselle soon rose and withdrew with her pupils; Anthony was not showing himself a particularly sociable companion. He had not touched any dessert; but seemed to be drinking a good deal of wine.

As they were going out of the room, Herbert bustled in. "Now then, take care!" cried he, for Minny, paying little attention to her movements, had gone full tilt at him.

"Oh! Herbert, can't you see?" cried she, dolefully rubbing her head. "What made you so late? Dinner's gone away."

"It can be brought in again," replied Herbert carelessly. "Comme il est chaud! n'est-ce pas, mademoiselle?"

This last was addressed to the governess. Rosa screamed with laughter at his bad French, and mademoiselle smiled. "You get on in French as you do in Italian, Monsieur Herbert," cried she. "And that is what you call—backward."

Herbert laughed good-humouredly. He did not know what particular mistake he had made; truth to say, he did not care. They withdrew, and he rang the bell for his dinner.

"Mind, Herbert," cried Minny, putting in her head again at the door, "papa said you were not to quarrel."

Better, perhaps, that she had not said it! Who can tell?

The brothers remained alone. Anthony sullen, and, as yet, silent. He appeared to have emptied the port wine decanter, and to be beginning upon the sherry! Herbert strolled past him; supreme indifference in his manner—some might have said contempt—and stood just outside the window, whistling.

You have not forgotten that this dining-room window opened to the ground. The apartment was long and somewhat narrow, the window large and high, and opening in the centre, after the manner of a French one. The door was at one end of the room; the window at the other.

Anthony was in too quarrelsome a mood to remain silent long. He began the skirmish by demanding what Herbert meant by absenting himself from the office for the afternoon, and where he had been to. His resentful tones, his authoritative words, were not calculated to win a very civil answer.

They did not win one from Herbert. His tones were resentful, too; his words were coolly aggravating. Anthony was not his master; when he was, he might, perhaps, answer him. Such was their purport.

A hot interchange of words ensued. Nothing more. Anthony remained at the table; Herbert, half in, half out of the window, leaned against its frame. When Joseph returned to put things in readiness for Herbert's dinner, they had subsided into quietness. It was only a lull in the storm.

Joseph placed the dessert nearer Anthony's end of the table, and laid the cloth across the other end. Herbert came into the room. "What a time you are with dinner, Joseph!" cried he. "One would think it was being cooked over again."

"Cook's warming it, sir."

"Warming it!" echoed Herbert. "Why couldn't she keep it warm? She might be sure I should be home to dinner."

"She was keeping it warm, sir; but Mr. Anthony ordered it to be put away."

Now, the man had really no intention of making mischief when he said this: that it might cause ill-feeling between the brothers never crossed his mind. He was only anxious that he and the cook should stand free from blame; for the young Dares, when displeased with the servants, were not in the habit of sparing them. Herbert turned to Anthony.

"What business have you to interfere with my dinner? Or with anything else that concerns me?"

"I choose to make it my business," insolently retorted Anthony.

At this juncture Joseph left the room. He had laid the cloth, and had nothing more to stay for. Better perhaps that he had remained! Surely they would not have proceeded to extremities, the brothers, before their servant! In a short time, sounds, as if both were in a terrible state of fury, resounded through the house from the dining-room. The sounds did not reach the kitchen, which was partially detached from the house; but the young ladies heard them, and came running out of the drawing-room.

The governess was in the school-room. The noise penetrated even there. She also came forth, and saw her two pupils extended over the balustrades, listening. At any other time mademoiselle would have reproved them: now she crept down and leaned over in company.

"What can be the matter?" whispered she.

"Papa told them not to quarrel!" was all the answer, uttered by Minny.

It was a terrible quarrel—there was little doubt of that; no child's play. Passionate bursts of fury rose incessantly, now from one, now from the other, now from both. Hot recrimination; words that were not suited to unaccustomed ears—or to any ears, for the matter of that—rose high and loud. The governess turned pale, and Minny burst into tears.

"Some one ought to go into the room," said Rosa. "Minny, you go! Tell them to be quiet."

"I am afraid," replied Minny.

"So am I."

A fearful sound: an explosion louder than all the rest. A noise as if some heavy weight had been thrown down. Had it come to blows? Minny shrieked, and at the same moment Joseph was seen coming along with a tray, Herbert's dinner upon it.

His presence seemed to bring with it a sense of courage, and Rosa and Minny flew down followed by the governess. Herbert had been knocked down by Anthony. He was gathering himself up when Joseph opened the door. Gathering himself up in a tempest of passion, his white face a livid fury, as he caught hold of a knife from the table and rushed upon Anthony.

But Joseph was too quick for him. The man dashed his tray on the table, seized Herbert, and turned the uplifted knife downwards. "For Heaven's sake, sir, recollect yourself!" said he.

Recollect himself then? No. Persons, who put themselves into that mad state of passion, cannot "recollect" themselves. Joseph kept his hold, and the dining-room resounded with shrieks and sobs. They proceeded from Rosa and Minny. They pulled their brothers by the coats, they implored, they entreated. The women servants came flying from the kitchen, and the Italian governess asked the two gentlemen in French whether they were not ashamed of themselves.

Perhaps they were. At any rate the quarrel was, for the time, ended. Herbert flung the knife upon the table and turned his white face upon his brother.

"Take care of yourself, though!" cried he, in marked tones: "I swear you shall have it yet."

They pulled Anthony out of the room, Rosa and Minny; or it is difficult to say what rejoinder he might have made, or how violently the quarrel might have been renewed. It was certain that he had taken more wine than was good for him; and that, generally speaking, did not improve the temper of Anthony Dare. Mademoiselle Varsini walked by his side, talking volubly in French. Whether she was sympathizing or scolding, Anthony did not know. Not particularly bright at understanding French at the best of times, even when spoken slowly, he could not, in his present excitement, catch the meaning of a single word. Entering the drawing-room, he threw himself upon the sofa, intending to smooth down his ruffled plumage by taking a nap.

Herbert meanwhile had remained in the dining-room, smoothing down his ruffled plumage. Joseph and the cook were bending over the débris on the carpet. When Joseph dashed down his tray on the table, a dish of potatoes had bounded off; both dish and potatoes thereby coming to grief. Herbert sat down and made an excellent dinner. He was not of a sullen temper; and, unlike Anthony, the affair once over he was soon himself again. Should they come into contact again directly, there was no saying how it would end or what might ensue. His dinner over, he went by-and-by to the drawing-room. Joseph had just entered, and was arousing Anthony from the sleep he had dropped into. "One of the waiters from the Star-and-Garter has come, sir. He says Lord Hawkesley has sent him to say that the gentlemen are waiting for you."

"I can't go, tell him," responded Anthony, speaking as he looked, thoroughly out of sorts. "I am not going out to-night. Here! Joseph!" for the man was turning away with the message.

"Sir?"

"Take these, and bring me my slippers."

"These" were his boots, which he, not very politely, kicked off in the ladies' presence, and sent flying after Joseph. The man stooped to pick them up and was carrying them away.

"Here!—what a hurry you are in!" began Anthony again. "Take lights up to my chamber, and the brandy, and some cold water. I shall make myself comfortable there for the night. This room's unbearable, with its present company."

The last was a shaft levelled at Herbert. He did not retort, for a wonder. In fact, Anthony afforded little time for it. Before the words had well left his lips, he had left the room. Herbert began to whistle; its very tone insolent.

It appeared almost certain that the unpleasantness was not yet over; and Rosa audibly wished her papa was at home. Joseph carried to Anthony's room what he required, and then brought the tea to the drawing-room. Herbert said he should take tea with them. It was rather unusual for him to do so; it was very unusual for Anthony not to go out. Their sisters felt sure that they were only staying in to renew hostilities; and again Rosa almost passionately wished for the presence of her father.

It was dusk by the time tea was over. Herbert rose to leave the room. "Where are you going?" cried mademoiselle sharply after him.

"That's my business," he replied, not in too conciliatory a tone. Perhaps he thought the question proceeded from one of his sisters, for he was outside the door when it reached him.

"He is going into Anthony's room!" cried Rosa, turning pale, as they heard him run upstairs. "Oh, mademoiselle! what can be done? I think I'll call Joseph."

"Hush!" cried mademoiselle. "Wait you here. I will go and see."

She stole out of the room and up the stairs, intending to reconnoitre. But she had no time to do so. Herbert was coming down again, and she could only slip inside the school-room door, and peep out. He had evidently been upstairs for his cloak, for he was putting it on as he descended.

"The cloak on a hot night like this!" said mademoiselle mentally. "He must want to disguise himself!"

She stopped to listen. Joseph had come up the stairs, bringing something to Anthony, and Herbert arrested him, speaking in low tones.

"Don't make any mistake to-night about the dining-room window, Joseph. I can't think how you could have been so stupid last night!"

"Sir, I assure you I left it undone, as usual," replied Joseph. "It must have been master who fastened it."

"Well, take care that it does not occur again," said Herbert. "I expect to be in between ten and eleven; but I may be later, and I don't want to ring you up again."

Herbert went swiftly downstairs and out, choosing to depart by the way, as it appeared, that he intended to enter—the dining-room window. Joseph proceeded to Anthony's chamber: and the governess returned to her frightened pupils in the drawing-room.

"A la bonne heure!" she said to them. "Monsieur Herbert has gone out, and I heard him say to Joseph that he had gone for the evening."

"Then it's all safe!" cried Minny. And she began dancing round the room. "Mademoiselle, how pale you look!"

Mademoiselle had sat down in her place before the tea-tray, and was leaning her cheek upon her hand. She was certainly looking unusually pale. "Enough to make me!" she said, in answer to Minny. "If there were to be this disturbance often in the house, I would not stop in it for double my appointements. It has given me one of those vilaine headaches, and I think I shall go to bed. You will not be afraid to stay up alone, mesdemoiselles?"

"There is nothing to be afraid of now," promptly answered Rosa, who had far rather be without her governess's company than with it. "Don't sit up for us, mademoiselle."

"Then I will go at once," said mademoiselle. And she wished them good night, and retired to her chamber.

PART THE THIRD

CHAPTER I

ANNA LYNN'S DILEMMA

It was a lovely evening. One of those warm, still evenings that May sometimes brings us, when gnats hum in the air, and the trees are at rest. The day had been intensely hot: the evening was little less so, and Anna Lynn leaned over the gate of their garden, striving to catch what of freshness there might be in the coming night. The garish day was fading into moonlight; the distant Malvern hills grew fainter and fainter on the view; the little lambs in the field—growing into great lambs now, some of them—had long lain down to rest; and the Thursday evening bells came chiming pleasantly on the ear from Helstonleigh.

"How late he is to-night!" murmured Anna. "If he does not come soon, I shall not be able to stay out."

Even as the words passed her lips, a faint movement might be distinguished in the obscurity of the night, telling of the advent of Herbert Dare. Anna looked round to see that the windows were clear from prying eyes, and went forth to meet him.

He had halted at the usual place, under cover of the hedge. The hedge of sweetbriar, skirting that side garden into which Signora Varsini had made good her entrée, in the gratification of her curiosity. A shaded walk and a quiet one: very little fear there, of overlookers.

"Herbert, thee art late!" cried Anna.

"A good thing I was able to come at all," responded Herbert, taking Anna's arm within his own. "I thought at one time I must have remained at home, to chastise my brother Anthony."

"Chastise thy brother Anthony!" repeated Anna in astonishment.

Herbert, for the first time, told her of the unpleasantness that existed between his brother and himself. He did not mention the precise cause; but simply said Anthony had behaved ill to him, and drawn down upon him trouble and vexation. Anna was all sympathy. Had Herbert told her the offence had lain on his side, not on Anthony's, her entire sympathy had still been his. She deemed Herbert everything that was good and great and worthy. Anthony—what little she knew of him—she did not like.

"Herbert, maybe he will be striking thee in secret, when thee art unprepared."

"Let him!" carelessly replied Herbert. "I can strike again. I am stronger than he is. I know one thing: either he or I must leave my father's house and take lodgings; we can't remain in it together."

"It would be he to leave, would it not, Herbert? Thy father would not be so unjust as to turn thee out for thy brother's fault."

"I don't know about that," said Herbert. "I expect it is I who would have to go. Anthony is the eldest, and my mother's favourite."

Anna lifted her hand, in her innocent surprise. Anthony the favourite by the side of Herbert? She could not understand how so great an anomaly could exist.

Interested in the topic, the time slipped on. During a moment of silence, when they had halted in their walk, they heard what was called the ten o'clock bell strike out from Helstonleigh: a bell that boomed out over the city every night for ten minutes before ten o'clock. The sound startled Anna. She had indeed overstayed her time.

"One moment, Anna!" cried Herbert, as she was preparing to fly off. "There can't be any such hurry. Hester will not be going to bed yet, on a hot night like this. I wanted you to return me that book, if you have done with it. It is not mine, and I have been asked for it."

Truth to say, Anna would be glad to return it. The book was Moore's "Lalla Rookh," and Anna had been upon thorns all the time she had been reading it, lest by some unlucky mishap it might reach the eyes of Patience. She thought it everything that was beautiful; she had read pages of it over and over again; they wore for her a strange enchantment; but she had a shrewd suspicion that neither book nor reading would be approved by Patience.

"I'll bring it out to thee at once, Herbert, if I can," she hastily said. "If not, I will give it thee to-morrow evening."

"Not so fast, young lady," said Herbert, laughing, and detaining her. "You may not come back again. I'll wish you good night now."

"Nay, please thee let me go! What will Hester say to me?"

Scarcely giving a moment to the adieu, Anna sped with swift feet to the garden gate. But the moment she was within the barrier, and had turned the key, she began—little dissembler that she was!—to step on slowly, in a careless, nonchalant manner, looking up at the sky, turning her head to the trees, in no more hurry apparently than if bedtime were three hours off. She had seen Hester Dell standing at the house door.

"Child," said Hester gravely, "thee shouldst not stay out so late as this."

"It is so warm a night, Hester!"

"But thee shouldst not be beyond the premises. Patience would not like it. It is past thy bedtime, too. Patience's sleeping-draught has not come," she added, turning to another subject.

"Her sleeping-draught not come!" repeated Anna in surprise.

"It has not. I have been expecting the boy to knock every minute, or I should have come to see after thee. Friend Parry may have forgotten it."

"Why, of course he must have forgotten it," said Anna, inwardly promising the boy a sixpence for his forgetfulness. "The medicine always comes in the morning. Will Patience sleep without it?"

"I fear me not. What dost thee think? Suppose I were to run for it?"

"Yes, do, Hester."

They went in, Hester closing the back door and locking it. She put on her shawl and bonnet, and was going out at the front door when the clock struck ten.

"It is ten o'clock, child," she said to Anna. "Thee go to bed. Thee needst not sit up. I'll take the latch-key with me and let myself in."

"Oh, Hester! I don't want to go to bed yet," returned Anna fretfully. "It is like a summer's evening."

"But thee hadst better, child," urged Hester. "Patience has been angry with me once or twice, saying I suffer thee to sit up late. A pretty budget she will be telling thy father on his return! Thee go to bed. Thy candle is ready here on the slab. Good night."

Hester departed, shutting fast the door, and carrying with her the latch-key. Anna, fully convinced that friend Parry's forgetfulness, or the boy's, must have been designed as a special favour to herself, went softly into the best parlour to take the book out of her pretty work-table.

But the room was dark, and Anna could not find her keys. She believed she had left her keys on the top of this very work-table; but feel as she would she could not place her hands upon them. With a word of impatience, lest, with all her hurry, Herbert Dare should be gone before she could return to him with the book, she went to the kitchen, lighted the chamber candle spoken of by Hester as placed ready for her use, and carried it into the parlour.

Her keys were found on the mantel-piece. She unlocked the drawer, took from it the book, blew out the candle, and ran through the garden to the field.

Another minute, and Herbert would have left. He was turning away. In truth, he had not in the least expected to see Anna back again. "Then you have been able to come!" he exclaimed, in his surprise.

"Hester is gone out," explained Anna. "Friend Parry has forgotten to send Patience's medicine, and Hester has gone for it. Herbert, thee only think! But for Hester's expecting Parry's boy to knock at the door, she would have come out here searching for me! She said she would. I must never forget the time again. There's the book, and thank thee. I am sorry and yet glad to give it thee back."

"Is that not a paradox?" asked Herbert, with a smile. "I do not know why you should be either sorry or glad: to be both seems inexplicable."

"I am sorry to lose it: it is the most charming book I have read, and but for Patience I should like to have kept it for ever," returned Anna with enthusiasm. "But I always felt afraid of Hester's finding it and carrying it up to Patience. Patience would be angry; and she might tell my father. That is why I am glad to give it back to thee."

"Why did you not lock it up?" asked Herbert.

"I did lock it up. I locked it in my work-table drawer. But I forget to put my keys in my pocket; I leave them about anywhere. I should have been out with it sooner, but that I could not find the keys."

Anna was in no momentary hurry to run in now. Hester was safe for full twenty minutes to come, therefore her haste need not be so great. She knew that it was past her bedtime, and that Patience would be wondering (unless by great good-fortune Patience should have dropped asleep) why she did not go in to wish her good night. But these reflections Anna conveniently ignored, in the charm of remaining longer to talk about the book. She told Herbert that she had been copying the engravings, but she must put the drawings in some safe place before Patience was about again. "Tell me the time, please," she suddenly said, bringing her chatter to a standstill.

Herbert took out his watch, and held its face towards the moon. "It is twelve minutes past ten."

"Then I must be going in," said Anna. "She could be back in twenty minutes, and she must not find me out again."

Herbert turned with her, and walked to the gate; pacing slowly, both of them, and talking still. He turned in at the gate with her, and Anna made no demur. No fear of his being seen. Patience was as safe in bed as if she had been chained there, and Hester could not be back quite yet. Arrived at the door, closed as Anna had left it, Herbert put out his hand. "I suppose I must bid you a final good night now, Anna," he said in low tones.

"That thee must. I have to come down the garden again to lock the gate after thee. And Hester may not be more than three or four minutes longer. Good night to thee, Herbert."

"Let me see that it is all safe for you, against you do go in," said Herbert, laying his hand on the handle of the door to open it.

To open it? Nay: he could not open it. The handle resisted his efforts. "Did you lock it, Anna?"

Anna smiled at what she thought his awkwardness. "Thee art turning it the wrong way, Herbert. See!"

He withdrew his hand to give place to hers, and she turned the handle softly and gently the contrary way; that is, she essayed to turn it. But it would not turn for her, any more than it had turned for

Herbert Dare. A sick feeling of terror rushed over Anna, as a conviction of the truth grew upon her. Hester Dell had returned, and she was locked out!

In good truth, it was no less a calamity. Hester Dell had not gone far from the door on her errand, when she met the doctor's boy with his basket, hastening up with the medicine. "I was just coming after it," said Hester to him. "Whatever brings thee so late?"

"Mr. Parry was called out this morning before he had time to make it up, and he has only just come home," was the boy's reply.

"Better late than never," he somewhat saucily added.

"Well, so it is," acquiesced Hester, who rarely gave anything but a meek retort. And she turned back home, letting herself in with the latch-key. The house appeared precisely as she had left it, except that Anna's candle had disappeared from the mahogany slab in the passage. "That's right! the child's gone to bed," soliloquised she.

She proceeded to go to bed herself. The Quaker's was an early household. All Hester had to do now, was to give Patience her sleeping-draught. "Let me see," continued Hester, still in soliloquy, "I think I did lock the back door."

To make sure, she tried the key and found it was not locked. Rather wondering, for she certainly thought she had locked it, but dismissing the subject the next minute from her thoughts, she locked it now and took the key out. Then she continued her way up to Patience. Patience, lying there lonely and dull with her night-light, turned her eyes on Hester.

"Did thee think we had forgotten thee, Patience? Parry has been out all day, the boy says, and the physic is but this minute come."

"Where's Anna?" inquired Patience.

"She is gone to bed."

"Why did she not come to me as usual?"

"Did she not come?" asked Hester.

"I have seen nothing of her all the evening."

"Maybe she thought thee'd be dozing," observed Hester, bringing forward the sleeping-draught which she had been pouring into a wine-glass. She said no more. Her private opinion was that Anna had purposely abstained from the visit lest she should receive a scolding for going to bed late, her usual hour being half-past nine. Neither did Patience say any more. She was feeling that Anna might be a little less ungrateful. She took the draught, and Hester went to bed.

And poor Anna? To describe her dismay, her consternation, would be a useless attempt. The doors were fast—the windows were fast also. Herbert Dare essayed to soothe her, but she would not be soothed. She sat down on the step of the back door and cried bitterly: all her apprehension being for the terrible scolding she should have from Patience, were it found out; the worse than scolding if Patience told her father.

To give Herbert Dare his due, he felt truly vexed at the dilemma for Anna's sake. Could he have let her in by getting down a chimney himself, or in any other impromptu way, and so opened the door for her, he would have done it. "Don't cry, Anna," he entreated, "don't cry! I'll take care of you. Nothing shall harm you. I'll not go away."

The more he talked, the more she cried. Very like a little child. Had Herbert Dare known how to break the glass without noise he would have taken out a pane in the kitchen window, and so reached the fastening and opened it. Anna, in worse terror than ever, begged him not to attempt it. It would be sure to arouse Hester.

"But you'll be so cold, child, staying here all night!" he urged. "You are shivering now."

Anna was shivering: shivering with vexation and fear. Herbert thought it would be better that he should boldly knock up Hester; and he suggested it: nay, he pressed it. But the proposal sounded more alarming to Anna than any that had gone before it. It seemed that there was nothing to be done.

How long she sat there, crying and shivering and refusing to be comforted or to hear reason, she could not tell. Half the night, it seemed. But Anna, you must remember, was counting time by her own state of mind, not by the clock. Suddenly a bright thought, as a ray of light, flashed into her brain.

"There's the pantry window," she cried, arresting her tears. "How could I ever have forgotten it? There is no glass, and thee art strong enough to push in the wire."

This pantry window Herbert Dare had known nothing about. It was at the side of the house, thickly surrounded by shrubs; a square window frame, protected by wire. He fought his way to it amidst the shrubs; but to get in proved a work of time and difficulty. The window was at some height from the ground, the wire was strong. Anna sat on the door-step, never stirring, leaving him to get in if he could, her tears falling, and terrific visions of Patience's anger chasing each other through her mind. And the night went on.

"Anna!"

She could have shouted forth a cry of delight as she leaped up. He had entered, had found his way to the kitchen window, had gently raised it, and was softly calling to her. Some little difficulty still, but with Herbert's assistance she was safely landed, a great tear in her dress the only damage. He had managed to obtain a light by means of some fusees in his pocket, and had lighted a candle. Anna sat down on a chair, her face radiant through her tears. "How shall I ever thank thee?"

He was looking at his fingers with a half-serious, half-mocking expression of dismay. The wire had torn them in many places, and they were bleeding. "I could have got in quicker had I forced the wire out in the middle," he observed, "but that would have told tales. I pushed it away from the side, and have pushed it back again into its place as well as I could. Perhaps it may escape notice."

"How shall I ever thank thee?" was all Anna could repeat in her gratitude.

"Now you know what you must do, Anna," said he. "I am going to jump out through the window, and be off home. You must shut it and fasten it after me: I'd shut it myself, after I'm out, but that these stains on my fingers would be transferred to the frame. And when you leave the kitchen, remember to turn the key of the door outside. I found it turned. Do you understand? And now farewell, my little locked-out princess. Don't say I have not worked wonders for you, as the good spirits do in the fairy tales."

She caught his hand in her glad delight. She looked at him with a face full of gratitude. Herbert Dare bent down and took a kiss from the up-turned face. Perhaps he thought he had fairly earned the reward. Then he proceeded to swing himself through the window, feeling delighted that he had been able to free Anna from her dilemma.

Before Helstonleigh arose next morning, a startling report was circulating through the city, the very air teeming with it. A report that Anthony Dare had been killed in the night by his brother Herbert.

CHAPTER II

COMMOTION

The streets of Helstonleigh, lying so still and quiet in the moonlight, were broken in upon by the noisy sound of a carriage, bowling through them. A carriage that was abroad late. It wanted very little of the time when the church clocks would boom out the two hours after midnight. Time, surely, for all sober people to be in bed!

The carriage contained Mr. Dare, his wife and daughter. They went, as you may remember, to a dinner party in the country. The dinner was succeeded by an evening gathering, and it was nearly one o'clock when they left the house to return. It wanted only five minutes to two when the carriage stopped at their own home, and sleepy Joseph opened the door to them.

"All in bed?" asked Mr. Dare, as he bustled into the hall.

"I believe so, sir," answered Joseph, as carelessly as he could speak. Mr. Dare, he was aware, alluded to his sons; and not being by any means sure upon the point, Joseph was willing to escape further questioning.

Two of the maids came forward—the lady's maid, as she was called in the family, and Betsy. Betsy was no other than our old friend Betsy Carter: once the little maid-of-all-work at Mrs. Halliburton's; risen now to be a very fine housemaid at Mrs. Dare's. They had sat up to attend upon Mrs. Dare and Adelaide.

Mr. Dare had been for a long while in the habit of smoking a pipe before he went to bed. He would have told you that he could not do without it. If business or pleasure took him out, he must have his pipe when he returned, however late it might be.

"How hot it is!" he exclaimed, throwing back his coat. "Leave the hall door open, Joseph: I'll sit outside. Bring me my pipe."

Joseph looked for the pipe in its appointed resting-place, and could not see it. It was a small, handsome pipe, silver-mounted, with an amber mouth-piece. The tobacco-jar was there, but Joseph could see nothing of the pipe.

"Law! I remember!" exclaimed Betsy. "Master left it in the dining-room last night, and I put it under the sideboard when I was doing the room this morning, intending to bring it away. I'll go and get it."

Taking the candle from Joseph's hand, she turned hastily into the dining-room. Not, however, as hastily as she came out of it. She rushed out, uttering a succession of piercing shrieks, and seized upon Joseph. The shrieks echoed through the house, upstairs and down, and Mr. Dare came in.

"Why, what on earth's the matter, girl?" cried he. "Have you seen a ghost?"

"Oh, sir! Oh, Joseph, don't let go of me; Mr. Anthony's lying in there, dead!"

"Don't be a simpleton," responded Mr. Dare, staring at Betsy.

Joseph gave a rather less complimentary reprimand, and shook the girl off. But suddenly, even as the words left his lips, there rose up before his mind's eye the vision of the past evening: the quarrel, the threats, the violence between Anthony and Herbert. A strange apprehension seated itself in the man's mind.

"Be still, you donkey!" he whispered to Betsy, his voice scarcely audible, his manner subdued. "I'll go in and see."

Taking the candle, he went into the dining-room. Mr. Dare followed. The worst thought that occurred to Mr. Dare was, that Anthony might have taken more wine than was good for him, and had fallen down, helpless, in the dining-room. Unhappily, Anthony had been known so to transgress. Only a week or two before—but let that pass: it has nothing to do with us now.

Mr. Dare followed Joseph in. At the upper end of the room, near the window, lay some one on the ground. It was surely Anthony. He was lying on his side, his head thrown back, his face up-turned. A ghastly face, which sent poor Joseph's pulses bounding on with a terrible fear as he looked down at it. The same face which had scared Betsy when she looked down.

"He is stark dead!" whispered Joseph, with a shiver, to Mr. Dare.

Mr. Dare, his own life-blood seeming to have stopped, bent over his son by the light of the candle. Anthony appeared to be not only dead, but cold. In his terrible shock, his agitation, he still remembered that it was well, if possible, to spare the sight to his wife and daughter. Mrs. Dare and Adelaide, alarmed by Betsy's screams, had run downstairs, and were now hastening into the room.

"Go back! go back!" cried Mr. Dare, fencing them away with his hands. "Adelaide, you must not come in! Julia," he added to his wife, in tones of imploring entreaty, "go upstairs, and keep back Adelaide."

He half led, half pushed them across the hall. Mrs. Dare had never in all her life seen his face as she saw it now—a face of terror. She caught the fear; vaguely enough, it must be confessed, for she had not heard Anthony's name, as yet, mentioned in connection with it.

"What is it?" she asked, holding on by the balustrades. "What is there in the dining-room?"

"I don't know what it is," replied Mr. Dare, from between his white lips. "Go upstairs! Adelaide, go up with your mother."

Mr. Dare was stopped by more screams. Whilst he was preventing immediate terror to his wife and daughter, the lady's maid, her curiosity excited beyond repression, had slipped into the dining-room, and peeped over Joseph's shoulder. What she had expected to see she perhaps could not have stated; what she did see was so far worse than her wildest fears, that she lost sense of everything, except the moment's fear; and shriek after shriek echoed from her.

A scene of confusion ensued. Mrs. Dare tried to force her way to the room; Adelaide followed her; Betsy began bewailing Mr. Anthony, by name, in wild words. And the sleepers, above, came flocking out of their chambers, with trembling limbs and white faces.

Mr. Dare put his back against the dining-room door. "Girls, go back! Julia, go back, for the love of Heaven! Mademoiselle, is that you? Be so good as to stay where you are, and keep Rosa and Minny with you."

"Mais, qu'est-ce que c'est, donc?" exclaimed mademoiselle, speaking, in her wonder, in her most familiar tongue, and, truth to say, paying little heed to Mr. Dare's injunction. "Y a-t-il du malheur arrivé?"

Betsy went up to her. Betsy recognised her as one not of the family, to whom she could ease her overflowing mind. The same thought had occurred to Betsy as to Joseph. "Poor Mr. Anthony's lying in there dead, mamzel," she whispered. "Mr. Herbert must have killed him."

Unheeding the request of Mr. Dare, unmindful of the deficiences or want of elegance in her costume, which consisted of what she called a peignoir, and a borderless calico nightcap, mademoiselle flew down to the hall and slipped into the dining-room. Some of the others slipped in also, and a sad scene ensued. What with wife, governess, servants, and children, Mr. Dare was powerless to end it. Mademoiselle went straight up, gave one look, and staggered back against the wall.

"C'est vrai!" she muttered. "C'est Monsieur Anthony."

"It is Anthony," shivered Mr. Dare, "I fear—I fear violence has been done him."

The governess was breathing heavily. She looked quite as ghastly as did that up-turned face. "But why should it be?" she asked, in English. "Who has done it?"

Ah, who had done it! Joseph's frightened face seemed to say that he could tell if he dared, Cyril bounded into the room, and clasped one of the arms. But he let it fall again. "It is rigid!" he gasped. "Is he dead? Father! he can't be dead!"

Mr. Dare hurried Joseph from the room—hurried him across the hall to the door. He, Mr. Dare, seemed so agitated as scarcely to know what he was about. "Make all haste," he said; "the nearest surgeon."

"Sir," whispered Joseph, turning when he was outside the door, his agitation as great as his master's: "I'm afraid it's Mr. Herbert who has done this."

"Why?" sharply asked Mr. Dare.

"They had a dreadful quarrel this evening, sir, after you left. Mr. Herbert drew a knife upon his brother. I got in just in time to stop bloodshed, or it might have happened then."

Mr. Dare suppressed a groan. "Go off, Joseph, and bring a doctor here. He may not be past reviving, Milbank is the nearest. If he is at home, bring him; if not, get anybody."

Joseph, without his hat, sped across the lawn, and gained the entrance gate at the very moment that a gig was passing. By the light of a lamp, Joseph saw that it contained Mr. Glenn, the surgeon, driven by his servant. He had been on a late professional visit into the country. Joseph shouted running before the horse in his excitement, and the man pulled up.

"What's the matter, Joseph?" asked Mr. Glenn. "Any one ill?"

Somewhat curious to say, Mr. Glenn was the usual medical attendant of the Dares. Joseph explained as well as he could. Mr. Anthony had been found lying on the dining-room carpet, to all appearance dead. Mr. Glenn descended.

"Anything up at your place?" asked a policeman, who had just come by, on his beat.

"I should think there is," returned Joseph. "One of the gentlemen's been found dead."

"Dead!" echoed the policeman. "Which of them is it?" he asked, after a pause.

"Mr. Anthony."

"Why, I saw him turn in here about half-past eleven!" observed the officer, "He is in a fit, perhaps."

"Why do you say that?" asked Joseph.

"Because he had been taking a drop too much. He could hardly walk. Somebody brought him as far as the gate."

Mr. Glenn had hastened on. The policeman followed with Joseph. Followed, possibly, to gratify his curiosity; possibly, because he thought his services might be in some way required. When the two entered the dining-room, Mr. Glenn was kneeling down to examine Anthony, and sounds of distress came on their ears from a distance. They were caused by the hysterics of Mrs. Dare.

"Is he dead, sir?" asked the policeman, in a low tone.

"He has been dead these two or three hours," was Mr. Glenn's reply.

But it was not a fit. It was not anything so innocent. Mr. Glenn found that the cause of death was a stab in the side. Death, he believed, must have been instantaneous: and the hemorrhage was chiefly internal. There were very few stains on the clothes.

"What's this!" cried Mr. Glenn.

He was pulling at some large substance on which Anthony had fallen. It proved to be a cloak. Cyril—and some others present—recognised it as Herbert's cloak. Where was Herbert? In bed? Was it possible that he could sleep through the noise and confusion that the house was in?

"Can nothing be done?" asked Mr. Dare of the surgeon.

Mr. Glenn shook his head. "He is stone dead, you see; dead, and nearly cold. He must have been dead more than two hours. I should say nearer three."

From two to three hours! Then that would bring the time of his death to about half-past eleven o'clock; close upon the time that the policeman saw him returning home. Some one turned to ask the policeman a question, but he had disappeared. Mr. Glenn went to see what he could do for Mrs. Dare, whose cries had been painful to hear, and Mr. Dare drew Joseph aside. Somehow he felt that he dared not question him in the presence of witnesses, lest any condemnatory fact should transpire to bring the guilt home to his second son. In spite of the sight of Anthony lying dead before him, in spite of what he had heard of the quarrel, he could not bring his mind to believe that Herbert had been guilty of this most dastardly deed.

"What time did you let him in?" asked Mr. Dare, pointing to his ill-fated son.

Joseph answered evasively. "The policeman said it was about half after eleven, sir."

"And what time did Mr. Herbert come home?"

In point of fact, but for seeing the cloak where he did see it, Joseph would not have known whether Mr. Herbert was at home yet. He felt there was nothing for it but to tell the simple truth to Mr. Dare—that the gentlemen had been in the habit of letting themselves in at any hour they pleased, the dining-room window being left unfastened for them. Joseph made the admission, and Mr. Dare received it with anger.

"I did it by their orders, sir," the man said, with deprecation. "If you think it was wrong, perhaps you'll put things on a better footing for the future. But, to wait up every night till its pretty near time to rise again, is what I can't do, or anybody else. Flesh and blood is but mortal, sir, and couldn't stand it."

"But you were not kept up like that?" cried Mr. Dare.

"Yes, sir, I was. If one of the gentlemen wasn't out, the other would be. I told them it was impossible I could be up nearly all night and every night, and rise in the morning just the same, and do my work in the day. So they took to have the dining-room window left open, and came in that way, and I went to rest at my proper hour. Mr. Cyril and Mr. George, too, they are taking to stay out."

"The house might have been robbed over and over again!" exclaimed Mr. Dare.

"I told them so, sir. But they laughed at me. They said who'd be likely to come through the grounds and up to the windows and try them? At any rate, sir," added Joseph, as a last excuse, "they ordered it done. And that's how it is, sir, that I don't know what time either Mr. Anthony or Mr. Herbert came in last night."

Mr. Dare said no more. The fruits of the way in which his sons had been reared were coming heavily home to him. He turned to go upstairs to Herbert's chamber. On the bottom stairs, swaying herself to and fro in her peignoir, a staring print, all the colours of the rainbow, sat the governess. She lifted her white face as Mr. Dare approached.

"Is he dead?"

Mr. Dare shook his head. "The surgeon says he has been dead ever since the beginning of the night."

"And Monsieur Herbert? Is he dead?"

"He dead!" repeated Mr. Dare in an accent of alarm, fearing possibly she might have a motive for the question. "What should bring him also dead? Mademoiselle, why do you ask it?"

"Eh, me, I don't know," she answered. "I am bewildered with it all. Why should he be dead, and not the other? Why should either be dead?"

Mr. Dare saw that she did look bewildered; scarcely in her senses. She had a white handkerchief in her hand, and was wiping the moisture from her scarcely less white face. "Did you witness the quarrel between them?" he inquired, supposing that she had done so by her words.

"If I did, I not tell," she vehemently answered, her English less clear than usual. "If Joseph say—I hear him say it to you just now—that Monsieur Herbert took a knife to his brother, I not give testimony to it. What affair is it of mine, that I should tell against one or the other? Who did it?—who killed him?"—she rapidly continued. "It was not Monsieur Herbert. No, I will say always that it was not Monsieur Herbert. He would not kill his brother."

"I do not think he would," earnestly spoke Mr. Dare.

"No, no, no!" said mademoiselle, her voice rising with her emphasis. "He never kill his brother; he not enough méchant for that."

"Perhaps he has not come in?" cried Mr. Dare, catching at the thought.

Betsy Garter answered the words. She had stolen up in the general restlessness, and halted there. "He must be come in, sir," she said; "else how could his cloak be in the dining-room? They are saying that it's Mr. Herbert's cloak which was under Mr. Anthony."

"What has Mr. Herbert's cloak to do with his coming in or not coming in?" sharply asked Mr. Dare. "He would not be wearing his cloak this weather."

"But he does wear it, sir," returned Betsy. "He went out in it to-night."

"Did you see him?" sternly asked Mr. Dare.

"If I hadn't seen him, I couldn't have told that he went out in it," independently replied Betsy, who, like her mother, was fond of maintaining her own opinion. "I was looking out of the window in Miss Adelaide's room, and I saw Mr. Herbert go out by way of the dining-room window towards the entrance-gate."

"Wearing his cloak?"

"Wearing his cloak," assented Betsy, "I hoped he was hot enough in it."

The words seemed to carry terrible conviction to Mr. Dare's mind. Unwilling to believe the girl, he sought Joseph and asked him.

"Yes, for certain," Joseph answered. "Mr. Herbert, as he was coming downstairs to go out, stopped to speak to me, sir, and he was fastening his cloak on then."

Minny ran up, bursting with grief and terror as she seized upon Mr. Dare. "Papa! papa! is it true?" she sobbed.

"Is what true, child?"

"That it was Herbert? They are saying so."

"Hush!" said Mr. Dare. Carrying a candle, he went up to Herbert's room, his heart aching. That Herbert could sleep through the noise was surprising; and yet, not much so. His room was more remote from the house than were the other rooms, and looked towards the back. But, had he slept through it? When Mr. Dare went in, he was sitting up in bed, awaking, or pretending to awake, from sleep. The window, thrown wide open, may have contributed to deaden any sound in the house. "Can you sleep through this, Herbert?" cried Mr. Dare.

Herbert stared, and rubbed his eyes, and stared again, as one bewildered. "Is that you, father?" he presently cried. "What is it?"

"Herbert," said his father, in low tones of pain, of dread; "what have you been doing to your brother?"

Herbert, as if not understanding the drift of the question, stared more than ever. "I have done nothing to him," he presently said. "Do you mean Anthony?"

"Anthony is lying on the dining-room floor killed—murdered. Herbert, who did it?"

Herbert Dare sat motionless in bed, looking utterly lost. That he could not understand, or was affecting not to understand, was evident. "Anthony is—what do you say, sir?"

"He is dead; he is murdered," replied Mr. Dare. "Oh, my son, my son, say you did not do it! for the love of heaven, say you did not do it!" And the unhappy father burst into tears and sank down on the bed, utterly unmanned.

CHAPTER III

ACCUSED

The grey dawn of the early May morning was breaking over the world—over the group gathered in Mr. Dare's dining-room. That gentleman, his surviving sons, a stranger, a constable or two; and Sergeant Delves, who had been summoned to the scene. Sundry of the household were going in and out, of their own restless, curious accord, or by summons. The sergeant was making inquiries into the facts and details of the evening.

Anthony Dare—as may be remembered—had sullenly retired to his room, refusing to go out when the message came to him from Lord Hawkesley. It appeared, by what was afterwards learnt, that he, Anthony Dare, had made an appointment to meet Hawkesley and some other men at the Star-and-Garter hotel, where Lord Hawkesley was staying; the proposed amusement of the evening being cards. Anthony Dare remained in his chamber, solacing his chafed temper with brandy-and-water, until the waiter from the Star-and-Garter appeared a second time, bearing a note. This note Sergeant Delves had found in one of the pockets, and had it now open before him. It ran as follows:—

"DEAR DARE,—We are all here waiting, and can't make up the tables without you. What do you mean by shirking us? Come along, and don't be a month over it.—Yours,

"HAWKESLEY."

This note had prevailed. Anthony, possibly repenting of the solitary evening to which he had condemned himself, put on his boots again and went forth: not—it is not pleasant to have to record it, but it cannot be concealed—not sober. He had taken ale with his dinner, wine after it, and brandy-and-water in his room. The three combined had told upon him.

On his arrival at the Star-and-Garter, he found six or seven gentlemen assembled. But, instead of sitting down there in Lord Hawkesley's room, it was suddenly decided to adjourn to the lodgings of a Mr. Brittle, hard by; a young Oxonian, who had been plucked in his Little Go, and was supposed to be reading hard to avoid a second similar catastrophe. They went to Mr. Brittle's and sat down to cards, over which brandy-and-water and other drinks were introduced. Anthony Dare, by way of quenching his thirst, did not spare them, and was not particular as to the sorts. The consequence was that he soon became most disagreeable company, snarling with all around; in short, unfit for play. This contretemps put the rest of the party out of sorts, and they broke up. But for that, they might probably have sat on, until morning, and that poor unhappy life have been spared. There was no knowing what might have been. Anthony Dare was in no fit state to walk alone, and one of them, Mr. Brittle, undertook to see him home. Mr. Brittle left him at the gate, and Anthony Dare stumbled over the lawn and gained the house. After that, nothing further was known. So much as this would not have been known, but that, in hastening for Delves, the policeman had come across Mr. Brittle. It was only natural that the latter, shocked and startled, should bend his steps to the scene; and from him they gathered the account of Anthony's movements abroad.

But now came the difficulty. Who had let Anthony in? No one. There was little doubt that he had made his way through the dining-room window. Joseph had turned the key of the front door at eleven o'clock, and he had not been called upon to open it until the return of Mr. and Mrs. Dare. The policeman who happened to be passing when Anthony came home—or it may be more correct to say, was brought home—testified to the probable fact that he had entered by means of the dining-room window. The man had watched him: had seen that, instead of making for the front door, which faced the road and was in view, he had stumbled across the grass, and disappeared down by the side of the house. On this side the dining-room window was situated; therefore it was only reasonable to suppose that Anthony had so entered.

"Had you any motive in watching him?" asked Sergeant Delves of this man.

"None, except to see that he did not fall," was the reply. "When the gentleman who brought him home loosed his arm, he told him, in a joking way, not to get kissing the ground as he went in; and I thought I'd watch him that I might go to his assistance if he did fall. He could hardly walk: he pitched about with every step."

"Did he fall?"

"No; he managed to keep up. But I should think he was a good five minutes getting over the grass plat."

"Did the gentleman remain to watch him?"

"No, not for above a minute. He just waited to see that he got safe over the gravel path on to the grass, and then he went back."

"Did you see anyone else come in? About that time?—or before it?—or after it?"

The man shook his head. "I didn't see anyone else at all. I shut the gate after Mr. Anthony, and I didn't see it opened again. Not but what plenty might have opened and shut it, and gone in, too, when I was higher up my beat."

Sergeant Delves called Joseph. "It appears uncommonly odd that you should have heard no noise whatever," he observed. "A man's movements are not generally very quiet when in the state described as being that of young Mr. Dare's. The probability is that he would enter the dining-room noisily. He'd be nearly sure to fall against the furniture, being in the dark."

"It's certain that I never did hear him," replied Joseph. "We was shut up in the kitchen, and I was mostly nodding from the time I locked up at eleven till master came home at two. The two girls was chattering loud enough; they was at the table, making-up caps, or something of that. The cook went to bed at ten; she was tired."

"Then, with the exception of you three, all the household were in bed?"

"All of 'em—as was at home," answered Joseph. "The governess had gone early, the two young ladies went about ten, Mr. Cyril and Mr. George went soon after ten. They came home from cricket 'dead beat' they said, had supper, and went to bed soon after it."

"It's not usual for them—the young men, I mean—to go to bed so early, is it?" asked Sergeant Delves.

"No, except on cricket nights," answered Joseph. "After cricket they generally come home and have supper, and don't go out again. Other nights they are mostly sure to be out late."

"And you did not hear Mr. Herbert come in?"

"Sergeant Delves, I say that I never heard nothing nor nobody from the time I locked the front door till master and missis came home," reiterated Joseph, growing angry. "Let me repeat it ten times over, I couldn't say it plainer. If I had heard either of the gentlemen come in, I should have gone to 'em to see if anything was wanted. Specially to Mr. Anthony, knowing that he was not sober when he went out."

Two points appeared more particularly to strike Sergeant Delves. The one was, that no noise should have been heard; that a deed like this could have been committed in, as it appeared, absolute silence. The other was, that the dining-room window should have been found fastened inside. The latter fact confirmed the strong suspicion that the offender was an inmate of the house. A person, not an inmate of the house, would naturally have escaped by the open dining-room window; but to do this, and to fasten it inside after him was an impossibility. Every other window in the house, every door, had been securely fastened; some in the earlier part of the evening, some at eleven o'clock by Joseph. Herbert Dare voluntarily acknowledged that it was he who had fastened the dining-room window. His own account was—and the sergeant looked at him narrowly while he gave it—that he had returned home late, getting on for two o'clock; that he had come in through the dining-room, and had put down the window fastening. He declared that he had not seen Anthony. If Anthony had been lying there, as he was afterwards found, he, Herbert, had not observed him. But, he said, so far as he remembered, he never glanced to that part of the room at all, but had gone straight through on the other side, between the table and the fireplace. And if he had glanced to it he could have seen nothing, for the room was dark. He had no light, and had to feel his way.

"Was it usual for the young gentlemen to fasten the window?" Sergeant Delves asked of Joseph. And Joseph replied that they sometimes did, sometimes did not. If by any chance Mr. Anthony and Mr. Herbert came in together, then they would fasten it; or if, when the one came in, he knew that the other was not out, he would equally fasten it. Mr. Cyril and Mr. George did not often come in that way; in fact, they were not out so late, generally speaking, as were their brothers.

"Precisely so," Herbert assented, with reference to the fastening. He had fastened it, believing his brother Anthony to be at home and in bed. When he went out the previous evening, Anthony had already gone to his room, expressing his intention not to leave it again that night.

Sergeant Delves inquired—no doubt for reasons of his own—whether this expressed intention on the part of Anthony could be testified to by any one besides Herbert. Yes. By Joseph, by the governess, by Rosa and Minny Dare; all four had heard him say it. The sergeant would not trouble the young ladies, but requested to speak to the governess.

The governess was indignant at the request being made. She was in and out amongst them with her white face, in her many-coloured peignior. She had been upstairs and partially dressed herself; had discarded the calico nightcap and done her hair, put on the peignior again, and come down to see and to listen. But she did not like being questioned.

"I know nothing about it," she said to the sergeant, speaking vehemently. "What should I know about it? I will tell you nothing. I went to bed before it was well nine o'clock; I had a headache; and I never heard anything more till the commotion began. Why you ask me?"

"But you can surely tell, ma'am, whether or not you heard Mr. Anthony say he was going to his chamber for the night?" remonstrated the sergeant.

"Yes, he did say it," she answered vehemently. "He said it in the salon. He kicked off his boots, and told Joseph to bring his slippers, and to take brandy-and-water to his room, for he should not leave it again that night. I never thought or knew that he had left it until I saw him lying in the dining-room, and they said he was dead."

"Was Mr. Herbert present when he said he should go to his room for the night?"

"He was present, I think: I think he had come in then to the salon. That is all I know. I made the tea, and then my head got bad, and I went to bed. I can tell you nothing further."

"Did you hear any noise in the house, ma'am?"

"No. If there was any noise I did not notice it. I soon went to sleep. Where is the use of your asking me these things? You should ask those who sat up. I shall be sick if you make me talk about it. Nothing of this ever arrived in any family where I have been before."

The sergeant allowed her to retire. She went to the stairs and sat down on the lower step, and leaned her cheek upon her hand, all as she had done previously. Mr. Dare asked her why she did not go upstairs, away from the confusion and bustle of the sad scene; but she shook her head. She did not care to be in her chamber alone, she answered, and her pupils were shut in with Madame Dare and Mademoiselle Adelaide.

It is possible that one thing puzzled the sergeant: though what puzzled him and what did not puzzle him had to be left to conjecture, for he said nothing about it. No weapon had been found. The policemen had been searching the room thoroughly, had partly searched the house; but had come upon no instrument likely to have inflicted the wound. A carving-knife or common table-knife had been suggested, remembering the previous occurrences of the evening; but Mr. Glenn's decided opinion was, that it must have been a very different instrument; some slender, sharp-pointed, two-edged blade, he thought, about six inches in length.

The most suspicious evidence, referring to Herbert, was the cloak. The sergeant had examined it curiously, with compressed lips. Herbert disposed of this, so far as he was concerned—that is, if he was to be believed. He said that he had put his cloak on, had gone out in it as far as the entrance gate; but finding it warmer than was agreeable, he had turned back, and flung it on to the dining-room table, going in, as he had come out, through the window. He added, as a little bit of confirmatory evidence, that he remembered seeing the cloak begin to slide off the table again, that he saw it must fall to the ground; but, being in a hurry, he would not stop to prevent its doing so, or to pick it up.

The sergeant never seemed to take his sidelong glance from Herbert Dare. He had gone to work in his own way; hearing the different accounts and conjectures, sifting this bit of evidence, turning about that, holding a whispered colloquy with the man who had been sent to examine Herbert's room: holding a longer whispered colloquy with Herbert himself. On the departure of the surgeon and Mr. Brittle, who had gone away together, he had marched to the front and side doors of the house, locked them, and put the keys into his pocket. "Nobody goes out of this without my permission," quoth he.

Then he took Mr. Dare aside. "There's no mistake about this, I fear," said he gravely.

Mr. Dare knew what he meant. He himself was growing grievously faint-hearted. But he would not say so; he would not allow it to be seen that he cast, or could cast, a suspicion on Herbert. "It appears to me that—that—if poor Anthony was in the state they describe, that he may have sat down or laid down after entering the dining-room, and dropped asleep," observed Mr. Dare. "Easy, then—the window being left open—for some midnight housebreaker from the street to have come in and attacked him."

"Pooh!" said Sergeant Delves. "It is no housebreaker that has done this. We have a difficult line of duty to perform at times, us police; and all we can do to soften matters, is to go to work as genteelly as is consistent with the law. I'm sorry to have to say it, Mr. Dare, but I have felt obliged to order my men to keep a look-out on Mr. Herbert."

A chill ran through Mr. Dare. "It could not have been Herbert!" he rejoined, his tone one of pain, almost of entreaty. "Mr. Glenn says it could not have been done later than half-past eleven, or so. Herbert never came home until nearly two."

"Who is to prove that he was not at home till near two?"

"He says he was not. I have no doubt it can be proved. And poor Anthony was dead more than two hours before."

"Now, look you here," cried Sergeant Delves, falling back on a favourite phrase of his. "Mr. Glenn is correct enough as to the time of the occurrence: I have had some experience in death myself, and I'm sure he is not far out. But let that pass. Here are witnesses who saw him alive at half-past eleven o'clock, and you come home at two and find him dead. Now, let your son Herbert thus state where he was from half-past eleven till two. He says he was out: not near home at all. Very good. Only let him mention the place, so that we can verify it, and find, beyond dispute, that he was out, and the suspicion against him will be at an end. But he won't do this."

"Not do it?" echoed Mr. Dare.

"He tells me point-blank that he can't and he won't. I asked him."

Mr. Dare turned impetuously to the room where he had left his second son—his eldest son now. "Here, Herbert"—he was beginning. But the officer cut short the words by drawing him back.

"Don't go and make matters worse," whispered he: "perhaps they'll be bad enough without it. Now, Lawyer Dare, you'll do well not to turn obstinate, for I am giving you a bit of friendly advice. You and I have had many a transaction together, and I don't mind going a bit out of my way for you, as I wouldn't do for other people. The worst thing your son could do, would be to say before those chattering servants that he can't or won't tell where he has been all night, or half the night. It would be self-condemnation at once. Ask him in private, if you must ask him."

Mr. Dare called his son to him, and Herbert answered to it. A policeman was sauntering after him, but the sergeant gave him a nod, and the man went back.

"Herbert, you say you did not come in until near two this morning."

"Neither did I. It wanted about twenty minutes to it. The churches struck half-past one as I came through the town."

"Where did you stay?"

"Well—I can't say," replied Herbert.

Mr. Dare grew agitated. "You must say, Herbert," he hoarsely whispered, "or take the consequences."

"I can't help the consequences," was Herbert's answer. "Where I was last night is no matter to any one, and I shall not say."

"Your not saying—if you can say—is just folly," interposed the sergeant. "It's the first question the magistrates will ask when you are placed before them."

Herbert looked up angrily. "Place me before the magistrates!" he echoed. "What do you mean? You will not dare to take me into custody!"

"You have been in custody this half-hour," coolly returned the sergeant.

Herbert looked terribly fierce.

"I will not submit to this indignity," he exclaimed. "I will not. Sergeant Delves, you are overstepping—"

"Look here," interrupted the sergeant, drawing something from some unseen receptacle; and Mr. Herbert, to his dismay, caught sight of a pair of handcuffs. "Don't you force me to use them," said the officer. "You are in custody, and must go before the magistrates; but now, you be a gentleman, and I'll use you as one."

"I protest upon my honour that I have had neither act nor part in this crime!" cried Herbert, in agitation. "Do you think I would stain my hand with the sin of Cain?"

"What is that on your hand?" asked the sergeant, bending forward to look more closely at Herbert's fingers.

Herbert held them out openly enough. "I was doing something last night which tore my fingers," he said. "I was trying to undo the fastenings of some wire. Sergeant Delves, I declare to you solemnly, that from the moment when my brother went to his chamber, as witnesses have stated to you, I never saw him until my father brought me down from my bed to see him lying dead."

"You drew a knife on him not many hours before, you know, Mr. Herbert!"

"It was done in the heat of passion. He provoked me very much; but I should not have used it. No, poor fellow! I should never have injured him."

"Well, you only make your tale good to the magistrates," was all the sergeant's answer. "It will be their affair as soon as you are before them—not mine."

Herbert Dare was handed back to the constable; and, as soon as the justice-room opened, was conveyed before the magistrates—all, as the sergeant termed it, in a genteel, gentlemanly sort of way. He was charged with the murder of his brother Anthony.

To describe the commotion that spread over Helstonleigh would be beyond any pen. The college boys were in a strange state of excitement: both Anthony and Herbert Dare had been college boys themselves not so very long ago. Gar Halliburton—who was no longer a college boy, but a supernumerary—went home full of it. Having imparted it there, he thought he could not do better than go in and regale Patience with the news, by way of divertissement to her sick bed. "May I come up, Patience?" he called out from the foot of the stairs. "I have something to tell you."

Receiving permission, up he flew. Patience, partially raised, was sewing with her hands, which she could just contrive to do. Anna sat by the window, putting the buttons on some new shirts.

"I have finished two," cried she, turning round to Gar in great glee. "And my father's coming home next week, he writes us word. Perhaps thy mother has had a letter from William. Look at the shirts!" she continued, exhibiting them.

"Never mind bothering about shirts, now, Anna," returned Gar, losing sight of his gallantry in his excitement. "Patience, the most dreadful thing has happened. Anthony Dare's murdered!"

Patience, calm Patience, only looked at Gar. Perhaps she did not believe it. Anna's hands, holding out the shirts, were arrested midway: her mouth and blue eyes alike opening.

"He was murdered in their dining-room in the night," went on Gar, intent only on his tale. "The town is all up in arms; you never saw such an uproar. When we came out of school just now, we thought the French must have come to invade us, by the crowds there were in the street. You couldn't get near the Guildhall, where the examination was going on. Not more than half a dozen of us were able to fight our way in. Herbert Dare looked so pale; he was standing there, guarded by three policemen—"

"Thee hast a fast tongue, Gar," interrupted Patience. "Dost thee mean to say Herbert Dare was in custody?"

"Of course, he was," replied Gar, faster than before. "It is he who has done it. At least, he is accused of it. He and Anthony had a quarrel yesterday, and it came to knives. They were parted then; but he is supposed to have laid wait for Anthony in the night and killed him."

"Is Anthony dead? Is he—Anna! what hast thee—?"

Anna had dropped the shirts and the buttons. Her blue eyes had closed, her lips and cheeks had grown white, her hands fell powerless. "She is fainting!" shouted Gar, as he ran to support her.

"Gar, dear," said Patience, "thee shouldst not tell ill news quite so abruptly. Thee hast made me feel queer. Canst thee stretch thy hands out to the bell? It will bring up Hester."

Helstonleigh could not recover its equanimity. Never had it been so rudely shaken. Incidents there had been as startling; crimes of as deep a dye; but, taking it with all its attendant circumstances, no occurrence, in the memory of the oldest inhabitant, had excited the interest that was attaching to the death and assumed murder of Anthony Dare.

The social standing of the parties, above that in which such unhappy incidents are more generally found; the conspicuous position they occupied in the town, and the very uncertainty—the mystery, it may be said—in which the affair was wrapped, wrought local curiosity to the highest point.

Scarcely a shadow of doubt rested on the public mind that the deed had been done by Herbert Dare. The Police force, actively engaged in searching out all the details, held the same opinion. In one sense, this was, perhaps, unfortunate; for, when strong suspicion, whether of the police or of the public, is especially directed to one isolated point, it inevitably tends to keep down doubts that might arise in regard to other quarters.

It seemed scarcely possible to hope that Herbert was not guilty. All the facts tended to the assumption that he was so. There was the ill-feeling known to have existed between himself and his brother: the quarrel and violence in the dining-room not many hours before, in which quarrel Herbert had raised a knife upon him. "But for the entrance of the servant Joseph," said the people, one to another, "the murder might have been done then." Joseph had stopped evil consequences at the time, but he had not stopped Herbert's mouth—the threat he had uttered in his passion—still to be revenged. Terribly those words told now against Herbert Dare.

Another thing that told against him, and in a most forcible manner, was the cloak. That he had put it on to go out; nay, had been seen to go out in it by the housemaid, was indisputable; and his brother was found lying on this very cloak. In vain Herbert protested, when before the magistrates and at the coroner's inquest, that he returned before leaving the gates, and had flung this cloak into the dining-room, finding it too hot that evening to wear. He obtained no credit. He had not been seen to do this; and the word of an accused man goes for little. All ominous, these things—all telling against him, but nothing, taking them collectively, as compared with his refusal to state where he was that night. He left the house between eight and nine, close upon nine, he thought; he was not sure of the exact time to a quarter of an hour; and he never returned to it until nearly two. Such was his account. But, where he had been in the interim, he positively refused to state.

It was only his assertion, you see, against the broad basis of suspicion. Anthony Dare's death must have taken place, as testified by Mr. Glenn, somewhere about half-past eleven; who was to prove that Herbert at that time was not at home? "I was not," Herbert reiterated, when before the coroner. "I did not return home till between half-past one and two. The churches struck the half-hour as I was coming through the town, and it would take me afterwards some ten minutes to reach home. It must have been about twenty minutes to two when I entered."

"But where were you? Where had you been? Where did you come from?" he was asked.

"That I cannot state," he replied. "I was out upon a little business of my own; business that concerns no one but myself; and I decline to make it public."

On that score nothing more could be obtained from him. The coroner drew his own conclusions; the jury drew theirs; the police had already drawn theirs, and very positive ones.

These were the two facts that excited the ire of Sergeant Delves and his official colleagues: with all their searching, they could find no weapon likely to have been the one used; and they could not discover where Herbert Dare had gone to that evening. It happened that no one remembered to have seen him passing in the town, early or late; or, if they had seen him, it had made no impression on their memory. The appearance of Mr. Dare's sons was so common an occurrence that no especial note was likely to have been taken of it. Herbert declared that in passing through West Street, Turtle, the auctioneer, was leaning out at his open bedroom window, and that he, Herbert, had called out to him, and asked whether he was star-gazing. Mr. Turtle, when applied to, could not corroborate this. He believed that he had been looking out at his window that night; he believed that it might have been about the hour named, getting on for two, for he was late going to bed, having been to a supper party; but he had no recollection whatever of seeing Mr. Herbert pass, or of having been spoken to by him, or by any one else. When pressed upon the point, Mr. Turtle acknowledged that his intellects might not have been in the clearest state of perception, the supper party having been a jovial one.

One of the jury remarked that it was very singular the prisoner could go through the dining-room, and not observe his brother lying in it. The prisoner replied that it was not singular at all. The room was in darkness, and he had felt his way through it on the opposite side of the table to that where his brother was afterwards found. He had gone straight through, and up to his chamber, as quietly as possible, not to disturb the house; and he dropped asleep as soon as he was in bed.

The verdict returned was "Wilful murder against Herbert Dare," and he was committed to the county gaol to take his trial at the assizes. Mr. Dare's house was beyond the precincts of the city. Sergeant Delves and his men renewed their inquiries; but they could discover no trace, either of the weapon, or of where Herbert Dare had passed the suspicious hours. The sergeant was vexed; but he would not allow that he was beaten. "Only give us time," said he, with a characteristic nod. "The Pyramids of Egypt were only built up stone by stone."

Tuesday morning—the morning fixed for the funeral of Anthony Dare. The curious portion of Helstonleigh wended its way up to the churchyard; as it is the delight of the curious portion of a town to do. What a sad sight it was! That dark object, covered by its pall, carried by its attendants, followed by the mourners; Mr. Dare, and his sons Cyril and George. He, the father, bent his face in his handkerchief, as he walked behind the coffin to the grave. Many a man in Helstonleigh enjoyed a higher share of esteem and respect than did Lawyer Dare; but not one present in that crowded churchyard that did not feel for him in his bitter grief. Not one, let us hope, that did not feel to his heart's core the fate of the unhappy Anthony, now, for weal or for woe, to answer before his Maker for his life on earth.

That same day, Tuesday, witnessed the return of Samuel Lynn and William Halliburton. They arrived in the evening, and of course the first news they were greeted with was the prevailing topic. Few things caused the ever-composed Quaker to betray surprise; but William was half-stunned with the news. Anthony Dare dead—murdered—buried that very day; and Herbert in prison, awaiting his trial for the offence! To William the whole affair seemed more incredible than real.

"Sir," he said to his master, when, the following morning, they were alone together in the counting-house at the manufactory, "do you believe Herbert Dare can be guilty?"

Mr. Ashley had been gazing at William, lost in thought. The change we often see, or fancy we see, in a near friend, after a few weeks' absence, was apparent in William. He had improved in looks; and yet those looks, with their true nobility, both of form and intellect, had been scarcely capable of improvement. Nevertheless, it was there, and Mr. Ashley had been struck with it.

"I cannot say," he replied, aroused by the question. "Facts appear conclusively against him; but it seems incredible that he should so have lost himself. To be suspected and committed on such a charge is grief enough, without the reality of guilt."

"So it is," acquiesced William.

"We feel the disgrace very keenly—as all must who are connected with the Dares in ever so remote a degree. I feel it, William; feel it as a blow; Mrs. Ashley is the cousin of Anthony Dare."

"They are relatives of ours also," said William in a low tone. "My father was first cousin to Mrs. Dare."

Mr. Ashley looked at him with surprise. "Your father first cousin to Mrs. Dare!" he repeated. "What are you saying?"

"Her first cousin, sir. You have heard of old Mr. Cooper, of Birmingham?"

"From whom the Dares inherited their money. Well?"

"Mr. Cooper had a brother and a sister. Mrs. Dare was the daughter of the brother; the sister married the Reverend William Halliburton, and my father was their son. Mrs. Dare, as Julia Cooper, and my father, Edgar Halliburton, both lived together for some time under their uncle's roof at Birmingham."

A moment's pause, and then Mr. Ashley laid his hand on William's shoulder. "Then that brings a sort of relationship between us, William. I shall have a right to feel pride in you now."

William laughed. But his cheek flushed with the pleasure of a more earnest feeling. His greatest earthly wish was to be appreciated by Mr. Ashley.

"How is it I never heard of this relationship before?" cried Mr. Ashley. "Was it purposely concealed?"

"It is only within a year or two that I have known of it," replied William. "Frank and Gar are not aware of it yet. When we first came to Helstonleigh, the Dares were much annoyed at it; and they made it known to my mother in so unmistakable a manner, that she resolved to drop all mention of the relationship; she would have dropped the relationship itself if she could have done so. It was natural, perhaps, that they should feel annoyed," continued William, seeking to apologize for them. "They were rich and great in the eyes of the town; we were poor and obscure."

Mr. Ashley was casting his recollections backwards. A certain event, which had always somewhat puzzled him, was becoming clear now. "William, when Anthony Dare—acting, as he said, for me—put that seizure into your house for rent, it must have been done with the view of driving you from the town?"

"My mother says she has always thought so, sir."

"I see; I see. Why, William, half the inheritance, enjoyed by the Dares, ought justly to have been your father's!"

"We shall do as well without it, in the long-run, sir," replied William, a bright smile illumining his face. "Hard though the struggle was at the beginning!"

"Ay, that you will!" warmly returned Mr. Ashley. "The ways of Providence are wonderful! Yes, William—and I know you have been taught to think so—what men call the chances of the world, are all God's dealings. Reflect on the circumstances favouring the Dares; reflect on your own drawbacks and disadvantages! They had wealth, position, a lucrative profession; everything, in fact, to help them on, that can be desired by a family in middle-class life; whilst you had poverty, obscurity, and toil to contend with. But now, look at what they are! Mr. Dare's money is dissipated; he is overwhelmed with embarrassment—I know it to be a fact, William; but this is for your ear alone. Folly, recklessness, irreligion, reign in his house; his daughters lost in pretentious vanity; his sons in something worse. In a few years they will have gone down—down. Yes," added Mr. Ashley, pointing with his finger to the floor of his counting-house, "down to the dogs. I can see it coming, as surely as that the sun is in the heavens. You and they will have exchanged positions, William; nay, you and yours, unless I am greatly mistaken, will be in a far higher position than they have ever occupied; for you will have secured the favour of God, and the approbation of all good men."

"That Frank and Gar will attain to a position in time, I should be worse than a heathen to doubt, looking back on the wonderful manner in which we have been helped on," thoughtfully observed William. "For myself I am not sanguine."

"Do you never cherish dreams on your own account?" inquired Mr. Ashley.

"If I do, sir, they are vague dreams. My position affords no scope for ambition."

"I don't know that," said Mr. Ashley. "Would you not be satisfied to become one of the great manufacturers of this great city?" he continued, laughing.

"Not unless I could be one of the greatest. Such as—" William stopped.

"Myself, for instance?" quietly put in Mr. Ashley.

"Yes, indeed," answered William, lifting his earnest eyes to his master. "Were it possible that I could ever attain to be as you are, sir, in all things—in character, in position, in the estimation of my fellow-citizens—it would be sufficient ambition for me, and I should sit down content."

"Not you," cried Mr. Ashley. "You would then be casting your thoughts to serving your said fellow-citizens in Parliament, or some such exalted vision. Man's nature is to soar, you know; it cannot rest. As soon as one object of ambition is attained, others are sought after."

"So far as I go, we need not discuss it," was William's answer. "There's no chance of my ever becoming even a second-rate manufacturer; let alone what you are, sir."

"The next best thing to being myself, would perhaps be that of being my partner, William."

The voice in which his master spoke was so significant, that William's face flushed to crimson. Mr. Ashley noticed it.

"Did that ambition ever occur to you?"

"No, sir, never. That honour is looked upon as being destined for Cyril Dare."

"Indeed!" calmly repeated Mr. Ashley. "If you could transform your nature into Cyril, I do not say but that it might be so in time."

"He expects it himself, sir."

"Would he be a worthy associate for me, think you?" inquired Mr.

Ashley, bending his gaze full on William.

William made no reply. Perhaps none was expected, for his master resumed:

"I do not recommend you to indulge that particular dream of ambition; I cannot see sufficiently into the future. It is my intention to push you somewhat on in the world. I have no son to advance," he added, an expression of sadness crossing his face. "All I can do for my boy is to leave him at ease after me. Therefore I may, if I live, advance you in his stead. Provided, William, you continue to deserve it."

A smile parted William's lips. That, he would ever strive for, heaven helping him.

Mr. Ashley again laid his hand on William, and gazed into his face. "I have had a wonderful account of you from Samuel Lynn. And it is not often the Friend launches into decided praise."

"Oh, have you, sir?" returned William with animation. "I am glad he was pleased with me."

"He was more than pleased. But I must not forget that I was charged with a message from Henry. He is outrageous at your not having gone to him last night. I shall be sending him to France one of these days, under your escort, William. It may do him good, in more ways than one."

"I will come to Henry this evening, sir. I must leave him, though, for half an hour, to go round to East's."

"Your conscience is engaged, I see. You know what Henry accused you of, the last time you left him to go to East's?"

"Of being enamoured of Charlotte," said William, laughing in answer to Mr. Ashley's smile. "I will come, at any rate, sir, and battle the other matter out with Henry."

CHAPTER V

A BRUISED HEART

If it were a hopeless task to attempt to describe the consternation of Helstonleigh at the death of Anthony Dare, far more difficult would it be to picture that of Anna Lynn. Believe Herbert guilty, Anna did not; she could scarcely have believed that, had an angel come down from heaven to affirm it. Her state of mind was not to be envied; suspense, sorrow, anxiety filled it, causing her to be in a grievous state of restlessness. She had to conceal this from the eyes of Patience; from the eyes of the world. For one thing, she could not get at the correct particulars; newspapers did not come in her way, and she shrank, in her self-consciousness, from asking. Her whole being—if we may dare to say it here—was wrapt in Herbert Dare; father, friends, home, country; she could have sacrificed them all to save him. She would have laid down her life for his. Her good sense was distorted, her judgment warped; she saw passing events, not with the eye of dispassionate fact, or with any fact at all, but through the unhealthy tinge of fond, blind prejudice. The blow had almost crushed her; the dread suspense was wearing out her heart. She seemed no longer the same careless child as before; in a few hours she had overstepped the barrier of girlish timidity, and had gained the experience which is bought with sorrow.

On the evening mentioned in the last chapter, just before William went out to keep his appointment with Henry Ashley, he saw from the window Anna in his mother's garden, bending over the flowers, and glancing up at him. Glancing, as it struck William, with a strangely wistful expression. He went out to her.

"Tending the flowers, Anna?"

She turned to him, her fair young face utterly colourless. "I have been so wanting to see thee, William! I came here, hoping thee wouldst come out. At dinner time I was here, and thee only nodded to me from the window. I did not like to beckon to thee."

"I am sorry to have been so stupid, Anna. What is it?"

"Thee hast heard what has happened—that dreadful thing! Hast thee heard it all?"

"I believe so. All that is known."

"I want thee to tell it me. Patience won't talk of it; Hester only shakes her head; and I am afraid to ask Gar. Thee tell it to me."

"It would not do you good to know, Anna," he gravely said. "Better try and not think—"

"William, hush thee!" she feverishly exclaimed. "Thee knew there was a—a friendship between me and him. If I cannot learn all there is to be learnt, I shall die."

William looked down at the changing cheek, the eyes full of pain, the trembling hands, clasped in their eagerness. It might be better to tell her than to leave her in this state of suspense.

"William, there is no one in the wide world that knows he cared for me, but thee," she imploringly resumed. "Thee must tell me; thee must tell me!"

"You mean that you want to hear the particulars of—of what took place on Thursday night?"

"Yes. All. Then, and since. I have but heard snatches of the wicked tale."

He obeyed her: telling her all the broad facts, but suppressing a few of the details. She leaned against the garden-gate, listening in silence; her face turned from him, looking through the bars into the field.

"Why do they not believe him?" was her first comment, spoken sharply and abruptly. "He says he was not near the house at the time the act must have been done: why do they not believe him?"

"It is easy to assert a thing, Anna. But the law requires proof."

"Proof? That he must declare to them where he has been?"

"Undoubtedly. And corroborative proof must also be given."

"But what sort of proof? I do not understand their laws."

"Suppose Herbert Dare asserted that he had spent those hours with me, for instance; then I must go forward at the trial and confirm his assertion. Also any other witnesses who may have seen him with me, if there were any. It would be establishing what is called an alibi."

"And would they acquit him then? Suppose there were only one witness to speak for him? Would one be sufficient?"

"Certainly. Provided the witness were trustworthy."

"If a witness went forward and declared it now, would they release him?"

"Impossible. He is committed to take his trial at the assizes, and he cannot be released beforehand. It is exceedingly unwise of him not to declare where he was that evening—if he can do so."

"Where do the public think he was? What do they say?"

"I am afraid the public, Anna, think that he was not out anywhere. At any rate, after eleven or half-past."

"Then they are very cruel!" she passionately exclaimed. "Do they all think that?"

"There may be a few who judge that it was as he says; that he was really away, and is, consequently, innocent."

"And where do they think he was?" eagerly responded Anna again. "Do they suspect any place where he might have been?"

William made no reply. It was not at all expedient to impart to her all the gossip or surmises of the town. But his silence seemed to agitate her more than any reply could have done. She turned to him, trembling with emotion, the tears streaming down her face.

"Oh, William! tell me what is thought! Tell me, I implore thee! Thee cannot leave me in this trouble. Where is it thought he was?"

He took her hands; he bent over her as tenderly as any brother could have done; he read all too surely how opposite to the truth had been her former assertion to him—that she did not care for Herbert Dare.

"Anna, child, you must not agitate yourself in this way: there is no just cause for doing so. I assure you I do not know where it is thought Herbert Dare may have been that night; neither, so far as can be learnt, does any one else know. It is the chief point—where he was—that is puzzling the town."

She laid her head down on the gate again, closing her eyes, as in very weariness. William's heart ached for her.

"He may not be guilty, Anna," was all the consolation he could find to offer.

"May not be guilty!" she echoed in a tone of pain. "He is not guilty. William, I tell thee he is not. Dost thee think I would defend him if he could do so wicked a thing?"

He did not dispute the point with her; he did not tell her that her assumption of his innocence was inconsistent with the facts of the case. Presently Anna resumed.

"Why must he remain in gaol till the trial? There was that man who stole the skins from Thomas Ashley—they let him out, when he was taken, until the sessions came on, and then he went up for trial."

"That man was out on bail. But they do not take bail in cases so grave as this."

"I may not stay longer. There's Hester coming to call me in. I rely upon thee to tell me anything fresh that may arise," she said, lifting her beseeching eyes to his.

"One word, Anna, before you go. And yet, I see how worse than useless it is to say it to you now. You must forget Herbert Dare."

"I shall forget him, William, when I cease to have memory," she whispered. "Never before. Thee wilt keep my counsel?"

"Truly and faithfully."

"Fare thee well, William; I have no friend but thee."

She ran swiftly into their own premises. William turned to pursue his way to Mr. Ashley's, the thought of Henry Ashley's misplaced attachment lying on his mind as an incubus.

CHAPTER VI

ONE DYING IN HONEY FAIR

Mrs. Buffle stood in what she called her "back'us," practically superintending a periodical wash. The day was hot, and the steam was hot, and, as Mrs. Buffle rubbed away, she began to think she should never be cool again.

"Missis," shrieked out a young voice from the precincts of the shop, "Ben Tyrrett's wife says will you let her have a gill o' vinegar? Be I to serve it?"

The words came from the small damsel who was had in to help on cleaning and washing days. Mrs. Buffle kept her hands still in the soapsuds, and projected her hot face over the tub to answer.

"Matty, tell Mary Ann Tyrrett as she promised faithful to bring me something off her score this week, but I've not seen the colour of it yet."

"She says as it's to put to his head," called back Matty, alluding to the present demand. "He's bad a-bed, and have fainted right off."

"Serve him right," responded Mrs. Buffle. "You may give her the vinegar, Matty. Tell her as it's a penny farthing. I heered he had been drinking again," she added to herself and the washing tub, "and laid hisself down in the wet road the night afore last, and was found there in the morning."

Later in the day, it happened that William Halliburton was passing through Honey Fair, and met Charlotte East. She stopped him. "Have you heard, sir, that Tyrrett is dying?" she asked.

"Tyrrett dying!" repeated William in amazement. "Who says he is?"

"The doctor says it, I believe, sir. I must say he looks like it. Mary Ann sent for me, and I have been down to see him."

"Why, what can be the matter with him?" asked William. "He was at work the day before yesterday!"

"He was at work, sir, but he could not speak, they tell me, for that illness that has been hanging about him so long, and had settled on his chest. That night, after leaving work, instead of going home and getting a basin of gruel, or something of that sort, he went to the Horned Ram, and drank there till he couldn't keep upright."

"With his chest in that state!"

"And that was not the worst," resumed Charlotte. "It had been a wet day, if you remember, sir, and he somehow strayed into Oxlip Lane, and fell down, and lay there till morning. What with drink, and what with exposure to the wet, his chest grew dangerously inflamed, and now the doctor says he has not many hours to live."

"I am sorry to hear it," cried William. "Is he sensible?"

"Too sensible, sir, in one sense," replied Charlotte. "His remorse is dreadful. He is saying that if he had not misspent his life, he might have died a good man, instead of a bad one."

William passed on, much concerned at the news. His way led him past Ben Tyrrett's lodgings, and he turned in. Mary Ann was sobbing and wailing, in the midst of as many curious and condoling neighbours as the kitchen would contain. All were in full gossip—as might be expected. Mrs. Cross had taken home the three little children, by way of keeping the place quiet; and the sick man was lying in the room above, surrounded by several of his fellow-workmen, who had heard of his critical state.

Some of the women sidled off when William entered, rather ashamed of being caught chattering vehemently. It was remarkable the deference that was paid him, and from no assumption of his own— indeed, the absence of assumption may have partially accounted for it. But, though ever courteous and pleasant with them all, he was a thorough gentleman: and the working classes are keen to distinguish this.

"Why, Mrs. Tyrrett, this is sad news!" he said. "Is your husband so ill?"

"Oh, he must die, he must die, sir!" she answered in a frantic tone. Uncomfortably as they had lived together, the man was still her husband, and there is no doubt she was feeling the present crisis; was shrinking with dread from the future. A widow with three young children, and the workhouse for an asylum! It was the only prospect before her. "He must die, anyways; but he might have lasted a few hours longer, if I could have got what the doctor ordered."

William did not understand.

"It was a blister and some physic, sir," explained one of the women. "The doctor wrote it on a paper, and said it was to be took to the nearest druggist's. But when they got it there, Darwin said he couldn't trust the Tyrretts, and they must send the money if they wanted the things."

"It was not Mr. Parry, then, who was called in?"

"It were a strange doctor, sir, as was fetched. There was Tyrrett's last bout of illness owing for to Parry, and so they didn't like to send for him. As to them druggists, they be some of 'em a cross-grained set, unless you goes with the money in your hand."

William asked to see the prescription. It was produced, and he read its contents—he was as capable of doing so and of understanding it as the best doctor in Helstonleigh. He tore a leaf from his pocket-book, wrote a few words in pencil, folded it with the prescription, and desired one of the women to take it to the chemist's again. He then went up to the sick room.

Tyrrett was lying on a flock mattress, on an ugly brown bedstead, the four posts upright and undraped. A blanket and a checked blue cotton quilt covered him. His breathing was terribly laboured, his face painfully anxious. William approached him, bending his head, to avoid contact with the ceiling.

"I'm a-going, sir," cried the man, in tones as anxious as his face. "I'm a-going at last."

"I hope not," said William. "I hope you will get better. You are to have a blister on your chest, and—"

"No he ain't, sir," interrupted one of the men. "Darwin won't send it."

"Oh yes, he will, if he is properly asked. They have gone again to him. Are you in much pain, Tyrrett?"

"I'm in an agony of pain here, sir," pointing to his chest. "But that ain't nothing to my pain of mind. Oh, Mr. Halliburton, you're good, sir; you haven't nothing to reproach yourself with; can't you do nothing for me? I'm going into the sight of my Maker, and He's angry with me!"

In truth, William knew not what to answer. Tyrrett's voice was as a wail of anguish; his hands were stretched out beseechingly.

"Charlotte East were here just now, and she told me to go to Christ—that He was merciful and forgiving. But how am I to go to Him? If I try, sir, I can't, for there's my past life rising up before me. I have been a bad man: I have never once in all my life tried to please God."

The words echoed through the stillness of the room; echoed with a sound that was terribly awful. Never once to have tried to please God! Throughout a whole life, and throughout all its blessings!

"I have never thought of God," he continued to reiterate. "I have never cared for Him, or tried to please Him, or done the least thing for Him. And now I'm going to face His wrath, and I can't help myself!"

"You may be spared yet," said William; "you may indeed. And your future life must atone for the past."

"I shan't be spared, sir; I feel that the world's all up with me," was the rejoinder. "I'm going fast, and there's nobody to give me a word of comfort! Can't you, sir? I'm going away, and God's angry with me!"

William leaned over him. "I can only say as Charlotte East did," he whispered. "Try and find your Saviour. There is mercy with Him at the eleventh hour."

"I have not the time to find Him," breathed forth Tyrrett, in agony. "I might find Him if I had time given me; but I have not got it."

William, shrinking in his youth and inexperience from arguing upon topics so momentous, was not equal to the emergency. Who was? He did what he could; and that was to despatch a message for a clergyman, who answered the summons with speed.

The blister also came, and the medicine that had been prescribed. William went home, hoping all might prove as a healing balm to the sick man.

A fallacious hope. Tyrrett died the following morning. When William went round early on his mission of inquiry, he found him dead. Some of the men, whom he had seen with Tyrrett the previous night, were assembled in the kitchen.

"He is but just gone, sir," they said, "The women be up with him now. They have took his wife round screeching to her mother's. He died with that there blister on his chest."

"Did he die peacefully?" was William's question.

"Awful hard, sir, toward the last; moaning, and calling, and clenching his hands in mortal pain. His sister, she come round—she's a hard one, is that Liza Tyrrett—and she set on at the wife, saying it was her fault that he'd took to go out drinking. That there parson couldn't do nothing with him," concluded the speaker, lowering his voice.

William's breath stood still. "No!"

The man shook his head. "Tyrrett weren't in a frame o' mind for it, sir. He kep' crying out as he had led a bad life, and never thought of God—and them was his last words. It ain't happy, sir, to die like that. It have quite cowed down us as was with him: one gets thinking, sir, what sort of a place it may be, t'other side, where he's gone to."

William lifted his head, a sort of eager hope on his countenance, speaking cheerily. "Could you not let poor Tyrrett's death act as a warning to you?"

There was a dead silence. Five men were present; every one of them leading careless lives. Somehow they did not much like to hear of "warning," although the present moment was one of unusual seriousness.

"Religion is so dreadful dull and gloomy, sir."

"Religion dull and gloomy!" echoed William. "Well, perhaps some people do make a gloomy affair of it; but then I don't think theirs can be the right religion. I do not believe people were sent into the world to be gloomy: time enough for that when troubles come."

"What is religion?" asked one of the men.

"It is a sort of thing that's a great deal better to be felt than talked about," answered William. "I am no parson, and cannot pretend to enlighten you. We might never come to an understanding over it, were we to discuss it all day long. I would rather talk to you of life, and its practical duties."

"Tyrrett said as he had never paid heed to any of his duties. It were his cry over and over again, sir, in the night. He said he had drunk, and swore, and beat his wife, and done just what he oughtn't to ha' done."

"Ay, I fear it was so," replied William. "Poor Tyrrett's existence was divided into three phrases—working, drinking, quarrelling: dissatisfaction attending all. I fear a great many more in Honey Fair could say the same."

The men's consciences were pricking them; some of them began to stand uncomfortably on one leg. They tippled; they quarrelled; they had been known to administer personal correction to their wives on provocation.

"Times upon times I asked Tyrrett to come round of an evening to Robert East's," continued William. "He never did come. But I can tell you this, my men; had he taken to pass his evenings there twelve months ago, when the society—as they call it—was first formed, he might have been a hale man now, instead of lying there, dead."

"Do you mean that he'd have growed religious, sir?"

"I tell you we will put religion out of the discussion: as you don't seem to like the word. Had Tyrrett taken to like rational evenings, instead of public-houses, it would have made a wonderful difference in his mode of thought, and difference in conduct would have followed. Look at his father-in-law, Cross. He was living without hope or aim, at loggerheads with his wife and with the world, and rather given to wishing himself dead. All that's over. Do you think I should like to go about with a dirty face and holes in my coat?"

The men laughed. They thought not.

"Cross used to do so. But you see nothing of that now. Many others used to do so. Many do so still."

Rather conscience-stricken again, the men tried to hide their elbows. "It's true enough," said one. "Cross, and some more of 'em, are getting smart."

"Smart inside as well as out," said William. "They are acquiring self-respect; one of the best qualities a man can find. They wouldn't be seen in the street now in rags, or the worse for drink, or in any other degrading position; no, not if you bribed them with gold. Coming round to East's has done that for them. They are beginning to see that it's just as well to lead pleasant lives here, as unpleasant ones. In a short time, Cross will be getting furniture about him again, towards setting up the home he lost. He—and many more—will also, as I truly believe, be beginning to set up furniture of another sort."

"What sort's that, sir?"

"The furniture that will stand him in need for the next life; the life that Tyrrett has now entered upon," replied William in deeper tones. "It is a life that must come, you know; our little span of time here, in comparison with eternity, is but as a drop of water to the great river that runs through the town; and it is as well to be prepared for it. Now, the next five I am going to get round to East's are you."

"Us, sir?"

"Every one of you; although I believe you have been in the habit of complimenting your friends who go there with the title of 'milksops.' I want to take you there this evening. If you don't like it, you know you need not repeat the visit. You will come, to oblige me, won't you?"

They said they would. And William went out satisfied, though he hardly knew how Robert East would manage to stow away the new comers. Not many steps from the door he encountered Mrs. Buffle. She stopped him to talk of Tyrrett.

"Better that he had spent his loose time at East's than at the publics," remarked that lady.

"It is the very thing we have been saying," answered William. "I wish we could get all Honey Fair there; though, indeed there's no room for more than we have now. I cast a longing eye sometimes to that building at the back, which they say was built for a Mormon stronghold, and has never been fitted up, owing to a dispute among themselves about the number of wives each elder might appropriate to his own share."

"Disgraceful pollagists!" struck in Mrs. Buffle, apostrophizing the Mormon elders. "One husband is enough to have at one's fireside, goodness knows, without being worried with an unlimited number."

"That is not the question," said William, laughing. "It is, how many wives are enough? However, I wish we could get the building. East will have to hold the gathering in his garden soon."

"There's no denying that it have worked good in Honey Fair," acknowledged Mrs. Buffle. "It isn't alone the men that have grown more respectable, them as have took to go, but their wives too. You see, sir, in sitting at the public-houses, it wasn't only that they drank themselves quarrelsome, but they spent their money. Now their tempers are saved, and their money's saved. The wives see the benefit of it, and of course try to be better-behaved theirselves. Not but what there's plenty of room for improvement still," added Mrs. Buffle, in a tone of patronage.

"It will come in time," said William.

"What we must do now, is to look out for a larger room."

"One with a chimbley in it, as'll draw?" suggested Mrs. Buffle.

"Oh yes. What would they do without fire on a winter's night? The great point is, to have things thoroughly comfortable."

"If it hadn't been for the chimbley, I might have offered our big garret, sir. But it's the crankiest thing ever built, is that chimbley; the minute a handful of fire's lighted, the smoke puffs it out again. And then again—there'd be the passing through the shop, obstructing the custom."

"Of course there would," assented William. "We must try for that failure in the rear, after all."

CHAPTER VII

COMING HOME TO THE DARES

The Pyramids of Egypt grew, in the course of time, into pyramids, as was oracularly remarked by Sergeant Delves; but that official's exertions, labour as hard as he would, grew to nothing—when applied to the cause with which he had compared the pyramids. All inquiry, all searching brought to bear upon it by him and his co-adherents, did not bring anything to light of Herbert Dare's movements on that fatal night. Where he had passed the hours remained an impenetrable mystery; and the sergeant had to confess himself foiled. He came, not unnaturally, to the conclusion that Herbert Dare was not anywhere, so far as the outer world was concerned: that he had been at home, committing the mischief. A conclusion the sergeant had drawn from the very first, and it had never been shaken.

Nevertheless, it was his duty to put all the skill and craft of the local police force into action; and very close inquiries were made. Every house of entertainment in the city, of whatever nature—whether a billiard-room or an oyster-shop; whether a chief hotel or an obscure public-house—was visited and keenly questioned; but no one would acknowledge to having seen Herbert Dare on the particular evening. In short, no trace of him could be unearthed.

"Just as much out as I was," said the sergeant to himself. And

Helstonleigh held the same conviction.

Pomeranian Knoll was desolate: with a desolation it had never expected to fall upon it. A shattering blow had been struck to Mr. and Mrs. Dare. To lose their eldest son in so terrible a manner, seemed, of itself, sufficient agony for a whole lifetime. Whatever may have been his faults—and Helstonleigh knew that he was somewhat rich in faults—he was dear to them; dearer than her other children to Mrs. Dare. Herbert had remarked, in conversing with Anna Lynn, that Anthony was his mother's favourite. It was so. She had loved him deeply, had been blind to his failings. Neither Mr. Dare nor his wife was amongst the religious of the world. Religious thoughts and reflections, they, in common with many others in Helstonleigh, were content to leave to a remote death-bed. But they had been less than human, worse than heathen, could they be insensible to the fate of Anthony—hurled away with his sins upon his head. He was cut off suddenly from this world, and—what of the next? It was a question, an uncertainty, that they dared not follow; and they sat, one on each side their desolate hearth, and wailed forth their vain anguish.

This would, in truth, have been tribulation enough to have overshadowed a life; but there was more beyond it. Hemmed in by pride, as the Dares had been, playing at being great and grand in Helstonleigh, the situation of Herbert, setting aside their fears or their sympathy for himself, was about the most complete checkmate that could have fallen upon them. It was the cup of humiliation drained to its dregs. Whether he should be proved guilty or not, he was thrown into prison as a common felon, awaiting his trial for murder; and that disgrace could not be wiped out. Did they believe him guilty? They did not know themselves. To suspect him of such a crime was painful in the last degree to their feelings; but why did he persist in refusing to state where he was on the eventful night? There was the point that staggered them.

A deep gloom overhung the house, extending to all its inmates. Even the servants went about with sad faces and quiet steps. The young ladies knew that a calamity had been dealt to them from which they should never wholly recover. Their star of brilliancy, in its little sphere of light at Helstonleigh, had faded into dimness, if not wholly gone down below the horizon. Should Herbert be found guilty, it could never rise again. Adelaide rarely spoke; she appeared to possess some inward source of vexation or grief, apart from the general tribulation. At least, so judged Signora Varsini; and she was a shrewd observer. She, Miss Dare, spent most of her time shut up in her own room. Rosa and Minny were chiefly with their governess. They were getting of an age to feel it in an equal degree with the rest. Rosa was eighteen, and had begun to go out with Mrs. Dare and Adelaide: Minny was anticipating the same privilege. It was all stopped now—visiting, gaiety, pleasure; and it was felt as a part of the misfortune.

The first shock of the occurrence subsided, the funeral over, and the family settled down in its mourning, the governess exacted their studies from her two pupils as before. They were loth to recommence them, and appealed to their mother. "It was cruel of mademoiselle to wish it of them," they said. Mademoiselle rejoined that her motive was anything but cruel: she felt sure that occupation for the mind was the best counteraction to grief. If they would not study, where was the use of her remaining, she demanded. Madame Dare had better allow her to leave. She would go without notice, if madame pleased. She should be glad to get back to the Continent. They did not have murders there in society; at least, she, mademoiselle, had never encountered personal experience of it.

Mrs. Dare did not appear willing to accede to the proposition. The governess was a most efficient instructress; and six or twelve months more of her services would be essential to her pupils, if they were to be turned out as pupils ought to be. Besides, Sergeant Delves had intimated that the signora's testimony would be necessary at the trial, and therefore she could not be allowed to depart. Mr. Dare thought if they did allow her to depart, they might be accused of wishing to suppress evidence, and it might tell against Herbert. So mademoiselle had to resign herself to remaining. "Très bien," she equably said; "she was willing; only the young ladies must resume their lessons." A mandate in which Mrs. Dare acquiesced.

Sometimes Minny, who was given to be incorrigibly idle, would burst into tears over the trouble of her work, and then lay it upon her distress touching the uncertain fate of Herbert. One day, upon doing this, the governess broke out sharply.

"He deserves to lie in prison, does Monsieur Herbert!"

"Why do you say that, mademoiselle?" asked Minny resentfully.

"Because he is a fool," politely returned mademoiselle. "He say, does he not, that he was not home at the time. It is well; but why does he not say where he was? I think he is a fool, me."

"You may as well say outright, mademoiselle, that you think him guilty!" retorted Minny.

"But I not think him guilty," dissented mademoiselle. "I have said from the first that he was not guilty. I think he is not one capable of doing such an injury, to his brother or to any one else. I used to be great friends with Monsieur Herbert once, when I gave him those Italian lessons, and I never saw to make me believe his disposition was a cruel."

In point of fact, the governess, more explicitly than any one else in the house, had unceasingly declared her belief in Herbert's innocence. Truly and sincerely she did not believe him capable of so grievous a crime. He was not of a cruel or revengeful disposition: certainly not one to lie in wait, and attack another savagely and secretly. She had never believed that he was, and would not believe it now. Neither had his family. Sergeant Delves' opinion was, that whoever had attacked Anthony had lain in wait for him in the dining room, and had sprung upon him as he entered. It is possible, however, that the same point staggered mademoiselle that staggered the rest—Herbert Dare's refusal to state where he was at the time. Believing, as she did, that he could account for it if he chose, she deemed herself perfectly justified in applying to him the complimentary epithet you have just heard. She expressed true sympathy and regret at the untimely fate of Anthony, lamenting him much and genuinely.

Upon Cyril and George the punishment also fell. With one brother not cold in his grave, and the other thrown into gaol to await his trial for murder, they could not, for shame, pursue their amusements as formerly; and amusements to Cyril and George Dare had become a necessity of daily life. Their friends and companions were growing shy of them—or they fancied it. Conscience is all too suggestive. They fancied people shunned them when they walked along the street: Cyril, even, as he stood in Samuel

Lynn's room at the manufactory, thought the men, as they passed in and out, looked askance at him. Very likely it was only imagination. George Dare had set his heart upon a commission; one of the members for the city had made a half-promise to Mr. Dare that he would "see what could be done at the Horse Guards." Failing available interest in that quarter, George was in hope that his father would screw out money to purchase one. But, until Herbert was proved innocent (if that time should ever arrive), the question of his entering the army must remain in abeyance. This state of things altogether did not give pleasure to Cyril and George Dare. But there was no remedy for it, and they had to content themselves with sundry private explosions of temper, by way of relief to their minds.

Yes, the evil fell upon all; upon the parents and upon the children. Of course, the latter suffered nothing in comparison with Mr. and Mrs. Dare. Unhappy days, restless nights, were their portion now: the world seemed to be growing too miserable to live in.

"There must be a fatality upon the boys!" Mr. Dare exclaimed one day, in the bitterness of his spirit, as he paced the room with restless steps, his wife sitting moodily, her elbow on the centre-table, her cheek pressed upon her hand. "Unless there had been a fatality upon them, they never could have turned out as they have."

Mrs. Dare resented the speech. In her unhappy frame of mind, which told terribly upon her temper, it seemed a sort of relief to resent everything. If Mr. Dare spoke against their sons, she stood up for them. "Turned out!" she repeated angrily.

"Let us say, as things have turned out, then, if you will. They appear to be turning out pretty badly, as it seems to me. The boys have had every indulgence in life: they have enjoyed a luxurious home; they have ruined me to supply their extravagances—"

"Ruined you!" again resented Mrs. Dare.

"Ay; ruined. It has all but come to it. And yet, what good has the indulgence or have the advantages brought them? Far better—I begin to see it now—that they had been reared to self-denial; made to work for their daily bread."

"How can you give utterance to such things!" rejoined Mrs. Dare, in a chafed tone.

Mr. Dare stopped in his restless pacing, and confronted his wife. "Are we happy in our sons? Speak the truth."

"How could any one be happy, overwhelmed with a misfortune such as this?"

"Put that aside: what are they without it? Rebellious to us; badly conducted in the sight of the world."

"Who says they are badly conducted?" asked Mrs. Dare, an undercurrent of consciousness whispering that she need not have made the objection. "They may be a little wild; but it is a common failing with those of their age and condition. Their faults are only faults of youth and of uncurbed spirits."

"I wish, then, their spirits had been curbed," was Mr. Dare's reply. "It is useless now to reproach each other," he continued, resuming his walk; "but there must have been something radically wrong in their bringing-up. Anthony, gone: Herbert, perhaps, to follow him by almost a worse death, certainly a more disgraceful one: Cyril—" Mr. Dare stopped abruptly in his catalogue, and went on more generally. "There is no comfort in them for us: there never will be any."

"What can you bring against Cyril?" sharply asked Mrs. Dare. It may be, that these complaints of her husband fretted her temper; chafed, perhaps, her conscience. Certain it was, they rendered her irritable; and Mr. Dare had latterly indulged in them frequently. "If Cyril is a little wild, it is a gentlemanly failing. There's nothing else to urge against him."

"Is theft gentlemanly?"

"Theft!" repeated Mrs. Dare.

"Theft. I have concealed many things from you, Julia, wishing to spare your feelings. But it may be as well now that you should know a little more of what your sons really are. Cyril might have stood where Herbert will stand—at the criminal bar; though for a crime of lesser degree. For all I can tell, he may stand at it still."

Mrs. Dare looked scared. "What has he done?" she asked, her tone growing timid.

"I say that I have kept these things from you. I wish I could have kept them from you always; but it seems to me that exposure is arising in many ways, and it is better that you should be prepared for it, if it must come. I awake now in the morning to apprehension; I am alarmed throughout the day at my own shadow, dreading what unknown fate may not be falling upon them. Herbert in peril of the hangman: Cyril in peril of a forced voyage to the penal settlements."

A sensation of utter fear stole over Mrs. Dare. For the moment, she could not speak. But she rallied her powers to defend Cyril.

"I think Cyril is hardly used, what with one thing and another. He was to have gone on that French journey, and at the last moment was pushed out of it for Halliburton. I felt more vexed at it, almost, than Cyril himself, and I spoke a word of my mind to Mrs. Ashley."

"You did?"

"Yes. I did not speak of it in the light of disappointment to Cyril; the actual fact of not taking the journey; so much as of the vexation he experienced at being supplanted by one whom he—whom we all— consider inferior to himself, William Halliburton. I let Mrs. Ashley know that we regarded it as a most unmerited and uncalled-for slight; and I took care to drop a hint that we believed Halliburton to have been guilty in that cheque affair."

Mr. Dare paused. "What did Mrs. Ashley say?" he presently asked.

"She said very little. I never saw her so frigid. She intimated that Mr. Ashley was a competent judge of his own business—"

"I mean as to the cheque?" interrupted Mr. Dare.

"She was more frigid over that than over the other. She preferred not to discuss it, she answered; who might have stolen it; or who not."

"I can set you right on both points," said Mr. Dare. "Cyril came to me, complaining of being superseded in this French journey, and I complied with his request, that I should go and remonstrate with Mr. Ashley—being a simpleton for my pains. Mr. Ashley informed me that he never had entertained the slightest intention of despatching Cyril, and why Cyril should have taken up the notion, he could not tell. Mr. Ashley went on to say that he did not consider Cyril sufficiently steady to be intrusted abroad alone—"

"Steady!" echoed Mrs. Dare. "What has steadiness to do with executing business? And, as to being alone, Quaker Lynn went over also."

"But at the outset, which was the time I spoke to him, Mr. Ashley's intention was to dispatch only one—Halliburton. He said that Cyril's want of steadiness would always have been a bar to his thinking of him. Shall I go on and enlighten you on the other point—the cheque?" Mr. Dare added, after a pause.

"Y—es," she answered, a nervous dread causing her to speak with hesitation. Had she a foreshadowing of what was coming?

"It was Cyril who took it," said Mr. Dare, dropping his voice to a whisper.

"Cyril!" she gasped.

"Our son, Cyril. No other."

Mrs. Dare took her hand from her cheek, and leaned back in the chair. She was very pale.

"He was traced to White's shop, where he changed the cheque for gold. He had put on Herbert's cloak, the plaid lining outside. When he began to fear detection, he ripped the lining out, and left the cloak in the state it is; now in the possession of the police. Some of the jags and cuts have been sewn up, I suppose by one of the servants: I made no close inquiries. That cloak," he added, with a passing shiver, "might tell queer tales of our sons, if it were able to speak."

"How did you know it was Cyril?" breathed Mrs. Dare.

"From Delves."

"Delves! Does he know it?"

"He does. And the man is keeping the secret out of consideration for us. Delves is good-hearted at bottom. Not but that I spoke a friendly word for him when he was made sergeant. It all tells."

"And Mr. Ashley?" she asked.

"There is no doubt that Ashley has some suspicion: the very fact of his not making a stir in it proves that he has. It would not please him that a relative—as Cyril is—should stand his trial for felony."

"How harshly you put it!" exclaimed Mrs. Dare, bursting into tears. "Felony."

"Nay; what else can I call it?"

A pause ensued. Mr. Dare resumed his restless pacing. Mrs. Dare sat with her handkerchief to her face. Presently she looked up.

"They said it was Halliburton's cloak that the person wore who went to change the cheque."

"It was not Halliburton's. It was Herbert's turned inside out. Herbert knew nothing about it, for I questioned him. He had gone out that night, leaving his cloak hanging in his closet. I asked him how it happened that his cloak, on the inside, should resemble Halliburton's, and he said it was a coincidence. I don't believe him. I entertain little doubt that it was so contrived with a view to enacting some mischief. In fact, what with one revelation and another, I live, as I say, in constant dread of new troubles turning up."

Bitter, most bitter were these revelations to Mrs. Dare; bitter had they been to her husband. Too swiftly were the fruits of their children's rearing coming home to them, bringing their recompense. "There must be a fatality upon the boys!" he reiterated. Possibly. But had neither parents nor children done aught to invoke it?

"Since these evils have come upon our house—the fate of Anthony, the uncertainty overhanging Herbert, the certain guilt of Cyril," resumed Mr. Dare: "I have asked myself whether the money we inherited from old Mr. Cooper may not have wrought ill for us, instead of good."

"Have wrought ill?"

"Ay! Brought with it a curse, instead of a blessing."

She made no remark.

"He warned us that if we took Edgar Halliburton's share it would not bring us good. Do you remember how eagerly he spoke it? We did take it," Mr. Dare added, dropping his voice to the lowest whisper. "And I believe it has just acted as a curse upon us."

"You are fanciful!" she cried, her hands shivering, as she raised her handkerchief to her pale face.

"No; there's no fancy in it. We should have done well to attend to the warning of the dying. Heaven is my witness that at the time, such a thought as that of appropriating it ourselves never crossed my mind. We launched out into expense, and the other share became a necessity to us. It is that expense which has ruined our children."

"How can you say it?" she rejoined, lifting her hands in a passionate sort of manner.

"It has been nothing else. Had they been reared more plainly, they would not have acquired those extravagant notions which have proved their bane. Without that inheritance and the style of living we allowed it to entail upon us, the boys must have understood that they would have to earn money before they spent it, and they would have put their shoulders to the wheel. Julia," he continued, halting by her, and stretching forth his troubled face until it nearly touched hers, "it might have been well now, well with them and with us, had our children been obliged to battle with the poverty to which we condemned the Halliburtons."

Mr. Dare had not taken upon himself the legal conduct of his son Herbert's case. It had been intrusted to the care of a solicitor in Helstonleigh, Mr. Winthorne. This gentleman, more forcibly than any one else, urged upon Herbert Dare the necessity of declaring—if he could declare—where he had been on the night of the murder. He clearly foresaw that, if his client persisted in his present silence, there was no chance of any result but the worst.

He could obtain no response. Deaf to him, as he had been to others, Herbert Dare would disclose nothing. In vain Mr. Winthorne pointed to consequences; first, by delicate hints; next, by hints not delicate; then, by speaking out broadly and fully. It is not pleasant to tell your client, in so many words, that he will be hanged and nothing can save him, unless he compels you to it. Herbert Dare so compelled Mr. Winthorne. All in vain. Mr. Winthorne found he might just as well talk to the walls of the cell. Herbert Dare declared, in the most positive manner, that he had been out the whole of the time stated; from half-past eight o'clock, until nearly two; and from this declaration he never swerved.

Mr. Winthorne was perplexed. The prisoner's assertions were so uniformly earnest, bearing so apparently the stamp of truth, that he could not disbelieve him; or rather, sometimes he believed and sometimes he doubted. It is true that Herbert's declarations did wear an air of entire truth; but Mr. Winthorne had been engaged for criminal offenders before, and knew what the assertions of a great many of them were worth. Down deep in his heart he reasoned very much after the manner of Sergeant Delves: "If he had been absent, he'd confess it to save his neck." He said so to Herbert.

Herbert took the matter, on the whole, coolly; he had done so from the beginning. He did not believe that his neck was really in jeopardy. "They'll never find me guilty," was his belief. He could not avoid standing his trial: that was a calamity from which there was no escape: but he steadily refused to look at its results in a sombre light.

"Can you tell me where you were?" Mr. Winthorne one morning impulsively asked him, when June was drawing to its close.

"I could if I liked," replied Herbert Dare. "I suppose you mean by that, to throw discredit on what I say, Winthorne; but you are wrong. I could point out to you and to all Helstonleigh where I was that night; but I will not do so. I have my reasons, and I will not."

"Then you will fall," said the lawyer. "The very fact of there being no other quarter than yourself on which to cast a shadow of suspicion, will tell against you. You have been bred to the law, and must see these things as plainly as I can put them to you."

"There's the point that puzzles me—who it can have been that did the injury. I'd give half my remaining life to know."

Mr. Winthorne thought that the whole of it, to judge by present appearances, might not be an inconveniently prolonged period; but he did not say so. "What is your objection to speak?" he asked.

"You have put the same question about fifty times, Winthorne, and you'll never get any different answer from the one you have had already—that I don't choose to state it."

"I suppose you were not committing murder in another quarter of the town, were you?"

"I suppose I was not," equably returned Herbert.

"Then, failing that crime, there's no other in the decalogue that I'd not confess to, to save my life. Whether I was robbing a bank, or setting a church on fire, I'd tell it out rather than be hanged by the neck until I was dead."

"Ah, but I was not doing either," said Herbert.

"Then there's the less reason for your persisting in the observance of so much mystery."

"My doing so is my own business," returned Herbert.

"No, it is not your own business," objected Mr. Winthorne. "You assert that you are innocent of the crime with which you are charged—"

"I assert nothing but the truth," interrupted Herbert.

"Good. Then, if you are innocent, and if you can prove your innocence, it is your duty to your family to do it. A man's duties in this life are not owing to himself alone: above all, a son's. He owes allegiance to his father and mother; his consideration for them should be above his consideration for himself. If you can prove your innocence it will be an unpardonable sin not to do it; a sin inflicted on your family."

"I can't help it," replied Herbert in his obstinacy. "I have my reasons for not speaking, and I shall not speak."

"You will surely suffer the penalty," said Mr. Winthorne.

"Then I must suffer it," returned the prisoner.

But it is one thing to talk, and another to act. Many a brave spirit, ready and willing to undergo hanging in theory, would find his heart fail and his bravery altogether die out, were he really required to reduce it to practice.

Herbert Dare was only human. After July had come in and the time for the opening of the assizes might be counted by hours, then his courage began to flinch. He spent a night in tossing from side to side on his pallet (a wide difference between that and his comfortable bed at home), during which a certain ugly apparatus, to be erected for his especial use within the walls of the prison some fine Saturday morning, on which he might figure by no means gracefully, had mentally disturbed his rest.

He arose unrefreshed. The vision of that possible future was not a pleasant one. Herbert remembered once, when he had been a college boy, that the Saturday morning's occasional drama had been enacted for the warning and edification of the town, and of the country people flocking into it for market. The college boys had determined for once in their lives to see the sight—if they could accomplish it. The ceremony was invariably performed at eight o'clock; the exhibition closed at nine; and the boys' difficulty was, how to arrive at the scene in time, considering that it was only at the striking of the latter hour that they were let loose down the steps of the school. They had tried the time between the cloisters and the county prison; and found that by dint of taking the shorter way through the back streets, tearing along at the fleetest pace, and knocking over every obstruction—human, animal, or material—that might unfortunately be in their path, they could do the distance in four minutes. Arriving rather out of wind, it's true: but that was nothing.

Four minutes! they did not see their way. If the curtain descended at nine, sharp, as good be forty minutes after the hour, as four, in point of practical effect. But the Helstonleigh college boys—as you may sometimes have heard remarked before—were not wont to allow difficulties to overmaster them. If there was a possible way of overcoming obstacles, they were sure to find it. Consultations had been anxious. To request the head-master to allow them as a favour to depart five or ten minutes before the usual time, would be worse than useless. It was a question whether he ever would have accorded it; but there was no chance of it on that morning. Neither could the whole school be taken summarily with spasms, or croup, or any other excruciating malady necessitating compassion and an early dismissal.

They came to the resolve of applying to the official who had the cathedral clock under his charge: or, as they phrased it, "coming over the clock-man." By dint of coaxing, or bribery, or some other element of persuasion, they got this functionary to promise to put the clock on eight minutes on that particular morning. And it was done. And at eight minutes before nine by the sun, the cathedral clock rang out its nine strokes. But, instead of the master lifting his finger—the signal for the boys to tear forth—the master sat quiet at his desk, and never gave it. He sat until the eight minutes had gone by, when the other churches in the town gave out their hour; he sat four minutes after that: and then he nodded them their dismissal.

The twelve minutes had seemed to the boys like twelve hours. Where the hitch was, they never knew; they never have known to this day; as they would tell you themselves. Whether the master had received an inkling of what was in the wind; or whether, by one of those extraordinary coincidences that sometimes occur in life, he, for that one morning, allowed the hour to slip by unheeded—had not heard it strike—they could not tell. He gave out no explanation, then or afterwards. The clock-man protested that he had been true; had not breathed a hint to any one living of the purposed advancement; and the boys had no reason to disbelieve him.

However it might have been, they could not alter it. It was four minutes past nine when they clattered pêle-mêle down the school-room steps. Away they tore, full of fallacious hope, out at the cloisters, through the cathedral precincts, along the nearest streets, and arrived within the given four minutes, rather than over it.

Alas, for human expectations! The prison was there, it is true, formidable as usual; but all trace of the morning's jubilee had passed away. Not only had the chief actor been removed, but also that ugly apparatus which Herbert Dare had dreamt of. That might have afforded them some gratification to contemplate, failing the greater sight. The college boys, dumb in the first moment of their disappointment, gave vent to it at length with three dismal groans, the echoes of which might have been heard as far off as the cathedral. Groans not intended for the unhappy mortal, then beyond hearing of that or any other earthly sound; not for the officials of the county prison, all too quick-handed that morning; but given as a compliment to the respected gentleman at that time holding the situation of head-master.

Herbert Dare remembered this: it was rising up in his mind with strange distinctness. He himself had been one of the deputation chosen to "come over" the clock-man; had been the chief persuader of that functionary. Would the college boys hasten down if he were to—In spite of his bravery, he broke off the speculation with a shudder; and, calling the turnkey to him, he despatched a message for Mr. Winthorne. Was it the remembrance of his old school-fellows, of what they would think of him, that brought about what no other consideration had been able to effect?

As much indulgence as it was possible to allow a prisoner was accorded to Herbert Dare. Indeed, it may be questioned whether any previous prisoner, incarcerated within the walls of the county prison, had ever enjoyed so much. The governor of the prison and Mr. Dare had lived on intimate terms. Mr. Dare and his two elder sons had been familiar, in their legal capacity, with both its civil and criminal prisoners; and the turnkeys had often bowed Herbert in and out of cells, as they now bowed out Mr. Winthorne. Altogether, what with the governor's friendly feeling, and the turnkey's reverential one, Herbert Dare obtained more privileges than the ordinary run of prisoners. The message was at once taken to Mr. Winthorne, and it brought that gentleman back again.

"I have made up my mind to tell," was Herbert's brief salutation when he entered.

"A very sensible resolution," replied the lawyer. Doubts, however, crossed his mind as he spoke, whether the prisoner was not about to set up some plea which had never had place in fact. In like manner to Sergeant Delves, Mr. Winthorne had arrived at the firm belief that there was nothing to tell. "Well?" said he.

"That is, conditionally," resumed Herbert Dare. "It would be of little use my saying I was at such and such a place, unless I could bring forward confirmatory evidence."

"Of course it would not."

"Well; there are witnesses who could give this satisfactory evidence: but the question is, will they be willing to do it?"

"What motive or excuse could they have for refusing?" returned Mr. Winthorne. "When a fellow-creature's life is at stake, surely there is no man so lost to humanity as not to come forward and save it, if it be in his power."

"Circumstances alter cases," was the curt reply of Herbert Dare.

"Was it your doubt, as to whether they would come forward, that caused your hesitation to call on them to do so?" asked Mr. Winthorne, something not pleasant in his tones.

"Not altogether. I foresaw a difficulty in it; I foresee it still. Winthorne, you look at me with a face full of doubt. There is no need for it—as you will find."

"Well, go on," said the lawyer; for Herbert had stopped.

"The thing must be gone about in a very cautious manner; and I don't quite see how it can be done," resumed Herbert slowly. "Winthorne, I think I had better make a confidant of you, and tell you the whole story from beginning to end."

"If I am to do you any good, I must hear it, I expect. A man can't work in the dark."

"Sit down then, and I'll begin. Though, mind—I tell it you in confidence. It's not for Helstonleigh. But you will see the expediency of being silent when you have heard it."

CHAPTER IX

SERGEANT DELVES "LOOKS UP"

The following Saturday was the day fixed for the opening of the commission at Helstonleigh. It soon came round, and the streets in the afternoon wore their usual holiday appearance. The high sheriff's procession went out to meet the judges, and groups stood about, waiting and watching for its return. Amongst other people blocking up the way, might be observed the portly person of Sergeant Delves. He strolled along, seeming to look at nothing, but his keen eye was everywhere. It suddenly fell upon Mr. Winthorne, who was picking his way through the crowd as fast as he could do so, apparently in a hurry. Hurry or not, Sergeant Delves stopped him, and drew him to a safe spot beyond the reach of curious ears.

"I was looking for you, Mr. Winthorne," said Delves in a confidential tone. "I say—this tale, that Dare will succeed in establishing an alibi, is it reliable?"

"Why—who the mischief can have been setting that afloat?" returned the lawyer, in tones of the utmost astonishment, not unmixed with vexation.

"Dare himself was my informant," replied the sergeant. "I was in the prison just now, and saw him in the yard with the turnkey. He called me aside, and told me he was as good as acquitted."

"Then he is an idiot for his pains. He had no right to talk of it, even to you."

"I am dark," carelessly returned Delves. "I don't wish ill to the Dares, and wouldn't work it to them; as perhaps some of them could tell you," he added significantly. "What about this acquittal that he talks of?"

"There's no doubt he will be acquitted. He will prove an alibi."

"Is it a got-up alibi?" asked the plain-speaking sergeant.

"No. And as far as I go, I would not lend myself to getting up anything false," observed the solicitor. "He has said from the first, you know, that he was not near the house at the time, and so it will turn out."

"Has he confessed where he was, after all his standing out?"

"Yes; to me: it will be disclosed at the trial."

"He was after no good, I know," nodded the sergeant oracularly.

Mr. Winthorne raised his eyebrows, and slightly jerked his shoulders. The movement may have meant anything or nothing. He did not reply in words.

Sergeant Delves fell into a reverie. He roused himself from it to take a searching gaze at the lawyer. "Sir," said he, and he could hardly have spoken more earnestly had his life depended on it, "tell me the truth out-and-out. Do you, yourself, from the depths of your own judgment, believe Herbert Dare to have been innocent?"

"Delves, as truly as that you and I now stand here, I honestly believe that he had no more to do with his brother's death than we had."

"Then I'm blest if I don't take up the other scent!" exclaimed Mr. Delves, slapping his thigh. "I did think of it once, but I dropped it again, so sure was I that it was Master Herbert."

"What scent is that?"

"Look here," said the sergeant—"but now it's my turn to warn you to be dark. There was a young woman met Anthony Dare the night of the murder, when he was going down to the Star and Garter. It's a young woman he did not behave genteel to some time back, as the ghost says in the song. She met him that night, and she gave him a bit of her tongue; not much, for he wouldn't stop to listen. But now, Mr. Winthorne, it has crossed my mind many times whether she might not have watched for his going home again, and followed him; followed him right into the dining-room, and done the mischief. I'll lay a guinea it was her!" added the sergeant, arriving at a hasty conclusion. "I shall look up again now."

"Do you mean that young woman in Honey Fair?" asked Mr. Winthorne.

"Just so. Her, and nobody else. The doubt has crossed me; but, as I say, I was so certain it was the brother, that I did not follow it up."

"Could a woman's feeble hand inflict such injuries?" debated the solicitor.

"'Feeble' be hanged!" politely rejoined the sergeant. "Some women have the fists of men; and the strength of 'em, too. You don't know 'em as we do. A desperate woman will do anything. And Anthony Dare, remember, had not his strength in him that night."

Mr. Winthorne shook his head. "That girl has no look of ferocity about her. I should question it being her. Let's see—what is her name?"

"Listen!" returned the sergeant. "When you have had half as much to do with people as I have, you'll have learnt not to go by looks. Her name is Caroline Mason."

At that moment the cathedral bells rang out, announcing the return of the procession, the advent of the judges. As if the sound reminded the lawyer of the speed of time, he hastily went on his way; leaving the sergeant to use his eyes and ears at the expense of the crowd.

"I wonder how the prisoners in the gaol feels?" remarked a woman whom the sergeant recognised as being no other than Mrs. Cross. She had just come out of a warehouse with her supply of work for the ensuing week.

"Ah, poor creatures!" responded another of the group, and that was Mrs. Brumm. "I wonder how young Dare likes it!"

"Or how old Dare likes it—if he can hear 'em all the way up at his office. They'll know their fate soon, them two."

In close vicinity to this colloquy was a young woman, drawn against the wall, under shelter of a projecting doorway. Her once good-looking face was haggard, and her clothes were scanty. It was for this reason, perhaps, that she appeared to shun observation. Sergeant Delves, apparently without any other design than that of working his way leisurely through the throng, edged himself up to her.

"Looking out for the show, Miss Mason?"

Caroline turned her spiritless eyes upon him. "I'm waiting till there's a way cleared for me to get through, without pushing against folks and contaminating 'em. What's the show to me, or me to it?"

"At the last assizes, in March, when the judges came in, young Anthony Dare made one in the streets, looking on," resumed the sergeant, chatting affably. "I saw him and spoke to him. And now he is gone where there's no shows to see."

She made no reply.

"The women there," pointing his thumb at the group of talkers hard by, "are saying that Herbert Dare won't like the sound of the college bells.—Hey, me! Look at those young toads of college boys, just let out of school!" broke off the sergeant, as a tribe of some twenty of the king's scholars came fighting and elbowing their way through the throng to the front. "They are just like so many wild colts! Maybe the prisoner, Herbert Dare, is now casting his thoughts back to the time when he made one of the band, and was as free from care as they are. It's not so long ago."

Caroline Mason asked a question somewhat abruptly. "Will he be found guilty, sir, do you think?"

The sergeant turned the tail of his keen eye upon her, and answered the question by asking another. "Do you?"

She shook her head. "I don't think he was guilty."

"You don't?"

"No, I don't. Why should one brother kill another?"

"Very true," coughed the sergeant. "But somebody must have done it. If Herbert Dare did not, who did?"

"Ah! who did? I'd like to know," she passionately added. "He had folks in this town that owed him grudges, had Mr. Anthony Dare."

"If my vision didn't deceive me, I saw you talking to him that very same night," carelessly observed the sergeant.

"Did you see me?" she rejoined, apparently as much at ease as the sergeant himself. "I had to do an errand at that end of the town, and I met him, and told him what he was. I hadn't spoke to him for months and months; for years, I think. I had slipped into doors, down entries, anywhere to avoid him, if I saw him coming; but a feeling came over me to speak to him then. I'm glad I did. I hope the truths I said to him went along with him to enliven him on his journey!"

"Did you see him after that, later in the evening?" resumed the inspector, putting the question sociably, and stretching his neck up to obtain a view of something at a distance.

"No, I didn't," she replied. "But I would, if I had thought it was going to be his last. I'd have bade him remember all his good works where he was going to. I'd almost have went with him, I would, to have heard how he answered for them, up there."

Caroline Mason glanced upwards to indicate the sky, when a loud flourish of trumpets from the advancing heralds sounded close upon them. As they rode up at a foot pace, they dropped their trumpets, and the mounted javelin-men quickly followed, their javelins in rest. A carriage or two; a few more officials; and then advanced the equipage of the high sheriff. Only one of the judges was in it, fully robed: a fine man, with a benign countenance. A grave smile was on it as he spoke to the sheriff, who sat opposite to him, his chaplain by his side.

Sergeant Delves's attention was distracted for an instant, and when he looked round again, Caroline Mason had disappeared. He just caught sight of her in the distance, winding her way through the crowd, her head down.

"Did she do it, or did she not?" cried the sergeant, in soliloquy. "Go on, go on, my lady, for the present; you are about to be a bit looked after."

How did the prisoners feel, and Herbert Dare amongst them, as the joyous sounds, outside, fell upon their ears; the blast of the trumpets, the sweetness of the bells, the stir of life: penetrating within the walls of the city and county prisons? Did they feel that the pomp and show, run after as a holiday sight, was only a cruel advent to them?—that the formidable and fiery vision in the scarlet robe and flowing wig, who sat in the carriage, bending his serene face upon the mob, collected to stare and shout, might prove the pronouncer of their doom?—a doom that should close the portals of this world upon them, and open those of eternity!

Tuesday morning was the day fixed for the trial of Herbert Dare. You might have walked upon the people's heads in the vicinity of the Guildhall, for all the town wished to get in to hear it. Of course only a very small portion of the town, relatively speaking, could have its wish, or succeed in fighting a way to a place. Of the rest, some went back to their homes, disappointed and exploding; and the rest collected outside and blocked up the street. The police had their work cut out that day; whilst the javelin-men, heralding in the judges, experienced great difficulty in keeping clear the passages. The heat in court would be desperate as the day advanced.

Sir William Leader, as senior judge, took his seat in the criminal court. It was he whom you saw in the sheriff's carriage on Saturday. The same benignant face was bent upon the crowded court that had been bent upon the street mob; the same penetrating eye; the same grave, calm bearing. The prisoner was immediately placed at the bar, and all eyes, strange or familiar, were strained to look at him. They saw a tall, handsome young man, looking too gentlemanly to stand in the felon's dock. He was habited in deep mourning. His countenance, usually somewhat conspicuous for its bright complexion, was pale, probably from the moment's emotion, and his white handkerchief was lifted to his mouth as he moved forward; otherwise he was calm. Old Anthony Dale was in court, looking far more agitated than his son. Preliminaries were gone through, and the trial began.

"Prisoner at the bar, how say you? Are you guilty, or not guilty?"

Herbert Dare raised his eyes fearlessly, and pleaded in a firm tone:

"Not Guilty!"

The leading counsel for the prosecution, Serjeant Seeitall, stated the case. His address occupied some time, and he then proceeded to call witnesses. One of the first examined was Betsy Carter. She deposed to the facts of having sat up with the lady's-maid and Joseph, until the return of Mr. and Mrs. Dare and their daughter; to having then gone into the dining-room with a light to look for Mr. Dare's pipe, which she had left there in the morning, when cleaning the room. "In moving forward with the candle, I saw something dark on the ground," continued Betsy, who, when her first timidity had gone off, seemed inclined to be communicative. "At the first glance, I thought it was one of the gentlemen gone to sleep there; but when I stooped down with the light, I saw it was the face of the dead. Awful, it looked!"

"What did you next do?" demanded the examining counsel.

"Screeched out, gentlemen," responded Betsy.

"What else?"

"I went out of the room, screeching to Joseph in the hall, and master came in from outside the front door, where he was waiting, all peaceful and ignorant, for his pipe, little thinking what there was so close to him. I screeched out all the more, gentlemen, when I remembered the quarrel that had took place at dinner that afternoon, and I knew it was nobody but Mr. Herbert that had done the murder."

The witness was sharply told to confine herself to evidence.

"It couldn't be nobody else," retorted Betsy, who, once set going, was a match for any cross-examiner. "There was the cloak to prove it. Mr. Herbert had gone out in the cloak that very night, and the poor dead gentleman was lying on it. Which proves it must have come off in the scuffle between 'em."

The fact of the quarrel, the facts connected with the cloak, as well as all other facts, had been mentioned by the learned Serjeant Seeitall in his opening address. The witness was questioned as to what she knew of the quarrel: but it appeared that she had not been present; consequently could not testify to it. The cloak she could say more about, and spoke of it confidently as Mr. Herbert's.

"How did you know the cloak, found under the dead man, was Mr. Herbert's?" interposed the prisoner's counsel, Mr. Chattaway.

"Because I did," returned the witness.

"I ask you how you knew it?"

"By lots of tokens," she answered. "By the shining black clasp, for one thing, and by the tears and jags in it, for another. Nobody has ever pretended it was not the cloak. I have seen it fifty times hanging up in Mr. Herbert's closet."

"You saw the prisoner going out in it that evening?"

"Yes, I did," she answered. "I was looking out at Miss Adelaide's chamber window, and I saw him come out of the dining-room window, and go off towards the front gates. The gentlemen often went out through the dining-room window, instead of at the hall door."

"The prisoner says he came back immediately, and left his cloak in the dining-room, going out finally without it. Did you see him come back?"

"No, I didn't," replied Betsy.

"How long did you remain at the window?"

"Not long."

"Did you remain long enough for him to cross the lawn to the front entrance gates, and come back again?"

"No, I don't think I did, sir."

"The court will please take note of that answer," said Mr. Chattaway, who was aware that a great deal had been made of the fact of the housemaid's having seen him go out in the cloak. "You left the window then, immediately?"

"Pretty near immediately. I don't think I stayed long enough at it for him to come back from the front gates—if he did come. I have never said I did," she resentfully continued.

"What time was it that you saw him go out?"

"I hadn't took particular notice of the time. It was dusk. I was turning down my beds; and I generally do that a little before nine. The next room I went into was Mr. Anthony's."

"The deceased was in it, was he not?"

"He was in it, stretched full length upon the sofa. He had his head down on the cushion, and his feet up over the arm at the foot, all comfortable and easy, with a cigar in his mouth, and some glasses and things on the table near him. 'What are you come bothering in here for?' he asked. So I begged his pardon; for you see, gentlemen, I didn't know he was there, and I went out again, and met Joseph carrying up a note to him. A little while after that, he went out."

The witness's propensity to degenerate into gossip appeared irrepressible. Several times she was stopped; once by the judge.

"Of how many servants did the household of Mr. Dare consist?" she was asked.

"There were four of us, gentlemen."

"Did you all sit up that night?"

"All but the cook. She went to bed."

"And the family, those who were at home, went to bed?"

"All of them, sir. The governess went early; she was not well; and Miss Rosa and Miss Minny went, and the two young gentlemen went when they came home from playing cricket."

"In point of fact, then, no one was up except you three servants in the kitchen?"

"Nobody, sir."

"And you heard no noise in the house until the return of Mr. and Mrs. Dare?"

"We never heard nothing," responded Betsy. "We were sitting quietly in the kitchen; me and the lady's-maid at work, and Joseph asleep. We never heard any noise at all."

This was the substance of what was asked her. Joseph was next called, and gave his testimony. He deposed to having fastened up the house at eleven o'clock, with the exception of the dining-room window: that was left open in obedience to orders. All other facts within his knowledge he also testified to. The governess, Signorina Varsini, was called, and questioned upon two points: what she had seen and heard of the quarrel, and of the subsequent conduct of Anthony and Herbert to each other in the drawing-room. But her testimony amounted to nothing, and she might as well not have been troubled. She was also asked whether she had heard any noise in the house between eleven o'clock and the return of Mr. and Mrs. Dare. She replied that she did not hear any, for she had been asleep. She went to sleep long before eleven, and did not wake up until aroused by the commotion caused by the finding of the body. The witness was proceeding to favour the court with her own conviction that the prisoner was innocent, but was brought up with a summary notice that that was not evidence, and that, if she knew nothing more, she might withdraw. Upon which, she honoured the bench with an elaborate curtsey, and retired. Not a witness throughout the day gave evidence with more absolute equanimity.

Lord Hawkesley was examined; also Mr. Brittle—the latter coming to Helstonleigh on his subpoena. But to give the testimony of all the witnesses in length, would only be to repeat what has already been related. It will be sufficient to extract a few questions here and there.

"What were the games played in your rooms that evening?" was asked of Mr. Brittle.

"Some played whist; some écarté."

"At which did the deceased play?"

"At whist."

"Was he a loser, or a gainer?"

"A loser; but to a very trifling amount. We were playing half-crown points. He and myself played against Lord Hawkesley and Captain Bellew. We broke up because he, the deceased, was not sufficiently sober to play."

"Was he sober when he joined you?"

"By no means. He appeared to have been drinking rather freely; and he took more in my rooms, which made him worse."

"Why did you accompany him home?"

"He was scarcely in a state to proceed alone: and I felt no objection to a walk. It was a fine night."

"Did he speak, during the evening, of the dispute which had taken place between him and his brother?" interposed the judge.

"He did not, my lord. A slight incident occurred, as we were going to his home, which it may be perhaps as well to mention—"

"You must mention everything which bears upon this unhappy case, sir," interrupted the judge. "You are sworn to tell the whole truth."

"I do not suppose it does bear upon it directly, my lord. Had I attached importance to it, I should have spoken of it before. In passing the turning which leads to the race-course, a man met us, and began to abuse the deceased. The deceased was inclined to stop and return it, but I drew him on."

"Of what nature was the abuse?" asked the counsel.

"I do not recollect the precise terms. It was to the effect that he, the deceased, tippled away his money instead of paying his debts. The man backed against the wall as he spoke: he appeared to have had rather too much himself. I drew the deceased on, and we were soon out of hearing."

"What became of the man?"

"I do not know. We left him standing against the wall. He called loudly after the deceased to know when his bill was to be paid. I judged him to be some petty tradesman."

"Did he follow you?"

"No. At least, we heard no more of him afterwards. I saw the deceased safely within his own gate, and left him."

"What state, as to sobriety, was the deceased in then?"

"He was what may be called half-seasover," replied the witness. "He could talk, but his words were not very distinct."

"Could he walk alone?"

"After a fashion. He stumbled as he walked."

"What time was this?"

"About half-past eleven. I think the half-hour struck directly after I left him, but I am not quite sure."

"As you returned, did you see anything of the man who had accosted the deceased?"

"Not anything."

Strange to say the very man thus spoken of was in court, listening to the trial. Upon hearing the evidence given by Mr. Brittle, he voluntarily came forward as a witness. He said he had been "having a drop," and it had made him abusive, but that Anthony Dare had owed him money long for work done, mending and making. He was a jobbing tailor, and the bill was a matter of fourteen pounds. Anthony Dare had only put him off and off; he was a poor man, with a wife and family to keep, and he wanted the money badly; but now, he supposed, he should never be paid. He lived close to the spot where he met the deceased and the gentleman who had just given evidence, and he could prove that he went home as soon as they were out of sight, and was in bed at half-past eleven. What with debts and various other things, he concluded the town had had enough to rue in young Anthony Dare. Still, the poor fellow didn't deserve such a shocking fate as murder, and he would have been the first to protect him from it.

That the evidence was given in good faith, was undoubted. He was known to the town as a harmless, inoffensive man, addicted, though upon rare occasions, to taking more than was good for him, when he was apt to dilate upon his grievances.

The constable who had been on duty that night near Mr. Dare's residence was the next witness called. "Did you see the deceased that night?" was asked of him.

"Yes, sir, I did," was the reply. "I saw him walking home with the gentleman who has given evidence—Mr. Brittle. I noticed that young Mr. Dare talked thick, as if he had been drinking."

"Did they appear to be on good terms?"

"Very good terms, sir. Mr. Brittle was laughing when he opened the gate for the deceased, and told him to mind he did not kiss the grass; or something to that effect."

"Were you close to them?"

"Quite close, sir. I said 'Good night' to the deceased, but he seemed not to notice it. I stood and watched him over the grass. He reeled as he walked."

"What time was this?"

"Nigh upon half-past eleven, sir."

"Did you detect any signs of people moving within the house?"

"Not any, sir. The house seemed quite still, and the blinds were down before the windows."

"Did you see any one enter the gate that night besides the deceased?"

"Not any one."

"Not the prisoner?"

"Not any one," repeated the policeman.

"Did you see anything of the prisoner later, between half-past one and two, the time he alleges as that of his going home?"

"I never saw the prisoner at all that night, sir."

"He could have gone in, as he states, without your seeing him?" interposed the prisoner's counsel.

"Yes, certainly, a dozen times over. My beat extended to half-a-mile beyond Mr. Dare's."

One witness, who was placed in the box, created a profound sensation: for it was the unhappy father, Anthony Dare. Since the deed was committed, two months ago, Mr. Dare had been growing old. His brow was furrowed, his cheeks were wrinkled, his hair was turning white, and he looked, as he obeyed the call to the witness-box, as a man sinking under a heavy weight of care. Many of the countenances present expressed deep commiseration for him.

He was sworn, and various questions were asked him. Amongst others, whether he knew anything of the quarrel which had taken place between his two sons.

"Personally, nothing," was the reply. "I was not at home."

"It has been testified that when they were parted, your son Herbert threatened his brother. Is he of a revengeful disposition?"

"No," replied Mr. Dare, with emotion; "that, I can truly say, he is not. My poor son, Anthony, was somewhat given to sullenness; but Herbert never was."

"There had been a great deal of ill-feeling between them of late, I believe."

"I fear there had been."

"It is stated that you yourself, upon leaving home that evening, left them a warning not to quarrel. Was it so?"

"I believe I did. Anthony entered the house as we were leaving it, and I did say something to him to that effect."

"The prisoner was not present?"

"No. He had not returned."

"It is proved that he came home later, dined, and went out again at dusk. It does not appear that he was seen afterwards by any member of your household, until you yourself went up to his room and found him there, after the discovery of the body. His own account is, that he had only recently returned. Do you know where he was, during his absence?"

"No."

"Or where he went to?"

"No," repeated the witness in sadly faltering tones, for he knew that this was the one weak point in the defence.

"He will not tell you?"

"He declines to do so. But," the witness added, with emotion, "he has denied his guilt to me from the first, in the most decisive manner: and I solemnly believe him to be innocent. Why he will not state where he was, I cannot conceive; but not a shade of doubt rests upon my mind that he could state it if he chose, and that it would be the means of establishing the fact of his absence. I would not assert this if I did not believe it," said the witness, raising his trembling hand. "They were both my boys: the one destroyed was my eldest, perhaps my dearest; and I declare that I would not, knowingly, screen his assassin, although that assassin were his brother."

The case for the prosecution concluded, and the defence was entered upon. The prisoner's counsel—two of them eminent men, Mr. Chattaway himself being no secondary light in the forensic world—laboured under one disadvantage, as it appeared to the crowded court. They exerted all their eloquence in seeking to divert the guilt from the prisoner: but they could not—distort facts as they might, call upon imagination as they would—they could not conjure up the ghost of any other channel to which to direct suspicion. There lay the weak point, as it had lain throughout. If Herbert Dare was not guilty, who was? The family, quietly sleeping in their beds, were beyond the pale of suspicion; the household equally so; and no trace of any midnight intruder to the house could be found. It was a grave stumbling-block for the prisoner's counsel; but such stumbling-blocks are as nothing to an expert pleader. Bit by bit Mr. Chattaway disposed, or seemed to dispose, of every argument that could tell against the prisoner. The presence of the cloak in the dining-room, from which so much appearance of guilt had been deduced, he converted into a negative proof of innocence. "Had he been the one engaged in the struggle," argued the learned Q.C., "would he have been mad enough to leave his own cloak there, underneath his victim, a damning proof of guilt? No! that, at any rate, he would have taken away. The very fact of the cloak being under the murdered man was a most indisputable proof, as he regarded it, that the prisoner remained totally ignorant of what had happened—ignorant of his unfortunate brother's being at all in the dining-room. Why! had he only surmised that his brother was lying, wounded or dead, in the room, would he not have hastened to remove his cloak out of it, before it should be seen there, knowing, as he must know, that, from the very terms on which he and his brother had been, it would be looked upon as a proof of his guilt?" The argument told well with the jury—probably with the judge.

Bit by bit, so did he thus dispose of the suspicious circumstances: of all, except one. And that was the great one, the one that nobody could get over: the refusal of the prisoner to state where he was that night. "All in good time, gentlemen of the jury," said Mr. Chattaway, some murmured words reaching his ear that the omission was deemed ominous. "I am coming to that later; and I shall prove as complete and distinct an alibi as it was ever my lot to submit to an enlightened court."

The court listened, the jury listened, the spectators listened, and "hoped he might." He had spoken, for the most part, to incredulous ears.

CHAPTER XI

THE WITNESSES FOR THE ALIBI

When the speech of the counsel ended, and the time came for the production of the witness or witnesses who were to prove the alibi, there appeared to be some delay. The intense heat of the court had been growing greater with every hour. The rays of the afternoon sun, now sinking lower and lower in the heavens, had only brought with them a more deadly feeling of suffocation. But, to go out for a breath of air, even had the thronged state of the passages permitted the movement, appeared to enter into no one's thoughts. Their suspense was too keen, their interest too absorbing. Who were those mysterious witnesses, that would testify to the innocence of Herbert Dare?

A stir at the extreme end of the court, where it joined the other passage. Every eye was strained to see, every ear to listen, as an usher came clearing the way. "By your leave there—by your leave; room for a witness!"

The spectators looked, and stretched their necks, and looked again. A few among them experienced a strange thrill of disappointment, and felt that they should have much pleasure in being allowed the privilege of boxing the usher's ears, for he preceded no one more important than Richard Winthorne, the lawyer. Ah, but wait a bit! What short and slight figure is it that Mr. Winthorne is guiding along? The angry crowd have not caught sight of her yet.

But, when they do—when the drooping, shrinking form is at length in the witness-box; her eyes never raised, her lovely face bent in timid dread—then a murmur arises, and shakes the court to its foundation. The judge feels for his glasses—rarely used—and puts them across his nose, and gazes at her. A fair girl, attired in the simple, modest garb peculiar to the sect called Quakers, not more modest than the lovely and gentle face. She does not take the oath, only the affirmation peculiar to her people.

"What is your name?" commenced the prisoner's counsel.

That she spoke words in reply, was evident, by the moving of her lips: but they could not be heard.

"You must speak up," interposed the judge, in tones of kindness.

A deep struggle for breath, an effort of which even those around could see the pain, and the answer came. "They call me Anna. I am the daughter of Samuel Lynn."

"Where do your live?"

"I live with my father and Patience, in the London Road."

"What do you know of the prisoner at the bar?"

A pause. She probably did not understand the sort of answer required. One came that was unexpected.

"I know him to be innocent of the crime of which he is accused."

"How do you know this?"

"Because he could not have been near the spot at the time."

"Where was he then?"

"With me."

But the reply came forth in so faint a whisper that again she had to be enjoined to speak louder, and she repeated it, using different words.

"He was at our house."

"At what hour did he go to your house?"

"It was past nine when he came up first."

"And what time did he leave?"

"It was about one in the morning."

The answer appeared to create some stir. A late hour for a sober little Quakeress to confess to.

"Was he spending the evening with your friends?"

"No."

"Did they not know he was there?"

"No."

"It was a clandestine visit to yourself, then? Where were they?"

A pause, and a very trembling answer. "They were in bed."

"Oh! You were entertaining him by yourself, then?"

She burst into tears. The judge let fall his glasses as though under the pressure of some annoyance, every feature of his fine face expressive of compassion: it may be, his thoughts had flown to daughters of his own. The crowd stood with open mouths, gaping with undisguised astonishment, and the burly Queen's counsel proceeded.

"And so he prolonged his visit until one o'clock in the morning?"

"I was locked out," she sobbed. "That is how he came to stay so late."

Bit by bit, with question and cross-questioning, it all came out: that Herbert Dare had been in the habit of paying stolen visits to the field, and that Anna had been in the habit of meeting him there. That she had gone in on this night just before ten, which was later than she had ever stayed out before: but, finding Hester had to go out for medicine for Patience, she had run to the field again to take a book to the prisoner; and that upon attempting to enter soon afterwards, she found the door locked, Hester having met the doctor's boy, and come back at once. She told it all, as simply and guilelessly as a child.

"What were you doing all that time? From ten o'clock until one in the morning?"

"I was sitting on the door-step, crying."

"Was the prisoner with you?"

"Yes. He stood by me part of the time, telling me not to be afraid; and the rest of the time—more than an hour, I think—he was working at the wires of the pantry window, to try to get in."

"Was he all that time at the wires?"

"It was a long time before I remembered the pantry window. He wanted to knock up Hester, but I was afraid to let him. I feared she might tell Patience, and they would have been so angry with me. He got in, at last, at the pantry window, and he opened the kitchen window for me, and I went in by it."

"And you mean to say he was all that time, till one o'clock in the morning, forcing the wires of a pantry window?" cried Sergeant Seeitall.

"It was nearly one. I am telling thee the truth."

"And you did not lose sight of the prisoner from the time he first came to the field, at nine o'clock, until he left you at one?"

"Only for the few minutes—it may have been four or five—when I ran in and came out again with the book. He waited in the field."

"What time was that?"

"The ten o'clock bell was going in Helstonleigh. We could hear it."

"He was with you all the rest of the time."

"Yes, all. When he was working at the pantry window I could not see him, because he was round the angle of the house, but I could hear him at the wires. Not a minute of the time but I heard him. He was more than an hour at the wires, as I have told thee."

"And until he began at the wires?"

"He was standing up by me, telling me not to be afraid."

"All the time? You affirm this?"

"I am affirming all that I say to thee. I am speaking as before my Maker."

"Don't you think it is a pretty confession for a young lady to make?"

She burst into fresh tears. The judge turned his grave face upon Sergeant Seeitall. But the sergeant had impudence enough for ten.

"Pray, how many times had that pretty little midnight drama been enacted?" he continued, whilst Anna sobbed in distress.

"Never before," burst forth a deep voice. "Don't you see it was a pure accident, as she tells you? How dare you treat her as you might a shameless witness?"

The interruption—one of powerful emotion—had come from the prisoner. At the sound of his voice, Anna started, and looked round hurriedly to the quarter whence it came. It was the first time she had raised her eyes to the court since entering the witness-box. She had glanced up to answer whoever questioned her, and that was all.

"Well?" said Sergeant Seeitall, as if demanding what else she might have to communicate.

"I have no more to tell. I have told thee all I know. It was nearly one o'clock when he went away, and I never saw him after."

"Did the prisoner wear a cloak when he came to the field that night?"

"No. He wore one sometimes, but he did not have it on that night. It was very warm—"

But, at that moment, Anna Lynn became conscious that a familiar face was strained upon her from the midst of the crowd: familiar, and yet not familiar; for the face was distorted from its natural look, and was blanched, as of one in the last agony—the face of Samuel Lynn. With a sharp cry of pain—of dread—Anna fell on the floor in a fainting fit. What the shame of being before that public court, of answering the searching questions of the counsel, had failed to take away—her senses—the sight of her father, cognizant of her disgrace, had effected. Surely it was a disgrace for a young and guileless maiden to have to confess to such an escapade—an escapade that sounded worse to censuring ears than it had been in reality. Anna fainted. Mr. Winthorne stepped forward, and she was borne out.

Another Quakeress was now put into the witness-box, and the court looked upon a little middle-aged woman, whose face was sallow, and who showed her defective teeth as she spoke. It was Hester Dell. She wore a brown silk bonnet, lined with white, and a fawn-coloured shawl. She was told that she must state what she knew, relative to the visit of Herbert Dare that night.

"I went to rest at my usual hour, or, maybe, a trifle later, for I had waited for the arrival of some physic, never supposing but that the child, Anna, had gone to her room before me, and was safe in bed. I had been asleep some considerable time, as it seemed, when I was awakened by what sounded like the raising of the kitchen window underneath. I sat up in bed and listened, and was convinced that the window was being raised slowly and cautiously, as if the raiser did not want it to be heard. I was considerably startled, the more so as I knew I had left the window fastened: and my thoughts turned to house-breakers. While I deliberated what to do, seeing I was but a lone woman in the house, save for the child Anna, and Patience who was disabled in her bed, I heard what appeared to be the voice of the child, and it sounded in the yard. I went to my window, but I could not see anything, it being right over the kitchen, and I not daring to open it. But I still heard Anna's voice: she was speaking in a low tone, and I believed I caught other tones also—those of a man. I thought I must be asleep and dreaming: next I thought it must be young Gar from the next door, Jane Halliburton's son. Her other sons I knew to be not at home; the one being abroad, the other at the University of Oxford. I deliberated, could anything be the matter at their house, and the boy have come for help. Then I reflected that that was most unlikely, for why should he be stealthily opening the kitchen window, and why should Anna be whispering with him? In short, to tell thee the truth"—raising her eyes to the judge, whom she appeared to address, to the ignoring of everyone else—"I did not know what to think, and I grew more disturbed. I quietly put on a few things, and went softly down the stairs, deeming it well, for my own sake, to feel my way, as it were, and not to run headlong into danger. I stood a moment at the kitchen door, listening; and there I distinctly heard Anna laugh—a little, gentle laugh. It reassured me, though I was still puzzled; and I opened the door at once."

Here the witness made a dead pause.

"What did you see when you opened the door?" asked the judge.

"I would not tell thee, but that I am bound to tell thee," she frankly answered. "I saw the prisoner, Herbert Dare. He appeared to have been laughing with Anna, who stood near him, and he was preparing to get out at the window as I entered."

"Well? what next?" inquired the counsel in an impatient tone; for Hester had stopped again.

"I can hardly tell what next," replied the witness. "Looking back, it appears nothing but confusion in my mind. It seemed nothing but confusion at the time. Anna cried out, and hid her face in fear; and the prisoner attempted some explanation, which I would not listen to. To see a son of Anthony Dare's in the house with the child at that midnight hour, filled me with anger and bewilderment. I ordered him away; I believe I pushed him through the window; I threatened to call in a policeman. Finally he went away."

"Saying nothing?"

"I tell you all, I would not listen to it. I remembered scraps of what he said afterwards. That Anna was not to blame—that I had no cause to scold her or to acquaint Patience with what happened—that the fault, if there was any fault, was mine, for locking the back door so quickly. I refused to hear farther, and he departed, saying he would explain when I was less angry. That is all I saw of him."

"Did you mention this affair to anyone?" asked the counsel for the prosecution.

"No."

"Why not?"

"The child clung about me in tears after he was gone, giving me the explanation that I would not hear from him, and beseeching me not to acquaint Patience. She told me how it had happened. That upon my going out to see after the sleeping-draught for Patience, she had taken the opportunity to run to the field with a book, where Herbert Dare waited: and that upon attempting to come in again she found the door locked."

"You returned sooner than she expected?"

"Yes. I met the doctor's boy near our house, bringing the physic, and I took it from him and went home again directly. Not seeing Anna about, I never thought but that she had retired to bed. I went up also, trying the back door as I passed it, which to my surprise I found unfastened."

"Why to your surprise?"

"Because I had, as I believed, previously turned the key of it. Finding it unlocked, I concluded I must have been mistaken. Afterwards, when the explanation came, I learnt that Anna had undone it. She clung about me, as I tell thee, sobbing and crying, saying, as he had said, that there was no cause to be angry with her: that she could not help what had happened; and that she had sat crying on the door-step the whole of the time, until he had effected an entrance for her. I went to the pantry window, and saw where the wires had been torn away, not roughly, but neatly; and I knew it must have taken a long time to accomplish. I fell in with the child's prayer, and did not speak of what had occurred; not even to Patience. This is the first time it has escaped my lips."

"So you deemed it desirable to conceal such an adventure, and give the prisoner opportunity to renew his midnight visits?" retorted the counsel for the prosecution.

"What was done could not be undone," said the witness. "I was willing to spare the scandal to the child, and not be the means of spreading it abroad. While I was deliberating whether to tell Patience, seeing she was in so suffering a state, news came that Herbert Dare was a prisoner. He had been arrested the following morning, on the accusation of murdering his brother, and I knew that he was safe for several weeks to come. Hence I held my tongue."

The witness had given her evidence in a clear, straightforward, uncompromising manner, widely at variance with the distressed timidity of Anna. Not a shade of doubt rested on the mind of any person in court that both had spoken the exact truth. But the counsel seemed inclined to question still.

"Since when did you know you were coming here to give this evidence?"

"Only when I did come. Richard Winthorne, the man of law, came to our house in a fly this afternoon, and brought us away with him. By some remarks he exchanged with Anna when we were in it, I found that she had known of it this day or two. They feared to avert me, I suppose, lest, maybe, I might refuse to attend."

"One question more, witness. Did the prisoner wear a cloak that night?"

"No; I did not see any."

This closed the evidence, and the witness was allowed to withdraw. Richard Winthorne went in search of Samuel Lynn, and found him seated on a bench in the outer hall surrounded by gentlemen of his persuasion, many of them of high standing in Helstonleigh. Tales of marvel, you know, never lose anything in spreading; neither are people given to placing a light construction on public gossip, when they can, by any stretch of imagination, give it a dark one. In this affair, however, no very great stretch was required. The town jumped to the charitable conclusion that Anna Lynn must be one of the naughtiest girls under the sun; imprudent, ungrateful, disobedient; I don't know what else. Had she been guilty of scattering poison in Atterly's field, and so killed all the lambs, they could not have said, or thought, worse than they did. All joined in it, charitable and uncharitable; all sorts of evil notions were spread, and were taken up. Herbert Dare, you may be very sure, came in for his share.

The news had been taken to Mr. Ashley's manufactory, sent by the astounded Patience, that Richard Winthorne had come and taken away Anna and Hester Dell to give testimony at the trial of Herbert Dare. The Quaker, perplexed and wondering, believed Patience must be demented; that the message could have no foundation in truth. Nevertheless, he bent his steps to the Guildhall, accompanied by William Halliburton, and was witness to the evidence. He, strict and sober-minded, was not likely to take up a more favourable construction of the general facts than the town was taking up. It may be guessed what it was for him.

He sat now on a bench in the outer hall, surrounded by friends, who, on hearing the crying scandal whispered, touching a young member of their body, had come flocking down to the Guildhall. When they spoke to him, he did not appear to hear; he sat with his hands on his knees, and his head sunk on his breast, never raising it. Richard Winthorne approached him.

"Miss Lynn and her servant will not be wanted again," said the lawyer. "I have sent for a fly."

The fly came. Anna was placed in it by Mr. Winthorne; Hester Dell followed; and Samuel Lynn came forward and stumbled into it. It is the proper word. He appeared to have no power left in his limbs.

"Thou wilt not be harsh with her, Samuel," whispered an influential Friend, who had a benevolent countenance. "Some of us will confer with thee to-morrow; but, meanwhile, do not be harsh with her. Thou wilt call to mind that she is thy child, and motherless."

Samuel Lynn made no reply. He did not appear to hear. He sat opposite his daughter, his eyes never lifted, and his face assuming a leaden hue. Hester suddenly leaned from the door, and beckoned to William Halliburton.

"Will thee please be so obliging as go up with us in the fly?" she said in his ear. "I do not like his look."

William stepped in, and the fly drove away with closed blinds, to the intense chagrin of the curious mob. Before it was out of the town, William and Hester, with a simultaneous movement, supported the Quaker. Anna screamed. "What is it?" she uttered, terrified at the sight of his drawn, distorted face.

"It is thy work," said Hester, less placidly than she would have spoken in a calmer moment. "If thee hast saved the life of thy friend, Herbert Dare, thee hast probably destroyed that of thy father."

They were close to the residence of Mr. Parry, and William ordered the fly to stop. The surgeon was at home, and took William's place in it. Samuel Lynn had been struck down with paralysis.

William was at the house before they were, preparing Patience. Patience was so far restored to health herself as to be able to walk about a little; she was very lame still.

They carried Mr. Lynn to his room. Anna in her deep humiliation and shame—having to give evidence, and such evidence, in the face of that open court, had been nothing less to her—flew to her own chamber, and flung herself, dressed as she was, on the carpet, in desperate abandonment. William saw her there as he passed it from her father's room. There was no one to attend to her, for they were occupied with Mr. Lynn. It was no moment for ceremony, and William entered and attempted to raise her.

"Let me be, William; let me be! I only want to die."

"Anna, child, this will not mend the past. Do not give way like this."

But she resolutely turned from him, sobbing more wildly. "Only to die! only to die!"

William went for his mother, and gave her the outline of the tale, asking her to go to the house of distress and see what could be done. Jane, in utter astonishment, sought further explanation. She could not understand him in the least.

"I assure you, I understand it nearly as little," replied William. "Anna was locked out through some mistake of Hester's, it appears, and Herbert Dare stayed with her. That it will be the means of acquitting him, there is no doubt; but Helstonleigh is making its comments very freely."

Jane went in, her senses bewildered. She found Patience in a state not to be described; she found Anna where William had left her, reiterating the same cry, "Oh, that I were dead! that I were dead!"

Meanwhile, the trial at the Guildhall was drawing to its close, and the judge proceeded to sum up. Not with the frantic bursts of oratory indulged in by those eloquent gentlemen, the counsel, but in a tone of dispassionate reasoning. He placed the facts concisely before the jury, not speaking in favour of the prisoner, but candidly avowing that he did not see how they could get over the evidence of the prisoner's two witnesses, the young Quaker lady and her maid. If that was to be believed—and for himself he fully believed it—then the prisoner could not have been guilty of the murder, and was clearly entitled to an acquittal. It was six o'clock when the jury retired to deliberate.

The judge, the bar, the spectators, sat on, or stood, with what patience they might, in the crowded and heated court. On the fiat of those twelve men hung the life of the prisoner: whether he was to be discharged an innocent man, or hanged as a guilty one. Reposing in the pocket of Sir William Leader was a certain little cap, black in colour, innocuous in itself, but of awful significance when brought forth by the hand of the presiding judge. Was it destined to be brought forth that night?

The jury were coming in at last. Only an hour had they remained in deliberation, for seven o'clock was booming out over the town. It had seemed to the impatient spectators more than two hours. What must it have seemed to the prisoner? They ranged themselves in their box, and the crier proclaimed silence.

"Have you agreed upon your verdict, gentlemen of the jury?"

"We have."

"How say you, gentlemen, guilty or not guilty?"

The foreman advanced an imperceptible step and looked at the judge, speaking deliberately:

"My lord, we find the prisoner NOT GUILTY."

CHAPTER XII

A COUCH OF PAIN

"William, I have had my death-blow! I have had my death-blow!"

The speaker was Henry Ashley. Four days had elapsed since the trial of Herbert Dare, and William Halliburton saw him now for the first time after that event. What with mind and body, Henry was in a grievous state of pain: all William's compassion was called forth, as he leaned over his couch.

It has been hinted that Helstonleigh, in its charity, took up the very worst view of the case that could be taken up, with regard to Anna Lynn. Had she gone about with a blazing torch and set all the houses on fire, their inhabitants could not have mounted themselves on higher stilts. Somehow, everybody took it up. It was like those apparently well-authenticated political reports that arrive now and then by telegram, driving the Stock Exchange, or the Paris Bourse, into a state of mad credulity. No one thought to doubt it; people caught up the notion from one another as they catch a fever. If even Samuel Lynn had looked upon it in the worst light, bringing to him paralysis, little chance was there that others might gaze through a brighter glass. It had half killed Henry Ashley: and the words were not, in point of fact, so wild as they sounded. "I have had my death-blow! I have had my death-blow!"

"No, you have not," was William's answer. "It is a blow—I know it—but not one that you cannot outlive."

"Why did you not come to me? Four whole days, and you have never been near the house!"

"Because I feared that you would be throwing yourself into the state of agitation that you are now doing," replied William, candidly. "Mr. Ashley said to me on the Wednesday, 'Henry has one of his bad attacks again.' I knew it to be more of mind than body this time, and I thought it well that you should be left in quiet. There's no one you can talk about it to, except me."

"Your staying away has not served your purpose, then. My father came to me with the details, thinking to divert me for a moment from my physical pain; never supposing that each word was a dagger plunged into my very being. My mother came, with this scrap of news, or the other scrap. Mary came, wondering and eager, asking information at second-hand: mamma was mysterious over it, and would not tell her. Mary cannot credit ill of Anna: she has as great a trust in her still as I had. As I had! Oh, William! she was my object in life. She was all my future—my world—my heaven!"

"Now you know you will suffer for this excitement," cried William, almost as he would have said it to a wayward child.

He might as well have talked to the wind. Henry neither heard nor heeded him. He continued, his manner as full of agitation as his mind.

"I am not as other men. You can go forth, all of you, into the world, to your pleasures, your amusements. I am confined here. But what mattered it? Did I envy you? No. While I had her to think of, I was happier than you."

"Had this not happened, you might have been crossed in some other way, and so it would have come to the same thing."

"And now it is over," reiterated Henry, paying no attention to the remark. "It is over, and gone; and I—I wish, William, I had gone with it."

"I wish you would be reasonable."

"Don't preach. You active men, with your innumerable objects and interests in life, cannot know what it is for one like me, shut out from the world, to love. I tell you, William, it was literally my life; the core of my life; my all. I am not sure but that I have been mad ever since."

"I am not sure but that you are mad now," returned William, believing that to humour him might be the worst plan he could adopt.

"I dare say I am," was the unsatisfactory answer. "Four days, and I have had to bury it all within me! I could not wail it out to my own pillow at night; for they concluded it was one of my bad attacks, and old nurse was posted in the bed in the next room with the door open. There's no one I can rave to but you, and you must let me do it, unless you would have me go quite mad, I hope I shan't be here long to be a trouble to any of you."

William did not know what to say. He believed there was nothing for it at present but to let him "rave himself out." "But I wish," he said, aloud, continuing the bent of his own thoughts, "that you would be a little rational over it."

"Stop a bit. Did you ever experience a blow such as this?"

"No indeed."

"Then don't hold forth to me, I say. You do not understand. It was all the joy I had on earth."

"You must learn to find other joys, other—"

"The despicable villain!" broke forth Henry, the heat-drops welling to his brow, as they had welled to Anna's when before the judge. "The shame-faced, cowardly villain! Was she not Samuel Lynn's child, and my sister's friend? What possessed the jury to acquit him? Did they think a rope's-end too good for his neck?"

"He was proved innocent of the murder. If he has any conscience—"

"What?" fiercely interrupted Henry Ashley. "He a conscience! I don't know what you are dreaming of. Is he going to stop in Helstonleigh?"

"I conclude so. He resumed his place quietly in his father's office the day after the trial. He is in London now, but only temporarily."

"Resumed his place quietly! What was the mob about, then?"

The question was put so quaintly, in such confiding simplicity, that a smile rose to William's face. "In awe of the police, I expect," he answered. "The Dares, while his fate was uncertain, have been rusticating. Cyril told me to-day, that now that the accusation was proved to have been false, they were 'coming out' again."

"Coming out in what? Villainy?"

"He left the 'what' to be inferred. In grandeur, I expect. The established innocence of Herbert—"

"If you apply that word to the man, William Halliburton, you are as black as he is."

William remembered Henry's tribulation both of mind and body, and went on without the shadow of a retort.

"I apply it to him in relation to the crime of which he was charged. His acquittal and release have caused the Dares to hold up their heads again. But they have lost caste in Helstonleigh."

"Caste!" was the scornful ejaculation of Henry Ashley. "They never had any caste to lose. Does the master intend to retain Cyril in the manufactory?"

"I have heard nothing to the contrary. If he retained him whilst the accusation was hanging over Herbert Dare's head, he will not be likely to discard him now it is removed."

"Removed!" shrieked Henry. "If one accusation has been removed, has not a worse taken its place?"

"Would it be just to visit on one brother the sins of another?"

"A nice pair of brothers they are!" cried Henry in the sharp, petulant manner habitual to him, when racked with pain. "How will Samuel Lynn like the company of Cyril Dare by his side in the manufactory, when he gets well again?"

William shook his head. These considerations were not for him. They were Mr. Ashley's.

"You heard her give her evidence?" resumed Henry, breaking a pause.

"Most of it."

"Tell it me."

"No, Henry; it would not do you good to hear it."

"Tell it me, I say," persisted Henry wilfully. "I know it in substance. I want to have it repeated over to me, word for word."

"But—"

Henry suddenly raised his hand and laid it on William's lips, with a warning movement. He turned and saw Mary Ashley.

"Take her back to the drawing-room, William," he whispered. "I can bear no one but you about me now. Not yet, Mary," he added aloud, motioning his sister away with his hand. "Not now."

Mary halted in indecision. William advanced, placed her hand within his arm, and led her, somewhat summarily, from the room.

"I am only obeying orders, Miss Ashley," said he. "They are to see you back to the drawing-room."

"If Henry can bear you with him, he might bear me."

"You know what his whims and fancies are, when he is suffering."

"Is there not a particularly good understanding between you and Henry?" she pointedly asked.

"Yes; we understand each other perfectly."

"Well, then, tell me—what is it that is the matter with him this time? I do not like to say so to mamma, because she might call me fanciful, but it appears to me that Henry's illness is more on the mind than on the body."

William made no reply.

"And yet, I cannot imagine it possible for Henry to have picked up any annoyance or grief," resumed Mary. "How can he have done so? He is not like one who goes out into the world—who has to meet with cares and cheeks. You do not speak," she added, looking at William. "Is it that you will not tell me? or do you know nothing?"

William lowered his voice. "I can only say that, should there be anything of the sort you mention, the kinder course for Henry—indeed the only course—will be, not to allow him to perceive that you suspect it. Conceal the suspicion both from him and from others. Remember his excessive sensitiveness. When he sees cause to hide his feelings, it would be almost death to him to have them scrutinized."

"I think you must be in his full confidence," observed Mary, looking at William.

"Pretty well so," he answered, with a passing smile.

"Then, if he has any secret grief, will you try and soothe it to him?"

"With all my best endeavours," earnestly spoke William. But there was not the least apparent necessity for his taking Mary Ashley's hand between his own, and pressing it there while he said it, any more than there was necessity for that vivid blush of hers, as she turned into the drawing-room.

But you must be anxious to hear of Anna Lynn. Poor Anna! who had fallen so terribly into the black books of the town, without really very much deserving it. It was a most unlucky contretemps, having been locked out; it was a still more unfortunate sequel, having to confess to it at the trial. She was not a pattern of goodness, it must be confessed: had not yet attained to that perfect model, which expects, as of a right, a niche in the saintly calendar. She was reprehensibly vain; she delighted in plaguing Patience; and she took to running out into the field, when it had been far better that she had remained at home. That running out entailed deceit and some stories: but it entailed nothing worse, and Helstonleigh need not have been so very severe in its judgment.

Never had there been a more forcible illustration of the old saying, "Give a dog a bad name, and hang him," than in this instance. When William Halliburton had told Anna that Herbert Dare was not a good man, and did not bear a good name, he had told her the strict truth. For that very reason a secret intimacy with him was undesirable, however innocent it might be, however innocent it was, in itself: and for that very reason did Helstonleigh look at it through clouded spectacles. Had she been locked out all night, instead of half a one, with some one in better odour, Helstonleigh had not set up its scornful crest. It is quite impossible to tell you what Herbert Dare had done, to have such a burden on his back as people seemed inclined to lay there. Perhaps they did not know themselves. Some accused him of one thing, some of another; ill reports never lose by carrying: the two cats on the tiles, you know, were magnified into a hundred. No one is as black as he is painted—there's a saying to that effect—neither, I dare say, was Herbert Dare. At any rate—and that is what we have to do with—he was not so in this particular instance. He was as vexed at the locking out as any one else could have been; and he did the best (save one thing) that he could for Anna, under the circumstances, and got her in again. The only proper thing to have done, was to knock up Hester. He had wished to do it, but had yielded to Anna's entreaties, that were born of fear.

Not a soul seemed to cast so much as a good word or a charitable thought to him in the matter. Did he deserve none? However thoughtless or reprehensible his conduct was, in drawing Anna into those field excursions, when the explosion came, he met it as a gentleman. Many a one, more renowned for the cardinal graces than was Herbert Dare, might have spoken out at once, and cleared himself at the expense of making known Anna's unlucky escapade. Not so he. A doubt may have been upon him that were it betrayed Helstonleigh might cast a taint on her fair name: and he strove to save it. He suffered the brand of a murderer to be attached to him—he languished for many weeks in prison as a criminal— all to save it. He all but went to the scaffold to save it. He might have called Anna and Hester Dell forward at the inquest, at the preliminary examination before the magistrates, and thus have cleared himself; but he would not do so. Whilst there was a chance of his innocence being brought to light in any other manner, he would not call on Anna. He allowed the odium to settle upon his own head. He went to prison, hoping that he should be cleared in some other way. There was a generous, chivalric feeling in this, which Helstonleigh could not understand when emanating from Herbert Dare, and they declined to give him credit for it. They preferred to look at the affair altogether in a different light, and to lavish hard names upon it. Every soul was alike: there was no exception: Samuel Lynn, and all else in Helstonleigh. They caught the epidemic, I say, one from another.

CHAPTER XIII

A RAY OF LIGHT

The first sharpness of the edge worn off, Anna grew cross. She did not see why every one should be blaming her. What had so sadly prostrated herself was the shame of having to appear before the court; to stand in it and give her evidence. The excitement, the shame, combined with the terrifying illness of her father, brought on, as Hester told her, through her, had sent her into a wild state of contrition and alarm. Little wonder that she wished herself dead! The mood passed away as the days went on, and Anna became tolerably herself again. When Friends called at the house to inquire after or to see her father, she ran and hid herself in her room, fearful lest a lecture on those field recreations might be delivered to her gratuitously. She shunned Patience, too, as much as she could. Patience had grown cold and silent; and Anna rather liked the change.

She sat for the most part in her father's room, never moving from his bedside, unless disturbed from it; never speaking; eating only when food was placed before her. Anna was in grievous fear lest a public reprimand should be in store for her, delivered at meeting on First Day: but she saw no reason why every one should continue to be cross with her at home.

She happened to be alone with her father when he first recovered consciousness. Some fifteen days had elapsed since the trial. But for the fact of her being with him, a difficulty might have been experienced to get her there. She dreaded his anger, his reproach, more than anything. So long as he lay without his senses, knowing her not, so long was she content to sit, watching. She was seated by the bedside in her usual listless attitude, head and eyes cast down, when her father's hand, not the one affected, was suddenly lifted and laid upon hers, which rested on the counterpane. Startled, Anna turned her gaze upon him, and she saw that his intellects were restored. With a suppressed cry of dismay she would have flown away, but he clasped his fingers round hers.

"Anna!"

She sank down on her knees, shaking as if with ague, and buried her face in the clothes. Samuel Lynn stretched forth his hand and put it on her head.

"Thou art my own child, Anna; thy mother left thee to me for good and for ill; and I will stand by thee in thy sorrow."

She burst into a storm of hysterical tears. He let it have its course; he drew her wet face to his and kissed it; he talked to her soothingly, never speaking a single word of reproach; and Anna overcame her fear and her sobs. She knelt down by the bed still, and let her cheek rest on the counterpane.

"It has nearly killed me," he murmured, after a while. "But I pray for life: I will struggle hard to live, that thee mayst have one protector. Friends and foes may cast reproach to thee, but I will not."

"Why should they cast reproach to me, father?" returned Anna, with a little spice of resentment. "I have not harmed them."

"No, child; thee hast not; only thyself. I will help thee to bear the reproach. Thou art my own child."

"But there's nothing for them to reproach me with," she reiterated, her face buried deeper in the counterpane. "It was not pleasant to stand there; but it is over. And they need not reflect upon me for it."

"What is over? To stand where?" he asked.

"At the Guildhall, on the trial."

"It is not that that people will reproach thee with, Anna. It was not a nice thing for thee; but that, in itself, brings no reproach."

Anna lifted her head wonderingly. "What does, then?" she uttered.

He did not answer. He only closed his eyes, a deep groan bursting from the very depths of his heart. It came into Anna's mind that he must be thinking of her previous acquaintance with Herbert Dare; of her stolen meetings in the field by twilight.

"Oh, father, don't thee be angry with me!" she implored, the tears streaming from her eyes. "It was no harm; it was not indeed. Thee mightst have been present always, for all the harm there was, and I wish thee hadst been. Why should thee think anger of it? There was no more harm in my talking with him now and then in the field, than there was in my talking with him in Margaret Ashley's drawing-room."

Something in the simple words, in the tone, in the manner altogether, caused the Quaker's heart to leap within him. Had he been making a molehill into a mountain? Surely, yes! But what else he would have said or done, what questions asked, cannot be known, for they were interrupted by a visit from William Halliburton. Anna stole away.

William was full of hearty congratulation on the visible improvement—the, so far, restoration to health. The Quaker murmured some half-inarticulate words, indicating something to the effect that he might not have been ill, but for taking up a worse view of the case than, as he believed now, it really merited.

William leaned over him; a glad look in his eye; a glad sound in his low voice.

"My mother has been telling Patience so to-day. She, my mother, is convinced now that very exaggerated blame was cast upon Anna. It was foolish of her, of course, to fall into the habit of running to the field; but the locking out might have happened to anyone. My mother told me this not half an hour ago. She has seen and talked to Anna frequently this last day or two, and has drawn her own positive deductions. My mother is vexed with herself for having fallen into the popular condemnation."

"Ay!" uttered Samuel Lynn. "There is condemnation abroad, then? I thought there was."

"People will come to their senses in good time," was William's answer. "Never doubt it."

The Quaker raised his feeble hand, and laid it upon William's. "The Ashleys—have they blamed her?"

"I fear they have," was the only reply he could make, in his strict truth.

"Then, William, thee go to them. Go to them now, and set them right."

He was already going, for he was engaged to the Ashleys that evening. Between Henry Ashley, the men at East's, and his own studies, which he would not wholly neglect, William's evenings had a tolerably busy time of it. He had assumed Samuel Lynn's place in the manufactory by Mr. Ashley's orders, head of all things, under the master. Cyril ground his teeth at this; he looked upon it as a slight to himself; but Cyril had no power to alter it.

William found Mr. and Mrs. Ashley alone. Mary was out. He sat with them for a few minutes, talking of Anna, and then rose to go to Henry. "How is he this evening?" he inquired.

"Ill and very fractious," was Mr. Ashley's reply. "William, you have great influence over him. I wish you could persuade him to give way less. He is not ill enough, so far as we can see, to keep his room; but we cannot get him out of it."

Henry was in one of his depressed moods, excessively dispirited and irritable. "Oh! so you have come!" he burst forth as William entered. "I should be ashamed to neglect a sick fellow as you neglect me. If I were well and strong, and you ill, you would find it different."

"I know I am late," acknowledged William. "Samuel Lynn took up a little of my time; and I have been sitting some minutes in the drawing-room."

"Of course!" was the fractious answer. "Any one before me."

"Samuel Lynn is a great deal better," continued William. "His mind is restored."

Henry received the news ungraciously, making no rejoinder; but his side was twitching with pain. "How is she?" he asked. "Is the shame fretting out her life?"

"Not at all. She is very well. As to shame—as you call it—I believe she has not taken much to herself."

"It will kill her: you'll see. The sooner the better for her I should say."

William sat down on the edge of the sofa, on which the invalid was lying. "Henry, I would set you right upon a point, if I thought it would be expedient to do so. You do go into fits of excitement so great, that it is dangerous to speak."

"Tell out anything you have to tell. Tell me, if you choose, that the house is on fire, and I must be pitched out of window to escape it. It would make no impression upon me. My fits of excitement have passed away with Anna Lynn."

"My news relates to Anna."

"What if it does? She has passed away for me."

"Helstonleigh, in its usual hasty fashion of jumping to conclusions, has jumped to a false one," continued William. "There have been no grounds for the great blame cast to Anna; except in the minds of a charitable public."

"A fact?" asked Henry, after a pause.

"There's not a shade of doubt about it."

He received the answer with equanimity; it may be said, with apathy. And turning on his couch, he drew the cover over him, repeating the words previously spoken: "She has passed away for me."

CHAPTER XIV

MR DELVES ON HIS BEAM ENDS

Samuel Lynn grew better, and Mr. Ashley, in his considerate kindness, proposed that he should reside abroad for a few months in the neighbourhood of Annonay, to watch the skin market, and pick up skins that would be suitable for their use. Anna and Patience were to accompany him. Anna had somewhat regained her footing in the good graces of the gossipers. That she did so, was partly owing to the indignant defence of her, entered upon by Herbert Dare. Herbert did behave well in this case, and he must have his due. Upon his return from London, whither he had gone soon after the termination of the trial, remaining away a week or two, he found what a very charitable ovation Helstonleigh was bestowing upon Anna Lynn. He met it with a storm of indignation; he bade them think as badly of him as they chose; believe him a second Burke if they liked; but to keep their mistaken tongues off Anna. What with one thing and another, some of the scandal-mongers did begin to think they had been too hasty, and withdrew their censure. Some (as a matter of course) preferred to doubt still; and opinions remained divided.

Helstonleigh took up the gossip on another score—that of Mr. Ashley's sending Samuel Lynn abroad, as his skin-buyer, for an indefinite period. "A famous trade Ashley must be doing, to go to that expense!" grumbled some of the envious manufacturers. True; he had a famous trade. And if he had not had one, he might have sent him all the same. Helstonleigh never knew the benevolence of Thomas Ashley's heart. The journey was fully decided upon; and Samuel Lynn had an application from a member of his own persuasion, to rent his house, furnished, for the term of his absence. He was glad to accept the accommodation.

But, before Mr. Lynn and his family started, Helstonleigh was fated to sustain another loss, in the person of Herbert Dare. Herbert contrived to get some sort of mission entrusted to him abroad, and made rather a summary exit from Helstonleigh to enter upon it. A friend of Herbert's, who had gone over to live in Holland, and with whom he was in frequent correspondence, wrote and offered him a situation in a merchant's house in Rotterdam, as "English clerk." The offer came in answer to a hint, or perhaps more than a hint, from Herbert, that a year or two's sojourn abroad would be acceptable to him. He would receive a good salary, if he proved himself equal to the duties, the information stated, and might rise in it, if he chose to remain. Herbert wrote off-hand to secure it, and then told his father what he had done.

"Enter a house at Rotterdam, as English clerk!" repeated Mr. Dare, unable to credit his own ears. "You a clerk!"

"What am I to do?" asked Herbert. "Since I came out of there," pointing in the direction of the county prison, "claims have thickened upon me. I do owe a good deal, and that's a fact—what with my own scores, and that for which I am liable for—for poor Anthony. People won't wait much longer; and I have no fancy to try the debtor's side of the prison."

They were standing in the front room of the office. Mr. Dare's business appeared to be considerably falling off, and the office had often leisure on its hands now. Of the two clerks kept, one had holiday, the other was out. Somehow, what with one untoward thing and another, people were growing shy of the Dares. Mr. Dare leaned against the corner of the window-frame, watching the passers-by, his hands in his pockets, and a blank look on his face.

"You say you can't help me, sir?" Herbert continued.

"You know I can't; sufficiently to do any good," returned Mr. Dare. "I am too much pressed for money myself. Look at the expenses attending the trial: and I was embarrassed enough before. I cannot help you."

"It seems to me, too, that you want me gone from here."

"I have not said so," curtly responded Mr. Dare.

"You told me the other day that it was my presence in the office which scared clients from it."

Mr. Dare could not deny the fact. He had said it. What's more, he had thought it; and did so still. "I cannot tell what else it is that is keeping clients away," he rejoined. "We have not had a dozen in since the trial."

"It is a slack season of the year."

"Maybe," shortly answered Mr. Dare. "Slack as it is, there's some business astir, but people are going elsewhere to get it done; those, too, who have never for years been near anyone but us. The truth is, Herbert, you fell into bad odour with the town on the day of the trial; and that you must know. Though acquitted of the murder, all sorts of other things were laid to your charge. Quaker Lynn's stroke amongst the rest."

"Carping sinners!" ejaculated Herbert.

"And I suppose it turned people against the office," continued Mr. Dare. "My belief is, they won't come back again as long as you are in it."

"That's precisely what I meant you had hinted to me" said Herbert. "Therefore, I thought I had better leave it. Pattison says he can get me this berth, and I should like to try it."

"You'll not like to turn merchant's clerk," repeated Mr. Dare with emphasis.

"I shall like it better than being nailed for debt here," somewhat coarsely answered Herbert. "It is not so agreeable at home now, especially in this office, that I should cry to stay in it. You have changed, sir, amongst the rest: many a day through, you don't give me a civil word."

Again Mr. Dare felt that he had changed to Herbert. When he found that he—Herbert—might have cleared himself at first from the terrible accusation of fratricide, had he so chosen, instead of allowing the obloquy to rest upon himself and his family for so long a period, he had become bitterly angry. Mrs. Dare and the whole family joined in the feeling, and Herbert suffered.

"As to civility, Herbert, I must first get over the soreness left by your conduct. You acted very badly in allowing the case to go on to trial. If you had no objection to sit down quietly under the crime yourself, you had no right to throw the disgrace and expense upon your family."

"If it were to come over again, I would not do so," acknowledged Herbert. "I thought then I was acting for the best."

"Pshaw!" was the peevish ejaculation of Mr. Dare.

"Altogether," resumed Herbert, "I think I had better go away. After a time, something or other may turn up to make things smoother here, and then I can come home again; unless I find a better opening abroad. I may do so; and I believe I shall like living there."

"Very well," said Mr. Dare, after some minutes' silence. "It may be for the best. At all events, it will give time for things here to blow over. If you don't find it what you like, you can only return."

"I shall be sure not to return, unless I can square up some of my liabilities here," returned Herbert. "You must help me to get there, sir."

"What do you want?" asked Mr. Dare.

"Fifty pounds."

"I can't do it, Herbert," was the prompt answer.

"I must have it if I am to go," was Herbert's firm reply. "There are two or three trifles here which I will not leave unsettled, and I cannot go over there with pockets absolutely empty. Fifty pounds is not so great a sum, sir, to pay to get rid of me."

Old Anthony Dare knit his brow in perplexity. He supposed he must furnish the money, though he did not in the least see how it was to be done.

The matter settled, Herbert took his hat and went out. The first object his eyes alighted on outside was Sergeant Delves. That worthy, pacing through the town, had brought himself to an anchor opposite the office of Mr. Dare, and was regarding it, lost in a brown study. The sergeant was in a state of discomfiture, touching the affair of the late Anthony Dare. He had lost no time in "looking after" Miss Caroline Mason, as he had promised himself; and the sequence had been—defeat. Without any open stir on the part of the police—without allowing Caroline herself to know that she was doubted—the sergeant contrived to put himself in full possession of her movements on that night. The result proved that she must be exempt from the suspicion; or, as the sergeant expressed it, "was out of the hole;" and that gentleman remained at fault again.

Herbert crossed over to him. "What are you looking at, Delves?"

"I wasn't looking at anything in particular," was the answer. "Coming in sight of your office naturally brought my thoughts back to that unsatisfactory business. I never was so baffled before."

"It is very strange who it could have been," observed Herbert. "I often think of it."

"Never so baffled before," continued the sergeant, as if there had been no interruption to his own words. "I could almost have been upon oath at the time, that the murderer was in the house; hadn't left it. And yet—"

"You could have been upon oath that it was I," interrupted Herbert.

"That's true. I could. But you had yourself chiefly to thank for it, Mr. Herbert Dare, through making a mystery of your movements that night. After you were cleared, my mind turned to that girl; and that, I found, was no go."

"What girl?" interrupted Herbert.

"The one in Honey Fair: your brother Anthony's old sweetheart. It wasn't her, though; I have proofs. Charlotte East had her at her house that evening, and kept her till twelve o'clock, when she went home to bed in her garret. Charlotte's going to try to make something of her again. And now I am baffled, and I don't deny it."

"To suspect any girl is ridiculous," observed Herbert Dare. "No girl, it is to be hoped, would possess the courage or the strength to accomplish such a deed as that."

"You don't know 'em as we police do," nodded the sergeant. "I was asking your father only a day or two ago, whether he could make sure of his servants, that they had not been in it—"

"Of our servants?" interrupted Herbert, in surprise. "What an idea!"

"Well, I have gone round to my old opinion—that it was some one in the house," returned the sergeant. "But it seems the servants are all on the square. I can't make it out."

"Why on earth should you suppose it to be any one in the house?" questioned Herbert, in considerable wonderment.

"Because I do," was the answer. "We police see and note down what others pass over. There was odds and ends of things at the time that made us infer it; and I can't get it out of my mind."

"It is an impossibility that it could have been a resident of the house," dissented Herbert. "Every one in it is above suspicion."

"Who do you fancy it might have been?" asked the sergeant, abruptly, almost as if he wished to surprise Herbert out of an incautious answer.

But Herbert had nothing to tell him; no suspicion was on his mind to be surprised out of. "If I could fancy it was, or might be, any particular individual, I should come to you and say so, without asking," he replied. "I am as much at fault as you can be. Anthony may have made slight enemies in the town, what with his debts and his temper, and one thing or another; but no enemies of that terrible nature—capable of killing him. I wish I could see cause for a reasonable suspicion," he added with emotion. "I would give my right arm"—stretching it out—"to solve the mystery. As well for my sake as for my dead brother's."

"Well, all I can say is, that I am down on my beam ends," concluded the sergeant.

Meanwhile Henry Ashley was getting little better. He had fallen into a state of utter prostration. Mental anguish had told upon him physically, and his bodily weakness was no doubt great: but he made no effort to rouse himself. He would lie for hours, his eyes half-closed, noticing no one. The medical men said they had seen nothing like it, and Mr. and Mrs. Ashley grew alarmed. The only one to remonstrate with him—he alone held the key to its cause—was William Halliburton.

William's influence over him was very great: he yielded to no one, not even to his father, as he would yield to William. Henry gave the reins to his tongue, and said all sorts of irritating things to William, as he did to every one else. It only masked the deep affection, the lasting friendship, which had taken possession of his heart for William.

"Let me be; let me be," he said to William one day, in answer to a remonstrance that he should rouse himself. "I told you that my life had passed out with her."

"But your life has not passed out with her," argued William; "your life is in you, just as much as it ever was. And it is your duty to make some use of your life; not to let it run to waste—as you are doing."

"It does not affect you," was the tart reply.

"It does very much affect me. I am grieved to see you hug your pain, instead of shaking it off; vexed to think that a man should so bury his days. It is an unfortunate thing that no one is cognizant of this matter but myself."

"Is it though!" retorted Henry. "You are a fine Job's comforter!"

"Yes, it is. Were it known to those about you, you would not for shame lie here, and indulge regrets after an imprudent and silly girl."

Henry flashed an angry glance at him from his soft dark eyes. "Take care, my good fellow! I can stand some things; but I don't stand all."

"An imprudent, silly girl, who does not care a rush for you," emphatically repeated William: "whose wild and ill-judged affection is given to another. Was ever infatuation like unto yours!"

"Have a care, I tell you!" burst forth Henry. "By what right do you say these things to me?"

"I say them for your good—and I intend that you should feel them. When a surgeon's knife probes a wound, the patient groans and winces; but it is done to cure him."

"You are a man of eloquence!" sarcastically rejoined Henry. "Pity but you could flourish at the Bar, and take the anticipated shine out of Frank!"

"Answer me one plain question, Henry. Do you still indulge a hope towards Anna Lynn?—to her becoming your wife?"

With a shriek of anger, Henry caught up his slipper, and sent it flying through the air at William's head.

"What's that for?" equably demanded William, dodging his head out of the way.

"How dare you hint at such a thing? I told you there were some things I wouldn't stand. Is it fitting that one who has figured in such an escapade should be made the wife of an Ashley? If we were left by our two selves upon the earth, all else gone dead and out of it, I wouldn't marry her."

"Precisely so. I have judged you rightly. Then, under this state of things, what in the name of fortune is the use of your lying here and thinking about her?"

"I don't think about her," fractiously returned Henry. "You are always fancying things."

"You do think about her. I can see that you do. I should be above it," quaintly continued William.

"Go and pick up my slipper."

"Will you come down to tea this evening?"

"No, I won't. You come here and preach up this morality, or divinity, or whatever you may please to term it, to me; but, wait and see how you'd act, if you should ever get struck on the keen edge as I have been."

"Come! let me help you up."

"Don't bother. I am not going to get up. I—"

At that moment, Mr. Ashley opened the door. His errand likewise was to induce Henry to leave his sofa and his room, and join them below. Henry could not be brought to comply.

"No. I have just told William. I cannot think why he did not go back and say so. He only stops here to worry me. There! get along, William; and come back when you have swallowed enough tea."

Mr. Ashley laid his hand on William's arm, as they walked together along the corridor, and brought him to a halt. "What is this illness of Henry's? There is some secret connected with it, I am sure, and you are cognizant of it. I must know what it is."

Mr. Ashley's tone was a decided one; his manner firm. William made no reply.

"Tell me what it is, William."

"I cannot," said William. "Certainly not without Henry's permission; and I do not think he will give it. If it were my secret, sir, instead of his, I would tell it at your bidding."

"Is it of the mind or the body?"

"The mind. I think the worst is over. Do not speak to him about it, I pray you, sir."

"William, is it anything that can be remedied? By money?—by any means at command?"

"It can never be remedied," replied William earnestly, "Were the whole world brought to bear upon it, it could do nothing. Time and his own good sense must effect the cure."

"Then I may as well not ask about it if I cannot aid. You are fully in his confidence."

"Yes. And all that another can do, I am doing. We have a daily battle. I want to rouse him out of his apathy."

"Oh, that you could!" aspirated Mr. Ashley.

CHAPTER XV

A LOSS FOR POMERANIAN KNOLL

Pomeranian Knoll had scarcely recovered its equanimity after the shock of the departure of Herbert Dare for foreign parts, when it found itself about to be shorn of another inmate. The word "shock" is used to express the suddenness of the affair, rather than in its enlarged and more ordinary sense. Herbert, what with one thing and another, had brought a good deal of vexation upon the paternal home; Helstonleigh also had not been holding him in extensive favour since the trial; and that home was not sorry that he should absent himself from it for a time. But it certainly did not bargain for his announcing his departure one night, and being off the next morning. Yet such was the course he pursued: and in that light his departure may be said to have been a shock to the town. Mr. Dare had known of it longer; but he had not proclaimed it any more than Herbert had: it may be that Herbert feared being stopped, if the intended journey got wind.

A week or two after this, Signora Varsini received a letter with a foreign post-mark on it. The fact was nothing extraordinary in itself: the signora did occasionally receive letters bearing foreign post-marks; but this one threw her into a state of commotion, the like of which had never been witnessed. Thrusting the letter into the deepest pocket of her dress when it was delivered to her, she finished giving the music lesson to Minny, which she was occupied upon, and then retired to her room to peruse it. From this she emerged a short time after, with a long face of consternation, uttering frantic ejaculations. Mrs. Dare was quite alarmed. What was the matter with mademoiselle?

"Ah, what misère! what désolation! what tristes nouvelles!" The letter was from her aunt in Paris, who was thrown upon her death-bed; and she, mademoiselle, must hasten thither without delay. If she could not start by a train that day, she must go by the first one the next. She was désolée to leave madame at a coup; her heart would break in bidding adieu to the young ladies; but necessity was stern. She must make her baggage forthwith, and would be obliged to madame for her salary.

Mrs. Dare was taken—as the saying runs—all of a heap. She had not cared to part with mademoiselle so soon, although the retaining her entailed an additional expense, which they could ill afford in their gradually increasing embarrassments and straitening means: but the chief point that puzzled her was the paying up of the salary. Between thirty and forty pounds were due. There appeared, however, to be no help for it, and she applied to Mr. Dare.

"You may as well ask me for my head as for that sum to-day," was that gentleman's reply, thinking he was destined never to find peace on earth. "Tell her you will send it after her, if she must go."

Mrs. Dare shook her head. It would not be of the least use, she was sure. Mademoiselle was not one to be put off in that way, or to depart without her money.

How Mr. Dare managed it he perhaps hardly knew himself; but he brought home the money at night, and the governess was paid in full. On the following morning there was a ceremonious leave-taking, loud and suggestive on the part of mademoiselle. She saluted them all on both cheeks, and promised to write every week, at least. A fly came to the door for her and her luggage, and George Dare mounted the box to escort her to the station. Mademoiselle politely invited him inside; but he had just lighted a cigar, and preferred to stop where he was.

"I say, mademoiselle," cried he, after she was seated in the railway carriage, "if you should happen to come across Herbert, I wish you'd tell him—"

Mademoiselle interrupted with a burst of indignation. She come across Monsieur Herbert! What should bring her coming across him? Monsieur George must be fou to think it. Monsieur Herbert was not in Paris, was he? She had understood he was in Holland.

"Oh, well, it's all on the other side of the Channel," answered George, whose geographical notions of the Continent were not very definite. "Perhaps you won't see him, though, mademoiselle; so never mind."

Mademoiselle replied by telling him to take care of himself; for the whistle was sounding. George drew back, and watched the train off; mademoiselle nodding her farewell to him from the window.

And that was the last that Helstonleigh saw of Mrs. Dare's Italian governess, the Signora Varsini. Helstonleigh might not have been any the worse had it never seen the first of her. Mrs. Dare, after her departure, suddenly remembered that mademoiselle had once told her she had not a single relative in the world. Who could this aunt be, to whom she was hastening?

And Henry Ashley? As the weeks and the months went on, Henry began to rouse himself from his prostration; his apathy. William Halliburton made no secret of it to Henry that it was suspected he was suffering from some inward grief which he was concealing, and that he had been questioned on the point by Mr. Ashley. "You know," said William, "I shall have no resource but to tell, unless you show yourself a sensible man, and come out of this nonsense."

It alarmed Henry; rather than have his secret feelings betrayed for the family benefit, he could have died. In a grumbling and discontented sort of mood, he went about again, and resumed his idle occupations (such as they were) as usual. One evening William enticed him out for a walk, took possession of his arm, and pounced into Robert East's, before Henry well knew where he was. He sat down, apathetic and indifferent, after nodding carelessly to the respectful salutation of the men. "I must give just ten minutes to them, as I am here," observed William. "You can go to sleep the while."

The ten minutes lengthened into twenty, and Henry's attention was so far roused that he came to the table in his impulsive way, and began talking on his own account. When William was ready to go, he was not; and he actually told the men that he would come round again. It was a great point gained.

Small beginnings, it has been remarked, lead to great endings. The humble, confined way in which the class had begun at Robert East's; the vague ideas of William upon the subject; the doubtings of East and Crouch, were looked back upon with a smile. For the little venture had swollen itself into a great undertaking—an undertaking that was destined to effect a revolution throughout the whole of Honey Fair, and might probably even extend to Helstonleigh itself. The drawback now was want of room; numbers were being kept away by it. Henry Ashley did go again; and finding that books of the right kind ran short, he, the day after his second visit, wrote off an order for a whole cargo.

Mr. Ashley was in a state of inward delight. Anything to rouse him! "You think it will succeed, that movement, do you, Henry?" he carelessly observed.

"It's safe to succeed," was the answer. "William, with his palavering, has gained the ear of the fellows. I don't believe there's William Halliburton's equal in the whole world!" he added, with enthusiasm. "Fancy his sacrificing his time to such a thing, and for no benefit to himself! It will bear a rich crop of fruit too. If I have the gift—I'll give you a long word for once—of ratiocination, this reform of William's will be more extensive than we now foresee."

The chief thing in these evenings was to keep alive the interest of the men. Not to lead them to abstruse things, which they had a difficulty in understanding, and remained strange to at best; but rather to plunge them into familiar home topics—the philosophy, if you will, of everyday life. There is a right and a wrong way of doing most things, and it often happens that people, from ignorance, pursue the wrong. Of the plain sanitary laws, relating to physical health, Honey Fair was intensely ignorant: of the ventilation of rooms, of cleanliness, of the most simple rules by which the body can be kept in order, they knew no more than they did of the moon. When a man was, to use Honey Fair phraseology, "took bad," he generally neglected the symptoms altogether, thereby laying the foundation of worse illness: or else he went to a doctor, and ran himself into expense. A little familiarity with ordinary complaints and ordinary antidotes would have remedied this. An acquaintance with sanitary laws would have prevented it. When children were down with measles or scarlatina, the careless of the land allowed the maladies to take their own course, and the sufferers to air themselves in the gutters, as usual. The cautious ones smothered the patients in a hot room, keeping up a fire as large as the stock of coals would allow, and borrowing all the blankets from the houses on either side, to heap upon them. No wonder the supply of little coffins was great to Honey Fair.

All these things would be talked of and discussed, and a little enlightenment imparted to the men, as a guidance for the future. No one who did not witness it can imagine the delighted satisfaction with which these and similar practical topics were welcomed; for they bore for them a personal interest—they concerned themselves, their families, and their homes.

One evening the way in which Honey Fair rather liked to spend its Sundays was under discussion; namely, the men in smoking; the women slatternly and dirty; the children fighting and quarrelling in the dirt outside.

William Halliburton was asking them in a half-earnest, half-joking manner, what particular benefit they found in it, that it should not be remedied? Could they impart its pleasures to him? If so—

His voice suddenly faltered and stopped. Standing just inside the door of the room, a quiet spectator and listener of the proceedings, was Thomas Ashley. The men followed William's gaze, saw who was amongst them, and rose in respectful silence.

Mr. Ashley came forward, signing to William to continue. But William's eloquence had died out, leaving only a heightened colour in its place. In the presence of Mr. Ashley, whom he so loved and respected, he had grown timid as a child.

"Do you know," said Mr. Ashley, addressing the men, "it gives me greater pleasure to see you here than it would do were I to hear that you had come into a fortune."

They smiled and shook their heads. "Fortunes didn't come to the like o' them."

"Never mind," replied Mr. Ashley: "fortunes are not the best gifts in life."

He stayed talking with them some little time, quiet words of encouragement, and then withdrew, wishing them good luck. William left with him: and as they passed through Honey Fair, the women ran to their doors to gaze after them. Mr. Ashley, slightly bent with his advancing years, leaned upon William's arm, but his face was fresh as ever, and his dark hair showed no signs of age. William erect, noble; his height greater than Mr. Ashley's, his forehead broader, his deep grey eyes strangely earnest and sincere; and a flitting smile playing on his lips. He was listening to Mr. Ashley's satisfaction at what he had witnessed.

"How long do you intend to sacrifice your evenings to them?"

"It is no sacrifice, Mr. Ashley. I am glad to do it. I consider it one of the best uses to which my evenings could be given. I intend to enlist Henry for good in the cause, if I can do so."

"You will be an ingenious persuader if you do," returned Mr. Ashley. "I would give half I am worth," he abruptly added, "to see the boy take an interest in life."

"It will be sure to come, sir. One of these days I shall surprise him into reading a good play to the men. Something to laugh at. It will be a beginning."

"He is very much better," observed Mr. Ashley. "All that listless apathy is going."

"Oh yes. He is all but cured."

"What was it, William?"

William was taken by surprise. He did not answer, and Mr. Ashley repeated the question.

"It is his secret, sir, not mine."

"You must confide it to me," said Mr. Ashley, in his tone of quiet firmness. "You know me, William. When I promise that neither it nor the fact of its having been disclosed to me, shall ever escape me, directly or indirectly, to any living person, you know that you may depend upon me."

He paused. William did not speak: he was debating with himself what he ought to do.

"William, it is a relief that I must have. Since my suspicions, that there was a secret, were confirmed, I cannot tell you what improbable fancies and fears have not run riot in my brain. For prostration so excessive to have overtaken him, one would almost think he had been guilty of murder, or some other unaccountable crime. You must relieve my mind: which, in spite of my uncontrollable fancies, I do not doubt the truth will do. It will make no difference to any one; it will only be an additional bond between myself and you; and you, my almost son."

William's duty rose before him, clear and distinct. But when he spoke, it was in a whisper.

"He loved Anna Lynn."

Mr. Ashley walked on without comment. William resumed.

"Had that unhappy affair not taken place, Henry's intention was to make her his wife, provided you could have been brought to consent to it. His whole days used to be spent, I believe, in planning how he could best invent a chance of obtaining it."

"And now?" very sharply asked Mr. Ashley.

"Now the thing is at an end for ever. Henry's good sense has come to his aid; I suppose I may say his pride; his self-esteem. Innocent of actual ill as Anna was in the affair, there was sufficient reflection cast upon her to prove to Henry that his hopeful visions could never be carried out. That was Henry's secret, sir: and I almost feared the blow would have killed him. But he is getting over it."

Mr. Ashley drew a deep breath. "William, I thank you. You have relieved me from a nightmare: and you may forget having given me the confidence if you like, for it will never be abused. What are you going to do about space?" he continued, in a different tone.

"About space, sir?"

"For those protégés of yours, at East's. They seem to me to be tolerably confined for it, there?"

"Yes, and that is not the worst," said William. "Men are asking to join every day, and they cannot be taken in."

"I can't think how you manage to get so many—and to keep them."

"I suppose the chief secret is, that their interest enters into it. We contrive to keep that up. Most of them would not go back to the Horned Ram for the world."

"Well, where shall you stow them?"

"It is more than I can say, sir. We must manage it somehow."

"Henry told me you were ambitious enough to aspire to the Mormon failure."

"I was foolish enough to do so," replied William, with a laugh. "Seeing it was very much in the condition of the famed picture taken of the good Dr. Primrose and his family—useless—I went and offered a rent for it—only a trifling sum, it is true; but if our fires only kept it from damp, one would think the builder might have been glad to let it, thrown as it is upon his hands. I told him so."

"What did he say?"

"He stood out for thirty pounds. But that's more than I—than we can afford."

"And who was going to find the money? You?"

William hesitated; but did not see any way out of the dilemma.

"Well, sir, you know it is a sad pity for the good work to be stopped, through so insignificant a trifle as want of room."

"I think it is," replied Mr. Ashley. "You can hire it to-morrow, and move your forms and tables and books into it as soon as you like. I will find the rent."

The words took William by surprise. "Oh, Mr. Ashley, do you really mean it?"

"Really mean it? It is little enough, compared with what you are doing. A few years, William, and your name may be great in Helstonleigh. You are working on for it."

William walked with Mr. Ashley as far as his house, and then turned back to his own. He found sorrow there. Not having been home since dinner-time, for he had taken tea at Mr. Ashley's, he was unconscious of some tidings which had been brought by the afternoon's post. Jane sat and grieved while she told him. Her brother Robert was dead. Very rarely indeed did she hear from the New World; Margaret appeared to be too full of cares and domestic bustle to write often. She might not have written now, but to tell of the death of Robert.

"I have lost myself sometimes in a vision of seeing Robert home again," said Jane, with a sigh. "And now he is gone!"

"He was not married, was he?" asked William.

"No. I fear he never got on very well. Never to be at his ease."

Gar came in noisily, and interrupted them. The death of an uncle whom he had never seen, and who had lived thousands of miles away, did not appear to Gar to be a matter calling for any especial amount of grief. Gar was in high spirits on his own account; for Gar was going to Cambridge. Not in all the pomp and pride of an unlimited purse, however, but as a humble sizar.

Gar, not seeing his way very clearly, had been wise enough to pluck up courage and apply for counsel to the head master of the college school. He had told him that he meant to go to college, and how he meant to go, and he asked Mr. Keating if he could help him to a situation, where he might be useful between terms. "A school where I might become a junior assistant," suggested Gar. "Or any family who would take me to read with their sons? If I only earned my food, it would be so much the less weight upon my mother," added he, in the candid spirit peculiar to the family.

"Have you forgotten that you ought to work, yourself, out of terms, nearly as hard as in them?" asked Mr. Keating.

"Oh, no, sir, I have not forgotten it. I will take care to accomplish my own work as well. That should not suffer."

Mr. Keating looked at the cheerful, hopeful face, a sure index of the brave hopeful spirit. He had taken unusual interest in the two Halliburtons, so clever and persevering. It had been impossible for him not to do so; for, if Mr. Keating had a weakness, it was for a good classical scholar.

"I'll see about it, Gar," said he. "But you are rather young to read with students. And I do not suppose any school would be willing to engage you on account of the interruption that keeping your terms would cause. If nothing better turns up, you can remain in the college school-room here, and undertake one of the junior desks. I should give you nothing for it," added the master, "except your meals. Those you would be welcome to take at my house with my private pupils, sleeping at your own home. And I think that, for you, it would be a better arrangement than any other, for it would leave you plenty of time for your own studies, and I could still superintend them."

Gar thought the arrangement would be first-rate. It would be the very thing. "Not that I ever thought of it," he ingenuously said. "I did not know the college school admitted assistants."

"Neither does it," replied the master. "You would be ostensibly my private pupil. And if I choose to set a private pupil to keep the desks to their work, that is my affair."

Gar could only reiterate his thanks.

"I am pleased to give you this little encouragement," remarked Mr. Keating. "When I see boys hopefully plodding on in the teeth of difficulties, of brave heart, of sterling conduct, they deserve all the encouragement that can be given to them. If you and your brothers only go on as you have hitherto gone on, you will stand in after-years as bright examples of what industry and perseverance can achieve."

So that, altogether, Gar was in spirits, and did not by any means put on superfluous mourning for a gentleman who had died in the backwoods of Canada, although he was his mother's brother.

CHAPTER XVI

AN OFFER OF MARRIAGE

"Mary," said Mr. Ashley, "I have received an offer of marriage for you."

A somewhat abrupt announcement to make to a young lady, and Mr. Ashley spoke in the gravest tone. They were seated round the breakfast table, Mary by her mother's side, who was pouring out the coffee. Mary looked surprised, rather amused; but that was the only emotion discernible in her countenance.

"It is fine to be you, Miss Mary!" struck in Henry, before anyone could speak. "Pray, sir, who is the venturer?"

"He assures me that his happiness is bound up in his offer being accepted," resumed Mr. Ashley. "I fancy he felt inclined to assure me that Mary's was also. Of course, all I can do, is, to lay the proposal before her."

"What is it that you are talking about, Thomas?" interposed Mrs. Ashley, unable until then to say a word, and speaking with some irritability. "I do not consider Mary old enough to be married. How can you think of saying such things to her?"

"Neither do I, mamma," said Mary, with a laugh. "I like my home too well to leave it."

"And while you are talking sentiment, my curiosity is on the rack," cried Henry. "I have inquired the name of the bridegroom, and I should like to be answered."

"The would-be bridegroom," put in Mary.

"Mary, I am ashamed of you!" went on Henry. "I blush for your manners. Nice credit she does to your bringing up, mamma! When young ladies of condition receive a celestial offer, they behave with due propriety, hang their heads with a blush, and subdue their voice to a whisper. And here's Mary—look at her!—talking quite loudly and making merry over it. Once more, sir, who is the adventurous gentleman? Is it good old General Wells, our gouty neighbour opposite, who is lifted in and out of his chariot for his daily airing? I have told Mary repeatedly that she was setting her cap at him."

"It is not so advantageous a proposal in a financial point of view," observed Mr. Ashley, maintaining his impassibility. "It proceeds from one of my dependents at the manufactory."

Mary had the sugar-basin in her hand at the moment, and a sudden tremor seemed to seize her. She set it down; but so clumsily, that half the lumps fell out. Her face had turned to a glowing crimson. Mr. Ashley noticed it.

Mrs. Ashley only noticed the sugar. "Mary, how came you to do that? Very careless, my dear."

Mary began meekly to pick up the sugar, the flush giving way to pallor. She lifted her handkerchief to her face and held it there, as if she had a cold.

"The honour comes from Cyril Dare," said Mr. Ashley.

"Cyril Dare!"

"Cyril Dare!"

In different tones of scorn, but each expressing it most fully, the repetition broke from Mrs. Ashley and Henry. Mary, on the contrary, recovered her equanimity and her countenance. She laughed out, as if she were glad.

"What did you say to him, papa?"

"I gave him my opinion only. That I thought he had mistaken my daughter, if he entertained hopes that she would listen to his suit. The question rests with you, Mary."

"Oh papa, what nonsense! rests with me! Why you know I would never have Cyril Dare."

A smile crossed Mr. Ashley's face. He probably had known it.

"Cyril Dare!" repeated Mary, as if unable to overcome her astonishment. "He must have turned silly. I would not have Cyril Dare if he were worth his weight in gold."

"And he must be worth a great deal more than his weight in gold, Mary, before I would consent to your having him," quietly rejoined Mr. Ashley.

"Have him!" echoed Henry. "If I feared there was a danger of the daughter of all the Ashleys so degrading herself, I should bribe cook to make an arsenic cake, cut the young lady a portion myself, and stand by while she ate it."

"Don't talk foolishly, Henry," rebuked Mrs. Ashley.

"Mamma, I must say I do not think it would be half so foolish as Cyril Dare was," cried Mary, with spirit.

Mrs. Ashley, relieved from any temporary fear of losing Mary, was comfortably going on with her breakfast. "Did Cyril say how he meant to provide for Mary, if he obtained her?" asked she, with an amused look.

"He did not touch upon ways and means. I conclude that he intended I should have the honour of keeping them both."

Henry Ashley leaned back in his chair, and laughed. "If this is not the richest joke I have heard for a long while! Cyril Dare! the kinsman of Herbert the beautiful! Confound his im-pu-dence!"

"Then you decline the honour of the alliance, Mary?" said Mr. Ashley. "What am I to tell him?"

"What you please, papa. Tell him, if you like, that I would rather marry a chimney-sweep. I would, if it came to a choice between the two. How very senseless of Cyril to think of such a thing!"

"How very shrewd, I think, Mary—if he could only have got you," was the reply of Mr. Ashley.

"If!" saucily put in Mary.

Henry bent over the table to his sister. "I tell you what, Mary. You go this morning and offer yourself to our gouty friend, the general. He will jump at it, and we'll have the banns put up. We cannot, you know, be subjected to such shocks as these, on your account; it is unreasonable to expect it. I assure you it will be the most effectual plan to set Cyril Dare, and those of his tribe, at rest. No, thank you, ma'am," turning to Mrs. Ashley—"no more coffee. This has been enough breakfast for me."

"Who is this?" asked Mr. Ashley, as footsteps were heard on the gravel-walk.

Mrs. Ashley lifted her eyes. "It is William Halliburton."

"William Halliburton!" echoed Henry. "Ah! if you could have put his heart and intellect into Cyril's form, now, it might have done."

He spoke with that freedom of speech which characterized him, and in which, from his infirmity, he had not been checked. No one made any remark in answer, and William entered. He had come to ask some business question of Mr. Ashley.

"I will walk down with you," said Mr. Ashley, "and see to it. Take a seat, William."

"It is getting late, sir."

"Well, I suppose you can afford to be late for once," replied Mr. Ashley. And William smiled as he sat down.

"We have had a letter from Cambridge, this morning. From Gar."

"And how does Mr. Gar get on?" asked Henry.

"First rate. He takes a leaf out of Frank's book; determined to see no difficulties in his way. Frank's letters are always cheering. I really believe he cares no more for being a servitor than he would for wearing a hat at Christchurch. All his wish is to get on: he looks to the future."

"But he does his duty in the present," quietly remarked Mr. Ashley.

William smiled. "It is the only way to insure the future, sir. Frank and Gar have been learning that all their lives."

Mr. Ashley, telling William not to get the fidgets, for he was not ready yet, withdrew to the next room with his wife. They had some weighty domestic matter to settle, touching a dinner party. Henry linked his arm within William's and drew him to the window, throwing it open to the early spring sunshine. Mary remained at the breakfast table.

"What do you think Cyril Dare, the presuming, has had the conscience to ask?" began he.

"I know," replied William. "I heard him say he should ask it yesterday."

"The deuce you did?" uttered Henry. "And you did not knock him down?"

"Knock him down! Was it any business of mine?"

"You might have done it as my friend, I think. A slight correction of his impudence."

"I do not see that it is your business either," returned William. "It is Mr. Ashley's."

"Oh, indeed! Perhaps you would like it carried out?"

"I have no right to say it shall not be."

"Thank you!" chafed Henry. "Mary," he called out to his sister, "here's Halliburton recommending that that business we know of shall be carried out."

William only laughed. He was accustomed to Henry's exaggerations. "It is what Cyril has been expecting for years," said he.

Henry gazed at him. "What is? What are you talking of?"

"Being taken into partnership by Mr. Ashley."

"Is it that you are blundering over? Does he expect it?" continued Henry, after a pause.

"Cyril said, yesterday, the firm would soon be Ashley and Dare."

"Did he indeed! He had better not count upon it so as to disturb his digestion. That's presumption enough, goodness knows; but it is a mere flea-bite compared with the other. He has asked for Mary. It is true as that we are standing here."

William turned his questioning gaze on Henry. He did not understand. "Asked for her for what? What to do?"

"To be his wife."

"Oh!" The strange sound was not a burst of indignation, or a groan of pain: it was a mixture of both. William thrust his head out of the window.

"He actually asked the master for her yesterday!" went on Henry. "He said his heart, or liver, or some such part of him was bound up in her: as she was bound up in him. Fancy the honour of her becoming Mrs. Cyril!"

William did not turn his head: not a glimpse of his face could be caught. "Will she have him?" he asked, at length.

The question exasperated Henry. "Yes, she will. There! Go and congratulate her. You are a fool, William."

The sound of his angry voice, not his words, reached Mary's ears. She came forward. "What is the matter, Henry?"

"So he is a fool," was Henry's answer. "He wants to know if you are going to marry Cyril Dare. I tell him yes. No one but an idiot would have asked it."

William turned, his face full of an emotion that Henry had never seen there: a streak of scarlet on his cheeks, his earnest eyes strangely troubled. And Mary?—her face seemed to have borrowed the same flush, as she stood there, her head and eyelashes bent.

Henry Ashley gazed, first at one, next at the other, and then turned and leaned from the window himself. In contrition for having spoken so openly of his sister's affairs? Not at all. Whistling the bars of a renowned comic song of the day called "The Steam Arm."

Mr. Ashley put in his head. "I am ready, William."

William touched Mary's hand in silence by way of adieu, and halted as he passed Henry. "Shall you come round to the men to-night?"

"No, I shan't," retorted Henry. "I am upset for the day."

He was halfway down the path when he heard himself called by Henry, still leaning from the window. He went back to him.

"She said she'd rather have a chimney-sweep than Cyril Dare. Don't go and make a muff of yourself again."

William turned away without any answer. Mr. Ashley, who had waited, put his arm within his, and they proceeded to the manufactory.

"Have you heard this rumour, respecting Herbert Dare, that has been wafted over from Germany within the last day or two?" inquired Mr. Ashley, as they walked along.

"Yes, sir," replied William.

"I wonder if it is true?"

William did not answer. William's private opinion was, that it was true. It had been tolerably well authenticated. A rumour that need not be very specifically enlarged upon here. Helstonleigh never came to the bottom of it: never knew for certain how much of it was true, and how much false, and we cannot expect to be better favoured than Helstonleigh, in the point of enlightenment. It was not a pleasant rumour, and the late governess's name was unaccountably mixed up in it. For one thing, it said that Herbert Dare, finding commercial pursuits not congenial to his taste, had given them up, and was roaming about Germany. Mademoiselle also. It was a report that did not do credit to Herbert, or tend to reflect respectability on his family; yet Mr. Ashley fully believed that to that report he owed the application of Cyril with regard to Mary, strange as it may appear at a first glance, to say it. The application had astonished Mr. Ashley beyond expression. He could only come to the conclusion that Cyril must have entertained the hope for some time, but had been induced to disclose it prematurely. So prematurely—even allowing that other circumstances favoured it—that Mr. Ashley was tempted to laugh. A man without means, without a home, without any definite prospects, merely a workman, as might be said, in his manufactory, upon a very small salary; it was ridiculous in the extreme for him to offer marriage to Miss Ashley. Mr. Ashley, of upright conduct in the sight of day, was not one to wink at folly; any escapade such as that, now flying about Helstonleigh as attributed to Herbert, would not be an additional recommendation in Cyril's favour. Had he hastened to speak before it should reach Mr. Ashley's ears? Mr. Ashley thought so. An hour after Cyril had spoken, he heard the scandal; and it flashed over his mind that to that he was indebted for the premature honour. Cyril would have liked to secure his consent before anything unpleasant transpired.

As Mr. Ashley came in view of the manufactory, Cyril Dare observed him. Cyril was lounging in an indolent manner at the entrance doors, exchanging greetings with the various passers-by. He ought to have been inside at his business; but oughts went for little with Cyril. Since Samuel Lynn's departure, Cyril had been living in clover; enjoying as much idleness as he liked. William assumed no authority over him, though full authority had been given to William over the manufactory in general; and Cyril, except when he just happened to be under Mr. Ashley's eye, passed his time agreeably. Cyril stared as he caught sight of the master, and then went in, his spirits going down a little. To see the master thus walking confidentially with William, seemed to argue unfavourably for his suit; though why it should seem so, Cyril did not know. Cyril's staring was occasioned by that fact. He had never been promoted to the honour of thus walking familiarly with Mr. Ashley. In fact, for the master, a reserved and proud man with all his good qualities, to link his arm within a dependant's, astonished Cyril considerably.

When they entered, Cyril was at work in his apron, standing at the counter in the master's room, steady and assiduous, as though he had been there for the last half-hour. The master came in, but William remained in Mr. Lynn's room.

"Good morning, sir," said Cyril.

"Good morning," replied the master.

He sat down to his desk, and opened a letter that was lying on it. Presently he looked up.

"Cyril!"

"Yes, sir."

"Step here."

Cyril approached the desk, feeling what a lady might call nervous. The decisive moment had come: should he be provided for, for life; enjoy a good position and the means of living as a gentleman? Or would his unlucky star prevail, and consign him to—he did not quite foresee to what?

"I have spoken to Miss Ashley. She was excessively surprised at your application, and begs to decline it in the most unequivocal manner. Allow me to add a recommendation from myself, that you bury in oblivion the fact of your having made it."

Cyril hesitated for a moment, and looked foolish. "Why?" he asked.

"Why?" repeated Mr. Ashley. "I think you could answer that query for yourself, and save me the trouble. I do not wish to go too closely into facts and causes, past and present, unless you desire it. One thing you must be aware of, Cyril, that such a proposition from you to my daughter was utterly out of place. I should have rejected it point-blank yesterday; in fact, in the surprise of the moment, I almost spoke out more plainly than you would have liked, but that I thought it as well for you to have Miss Ashley's opinion as well as my own."

"Why am I rejected, sir?" continued Cyril.

Mr. Ashley waved his hand with dignity. "Return to your employment, Cyril. It is quite sufficient for you to know that you are rejected, without my going into motives and reasons. They might not, I say, be palatable to you."

Cyril did not venture to press it further. He returned to the counter, and stood there, ostensibly going on with his work, and boiling over with rage. The master sat some little time longer and then left the room. Soon after, William came in. His eye caught Cyril's employment.

"Cyril," cried he, hastily advancing to him, "you must not make up those gloves. I told you yesterday not to touch them."

A dangerous speech. Cyril was not unlike touchwood at that moment, liable to go off at the slightest contact. "You told me!" he burst forth. "Do you think I am going to do what you choose to tell me? Try it on for the future, that's all. You tell me!"

"They are the very best gloves, and must be sorted with nicety," returned William. "Don't you know that the sorting of the last parcel was found fault with in London? It vexed the master; and he desired me to do all the sorting myself, until Mr. Lynn should be at home."

"I choose to sort," returned Cyril.

"But you must not sort in the face of the master's orders; or, if you do, I must go over them again."

"That's right; praise up yourself!" foamed Cyril. "Of course you are an efficient sorter, and I am a bad one."

"You might be as good a sorter as any one, if you chose to give it proper time and attention. What a temper you are in this morning! What's the matter?"

"The matter is, that I have submitted to your rule long enough, but I'll do it no longer," was the reply of Cyril, whose anger was gathering strength, and whose ill feeling towards William, deep down in his heart from long ago, had had envy added to it of late.

William made no reply. He carefully swept the dozens that Cyril had made up, farther down the counter, that they might be in a stronger light.

"What's that for?" cried Cyril. "How dare you meddle with my work? They are done as well as you can do them, any day."

"Now, where's the use of flying into this passion, Cyril? What's it for? Do you suppose I go over your work again for pleasure, or to find fault with it? I do it because the master has ordered me to make up every dozen that goes out; and if you do it first of all, it is sheer waste of time. See here," added William, holding two or three pairs towards him, "these will not do for firsts."

Angry Cyril! He was quite beside himself with anger. It was not this trifling matter in the daily business that would have excited him; but Mr. Ashley's rejection, his words altogether, had turned Cyril's blood into gall; and this was made the outlet. He dashed the gloves out of William's hand to the farthest corner of the room, and struck him a powerful blow on the chest. It caused William to stagger: he was unprepared for it; but whether he would have returned it must remain uncertain. Before there was time or opportunity, Cyril found himself whirled backwards by a hand as powerful as his own; and a voice of stern authority was demanding the meaning of the scene.

The hand, the voice, were those of the master.

CHAPTER XVII

"What is the meaning of this, Cyril Dare?"

Had Cyril supposed that the master was so close at hand, he had subdued his passion to something short of striking a blow. He stood against the counter, his brow lowering, his eye furious; William looked angry too. Mr. Ashley, calm and dignified, waited for an answer.

None came. Cyril was too excited to speak.

"Will you explain it?" said the master, turning to William. "Fighting in my counting-house!"

"I cannot, sir," replied William, recovering his equanimity. "I do not understand it. I did nothing to provoke him, that I am aware of. It is true I said I must go over the gloves again that he had made up."

"What are those gloves flung there?"

"I was showing them to him—that they were not fit for firsts."

"They are fit for firsts!" retorted Cyril, breaking his silence. "I know I did put a pair in that was not up to the mark."

The master went and picked up the gloves himself. Taking them to the light, he turned them about in his hands.

"I should put two of these pairs as seconds, and one as thirds," remarked he. "You must have been asleep when you put this one among the firsts," he continued, indicating the latter pair, and speaking to Cyril Dare. "It has a flaw in it."

"Of course you will uphold Halliburton, sir, whatever he may say. That has been the case for a long time past."

He spoke in an insolent tone; such as none within the walls of that manufactory had ever dared to use to the master. The master turned upon him, speaking quietly and significantly.

"You forget yourself, Cyril Dare."

"All he does is right, and all I do is wrong," persisted Cyril. "You treat him, sir, just as though you considered him the gentleman, instead of me."

A half-smile, which had too much mockery in it to please Cyril, crossed the lips of Mr. Ashley. "What's that you say about being a gentleman, Cyril? Repeat it, will you? I should like to hear it again."

Mockery and double mockery! Cyril's suggestive ears detected it in the tone, if no other ears could do so. It did not improve his temper. "The thing is this, sir: I won't submit to this state of affairs any longer. I was not placed here to be ruled over by him; and if things can't be put upon a better footing, one of us must leave."

"Then, as it has come to this explosion, I say the same," struck in William. "It is high time that things were put upon a better footing. Cyril, you have forced me to speak, and you must take the consequences. Sir," turning to the master, "my authority over the men is ridiculed in their hearing. It ought not to be so."

"By whom?" demanded the master.

"You can ask that question of Cyril, sir."

The master did ask it of Cyril. "Have you done this?"

"Possibly I have," innocently returned Cyril.

"You know you have," rejoined William.

"Only yesterday, when I was giving directions to the stainers, he derided all I said, and one of them inquired whether I had received orders for what I was telling them. If the authority vested in me is to be undermined, the men will soon set it at naught."

Mr. Ashley looked provoked; more so than William ever remembered to have seen him. He paused a moment, his lips quivering angrily, and then flung open the counting-house door.

"Dick!"

Dick, a young tinker of ten, black in clothes and in skin, came flying at the summons and its unusually stern tone. "Please, sir?"

"Ring the large bell."

Dick stared with all his eyes at hearing the words. To ring the large bell between ten and eleven o'clock in the morning was a marvel that had never happened in Dick's experience. But the master's orders were to be obeyed, not questioned; and Dick, rang out a prolonged peal. The master looked into the serving-room.

"James Meeking, I have ordered the bell rung for the men. Pass the word for them to come into my room; and do you and East come with them."

The men appeared, flocking from all parts of the premises, their astonishment certainly not inferior to Dick's. What could be the meaning of the wholesale summoning to the presence of the master? They stood there crowding, a sea of curious faces. Dick, consigned to the background, climbed up the door-post, and held on by it in a mysterious manner.

Mr. Ashley drew William to his side, and laid his hand upon him.

"It has been told to me that the authority vested in Mr. Halliburton has not been implicitly obeyed by every one in the manufactory. I have called you before me to give you my instructions personally upon the point, that there may be no misunderstanding in the future. Whatever directions he may see well to give, you will receive them from him, as you would from myself. I invest him with full and complete power. And in all my absences from the manufactory, whether they may be of an hour's, a day's, or any longer duration, Mr. Halliburton is its master."

They touched their hair, turned and went out as far as the serving-room, collecting there to talk. In a short time, one of them was seen coming back again; a grey-haired man, a sorter of leather. He addressed himself to Mr. Ashley.

"We have not disputed his orders, please, sir, that we can call to mind; and if we have done it unintentional, we'd ask pardon for it, for it's what we never thought to do. Next to yourself, sir, we couldn't wish for a better master than young Mr. Halliburton. We think as much of him, sir, as we should if he was your own son."

"All right, my men," cheerfully responded Thomas Ashley.

But was not Cyril put in the background by this? As badly as Dick had been; and Cyril had no door-post to climb, and so obtain vantage ground. He had stood with his back to the crowd and his face to the counter. When the men were out of hearing, he turned and walked up to the master.

"It is the place I thought to fill," said he. "It is the place that was promised me."

"Not promised," replied Mr. Ashley. "Not thought to be promised. A very long time ago, you may have been spoken of conditionally, as likely to fill it. Conditionally, I say."

"Conditionally on what, sir?"

"On your fitness for it. By conduct and by capability."

"What is the matter with my conduct, sir?" returned Cyril, his tone a sharp one.

"It is bad," curtly replied Mr. Ashley. "Deceitful in public; bad in private. I have told you once before this morning, that I do not care to go into details; you must know that there is no necessity for my doing so."

Cyril paused. "I have been led to expect, sir, that you would take me into partnership."

"Not by me," said the master.

"My father and mother had given me the hope ever since I came here."

"I cannot help that. They had no authority for it from me."

"They have always said I should be made your partner and son-in-law," persisted Cyril.

"They have! It is very obliging of them, I am sure, to settle my affairs for me, even to the disposal of my daughter! Pray what nice little destiny may they have carved out for Mrs. Ashley or for my son?"

Cyril chafed at the words. He would have liked, just then, to strike Mr. Ashley, as he had struck William. "Would I ever have demeaned myself to enter a glove manufactory, disgracing my family, had I known I was to be only a workman in it?" he cried. "No, sir, that I never would. I am rightly served, for putting myself out of my position as a gentleman."

Mr. Ashley, but for the pity he felt, could have laughed outright. He really did feel pity for Cyril. He believed that the unhappy way in which the young Dares were turning out might be laid to the fault of their rearing, and this had rendered him considerate to Cyril. How considerate he had for a long while been, he himself alone knew: Cyril perhaps suspected.

"It is a shame!" cried Cyril. "To be dealt with in this way is nothing less than a fraud upon me. I was led to expect that I should be made your partner."

"Wait a bit, Cyril. I am willing to put you right upon the point. The proposal, that you should be placed here, emanated in the first instance from your father. He came to me one day, here, in this very room, saying that he concluded I should not put Henry to business, and thought it would be a fine opening for his son Cyril. He hinted that I should want some one to succeed me; and that you might come to it with that view. But I most distinctly disclaimed endorsing that hint in the remotest degree. I would not subscribe to it so much as by a vague 'Perhaps it may be so.' All that I conceded upon the point was this. I told Mr. Dare that when the time came for me to be looking out for some one to succeed me—if it ever did come—and I found his son—you—had served me faithfully, was upright in conduct and in heart— one, in short, whom I could thoroughly confide in—why, then he should have the preference over any other. So much I did say, Cyril, but no more."

"And why won't you give me the preference, sir?"

Mr. Ashley looked at him, apparently in surprise that he could ask the question. He bent his head forward, and spoke in a low tone, but one full of meaning.

"Upright in conduct and in heart, I said, Cyril. It was an absolute condition."

Cyril's gaze fell before Mr. Ashley's. His conscience may have pricked him, and he had the grace to look ashamed of himself. There ensued a pause.

Presently Cyril looked up. "Then I am to understand, sir, that all hope of being your partner and successor is over?"

"It is. It has been over this many a year, Cyril. I should do wrong to deal otherwise than perfectly plainly with you. Were you to reform anything there may have been amiss in your conduct, to become a model of excellence in the sight of Helstonleigh, I could never admit your name to be associated with mine. The very notion is offensive to me."

Cyril—it was a great wonder—restrained his passion. "Perhaps I had better leave, then?" he said.

"You are welcome to stay until you can find a situation more agreeable to you," replied Mr. Ashley. "Provided you undertake to behave yourself."

"Stay! and for nothing in the end!" echoed Cyril. "No, that I never will! If I must remain a dependant, I'll try it on at something else. I am sick of this."

He untied his apron, dashed it on to the floor, and went out without another word. So furiously did he stamp through the serving-room, that James Meeking turned round to look at him, and Dick, taking a recreative balance at that moment on the edge of an upright coal-scuttle, thought he must be running for the fire-engines. Dick's speculations were disturbed by the sound of the master's voice, calling to him.

He hastened to the counting-house, and was ordered to "take that apron away." Dick picked it up and withdrew with it, folding it carefully against Mr. Cyril should come in. Dick little thought the manufactory had seen the last of him.

Mr. Ashley was indulging in a quiet laugh. "Demeaning himself by entering my manufactory! Disgracing his family—the high blood of the Dares! Poor Cyril! William, do you look at it in the same light?"

William had remained in the room, taking no part whatever in the final contest. He had stood with his back to them, following his occupation. He turned round now.

"Sir, you know I do not."

"You once told me it presented no field for getting on. What was the word you used?—was it ambition? Truly, there's not much ambition attached to it. Nevertheless, I am satisfied with my career, William, although I am only the glove manufacturer, Thomas Ashley."

He satisfied! How many a one would be proud to be in the position of Thomas Ashley! William did not say so. He began to speak of Cyril Dare.

"Do you think he will come back again, sir?"

"I do not think he will. Should he do so, the doors are closed to him. He has left of his own accord, and I shall not allow him to return."

"I am very sorry," remarked William. "It has been partly my fault."

"Do not make yourself uneasy. I have tolerated Cyril Dare here; have allowed him to remain on sufferance: and that is the best that can be said of it."

"He may feel it as a blow."

"As a jubilee, you mean. It will be nothing less to him. He has hated the manufactory with all his heart from the moment he first entered it, and is now, if we could see him, kicking up his heels with delight at the emancipation. Cyril Dare my partner!"

William continued his work, saying nothing. Mr. Ashley resumed:

"I must be casting my thoughts around for a fitting substitute to succeed to the post of ambition Cyril coveted. Can you direct me to any quarter, William?"

Mr. Ashley was now standing at William's side, looking at him as he went over the gloves left by Cyril. He saw the red flush mount to his face. Mr. Ashley laid his hand on William's shoulder, and spoke in low tones, full of emotion.

"It may come, my boy; my almost son! And when Thomas Ashley's head shall be low in the grave, the leading manufacturer of this city may be William Halliburton."

A loud rapping at the door with a thick stick interrupted the master's words. He turned to behold Mr. Dare. It appeared that Cyril had by chance met his father in the street almost immediately after going out; he had volunteered to him a most exaggerated account, and Mr. Dare had come, as he said, to learn the rights of it.

William left the room. He could not avoid remarking the bowed, broken appearance of the man. Mr. Ashley related the particulars, and the listener was obliged to acknowledge that Cyril had been to blame—had been too hasty.

"I confess it appears so," he said. "He must have been led away by temper. But, Mr. Ashley, you ought to stretch a point, and make a concession. We are kinsmen."

"What concession?"

"Discharge William Halliburton. Things can never go on smoothly between him and Cyril. Stretch a point to oblige us, and send him away."

"Discharge William Halliburton!" echoed Mr. Ashley in surprise. "I could as soon discharge myself. William is the right hand of the business. It could go on without me, but I am not sure that it could do so without him."

"Cyril can take his place."

"Cyril is not qualified for it. And—"

"Cyril declares he will never enter the place again, so long as Halliburton is in it."

"Cyril never will enter it again," quietly rejoined Mr. Ashley. "Cyril and I have parted. I will give you his wages for this week, now that you are here; legally, though, he could not claim them."

Mr. Dare looked sad—gloomy. It was only what he had expected for some time past. "You promised to do well by him, Mr. Ashley; to take him into partnership."

"You must surely remember that I promised nothing of the sort," said Mr. Ashley. "I have been telling the same thing to Cyril. All I said—and a shrewd, business man, as you are, could not fail thoroughly to understand me," he pointedly added—"was, that I would choose Cyril in preference to others, provided he proved himself worthy of the preference. Circumstances appear to have worked entirely against carrying out that idea, Mr. Dare."

"What circumstances?"

Mr. Ashley did not immediately reply, and the question was repeated in a hasty, almost an imperative tone. Then Mr. Ashley answered it.

"I do not wish to say a word that should unnecessarily hurt your feelings; but in a matter of business I believe there is no resource but to speak plainly. The unfortunate notoriety acquired, in one way or other, by your sons, has rendered the name of Dare so conspicuous, that, were there no other reason, it could never be associated with mine."

"Conspicuous? How?" interposed Mr. Dare.

Mr. Ashley would not have believed the words were uttered as a question, but that the answer was evidently waited for. "You ask how," he said. "Surely I need not remind you. The scandal which, in more ways than one, attached to Anthony—though I am sorry to allude to him, poor fellow, in any such way; the circumstances attending the trial of Herbert; the—"

"Herbert was innocent," interrupted Mr. Dare.

"Innocent of the murder, no doubt; as innocent as you or I. But people made free with his name in other ways; had often made free with it. And look at this last report, wafted over to us from Germany, that is just now astonishing the city!"

"Hang him for a simpleton!" burst forth Mr. Dare.

"It is all so much discredit to the name—to the family altogether," concluded Mr. Ashley, as if his sentence had not been interrupted.

"The faults of his brothers ought to be no good reason for your rejecting Cyril."

"They are not my reason for rejecting him," quietly returned Mr. Ashley.

"No? You have just said they were."

"I said the notoriety given by your sons to the name of Dare would bar its association with mine. In saying 'your sons,' I included Cyril himself. He interposes the greatest barrier of all. Were the rest of them of good report in the sight of day, Cyril is not so."

"What's the matter with him?" asked Mr. Dare.

"I do not care to tell you. A great deal of it you must know."

"Go on," cried Anthony Dare, who was leaning forward in his chair, his chin resting on his stick, as one who sets himself calmly to hear the whole.

"Cyril's private conduct is bad. He—"

"Follies of youth only," cried old Anthony. "He will outlive them."

"Youth's follies sometimes end in manhood's crimes," was the reply. "I am thankful that my son is free from them."

"Your son!" returned Anthony Dare, coughing down his slighting tone. "Your son is one apart. He has not the health to be knocking about. If young men are worth anything, they are sure to be a bit wild."

A frown passed over the master's brow. "You are mistaken, Mr. Dare. Young men who are worth anything keep themselves from such folly. Opinions have taken a turn. Society is becoming more sensible of the world's increased enlightenment; and ill conduct, although its pursuer may be a fashionable young man, is beginning to be called by its right name. Would you believe that Cyril has, more than once, come here—I hesitate to say the word, it is so ugly a one—drunk? Drunk, Mr. Dare!"

"No!"

"He has."

"Then he must have been a fool for his pains," was the angry retort of old Anthony.

"He is untruthful; he is idle; he is deceitful—but I do not, I say, care to go into this. Were you cognizant of the application Cyril made to me yesterday, respecting my daughter?"

"I don't know of any application."

"He did me the honour to make her an offer of marriage."

Old Anthony lifted his head sharply, not speaking. The master continued:

"He said yesterday that he was acting by your advice. He repeated to-day, that you and Mrs. Dare had led him to look to Mary."

"Well?" returned Mr. Dare. "But I did not know he had spoken."

"How could you—excuse me, I again say, if I am to speak plainly—how could you ever have entertained so wild an idea?"

"Perhaps you would like to call it a presumptuous one?" chafed Mr. Dare.

"I do call it so," returned Mr. Ashley. "It can be regarded as nothing less; any impartial person would tell you so. I put out of the discussion altogether the want of means on the part of Cyril; I speak of its suitability. That Cyril should have aspired to an alliance with Mary Ashley was presumption in the highest degree. It has displeased me very much, and Henry looks upon it in the light of an insult."

"Who's Henry?" scornfully returned Mr. Dare. "A dreamy hypochondriac! Pray is Cyril not as well born as Mary Ashley?"

"Has he been as well reared? Is he proving that he has been? A man's conduct is of far more importance than his birth."

"It would seem that you care little about birth, or rearing either, or you would not exalt Halliburton to a level with yourself."

The master fixed his expressive eyes on Anthony Dare. "Halliburton's birth is, at any rate, as good as your family's and mine. His father's mother and your wife's father were brother and sister."

Old Anthony looked taken by surprise. "I don't know anything about it," said he, somewhat roughly. "I know a little of how he has been bred, he and his brothers."

"So do I," said Mr. Ashley. "I wish a few more in the world had been bred in the same way."

"Why! they have been bred to work!" exclaimed old Anthony, in astonishment. "They have not been bred as gentlemen. They have not had enough to eat."

The concluding sentence elicited an involuntary laugh from the master. "At any rate, the want does not appear to have stinted their growth, or injured them in a physical point of view," he rejoined, a touch of sarcasm in his tone. "They are fine-grown men; and, Mr. Dare, they are gentlemen, whether they have been bred as such or not. Gentlemen in looks, in manners, and in mind and heart."

"I don't care what they are," again repeated old Anthony. "I did not come here to talk about them, but about Cyril. Your exalting Halliburton into the general favour that ought legitimately to have been Cyril's is a piece of injustice. Cyril says you have this morning announced publicly that Halliburton is master, under you. It is flagrant injustice."

"No man living has ever had cause to tax me with injustice," impressively answered Thomas Ashley. "I have been far more just to Cyril than he deserves. Stay: 'just' is a wrong word. I have been far more lenient to him. Shall I tell you that I have kept him on here out of compassion, in the hope that the considerate way in which I treated him might be an inducement to him to turn over a new leaf, and discard his faults? I would not turn him away to be a town's talk. Deep down within the archives of my memory, my own sole knowledge, I buried the great fault of which he was guilty here. He was young; and I would not take from him his fair fame on the very threshold of his commercial life."

"Great fault?" hesitated Mr. Dare, looking half frightened.

Thomas Ashley inclined his head, and lowered his voice to a deeper whisper.

"When he robbed my desk of the cheque, I fancy your own suspicions of him were to the full as much awakened as mine."

There was no reply, unless a groan from Anthony Dare could be called one. His hands, supporting his chin, rested on his stick still. Mr. Ashley resumed:

"I became convinced, though not in the first blush of the affair that the transgressor was no other than Cyril; and I deliberated what my course should be. Natural impulse would have led me to turn him away, if not to prosecute. The latter would scarcely have been palatable towards one of my wife's kindred. What was I to do with him? Turn him adrift without a character? and a character that would get him any other situation of confidence, I could not give him. I resolved to keep him on. For his own sake I would give him a chance of redeeming what he may have done in a moment's thoughtless temptation. I spoke to him privately. I did not tell him in so many words that I knew him to be guilty; but he could not well misunderstand that my suspicions were awakened. I told him his conduct had not been good—not such that I could approve; but that I was willing, for his own sake, to bury the past in silence, and retain him, as a last chance. I very distinctly warned him what would be the consequences of the smallest repetition of his fault: that no consideration for myself or for him would induce me to look over it a second time. Thus he stayed on: I, continually giving an eye to his conduct, and taking due precautions for the protection of my property, and keeping fast my keys. James Meeking received my orders that Mr. Cyril should never be called upon to help pay the men, or to count the packets of halfpence; and when the man looked wonderingly at me in return, I casually added that there was no necessity to put Mr. Cyril to an employment he particularly disliked, while he could call upon East to help him, or in case of need, upon Mr. Halliburton. Never think again, Mr. Dare, that I have been unjust to your son. If I have erred at all, it has been on the side of kindness."

There was a long pause. Anthony Dare probably was feeling the kindness, in spite of himself.

"What have you had to complain of in him since?" he asked.

"Not of any more robbery: but of his general conduct a great deal. He is deceitful: he has appeared here in the state I have hinted to you; he is incorrigibly idle. He probably fancies, because I do not take a very active part in the management of my business and my workpeople, that I sit here with my eyes shut, seeing little and knowing less of what goes on around me. He is essentially mistaken: I am cognizant of all; as much so, or nearly as much so, as Samuel Lynn would be, were he at his post again. Look at his sorting of gloves, for instance—the very thing about which the disturbance occurred just now. Cyril can sort if he pleases; he is as capable of sorting them properly as I should be; perhaps more so: but he does not do it; and every dozen he attempts to make up has to be done over again. In point of fact, he has been of no real use here; for nothing that he attempts to do will he do well. A fitting hand to fill the post of manager! Taking all these facts into consideration," added the master, "you will not be surprised that an offer of marriage from Cyril Dare to my daughter bears an appearance little removed from insult."

So it was all known to Mr. Ashley, and there was an end of Cyril and his hopes! It may be said of his prospects.

"What is he to do now?" broke from the lips of Anthony Dare.

"Indeed I do not know. Unless he changes his habits, he will do no good at anything."

"Won't you take him back again?"

"No," unequivocally pronounced Mr. Ashley. "He has left of his own accord, and he must abide by it. Stay—hear me out. Were I to allow him to return, he would not remain here a week; I am certain of it. That Cyril has been acting a part, to beguile me of my favour with regard to those foolish hopes of his, there is no doubt. The hopes gone, he would not keep up even the semblance of good conduct; neither would he submit to the rule of William Halliburton. It is best as it is; he is gone, and he cannot return. My opinion is, that were the offer of return made to him, he would reject it."

Mr. Dare's opinion was not far different, although he had pleaded for the concession.

"Then you will not make him your partner?" he resumed.

"Mr. Dare!"

"I suppose you will take in Halliburton?"

"It is very probable. Whoever I take must be a man of probity and honour: and a gentleman," he added, with a stress upon the word. "William Halliburton is all that."

Anthony Dare rose with a groan. He could contend no longer.

"My sons have been my bane," he uttered from between his bloodless lips. "I wonder, sometimes, whether they were born bad."

"No," said Thomas Ashley. "The badness has come with their training."

CHAPTER XVIII

"CALLED"

And now there occurs another gap in the story—a gap of years, and we have entered on the third and last part.

The patient well-doing of the Halliburtons was approaching fruition, their struggles were well-nigh over, and they were ready to play their part, for success or for failure, in the great drama of life. Jane's troubles were at an end.

Did you ever remark how some things, when they draw towards a close, seem to advance with rapid strides, unlike the slow, crawling pace that characterized their beginning? Life: in its childhood, its youth, nay, in its middle age, how slowly it seems to pass! how protracted its distinctive periods appear to be! But when old age approaches then time moves with giant strides. Undertake a work, whether of the hands or the head, very, very slow does the progress appear to be, until it is far advanced; and then the conclusion is attained fast and imperceptibly. Thus does it seem to be in the history of the young Halliburtons. To them the race may have been tedious, the labour as hard at the close of their preparatory career as at its commencement; but not so to those who were watching them.

There has not been space to trace the life of Frank and Gar at the Universities, to record word by word how they bore onward with unflinching perseverance, looking towards the goal in view. Great praise was due to them; and they won it from those who knew what hard work meant. Patiently and steadily had they laboured on, making of themselves sound and brilliant scholars, resisting temptations that lead so many astray, and bearing the slights and mortifications incidental to their subordinate position. "I'll take it all out, when I am Lord Chancellor of England," Frank would say, in his cheery way. Of course Frank had always intended to go up for honours; and of course Frank gained them. He went to Oxford as a humble servitor, and he left it a man of note. Francis Halliburton had obtained a double-first, and gained his fellowship.

He had entered himself a student of the Middle Temple long before his college career was over. The expenses of qualifying for the Bar are considerable, and Frank's fellowship did not suffice for all. He procured literary employment: writing a leading article for one of the daily papers, and contributing to sundry reviews.

Gar, too, had quitted Cambridge with unusual credit, though he was not senior wrangler. No one but Gar, perhaps, knew that he had aspired to that proud distinction, so it did not signify. A more solid scholar, or one with a higher character in the best sense of the term, never left the University to be ordained by the Bishop of Helstonleigh—or by any other prelate on the bench. He had a choice of a title to orders. His uncle, the Reverend Francis Tait—who, like his father before him, had, after many years' service, obtained a living—had offered Gar his title. But a clergyman in the county of Helstonleigh had also offered him one, and Gar, thanking his uncle, chose Helstonleigh.

William's dream of ambition was fulfilled; the dream which he had not indulged; for it had seemed all too high and vague for possibility. He was Mr. Ashley's partner. The great firm in Helstonleigh was Ashley and Halliburton.

Ashley and Halliburton! And the event had been so gradually, so naturally led up to, that Helstonleigh was not surprised when it was announced. Of course William received as yet only a small share of the profits: how small or how large was not known. Helstonleigh racked its curiosity to learn particulars, and racked it in vain. One fact was assumed beyond doubt: that a portion of the profits was secured to Henry in the event of Mr. Ashley's death.

William was now virtually sole master of the business. Mr. Ashley had partially retired from the manufactory: at least, his visits to it were of occurrence so rare as almost to amount to retirement. Samuel Lynn was manager, as of old; William had assumed Mr. Ashley's place and desk in the counting-house—as master. Mr. Ashley had purchased an estate, Deoffam Hall, some two to three miles distant from the city, close to the little village of Deoffam: and there he and his family had gone to reside. He retained his old house in the London Road, and they would visit it occasionally, and pass a week there. The change of abode did not appear to give unqualified gratification to Henry Ashley. He had become so attached to William that he could not bear to be far away from him. In the old home William's visits had been daily; or rather, nightly: in this he did see him so often. William contrived to go over twice or thrice a week; but that did not appear to be often enough for Henry. Mary Ashley was not married; to the surprise of Helstonleigh: but Mary somewhat obstinately refused to leave the paternal home. William and his mother lived on together in the old house. But they were alone now: for he could afford to keep up its expenses, and he had insisted upon doing so; insisted that she who had worked so hard for them, should have rest, now they could work for her.

Yes, they had all worked; worked on for the end, and gained it. Looking back, Jane wondered how she had struggled on. It seemed now next to an impossibility that she could have done it. Verily and truly she believed that God alone had borne her up. Had it been a foreshadowing of what was to come, when her father, years back, had warned her, on the very day of her marriage with Mr. Halliburton had been decided, that it might bring many troubles upon her? Perhaps so. One thing was certain: that it had brought them, and in no common degree. But the troubles were surmounted now: and Jane's boys were turned out just as well as though she had had thousands a year to bring them up upon. Perhaps better.

Perhaps better! How full of force is the suggestion! I wonder if no one will let this history of the young Halliburtons read a lesson to them? Many a student, used worse by fortune and the world than he thinks he deserves, might take it to himself with profit. Do not let it be flung away as a fancy picture; endeavour to make it your reality. A career, worked out as theirs was, insures success as a necessity. "Ah!" you may think, "I am poor; I can't hope to achieve such things." Poor! What were they? What's that you say? "There are so many difficulties in the way!" Quite true; there are difficulties in the way of attaining most things worth having; but they are only placed there to be overcome. Like the hillocks and stumbling-blocks in that dream that came to Mr. Halliburton when he was dying, they are placed there to be subdued, not to be shunned in fear, or turned from in idleness. Whatever may be your object in life, work on for it. Be you heir to a dukedom, or be your heritage that of daily toil, an object you must have: a man who has none is the most miserable being on the face of the earth. Bear manfully onward and attain the prize. Toil may be hard, but it will grow lighter as you advance; impediments may be disheartening, but they are not insurmountable; privations may be painful, but you are working on to plenty; temptations to indolence, to flagging, to that many-headed monster, sin, may be pulling at you; but they will not stir you from your path an inch, unless you choose to let them do so. Only be resolute; only regard trustingly the end, and labour for it; and it will surely come. It may look in the distance so far off that the very hope of attaining it seems but a chimera. Never mind; bear hopefully on, and the distance will lessen palpably with every step. No real good was ever attained to in this world without working for it. No real good, as I honestly believe, was ever gained, unless God's blessing went with the endeavours to attain it. Make a friend of God. Do that, and fight your way on, doing your duty, and you will find the goal: as the sons of Mrs. Halliburton did.

Jane was sitting alone one afternoon in her parlour. She was little changed. None, looking at her, could believe her old enough to be the mother of those three great men, her sons. Not that Gar was particularly great; he was only of middle height. Jane wore a shaded silk dress; and her hair looked as smooth and abundant as in the old days of her girlhood. It was remarkable how little her past troubles had told upon her good looks; how little she was aging.

She saw the postman come to the door, and Dobbs brought in a letter. "It's Mr. Frank's writing," growled Dobbs.

Jane opened it, and found that Frank had been "called." Half his care was over.

"MY DARLING MOTHER,—I am made a barrister at last. I really am; and I beg you will all receive the announcement with appropriate awe and deference. I was called to-day: and I intend to have a photograph taken of myself in my wig and gown, and send it down to you as a confirmation of the fact. When you see the guy the wig makes of me, you will say you never saw an ugly man before. Tell Dobbs so; it will gladden her heart: don't you remember how she used to assure us, when boys, that we ought to be put under a glass case, as three ultra specimens of ugliness?

"I shall get on now, dearest mother. It may be a little up-hill work at first: but there's no fear. A first-rate law firm has promised me some briefs: and one of these speedy days I shall inevitably take the ears of some court by storm—the jury struck into themselves with the learned counsel's astounding eloquence, and the bar dumb—and then my fortune's made. I need not tell you what circuit I shall patronize, or in how short a time afterwards I intend to be leading it: but I will tell you that my first object in life, when I am up in the world, shall be the ease and comfort of my dear mother. William is not going to do everything, and have you all to himself.

"Talking about William, ask him if he cannot get up some chance litigation, that I may have the honour of appearing for him next assizes. I'll do it all free, gratis, for nothing. Ever your own son,

"FRANK."

Jane started up from her chair at the news, almost as a glad child. Who could she find to share it with her? She ran into the next house to Patience. Patience limped a little in her walk still; she would limp always. Anna, in her sober Quaker's cap, the border resting on her fair forehead, looked up from her drawing, and Jane told them the news, and read the letter.

"That is nice," said Patience. "It must be a weight off thy mind."

"I don't know that it is that," replied Jane. "I have never doubted his success. I don't doubt it still. But I am very glad."

"I wish I had a cause to try," cried Anna, who had recovered all her old spirits and her love of chatter. "I would let Frank plead it for me."

"Will you come back with me, Anna, and take tea?" said Jane. "I shall be alone this evening. William is going over to Deoffam Hall."

"I'll come," replied Anna, beginning to put up her pencils with alacrity. Truth to say, she was just as fond of going out and of taking off her cap, that her curls might fall, as she used to be. She had quite recovered caste in the opinion of Helstonleigh. In fact, when the reaction set in, Helstonleigh had been rather demonstrative in its expression of repentance for having taken so harsh a view of the case. Nevertheless, it had been a real lesson to Anna, and had rendered her more sober and cautious in conduct.

Dobbs was standing at the kitchen door as they went in. "Dobbs," said Jane, in the gladness of her heart, "Mr. Frank is called."

"Called?" responded Dobbs, staring with all her might.

"Yes. He was called yesterday."

"Him called!" repeated Dobbs, evidently doubting the fact. "Then, ma'am you'll excuse me, but I'm not a-going to believe it. It's a deal more likely he's gone off t'other way, than that he's called to grace."

Anna nearly choked with laughter. Jane laughed so that she could not at once speak. "Oh, Dobbs, I don't mean that sort of calling. He is called to the Bar. He has become a barrister."

"Oh—that," said Dobbs ungraciously. "Much good may it do him, ma'am!"

"He wears a wig and gown now, Dobbs," put in Anna. "He says his mother is to tell thee that it makes a guy of him, and so gladden thy heart."

"Ugh!" grunted Dobbs.

"We will make him put them on when he comes down, won't we! Dobbs, if thee'd like his picture in them, he'll send it thee."

"He'd better keep it," retorted Dobbs. "I never yet saw no good in young chaps having their picturs took, Miss Anna. They're vain enough without that. Called! That would have been a new flight for him."

CHAPTER XIX

A GLIMPSE OF A BLISSFUL DREAM

A prettier place than Deoffam Hall could not well be conceived. "For its size," carping people would add. Well, it was not so large as Windsor Castle; but it was no smaller than the bishop's palace at Helstonleigh—if it has been your good fortune to see that renowned edifice. Deoffam Hall was a white, moderate-sized, modern villa, rising in the midst of charming grounds; grassy lawns smooth as velvet, winding rivulets, groves of trees affording shelter on a summer's day. On the terrace before the windows a stately peacock was fond of spreading its plumes, and in the small park—it was only a small one—the deer rubbed their antlers on the fine old trees. The deer and the peacock were the especial pets of Henry Ashley. Deoffam itself was an insignificant village; a few gentlemen's houses and a good many cottages comprised it. It was pleasantly and conveniently situated; within a walk of Helstonleigh for those who liked walking, or within a short drive. But, desirable as it was as a residence, Henry Ashley was rather addicted to grumbling at it. He would often wish himself back in his old home.

One lovely morning in early summer, when they were assembled together discussing plans for the day, he suddenly broke into one of his grumbling humours. "You bought Deoffam for me, sir," he was beginning, "but—"

"I bought it for myself and your mother," interposed Mr. Ashley.

"Of course. But to descend to me afterwards—you know what I mean. I have made up my mind, when that time shall come, to send gratitude to the winds, and sell it. Stuck out here, alone with the peacock, you and the mother gone, I should—I don't like to outrage your feelings by saying what I might do."

"There's Mary," said Mrs. Ashley.

"Mary! I expect she'll have gone into fresh quarters by that time. She has only stopped here so long out of politeness to me."

Mary lifted her eyes, a smile and a glow on her bright face. A lovely picture, she, in her delicate summer muslin dress.

"I tell every one she is devoted to me," went on Henry, in his quaint fashion. "'Very strange that handsome girl, Mary Ashley, does not get married!' cries Helstonleigh. Mary, my dear, I know your vanity is already as great as it can be, so I don't fear to increase it. 'My sister get married!' I say to them. 'Not she; she has resolved to make a noble sacrifice of herself for my sake, and live at home with me, a vestal virgin, and see to the puddings.'"

The smile left Mary's face—the glow remained. "I do wish you would not talk nonsense, Henry! As if Helstonleigh troubled itself to make remarks upon me. It is not so rude as you are."

"Just hark at her!" returned Henry. "Helstonleigh not trouble itself to make remarks! When you know the town was up in arms when you refused Sir Harry Marr, and sent him packing. Such an honour had never fallen to its luck before—that one of its fair citizens, born and bred, should have the chance of becoming a real live My Lady."

Mary was cutting a pencil at the moment, and broke the point off. "Papa," cried she, turning her hot face to his, "can't you make Henry talk sense?—if he must talk at all."

Mrs. Ashley interposed. It was quite true that Mary had had, as Henry phrased it, a chance of becoming a "real live My Lady"; and there lurked in Mrs. Ashley's heart a shadow of grievance, of disappointment, that she should have refused the honour. She spoke rather sharply, taking Henry's part, not Mary's.

"Henry is talking nothing but sense. My opinion is that you behaved quite rudely to Sir Harry. It is an offer you will not have again, Mary. Still," added Mrs. Ashley, subduing her tone a little, "it is no business of Helstonleigh's; neither do I see whence the town could have derived its knowledge."

"As if any news could be stirring, good or bad, that Helstonleigh does not ferret its way to!" returned Henry.

"My belief is that Henry went and told," retorted Mary.

"I! what next?" cried Henry. "As if I should tell of the graceless doings of my sister; it is bad enough to lie under the weighty knowledge one's self."

"And as if I should ever consent to marry Sir Harry Marr!" returned Mary, with a touch of her brother's spirit.

"Mary," said Mr. Ashley, quietly, "you seemed to slip out of that business, and of all questioning over it, as smoothly as an eel. I never came to the bottom of it. What was your objection to Sir Harry?"

"Objection, papa?" she faltered, with a crimsoned face. "I—I did not care for him."

"Oh, that was it, was it?" returned Mr. Ashley.

"Is it always to go on so, my dear?" asked her mother.

Poor Mary was in sad confusion, scarcely knowing whether to burst into anger or into tears. "What do you mean, mamma? How 'go on'?"

"This rejection of every one. You have had three good offers—"

"Not counting the venture of Cyril Dare," put in Henry.

"And you say 'No' to all," concluded Mrs. Ashley. "I fear you must be very fastidious."

"And she's growing into an old maid, and—"

"Be quiet, Henry. Can't you leave me in peace?"

"My dear, it is true," cried Henry, who was in one of his teasing moods. "Of course I have not kept count of your age since you were eighteen—it wouldn't be polite to do so; but my private conviction is that you are four-and-twenty this blessed summer."

"If I were four-and-thirty," answered Mary, "I wouldn't marry Sir Harry Marr. I am not obliged to marry, I suppose, am I?"

"My dear, no one said you were," said Henry, flinging a rose at her, which he took from his button-hole. "But don't you see that this brings round my argument, that you have resolved to make yourself a noble sisterly sacrifice, and stop at home with me? Don't you take to cats yet, though!"

Mary thought she was getting the worst of it, and left the room. Soon afterwards Mrs. Ashley was called out by a servant.

"Did you receive a note from William this morning, sir?" asked Henry.

"Yes," replied Mr. Ashley, taking it from his pocket. "He mentions in it that there is a report in the town that Herbert Dare is dead."

"Herbert Dare! I wonder if it's true?"

"It is to be hoped not. I fear he was not very fit to die. I am going into Helstonleigh, and shall probably hear more."

"Oh! are you going in to-day, sir? Despatch William back, will you?"

"I don't know, Henry. They may be busy at the manufactory. If so, I am sure he will not leave it."

"What a blessing if that manufactory were up in the clouds!" was Henry's rejoinder. "When I want William particularly, it is sure to be—that manufactory!"

"It is well William does not think as you do," remarked Mr. Ashley.

"Well, sir, he must certainly think Samuel Lynn a nonentity, or he would not stick himself so closely to business. You never applied yourself in such a way."

"Yes, I did. But you must please to remember, Master Henry, that the cases are not on a parallel. I was head and chief of all, accountable to none. Had I chosen to take a twelvemonth's holiday, and let the business go, it would have been my own affair exclusively. Whether the business went right, or whether it went wrong, I was accountable to none. William is not in that position."

"I know he is often in the position of not being to be had when he is wanted," was Henry's reply, as he listlessly turned over some books that lay on the table.

"Will you go into town with me?"

"I could not stand it to-day. My hip is giving me twinges."

"Is it? I had better bring back Parry."

"No. I won't have him, unless I find there's actual need. The mother knows what to do with me. I don't suppose it will come to anything; and I have been so much better of late."

"Yes, you have. Although you quarrel with Deoffam, it is the change to it—the air of the place—that has renewed your health, you ungrateful boy!"

Mr. Ashley's eyes were bent lovingly on Henry's as he said it. Henry seized his father's hands, his half-mocking tone exchanged for one of earnestness.

"Not ungrateful, sir—far from it. I know the value of my dear father: that a kinder or a better one son could not possess. I shall grumble on to my life's end. It is my amusement. But the grumbling is from my lips only: not from my fractious spirit, as it was in days gone by."

"I have remarked that: remarked it with deep thankfulness. You have acquired a victory over that fractious spirit."

"For which the chief thanks are due to William Halliburton. Sir, it is so. But for him, most probably I should have gone, a discontented wretch, to the—let me be poetical for once—silent tomb: never seeking out either the light or the love that may be found in this world."

Mr. Ashley glanced at his son. He saw that he was contending with emotion, although he had reassumed his bantering tone.

"Henry, what light—what love?"

"The light and the love that a man may take into his own spirit. He—William—told me, years ago, that I might make even my life a pleasant and a useful one; and measureless was the ridicule I gave him for it. But I have found that he was right. When William came to the house one night, a humble errand-boy, sent by Samuel Lynn with a note—do you remember it, sir?—and offered to help me, dunce that I was, with my Latin exercise—a help I graciously condescended to accept—we little thought what a blessing had entered the dwelling."

"We little thought what a brave, honest, indomitable spirit was enshrined in the humble errand-boy," continued Mr. Ashley.

"He has got on as he deserved. He will be a worthy successor to you, sir: a second Thomas Ashley; a far better one than I should ever have been, had I possessed the rudest health. There's only one thing more for William to gain, and then I expect he will be at rest."

"What's that?"

"Oh, it's no concern of mine, sir. If folks can't manage for themselves, they need not come to me to help them."

Mr. Ashley looked keenly at his son. Henry passed to another topic.

"Do send him here, sir, when you get in; or else drive him back with you."

"I shall see," said Mr. Ashley. "Do you know where your mother went to?"

"After some domestic catastrophe, I expect. Martha came to the door, with a face as green as the peacock's tail, and beckoned her out. The best dinner-service come to grief, perhaps."

Mr. Ashley rang, and ordered the pony-carriage to be got ready: one bought chiefly for Henry, that he might drive into town. Before he started, he came across Mary, who stood at one of the corridor windows upstairs, and had evidently been crying.

"What is your grief, Mary?"

She turned to the sheltering arm open to her, and tried to choke the tears down, which were again rising. "I wish you and mamma would not keep so angry at my refusing Sir Harry Marr."

"Who told you I was angry, Mary?"

"Oh, papa, I fancied so this morning. Mamma is angry about it, and it pains me. It is as though you wanted me gone."

"My dear child! Gone! For our comfort I should wish you might never go, Mary. But for your own, it may be different."

"I do not wish to go," she sobbed. "I want to stay at home always. It was not my fault, papa, if I could not like Sir Harry."

"You should never, with my consent, marry any one you did not like, Mary; not if it were the greatest match in the three kingdoms. Why this distress, my dear? Mamma's vexation will blow over. She hoped—as Henry tells us—to see you converted into a 'real live My Lady.' 'My daughter, Lady Marr!' It will blow over, child."

Mary cried in silence. "And you will not let me be driven away, papa? You will keep me at home always?"

Mr. Ashley shook his head. "Always is a long day, Mary. Some one may be coming, less distasteful than Sir Harry Marr, who will induce you to leave it."

"No, never!" cried she, somewhat more vehemently than the case seemed to warrant. "Should any one be asking you for me, you can tell them 'No,' at once; do not trouble to bring the news to me."

"Any one, Mary?"

"Yes, papa, no matter who. Do not drive me away from you."

He stooped and kissed her. She stood at the window still, in a dreamy attitude, and watched the carriage drive off with Mr. Ashley. Presently Henry passed.

"Has the master gone, do you know, Mary?"

"Five minutes ago."

"I hope and trust he'll send back William."

It was striking half-past two when Mr. Ashley entered the manufactory. Samuel Lynn was in his own room, sorting gloves; William was in the counting house, seated at his desk. His, now; formerly Mr. Ashley's; the very desk from which the cheque had disappeared; but William took a more active part in the general management than Mr. Ashley had ever done. He rose, shook hands with the master, and placed a chair for him. The "master" still he was called; indeed, he actually was so; William, "Mr. Halliburton."

A short time given to business details, and then Mr. Ashley referred to the report of Herbert Dare's death. Poor Herbert Dare had never returned from abroad, and it was to be feared he had been getting lower and lower in the scale of society. Under happier auspices, and with different training, Herbert might have made a happier and a better man. Helstonleigh did not know how he lived abroad, or why he stayed there. Possibly the free and easy continental life had become necessary to him. Homburg, Baden-Baden, Wiesbaden, wherever there were gaming-tables, there might be found Herbert Dare. That he must find a living at them in some way seemed pretty evident. It was a great pity.

"How did you hear that he was dead?" inquired Mr. Ashley.

"From Richard Winthorne," replied William. "I met him yesterday evening in Guild Street, and he told me a report had come over that Herbert Dare had died of fever."

As William spoke, a gentleman entered the room, and interrupted them; a Captain Chambers. "Have you heard that Herbert Dare's dead?" was his first greeting.

"Is it certain?" asked Mr. Ashley.

"I don't know. Report says it is certain; but report is not always to be believed. How that family has gone down!" continued Captain Chambers. "Anthony first; now Herbert; and Cyril will be next. He will go out of the world in some discreditable way. A wretched scamp! Shocking habits! Old Dare, too, unless I am mistaken, is on his last legs."

"Is he ill?" inquired Mr. Ashley.

"No; no worse than usual; but I never saw a man so broken. I alluded to the legs of prosperity. Talk about reports, though," and Captain Chambers suddenly wheeled round on William, "there's one going the round of the town to-day about you."

"What's that?" asked William. "Not that I am dead, I suppose, or on my last legs?"

"Something better. That you are going to marry Sophy Glenn."

William looked all amazement, an amused smile stealing over his lips. "Well, I never!" uttered he, using a phrase just then in vogue in Helstonleigh. "What has put that into the town's head?"

"You should best know that," said Captain Chambers. "Did you not, for one thing, beau Miss Sophy to a concert last night? Come, Master William! guilty or not guilty?"

"Guilty of the beauing," answered William. "I called on the Glenns yesterday evening, and found them starting for the concert; so I accompanied them. I did give my arm to Sophy."

"And whispered the sweet words, 'Will you be my charming wife?'"

"No, that I did not," said William, laughing. "And I dare say I shall never whisper them to any woman yet born: if it will give Helstonleigh satisfaction to know so much."

"You might go farther and fare worse, than in taking Sophy Glenn, I can tell you that, Master William," returned Captain Chambers. "Remember, she is the lucky one of three sisters, and had the benignant godmother. Sophy Glenn counts five thousand pounds to her fortune."

When Captain Chambers took his departure, Mr. Ashley looked at William. "I have heard Henry joke you about the Glenn girls—nice little girls they are too! Is there anything in it, William?"

"Sir! How can you ask such a thing?"

"I think, with Chambers, that a man might do worse than marry Sophy Glenn."

"So do I, sir. But I shall not be the man."

"Well, I think it is time you contemplated something of the sort. You will soon be thirty years of age."

"Yes, sir, but I do not intend to marry."

"Why not?" asked Mr. Ashley.

"Because—I fear my wishes would lead me to soar too high. That is, I—I—mean—" He stopped; and seemed to be falling into inextricable confusion. A notable thing for the self-possessed William Halliburton.

"Do you mean that you have an attachment in some quarter?" resumed Mr. Ashley.

William's face turned fiery red. "I cannot deny it, sir," he answered, after considerable hesitation.

"And that she is above your reach?"

"Yes."

"In what manner? In position?—or by any insurmountable obstacle? I suppose she is not some one else's wife?"

William smiled. "Oh, no. In position."

"Shall I give you my opinion, William, without knowing the case in detail?"

William was standing at one corner of the mantel-piece, his arm leaning on its narrow shelf. He did not lift his eyes. "Yes, sir, if you please."

"Then I think there is scarcely any marriageable girl in the county, to whom you might not aspire, and in time win."

"Oh, Mr. Ashley!"

"Is it the daughter of the lord-lieutenant?"

William laughed.

"Is it the bishop's daughter?"

William shook his head. "She seems to be quite as far removed from me."

"Come, I must know. Who is it?"

"It is impossible that I can tell you, sir."

"I must know. I don't think I have ever asked you in vain, since the time when, a boy, you confessed your thoughts about the found shilling. Secrets from me! I will know, William!"

William did not answer. The upper part of his face was concealed by his hand; but Mr. Ashley marked the sweet smile that played around his mouth.

"Come, I will help you. Is it the charming Dobbs?"

Amused, he took his hand from his face. "Well, sir—no."

"It cannot be Charlotte East; because she is married."

William seemed as impervious as ever. The master suddenly laid his hand upon his shoulder, and confronted him face to face.

"Is it Mary Ashley?"

The burning flush of scarlet that dyed his face, even to the very roots of his hair, told Mr. Ashley the truth, far more effectually than words could have done. There ensued a pause. Mr. Ashley was the first to break it.

"How long have you loved her?"

"For years. That has been the wild dream of my aspirations: one that I knew would never be realized," he answered, suffering his eyes to meet for a moment Mr. Ashley's.

"Have you spoken to her of it?"

"Never."

"Or led her to believe you loved her?"

"No, sir. Unless my looks and tones may have betrayed me. I fear they have; but it was not intentionally done."

"Honest in this, as in all else," thought Mr. Ashley. "What am I to say to you?" he asked aloud.

"I do not know," sighed William. "I expect, of course, sir, that you will forbid me Deoffam Hall: but I can still meet Henry at the house in town. I hope you will forgive me!" he added in an impassioned tone. "I could not help loving her. Before I knew what my new feelings meant, love had come. Such love! Had I been in a position to marry her, I would have made her life one dream of happiness! When I awoke to it all—"

"What awoke you?" was the interruption.

"I think it was Cyril Dare's asking for her. I debated with myself then, whether I ought to give up going to your house; but I came to the conclusion that, so long as I was able to hide my feelings from her, I need not banish myself. My judgment was wrong, I know; but the temptation to see her occasionally was great, and I did not resist it."

"And so you continued to go, feeding the flame?"

"Yes. Feeding it passionately and hopelessly; never forgetting that the pain of separation must come!"

"Did you hear of Sir Harry Marr's offer?"

"Yes, I heard of it."

William swept his hand across his face as he spoke. It wore a wrung expression. Mr. Ashley changed his tone.

"William, I cannot decide this matter, one way or the other. You must ask Mary to do that!"

"Sir!"

"If Mary chooses to favour you more than she does other suitors, I will not forbid her doing it. Only this very day she begged me, with tears, to keep all such troublesome customers away from her; to refuse them of my own accord. But it strikes me that you may as well have an answer from herself!"

William, his whole soul in his eyes, was gazing at Mr. Ashley. He could not tell whether he might believe what he heard; whether he was awake or dreaming.

"Did I deliver you a message from Henry?"

"No, sir," was the abstracted response.

"He wants you to go over to him. I said I would send you if you were not busy. He is not very well to-day."

"But—Mr. Ashley—did you mean what you said?"

"Should I have said it had I not meant it?" was the quiet answer. "Have you a difficulty in believing it?"

The ingenuous light rose to William's eyes, as he raised them to his master's. "I have no money," he whispered. "I cannot settle a farthing upon her."

"You have something better than money, William—worth. And I can make settlements. Go and hear what Mary says. You will catch the half-past three o'clock coach, if you make haste."

William went out, believing still that he must be in a trance. His deeply buried dream of the long past years: was it about, indeed, to become reality?

But in the midst of it he could not help casting a thought to a less pleasing subject—the Dares. Herbert was young to die; he was, no doubt, unprepared to die; and William sincerely hoped that the report would prove untrue. The Dares were going down sadly in the social scale; Cyril especially. He was just what Captain Chambers had called him—a scamp. After leaving Mr. Ashley's, he had entered his father's office; as a temporary thing, it was said; but he had never left it for anything else. A great deal of his time was passed in public-houses. George, whose commission never came, had gone out, some two or three years ago, to Sydney. His sister Julia and her husband had settled there, and they had found an opening for George. William walked on, thinking of the Dares' position and of his own.

CHAPTER XX

WAYS AND MEANS

When William reached Deoffam Hall, he found Henry Ashley alone, lying in the drawing-room, the sofa near the open window.

"That's good!" cried he. "Good of the master for sending you, and of you for coming."

"You don't look well to-day," observed William. "Your brow has the old lines of pain in it."

"Thanks to my hip, which is giving me threatening twinges. What's this report about Dare? Is it confirmed?"

"Not absolutely. It was Winthorne told me. Captain Chambers came into the manufactory, and spoke of it this afternoon."

"I dare say it's true," said Henry. "I wonder if Anna Lynn will put on weeds for him?" he sarcastically added.

"Quakers don't wear weeds."

"Teach your grandmother," returned Henry, lapsing into one of those free, popular phrases he indulged in, and was indulged in. "How you stare at me! Do you think I am not cured? Ay; years ago."

"You'd have no objection to see Anna marry, I suppose?"

"She's welcome to marry, for me. You may go and propose to her yourself, if you like. I'll be groomsman at the wedding."

"Would the alliance give you pleasure?"

Henry laughed. "You'd deserve hanging in chains, if you did enter upon it; that's all."

"I have had one wife assigned to me to-day," remarked William.

"Whom may she be?"

"Sophy Glenn."

"Sophy Glenn?"

"Sophy Glenn. Chambers gravely assured me that Helstonleigh had settled the match. He, Chambers, considers that I may go farther and fare worse. Mr. Ashley said the same."

"But what do you say?" cried Henry, rising up on his sofa, and speaking quite sharply.

"I? Oh, I shall consider of it."

At that moment Mary Ashley appeared on the terrace outside; a small basket and a pair of scissors in her hand. Henry called to her. "Are you going to cut more flowers?"

"Yes. Mamma has sent the others away. She said they were fading." Seeing William there, she nodded to him, her colour rising.

"I say, Mary—he has come here to bring some news," went on Henry. "What do you suppose it is?"

"Mamma has told me. About Herbert Dare."

"Not that. He is going to make himself into a respectable man, and marry Sophy Glenn. He came here to announce it. Don't cut too much of that syringa; its sweetness is overpowering in a room."

Mary walked away. William felt excessively annoyed. "You are more dangerous than a child," he exclaimed. "What made you say that?"

And Henry, like a true child, fell back, laughing aloud. "I say, though, comrade, where are you off to?" he called after William, who was leaving the room.

"To cut the flowers for your sister, of course."

But when William reached Mary Ashley, she had apparently forgotten her errand. Standing in a dark spot against the trunk of the acacia tree, her face was white and still, and the basket lay on the ground. She picked it up, and would have hastened away, but William caught her hand and placed it within his arm, little less agitated than she was.

"Not to tell him that news," he whispered. "I did indeed come here, hoping to solicit one to be my wife; but it was not Sophy Glenn. Mary, you cannot mistake what my feelings have long been."

"But—papa?" she gasped, unable to control her emotion.

He looked at her; he made her look at him. What strange, happy light was that in his earnest eyes, causing her heart to bound? "Mr. Ashley sent me to you," he softly whispered.

Henry lay and waited till he was tired. No William; no Mary; no flowers; no anything. Had they both gone to sleep? He arose; and, taking his stick, limped away to see after them. But he searched the flower-garden in vain.

In the sheltered shrubbery, pacing it leisurely, as closely together as they could well be linked, were they; a great deal too much occupied with each other to pay attention to anything else. The basket lay on the ground, empty of all, except the scissors.

"Well, you two are a nice lot for a summer's day!" began Henry, after his old fashion, and using his own astonished eyes. "What of the flowers?"

Mary would have flown, but William held her tightly, and led her up to her brother. He strove to speak jestingly; but his voice betrayed his emotion.

"Henry, shall it be your sister, or Sophy Glenn?"

"So! you have been settling it for yourselves, have you! I would not be in your shoes, Miss Ashley, when the parental thunderbolts shall descend. Was this what you flung Sir Harry over for? There never was any accounting for taste in this world, and there never will be. I ask you where the flowers are, and I should like an answer."

"I will cut them now," said William. "Will you come?" he asked, holding out his arm to Henry.

"No," replied Henry, sitting down on the shrubbery bench, "I must digest this shock first. You two will be enough to cut them, I dare say."

They walked away towards the flower-garden. But ere they had gone many steps he called out; and they turned.

"Mary! before you tie yourself up irrevocably, I hope you will reflect upon the ignominy of his being nothing on earth but a manufacturer. A pretty come down, that, for the Lady Marr who might have been!"

He was in one of his most ironical moods; a sure sign that his inward state was that of glowing satisfaction. This had been his hope for years—his plan, it may be said; but he had kept himself silent and neutral. As he sat there ruminating, he heard the distant sound of the pony carriage; and, taking a short cut, met it in the park. Mr. Ashley handed the reins to his groom, got out, and gave his arm to Henry.

"How are you by this time?"

"Better, sir. Nothing much to brag of."

"I thought William would have been with you. Is he not come?"

"Yes, he is come. But I am second with him to-day. Miss Mary's first."

"Oh indeed!" returned Mr. Ashley.

"They are gone off somewhere, under the pretext of cutting flowers. I don't think the flowers were quite the object, though."

He stole a glance at his father as he spoke. But he gathered nothing. And he dashed at once into the subject he had at heart.

"Father, you will not stand in their light! It will be a crushing blow to both, if you do. Let him have her! There's not a man in the world half as worthy."

But still Mr. Ashley made no rejoinder. Henry scarcely gave him time to make one.

"I have seen it a long time. I have seen how Halliburton kept down his feelings, not being sure of the ground with you. I fear that to-day they must have overmastered him; for he has certainly spoken out. Dear father, don't make two of the best spirits in the world miserable, by withholding your consent!"

"Henry," said Mr. Ashley, turning to him with a smile, "do you fancy William Halliburton is one to have spoken out without my consent?"

Henry's thin cheek flushed. "Did you give it him? Have you already given it him?"

"I gave it him to-day. I drew from him the fact of his attachment to Mary: not telling him in so many words that he should have her, but leaving it for her to decide."

"Then it will be: for I have seen where Miss Mary's love has been. How immeasurably you have relieved me!" continued Henry. "The last half-hour I have been seeing nothing but perplexity and cross-grained guardians."

"Have you?" returned Mr. Ashley. "You should have brought a little common sense to bear upon the subject, Henry."

"But my fear was, sir, that you would not bring the common sense to bear," freely spoke Henry.

"You do not quite understand me. Had I entertained an insuperable objection to Mary's becoming his wife, do you suppose I should have been so wanting in prudence and forethought as to have allowed opportunity for an attachment to ripen? I have long believed that there was no man within the circle of my acquaintance, or without it, so deserving of Mary, except in fortune: therefore I suffered him to come here, with my eyes open as to what might be the result. A very probable result, it has appeared to me. I would forgive any girl who fell in love with William Halliburton."

"And what about ways and means?"

"William's share shall be increased, and Mary will not go to him dowerless. They must live in our house in Helstonleigh; and when we want to go there we must be their guests."

"It will be the working-out of my visions," said Henry in low deep tones. "I have seen them in it in fancy; in that very house; and myself with them, my home when I please. I think you have been planning for me, as much as for them."

"Not exactly, Henry. I have not planned. I have only let things take their course. It will be happier for you, my boy, than if she had gone from us to be Lady Marr."

"Oh! if ever I felt inclined to smother a man, it was that Marr. I never, you know, brought myself to be decently civil to him. There's no answering for the vanity of maidens, and I thought it just possible he might put William's nose out of joint. What will the mother say?"

"The mother will be divided," said Mr. Ashley, a smile crossing his face. "She likes William; but she likes a title. We must allow her a day or two to get over it. I will go and give her the tidings now, if Mary has not done so."

"Mary is with her lovier," returned Henry. "She can't have dragged herself away from him yet."

Mary, however, was not with her "lovier." As Mr. Ashley crossed the hall, he met her. She stopped in hesitation, and coloured vividly.

"Well, Mary, I soon sent you a candidate; though it was in defiance of your express orders. Did I do right?"

Mary burst into tears, and Mr. Ashley drew her face to him. "May God bless your future and his, my child!"

"I am afraid to tell mamma," she sobbed. "I think she will be angry. I could not help liking him."

"Why, that is the very excuse he made to me! Neither can I help liking him, Mary. I will tell mamma."

Mrs. Ashley received the tidings not altogether with equanimity. As Mr. Ashley had surmised, she was divided between conflicting opinions. She liked and admired William; but she equally liked and admired a title and fortune.

"Such a position to relinquish—the union with Sir Harry!"

"Had she married Sir Harry we should have lost her," said Mr. Ashley.

"Lost her!"

"To be sure we should. She would have gone to her new home, twelve miles on the other side of Helstonleigh, amidst her new connections, and have been lost to us, excepting for a formal visit now and then. As it is, we shall keep her; at her old home."

"Yes, there's a great deal to be said on both sides," acknowledged Mrs. Ashley. "What does Henry say?"

"That he thinks I have been planning to secure his happiness. Had Mary married away, we—when we quit this scene—must have left him to his lonely self: now, we shall leave him to them. Things are wisely ordered," impressively added Mr. Ashley: "in this, as in all else. Margaret, let us accept them, and be grateful."

Mrs. Ashley went to seek William. "You will be a loving husband to her," she said with agitation. "You will take care of her and cherish her?"

"With the best endeavours of my whole life," he fervently answered, as he took Mrs. Ashley's hands in his.

It was a happy group that evening. Henry lay on his sofa in complacent ease, Mary drawn down beside him, and William leaning over the back of it, while Mr. and Mrs. Ashley sat at a distance, partially out of hearing.

"Have you heard what the master says?" asked Henry. "He thinks you have been getting up your bargain out of complaisance to me. You are aware, I hope, Mr. William, that whoever takes Mary must take me?"

"I am perfectly willing."

"It is well you are! And—do you know where you are to live?"

William shook his head. "You can understand how all these future considerations have weighed me down," he said, glancing at Mary.

"You are to live at the house in Helstonleigh. It's to be converted into yours by some patent process. The master had an eye to this, I know, when he declined to take out any of the furniture, upon our removal here. The house is to be yours, and the run of it is to be mine; and I shall grumble away to my heart's content at you both. What do you answer to that, Mr. William? I don't ask her; she's nobody."

"I can only answer that the more you run into it, the better pleased we shall be. And we can stand any extent of grumbling."

"I am glad you can. You ought to by this time, for you have been pretty well seasoned to it. So, in the Helstonleigh house, remember, my old rooms are mine; and I intend to be the plague of your lives. After a time—may it be a long time!—I suppose it will be 'Mr. Halliburton of Deoffam Hall.'"

"What nonsense you talk, Henry!"

"Nonsense? I shall make it over to you. Catch me sticking myself out here in solitary state to the admiration of the peacock! What's the matter with you now, you two! Oh, well, if you turn up your noses at Deoffam, it shall never be yours. I'll leave it to the eldest chickabiddy. And mark you, please! I shall have him named 'Ashley,' and stand godfather to him; and, he'll be mine, and not yours. I shall do just as I like with the whole lot, if they count a score, and spoil them as much as I choose."

"What is the matter there?" exclaimed Mrs. Ashley, perceiving a commotion on the sofa.

Mary succeeded in freeing herself, and went away with a crimsoned face. "Mamma, I think Henry must be going out of his mind! He is talking so absurdly."

"Absurdly! Was what I said absurd, William?"

William laughed. "It was premature, at any rate."

Henry stretched up his hands and laid hold of William's. "It is true what Mary says—that I must be going out of my mind. So I am: with joy."

But the report of Herbert Dare's death proved to be a false one.

CHAPTER XXI

THE DREAM REALIZED

The approaching marriage of William Halliburton gave rise to a dispute. A dispute of love, though, not bitterness. Frank and Gar contended which should have their mother. William no longer wanted her; he was going to a home of his own. Frank wished to take larger chambers where she would find sufficient accommodation; he urged a hundred reasons; his grievances with his laundress, and his buttonless shirts. Gar, who was in priest's orders now, had remained in that same first curacy, at a hundred a year and the parsonage house to live in. He said he had been wanting his mother all along, and could not do without her.

Jane inclined to Gar. She said she had an idea that old ladies—how they would have rebelled at hearing her call herself old!—were out of place in a young barrister's chambers; and she had a further idea that chambers were comfortless quarters to live in. The question was to be decided when they met at William's wedding. Frank was getting on well; better than the ordinary run of aspirants; he had come through Helstonleigh two or three times on circuit, and had picked up odds and ends of briefs there.

Meanwhile William took possession of Mr. Ashley's old house, and the wedding day approached. Besides her boys, Jane had another visitor for the time; her brother Francis, who came down to marry them. Perhaps because the Vicar of Deoffam had recently died. He might have come all the same, had that gouty old gentleman been still alive.

All clear and cloudless rose the September sun on Deoffam; never a brighter sun shone on a wedding. It was a quiet wedding: only a few guests were invited to it. Mary, in her white lace robes and floating veil—flushed, timid, lovely—stood with her bridesmaids; not more lovely than one of those bridesmaids, for one was Anna Lynn.

Anna Lynn! Yes; Anna Lynn. To the lasting scandal of Patience, Anna stood in the open church, dressed in bridesmaid's attire. Mary, who had not been permitted the same intimacy with Anna since that marked and unhappy time, but who had loved her all along, had been allowed by Mrs. Ashley to choose her for one of her bridesmaids. The invitation was proffered, and Samuel Lynn did not see reason to decline it. Patience was indignantly rebellious; Anna, wild with delight. Look at her, as she stands there! flowing robes of white around her, not made after the primitive fashion of her robes, but in the fashion of the day. Her falling hair shades her carmine cheeks, and her blue eyes seek modestly the ground. A fair picture; and a dangerous one to Henry Ashley, had those old feelings of his remained in the ascendant. But he was cured; as he told William: and he told it in truth.

A short time, and Anna would want bridesmaids on her own account; though that may be speaking metaphorically of a Quakeress. Anna's pretty face had pierced the heart of one of their male body; and he had asked for Anna in marriage. A very desirable male was he, in a social point of view; and female Helstonleigh turned up its nose in envy at Anna's fortune. He was considerably older than Anna; a fine-looking man and a wealthy one, engaged in wholesale business. His name was Gurney; his residence, outside the city, was a handsome one, replete with every comfort; and he drove a carriage-and-pair. He had been for some time a visitor at Samuel Lynn's, and Anna had learned to like him. That his object in visiting there could only be Anna, every one had been sure of, his position being so superior to Samuel Lynn's. Every one but Anna. Somehow, since that past escapade, Anna had not cast a thought to marrying, or to the probability of anyone asking her; and she did not suspect his intentions. If she had suspected them, she might have set herself against him; for there was a little spice of opposition in her, which she loved to indulge. However, before that suspicion came to her she had grown to care for him too much to play the coquette. Strange to say, there was something in his figure and in the outline of his face, which reminded people of Herbert Dare; but his features and their expression were quite different.

It was a most excellent match for Anna; there was no doubt of that; but it did not afford complete satisfaction to Patience. Patience felt a foreboding that he would be a good deal more indulgent to Anna than she considered was wholesomely good for her: Patience had a misgiving that Anna would be putting off her caps as she chose, then, and would not be reprimanded for it. Not unlikely; could that future bridegroom, Charles Gurney, catch sight of Anna as she stands now! for a more charming picture never was seen.

William, quiet and self-possessed, received Mary from the hands of her father, who gave her away. The Reverend Francis Tait read the service, and Gar, in his white canonicals, stood with him, after the new fashion of the day. Jane's tears dropped on her pearl-grey damask dress; Frank made himself very busy amongst the bridesmaids; and Henry Ashley was in his most mocking mood. Thus they were made man and wife; and Mr. Tait's voice rose high and echoed down the aisles of the little old church at Deoffam, as he spoke the solemn injunction—"THOSE WHOM GOD HATH JOINED TOGETHER, LET NO MAN PUT ASUNDER."

Helstonleigh's streets were lined that day, and Helstonleigh's windows were alive with heads. It was known that the bride and bridegroom would pass through the town, on the first stage of their bridal tour, whose ultimate destination was to be the Continent. The whole crowd of the Ashley workpeople had gathered outside the manufactory, neglecting their afternoon's work; a neglect which Samuel Lynn not only winked at, but participated in, for he stood with them. As the carriage, which was Mr. Ashley's, came in sight, its four horses urged by the postillions to a sharp trot, one deafening cheer arose from the men. William laughed and nodded to them; but they did not get half a good view of the master's daughter beside him: nothing but a glimpse of a flushed cheek, and a piece of a white veil.

Slouching at the corner of a street, in a seedy coat, his eyes bloodshot, was Cyril Dare. Never did one look more of a mauvais sujet than he, as he watched the chariot pass. The place now occupied by William might have been his, had he so willed it and worked for it. Not, perhaps, that of Mary's husband; he could not be sure of that, but as Mr. Ashley's partner. A bitter cloud of disappointment, of repentance, crossed his face as he looked at them. They both saw him standing there. Did Mary think what a promising husband he would have made her? Cyril flung a word after them; and it was not a blessing.

Dobbs had also flung something after them, and in point of time and precedence this ought to have been mentioned first. Patience, watching from her window, curious as every one else, had seen Dobbs come out with something under her apron, and take up her station at the gate, where she waited patiently for just an hour and a quarter. As the carriage had come into view, Dobbs sheltered herself behind the shrubs, nothing to be seen of her above them, but her cap and eyes. The moment the carriage was past, out flew Dobbs to the middle of the road. Bringing forth from their hiding-place a pair of shoes considerably the worse for wear, the one possessing no sole, and the other no upper leather, Dobbs dashed them with force after the chariot, very much discomposing the manservant in the rear, whose head they struck.

"Nothing like old shoes to bring 'em luck," grunted Dobbs to Patience, as she retired indoors. "I never knew good come of a wedding that didn't get 'em."

"I wish them luck; the luck of a safe arrival home from those unpleasant foreign parts," emphatically remarked Patience, who had found her residence amongst the French nothing less than a species of terrestrial purgatory.

CHAPTER XXII

THE BISHOP'S LETTER

A day or two after the wedding, a letter was delivered at Mrs. Halliburton's residence, addressed to Gar. Its seal, a mitre, prepared Gar to find that it came from the Bishop of Helstonleigh. Its contents proved to be a mandate, commanding his attendance the following morning at the palace at nine o'clock. Gar turned nervous. Had he fallen under his bishop's displeasure, and was about to be reprimanded? Mr.

Tait had gone back to London; Gar was to leave on the following day, Saturday; Frank meant to stay on for a week or two. It was his vacation.

"That's Gar all over!" cried Frank, who had perched himself on a side table. "Gar is sure to look to the dark side of things, instead of the bright. If the Lord Chancellor sent for me, I should set it down that my fortune was about to be made. His lordship's going to present you with a living, Gar."

"That's good!" retorted Gar. "What interest have I with the bishop?"

"He has known you long enough."

"As he has many others. If the bishop interested himself for all the clergymen who have been educated at Helstonleigh college school, he would have enough upon his hands. I expect it is to find fault with me for some unconscious offence."

"Go it, Gar! You'll get no sleep to-night."

"Frank, I must say the note appears a peremptory one," remarked Jane.

"Middling for that. It's short, if not sweet."

Whether Gar had any sleep or not that night, he did not say; but he started to keep the appointment punctually. His mother and Frank remained together, and Jane fell into a bit of quiet talk over the breakfast table.

"Frank," said she, "I am often uneasy about you."

"About me!" cried Frank in considerable wonderment.

"If you were to go wrong! I know what the temptations of a London life must be. Especially to a young man who has, so to say, no home."

"I steer clear of them. Mother darling, I am telling you the truth," he added earnestly. "Do you think we could ever fall away from such training as yours? No. Look at what William is; look at Gar; and for myself, though I don't like to boast, I assure you, the Anti-evil-doing Society—if you have ever heard of that respected body—might hoist me on a pedestal at Exeter Hall as their choicest model. You don't like my joking! Believe me, then, in all seriousness, that your sons will never fail you. We did not battle on in our duty as boys, to forget it as men. You taught us the bravest lesson that a mother can teach, or a child learn, when you contrived to impress upon us the truth that God is our witness always, ever present."

Jane's eyes filled with tears: not of grief. She knew that Frank was speaking from his heart.

"And you are getting on well?"

"What with stray briefs that come to me, and my literary work, and the fellowship, I make six or seven hundred a year already."

"I hope you are not spending it all?"

"That I am not. I put by all I can. It is true that I don't live upon bread and potatoes six days in the week, as you know we have done; but I take care that my expenses are moderate. It is keeping hare-brained follies at arm's-length that enables me to save."

"And now, Frank, for another question. What made you send me that hundred-pound note?"

"I shall send you another soon," was all Frank's answer. "The idea of my gaining a superfluity of money, and sending none to my darling mother!"

"But indeed I don't know what to do with it, Frank. I do not require it."

"Then put it by to look at. As long as I have brains to work with, I shall think of my mother. Have you forgotten how she worked for us? I wish you would come and live with me?"

Jane entered into all her arguments for deeming that she should be better with Gar. Not the least of them was, that she should still be near Helstonleigh. Of all her sons, Jane, perhaps unconsciously to herself, most loved her eldest: and to go far away from him would have been another trouble.

By-and-by, they saw Gar coming back. And he did not look as if he had been receiving a reprimand: quite the contrary. He came in almost as impulsively as he used to do in his schoolboy days.

"Frank, you were right! The bishop is going to give me a living. Mother, it is true."

"Of course," said Frank. "I always am right."

"The bishop did not keep me waiting a minute, although I was there before my time. He was very kind, and—"

"But about the living?" cried impatient Frank.

"I am telling you, Frank. The bishop said he had watched us grow up—meaning you, as well—and he felt pleased to tell me that he had never seen anything but good in either of us. But I need not repeat all that. He went on to ask me whether I should be prepared to do my duty zealously in a living, were one given to me. I answered that I hoped I should—and the long and the short of it is, that I am going to be appointed to one."

"Long live the bishop!" cried Frank. "Where's the living situated! In the moon?"

"Ah, where indeed? Guess what living it is, mother."

"Gar, dear, how can I?" asked Jane. "Is it a minor canonry?"

They both laughed. It recalled Jane to her absence of mind. The bishop had nothing to do with bestowing the minor canonries. Neither could a minor canonry be called a "living."

"Mother, it is Deoffam."

"Deoffam! Oh, Gar!"

"Yes, it is Deoffam. You will not have to go far away from Helstonleigh, now."

"I'll lay my court wig that Mr. Ashley has had his finger in the pie!" cried quick Frank.

But, in point of fact, the gift had emanated from the prelate himself. And a very good gift it was: four hundred a year, and the prettiest parsonage house within ten miles. The brilliant scholarship of the Halliburtons, attained by their own unflagging industry, the high character they had always borne, had not been lost upon the Bishop of Helstonleigh. Gar's conduct as a clergyman had been exemplary; Gar's preaching was of no mean order, and the bishop deemed that such a one as Gar ought not to be overlooked. The day has gone by for a bishop to know nothing of the younger clergy of his diocese, and he of Helstonleigh had Gar Halliburton down in his preferment book. It is just possible that the announcement of his name in the local papers, as having helped to marry his brother at Deoffam, may have put that particular living into the bishop's head. Certain it was, that, a few hours after the bishop read it, he ordered his carriage, and went to pay a visit at Deoffam Hall. During his stay, he took Mr. Ashley's arm, and drew him out on to the terrace, very much as though he wished to take a nearer view of the peacock.

"I have been thinking, Mr. Ashley, of bestowing the living of Deoffam upon Edgar Halliburton. What should you say to it?"

"That I should almost feel it as a personal favour paid to myself," was the reply of Mr. Ashley.

"Then it is done," said the bishop. "He is young, but I know a great many older men who are less deserving than he."

"Your lordship may rely upon it that there are few men, young or old, who are so intrinsically deserving as the Halliburtons."

"I know it," said the bishop. "They interested me as lads, and I have watched them ever since."

And that is how Gar became Vicar of Deoffam.

"You will be trying for a minor canonry now, Gar, I suppose, living so near to it?" observed Jane.

"Mrs. Halliburton, will you be so kind as not to put unsuitable notions into his head?" interrupted Frank. "The Reverend Gar must look out for a canonry, not a minor. And he won't stop there. When I am on the woolsack, in my place in the Lords, Gar may be opposite to me, a spiritual peer."

Jane laughed, as did Frank. Who knew, though? It all lay in the future.

CHAPTER XXIII

A DYING CONFESSION

Meanwhile William Halliburton and his wife had crossed the Channel. Amongst other letters, written home to convey news of them, was the following. It was written by Mary to Mrs. Ashley, after they had been abroad a week or two.

"Hôtel du Chapeau Rouge, Dunkerque,

"September 24th.

"MY EVER DEAR MAMMA,

"You have heard from William how it was that we altered our intended route. I thought the sea-side so delightful that I was unwilling to leave it, even for Paris, and we determined to remain on the coast, especially as I shall have other opportunities of seeing Paris with William. Boulogne was crowded and noisy, so we left it for less frequented towns, staying a day or two in each place. We went to Calais and to Gravelines; also to Bourbourg, and to Cassel—the two latter not on the coast. The view from Cassel— which you must not confound with Cassel in Germany—is magnificent. We met some English people on the summit of the hill, and they told us the English called it the Malvern of France. I am not sure which affords the finer view, Cassel or Malvern. They say that eighty towns or villages may be counted from it; but I cannot say that we made out anything like so many. We can see the sea in the far distance—as we can, on a clear day, catch a glimpse from Malvern of the Bristol Channel. The view from some of the windows of the Hôtel de Sauvage was so beautiful that I was never tired of looking at it. William says he shall show me better views when he takes me to Lyons and Annonay, but I scarcely think it possible. At a short distance rises a monastery of the order of La Trappe, where the monks never speak, except the 'Memento mori' when they meet each other. Some of the customs of the hotel were primitive; they gave us tablespoons in our coffee-cups for breakfast.

"From Cassel we came to Dunkerque, and are staying at the Chapeau Rouge, the only large hotel in the place. The other large hotel was made into a convent some time back; both are in the Rue des Capucins. It is a fine and very clean old fortified town, with a statue of Jean Bart in the middle of the Place. Place Jean Bart, it is called; and the market is held in it on Wednesdays and Saturdays, as it is at Helstonleigh. Such a crowded scene on the Saturday! and the women's snow-white caps quite shine in the sun. I cannot tell you how much I like to look at these old Flemish towns! By moonlight, they look exactly like the towns you are familiar with in old pictures. There is a large basin here, and a long harbour and pier. One English lady, whom we met at the table d'hôte, said she had never been to the end of the pier yet, and she had lived in Dunkerque four years. It was too far for a walk, she said. The country round is flat and poor, and the lower classes mostly speak Flemish.

"On Monday we went by barge to a place called Bergues, four miles off. It was market day there, and the barge was crowded with passengers from Dunkerque. A nice old town, with a fine church. They charged us only five sous for our passage. But I must leave all these descriptions until I return home, and come to what I have chiefly to tell you.

"There is a piece of enclosed ground here, called the Pare. On the previous Saturday, which was the day we first arrived here, I and William were walking through it, and sat down on one of the benches facing the old tower. I was rather tired, having been to the end of the pier—for its length did not alarm us. Some one was seated at the other end of the bench, but we did not take particular notice of her. Suddenly she turned to me, and spoke: 'Have I not the honour of seeing Miss Ashley?' Mamma, you may imagine my surprise. It was that Italian governess of the Dares, Mademoiselle Varsini, as they used to call her. William interposed: I don't think he liked her speaking to me. I suppose he thought of that story about her, which came over from Germany. He rose and took me on his arm to move away. 'Formerly Miss Ashley,' he said to her: 'now Mrs. Halliburton.' But William's anger died away—if he had felt any—when he saw her face. I cannot describe to you how fearfully ill she looked. Her cheeks were white, and drawn, and hollow; her eyes were sunk within a dark circle, and her lips were open and looked black. 'Are you ill?' I asked her. 'I am so ill that a few days will be the finish of me,' she answered. 'The doctor gave me to the falling of the leaves, and many are already strewing the grass; in less than a week's time from this, I shall be lower than they are.' 'Is Herbert Dare with you?' inquired William—but he has said since that he spoke in the moment's impulse. Had he taken thought, he would not have put the question. 'No, he is not with me,' she answered, in an angry tone. 'I know nothing of him. He is just a vagabond on the face of the earth.' 'What is it that is the matter with you?' William asked her. 'They call it decay,' she answered. 'I was in Brussels, getting my living by daily teaching. I had to go out in all weathers, and I did not take heed to the colds I caught. I suppose they settled on my lungs.' 'Have you been in this town long?' we inquired of her. 'I came in August,' she answered. 'The Belgian doctor said if I had a change, it might do something for me, and I came here; it was the same to me where I went. But it did me harm instead of good. I grew worse directly I came; and the doctor here said I must not move away again; the travelling would injure me. What mattered it? As good die here as elsewhere.' That she had death written plainly in her face, was evident. Nevertheless, William tried to say a word of hope to her: but she interrupted him. 'There's no recovery for me; I am sure to die; and the time, it's to be hoped, will not be long in coming, or my money will not hold out.' She spoke in a matter-of-fact tone shocking to hear: and before I could call up any answer, she turned to William. 'You are the William Halli—I never could say the name—who was at Mr. Ashley's with Cyril Dare. May I ask where you have descended in Dunkerque?' 'At the Chapeau Rouge,' replied William. 'Then, if I should send there to ask you to come and speak with me, will you come?' she continued. 'I have something that I should like to tell you before I die.' William informed her that we should remain a week; and we wished her good morning and moved away into another walk. Soon afterwards, we saw a Sister of Charity, one of those who go about nursing the sick, come up to her and lead her away. She could scarcely crawl, and halted to take breath between every few steps.

"This, I have told you, was last Saturday. This evening, Wednesday, just as we were rising from table, a waiter came to William and called him out, saying he was wanted. It proved to be the Sister of Charity that we had seen in the park; she told William that Madame Varsini was near death, and had sent her for him. So William went with her, and I have been writing this to you since his departure. It is now ten o'clock, and he has not yet returned. I shall keep this open to tell you what she wanted with him. I cannot imagine.

"Past eleven. William has come in. He thinks she will not live over to-morrow. And I have kept my letter open for nothing, for William will not tell me. He says she has been talking to him about herself and the Dares; but that the tale is more fit for papa's ears than for yours or mine.

"My sincerest love to papa and Henry. We are so glad Gar is to be at Deoffam!—And believe me, your ever-loving child,

"MARY HALLIBURTON."

"Excuse the smear. I had nearly put 'Mary Ashley.'"

This meeting, described in Mary's letter, must have been one of those remarkable coincidences that sometimes occur during a lifetime. Chance encounters they are sometimes called. Chance! Had William and his wife not gone to Dunkerque—and they went there by accident, as may be said, for the original plan had been to spend their absence in Paris—they would not have met. Had the Italian lady not gone to Dunkerque when ordered change—and she chose it by accident, she said—they would not have met. But somehow both parties were brought there, and they did meet. It was not chance that led them there.

When William went out with the sister, she conducted him to a small lodging in the Rue Nationale, a street not far from the hotel. The accommodation appeared to consist of a small ante-room and a bed-chamber. Signora Varsini was in the latter, dressed in a peignoir, and sitting in an arm-chair, supported by cushions. A washed-out, faded peignoir, possibly the very one she had worn years ago, the night of the death of Anthony Dare. William was surprised; by the sister's account he had expected to find her in bed, almost in the last extremity. But hers was a restless spirit. She was evidently weaker, and her breath seemed to come irregularly. William sat down in a chair opposite to her: he could not see very much of her face, for the small lamp on the table had a green shade over it, which cast its gloom on the room.

The sister retired to the ante-room and closed the door between with a caution. "Madame was not to talk much." For a few moments after the first greeting, she, "Madame," kept silence; then she spoke in English.

"I should not have known you. I never saw much of you. But I knew Miss Ashley in a moment. You must have prospered well."

"Yes, I am Mr. Ashley's partner."

"So! That is what Cyril Dare coveted for himself. Miss Ashley also. 'Bah, Monsieur Cyril!' said I sometimes to my mind; 'neither the one nor the other for thee.' Where is he?"

"Cyril? He is at home. Doing no good."

"He never do good," she said with bitterness. "He Herbert's own brother. And the other one—George?"

"George is in Australia. He has a chance, I believe, of doing pretty well."

"Are the girls married?"

"No."

"Not Adelaide?"

"No."

Something like a smile curled her dark and fevered lips. "Mademoiselle Adelaide was trying after that vicomte. 'Bah!' I would say to myself as I did by Cyril, 'there's no vicomte for her; he is only playing his game.' Does he go there now?"

"Lord Hawkesley? Oh, no. All intimacy has ceased."

"They have gone down, have they not? They are very poor?"

"I fear they are poor now. Yes, they have very much gone down. May I inquire what it is you want with me?"

"You inquire soon," she answered in resentful tones. "Do you fear I should contaminate you?—as you feared for your wife on Saturday?"

"If I can aid you in any way I shall be happy and ready to do so," was William's answer, spoken soothingly. "I think you are very ill."

"The doctor was here this afternoon. 'Ma chère,' said he, 'to-morrow will about end it. You are too weak to last longer; the inside is gone.'"

"Did he speak to you in that way?—a medical man!"

"He is aware that I know as much about my own state as he does. He might not be so plain with all his patients. Then I said to the sister, 'Get me up and make the bed, for I must see a friend.'—And I sent her for you. I told you I wanted you to do me a little service. Will you do it?"

"If it is in my power."

"It is not much. It is this," she added, drawing from beneath the peignoir a small packet, sealed and stamped, looking like a thick letter. "Will you undertake to put this surely in the post after I am dead? I do not want it posted before."

"Certainly I will," he answered, taking it from her hand, and glancing at the superscription. It was addressed to Herbert Dare at Dusseldorf. "Is he there?" asked William.

"That was his address the last I heard of him. He is now here, now there, now elsewhere; a vagabond, as I told you, on the face of the earth. He is like Cain," she vehemently continued. "Cain wandered abroad over the earth, never finding rest. So does Herbert Dare. Who wonders? Cain killed his brother: what did he do?"

William lifted his eyes to her face; as much of it as might be distinguished under the dark shade cast by the lamp. That she appeared to be in a very demonstrative state of resentment against Herbert Dare was indisputable.

"He did not kill his brother, at any rate," observed William. "I fear he is not a good man; and you may have cause to know that more conclusively than I; but he did not kill his brother. You were in Helstonleigh at the time, mademoiselle, and must remember that he was cleared," added William, falling into the style of address used by the Dares.

"Then I say he did kill him."

She spoke with slow distinctness. William could only look at her in amazement. Was her mind wandering? She sat glaring at him with her light blue eyes, so glazed, yet glistening; just the same eyes that used to puzzle old Anthony Dare.

"What did you say?" asked William.

"I say that Herbert Dare is a second Cain," she answered.

"He did not kill Anthony," repeated William. "He could not have killed him. He was in another place at the time."

"Yes. With that Puritan child in the dainty dress—fit attire only for your folles in—what you call the place?—Bedlam! I know he was in another place," she continued: and she appeared to be growing terribly excited, between passion and natural emotion.

"Then what are you speaking of?" asked William. "It is an impossibility that Herbert could have killed his brother."

"He caused him to be killed."

William felt a nameless dread creeping over him. "What do you mean?" he breathed.

"I send that letter, which you have taken charge of, to Herbert the bad; but he moves about from place to place, and it may never reach him. So I want to tell you in substance what is written in the letter, that you may repeat it to him when you come across him. He may be going back to Helstonleigh some day; if he not die off first, with his vagabond life. Was it not said there, once, that he was dead?"

"Only for a day or two. It was a false report."

"And when you see him—in case he has not had that packet—you will tell him this that I am now about to tell you."

"What is its nature?" asked William.

"Will you promise to tell him?"

"Not until I first hear what it may be," fearlessly replied William. "Intrust it to me, if you will, and I will keep it sacred; but I must use my own judgment as to imparting it to Herbert Dare. It may be something that would be better left unsaid."

"I do not ask you to keep it sacred," she rejoined. "You may tell it to the world if you please; you may tell it to your wife; you may tell it to all Helstonleigh. But not until I am dead. Will you give that promise?"

"That I will readily give you."

"On your honour?"

William's truthful eyes smiled into hers. "On my honour—if that shall better satisfy you. It was not necessary."

She remained silent a few moments, and then burst forth vehemently. "When you see him, that cochon, that vaurien—"

"I beg you to be calm," interrupted William. "This excitement must be most injurious to one in your weak state; I cannot sit and listen to it."

"Tell him," said she, leaning forward, and speaking in a somewhat calmer tone, "tell him that it was he who caused the death of his brother Anthony."

William could only look at her. Was she wandering? "I killed him," she went on. "Killed him in mistake for Monsieur Herbert."

Barely had the words left her lips, when all that had been strange in that past tragedy seamed to roll away as a cloud from William's mind. The utter mystery there had been as to the perpetrator: the almost impossibility of pointing accusation to any, seemed now accounted for: and a conviction that she was speaking the dreadful truth fell upon him. Involuntarily he recoiled from her.

"He used me ill; yes, he used me ill, that wicked Herbert!" she continued in agitation. "He told me stories; he was false to me; he mocked at me! He had made me care for him; I cared for him—ah, I not tell you how. And then he turned round to laugh at me. He had but amused himself—pour faire passer la temps!"

Her voice had risen to a shriek; her face and lips grew ghastly, and she began to twitch as one falling into convulsion. William grew alarmed, and hastened to her support. He could not help it, much as his spirit revolted from her.

"Y a-t-il quelque chose qu'on peut donner à madame pour la soulager?" he called out hastily to the sister in his fear.

The woman glided in. "Mais oui, monsieur. Madame s'agite, n'est-ce pas?"

"Elle s'agite beaucoup."

The sister poured some drops from a phial into a wine-glass of water, and held it to those quivering lips. "Si vous vous agitez comme cela, madame, c'est pour vous tuer, savez-vous?" cried she.

"I fear so too," added William in English to the invalid. "It would be better for me not to hear this, than for you to put yourself into this state."

She grew calmer, and the sister quitted them. William resumed his seat as before; there appeared to be no help for it, and she continued her tale.

"I not agitate myself again," she said. "I not tell you all the details, or what I suffered: à quoi bon? Pain at morning, pain at midday, pain at night; I think my heart turned dark, and it has never been right again—"

"Hush, mademoiselle! The sister will hear you."

"What matter? She not speak English."

"I really cannot, for your sake, remain here, if you put yourself into this state," he rejoined.

"You must remain; you must listen! You have promised to do it," she answered.

"I will, if you will be calm."

"I'll be calm," she rejoined, the check having driven back the rising passion. "The worst is told. Or rather, I do not tell you the worst—that mauvais Herbert! Do you wonder that my spirit was turned to revenge?"

Perceiving somewhat of her fierce and fiery nature, William did not wonder at it. "I do not know what I am to understand yet?" he whispered. "Did you—kill—Anthony?"

She leaned back on her pillow, clasping her hands before her. "Ah me! I did! Tell him so," she continued again passionately; "tell him that I killed Anthony—thinking it was him."

"It is a dreadful story!" shuddered William.

"I did not mean it to be so dreadful," she answered, speaking quite equably. "No, I did not; and I am telling you as true as though it were my confession before receiving the bon dieu. I only meant to wound him—"

"Herbert?"

"Herbert! Of course; who else but Herbert?" she retorted, giving signs of another relapse. "Had I cause of anger against that pauvre Anthony? No; no. Anthony was sharp with the rest sometimes, but he was always civil to me; I never had a mis-word with him. I not like Cyril; but I not dislike George and Anthony. Why, why," she continued, wringing her hands, "did Anthony come forth from his chamber that night and go out, when he said he had retired to it for good? That is where all the evil arose."

"Not all," dissented William in low tones.

"Yes, all," she sharply repeated. "I had only meant to give Mr. Herbert a little prick in the dark, just to repay him, to stop his pleasant visits to that field for a term. I never thought to kill him. I liked him better than that, ill as he was behaving to me. I never thought to kill him; I never thought much to hurt him. And it would not have hurt Anthony; but that he was what you call tipsy, and fell on the point of the—"

"Scissors?" suggested William, for she had stopped. How could he, even with this confession before him, speak to a lady—or one who ought to have been a lady—of any uglier weapon?

"I had something by me sharper than scissors. But never you mind what. That, so far, does not matter. The little hurt I had intended for Herbert he escaped; and poor Anthony was killed."

There was a long pause. William broke it, speaking out his thoughts impulsively.

"And yet you went to Rotterdam afterwards to make friends with Herbert!"

"When he write and tell me there good teaching in the place, could I know it was untrue? Could I know that he would borrow all my money from me? Could I know that he turn out a worse—"

"Mademoiselle, I pray you, be calm."

"There, then. I will say no more. I have outlived it. But I wish him to know that that fine night's work was his. It was the right man who lay in prison for it. The letter I have given you may never reach him; and I ask you tell him, for his pill, should it not."

"Then you have never hinted this to him?" asked William.

"Never. I was afraid. Will you tell him?"

"I cannot make the promise. I must use my own discretion. I think it is very unlikely that I shall ever see him."

"You meet people that you do not look for. Until last Saturday, you might have said it was unlikely that you would meet me."

"That is true."

Now that the excitement of the disclosure was over, she lay back in a grievous state of exhaustion. William rose to leave, and she held out her hand to him. Could he shun it—guilty as she had confessed herself to him? No. Who was he, that he should set himself up to judge her? And she was dying!

"Can nothing be done to alleviate your sufferings?" he inquired in a kindly tone.

"Nothing. The sooner death comes to release me from them, the better."

He lingered yet, hesitating. Then he bent closer to her, and spoke in a whisper.

"Have you thought much of that other life? Of the necessity of repentance—of seeking earnestly the pardon of God?"

"That is your Protestant fashion," she answered with equanimity. "I have made my confession to a priest and he has given me absolution. A good fat old man; he was very kind to me; he saw how I had been tossed and turned about in life. He will bring the bon dieu to me the last thing, and cause a mass to be said for my soul."

"I thought I had heard that you were a Protestant."

"I was either. I said I was a Protestant to Madame Dare. But the Roman Catholic religion is the most convenient to take up when you are passing. Your priests say they cannot pardon sins."

The interview took longer in acting than it has in telling, and William returned to the hotel to find Mary tired, wondering at his absence, and a letter to Mrs. Ashley—with which you have been favoured—lying on the table, awaiting its conclusion.

"You are weary, my darling. You should not have remained up."

"I thought you were never coming, William. I thought you must have gone off by the London steamer, and left me here! The hotel omnibus took some passengers to it at ten o'clock."

William sat down on the sofa, and drew her to him; the full tide of thankfulness going up from his heart that all women were not as the one he had just left.

"And what did Mademoiselle Varsini want with you, William? Is she really dying?"

"I think she is dying. You must not ask me what she wanted, Mary. It was to tell me something—to speak of things connected with herself and the Dares. They would not be pleasant to your ears."

"But I have been writing an account of all this to mamma, and have left my letter open, to send word what the governess could have to say to you. What can I tell her?"

"Tell her as I tell you, my dearest: that what I have been listening to is more fit for Mr. Ashley's ears than for yours or hers."

Mary rose and wrote rapidly the concluding lines. William stood and watched her. He laughed at the "smear."

"I am not familiar with my new name yet: I was signing myself 'Mary Ashley.'"

"Would you go back to the old name, if you could?" cried he, somewhat saucily.

"Oh, William!"

Saturday came round again: the day they were to leave—just a week since they had come, since the encounter in the park. They were taking an early walk in the market, when certain low sounds, as of chanting, struck upon their ears. A funeral was coming along; it had just turned out of the great church of St. Eloi, at the other corner of the Place. Not a wealthy funeral—quite the other thing. On the previous day they had seen a grand interment, attended by its distinguishing marks; seven or eight banners, as many priests. Some sudden feeling prompted William to ask whose funeral this was, and he made inquiry of a shopkeeper, who was standing at her door.

"Monsieur, c'est l'enterrement d'une étrangère. Une Italienne, l'on dit: Madame Varsini."

"Oh, William! do they bury her already?" was Mary's shocked remonstrance. "It was only yesterday at midday the sister came to you to say she had died. What a shame!"

"Hush, love! Many of the people here understand English. They bury quickly in these countries."

They stood on the pavement, and the funeral came quickly on. One black banner borne aloft in a man's hand, two boys in surplices with lighted candles, and the priest chanting with his open book. Eight men, in white corded hats and black cloaks, bore the coffin on a bier, and there was a sprinkling of impromptu followers—as there always is at these foreign funerals. As the dead was borne past him on its way to the cemetery, William, following the usage of the country, lifted his hat, and remained uncovered until it had gone by.

And that was the last of Bianca Varsini.

CHAPTER XXIV

THE DOWNFALL OF THE DARES

It was a winter's morning, and the family party round the breakfast table at William Halliburton's looked a cheery one, with its adjuncts of a good fire and good fare. Mr. and Mrs. Ashley and Henry were guests. And I can tell you that in Mr. Ashley they were entertaining no less a personage than the high sheriff of the county.

The gentlemen nominated for sheriffs, that year, for the county of Helstonleigh, whose names had gone up to the Queen, were as follows:—

Humphrey Coldicott, Esquire, of Coldicott Grange;

Sir Harry Marr, Bart., of The Lynch;

Thomas Ashley, Esquire, of Deoffam Hall. And her Majesty had been pleased to pick the latter name.

The gate of the garden swung open, and some one came hastily round the gravel-path to the house. Mary, who was seated at the head of the table, facing the window, caught a view of the visitor.

"It is Mrs. Dare!" she exclaimed.

"Mrs. Dare!" repeated Mr. Ashley, as a peal at the hall-bell was heard. "Nonsense, child!"

"Papa, indeed it is."

"I think you must be mistaken, Mary," said her husband. "Mrs. Dare would scarcely be out at this early hour."

"Oh, you disbelievers all!" laughed Mary. "As if I did not know Mrs. Dare! She looked scared and flurried."

Mrs. Dare, looking indeed scared and flurried, came into the breakfast-room. The servant had been showing her into another room, but she put him aside, and appeared amidst them.

What brought her there? What had she come to tell them? Alas! of their unhappy downfall. How the Dares had contrived to go on so long, without the crash coming, they alone knew. They had promised to pay here, they had promised to pay there; and people, tradespeople especially, did not much like to begin compulsory measures with old Anthony Dare, who had so long held sway in Helstonleigh. His professional business had almost left him—perhaps because there was no efficient head to carry it on. Cyril was just what mademoiselle had called Herbert, a vagabond; and Cyril was an irretrievable one. No good to the business was he—not half as much good as he was to the public-houses. Mr. Dare, with white hair, bent form, and dim eyes, would go creeping to his office most days; but his memory was leaving him, and it was evident to all that he was relapsing into his second childhood. Latterly they had lived entirely by privately disposing of their portable effects—as Honey Fair used to do when it fell out of work. They owed money everywhere; rent, taxes, servants' wages, large debts, small debts—it was universal. And now the landlord had put in his claim after the manner of landlords, and it had brought on the climax. They were literally without resource; they knew not where to turn; they had not a penny, or the worth of it, in the wide world. Mrs. Dare, in the alarm occasioned by the unwelcome visitor—for the landlord's man had made good his entrance that morning—came flying off to Mr. Ashley, some extravagant hope floating in her mind that help might be obtained from him.

"Here's trouble! Here's trouble!" she exclaimed by way of salutation, wringing her hands frantically.

They rose in consternation, believing she must have gone wild. William handed her a chair.

"There, don't come round me," she cried, as she flung herself into it. "Go on with your breakfast. I have concealed our troubles until I am heart-sick, and now they can be concealed no longer, and I have come for help to you. Don't press anything upon me, Mrs. William Halliburton; to attempt to eat would choke me!"

She sat there and entered on her grievances. How they had long been without money, had lived by credit, and by pledging things out of their house; how they owed more than she could tell; how a "horrible man" had come into their house that morning, as an emissary of the landlord.

"What are we to do?" she wailed. "Will you help us? Mr. Ashley, will you?—your wife is my husband's cousin, you know. Mr. Halliburton, will you help us? Don't you know that I have a right to claim kindred with you? Your father and I were first cousins, and lived for some time under the same roof."

William remembered the former years when she had not been so ready to own the relationship. He remembered the day when Mr. Dare had put a seizure into their house, and his mother had gone, craving grace of him. Mr. Ashley remembered it, and his eye met William's. How marvellously had the change been brought round! the right come to light!

"What is it that you wish me to do?" inquired Mr. Ashley. "I do not understand."

"Not understand!" she sharply echoed, in her grief. "I want the landlord paid out. You have ample means at command, Mr. Ashley, and might do this much for us."

A modest request, certainly! The rent due was for three years: considerably more than two hundred pounds. Mr. Ashley replied to it quietly.

"A moment's reflection might convince you, Mrs. Dare, that to pay this money would be fruitless waste. The instant this procedure gets wind—and in all probability it has already done so—other claims, as pressing, will be enforced."

"Tradespeople must wait," she answered, with irritation.

"Wait for what?" asked Mr. Ashley. "Do you expect to drop into a fortune?"

Wait for what, indeed? For complete ruin? There was nothing else to wait for. Mrs. Dare sat beating her foot against the carpet.

"Mr. Dare has grown useless," she said. "What he says one minute, he forgets the next; he is almost in a state of imbecility. I have no one to consult with, and therefore I come to you. Indeed, you must help me."

"But I do not see what I can do for you," rejoined Mr. Ashley. "As to paying your debts, it is—it is—in fact, it is not to be thought of. I have my own payments to make, my expenses to keep up. I could not do it, Mrs. Dare."

She paused again, playing nervously with her bonnet strings. "Will you go back with me, and see what you can make of Mr. Dare? Perhaps between you something may be arranged. I don't understand things."

"I cannot go back with you," replied Mr. Ashley. "I must attend the meeting which takes place this morning at the Guildhall."

"In your official capacity," remarked Mrs. Dare in not at all a pleasant tone of voice. "I forgot that you preside at it. How very grand you have become!"

"Very grand indeed, I think, considering the lowly estimation in which you held the glove manufacturer, Thomas Ashley," he answered, with a good-humoured laugh. "I will call upon your husband in the course of the day, Mrs. Dare."

She turned to William. "Will you return with me? I have a claim on you," she reiterated eagerly.

He shook his head. "I accompany Mr. Ashley to the meeting."

She was obliged to be satisfied, turned abruptly, and left the room, William attending her to the door.

"What d'you call that?" asked Henry, lifting his voice for the first time.

"Call it?" repeated his sister.

"Yes, Mrs. Mary; call it. Cheek, I should say."

"Hush, Henry," said Mr. Ashley.

"Very well, sir. It's cheek all the same, though."

As Mr. Ashley surmised, the misfortune had already got wind, and the unhappy Dares were besieged that day by clamorous creditors. When Mr. Ashley and William arrived there, for they walked up at the conclusion of the public meeting, they found Mr. Dare seated alone in the dining-room; that sad dining-room which had witnessed the tragical end of Anthony. He cowered over the fire, his thin hands stretched out to the blaze. He was not altogether childish; but his memory failed, and he was apt to fall into fits of wandering. Mr. Ashley drew forward a chair and sat down by him.

"I fear things do not look very bright," he observed. "We called in at your office as we came by, and found a seizure was also put in there."

"There's nothing much for 'em to take but the desks," returned old Anthony.

"Mrs. Dare wished me to come and talk matters over with you, to see whether anything could be done. She does not understand them, she said."

"What can be done, when things come to such a pass as this?" returned Anthony Dare, lifting his head sharply. "That's just like women—'seeing what's to be done!' I am beset on all sides. If the bank sent me a present of three or four thousand pounds, we might go on again. But it won't, you know. The things must go, and we must go. I suppose they'll not put me in prison; they'd get nothing by doing it."

He leaned forward and rested his chin on his stick, which was stretched out before him as usual. Presently he resumed, his eyes and words alike wandering:

"He said the money would not bring us good if we kept it. And it has not: it has brought a curse. I have told Julia so twenty times since Anthony went. Only the half of it was ours, you know, and we took the whole."

"What money?" asked Mr. Ashley, wondering what he was saying.

"Old Cooper's. We were at Birmingham when he died, I and Julia. The will left it all to her, but he charged us—"

Mr. Dare suddenly stopped. His eye had fallen on William. In these fits of wandering he partially lost his memory, and mixed things and people together in the most inextricable confusion.

"Are you Edgar Halliburton?" he went on.

"I am his son. Do you not remember me, Mr. Dare?"

"Ay, ay. Your son-in-law," nodding to Mr. Ashley. "But Cyril was to have had that place, you know. He was to have been your partner."

Mr. Ashley made no reply. It might not have been understood. And Mr. Dare resumed, confounding William with his father.

"It was hers in the will, you know, Edgar, and that's some excuse, for we had to prove it. There was not time to alter the will, but he said it was an unjust one, and charged us to divide the money; half for us, half for you; to divide it to the last halfpenny. And we took it all. We did not mean to take it, or to cheat you, but somehow the money went; our expenses were great, and we had heavy debts, and when you came afterwards to Helstonleigh and died, your share was already broken into, and it was too late. Ill-gotten money brings nothing but a curse, and that money brought it to us. Will you shake hands and forgive?"

"Heartily," replied William, taking his wasted hand.

"But you had to struggle, and the money would have kept struggle from you. It was many thousands."

"Who knows whether it would or not?" cheerily answered William. "Had we possessed money to fall back upon, we might not have struggled with a will; we might not have put out all the exertion that was in us, and then we should never have got on as we have done."

"Ay; got on. You are looked up to now; you have become gentlemen. And what are my boys? The money was yours."

"Dismiss it entirely from your memory, Mr. Dare," was William's answer, given in true compassion. "I believe that our not having had it may have been good for us in the long-run, rather than a drawback. The utter want of money may have been the secret of our success."

"Ay," nodded old Dare. "My boys should have been taught to work, and they were only taught to spend. We must have our luxuries indoors, forsooth, and our show without; our servants, and our carriages, and our confounded pride. What has it ended in?"

What had it! They made no answer. Mr. Dare remained still for a while, and then lifted his haggard face, and spoke in a whisper, a shrinking dread in his face and tone.

"They have been nothing but my curses. It was through Herbert that she, that wicked foreign woman, murdered Anthony."

Did he know of that? How had the knowledge come to him! William had not betrayed it, except to Mr. Ashley and Henry. And they had buried the dreadful secret down deep in the archives of their breasts. Mr. Dare's next words disclosed the puzzle.

"She died, that woman. And she wrote to Herbert on her death-bed and made a confession. He sent a part of it on here, lest, I suppose, we might doubt him still. But his conduct led to it. It is dreadful to have such sons as mine!"

His stick fell to the ground. Mr. Ashley held him, while William picked it up. He was gasping for breath.

"You are not well," cried Mr. Ashley.

"No; I think I am going. One can't stand these repeated shocks. Did I see Edgar Halliburton here? I thought he was dead. Is he come for his money?" he continued in a shivering whisper. "We acted according to the will, sir: according to the will, tell him. He can see it in Doctors' Commons. He can't proceed against us; he has no proof. Let him go and look at the will."

"We had better leave him, William," murmured Mr. Ashley. "Our presence only excites him."

In the opposite room sat Mrs. Dare. Adelaide passed out of it as they entered. Never before had they remarked how sadly worn and faded she looked. Her later life had been spent in pining after the chance of greatness she had lost, in missing Viscount Hawkesley. Irrevocably lost to her; for the daughter of a neighbouring earl now called him husband. They sat down by Mrs. Dare, but could only condole with her: nothing but the most irretrievable ruin was around.

"We shall be turned from here," she wailed. "How are we to find a home—to earn a living?"

"Your daughters must do something to assist you," replied Mr. Ashley. "Teaching, or—"

"Teaching! in this overdone place!" she interrupted.

"It has been somewhat overdone in that way, certainly of late years," he answered. "If they cannot get teaching, they may find some other employment. Work of some sort."

"Work!" shrieked Mrs. Dare. "My daughters work!"

"Indeed, I don't know what else is to be done," he answered. "Their education has been good, and I should think they may obtain daily teaching: perhaps sufficient to enable you to live quietly. I will pay for a lodging for you, and give you a trifle towards housekeeping, until you can turn yourselves round."

"I wish we were all dead!" was the response of Mrs. Dare.

Mr. Ashley went a little nearer to her. "What is this story that your husband has been telling about the misappropriation of the money that Mr. Cooper desired should be handed to Edgar Halliburton?"

She threw her hands before her face with a low cry. "Has he been betraying that? What will become of us?—what shall we do with him? If ever a family was beaten down by fate, it is ours."

Not gratuitously by fate, thought Mr. Ashley. Its own misdoings have brought the evil upon it. "Where is Cyril?" he asked aloud. "He ought to bestir himself to help you, now."

"Cyril!" echoed Mrs. Dare, a bitter scowl rising to her face. "He help us! You know what Cyril is."

As they went out, they met Cyril. What a contrast the two cousins presented, side by side!—he and William might be called such. The one—fine, noble, intellectual; his countenance setting forth its own truth, candour, honour; making the best in his walk of life, of the talents entrusted to him by God. The other—slouching, untidy, all but ragged; his offensive doings too plainly shown in his bloated face, his inflamed eyes: letting his talents and his days run to worse than waste; a burden to himself and to those around him. And yet, in their boyhood days, how great had been Cyril's advantages over William Halliburton's!

They walked away arm-in-arm, William and Mr. Ashley. A short visit to the manufactory in passing, and then they continued their way home, taking it purposely through Honey Fair.

Honey Fair! Could that be Honey Fair? Honey Fair used to be an unsightly, inodorous place, where mud, garbage, and children ran riot together: a species, in short, of capacious pigsty. But look at it now. The paths are well kept, the road is clean and cared for. Her Majesty's state coach-and-eight might drive down it, and the horses would not have to tread gingerly. The houses are the same; small and large bear evidence of care, of thrift, of a respectable class of inmates. The windows are no longer stuffed with rags, or the palings broken. And that little essay—the assembling at Robert East's, and William Halliburton—had led to the change.

Men and women had been awakened to self-respect; to the duty of striving to live well and to do well; to the solemn thought that there is another world after this, where their works, good or bad, would follow them. They had learned to reflect that it might be possible that one phase of a lost soul's punishment after death, will lie in remembering the duties it ought to have performed in life. They knew, without any effort of reflection, that it is a remembrance which makes the sting of many a death-bed. Formerly, Honey Fair had believed (those who had thought about it) that their duties in this world and any duties which lay in preparing for the next, were as wide apart as the two poles. Of that they had now learned the fallacy. Honey Fair had grown serene. Children were taken out of the streets to be sent to school; the Messrs. Bankes had been discarded, for the women had grown wiser; and, for all the custom the "Horned Ram" obtained from Honey Fair, it might have shut itself up. In short, Honey Fair had been awakened, speaking from a moderate point of view, to enlightenment; to the social improvements of an advancing and a thinking age.

This was a grand day with Honey Fair, as Mr. Ashley and William knew, when they turned to walk through it. Mr. Ashley had purchased that building you have heard of, for a comparative trifle, and made Honey Fair a present of it. It was very useful. It did for their schools, their night meetings, their provident clubs; and to-night a treat was to be held in it. The men expected that Mr. Ashley would look in, and Henry Ashley had sent round his chemical apparatus to give them some experiments, and had bought a great magic-lantern. The place was now called the "Ashley Institute." Some thought—Mr. Ashley for one—that the "Halliburton Institute" would have been more consonant with fact; but William had resolutely withstood it. The piece of waste land behind it had been converted into a sort of playground and garden. The children were not watched in it incessantly, and screamed at:—"You'll destroy those flowers!" "You'll break that window!" "You are tearing up the shrubs!" No: they were made to understand that they were trusted not to do these things; and they took the trust to themselves, and were proud of it. You may train a child to this, if you will.

As they passed the house of Charlotte East, she was turning in at her garden gate; and, standing at the window, dandling a baby, was Caroline Mason. Caroline was servant to Charlotte now, and that was Charlotte's baby; for Charlotte was no longer Charlotte East, but Mrs. Thorneycroft. She curtsied as they came up.

"Good afternoon, gentlemen. I have been round to the rooms to show them how to arrange the evergreens. I hope they will have a pleasant evening!"

"They!" echoed Mr. Ashley. "Are you not coming yourself?"

"I think not, sir. Adam and Robert will be there, of course; but I can't well leave baby!"

"Nonsense, Charlotte!" exclaimed William. "What harm will happen to the baby? Are you afraid of its running away?"

"Ah, sir, you don't understand babies yet."

"That has to come," laughed Mr. Ashley.

"I understand enough about babies to pronounce that one a most exacting infant, if you can't leave it for an hour or two," persisted William. "You must come, Charlotte. My wife intends to be there."

"Well, sir,—I know I should like it. Perhaps I can manage to run round for an hour, leaving Caroline to listen."

"How does Caroline go on?" inquired Mr. Ashley.

"Sir, never a better young woman went into a house. That was a dreadful lesson to her, and it has taught her what nothing else could. I believe that Honey Fair will respect her in time."

"My opinion is, that Honey Fair would not be going far out of its way to respect her now," remarked William. "Once a false step is taken, it is very much the fashion to go tripping over others. Caroline, on the contrary, has been using all her poor endeavours ever since to retrieve that first mistake."

"I could not wish for a better servant," said Charlotte. "Of course, I could not keep a servant for housework alone, and Caroline nearly earns her food helping me at the gloves. I am pleased, and she is grateful. Yes, sir, it is as you say—Honey Fair ought to respect her. It will come in time."

"As most good things come, that are striven for in the right way," remarked Mr. Ashley.

CHAPTER XXV

ASSIZE TIME

Once more, in this, the almost concluding chapter of the history, are we obliged to take notice of Assize Saturday. Once more had the high sheriff's procession gone out to receive the judges; and never had the cathedral bells rung out more clearly, or the streets and windows been so thronged.

A blast, shrill and loud, from the advancing heralds, was borne on the air of the bright March afternoon, as the cavalcade advanced up East Street. The javelin-men rode next, two abreast, in the plain dark Ashley livery, the points of their javelins glittering in the sunshine, scarcely able to advance for the crowd. A feverish crowd. Little cared they to-day for the proud trumpets, the javelin-bearers, the various attractions that made their delight on other of those days; they cared only for that stately equipage in the rear. Not for its four prancing horses, its silver ornaments, its portly coachman on the hammer-cloth; not even for the very judges themselves; but for the master of that carriage, the high sheriff, Thomas Ashley.

He sat in it, its only plainly attired inmate. The scarlet robes, the flowing wigs of the judges, were opposite to him; beside him were the rich black silk robes of his chaplain, the vicar of Deoffam. A crowd of gentlemen on horseback followed—a crowd Helstonleigh had rarely seen. William was one of them.

The popularity of a high sheriff may be judged by the number of his attendants, when he goes out to meet the judges. Half Helstonleigh had placed itself on horseback that day, to do honour to Thomas Ashley.

Occupying a conspicuous position in the street were the Ashley workmen. Clean and shaved, they had surreptitiously conveyed their best coats to the manufactory; and, with the first peal of the college bells, had rushed out, dressed—every soul—leaving the manufactory alone in its glory, and Samuel Lynn to take care of it. The shout they raised, as the sheriff's carriage drew near, deafened the street. It was out of all manner of etiquette or precedence to cheer the sheriff when in attendance on the judges; but who could be angry with them? Not Mr. Ashley. Their lordships looked out astonished. One of the judges you have met before—Sir William Leader; the other was Mr. Justice Keene.

The judges gazed from the carriage, wondering what the shouts could mean. They saw a respectable-looking body of men—not respectable in dress only, but in face—gathered there, bareheaded, and cheering the carriage with all their might and main.

"What can that be for?" cried Mr. Justice Keene.

"I believe it must be meant for me," observed Mr. Ashley, taken by surprise as much as the judges were. "Foolish fellows! Your lordships must understand that they are the workmen belonging to my manufactory."

But his eyes were dim, as he leaned forward and acknowledged the greeting. Such a shout followed upon it! The judges, used to shouting as they were, had rarely heard the like, so deep and heartfelt was it.

"There's genuine good-feeling in that cheer," said Sir William Leader. "I like to hear it. It is more than lip deep."

The dinner party for the judges that night was given at the deanery. Not a more honoured guest had it than the high sheriff. His chaplain was with him, and William and Frank were also guests. What did the Dares think of the Halliburtons now?

The Dares, just then, were too much occupied with their own concerns to think of them at all. They were planning how to get out to Australia. Their daughter Julia, more dutiful than some daughters might prove themselves, had offered an asylum to her father and mother, if they would go out to Sydney. Her sisters, she wrote word, would find good situations there as governesses—probably in time find husbands.

They were wild to go. They wanted to get away from mortifying Helstonleigh, and to try their fortunes in a new world. The passage money was the difficulty. Julia had not sent it, possibly not supposing they were so very badly off; she did not know yet of the last touch to their misfortunes. How could they scrape together even enough for a steerage passage? Mr. Ashley's private opinion was that he should have to furnish it. Ah! he was a good man. Never a better, never a more considerate to others than Thomas Ashley.

Sunday morning rose to the ringing again of the cathedral bells—bells that do not condescend to ring except on rare occasions—telling that it was some day of note in Helstonleigh. It was a fine day, sunny, and very warm for March, and the glittering east window reflected its colours upon a crowd such as the cathedral had rarely seen assembled within its walls for divine service, even on those thronging days, Assize Sundays.

The procession extended nearly the whole way from the grand entrance gates to the choir, passing through the body and the nave. The high sheriff's men, standing so still, their formidable javelins in rest, had enough to do to retain their places, from the pressure of the crowd, as they kept the line of way. The bishop in his robes, the clergy in their white garments and scarlet or black hoods, the long line of college boys in their surplices, the lay-clerks, yet in white. Not (as you were told of yesterday) on them; not on the mayor and corporation, with their chains and gowns; not on the grey-wigged judges, their fiery trains held up behind, glaring cynosure of eyes on other days, was the attention of that crowd fixed; but on him who walked, calm, dignified, quiet, in immediate attendance on the judges—their revered fellow-citizen, Thomas Ashley. In attendance on him was his chaplain, his black gown, so contrasting with the glare and glitter, marking him out conspicuously.

The organ had burst forth as they entered the great gates, simultaneously with the ceasing of the bells which had been sending their melody over the city. With some difficulty, places were found for those of note; but many a score stood that day. The bishop had gone on to his throne; and opposite to him, in the archdeacon's stall, the appointed place for the preacher on Assize Sundays, sat the sheriff's chaplain. Sir William Leader was shown to the dean's stall; Mr. Justice Keene to the sub-dean's; the dean sitting next the one, the high sheriff next the other. William Halliburton was in a canon's stall; Frank— handsome Frank!—found a place amidst many other barristers. And in the ladies' pew, underneath the dean, seated with the dean's wife, were Mrs. Ashley, her daughter, and Mrs. Halliburton.

The Reverend Mr. Keating chanted the service, putting his best voice into it. They gave that fine anthem, "Behold, God is my salvation." Very good were the services and the singing that day. The dean, the prebendary in residence, and Mr. Keating went to the communion-table for the commandments, and thus the service drew to an end. As they were conducted back to their stall, a verger with his silver mace cleared a space for the sheriff's chaplain to ascend the pulpit stairs, the preacher of the day.

How the college boys gazed at him! Only a short time before (comparatively speaking) he had been one of them, a college boy himself; some of the seniors (juniors then) had been school-fellows with him. Now he was the Reverend Edgar Halliburton, chief personage for the moment in that cathedral. To the boys' eyes he seemed to look dark; except on Assize Sundays, they were accustomed to see only white robes in that pulpit.

"Too young to give us a good sermon," thought half the congregation, as they scanned him. Nevertheless, they liked his countenance; its grave earnest look. He gave out his text, a verse from Ecclesiastes:

"Whatsoever thy hand findeth to do, do it with thy might; for there is no work, nor device, nor knowledge, nor wisdom, in the grave, whither thou goest."

Then he leaned a little forward on the cushion; and, after a pause, began his sermon, which lay before him, and worked out the text.

It was an admirable discourse, clear and practical; but you will not care to have it recapitulated for you, as it was recapitulated in the local newspapers. Remembering what the bringing up of the Halliburtons had been, it was impossible that Gar's sermons should not be practical; and the congregation began to think they had been mistaken in their estimate of what a young man could do. He told the judges where their duty lay, as fearlessly as he told it to the college boys, as he told it to all. He told them that the golden secret of success and happiness in this life, lay in the faithful and earnest performance of the duties that crowded on their path, striving on unweariedly, whatsoever those duties might be, whether pleasant or painful; joined to implicit reliance on, and trust in God. A plainer sermon was never preached. In manner he was remarkably calm and impressive, and the tone of his voice was quiet and persuasive, just as if he were speaking to them. He was listened to with breathless interest throughout; even those gentry, the college boys, were for once beguiled into attending to a sermon. Jane's tears fell incessantly, and she had to let down her white veil to hide them; as on that day, years ago, when she had let down her black crape veil to conceal them, in the office of Anthony Dare. Different tears this time.

The sermon lasted just half an hour, and it had seemed only a quarter of one. The bishop then rose and gave the blessing, and the crowds began to file out. As the preacher was being marshalled by a verger through the choir to take his place in the procession next the high sheriff, Mr. Keating met him and grasped his hand.

"You are all right, Gar," he whispered, "and I am proud of having educated you. That sermon will tell home to some of the drones."

"I knew he'd astonish 'em!" ejaculated Dobbs, who had walked all the way from Deoffam to see the sight, to hear her master preach to the cathedral, and had fought out a standing-place for herself right in front of the pulpit. "His sermons aren't filled up with bottomless pits as are never full enough, like those of some preachers be."

That sermon and the Rev. Edgar Halliburton were talked of much in Helstonleigh that day.

But ere the close of another day the town was ringing with the name of Frank. He had led; he, Frank Halliburton! A cause of some importance was tried in the Nisi Prius Court, in which the defendant was Mr. Glenn the surgeon. Mr. Glenn, who had liked Frank from the hour he first conversed with him that evening at his house, now so long ago—a conversation at which you had the pleasure of assisting—who had also the highest opinion of Frank's abilities in his profession, had made it a point that his case should be intrusted to Frank. Mr. Glenn was not deceived. Frank led admirably, and his eloquence quite took the spectators by storm. What was of more importance, it told upon Mr. Justice Keene and the jury, and Frank sat down in triumph and won his verdict.

"I told you I should do it, mother," said he, quietly, when he reached Deoffam that night, after being nearly smothered with congratulations. "You will live to see me on the woolsack yet."

Jane laughed. She often had laughed at the same boast. She was alone that evening; Gar was attending the high sheriff at an official dinner at Helstonleigh. "Will no lesser prize content you, Frank?" asked she, jestingly. "Say, for example, the Solicitor-Generalship?"

"Only as a stepping-stone."

"And you still get on well? Seriously speaking now. Frank."

"First-rate," answered Frank. "This day's work will be the best lift for me, though, unless I am mistaken. I had two fresh briefs put into my hands as I sat down," he added, going off in a laugh. "See if I make this year less than a thousand!"

"And the next thing, I suppose, you will be thinking of getting married?"

The bold barrister actually blushed. "What nonsense, mother! Marry, and lose my fellowship!"

"Frank, it is so! I see it in your face. You must tell me who it is."

"Well, as yet it is no one. I must wait until my eloquence, as they called it to-day in court, is a more assured fact with the public, and then I may speak out to the judge. She means waiting for me, though, so it is all right."

"Tell me, Frank," repeated Jane; "who is 'she'?"

"Maria Leader."

Jane looked at him doubtingly. "Not Sir William's daughter?"

"His second daughter."

"Is not that rather too aspiring for Frank Halliburton?"

"Maria does not think so. I have been aspiring all my life, mother; and so long as I work on for it honourably and uprightly, I see no harm in being so."

"No, Frank; good instead of harm. How did you become acquainted with her?"

"Her brother and I are chums: have been ever since we were at Oxford. Bob is at the Chancery bar, but he has not much nous for it—not half the clever man that his father was. His chambers are next to mine, and I often go home with him. The girls make a great deal of us, too. That is how I first knew Maria."

"Then I suppose you see something of the judge?"

"Oh dear," laughed Frank, "the judge and I are upon intimate terms in private life; quite cronies. You would not think it, though, if you saw me bowing before my lord when he sits in his big wig. Sometimes I fancy he suspects."

"Suspects what?"

"That I and Maria would like to join cause together. But I don't mind if he does. I am a favourite of his. The very Sunday before we came on circuit he asked me to dine there. We went to church in the evening, and I had Maria under my wing; Sir William and Lady Leader trudging on before us."

"Well, Frank, I wish you success. I don't think you would choose any but a nice girl, a good girl—"

"Stop a moment, mother; you will meet the judge to-morrow night, and you may then draw a picture of Maria. She is as like him as two peas."

"How old is she, Frank?"

"Two-and-twenty. I shall have her. He was not always the great Judge Leader, you know, mother; and he knows it. And he knows that every one must have a beginning, as he and my lady had it. For years after they were married he did not make five hundred a year, and they had to live upon it. He does not fear to revert to it, either; often talks of it to me and Bob—a sort of hint, I suppose, that folk do get on in time, by dint of patience. You will like Sir William Leader."

Yes: Jane would meet Sir William on the following night, for that would be the evening of the entertainment given by the high sheriff to the judges at Deoffam Hall.

CHAPTER XXVI

THE HIGH SHERIFF'S DINNER PARTY

William Halliburton drove his wife over in the pony carriage in the afternoon; they would dress and sleep at Deoffam. They went early, and in driving past Deoffam Vicarage, who should be at the gate looking out for them, but Anna! Not Anna Lynn now, but Anna Gurney.

"William, William, there's Anna!" Mary exclaimed. "I will get out here."

He assisted her down, and they remained talking with Anna. Then William asked what he was to do. Wait with the carriage for Mary, or drive on to the hall, and walk back for her?

"Drive to the hall," said Mary, who wished to stay a little while with Anna. "But, William," she added, as he got in, "don't let my box go round to the stables."

"With all its finery!" laughed William.

"It contains my dinner dress," Mary explained to Anna. "Have you been here long?"

"This hour, I think," replied Anna. "My husband had business a mile or two further on, and drove me here. What a nice garden this is! See, I have been picking Gar's flowers."

"Where is Mrs. Halliburton?" asked Mary.

"Dobbs called her in to settle some dispute in the kitchen. I know Dobbs is a great tyrant over that new housemaid."

"But now tell me about yourself, Anna," said Mary, leading her to a bench. "I have scarcely seen you since you were married. How do you like being your own mistress?"

"Oh, it's charming!" replied Anna, with all her old childish, natural manner. "Mary, what dost thee think? Charles lets me sit without my caps."

Mary laughed. "To the great scandal of Patience!"

"Indeed, yes. One day, Patience called when we were at dinner. I had not so much as a bit of net on, and Patience looked so cross; but she said nothing, for the servants were in waiting. When they had left the room she told Charles that she was surprised at his allowing it; that I was giddy enough and vain enough, and it would only make me worse. Charles smiled; he was eating walnuts: and what dost thee think he answered? He—but I don't like to tell thee," broke off Anna, covering her face with her pretty hands.

"Yes, yes, Anna, you must tell me."

"He told Patience that he liked to see me without the caps, and there was no need for my wearing them until I should have children old enough to set an example to."

Anna took off her straw bonnet as she spoke, and her curls fell to shade her blushing cheeks. Mary wondered whether the "children" would have faces as lovely as their mother's. She had never seen Anna look so well. For one thing, she had rarely seen her so well dressed. She wore a stone-coloured corded silk, glistening with richness, and an exquisite white shawl that must have cost no end of money.

"I should always let my curls be seen, Anna," said Mary; "there can be no harm in it."

"No, that there can't, as Charles does not think so," emphatically answered Anna. "Mary," dropping her voice to a whisper, "I want Charles not to wear those straight coats any more. He shakes his head at me and laughs; but I think he will listen to me."

Seeing what she did of the change in Anna's dress, Mary thought so too. Not but that Anna's things were still cut sufficiently in the old form to bespeak her sect: as they, no doubt, always would be.

"When art thee coming to spend the day with me, as thee promised?" asked Anna.

"Very soon: when this assize bustle shall be over."

"How gay you will be to-night!"

"How formal you mean," said Mary. "To entertain judges when on circuit, and bishops, and deans, is more formidable than pleasant. It is a state dinner to-night. When I saw papa this morning, I inquired if we were to have the javelin-men on guard in the dining-room."

Anna laughed. "Do Frank and Gar dine there?"

"Of course. The high sheriff could not give a dinner party without his chaplain at hand to say grace," returned Mary, laughing.

William came back: and they all remained for almost the rest of the afternoon, Jane regaling them with tea. It was scarcely over when Mr. Gurney drove up in his carriage: a large, open carriage, the groom's seat behind, the horses very fine ones. He came in for a few minutes; a very pleasant man of nearly forty years; a handsome man also. Then he took possession of Anna, carefully assisted her up, took the seat beside her, and the reins, and drove off.

William started for the Hall with Mary, walking at a brisk pace. It was not ten minutes' distance, but the evening was getting on. Henry Ashley met them as they entered, and began upon them in his crossest tones.

"Now what have you two got to say for yourselves? Here, I expect you, Mr. William, to pass the afternoon with me: the mother expects Mary: and nothing arrives but a milliner's box! And you make your appearance when it's pretty nearly time to go up to embellish!"

"We stayed at the Vicarage, Henry; and I don't think mamma could want me. Anna Gurney was there."

"Rubbish! Who's Anna Gurney that she should upset things? I wanted William, and that's enough. Do you think you are to monopolize him, Mrs. Mary, just because you happen to have married him?"

Mary went behind her brother, and playfully put her arms round his neck. "I will lend him to you now and then, if you are good," she whispered.

"You idle, inattentive girl! The mother wanted you to cut some hot-house flowers for the dinner-table."

"Did she? I will do it now."

"Listen to her! Do it now! when it has been done this hour past. William, I don't intend to show up to-night."

"Why not?" asked William.

"It is a nuisance to change one's things: and my side's not over clever to-day: and the ungrateful delinquency of you two has put me out-of-sorts altogether," answered Henry, making up his catalogue. "Condemning one to vain expectation, and to fretting and fuming over it! I shan't show up. William must represent me."

"Yes, you will show up," replied William. "For you know that your not doing so would vex Mr. Ashley."

"A nice lot you are to talk about vexing! You don't care how you vex me."

William gently took him by the arm. "Come along to your room now, and I will help you with your things. Once ready, you can do as you like about appearing."

"You treat me just as a child," grumbled Henry. "I say, do the judges come in their wigs?"

Mary broke into a laugh.

"Because that case of stuffed owls had better be ordered out of the hall. The animals may be looked upon as personal."

"I hope there's a good fire in your room, Henry."

"There had better be, unless the genius that presides over the fires in this household would like to feel the weight of my displeasure."

Mary went to find her mother; she was in her chamber, dressing.

"My dear child, how late you are!"

"There's plenty of time, mamma. We stayed at the parsonage. Anna Gurney was there. Henry says he is not very well."

"He says that always when William disappoints him. He will be all right now you have come. Go to your room, my dear, and I will send Sarah to you."

Mary was ready, and the maid gone, before William left Henry to come and dress on his own account. Mary wore white silk, with emerald ornaments.

"Shall I do, William?" asked she, when William came in.

"Do!" he answered, running his eyes over her. "No!"

"Why, what's the matter with me?" she cried, turning hurriedly to the great glass.

"This." He took her in his arms, and kissed her passionately. "My darling wife! You will never 'do' without that."

It was not a formidable party at all, in defiance of Mary's anticipations. The judges, divested of their flowing wigs and flaming robes, looked just like other men. Jane liked Sir William Leader, as Frank had told her she would; and Mr. Justice Keene was an easy, talkative man, fond of a good joke and a good dinner. Mr. Justice Keene seemed excessively to admire Mary Halliburton; and—there could be no doubt about it, and I hope the legal bench won't look grave at the reflection—seemed very much inclined to get up a flirtation with her over the coffee. Being a judge, I think the bishop ought to have read him a reprimand.

Standing at one end of the room, coffee-cups in hand, were Sir William Leader, the Dean of Helstonleigh, Mr. Ashley, and his son. They were talking of the Halliburtons. Sir William knew a good deal of their history from Frank.

"It is most wonderful!" Sir William was remarking. "Self-educated, self-supporting, and to be what they are!"

"Not altogether self-educated," dissented the dean; "for the two younger, the barrister and clergyman, were in the school attached to my cathedral; but self-educated in a great degree. The eldest, my friend's son-in-law, never had a lesson in the classics after his father's death, and there's not a more finished scholar in the county."

"The father died and left them badly provided for," remarked Sir William.

"He did not leave them provided for at all, Sir William," corrected Mr. Ashley. "He left nothing, literally nothing, but the furniture of the small house they rented; and he left some trifling debts. Poor Mrs. Halliburton turned to work with a will, and not only contrived to support them, but brought them up to be what you see them—high-minded, honourable, educated men."

The judge turned his eyes on Jane. She was sitting on a distant sofa, talking with the bishop. So quiet, so lady-like, nay—so attractive—she looked still, in the rich pearl-grey dress warn at William's wedding; not in the least like one who had had to toil hard for bread.

"I have heard of her—heard of her worth from Frank," he said, with emphasis. "She must be one in a thousand."

"One in a million, Sir William," burst forth Henry Ashley. "When they were boys, you could not have bribed them to do a wrong thing: neither temptation nor anything else turned them from the right. And they would not be turned from the right now, if I know anything of them."

The judge walked up to Jane, and took the seat beside her just vacated by the bishop.

"Mrs. Halliburton," said he, "you must be proud of your sons."

Jane smiled. "I have latterly been obliged to take myself to task for being so, Sir William," she answered.

"To task! I wish I had three such sons to take myself to task for being proud of," was his answer. "Not that mine are to be found fault with; but they are not like these."

"Do you think Frank will get on?" she asked him.

"It is no longer a question of getting on. He has begun to rise in an unusually rapid manner. I should not be surprised if, in after-years, he may find the very highest honours opening to him."

Again Jane smiled. "He has been in the habit of telling us that he looks forward to ruling England as Lord Chancellor."

The judge laughed. "I never knew a newly-fledged barrister who did not indulge that vision," said he. "I know I did. But there are really not many Frank Halliburtons. So, sir," he continued, for Frank at that moment passed, and the judge pinned him, "I hear you cherish dreams of the woolsack."

"To look at it from a distance is not high treason, Sir William," was Frank's ready answer.

"Why, what do you suppose you would do on the woolsack, if you got there?" cried Sir William.

"My duty, I hope, Sir William. I would try hard for it."

Sir William loosed him with an amused expression, and Frank passed on. Jane began to think Frank's dream—not of the woolsack, but of Maria Leader—not so very improbable a one.

"I have heard of your early struggles," said the judge to her in low tones. "Frank has talked to me. How you could have borne up, and done long-continued battle with them, I cannot imagine!"

"I never could have done it but for one thing," she answered: "my trust in God. Times upon times, Sir William, when the storm was beating about my head, I had no help or comfort in the wide world: I had nothing to turn to but that. I never lost my trust in God."

"And therefore God stood by you," remarked the judge.

"And therefore God stood by me, and helped me on. I wish," she added earnestly, "the whole world could learn the same great lesson that I have learnt. I have—I humbly hope I have—been enabled to teach it to my boys. I have tried to do it from their very earliest years."

"Frank shall have Maria," thought the judge to himself. "They are an admirable family. The young chaplain should have another of the girls if he liked her."

What was William thinking of, as he stood a little apart, with his serene brow and his thoughtful smile? His mind was in the past. That long past night, following the day of his entrance to Mr. Ashley's manufactory, was present to him, when he had lain down in despair, and sobbed out his bitter grief. "Bear up, my child," were the words his mother had comforted him with: "only do your duty, and trust implicitly in God." And when she had gone down, and he could get the sobs away from his heart and throat, he made the resolve to do as she had told him—at any rate, to try and do it. And he kneeled down there and then, and asked to be helped to do it. And, from that hour to this, William had never known the trust to fail. Success? Yes, they had reaped success—success in no measured degree. Be very sure that it was born of that great trust. Oh!—as Jane had just said to Sir William Leader—if the world could only learn this wonderful truth!

"BECAUSE HE HATH SET HIS LOVE UPON ME, THEREFORE WILL I DELIVER HIM: I WILL SET HIM UP, BECAUSE HE HATH KNOWN MY NAME."

MRS HENRY WOOD (aka ELLEN WOOD) – A CONCISE BIBLIOGRAPHY

Danesbury House (1860)
East Lynne (1861)
The Elchester College Boys (1861)
A Life's Secret (1862)
Mrs. Halliburton's Troubles (1862)
The Channings (1862)
The Foggy Night at Offord: A Christmas Gift for the Lancashire Fund (1863)
The Shadow of Ashlydyat (1863)
Verner's Pride (1863)
Lord Oakburn's Daughters (1864)
Oswald Cray (1864)
Trevlyn Hold; or, Squire Trevlyn's Heir (1864)
William Allair; or, Running away to Sea (1864)
Mildred Arkell: A Novel (1865)
The Argosy (1865)
Elster's Folly: A Novel (1866)

St. Martin's Eve: A Novel (1866)
Lady Adelaide's Oath (1867)
Orville College: A Story (1867)
The Ghost of the Hollow Field (1867)
Anne Hereford: A Novel (1868)
Castle Wafer; or, The Plain Gold Ring (1868)
The Red Court Farm: A Novel (1868)
Roland Yorke: A Novel (1869)
Bessy Rane: A Novel (1870)
George Canterbury's Will (1870)
Dene Hollow (1871)
Within the Maze: A Novel (1872)
The Master of Greylands (1872)
Johnny Ludlow (1874)
Bessy Wells (1875)
Told in the Twilight: Containing 'Parkwater' and nine short stories (1875)
Adam Grainger: A Tale (1876)
Edina (1876)
Our Children (1876)
Parkwater: With four other tales (1876)
Pomeroy Abbey (1878)
Lady Adelaide (1879)
Johnny Ludlow, Second Series (1880)
A Tale of Sin and Other Tales (1881)
Court Netherleigh: A Novel (1881)
About Ourselves (1883)
Johnny Ludlow. Third Series (1885)
Lady Grace and Other Stories (1887)
The Story of Charles Strange (1888)
Featherston's Story. A Tale by Johnny Ludlow (1889)
The Unholy Wish and Other Stories (1890)
The House of Halliwell. A Novel (1890)
Ashley and Other Stories (1897)
Victor Serenus (1898)
Johnny Ludlow. Fifth series (1899)
Johnny Ludlow. Sixth series (1899)

Translations
Les Channing. Traduit de l'Anglais par Mme Abric-Encontre (1864)
Les Filles de Lord Oakburn: Roman traduit de l'anglais par L. Bochet (1876)
La Gloire des Verner: Roman traduit de l'anglais par L. de L'Estrive (1878)
Le Serment de Lady Adelaïde: Roman traduit de l'anglais par Léon Bochet (1878)